INTO THE
DARKNESS

INTO THE
DARKNESS

HARRY TURTLEDOVE

EARTHLIGHT

LONDON · SYDNEY · NEW YORK · TOKYO · SINGAPORE · TORONTO
www.earthlight.co.uk

First published in Great Britain by Earthlight, 1999
The paperback edition first published by Earthlight, 2000
An imprint of Simon & Schuster UK Ltd
A Viacom Company

1 3 5 7 9 10 8 6 4 2

Simon & Schuster UK Ltd
Africa House
64–78 Kingsway
London WC2B 6AH

Simon & Schuster Australia
Sydney

A CIP catalogue record for this book is available
from the British Library.

ISBN 0-671-022822

Typeset by SX Composing DTP, Rayleigh, Essex
Printed and bound in Great Britain by
Caledonian International Book Manufacturing, Glasgow

MAP

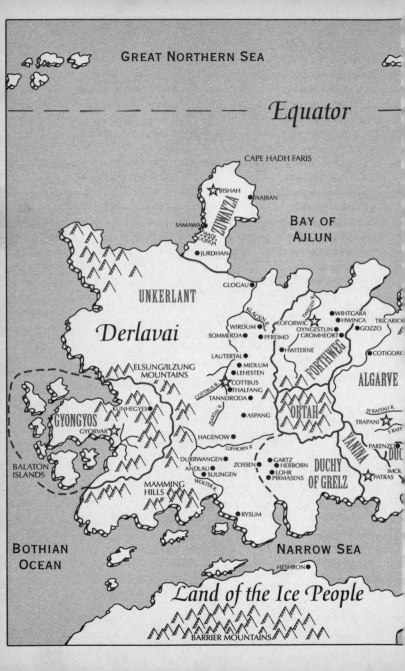

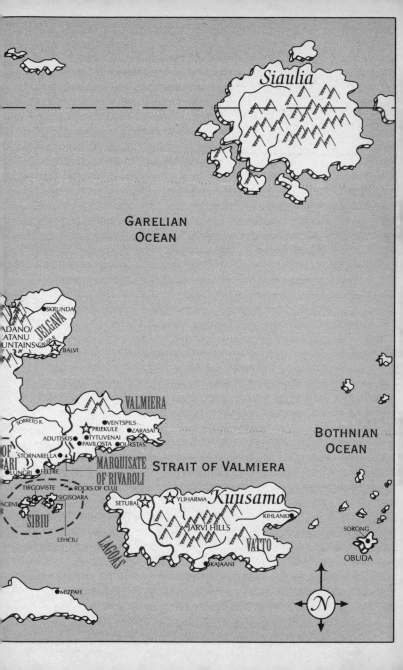

DRAMATIS PERSONAE

Algarve

Alardo	Duke of Bari
Alcina	Gardener in Tricarico
Balastro	Marquis; Algarvian minister to Zuwayza
Balozio	Man of Kaunian blood in Tricarico
Bembo★	Constable in Tricarico
Borso	Commandant of dragon farm outside Trapani
Cilandro	Colonel of footsoldiers near Tricarico
Corbeo	Dragonflier in Sabrino's wing
Dalinda	Gardener in Tricarico
Domiziano	Captain–squadron commander in Sabrino's wing
Dudone	King Mezentio's predecessor
Elio	Lieutenant in Tealdo's regiment
Evadne	Kaunian woman in Tricarico; Falsirone's wife
Falsirone	Kaunian hair stylist in Tricarico; Evadne's husband
Fiametta	Courtesan in Tricarico
Frontino	Warder in Tricarico
Gabrina	Slattern in Tricarico
Galafrone	Captain replacing Larbino
Ippalca	Algarvian noblewoman
Ivone	Grand duke commanding Algarvian forces in Valmiera
Larbino	Captain in Tealdo's regiment
Lurcanio	Count and colonel occupying Prickule
Mainardo	Mezentio's brother, named King of Jelgava
Martusino	Thief in Tricarico
Mezentio	King of Algarve
Mosco	Captain; Colonel Lurcanio's adjutant
Ombruno	Colonel commanding officer of Tealdo's regiment
Oraste	Constable in Tricarico

Orosio	Senior lieutenant in Sabrino's wing
Panfilo	Sergeant in Tealdo's regiment
Pesaro	Constabulary sergeant in Tricarico
Procla	Gardener in Tricarico
Sabrino★	Count and colonel of dragonfliers
Saffa	Constabulary sketch artist in Tricarico
Sasso	Constabulary captain in Tricarico
Spinello	Major commanding occupiers in Oyngestun
Tealdo★	Common soldier
Trasone	Common soldier; Tealdo's friend

Forthweg

Agmund	Master of Algarvian, Gromheort
Arnulf	Firstman in village in eastern Forthweg
Bede	Master of classical Kaunian, Gromheort
Beocca	Leofsig's squadmate
Brivibas	Vanai's grandfather
Brorda	Count of Gromheort
Burgred	Laborer in Leofsig's gang
Ceolnoth	Magecraft master at Ealstan and Sidroc's academy
Conberge	Ealstan and Leofsig's sister
Cynfrid	Brigadier; senior officer in captives' camp
Ealstan★	Student in Gromheort; Leofsig's younger brother
Elfryth	Ealstan and Leofsig, and Conberge's mother
Elfsig	Felgilde's father
Felgilde	Leofsig's girlfriend
Frithstan	Professor of ancient history
Gutauskas	Kaunian war captive
Hengist	Sidroc's father; Hestan's brother
Hestan	Ealstan, Leofsig, and Conberge's father – a bookkeeper
Leofsig★	Soldier in King Penda's levy; Ealstan's older brother
Merwit	War captive
Odda	One of Ealstan's classmates
Osgar	Master of herblore in Gromheort
Penda	King of Forthweg
Sidroc	Ealstan's first cousin
Swithulf	Headmaster of Ealstan and Sidroc's academy

Tamulis	Kaunian apothecary in Oyngestun
Vanai★	Young Kaunian woman in Forthweg
Womer	Linen merchant in Gromheort
Wulfher	Ealstan's uncle

Gyongyos
Arpad	Ekrekek (King) of Gyongyos
Borsos	Dowser on Obuda
Gergely	Borsos's wife
Horthy	Gyongyosian minister to Zuwayza
Istvan★	Common soldier on island of Obuda
Jokai	Sergeant in Istvan's company
Kisfaludy	Major in Istvan's battalion
Kun	Soldier on Obuda; former mage's apprentice
Szonyi	Soldier on Obuda
Turul	Dragonkeeper

The Ice People
| Doeg | Caravan master |

Jelgava
Adomu	Colonel of Talsu's regiment, replacing Dzirnavu
Ausra	Talsu's younger sister
Balozhu	Colonel commanding Talsu's regiment, replacing Adomu
Donalitu	King of Jelgava
Dzirnavu	Count and colonel of Talsu's regiment
Laitsina	Talsu's mother
Smilsu	Talsu's friend
Talsu★	Common soldier in Bratanu Mountains
Traku	Talsu's father, a tailor
Vartu	Colonel Dzirnavu's servant

Kuusamo
Alkio	Theoretical sorcerer; Raahe's husband
Elimaki	Pekka's sister
Ilmarinen	Raffish elderly master theoretical sorcerer
Joroinen	One of the Seven Princes of Kuusamo

Leino	Pekka's husband; a practical mage
Olavin	Elimaki's husband – a banker
Pekka★	Professor of theoretical sorcery, Kajaani City College
Piilis	Theoretical sorcerer
Raahe	Theoretical sorcerer; Alkio's wife
Risto	Admiral fighting in the Bothnian Ocean
Siuntio	Elderly master theoretical sorcerer
Uto	Pekka and Leino's son

Lagoas

Brinco	Secretary to Grandmaster of Lagoan Guild of Mages
Ebastiao	Naval captain in Setubal
Fernao★	First-rank mage
Pinhiero	Grandmaster of the Lagoan Guild of Mages
Ramalho	Naval lieutenant in Setubal
Ribiero	Naval commodore in Setubal
Rogelio	Captain of the *Leopardess*
Shelomith	A spy

Sibiu

Burebistu	King of Sibiu
Cornelu★	Commander and leviathan-rider, Sibian navy
Costache	Cornelu's wife
Delfinu	Commodore, Sibian navy
Propatriu	Captain of the *Impaler*
Vitor	King of Sibiu

Unkerlant

Agen	A peasant in Zossen
Annore	Garivald's wife
Ansovald	Unkerlanter minister to Zuwayza
Berthar	One of Leudast's squadmates
Dagulf	A peasant in Zossen; Garivald's friend
Droctulf	General commanding Unkerlanter attack on Zuwayza
Garivald★	Unkerlanter peasant in the village of Zossen
Gernot	Soldier in Leudast's squad in Forthweg
Gurmun	Droctulf's successor in command in Zuwayza

Herka	Firstman Waddo's wife
Herpo	A traveling spice seller
Huk	Soldier in Leudast's squad in Forthweg
Ibert	Deputy foreign minister
Kyot	Swemmel's deceased twin brother
Leuba	Garivald and Annore's baby daughter
Leudast★	Common soldier
Magnulf	Sergeant in Leudast's company
Merovec	Major; Marshal Rathar's adjutant
Nantwin	A soldier in Leudast's company
Rathar★	Marshal of Unkerlant
Roflanz	Colonel commanding regiment in western Forthweg
Swemmel	King of Unkerlant
Syrivald	Garivald and Annore's son
Trudulf	Soldier in Leudast's company in western Forthweg
Uote	An old peasant woman in Zossen
Urgan	Leudast's company commander
Waddo	Firstman of Zossen
Werpin	General in the attack over the Wadi Ugeiga
Wisgard	One of Leudast's squadmates
Zaban	Foreign ministry official

Valmiera

Bauska	Krasta's maidservant
Enkuru	Count in southern Valmiera
Erglyu	Public affairs officer in the war ministry
Gainibu	King of Valmiera
Gedominu	Elderly farmer near Pavilosta; Merkela's husband
Kestu	Valmieran duke
Krasta★	Marchioness in Priekule; Skarnu's sister
Marstalu	Duke of Klaipeda; commander of the Valmieran army
Merkela	Gedominu's young wife
Raunu	Senior sergeant in Skarnu's company
Rudninku	Captain fighting in southern Valmiera
Skarnu★	Marquis; captain; Krasta's brother
Valnu	Viscount in Priekule

Yanina

Cossos	One of Tsavellas's stewards
Gyzis	Varvakis's clerk
Tsavellas	King of Yanina
Varvakis	Purveyor of delicacies

Zuwayza

Hajjaj★	Foreign minister of Zuwayza
Hassila	Hajjaj's middle wife
Jamila	Hajjaj's daughter
Kolthoum	Hajjaj's senior wife
Lalla	Hajjaj's junior wife
Mithqal	Military mage of the second rank
Shaddad	Hijjaj's secretary
Shazli	King of Zuwayza
Tewfik	Hajjaj's elderly majordomo

★denotes a viewpoint character

1.

Ealstan's master of herblore droned on and on about the mystical properties of plants. Ealstan paid him no more attention than he had to, no more attention than any other fifteen-year-old boy would have given of a warm summer afternoon. He was thinking about stripping off his tunic and jumping in the stream that flowed past Gromheort, about girls, about what his mother would fix for supper, about girls, about the health of the distant and ancient Duke of Bari, about girls . . . about everything under the sun, in short, except herblore.

He was a little too obviously not thinking about herblore. The master's voice came sharp as a whipcrack: "Ealstan!"

He started, then sprang to his feet, almost knocking over the stool on which he'd been perched. "Master Osgar!" he said, while the other boys whom Osgar taught snickered at his clumsiness – and in relief because the master had caught him instead of them.

Osgar's gray-streaked beard seemed to quiver with indignation. Like most men of Forthweg – like Ealstan himself – he was strong and stocky and dark, with an imperiously curved nose and with eyes that, at the moment, flashed fire a wardragon might have envied. His voice dripped sarcasm. "Perhaps you will do me the honor, Ealstan, of reminding me of the chiefest property of the herb snake's-grass." He whacked a switch into the palm of his hand, a hint of what Ealstan would get if he did not do him that honor.

"Snake's-grass, Master Osgar?" Ealstan said. Osgar nodded, anticipation on his face: if Ealstan needed to repeat the question, he hadn't been listening. And so, indeed, he hadn't. But his uncle had used snake's-grass the year before, which meant he knew the answer: "May it please you, Master Osgar, if you set the powder of snake's-grass and three-leaved grass under a man's pillow, he will not dream of himself afterwards ever again."

It did not please the master of herblore. His expression made that plain. But it was the right answer. Reluctantly, Osgar nodded and said, "Resume your seat – without making the countryside fear an earthquake, if that be possible. And henceforth, make some effort to appear as if you care what passes here."

"Aye, Master Osgar. Thank you, Master Osgar." Ealstan sat as carefully as he could. For a little while, till the master of herblore stopped aiming glances sharp as a unicorn's horn his way, he paid attention to Osgar's words. There were apothecaries in his family, and he'd thought more than idly of going into that trade himself one day. But he had so many other things to think about, and . . .

Thwack! The switch came down, not on his back, but on that of his cousin Sidroc. Sidroc had been thinking of something else, too, and hadn't been lucky enough to get a question he could handle with what he already knew. All the boys in Osgar's class looked diligent then, whether they were or not.

After what seemed like forever, a brazen bell released them. As they filed out, Osgar said, "Study well. We meet again tomorrow afternoon." He contrived to make that sound like a threat.

To Ealstan, tomorrow afternoon felt a million miles away. So did his morning classes in Forthwegian literature and ciphering. So did the work he would have to do tonight for all of those classes and more besides. For now, as he left the gloomy corridors of the academy and stepped out into bright sunshine, the whole world seemed his – or, if not the whole world, at least the whole town of Gromheort.

He glanced back over his shoulder at the whitewashed stone keep where Count Brorda made his residence. As far as he was concerned, neither Brorda nor Gromheort got their due from King Penda, nor from anyone else in Eoforwic, the capital. To them, Gromheort was just a medium-sized town not far from the border with Algarve. They did not grasp its magnificent uniqueness.

That this was also Count Brorda's view of the situation, and one he assiduously cultivated in the folk of Gromheort, had never crossed Ealstan's mind.

It didn't cross his mind now, either. Sidroc made as if to hit him, saying, "Curse you, how did you come up with that about snake's-grass? When I strip off for the baths, everyone's going to tease me about the welt on my back."

"Uncle Wulfher used the stuff, remember, when he thought he

had a sending of nightmares," Ealstan replied.

Sidroc snorted. He didn't want an answer; he wanted sympathy. Ealstan was his cousin, not his mother, and had scant sympathy to give.

Bantering with their friends, they made their way through the streets of Gromheort toward their homes. Ealstan blinked against the impact of the strong northern sun against whitewash and red tile roofs. Until his eyes got used to the light, he sighed with relief whenever he ducked under an olive tree or one full of ripening almonds. Goodbyes came every couple of blocks as one boy after another peeled off from the group.

Ealstan and Sidroc were halfway home when one of Count Brorda's constables held up a ceremonial sword to halt foot traffic and wagons on their street. He shouted curses at a luckless man who didn't stop fast enough to suit him. "What's going on?" Sidroc asked, but Ealstan's ears had already caught the rhythmic clip-clop of cavalry.

Both boys shouted cheers as the unicorns trotted by. One of the officers made his mount rear for a moment. The sun shone bright as silver off its iron-shod horn and off its spotless white coat, a white that put whitewash to shame. Most of the troopers, though, had sensibly daubed their mounts with paint. Dun and sand and even muddy green were less likely to draw the notice of the foe and a streak of spurting fire, even if they seemed less magnificent than white.

A couple of slim, fair, trousered Kaunians, a man and a woman, cheered the cavalry along with everyone else. In their hatred of Algarve, they and the rest of the folk of the Kingdom of Forthweg agreed. After the constable waved traffic forward, Ealstan watched the woman's hips work in those revealing pants. He licked his lips. Forthwegian women went out in long, loose tunics that covered them from neck to ankles and kept their shapes decently disguised. No wonder people talked about Kaunians the way they did. And yet the woman strode along as if unaware of the spectacle she was creating, and chattered with her companion in their own sonorous language.

Sidroc watched her, too. "Disgusting," he said, but, by his avid voice and by the way he eyes kept following her, he was perhaps not altogether disgusted.

"Just because they dressed that way in the days of the Kaunian Empire, they think they have the right to keep on doing it," Ealstan agreed. "The Empire fell more than a thousand years ago, in case they hadn't noticed."

"Because the Kaunians de-gen-er-ated from wearing clothes like that." Sidroc pronounced with exaggerated care the long word he'd learned from the history master earlier in the year.

He and Ealstan had gone a couple of more blocks when someone came running up the street behind them shouting, "He's dead! He's dead!"

"Who's dead?" Ealstan called, but he was afraid he knew.

"Duke Alardo, that's who," the man answered.

"Are you sure?" Ealstan and Sidroc and several other people asked the question at the same time. Alardo of Bari had been at death's door more than once in the nearly thirty years since his domain was forcibly detached from Algarve in the aftermath of the Six Years' War. He'd been vigorous enough to pull through every time. *If only*, Ealstan thought, *he'd been vigorous enough to sire a son . . .*

But the man with the news was nodding vigorously. "I have it straight from my brother-in-law, who has it from Count Brorda's secretary, who heard the message with his own ears when it reached the keep by crystal."

Like everyone else in Gromheort, Ealstan fancied himself a connoisseur of rumors. This one sounded highly probable. "King Mezentio will claim Bari," he said grimly.

"If he does, we'll fight him." Sidroc sounded grim, too, grim and excited at the same time. "He can't fight Forthweg and Valmiera and Jelgava all at once. Not even an Algarvian would be crazy enough to try that."

"Nobody knows what an Algarvian is crazy enough to try," Ealstan said with conviction. "He may have more enemies than that, too – Sibiu doesn't like Algarve, either, and the islanders are supposed to be tough. Come on – let's hurry home. Maybe we can be first with the news." They both began to run.

As they ran, Sidroc said, "I bet your brother will be glad to get the chance to slaughter some stinking Algarvians."

"Not *my* fault Leofsig was born first," Ealstan panted. "If I were nineteen, I'd have gone into the King's levy, too." He pretended to spray fire around, so recklessly that, had it been real, he would have burned down half of Gromheort.

He dashed into his own house shouting that Duke Alardo was dead. "What?" His sister Conberge, who was a year older than he, came in from the courtyard, where she'd been trying to keep the flower garden flourishing despite Forthweg's savage summer heat. "What will Mezentio do now?"

"He will seize the Duchy." That wasn't Ealstan; it was his mother, Elfryth. She'd hurried out of the kitchen, and was wiping her hands on a linen towel. "He will seize it, and we will go to war." She did not sound excited, but about to burst into tears. After a moment, she gathered herself and went on, "I was about your age, Conberge, when the Six Years' War ended. I remember the uncles and cousins you never got to know because they didn't come home from the war." Her voice broke. She did begin to cry.

Ealstan said, "Leofsig will fight for Forthweg. He won't be dragooned into Algarve's army, or Unkerlant's, either, the way so many Forthwegians were in the last war."

His mother looked at him as if he'd suddenly started speaking the language of the Lagoans, whose island kingdom lay beyond the isles of Sibiu, far southeast of Forthweg. "I don't care under which banner he fights," she said. "I don't want him to fight at all."

"Losing the last war didn't teach the Algarvians their lesson," Ealstan said. "This time, we'll hit them first." He smacked a fist into the palm of the other hand. "They won't stand a chance." That should have convinced his mother; none of his masters could have faulted his logic. For some reason, though, Elfryth looked less happy than ever.

So did Hestan, his father, when he came home from casting accounts for one or another of Gromheort's leading merchants. He had already heard the news. By then, very likely, all of Gromheort, all of Forthweg but for a few peasants and herders, had heard the news. He didn't say much. He seldom said much. But his silence seemed . . . heavier than usual as he drank his customary evening glass of wine with Elfryth.

He had a second glass of wine with supper, something he rarely did. And, all through supper, he kept looking, not east toward Algarve but to the west. He had nearly finished his garlicky stew of mutton and eggplant when, as if unable to contain himself any longer, he burst out, "What will Unkerlant do?"

Ealstan stared at him, then started to laugh. "Your pardon, sir," he said at once; he was, on the whole, a well-mannered boy. "The Unkerlanters are still digging out from their Twinkings War, and trying to fight Gyongyos in the far west, and snapping and snarling at Zuwayza, too. Don't you think they have enough on their plate?"

"If they hadn't fought themselves in the Twinkings War, they would still rule most of Forthweg," Hestan pointed out. Ealstan knew that, but it felt like history as old as that of the Kaunian Empire to him. His father resumed: "Anyhow, what I think doesn't matter. What matters is what King Swemmel of Unkerlant thinks – and, by all I've heard, he doesn't know his own mind from day to day."

Tealdo studied himself in the little hand mirror. He muttered something vile under his breath: one of the spikes of his mustache was not all it might have been. He applied a little more orange-scented wax, twisted the mustachio between thumb and forefinger, and studied the result. *Better*, he decided, but kept fiddling with the mustache and with his imperial even so. *Better* wasn't good enough, not here, not now. Even perfection would be barely good enough.

Panfilo came swaggering up the aisle of the caravan coach. His own mustaches, even more fiery of hue than Tealdo's, swept up and out like the horns of a bull. Instead of a chin beard, he favored bushy side whiskers. He paused to nod at Tealdo's primping. "That's good," he said. "Aye, that's very good. All the girls in the Duchy will want to kiss you."

"Sounds fine to me, Sergeant," Tealdo said with a grin. He patted the sleeve of his drab tan uniform tunic. "I just wish we could wear something with a little style to it, the way our fathers and grandfathers did."

"So do I, and I'll not deny it," Panfilo said. "But our fathers went into the Six Years' War in gold tunics and scarlet kilts. They looked like they were already blazing, and they burned – how they burned!" The sergeant went on up the aisle, snarling at soldiers less fastidious than Tealdo.

The caravan hummed south along the ley line. A few minutes later, Lieutenant Elio came through the coach and snapped at a couple of men Panfilo had missed. A few minutes after that, Captain Larbino came through and growled at men Elio had missed – and at a couple he hadn't.

Nobody growled at Tealdo. He leaned back in his seat and whistled an off-color song and watched the Algarvian landscape flow by outside the coach. Red brick and timber had long since replaced whitewashed plaster; the southern part of the realm was cool and cloudy and not well suited to the airier forms of architecture in fashion farther north. Here, a man wanted to be sure he stayed warm of nights – and of days, too, a good part of the year.

Halfway through the afternoon, the almost subliminal hum of the caravan deepened as it drew less energy from the line over which it traveled. It slowed to a stop. Captain Larbino threw open the door to the coach. "Form up in order of march outside," he said. "Remember, King Mezentio has done us great honor by allowing this regiment to take part in the return of the Duchy of Bari to its rightful allegiance. Remember also, any man failing to live up to this honor will personally answer to me." He set a hand on the basket hilt of his officer's rapier; Tealdo did not doubt he meant that. The captain added, "And finally, remember that we are not marching into a foreign country. We are welcoming our brothers and sisters home."

"Hang our brothers," said the soldier next to Tealdo, a burly fellow named Trasone. "I want one of our sisters in Bari to welcome me home, and then screw me till I can't even walk."

"I've heard ideas I liked less," Tealdo said as he got to his feet. "Lots of them, as a matter of fact." He filed toward the door, then jumped down from the coach, which floated a couple of feet above the ground, and took his place in the ranks.

Captain Larbino's company was not the first in the regiment, but was the second, which let Tealdo see ahead well enough. In front of the first company stood the color guard. He envied them their gaudy ceremonial uniforms, from gilded helms to gleaming boots. The man in the middle of the color guard, who had surely been chosen for his great height, bore the banner of Algarve, diagonal slashes of red, green, and white. The soldier to his left carried the regiment pennon, a blue lightning bolt on gold.

Just ahead of the color guard stood a squat brick building also flying the Algarvian national banner: the customs house on the border –

what had been the border – between Algarve and Bari. Its turnstile was raised, inviting the Algarvian soldiers forward. An almost identical brick building stood a few feet farther south, on the other side of the border. Bari's banner, a white bear on orange, floated on a staff beside it. Its wooden turnstile still made as if to bar the road into the Duchy.

Out of that second building came a plump man in uniform. His tunic and kilt were of different color and cut from those of the Algarvians: not tan, but a brown with green mixed in. Duke Alardo, powers below curse his ghost, had *liked* running his own realm; he'd been the perfect cat's-paw for the victors of the Six Years' War.

But he was dead now, dead without an heir. As for what his people thought . . . The plump man in the mud-and-moss uniform bowed to the Algarvian banner as the color-bearer brought it up to the border. Then he turned and bowed to the Barian banner before running it down from the pole where it had floated for a generation and more. And *then* he let it fall to the ground and spurned it with his boots. He raised the turnstile, crying, "Welcome home, brothers!"

Tealdo shouted himself hoarse but could hardly hear himself, for every man in the regiment was shouting himself hoarse. Colonel Ombruno, who commanded the unit, ran forward, embraced the Barian – the former Barian – customs officer, and kissed him on both cheeks. Turning back to his own men, he said, "Now, sons of my fighting spirit, enter the land that is ours once more."

The captains began singing the Algarvian national hymn. The men joined them in a swelling chorus of joy and pride. They marched past the two customs houses now suddenly made useless. Tealdo poked Trasone in the ribs and murmured, "Now that we're entering the land, let's see if we can enter the women too, eh, like you said." Trasone grinned and nodded. Sergeant Panfilo looked daggers at both of them, but the singing was so loud, he couldn't prove they hadn't taken part. Tealdo did start singing again: lustily, in every sense of the word.

Parenzo, the Barian town nearest this stretch of the border with Algarve – no, nearest this stretch of the border with the rest of Algarve – lay a couple of miles south of the customs houses. Long before the regiment reached the town, people began streaming out of it toward them. Perhaps the fat Barian customs officer had used his crystal to let the baron in charge of the town know the reunion was now official. Or perhaps such news spread by magic less formal but no less effective than that by which crystals operated.

Whatever the reason, the road was lined with cheering, screaming men and women and children before the regiment got halfway to Parenzo. Some of the locals waved homemade Algarvian banners: homemade because Alardo had forbidden display or even possession of the Algarvian national colors in his realm while he lived. In the handful of days since the Duke's death, quite a few Barians had dyed white tunics and kilts with stripes of green and red.

The crowds didn't just line the road, either. In spite of Colonel Ombruno's indignant shouts, men dashed out to clasp the hands of the Algarvian soldiers and to kiss them on the cheeks, as he had done with the customs officers. Women ran out, too. They pressed flowers into the hands of the marching Algarvians, and national banners, too. And the kisses they gave were no mere pecks on the cheeks.

Tealdo did not want to let go of a sandy-haired beauty whose tunic and kilt, though of perfectly respectable cut, were woven of stuff so filmy, she might as well have been wearing nothing at all. "March!" Panfilo screamed at him. "You are a soldier of the Kingdom of Algarve. What will people think of you?"

"They will think I am a man, Sergeant, as well as a soldier," he replied with dignity. He gave the girl a last pat, then took a few steps double-time to resume his place in the ranks. He twirled his mustache as he went, in case the kisses had melted the wax out of it.

Because of such distractions, the two-mile march to Parenzo ended up taking twice as long as it should have. Colonel Ombruno went from apoplectic at the delay to placid when a statuesque woman in an outfit even more transparent than that of the girl who'd kissed Tealdo attached herself to him and showed no intention of letting go till she found a bed.

Trasone snickered. "The good colonel's wife will be furious if word of this ever gets back to her," he said.

"So will both his mistresses," Tealdo said. "The bold colonel is a man of parts – and I know the part he intends using tonight."

"The same one you do, once we billet ourselves in Parenzo," Trasone said.

"If I can find that same lady again – why not?" Tealdo asked. "Or even a different one."

A shadow flicked across his face, and then another. He craned his neck. A flight of dragons, their scaly hides painted red, green, and white, flew down from Algarve into Bari: one of many entering the Duchy, no doubt. High as they flew, the rhythmic whoosh of their wingbeats was easy to hear on the ground.

Tealdo made as if to clap his hands when the dragons flew past Parenzo. "Dragonfliers always get more than their share of women," he said. "For one thing, most of them are nobles. For another, they've got the lure of the beasts."

"Not fair," Trasone agreed.

"Not even close to fair," Tealdo said. "But if they don't land anywhere close to us, it doesn't matter."

In the town square of Parenzo, the local baron stood on a wooden rostrum. He had the intent look of a man who was either going to make a speech or run for the latrine. Tealdo knew which he would have preferred, but no one consulted him.

The speech, inevitably, was long and boring. It was also in the fast, clucking Barian dialect, so that Tealdo, who came from the foothills of northeastern Algarve, not far from the Jelgavan border, missed about one word every sentence. Duke Alardo had tried to make the Barian dialect into a language of its own, further sundering his people from the rest of Algarve. He'd evidently had some luck. But when the count led the regiment in singing the national hymn, he and King Mezentio's soldiers understood one another perfectly.

Colonel Ombruno ascended to the rostrum. "Noble Baron, I thank you for your gracious remarks." He looked out over the neat ranks of soldiers. "Men, I grant you permission to fraternize with your fellow countrymen of Parenzo, provided only that you return to this square for billeting before the chimes of midnight. For now – dismissed!"

He came down and slipped an arm around the waist of the woman in the filmy tunic and kilt. With whoops and cheers, the regiment dispersed. Tealdo did his share of backslapping and wrist clasping with his fellow countrymen, but that wasn't the only thing on his mind.

Having been blessed with a good sense of direction, he went

farther from the central square than did most of his comrades, thereby reducing his competition. When he walked into a cafe, he found himself the only soldier – indeed, the only customer – in the place. The serving girl was pretty, or even a little more than pretty. Her smile was friendly, or even a little more than friendly, as she came up to him. "What can I get you, hero?" she asked.

Tealdo glanced at the bill of fare on the wall. "We're not far from the sea," he answered, smiling back, "so how about the stewed eels with onions? And a yellow wine to go with them – and a glass for yourself, sweetheart, if you'd like one."

"I'd like one fine," she said. "And after supper, would you like to get your own eel stewed? I have a room upstairs." Her sigh was low and throaty. "It's so *good* to be in Algarve again, where we belong."

"I think it'll be good, coming into Bari," Tealdo said, and pulled the serving girl down on to his lap. Her arms twined around him. Suddenly, he didn't care whether he got supper or not.

Krasta peered into her closet, wondering what she had that was suitable to wear to a declaration of war. That problem had never before vexed the young marchioness, although her mother had surely had to make the same difficult choice at the outset of the Six Years' War, when Valmiera and her allies last sought to invade and subdue Algarve.

Her mouth thinned to a narrow line. She could not make up her mind. She picked up a bell and rang it. Let a servant figure out the permutations. That was what servants were for.

Bauska hurried in. She was wearing a sensible gray tunic and trousers: sensible and boring. "What shall I put on to go to the palace, Bauska?" Krasta asked. "Should I be cautious with a tunic, or show our grand Kaunian heritage by wearing trousers and blouse?" She sighed. "I really fancy a short tunic and kilt, but I don't suppose I can wear an Algarvian style when we're declaring war on that windbag, Mezentio."

"Not unless you care to be stoned through the streets of Priekule," Bauska replied.

"No, that wouldn't be good," Krasta said peevishly. She plucked a cinnamon-flavored sweet from a gold-chased bowl on the dresser and popped it into her mouth. "Now – what should I do?"

Not being a hereditary noble, Bauska had to make her wits work. She plucked at a loose wisp of pale hair – but not so pale as Krasta's – while she thought. At last, she said, "Tunic and trousers would show solidarity with Jelgava, and to some degree with Forthweg, though folk of Kaunian blood don't rule there—"

Krasta sniffed. "Kaunians in Forthweg bore me to tears, with their endless chatter about being oldest of the old."

"Those claims hold some truth, milady," Bauska said.

"I don't care," Krasta said. "I don't care at all. They're still dull."

"As you say, milady." Bauska held a finger in the air. "But tunic and trousers might offend the envoys from the islands of Sibiu and from Lagoas, for their ancestors have close ties to the ancestors of the Algarvians."

"They all spring from the same pack of barbarian dogs, you mean, even if some of them might be on our side now." Krasta barely refrained from boxing Bauska's ears. "You still haven't told me what I ought to wear!"

"You cannot know till you reach the palace whether or not you have made the perfect choice," her servant answered, mild as ever.

"It's not fair!" Krasta cried. "My brother doesn't have to worry about things like this. Why should I?"

"Lord Skarnu has no choice in his apparel because he wears King Gainibu's uniform," Bauska said. "I am sure he will make Valmiera proud of his brave service."

"I am sure I don't know what to put on, and you're no help at all," Krasta said. Bauska bowed her head. "Get out!" Krasta shouted, and the servant fled. That left Krasta alone with her choice. "I *can't* get good help," she fumed, taking gray wool trousers and a blue silk top from their hooks and putting them on.

She studied the effect in the mirror. It didn't satisfy her, but then very little satisfied her. A few pounds lighter, a couple of inches taller . . . and she probably would have remained dissatisfied, though she didn't think so. Grudgingly, she admitted to herself that the blue of her tunic set off the almost matching blue of her eyes. She belted the trousers with a rope of white gold and put a thinner rope around her neck. They played up the paleness of her hair.

She sighed. This would have to do. She went downstairs and called loudly for the carriage. Her estate had sat by the edge of Priekule for centuries, long before all the ley lines around the power point at the heart of the city were charted and exploited, and so stood near none of them. Even if it had, she would not have cared to ride a public caravan to the palace and subject herself to the stares of barmaids and booksellers and other vulgar, common folk.

She got more stares riding in the carriage, but she didn't have to notice those; they weren't so intimate as they would have been in the cramped confines of a caravan coach. The horses clopped along the cobblestones past square modern buildings of brick and glass (at which she sneered because they were modern); past others whose marble colonnades and painted statues imitated forms from the days of the Kaunian Empire (at which she sneered because they were imitations); past some a couple of hundred years old, when the ornate Algarvian architectural influence was strong (at which she sneered because they looked Algarvian); and past a few true Kaunian relics (at which she sneered because they were decrepit).

The carriage had just passed the famous Kaunian Column of Victory – now at last fully restored after fire damage during the Six Years' War – when a green-uniformed fellow held up a hand to bar the way. "What is the meaning of this?" Krasta demanded of her driver. "Never mind that oaf – go on through."

"Milady, I had better not," he answered cautiously.

She started to rage at him, but then the first Valmieran footsoldiers started tramping through the street from which she'd been barred. The river of men in dark green trousers and tunics seemed to take forever to flow past. "If I am late to the palace because of these soldiers, I shall be very unhappy – and so shall you," she told the driver, tapping her foot on the carpeted floor. She smiled to see him shiver; all her servants knew she meant what she said when she said things like that.

Great troops of horse cavalry and unicorn cavalry followed the infantrymen. Krasta curled her lip to see unicorns made as ugly as horses. And then she curled her lip again, for a squadron of behemoths followed the unicorns. They were ugly already, and thus did not need to be made so. Except for their horns – as long as those of the unicorns, but far thicker, and wickedly curved – they resembled nothing so much as great, hairy, thick-legged pigs. Their sole virtue was strength: each effortlessly carried not only several riders but also a heavy stick and a thick blanket of mail.

At last, men and beasts cleared the road. Without Krasta's having to say a word, the driver whipped the horses up into a gallop as soon as he could. The carriage shot through the narrow, winding streets of Priekule, almost mowing down a couple of women unwise enough to try to cross in front of it. They shrieked at Krasta. She angrily shouted back: had the carriage hit them, she might have been late to the palace.

As things were, she did arrive in good time. A bowing servant took charge of the carriage. Another helped her alight and said, "If milady the marchioness will be good enough to accompany me to the Grand Hall . . ."

"Thank you," Krasta said, words she seldom wasted on her own servitors. Here in the palace, though, she was not the ruler, nor even of more than slightly above middling rank. The gold and furs and splendid portraits of kings past reminded her of that. So did the princesses and duchesses who looked down their noses at her as she was accustomed to looking down on the rest of the world.

As soon as she saw a woman who outranked her wearing trousers, she relaxed: even if that proved a mistake, the duchess would get the blame, not she. But, in fact, more women in tunics looked nervous about their outfits than did women in trousers. Safe from censure, she let out a small, invisible sigh of relief.

Almost all the noblemen coming into the Grand Hall were in trousers and short tunics. Many of them were in uniform, with glittering badges showing both military and social rank. Krasta looked daggers at a man in a tunic and pleated kilt till she heard him speaking Valmieran with a rhythmic, trilling accent and realized he was the minister from Sibiu in his native costume.

A horn's clear note pierced the chatter. "Forth comes Gainibu III," a herald cried, "King of Valmiera and Emperor of the provinces and colonies across the seas. Give him great honor, as he deserves!"

Krasta rose from her seat and bowed very low, as did all the nobles and diplomats in the Great Hall. She remained standing till Gainibu had taken his place behind the podium at the front of the hall. Like so many of his nobles, he wore a uniform, the chest of which was almost hidden by a great profusion of medallions and ribbons. Some of those showed honorary affiliations. Some were true rewards for courage; while still Crown Prince, he had served with distinction against Algarve during the Six Years' War.

"Nobles and people of Valmiera," he said, while artists sketched his picture and scribes scribbled down his words for news sheets to reach the people whose villages were too poor and too far from a power point to boast even one crystal, "the Kingdom of Algarve, in willful violation of the terms of the Treaty of Tortush, has sent armed invaders into the sovereign Duchy of Bari. The Algarvian minister to Valmiera has stated that King Mezentio has no intention of withdrawing his men from the said Duchy, and has positively rejected my demand that Algarve do so. When this latest outrage is added to the many others Algarve has committed in recent years, it leaves me no choice but to declare that, from this moment forth, the Kingdom of Valmiera considers itself to be at war with the Kingdom of Algarve."

Along with the other nobles King Gainibu had summoned to the palace, Krasta applauded. "Victory! Victory! Victory!" The shout filled the Grand Hall, with occasional cries of "On to Trapani!" thrown in for good measure.

Gainibu held up his hand. Slowly, silence returned. Into it, he said, "Nor does Valmiera go to war alone. Our allies of old are our allies yet."

As if to prove as much, the minister from Jelgava came and stood beside the king. "We too are at war with Algarve," he said. Krasta understood his words with no trouble, though to her ear they had an odd accent: Jelgavan and Valmieran were so closely related, some reckoned them dialects rather than two separate languages.

The tunic the swarthy minister from Forthweg wore could not disguise his blocky build. Instead of Valmieran, he spoke in classical Kaunian: "Forthweg, free not least because of the courage of Valmiera and Jelgava, stands by her friends in bad times as well as good. We too war with Algarve." Formality fell from him like a mask. He abandoned the ancient tongue for the modern to roar, "On to Trapani!" The cheers were deafening.

"Bari in Algarvian hands is a dagger aimed at Sibiu's heart," the minister from the island nation said. "We shall also fight the common foe."

But the minister from Lagoas, which had been Valmiera's ally in the Six Years' War, stayed silent now. So did the slant-eyed envoy from Kuusamo, which ruled the eastern, and much larger, part of the island it shared with Lagoas. Lagoas was nervous about Kuusamo; Kuusamo was fighting a desultory naval war far to the east against Gyongyos – though not, strangely, in any real alliance with Unkerlant. The Unkerlanter minister also sat on his hands, as did the envoys from the minor powers between Unkerlant and Algarve.

Krasta hardly noticed the omissions. With her allies, Valmiera would surely punish the wicked Algarvians. They had brought the war on themselves – now let them see how they liked it. "On to Trapani!" she yelled.

Count Sabrino elbowed his way through the crowd in Trapani's Royal Square, toward the balcony from which King Mezentio would address the people and nobles of Algarve. He wanted to hear Mezentio's words with his own ears, not read them later on or, if he was lucky, catch them from a crystal some nearby sorcerer was holding.

People gave way before him, men with nods that would have to make do in the crush for bows, women, some of them, with inviting smiles. Those had nothing to do with his noble rank. They had everything to do with his tan uniform, with the three silver pips of a colonel on each shoulder strap, and, most of all, with the prominent Dragon Corps badge just above his heart.

Close by, a man with his mustache going from red to white spoke to a younger woman, perhaps a daughter, perhaps a mistress or new wife: "I was here, darling, right here, when King Dudone declared war on Unkerlant all those years ago."

"So was I," Sabrino said. He'd been a youth then, too young to fight until the Six Years' War had nearly run its course. "People were afraid then. Look now." He waved, ending with a typically flamboyant Algarvian twist of the wrist. "This might be a festival!"

"We're taking back our own this time, and everybody knows it," the older man said, and his female companion nodded vigorous agreement. Noticing the silver dragon coiled on Sabrino's chest, the man added, "And the greatest good luck to you in the air, sir. Powers above keep you safe."

"For which you have my thanks, poor though they be." Crush or no crush, Sabrino bowed to both the man and his lady before pressing on.

He brought a chunk of melon wrapped in a parchment-thin slice of ham from a vendor with an eye for the main chance, and advanced with only one elbow to clear his path while he ate. He hadn't come quite so far as he wanted when King Mezentio appeared on the balcony: a tall, lean man, his golden crown gleaming even more brightly in the noonday sun than his bald scalp would have.

"My friends, my countrymen, we are invaded!" he cried, and Sabrino, to his relief, found he had no trouble hearing. "All the Kaunian countries want to gnaw our bones. The Jelgavans are attacking us in the mountains, the Valmierans have swarmed out of the marquisate on this side of the Soretto they stole from us in the Treaty of Tortusso, and Forthweg's fierce cavalry sweeps over the plains in the northwest. Even Sibiu, our own blood kin, plunges the dagger into our back, assaulting our ships and burning our harbors. They think – they all think – we shall be meat for their butchering. My friends, my countrymen, what say you about that?"

"No!" Sabrino shouted it at the top of his lungs, along with everyone else. The roar was terrific, overpowering.

"No," Mezentio agreed. "We have done nothing but take back that which is rightfully ours. Even doing that, we were calm, we were reasonable. Did we war with the traitor Duke of Bari, Alardo the lickspittle? We had every reason to war with him, but we let him live out his long and worthless span of days. Only after the flames claimed his carcass did we reclaim the Duchy – and the people of Bari welcomed us with flowers and kisses and songs of joy. And for those songs of joy, we are plunged into a war we do not want.

"My friends, my countrymen, did we claim the Marquisate of Rivaroli, which Valmiera cut from the body of our kingdom after the Six Years' War for their foothold on this side of the Soretto? We did not. We do not, though King Gainibu's men mistreat the good Algarvians who live there. I thought no one could doubt the justice of our claim to Bari. It seems I was wrong.

"It seems I was wrong," Mezentio repeated, bringing his right fist down on the waist-high marble balustrade. "The Kaunians and their jackals sought any excuse for war, and now they think they have one. My countrymen, my friends, mark my words: if we lose this struggle, they will ruin us. Jelgava and Forthweg will join hands in the north across the corpse of our kingdom, cutting us off forevermore from the

Garelian Ocean. In the south, the Treaty of Tortusso gave barely a taste of what Valmiera and Sibiu, aye, and Lagoas, too, would do to us if only they could."

Sabrino frowned a little. Since the Lagoans had not declared war on Algarve, he would not have mentioned them. He did not for a moment think King Mezentio wrong about what Lagoas wanted, merely a trifle impolitic.

Mezentio went on, "As I speak here, our enemies burn our fields and farms and villages. Their dragons carry eggs of devastation and destruction and death to our towns and cities. My friends, my countrymen, shall we do what is in our poor power to throw them back?"

"Aye!" Again, Sabrino yelled as loud as he could. Again, he could hardly hear himself for the outcry around him.

"Valmiera has declared war on us. Jelgava has followed like a dog on a leash. Forthweg has declared war. So has Sibiu." This time, Mezentio raised his fist in the air. "They seek to chop us off at the knees. My friends, my countrymen, people of Algarve, here is my vow to you: *it shall not be!*"

Sabrino yelled yet again. He too pumped his fist in the air. A woman beside him stood up on tiptoe to kiss him on the cheek. He gathered her into his arms and made a proper job of the kiss.

King Mezentio held both hands high, palms out toward the crowd. After a little while, quiet returned. Into it, he spoke with simple determination: "We *shall* defend Algarve."

"Algarve! Algarve! Algarve!" The chant echoed through the square, through all of Trapani, and, Sabrino hoped, throughout the kingdom. Mezentio bowed stiffly from the waist, acknowledging in his own person the cheers for his kingdom. Then, with a final wave, he withdrew from the balcony. Sabrino saw one of his ministers come forward to clasp his wrist in congratulation.

"You'll help save us, Colonel," said the woman who'd kissed him.

"Milady, I shall do what I can," Sabrino answered. "And now, much as I would sooner linger with you" – she dropped him a curtsy for that – "I must go and do it."

The dragon farm lay well outside Trapani, so far outside that Sabrino had to take a horse-drawn carriage for the last leg of the journey, as no ley caravan reached such a distance from the power point at the heart of the capital. "Good of you to join us," said General Borso, the farm commandant, giving Sabrino a jaundiced stare.

"My lord, I am not tardy, not by my orders, and I had the honor of hearing with my own ears King Mezentio casting defiance in the face of all those who wrong Algarve," Sabrino said, respectfully defiant of higher authority.

Higher authority yielded, Borso saying, "Ah, my friend, in that case I envy you. Being confined here on duty, I heard him through the crystal. He spoke very well, I thought. The Kaunians and their friends would be wrong to take us lightly."

"That they would," Sabrino agreed. "The crystal is all very well when required, but everything in it is tiny and tinny. In person, the king was magnificent."

"Good, good." Borso bunched his fingertips and kissed them. "Splendid. If he was magnificent, we too must be magnificent, to live up to his example. In aid of which, my dear fellow, is your wing fully prepared for action?"

"My lord, you need have no doubts on that score," Sabrino said. "The fliers are in fine fettle, every one of them eager for duty. And we are well supplied with meat and brimstone and quicksilver for the dragons. My report of three days past goes into full detail on all these matters."

"Reports are all very well," Borso said, "but the impressions of the men who write them are better. And I have orders for you, since all is in such excellent readiness. You and your entire wing are ordered northwest to Gozzo, from which point you are to resist the invading Forthwegians with every power you command."

"Gozzo? If I remember the place rightly, it is a miserable excuse for a town," Sabrino said with a sigh. "Will they be able to keep us supplied there?"

"If they cannot, the count's head will roll, and so will the duke's, and so will the quartermaster's," Borso answered. "We are as ready for this war as we can be, I assure you of that."

"Our foes surround us," Sabrino said. "They tried to destroy us in the Six Years' War, and came too close to succeeding. We need to be ready, for we have always known they would try again."

He saluted the farm commandant, then went out to his wing. The dragons were tethered in long rows behind Borso's office. When they saw him, they hissed and raised their scaly crests – not in greeting, he knew, but in a dragonish mix of anger and alarm and hunger.

Some people romanticized unicorns, which were beautiful and quite bright as animals went. Some people romanticized horses, which were pretty stupid. And, sure as sure, some people romanticized dragons, which were not only stupid but vicious to boot. Sabrino chuckled. Nobody, as far as he knew, romanticized behemoths – and a good thing, too.

He shouted for an orderly. When the young subaltern came running up, Sabrino said, "Summon the men of my wing. We are ordered to Gozzo, to defend against the cursed Forthwegians, as soon as may be." The subaltern bowed and hurried away.

A moment later, a trumpeter blared out half a dozen harsh, imperative notes: the opening notes to the Algarvian national hymn. As he played them over and over again, men spilled from tan tents and ran, kilts flapping, to form an eight-by-eight square in front of Sabrino, four captains standing out ahead of it. The dragons hissed and moaned and spread their enormous wings. Stupid though they were, they'd learned an assembly meant they were likely to fly soon.

"It's war," Sabrino told the fliers in his wing. "We are ordered to Gozzo, to fight the Forthwegians. Is every man, is every beast, ready to depart within the hour?" A chorus of *Aye!* rang out, but one flier, misery on his face, raised a hand. Sabrino pointed to him. "Speak, Corbeo!"

"My lord," Corbeo said, "I regret to report that my dragon's torn wing membrane has not yet healed enough to let her fly." He hung his head in shame. "Had the war but waited another week—'

"It was not your fault, and it can't be helped," Sabrino said, adding, "Cheer up, man! A week's not such a long time. You'll see our share of action, never fear. They may even throw you aboard a fresh mount before then, if they decide they need trained fliers in a hurry."

Corbeo bowed. "May it be so, lord!"

Sabrino shook his head. "No, for that would show our beloved kingdom was in great danger. I hope you relax and drink wine and pinch the pretty girls till your dragon heals." Corbeo bowed again, grinning now. Pleased with himself, Sabrino addressed the whole wing: "Men, prepare to fly. My captains, to me."

One of the captains, Domiziano, asked the question Sabrino was about to address: "My lord, will we have force enough to turn back the invaders?"

"We must," Sabrino said simply. "Algarve depends on us. We yield as little ground as we can. Whatever we do" – he remembered Mezentio's words from the balcony – "we don't let Forthweg and Jelgava join hands. To block that, our lives mean nothing. Do you understand?" Domiziano and the other three squadron commanders nodded. Sabrino slapped each of them on the back. "Good. Splendid. And now we needs must ready ourselves as well."

When he was mounted at the join of his dragon's neck and shoulders, when he spurred the soft skin there and the beast sprang into the air, when the ground fell away beneath him and the dragon's wings thundered, he could understand for a moment why some people sighed over the great beasts. When the dragon twisted and tried to bite till he whacked it in the snout with a long-handled goad, he cursed those people, who knew nothing about real dragons, as a pack of fools.

The Elsung Mountains formed the land border between Unkerlant and Gyongyos. Precisely where they formed the border was a matter on which King Swemmel of Unkerlant and Ekrekek Arpad of Gyongyos had trouble agreeing. Because they had trouble agreeing, some thousands of young men from each of the two kingdoms were settling the question for them.

Leudast wished he were back on his farm, not far from the Forthwegian border, rather than sitting around a campfire here in the rock-strewn middle of nowhere. As far as he was concerned, Arpad was welcome to every one of these boulders if he was crazy enough to want them.

He didn't mention his opinion. Sergeants took a dim view of such sentiments. Officers took an even dimmer one. From what people said (whispered, actually), King Swemmel took the dimmest view of all. Having finally won the long civil war with his twin brother, Kyot, Swemmel thought anyone who disagreed with him a traitor. A lot of people had disappeared because Swemmel held that opinion. Leudast did not want to add his name to the list.

He leaned forward to toast a piece of sausage skewered on a stick over the fire. He twirled the stick between the palms of his hands to get the hard, peppery sausage done on all sides. His sergeant, a veteran named Magnulf, nodded approval, saying, "Very efficient, Leudast."

"Thank you, Sergeant." Leudast beamed. That was high praise. He'd never heard the word *efficiency* before the impressers pulled him off his farm and put him in a rock-gray uniform tunic, but King Swemmel was wild for it, which meant everyone beneath Swemmel was wild for it, too. Along with learning how to slaughter the foes of Unkerlant, Leudast had learned to mouth the phrases: "Time and motion – least and fewest."

"Least and fewest," Magnulf agreed around a mouthful of his own sausage. Leudast had a little trouble understanding him, but waiting to swallow would have been inefficient. Magnulf scratched his formidable nose – though it was less formidable than those of Leudast and half the other troopers in his squad – and went on, "The stinking Gongs are liable to try something tonight. That's what we hear from prisoners, anyhow."

Leudast wondered how they'd squeezed out the news. Efficiently, without a doubt. His stomach did a slow flipflop as he thought about how efficient interrogators could be.

One of his squadmates, a fellow named Wisgard who was slim by Unkerlanter standards, spoke up: "Back home, it would be midnight or so, and here the sun's barely down."

"We are a great kingdom." Magnulf thumped his broad chest with a big, thick-fingered fist. "And we are going to be a greater kingdom still, once we drive the Gongs off the mainland and over to the islands they've taken to infesting."

"That'd be easier if they hadn't stolen this stretch of land from us during the Twinkings War," a trooper named Berthar said.

"Proves how important efficiency is," Magnulf said. "A kingdom gets on fine with one king – that's efficient. Try to put two in the space meant for one, and everything goes to pieces."

That wasn't efficiency, not the way Leudast saw things. It was just common sense. If either Swemmel or Kyot had admitted he was the younger twin, Unkerlant would have been spared a lot of grief. Armies had marched and countermarched across Leudast's farm – it had been his father's then, for he'd been born just as the civil war was finally petering out – stealing what they could and burning a lot of what they couldn't. The countryside had been years recovering.

And now, when it finally had recovered, here was another war on the far frontier of the kingdom. For the life of him, Leudast couldn't see the efficiency of that. Again, though, he could see the inefficiency of saying so.

Captain Urgan came up to the fire and said, "Be alert, men. The Gyongyosians are planning something nasty."

"I've already warned them, sir," Magnulf said.

"Efficient," Urgan said crisply. "I have more news, too: over in the far east, all of Algarve's neighbors have jumped on her back."

"His Majesty was as efficient as all get-out to stand aside from that war," Magnulf said. "Let all those tall bastards kill each other."

"Forthwegians aren't tall bastards," Berthar said with fussy precision.

Magnulf gave him a glare undoubtedly practiced in front of a mirror. "They may not be tall bastards, but they're bastards just the same," the sergeant growled. "If they weren't bastards, they wouldn't have thrown off Unkerlanter suzerainty during the Twinkings War, now would they?"

His tone strongly suggested that giving any kind of answer would be inefficient. Berthar didn't need to be a first-rank mage to figure that out. He kept his mouth shut. Captain Urgan added, "And Forthweg has its own share of Kaunians. *They're* tall bastards, every bit as much as the lousy Algarvians."

Berthar did his best to look as if he'd never been so rash as to open his mouth. Leudast wouldn't have been so rash himself. He did ask, "Sir, any word on what the Gongs have in mind?"

"I'm afraid not," Urgan said. "I don't look for anything over-whelming, though – with so few ley lines charted in this powers-forsaken stretch of the world, and with even fewer properly improved, they have as much trouble moving men and supplies as we do. This isn't the most efficient war ever fought, but Gyongyos started it, so we've got to respond."

A brief hiss of cloven air was the only warning Leudast had before an egg burst about fifty yards from the campfire. The blast of light and heat from the energies it released knocked him off his feet and made him wonder if he'd been blinded: all he saw for a moment were purple smears in front of his eyes.

He did not need to hear the screech of a swooping dragon to know it would attack the men around the fire. Nor did he need to see it to know it would be able to see him if he stayed close by the flames. He rolled away, bumping over rocks and over little spiky-leafed mountain shrubs whose name he did not know: before the impressers took him away, he'd always been a man of the flatlands.

He saw the flame that burst from the dragon's jaw, saw it and smelled the brimstone reek, too. Somewhere behind him, Wisgard shrieked. A moment later, a pale, thin beam of light shot from the ground toward the dragon. Leudast wished he'd had his own stick slung on his back. Then he could have blazed at the enemy, too, instead of seeking only to hide.

But the Gyongyosians, like the folk of most other realms these days, were sly enough to silver their dragons' bellies and the undersides of their wings. The beam that would have burned a hole in man was harmlessly reflected away. The dragon belched forth fire again. Another scream arose. No one blazed back at the beast as it flew off to the west. The wind from its great wingbeats blew Leudast's hair all awry.

Blinking frantically, he scrambled toward the sticks. As he groped for his own, Magnulf and Berthar came crawling up. "Where's the captain?" Leudast asked.

"Back there, toasted like bread you forget over the fire," Magnulf answered. Somewhere west of them, someone kicked a rock. Magnulf cursed. "And here come the Gongs. Let's see how expensive we can make ourselves. Spread out — we don't want them getting around our flank."

Leudast scuttled toward a boulder fifteen or twenty feet away. A beam like the one poor Captain Urgan had aimed at the dragon zipped close to him, but did not strike. He dove behind the boulder, almost knocking the wind out of himself. Then, peering out into the night, he tried to find the spot from which the enemy had blazed at him.

The big disadvantage to using a stick at night was that, if you missed, the flash of light could tell the enemy where you were. If you were smart, you didn't stay there long. If you moved, though, you were liable to expose yourself, or to make some noise.

Leudast heard some noise off to his right: running footsteps. He whirled. Straight at him came a Gyongyosian trooper who must have noted the thud and clatter he'd made diving for cover. With a gasp, Leudast thrust his forefinger into the recess at the base of his stick.

As much by luck as by good aim, his beam caught the Gong square in the chest. Just for a moment, Leudast saw the enemy's broad, staring face, made animal-like – at least to a clean-shaven Unkerlanter – by a bushy yellow beard. The fellow let out a grunt, more of surprise than of pain, and toppled.

"The stick," Leudast muttered, and scurried over to grab it. He didn't know how much power his own had left. This far from a ley line, with no first-rank mage close by, when that power was gone, it was gone. Good to have a second stick handy.

He scowled at the Gyongyosian's body, from which rose a faint smell of burnt meat along with the latrine odor of suddenly loosed bowels. The bastard was already dead, sure as sure. A mage didn't have to be of the first rank to draw energy from a sacrifice. Soldiers who gave themselves up to power their comrades' sticks won the Star of Efficiency – posthumously, of course – but expending a captive was more efficient still.

It didn't matter, not here. For one thing, he had no captive, only a corpse. For another, no mages, first-rank or otherwise, were around. He crawled back behind his boulder and waited for the Gyongyosians to press the attack.

For several minutes, they didn't. Maybe they weren't sure how much damage the dragon attack had done. Or maybe they weren't any more enthusiastic about the war than Leudast was. He listened to somebody, presumably an officer, haranguing them in their unintelligible twittering language. Knowing what an Unkerlanter officer would say in such a spot, Leudast guessed the fellow was telling them they'd get worse from him than from their foes if they didn't start moving.

Here they came, the fuzzy bastards, some of them blazing, others darting forward while the rest made the Unkerlanters keep their heads down. Leudast popped up, took a couple of blazes with his beam, and then ducked again before the Gongs could puncture him as he'd punctured their trooper.

When he heard more of them getting around to his right, he fell back. A beam came horrifyingly close to him, lighting up a rock just in front of his face. But then he was in good cover again, and blazing back at the enemy.

And then, rather to his own surprise, more Unkerlanters came moving up from the rear, shouting King Swemmel's name as they advanced. The Gyongyosians shouted, too, in dismay. Their chance was gone, and they knew it. The reinforcements even had a small portable egg-tosser with them. How the Gongs howled when they were on the receiving end of eggshells full of light and fire!

"Forward, men!" an Unkerlanter officer shouted. "Let's drive them out of the mountains and into the flat. King Swemmel and efficiency!"

As far as Leudast was concerned, thinking a couple of platoons of soldiers could drive Gyongyos out of the Elsung Mountains wasn't very efficient. He lay panting behind his heap of rocks. He'd been in the mountains for a while. No overeager fool was going to get him killed, not when he'd just come through a skirmish in one piece. "Staying alive is efficient, too," he muttered, and sat tight.

Fernao stood at the bow of the *Leopardess* as she bounded north and west across the waves from Setubal, the capital of Lagoas, toward the Algarvian port of Feltre. The mage felt harassed. Not only did he have to bear in mind the pattern of ley lines on the sea – harder to read than they were on land – but he also had to be alert for any trace of Sibian warships, and perhaps for those of Valmiera, too.

Captain Rogelio came up to him. "Anything?" he asked.

"No, sir." Fernao shook his head, and felt the ponytail flip back and forth on his neck. Like most Lagoans, he was tall and on the lean side. In some lights, his hair was auburn; in others, a rich brown. His narrow eyes, with a fold of skin at the inner corners that made them look set at a slant, told of Kuusaman blood. "All seems as quiet as if we were still at peace."

Rogelio snorted. "Lagoas *is* at peace, I'll thank you to remember. It's all the other fools who've thrown the world into the fire." He twiddled at his mustache: he wore a big waxed swashbuckler, in Algarvian style.

"As if the world were at peace." Fernao accepted the correction; like any mage worth his salt, he craved precision. After a moment, he went on, "In the Six Years' War, we chose sides."

"And a whole great whacking lot of good it did us, too," the captain of the *Leopardess* said with another snort. "What did we get out of it? Thousands – tens, hundreds of thousands – dead, even more maimed, a war debt we're just now starting to get out from under, half our shipping sunk – and you want to do it again? Here's what I think of that." He spat – carefully, over the leeward rail.

"I never said I wanted to do it again," Fernao replied. "My older brother died in the woods in front of Priekule. I don't remember much about him; I was only six or seven. I lost an uncle – my mother's younger brother – and a cousin, and another cousin came home short a foot." He shrugged. "I know it's not anything special. Plenty of families in Lagoas have worse stories to tell. Too many families simply *aren't*, after the Six Years' War."

"*That's* the truth," Rogelio said with an emphatic nod. Everything he did was emphatic; he aped Algarvian style in more than his mustache. "So why do you sound so cursed glum about staying at peace, then?"

"I'm not glum about our staying at peace," Fernao said. "I'm glum about the rest of the world going back to war. All the kingdoms of eastern Derlavai suffered as much as we did."

"And Unkerlant," Rogelio put in. "Don't forget Unkerlant."

"Unkerlant *is* a kingdom of eastern Derlavai . . . in a manner of speaking," Fernao said with a thin smile. The smile soon slipped. "Thanks to the Twinkings War, they hurt themselves worse than Algarve ever managed, and Algarve hurt them plenty."

Rogelio's lip curled scornfully. "They were *efficient* at hurting themselves."

Fernao's chuckle had a bitter edge. "King Swemmel will make the Unkerlanters efficient about the time King Gainibu makes the Valmierans shy."

"But Gainibu has a little sense – as much as you can expect from a Valmieran, anyhow," Rogelio said. "He doesn't try to make his people into something they're not." The captain waved a hand. "There! You see, my friend? Between us, we've solved all the problems in the world."

"All but one: how to get the world to pay any attention to us," Fernao said. His sardonic streak made a good counter to Rogelio's extravagances.

When it came to running the *Leopardess*, though, the captain was all business. "If we are sailing an evasive course, my sorcerous friend, should we not be shifting ley lines soon?"

"If we really wanted an evasive course, we *would* sail, with canvas and masts, as they did in the days of the Kaunian Empire," Fernao said. "If we did that, we could slip by Sibiu close enough to spit, and we'd never be noticed."

"Oh, aye, no doubt," Rogelio said, arching his eyebrows. "And if a storm blew up at the wrong time, it'd fling us on to the Rocks of Cluj, too. No, thank you! They might have been men in those days, but they were madmen, if anybody wants to know what I think. Sailing by wind and by guess, without the earth's energy matrix to draw on? You'd have to be a madman to try that."

"No, just an ignorant man – or a yachtsman," Fernao said. "Not being either of those myself . . ." He drew from around his neck an amulet of lodestone and amber set in gold. Holding it between the palms of his hands, he felt of the energy flowing through the ley line along which the *Leopardess* cruised. He could not have put into words the sensation that passed through him, but he understood what it meant. "Three minutes, Captain, perhaps four, before our line intersects the next."

"Time enough for me to get to the wheel myself, then," Rogelio said. "That chucklehead of a helmsman we've got would likely be picking his nose or playing with himself when you signaled, and then we'd just keep barreling along, probably right down the Sibs' throats."

Without waiting for an answer, he hurried away. Fernao knew he was maligning the helmsman. He also knew Rogelio knew he was being outrageous, and that the captain always used the fellow with great courtesy when they were together. Extravagant Rogelio was; simple, no.

And then the mage forgot about Rogelio, forgot about everything but the sensation trickling out of the amulet and through him. He was not so much its interpreter as its conduit, in the same way that the ley line was a conduit for the energy the amulet sensed. He leaned a little as the trickle shifted, then thrust his right hand high into the air.

The *Leopardess* swung to starboard, the deck heeling under Fernao's feet. No mere sailing ship could have turned so sharply; the

motion was almost as if a geometer had scribed a right angle. Fernao
could not see the crossing of the ley lines, but he did not need to see
them. He had other senses.

As soon as he was sure the turn was good and true, he slid the
amulet's chain back over his head, returning the familiar weight to
where it normally rested, just above his heart. From the bridge,
Rogelio waved to him. He waved back. He took pride in what he
did, and in doing it well.

And then, suddenly, he frowned. He yanked out the amulet once
more and held it between his hands. He waved to the bridge again,
urgently this time. "Captain!" he shouted. "We're going to have
company."

"What's toward?" Rogelio shouted back, cupping his hands in
front of his mouth to make a megaphone.

"Quiver in the ley line, Captain – no, quivers." Fernao corrected
himself. "Two ships on this line, heading our way. Maybe an hour
out from us, maybe a little less."

Rogelio cursed. "They'll know we're here, too?" he demanded.

"Unless their mages are asleep, yes," Fernao answered.

More curses came from the captain of the *Leopardess*. Then he
grasped for a bright side to the unwelcome news. "They wouldn't by
any chance by Algarvian ships come to escort us into port?"

Fernao frowned once more; that hadn't occurred to him. He
concentrated on the amulet. "I don't *think* they're Algarvian," he said
at last, "but I can't be sure. Sibiu and Algarve use about the same ley
magic, not much different from ours. They aren't Valmierans; I'm
sure of that. Valmiera and Jelgava have their own style."

Rogelio came forward, to be able to talk without screaming.
"They're going to be Sibs, all right," he said. "Now life gets
interesting."

"We're neutrals," Fernao said. "Sibiu needs our trade more than
Algarve does: those islands don't come close to raising everything the
Sibians want. If they try to block us, they go under embargo. You'd
have to be a lackwit to think King Vitor would say something like
that without meaning it, and the Sibs aren't lackwits."

"They're in a war," Rogelio said. "You don't think straight when
you're in a war. Anyone who doesn't know that is a lackwit, too, my
dear mage."

"As may be." Fernao bowed with exquisite courtesy. "I tell you this, though, my dear captain: if Sibiu interferes very much with Lagoan shipping, Vitor won't just embargo them. He will go to war, and that fight is one Sibiu can't win."

"The Sibs against Algarve and us?" Rogelio pursed his lips, then nodded. "Well, you're right about that, though I'm hanged if I fancy the notion of allying with King Mezentio."

"We wouldn't be allies, just people with the same enemies," Fernao said. "Unkerlant and Kuusamo are both fighting the Gyongyos, but they aren't allies."

"Would *you* ally with the Unkerlanters? I'd almost sooner pucker up and kiss Mezentio's bald head," Rogelio returned. Then he bared his teeth in a horrible grimace. "If the Sibs could talk Kuusamo into jumping on our backs, though—"

"That won't happen," Fernao said, and hoped he was right. He had reason to think so, anyhow: "Kuusamo won't get into two wars at the same time."

Rogelio grunted. "Mm, maybe not. *I* wouldn't want to be in two wars at once. By the king's beard, I wouldn't even want to be in one war at once."

A hail from the crow's nest made him turn: "Two ships on the western horizon, sir! They look like Sibian frigates."

Rogelio dashed for the bridge. Fernao peered west. The lean shark shapes swelled rapidly: Sibian frigates sure enough, bristling with sticks and with egg-tossers whose glittering spheroids could disable a ship at a range of several miles. The *Leopardess* could neither fight them nor outrun them.

"Master mage, they're hailing us," Rogelio called. "You speak Sibian, don't you? Mine is foul, and the bastard I'm talking to doesn't know much Lagoan."

"Yes, I speak it." Fernao hurried toward the bridge. Sibian, Algarvian, and Lagoan were related tongues, but the first two were brothers, with Lagoan a distant cousin that had dropped inflections the others shared and borrowed words from both Kuusaman and the Kaunian languages. The mage stared into the *Leopardess*'s crystal at a man in a sea-green Sibian naval uniform. Fernao identified himself in Sibian, then asked, "Who are you, and what do you require?"

"I am Captain Propatriu of the *Impaler*, Royal Sibian Navy," the man replied, the words echoing from the glass. "You are to stop for boarding and inspection."

Rogelio shook his head when the mage translated. "No," Fernao said. "We are on our lawful occasions. You trifle with us at your peril."

"You are bound for Algarve," Captain Propatriu said. "We will search you."

"No," Fernao repeated. "King Vitor has ordered us to allow no interference with our commerce with *any* kingdom, on pain of embargo or worse against the violator. Can Sibiu afford that?"

"Stinking, arrogant Lagoans," Propatriu muttered. Fernao pretended not to hear. The Sibian naval officer gathered himself and spoke directly into the crystal once more: "You will wait." The polished gem went blank.

"What's he doing?" Rogelio asked.

"Calling home for instructions, unless I'm wrong," Fernao answered. If he *was* wrong, things were liable to get sticky in a hurry.

But Captain Propatriu reappeared in the crystal a couple of minutes later. "Pass on," he growled, looking and sounding as if he hated Lagoans. He added, "My curses go with you," and vanished once more. Rogelio and Fernao let out sighs of relief. The *Leopardess* slid between the two Sibian frigates and sped on toward Algarve.

2.

Hajjaj rode from King Shazli's palace to the Unkerlanter ministry in Bishah with all the eagerness of a man going to have a tooth pulled. He, like King Shazli, like all Zuwayzin with a barleycorn's weight of sense in their heads, regarded Zuwayza's immense southern neighbor with the wary attention any house cat might give a lion living next door.

The sun blazed down almost vertically from a blue enamel sky: Zuwayza projected farther north than any other kingdom of Derlavai. Despite that tropic brilliance, most of the men and women on the streets wore only sandals and broad-brimmed hats, with nothing in between. With their dark brown skins, they took even the fiercest sun in stride.

In deference to Unkerlanter sensibilities, Hajjaj had donned a cotton tunic that covered him from neck to knee. He'd never seen any sense to clothes till his first winter at the university in Trapani, before the Six Years' War broke out. He still didn't see any sense to them in Bishah's climate, but reckoned them part of the price he paid for being a diplomat.

Unkerlanter soldiers stood guard outside the ministry. They wore tunics, too, dull gray ones jarringly out of place in a city of whitewash and glowing golden sandstone. Sweat stained and darkened the tunics under the men's arms and across their chests. Though suffering in what was for them dreadful heat, they held themselves motionless – all but their eyes, which hungrily followed every pretty young Zuwayzi woman walking past. Hajjaj laughed, but only inside, where it did not show.

King Swemmel's minister to Zuwayza was a dour, middle-aged man named Ansovald. Maybe he had a magic that prevented sweat, or maybe he was just too stubborn to permit any such merely human failing. However he managed it, his tunic and his forehead remained dry.

"In the name of my king, I greet you," he said to Hajjaj after a servant had escorted the Zuwayzi foreign minister to his chamber. "That you are so punctual shows your efficiency."

"I thank you. And in the name of my king, I greet you in return," Hajjaj replied. He and Ansovald spoke Algarvian, in which they were both fluent. Hajjaj thought Swemmel would have been efficient to send to Bishah a minister who spoke Zuwayzi, but saying as much struck him as undiplomatic. He himself understood more of the Unkerlanter language than he let on. As would any Zuwayzi in similar circumstances, he thought, *I understand more Unkerlanter than I want.*

"Well, what is the point of this meeting?" Ansovald demanded.

Abrupt as an Unkerlanter was a common Zuwayzi phrase. Had Hajjaj been visiting one of his countrymen, they would have shared tea and wine and cakes and small talk before eventually getting down to business. Had Ansovald come to the palace, Hajjaj would also have gone through the leisurely rituals of hospitality, as much to annoy Swemmel's envoy as for the sake of form. Here, though, Unkerlanter rules prevailed. Hajjaj sighed, not quite invisibly.

"The point of this meeting, your Excellency, is to convey my sovereign's displeasure with recent provocations along the border between our two kingdoms," Hajjaj said. King Shazli was hopping mad and scared green, both at the same time. *Displeasure* suggested that as diplomatically as possible.

Ansovald's massive shoulders moved up and down in a shrug. "I deny that any such provocations have taken place," he said.

Hajjaj reached into a leather case and produced a short scroll. "Your Excellency, I have here a list of Zuwayzi border guards and soldiers killed, border guards and soldiers wounded, and Zuwayzi property on Zuwayzi territory destroyed during Unkerlanter incursions this season, and Unkerlanter buildings and encampments erected on land rightfully under the rule of King Shazli."

Ansovald read through the document – written, like most diplomatic correspondence, in classical Kaunian – and then shrugged again. "All of these alleged incidents took place on Unkerlanter soil," he said. "If anyone is the provocateur here, it is Zuwayza."

"Now really, your Excellency!" Hajjaj exclaimed, indignation overcoming diplomacy for a moment. He pointed to the map of

Zuwayza on the wall behind Ansovald. "Please look again. Some of these incidents occurred as much as ten or fifteen miles north of the border between our two kingdoms established by the Treaty of Bludenz."

"Ah, the Treaty of Bludenz." Ansovald's smile was anything but pleasant. "Kyot the traitor dickered the Treaty of Bludenz with you Zuwayzin, thinking to be efficient: by not fighting your secession, he had more resources to use against King Swemmel. Much good it did him." The unpleasant smile got broader. "Why should King Swemmel pay the least heed to anything the traitor did?"

Hajjaj was no longer indignant. He was appalled. He briefly wondered whether Unkerlant would have been a more pleasant neighbor had Kyot won the Twinkings War. He doubted it: Unkerlanters, worse luck, were Unkerlanters. Speaking now with great care, he said, "King Swemmel has conformed to the terms of the Treaty of Bludenz since gaining sole rule over Unkerlant. You would not be here as his minister, your Excellency, did he not recognize Zuwayza as a free and independent kingdom. Would it be efficient for him to overturn a policy that has given him good results?"

Not even the phrase that seemed so magic to Unkerlanter ears swayed Swemmel's envoy. Shrugging yet again, Ansovald said, "What is efficient changes with circumstances. In any case, the protest you have conveyed from King Shazli is rejected. Have you anything more, or are we through?"

Even by Unkerlanter standards, that was brusque to the point of rudeness. "Please inform King Swemmel that we shall defend our borders," Hajjaj said as he rose to go. He added a parting blaze: "Our *legitimate* borders."

Ansovald yawned. Legitimacy did not concern him. Spitefully, Hajjaj wondered if it had concerned his father.

Outside on the street, the Zuwayzi foreign minister almost stripped off his tunic right there in front of the Unkerlanter ministry. That wouldn't have shown the stolid, sweating guards anything they wanted to see, but it would have relieved his feelings. Not without regret, he restrained himself. As he rode back to the palace, he morosely watched sweat darken the cotton.

Once at the palace – a building whose thick walls of mud brick helped fight the heat – he did pull the tunic off over his head. King Shazli's guardsmen grinned sympathetically as he sighed with relief. "Out of the funeral wrappings, eh, your Excellency?" one of them said, white teeth shining in his dark face.

"Even so." Hajjaj rolled the tunic into a ball and stuffed it into his case. The breeze felt sweet on his skin. He waved to one of Shazli's servitors. "Can his Majesty see me now? I'm just back from consulting with Ansovald of Unkerlant." Neither by word nor by expression did he imply the meeting with Ansovald had gone anything but well. That was no one's business but the sovereign's.

"Of course, your Excellency," the servant answered. "He has been awaiting your return."

Shazli received his foreign minister in a chamber off the throne room. Hajjaj bowed low to the king of Zuwayza, who, without his golden circlet of rank, might have been anyone: in the absence of clothes, status could be hard to gauge. Shazli was a medium-sized, rather pudgy man in his early thirties, a bit less than half Hajjaj's age. His father had regained Zuwayza's freedom; some generations before, an Unkerlanter army that forced its way through the desert to Bishah had brought the land into the muscular embrace of its larger neighbor.

A serving woman carried in a jar of wine, a teapot, and a plate of honey cakes fragrant with cinnamon. She was comely; Hajjaj admired her as he admired the elegant ivory figurines adorning the chamber, and with hardly more desire. Being habitual to Zuwayzin, nudity did not inflame them.

Drinking and eating and chatting with the king helped Hajjaj relax; the thudding urgency he'd felt while meeting with the Unkerlanter minister receded, at least a little. After a while, Shazli said, "And how badly did Ansovald hurry you today? Efficiency." He rolled his eyes to show what he thought of the term, or at least of the way the Unkerlanters used it.

"Your Majesty, I have never known worse," Hajjaj said with feeling. "Never. And he rejected your protest out of hand. *And* he did something no Unkerlanter has ever done before: he questioned the legitimacy of the Treaty of Bludenz."

The king hissed like a sand viper. "No, Unkerlant has never presumed to do that before," he agreed. "I mislike the omen."

"As do I, your Majesty, as do I," Hajjaj said. "Up till now, we have been lucky in our relations with the Unkerlanters. They suffered hideously in the Six Years' War and then, as if they were not satisfied, they warred among themselves. That gave your father of splendid memory the chance to remind them we still remembered how to be our own masters. Afterwards, they were busy picking up the pieces they themselves had dropped."

"And after that, for good measure, they marched straight into a senseless war with Gyongyos," King Shazli added. "Were King Swemmel half as efficient as he thinks he is, he would be twice as efficient as he truly is."

"Even so, your Majesty, and elegantly phrased." Hajjaj smiled and sipped at his wine. "Of course, Ekrekek Arpad also took advantage of Unkerlant's internecine strife to make his own realm grow at Swemmel's expense."

"And Swemmel has spent the last several years trying to take his revenge," Shazli said. His eyes narrowed; he looked very crafty indeed. "Now, I appreciate revenge as much as the next man — I could scarcely be a Zuwayzi did I not, eh? But a man who does not weigh what he spends against what he gets is a fool."

"Seen through King Swemmel's eyes, Gyongyos is not the only kingdom against which Unkerlant needs to be avenged," Hajjaj said. "I suppose that explains some of Ansovald's insolence." He started to take another sip of wine, but paused with the goblet halfway to his lips. "I should attune my crystal to that of the Gyongyosian minister. No. I should pay a call on Horthy myself."

"Why say you that?" King Shazli asked.

"Because, your Majesty, if Unkerlant is seeking to patch up a truce in the far west — or if King Swemmel has already patched up such a truce — we may be next on the list for a visit from our friends," Hajjaj replied. "I don't think even Swemmel is stupid enough to get into two wars at once. Should he abandon one . . ."

Shazli's eyes widened. "Will Horthy tell you?"

"I don't see why he shouldn't," Hajjaj said. "By the very nature of things, Gyongyos and Zuwayza can hardly be enemies. We are too far apart; all we have in common is a border with Unkerlant." He opened his leather case and took out the tunic he'd stuffed into it. With a martyred sigh, he donned the garment once more. "I'd better go now, your Majesty. I don't think this will wait."

Skarnu stood against a tree to ease himself. Since the tree was a few miles inside Algarve, the young Valmieran marquis consoled himself by thinking he was pissing on the enemies of his kingdom. He would have felt more consolation, though, had the invasion pushed farther and done more.

After buttoning his fly, he rejoined his company. His noble birth made him an officer. Till he was mobilized, he'd thought his noble birth also prepared him for command. He was certainly used to giving orders, even if he didn't enjoy it quite so much as his sister Krasta did. But he'd soon discovered the difference between giving orders in a mansion and giving them to soldiers: the former sort merely required obedience from the servants, while the latter also needed to make sense.

"Where now, Captain?" asked Raunu, the company's senior sergeant. He was senior enough to have a lot of silver threads in the gold of his hair, senior enough to have fought as a youth in the Six Years' War. But his father sold sausages for a living, so he was unlikely ever to rise above senior sergeant. If he resented that, he hid it very well.

After scratching his head, Skarnu pointed west and answered, "Forward to the edge of open country. If there are any more Algarvians lurking here in the woods, we need to flush them out." He scratched again. He itched all the time. He wondered if he was lousy. The idea made his flesh crawl, but he knew it could happen to soldiers in wartime.

Raunu considered, then nodded. "Aye, about the best thing we can do, I reckon." He turned Skarnu's notion into precise, cautious reality, ordering scouts ahead and to either side and sending the rest of the company forward by sections along three different game tracks.

In fact, as Skarnu had quickly realized, Raunu ran the company. He knew how to do the job, whereas Skarnu's presence, while ornamental, was anything but necessary. That had mortified the marquis, seeming an offense against both propriety and honor.

"Don't fret yourself about it, lord," Raunu had said when he broached the issue. "There's three kinds of noble officers. Some don't know anything and stay out of their sergeants' way. They're harmless.

Some don't know anything and give forth with all sorts of orders anyhow." He'd shuddered. "They're dangerous. And some don't know anything and try and learn. Give 'em time, and they're apt to make pretty fair soldiers."

Skarnu had never before heard such a blunt appraisal of his class. None of the servants back at his mansion would have dared speak to him thus. But he was not Raunu's master and employer; King Gainibu was. That made the sergeant's relationship with a noble also serving the king different from that of a cook or butler. Skarnu was doing his best to fall into the third class of officer. He hoped he was succeeding, but hadn't had the nerve to ask.

Now, stick at the ready, he paced along the gloomy track. The Algarvians hadn't offered much resistance at the border, falling back before the advancing Valmierans toward the line of forts they'd built about twenty miles inside their territory. The Duke of Klaipeda, who commanded the Valmierans, was exultant; he'd published an order of the day reading, "The enemy, beset by many foes, ingloriously flees before our triumphant advance. Soon he must either give battle on our terms or yield his land to our victorious arms."

That sounded splendid to Skarnu till he thought about it for a little while. If the Algarvians were ingloriously fleeing, why didn't the illustrious Duke of Klaipeda put more pressure on them? Skarnu knew himself to be imperfectly trained in the military arts. He hoped the same did not hold true for the illustrious duke.

A beam from a stick struck the trunk of an elm a couple of feet above his head. Steam spurted from the tree, smelling of hot sap. Though imperfectly trained in the military arts, Skarnu knew what to do when people started blazing at him: he threw himself flat and crawled on his belly toward some bushes by the side of the track. If the Algarvian couldn't see him, he couldn't shoot.

Another Valmieran went down, too, this one with a harsh cry of pain. From cover, Skarnu shouted, "Hunt the enemy down!" He got up into a crouch and then dashed forward, diving down on to his belly behind a stout pine.

Another beam slammed into the tree. Its resinous sap had a tangy odor very different from that of the elm. Skarnu was glad the woods were moist; the fight would have fired drier country. He peered up over the top of a gnarled root. Spying a bit of tan among green bushes, he stuck his finger into the stick's recess and blazed away at it.

The leaves the beam touched went sere and brown in an instant, as if winter had come all at once to that corner of the world. An Algarvian soldier had been hiding in those bushes, too. He let out a horrible cry in his ugly, trilling native tongue. Another Valmieran blazed at him from off to one side of Skarnu. That cry abruptly cut off.

"Come on, men!" Skarnu shouted. "Forward! King Gainibu and victory!"

"Gainibu!" his men shouted. They did not rush straight at the Algarvians lurking among the trees. Such headlong dash was all very well in an entertainment. In real war, it brought nothing but gruesome casualties. The Valmierans darted from tree to tree, from bush to rock, one group blazing to make the enemy keep his head down while another advanced.

A couple of soldiers went staggering back with wounds, one with an arm over the shoulder of a healthy comrade. One or two men went down and would not get up again. The rest, though, drove the Algarvians, who did not seem present in any great numbers, before them. Once, by the shouts – no, the screams – the fighting came to such close quarters that it went on with knives and reversed sticks rather than with beams, but that did not last long. Valmieran voices soon rang out in triumph.

Pushing forward as he did, paying more heed to what the enemy soldiers in tan kilts were trying to do than to exactly where he was, Skarnu was surprised when he burst out of the woods. He stood a moment, blinking in the bright afternoon sun that beat into his face. Ahead lay fields of barley and oats going from green to gold, and beyond them an Algarvian farming village. The sturdy buildings would have looked more picturesque had he not been able to make out Algarvian troops moving among them.

Algarvian troops rather closer by could make him out. One of them blazed at him from the cover of the growing grain. The beam went wide. Cursing, Skarnu ducked back among the trees. He went some little distance along the edge of the forest before peering out again. This time, he was careful to keep a screen of leaves and branches in front of his face.

As if by sorcery, Sergeant Raunu silently materialized beside him. "Wouldn't want to try crossing that without a lot of friends along," Raunu remarked in matter-of-fact tones. "Truth is, I wouldn't want to cross that even with a lot of friends along, but some of us might get to the other side if we did it like that."

Skarnu's voice was dry: "I hadn't planned on ordering us to cross those fields and seize that village."

"Powers above and powers below be praised," Raunu muttered.

Not knowing whether he was supposed to have heard him, Skarnu pretended he hadn't. He pulled a map out of a tunic pocket. "That should be the village of Bonorva," he said. "It's past those woods on the other wide that the Algarvians are supposed to have their main belt of fortifications."

Raunu nodded. "Aye, that makes sense, lord. The forts are too far back for us to fling eggs at 'em from our side of the border."

Skarnu whistled thoughtfully. That hadn't occurred to him. Raunu might be a sausage-seller's son, but he was no fool. Many Valmieran nobles assumed all those below them to be fools: Skarnu chuckled, thinking of his sister. He had less of that attitude in him, but he wasn't free of it, either.

"They'll have to bring everyone up for the assault on the forts," he said. "That will make taking Bonorva look like a walk in Two Rivers Park by comparison."

"It'll cost a deal of blood, all right," Raunu agreed. "I wonder how many who hit the forts from this side will make it through to the other."

"However many they are, they'll be in position to peel the shell off Algarve, the way you do with a plump lobster," Skarnu said.

"I wouldn't know about that, sir," Raunu said. "It's bread and sausage and fruit for the likes of me. But you can't peel anything if you *don't* get through. Anybody who fought in the Six Years' War would tell you that."

All of Valmiera's generals, like those of any other kingdom, were veterans of the war a generation earlier. But Skarnu was not thinking of other kingdoms; he was thinking of his own. "*That's* why we haven't pressed our attacks harder!" he exclaimed with the air of a man who'd had a revelation. "The commanders dread the casualties they'd cost."

"Commanders who don't dread casualties don't stay in command, either," Raunu said. "After a while, the troops won't stand any more. Jelgava had mutinies during the Six Years' War. The Unkerlanter armies that were fighting Algarve mutinied so they could go off and fight each other – Unkerlanters are fools, you ask me. And finally the Algarvians mutinied, too. That's what won the war for us, more than anything else."

It was history to Skarnu; Raunu had lived it. Skarnu said, "May they mutiny again, then. If they didn't want a war, they shouldn't have gone tramping into Bari."

"I suppose that's so, sir." Raunu sighed, then chuckled. "I'm an old soldier at heart, and I make no bones about it. I'd sooner be back in the barracks drinking beer than here in the middle of this powersforsaken country."

"Can't blame you for that, but when the king and his ministers order, we obey," Skarnu said, and the sergeant nodded. Skarnu withdrew deeper into the woods, then scribbled a note describing his company's position and called for a runner. When a man came up, Skarnu gave him the note and said, "Take this back to headquarters. If they plan on bringing reinforcements forward, hurry back to let me know. That will tell me whether to prepare another attack or to settle in and defend what we've gained here."

"Aye, sir – just as you say." The runner hurried off.

"The Algarvians will have something to say about whether we attack or defend, too, sir," Raunu observed, pointing west.

"Mm, that's true," Skarnu said, not altogether happily. "That's one reason I wish we'd pressed this opening attack harder: the better to impose our will on the enemy."

Raunu grunted. "The Algarvians have plenty of will of their own. I'm surprised they haven't tried imposing theirs on us."

"They're beset from four sides at once," Skarnu said. "Before long, they'll break somewhere." Raunu grunted again. A few minutes later, the runner came back with orders for Skarnu's men to consolidate their position. He obeyed, as he was obliged to obey. If he muttered under his breath, that was his business, and no one else's.

High above Vanai's head, a dragon screamed. She craned her neck, trying to find the tiny dot in the sky. At last, she did. The dragon was flying from west to east, which meant it belonged to Forthweg, not Algarve. Vanai waved, though the man aboard the dragon could not possibly have seen her.

Brivibas walked on for several steps before realizing she was no longer beside him. He looked back over his shoulder. "The work won't wait," he snapped, exasperated enough to speak Forthwegian instead of Kaunian without even knowing he'd done it.

"I am sorry, my grandfather." Vanai spoke Kaunian. Her grand-father would have given her much more of the rough side of his tongue if she'd made his slip. He was so confident of his inalterable Kaunianity, he could slip its bounds now and then. If anyone younger slipped, though, he would fret for days about dilution.

Vanai hurried to catch up with him. Her short, tight tunic and close-fitting trousers rubbed at her as she ran. She envied the Forthwegian girls her age their comfortable, loose-fitting long tunics. Such clothes suited Forthweg's warm, dry climate far better than what she wore. But the folk of the Kaunian Empire had worn short, tight tunics and trousers, and so their descendants perforce did likewise.

"My grandfather, are you certain you know where this old power point lay?" she asked after a long, sweaty while. "We've walked more than halfway to Gromheort, or so it seems."

"Say not Gromheort," Brivibas replied. "Say rather Jekabpils, the name the city knew in more glorious times." On he went, tireless for an old man: he had to be nearly sixty. To Vanai, at sixteen, that certainly seemed ancient.

Her grandfather took from the pack he wore on his back an instrument of his own design: two wings of gold leaf suspended inside a glass sphere by gold wire. He murmured words of command in a Kaunian dialect archaic even when the Empire was at its height.

One of the wings twitched. "Ah, good. This way," Brivibas said, and set off across a meadow, through an almond grove, and then into a nasty stretch of bushes and shrubs, most of which proved well equipped with spines and thorns. At last, after what seemed to Vanai far too long, he stopped. Both gold wings were fluttering, neither higher than the other. Brivibas beamed. "Here we are."

"Here we are," Vanai agreed in a hollow voice. She had her doubts anyone else had ever been here before. In lieu of stating them more openly, she asked, "Did the ancient Kaunians truly know of this place?"

"I believe they did," Brivibas answered. "The evidence from inscriptions at the King's University in Eoforwic strongly suggests they did. But, so far as I know, no one has yet performed the sorcery which alone can transform supposition into knowledge. That is why we are here."

"Yes, my grandfather," Vanai said resignedly. He was very good to her; he'd raised her since her parents had died in a wrecked caravan when she was hardly more than a baby. He'd given her a splendid education in both Kaunian and modern subjects. She found his work as an archaeological mage interesting, sometimes even fascinating. *If only he didn't treat me like nothing but an extra pair of hands when we're in the field*, she thought.

He set down his pack. With a sigh of relief, she did the same with hers. "Now, my granddaughter," Brivibas said, "if you would be good enough to fetch me the green medius stone, we may begin."

You may begin, you mean, Vanai thought. But she rummaged through the pack till she found the weathered green stone. "Here you are," she said, and handed it to him.

"Ah, thank you, my granddaughter. The medius stone, when properly activated, removes the blindness from our eyes and lets us see what otherwise could no longer be seen," Brivibas said. But, as he chanted, and as Vanai unobtrusively wiped her hands on her trousers – handling the stone irritated her skin – she wondered if, when the spell was complete, it would show only ancient thorn bushes as opposed to modern ones. No matter what the fluttering gold leaves declared, she doubted any power point had ever existed here.

Her mind was elsewhere, anyhow. When Brivibas paused between spells, she asked, "My grandfather, how can you so calmly investigate the past when all the world around you is going up in flames?"

Brivibas shrugged. "The world will do as it will do, regardless of whether I investigate or not. And so – why should I not learn what I can? Adding some small bits to the total of human knowledge may perhaps keep us from going up in flames, as you put it, some time in the future." His mouth twisted. "I would have hoped it had done so already, but no one sees all his hopes granted." After fiddling with the latitude screw and the leveling vernier on his portable sundial, he grunted softly. "And now, back to it."

And now, Vanai, shut your trap, she thought. But her grandfather was expert at what he did. She watched closely as he evoked power from a power point forgotten since the days of the Empire. *It was here after all*, she thought. And then, at his word of command, the scene before her suddenly shifted. She clapped her hands together: she was looking back at the long-vanished days when the Kaunian Empire stretched over a great part of northeastern Derlavai.

Naturally, Brivibas's use of power had summoned up the image of another time when power was used here. Vanai stared at ancient Kaunians. They went on about their business; they could not sense her or her grandfather. If she walked over the front edge of the stretch of cleared ground that had appeared before her, she wouldn't be able to turn around and see the other side of the scene from long ago. She would just see the scrub through which she'd trudged to get here.

The ancient Kaunians wore woolen trousers, baggier than hers; some had on tunics of wool, too, others of linen. Some of the tunics and trousers were undyed, some dark blue or muddy brown: no bright colors anywhere. Almost all the clothes were visibly dirty, and so were a fair number of the Kaunians. People who'd worked with archaeological magic tended to be less romantic about the glories of the past than the bulk of the populace.

Brivibas sketched the scene, rapidly and accurately. Skill with a pencil was part of fieldwork. "The men are wearing beards," he remarked, "and the women have their hair piled high on their heads with curls," he remarked. "From what period would that make this scene date?"

Vanai frowned as she thought. "About the reign of Verigas II," she replied at last.

Her grandfather beamed. "Very good! Yes, about two hundred years before the Algarvian Irruption – so-called – wrecked the Empire. Ah!" He readied a new leaf for sketching. "Here we have the action, I think."

Four Kaunian men carried in a woman who was lying on a litter. She looked not far from the point of death. A fifth man, in cleaner clothes than the litter-bearers, led a sheep after them. He drew a knife from his belt and tested the edge with his thumb. Evidently being satisfied, he turned so that his back was to the modern observers and began magic of his own.

Brivibas exclaimed in frustration: "I wanted to read his lips!"

After raising one hand to the sky and pointing with the other – the one holding the knife – to the power point, the ancient medical mage cut the sheep's throat. As blood poured down, the woman rose from the litter. She still seemed less than perfectly well, but far better than she had a moment before. As she was bowing to the man who had helped her, the scene faded away, to be replaced once more by modern underbrush.

"Even then, they knew life force helps make sorcery stronger," Vanai said in musing tones. "But they didn't know about ley lines: they still traveled on horseback and carried things in oxcarts."

"Our ancestors were splendid intuitive sorcerers," Brivibas said. "They had no true understanding of the mathematical relationships by which magic is harnessed though. Ley lines being a far more subtle phenomenon than power points, it is no wonder they failed either to discover them or to predict their existence." He muttered something in Forthwegian that sounded angry, then returned to Kaunian: "A pity I could not learn more of the healing spell that fellow used." With what looked like deliberate effort, he forced himself back toward calm. "At the very least, though, I can now definitively document this power point and its use in imperial times. And let us see what the learned Professor Frithstan thinks of *that*!" He held out his hands in appeal to Vanai: "I ask you, have Forthwegians any business meddling in Kaunian history?"

"My grandfather, they say it is also the history of Forthweg," she answered. "Some of them, from the books and journals I have read, are scholars to be respected."

"A few," Brivibas sniffed. "A handful. Most write for the greater glory of Forthweg, a subject, believe me, of scant intrinsic value."

He fumed all the way back to the village of Oyngestun, about ten miles west of Gromheort, where he and Vanai made their home. Only when he started tramping along the dusty main street of the village did he fall silent; Forthwegians in Oyngestun outnumbered people of Kaunian blood four or five to one, and failed to appreciate the way the elder folk looked down on them as barbarians.

Falling silent didn't always help. A shopkeeper came out to stand on the board sidewalk in front of his sleepy place of business and call, "Hey, old man, have fun playing with your shadows and ghosts?" He set hands on hips and laughed.

"Yes, thank you," Brivibas answered in reluctant Forthwegian. He stalked along stiff-backed, like a cat with ruffled dignity.

That only made the shopkeeper laugh louder. He reached out with one of his big, beefy hands, palm up, fingers spread and slightly hooked, as if he were about to grab Vanai's backside. Rude Forthwegian men – often a redundancy – enjoyed aiming that gesture at trousered women of Kaunian blood. Vanai ignored it so ostentatiously, the shopkeeper had to lean against the whitewashed plaster of his front wall to keep from falling over with what he reckoned mirth.

Fewer young Forthwegian louts were on the streets and cluttering the taverns of Oyngestun than would have been true a few weeks earlier, though: the army had summoned them to fight the Algarvians. King Penda had also taken a fair number of men of Kaunian blood from Oyngestun into his service. As long as they dwelt in his realm and had blood in their veins, he didn't care what sort of blood it was.

Brivibas's house was in the middle of the Kaunian section, on the west side of the village. Not all Kaunians in Oyngestun dwelt there, and a few Forthwegians lived among them, but for the most part each of the two peoples followed its own path through the world.

Here and there, the two folk did mix. When Vanai saw a tall, lean man with a dark beard or a fair-haired woman who was built like a brick, she pitied their Kaunian ancestors. In a village like Oyngestun, such mingling was rare. It was not common in Gromheort, either. In worldly – Brivibas called it decadent – Eoforwic, though, from what Vanai had heard, it was in some circles taken for granted.

"My grandfather," she said suddenly as they went inside, "you could be a scholar at the King's University, did you so choose. Why have you been content to stay here in Oyngestun all your days?"

Brivibas stopped so abruptly, she almost ran into him. "Why?" he said, perhaps as much to himself as to Vanai. After a considerable pause for thought, he went on, "Here, at least, I know the Forthwegians who dislike me because I have light hair. In the capital, I would ever be taken by surprise. Some surprises are delightful.

Some, like that one, I would sooner do without."

At first, Vanai thought that was the most foolish answer she'd ever heard. The longer she thought about it, though, the more sense it made.

All things considered, Istvan could have liked the island of Obuda. The weather was mild, or at least he thought so: having grown up in the domain of the Hetman of Zalaber in central Gyongyos, his standards of comparison were not stringent. The soil was rich – again, by his standards. He did not mind military discipline; his father had clouted him harder than his sergeant did. The Obudans were friendly, the women often delightfully so. They said they preferred Arpad, the Ekrekek of Gyongyos, to the Seven Princes of Kuusamo as their overlord.

When Istvan remarked on that in the barracks one morning, Sergeant Jokai laughed at him. "They're whores, is what they are," Jokai said. "Two years ago, before we bounced the Kuusamans off this rock, you'd better believe the natives were telling *them* how wonderful they were, too."

"It could be, I suppose," Istvan said.

"Could be, nothing – it is." Jokai spoke with great assurance. "And if those slant-eyed whoresons throw us off of here again, the Obudans'll tell 'em what great heroes they are. And if any of our boys didn't get away, they'll tell the Kuusamans where they're hiding."

Arguing with a sergeant wasn't smart, not unless you were fond of latrine detail. Istvan wasn't. He poured down his morning beer – that was brought from home, for the stuff the natives brewed wasn't fit to drink; it was, in his view, barely fit for removing varnish – and went outside.

The barracks lay just outside of Sorong, the biggest town on the island, which didn't boast more than three, plus a couple of smaller villages. Sorong was halfway up a hill the Obudans called Mount Sorong. That made Istvan want to laugh. If the natives ever saw a real mountain, like the ones that towered above his own home village, they'd take that name and throw it into the sea: the stubby little hill didn't come close to deserving it.

But, since it was the highest ground on Obuda, though, Istvan could see a long way from where he stood. Down below were small patches of timber and long stretches of wheat and barley fields and vegetable gardens. Out past them, the surf rolled up the beach, then slid back down again.

Istvan had never seen the ocean before he went into the army. Its immensity fascinated him. He could spy a couple of other islands, blue and misty in the distance. Otherwise, the water went on forever: or as far as his eye could reach, which amounted to the same thing. He was used to looking *up* if he wanted to see the sky, not straight out.

When he did look up, he spied a couple of dragons circling overhead, so high that, even with their enormous wingspans, they seemed only dots, midges seen at arm's length. They floated as high as any of the peaks serrating the skyline back home. Up there, the air got cold and thin. The fliers swaddled themselves in furs and leather, the way hunters did when they went after snow leopards or marauding mountain apes.

His reveries were rudely interrupted when Sergeant Jokai came out behind him. Sergeants were unlikely to know any other way to interrupt a reverie. "Time on your hands, eh?" Jokai said. "That's a shame. That's a crying shame. Why don't you go police the dragon pens? The scouts won't be back for a while, that's plain."

"Have a heart, Sergeant," Istvan pleaded.

He might as well have asked for the moon. "Go draw your leathers and go get to work," Jokai said implacably. He hated idleness in any form. Poor Istvan hadn't yet perfected the art of looking busy even when he wasn't.

Cursing under his breath, he went over to the dragon pens – at the prescribed brisk march, because Jokai was watching – and pulled on elbow-length leather gauntlets and leather shin protectors that fit over the tops of his shoes. He grabbed a rake and a broom and a pail.

Turul, the head dragonkeeper, chuckled as Istvan donned the protective gear. "And how did you win the prize?" he asked.

"I was breathing," Istvan answered bitterly.

Turul chuckled again. "Don't do too much of that while you're working, or you'll be sorry afterwards."

"I'm already sorry," Istvan said. All that did was make the dragon-keeper laugh louder than ever. Istvan himself was something less than amused. Mucking out after horses or unicorns was nasty, smelly work. Mucking out after dragons was nasty, smelly, dangerous work.

He shoveled dung and raked foul straw, doing his best not to let any of the fetid stuff – and it was far more fetid than what horses and unicorns produced – touch bare skin. The brimstone and quicksilver dragons ate along with their meat made their wastes not just odorous but corrosive. They also made their wastes toxic, for those who dealt with them over years. *Mad as a dragonkeeper* was a common expression, but not one Istvan had the nerve to use around Turul.

Istvan cursed when a couple of drops of dragon piss splashed up and caught him on the arm above the gauntlet. The stuff burned like acid. It *was* acid. He snatched up some clean straw from a corner of the pen and scrubbed it off. It left behind a nasty red welt.

A copper-skinned Obudan boy watched him, wide-eyed. Dragons fascinated the locals. Even wild ones were rare all through the long reach of islands between Kuusamo and the western mainland of Derlavai. None of the islanders had ever imagined taming them. That a man could ride one high into the heavens left the locals astonished and awed.

No matter how astonished and awed they were, Istvan didn't feel like being watched right now. He grabbed a ball of dragon dung with his gauntleted hand and made as if to throw it at the Obudan boy. The boy fled, shrieking with laughter.

Istvan laughed a little himself, some of his good humor restored. He brought the tools back to Turul and dumped the contents of the pails in a special slit trench that had been dug even farther away from the streams than the Gyongyosian soldiers' latrines. Then, with a sigh of relief, he stripped off the gauntlets and the shin protectors and hung those up, too.

He hadn't even started to walk away when he saw one of the scout dragons spiralling down toward a pen he had just cleaned. He shook his fist at the great beast. "If you shit in there again, you can clean it up yourself," he called. Turul thought that was pretty funny. Istvan didn't. He meant it from the bottom of his heart.

Down came the dragon, with a great fluttering of wings as it landed. The blast of wind from them almost knocked Istvan off his feet. The flier sprang off the beast's neck, secured its chain to the iron post in the center of the pen, and started to dash away. "Who set fire to your breeks?" Turul asked.

"We're going to have company," the flier answered, and pointed west. He said no more, but hurried away to give his superiors a detailed account of what kind of company and how soon.

Only one kind of company mattered, though: the Kuusamans. Several ley lines converged on Obuda. That was why Gyongyos and Kuusamo kept fighting over the island. The natives' sorcerers hadn't discovered ley lines. They sailed by wind and paddle; several fishing boats bobbed in the ocean off the island.

"If we weren't fighting the Unkerlanters, too, we'd kick Kuusamo hard enough to make the Seven Princes leave us alone," Istvan said hotly.

Turul shrugged. "If all seven of the Princes ever walked in the same line, they might do the same to us. Nobody's giving this war everything he had – and a good thing, too, says I."

Being young and from the back country, Istvan said, "Not bloody likely!"

"I'll bet the recruiters smiled when they got their hands on you." Turul smiled, too, but not altogether pleasantly.

Drums started thudding an alarm. Istvan forgot about the cynical dragonkeeper and ran to snatch up his stick and to assemble so an officer could send him to a battle station. He almost collided with several of his squadmates, who were also doing their best to seem seasoned soldiers. None of them had yet seen combat. Istvan was half eager, half terrified.

The Obudans had seen combat, even if they hadn't taken part in it. They had their own strong opinion on the subject, and showed it by fleeing the town of Sorong. Some ran up toward the top of Mt. Sorong, others just headed off into the woods. A few carried sacks of coarse native cloth stuffed with their belongings; most didn't bother, and took off with nothing but the robes on their backs.

"Have no fear, fierce warriors of Ekrekek Arpad!" Major Kisfaludy cried. Every tawny strand of his beard seemed to quiver from great emotion. "We have a surprise in store for the Kuusamans, if those little slant-eyed demons ever dare set foot on the soil of this island." His grin was both fierce and conspiratorial. "They can have no notion of how many dragons we've flown into Obuda since we took it back from them."

In his mind's eye, Istvan saw dragons dropping eggs around and then on Kuusaman ships that presumed to approach Obuda. He saw some of those ships burning and others fleeing east down the ley lines as fast as they could go. He joined the rest of the squad, the rest of the whole unit, in a rousing cheer.

"And now, down toward the beach," Major Kisfaludy said. "If any Kuusamans are lucky enough to land on Obuda, we shall drive them back into the sea."

Along with his comrades, Istvan cheered again. Wings thundered, off in the distance, as dragons hurled themselves and their fliers into the air. Istvan laughed to think of the dreadful surprise the enemy would get when flame and raw energy consumed them. If they were rash enough to set themselves against the will of Arpad the ekrekek, they deserved nothing better, not as far as he was concerned.

He trotted down a path through the woods toward the beach. At the edge of the trees, sheltered among logs and rocks, stood egg-tossers and their crews, also ready to rain fire down on any Kuusamans who reached land. Istvan waved to the crews, then filed into a trench.

After that, he had nothing to do but wait. He watched the dragons wing their way east against targets they could see, but which the bulge of the earth hid from his eyes. And then he watched in some surprise as dragons came out of the east toward those that had flown from Obuda. He scratched his head. Was a flight returning already?

Sergeant Jokai cursed horribly. At last, the curses cooled to coherence: "The slant-eyes have gone and loaded a ship full of dragons. Life just got uglier, aye, it did."

Sure enough, while some of the Gyongyosian dragons arrowed down toward whatever Kuusaman ships lay below Istvan's horizon, others wheeled in a dance of death with the enemy's fliers. When a couple of the great beasts flew back toward Obuda, neither Istvan nor anyone else on the ground knew whether or not to blaze at them.

One was plainly laboring, doing more gliding than stroking with its left wing. It crashed down on to the sand not twenty feet in front of Istvan, which let him see how badly that wing was burned. The bloodied flier, a Gyongyosian, staggered toward the trench. "We drove 'em back!" he called, and fell on his face.

A couple of soldiers ran out and scooped him up. Sergeant Jokai cursed again. "We drove 'em back this time," he said, "on account of we had a surprise to match their surprise, and because we spotted 'em early. But flying dragons off a ship! The Kuusaman bastards have gone and complicated the war, curse 'em to powerloss." Istvan was suddenly just as well pleased not to have received his initiation into combat, at least from the receiving end.

Pekka looked out at the students filing into the auditorium. It was hardly the biggest hall at Kajaani City College, but that did not dismay her. Theoretical sorcery, unlike the more practical applications of the art, was not a ley line to fame or riches. Without theoretical sorcery, though, no one would ever have realized ley lines existed, let alone figured out how to use them.

She set her hands on the lectern, took a deep breath, and began: before anything else, ritual. "Before the Kaunians came, we of Kuusamo were here. Before the Lagoans came, we of Kuusamo were here. After the Kaunians departed, we of Kuusamo were here. We of Kuusamo are here. After the Lagoans depart, we of Kuusamo shall be here."

Softly, her students repeated the unadorned but proud phrases. A couple of the students *were* of Kaunian blood, from Valmiera or Jelgava; another handful were Lagoans. Their inches and beaky features and yellow and auburn hair set them apart from the Kuusaman majority (though some who served the Seven Princes, especially from the eastern part of the realm, might almost have been Lagoans by looks). Regardless of their homelands, they joined in the ritual. If they refused, they did not attend Pekka's lectures.

"Mankind has used the energies manifested and released at power points since long before the beginning of recorded history," she began. Her students scribbled notes. Watching them amused her. Most of them took down everything she said, even when it was something they already knew. For those who advanced in the discipline, that would end. Theoretical sorcery was, after all, about the essential, not the accidental in which it was surrounded.

"Only improvements in both the theoretical underpinnings of sorcery and in sorcerous instrumentation have enabled us to advance beyond what was known in the days of the Kaunian Empire," Pekka went on. She held up an amulet of amber and lodestone, such as a mage might use at sea. "Please note that these phenomena have gone hand in hand. Improved instruments of magecraft had yielded new data, which, in turn, have forced improvements in theory, making it correspond more closely to observed reality. And new theory has also led to new instruments to exploit and expand upon it."

She turned and wrote on a large sheet of slate behind her the law of similarity – *similar causes produce similar effects* – and the law of contagion – *objects once in contact continue to influence each other at a distance*. Like her body, her script was small and precise and elegant.

One of the students in the front row muttered discontentedly to her benchmate: "What does she think we are, morons? They knew that much back in the Kaunian Empire."

Pekka nodded. "Yes, they did know the two laws back in the days of the Empire. Our own ancestors" – like her, the student was of Kuusaman blood – "knew them before the Kaunians crossed the Strait of Valmiera and came to our island. The ancestors of the Gyongyosians discovered them independently. Some of the savages in the distant jungles of equatorial Siaulia and on the island of the Great North Sea know them, too. Even the shaggy Ice People know them, though they may have learned them from us or from the folk of Derlavai."

The student looked as if she wished she'd never opened her mouth. In her place, Pekka would have wished the same thing. But wishes had no place in theoretical sorcery. Pekka resumed:

"What we have here is qualitative, not quantitative. The laws of similarity and contagion state *that* these effects occur, but not *how* they occur or *to what degree* they occur. That is what we shall be contemplating during the rest of the term."

She covered the sheet of slate with symbols and numbers a couple of times before the lecture ended, pausing to use an old wool rag to wipe it clean before cluttering it once more. When she dismissed the students, one of them came up to her, bowed, and asked, "Mistress Pekka, could you not have cleansed the slate by magecraft instead of bothering with that rag?"

"A mage with a stronger practical bent than mine would have had an easier time of it, but yes, I could have done that." Pekka hid most of her amusement; she got this sort of question about every other term. She could see the followup gleaming in the young man's eyes, and forestalled it: "I use the rag instead of magic because using the rag is easier than any magic I could make. One thing a mage must learn is, that he *can* do something does not necessarily mean he *should* do it."

He stared at her, his eyes as wide as a Kuusaman's could be, nothing but incomprehension on his face. "What's the point of magic, if not doing things?" he asked.

"Knowing what things to do?" Pekka suggested gently. No, the student did not understand; she could see as much. Perhaps he would begin to by the end of the term. Perhaps not, too. He was very young. And, being a man, he was likelier to think of limits as things to be overcome than to be respected.

He went off shaking his head. Pekka permitted herself a small smile. She dealt with a couple of other questions of smaller import, though ones more immediately urgent to the students asking them: matters of text and examinations. And then, as a new group of chattering young men and women began coming into the auditorium for the lecture on crystallography that followed hers, Pekka neatly tucked her notes into a small leather valise and left the hall.

The sun had come out while she was speaking, and puddles from the previous night's rain sparkled, sometimes dazzlingly. Even in summer, though, the sunlight had a watery quality to it. Kuusamo was a land of mists and fogs and drizzles, a land where the sky went from gray to grayish blue and back again, a land where the rich and brilliant greens of forest and meadow and hillside had to make up for the drabness overhead.

And they did. So everyone in Kuusamo proudly boasted. Pekka was no different from her countrymen in that. But, four or five years before – no, it had to be five, because the war with Gyongyos hadn't started – she'd taken a holiday on the famous golden beaches of northern Jelgava. Her skin, not far from golden itself, withstood the fierce sun better than the pale hides of the Jelgavans who toasted themselves on the sand. That was one of the memories she'd brought home to Kajaani. Another – and she could still call it up whenever she chose, as if she lay naked on the beach again – was the astonishing color of the sky. Passages of Kaunian poetry that had been obscure suddenly took on new meaning for her.

Here, though, such colors, such heat, were only memories. Kajaani, on the southern coast of Kuusamo, looked out across the

Narrow Sea southeast toward the land of the Ice People and straight
south toward the endless ice floes at the bottom of the world. Pekka
straightened her slim shoulders. She enjoyed remembering Jelgava.
She would not have wanted to live there. Kajaani was *home*.

That mattered very much to a Kuusaman. Picking her way around
the puddles, Pekka really noticed the buildings that more often just
formed the backdrop before which she played out her life. Most of
them were wooden: Kuusamo was a land of wide forests. Some of the
timber was stained, some pale with weathering. Very little was
painted, not on the outside; gaudy display was alien to her people.
The handful of brick buildings harmonized with the rest. They were
brown or yellow-brown or tan – no reds or oranges to jar the eyes.

"No," she said softly, but with no less pride than that, "we are no
branch from the Algarvic stem, nor the Kaunian, either. Let them
swagger and preen. We endure."

She hardly knew when she left the college grounds and went into
Kajaani itself. The people on the streets here were a little older, a little
more sober looking. The Lagoans and men from the Kaunian
countries who leavened the mix were more apt to be sailors than
students. Shops showed their wares, but the shopkeepers didn't rush
out, grab her by the arm, and try to drag her inside, as happened in
Jelgava. That would have been gaudy display, too.

A public caravan hummed by her, the wind of its passage ruffling
the rainwater in the gutters. The two coaches were also of wood,
with their roofs overhanging the windows to either side to ward
against the weather. In Lagoas or Sibiu, they would have been metal.
In Valmiera or Jelgava, they would have been painted to look like
marble, whatever they were made of.

Pekka paid a couple of coppers for a news sheet and walked along
reading it. She made a clucking noise of dismay when she saw that
the Gongs had thrown back the fleet trying to retake Obuda. Admiral
Risto was quoted as saying, "They had more dragons up their sleeve
than we expected. We'll regroup and have another go at them
sometime later."

Swemmel of Unkerlant would have had Risto's head for a failure
like that. The Naval Ministry issued a statement over the signature
of the Seven Princes expressing full confidence in the admiral.
Lopping off heads was not the Kuusaman style. Pekka wondered,

just for a moment, whether the war would have gone better if it had been.

In the war on the mainland of Derlavai, Valmiera and Jelgava and Forthweg all claimed smashing victories over the Algarvians. Algarve reported smashing victories over her foes, too. Somebody was lying. Pekka smiled wryly. Maybe everybody was lying.

She walked up into the hills that rose swiftly from the gray, booming sea. Gulls wheeled screeching, high overhead. A jay in a pine sapling screeched, too, on a different note. A bright yellow brimstone butterfly fluttered past. This time, genuine pleasure filled Pekka's smile. Butter-flies had only a brief stretch of summer to be on the wing, down here in Kajaani.

Pekka turned off the road and down a narrower one. Her sister and brother-in-law dwelt next door to her, in a weathered wooden house with tall pines behind. Elimaki opened the door when she saw Pekka coming up the walk. Pekka's son dodged past her and ran to his mother with a shout of glee.

She stooped down and took him in her arms. "Were you good for Aunt Elimaki, Uto?" she demanded, doing her imperfect best to sound severe. Uto nodded with grave four-year-old sincerity. Elimaki rolled her eyes, which surprised Pekka not at all.

Pekka took the egg of terror disguised as a small boy by the hand and led him to their own home, making sure he did nothing too drastic along the way. When she went inside, she said, "Try to keep the house halfway clean until your father comes home from the college." Leino, her husband, was also a mage. This term, his last lecture came several hours later than hers.

Uto promised. He always promised. A four-year-old's oaths were written on the wind. Pekka knew it. She took a duck from the rest crate. The Kaunians had developed that spell, and used it for paralyzing their foes – till both they and their neighbors found countermeasures for it. After that, it lay almost forgotten for centuries until, with greater understanding of exactly how it worked, modern researchers began applying it both to medicine and to preserving food. In the rest box, the plucked and gutted duck would have stayed fresh for many weeks.

Glazed with cranberry jam, it had just gone into the oven when something fell over with a crash. Pekka shut the oven door, splashed water on her hands, and hurried off to see what sort of atrocity Uto had committed this time.

Garivald was weeding – exactly what he was supposed to be doing – when King Swemmel's inspectors paid his village a visit. The inspectors wore rock-gray tunics, as if they were Unkerlanter soldiers, and strode along as if they were kings themselves. Garivald knew what he thought of that, but letting them know wouldn't have been efficient. Very much the reverse, in fact.

One of the inspectors was tall, the other short. But for that, they might have been stamped from the same mold. "You!" the tall one called to Garivald. "What's the harvest going to look like here?"

"Still a little too early to tell, sir," Garivald answered, as any man with an ounce – half an ounce – of sense would have done. Rain as the barley and rye were being gathered would be a disaster. It would be an even worse disaster than it might have otherwise, because the inspectors and their minions would cart off Swemmel's share no matter what, leaving the village to get by on the remainder, if there was any.

"Still a little too early to tell," the short one repeated. His accent said he came right out of Cottbus, the capital. In Garivald's ears, it was harsh and choppy, well suited to its arrogant possessor. Southerners weren't in such a big hurry when they opened their mouths. By talking slower, they made asses of themselves less often, too – or so they said when their overlords weren't around to hear.

"If this whole Duchy of Grelz were more efficient all the way around, we'd be better off," the tall one said.

If Swemmel's men, and Kyot's, hadn't burned about every third village in the Duchy of Grelz back around the time Garivald was born, Unkerlant would have been better off. Being efficient was hard without a roof over your head in a southern winter. It was even harder with your fields trampled and your livestock stolen or killed. Even now, a generation later, the effects lingered.

The short inspector glared at Garivald, who had stayed on his knees and so was easy to look down on. "Don't think you can cheat us by lying about how much you bring in, either," he snapped. "We have ways of knowing. We have ways of making cheaters sorry, too."

Garivald had to answer that. "I am only one farmer in this village,

sir," he said, genuine alarm in his voice now. He knew villages had
vanished off the face of the earth after trying to hold out on Cottbus:
that was the excuse King Swemmel's men used once the dirty work
was done, anyhow. He went on, "I have no way of knowing how
much the whole village will bring in. The only one who could even
guess would be Waddo, the firstman." He'd never liked Waddo, and
didn't care what the inspectors did to him.

They both laughed, nastily. "Oh, he knows what we can do," the
tall one said. "Never fret yourself about that. But we want to make
sure everyone else knows, too. That's efficient, that is." He folded his
arms across his chest. "Everybody needs to know King Swemmel's
will, not just that ugly lump of a Waddo."

"Aye, sir," Garivald said, more warmly than he'd expected. If
Swemmel's inspectors could see that Waddo was an ugly lump,
maybe they weren't asses after all. No. That, surely, gave them too
much credit. Maybe they weren't such dreadful asses after all.

"A lot of men in this village," the short one remarked. "A lot of
young men in this village." He jotted a note, then asked Garivald,
"When did the impressers last visit here?"

"Sir, I don't really recall, I'm afraid." The peasant plucked a weed
from the ground with altogether unnecessary violence.

"Inefficient." The inspectors spoke together. Garivald didn't
know whether they meant him or the impressers or both at once.
He hoped the village wouldn't have to try to bring in the harvest
with half the young men dragged into the army to go off and fight
Gyongyos. He hoped even more that he wouldn't be one of those
young men.

"Does this powersforsaken place boast a crystal?" the tall inspector
asked. "I didn't see one in your firstman's shack."

Waddo owned the finest house in the village. Garivald wished his
own were half so large. Waddo had even added on half a second story
to give some of his children rooms of their own. Everyone thought
that a citified luxury – everyone but the inspector, evidently. Garivald
answered, "Sir, we don't. We're a long way from the closest ley line,
and—'

'We know *that*," the short inspector broke in. "I'm so saddle-sore,
I can hardly walk." He rubbed at his left buttock.

And we like it just fine, Garivald thought. That was one reason impressers and inspectors didn't come round very often. Nobody hereabouts missed them. Nobody hereabouts missed anyone from Cottbus. In the olden days, the Duchy of Grelz – the Kingdom of Grelz, it had been then, till the Union of Thrones – had been the most important part of Unkerlant. Now the men from the hot, dusty north lorded it over their southern cousins. As far as Garivald was concerned, they could go away and never come back. Bandits, that's what they were, nothing but bandits.

He wondered if they were efficient bandits. If they happened to suffer unfortunate accidents, would anyone track them down and take the kind of revenge for which Swemmel had become all too famous? His shoulders worked in a large shrug. He didn't think the chance worth taking, worse luck. Odds were no one else in the village would, either.

The inspectors went off to inflict themselves on someone else. As Garivald kept on pulling weeds, he imagined their stems were the inspectors' necks. That sent him back to the village at the close of day in a better mood than he would have thought possible while the inspectors raked him over the coals.

He never thought to wonder what the place looked like to the men from the capital. To him, it was simply home: three or four lines of wooden houses with thatched roofs, and a blacksmith's shop and a couple of taverns among them. Chickens roamed the dirt streets, pecking at whatever they could find. A sow in a muddy wallow between two houses looked out at Garivald and grunted. Dogs and children roamed the streets, too, sometimes chasing chickens, sometimes one another. He swatted at a fly that landed on the back of his neck. A moment later, another one bit him in the arm.

In winter, the flies died. In winter, though, the livestock would stay in the house with him and his family. That kept the beasts warm, and helped keep him and his wife and his boy and baby girl warm, too. Winters in Grelz were not for the fainthearted.

Annore was chopping up parsnips and rhubarb and throwing them into a stewpot full of barley and groats when he came into the house. "I'll put in the blood sausages in a little while," she said. When she smiled, he still saw some of the pert good looks that had drawn him to her half a dozen years before. Most of the time, though, she just looked tired.

Garivald understood that; he was bone-weary himself. "Any beer left in the bucket?" he asked.

"Plenty." Annore tapped it with her sandal. "Dip me up a mug, too, will you?" When her husband did, she murmured a word of thanks. Then she said, "People say the inspectors were buzzing around you out in the fields." The words came out with the usual mixture of hate and fear — and, as usual, fear predominated.

But Garivald shrugged his broad shoulders. "It wasn't too bad. They were being efficient" — he laced the catchword with scorn — " so they didn't spend too much of their precious time on me." He raised his wooden mug of beer to his lips and took a long pull. After wiping his upper lip on his sleeve, he went on, "The one bad part was when they asked if the impressers had been through this part of the Duchy any time lately."

"What did you tell them?" Annore asked. Yes, fear predominated.

He shrugged again. "Told 'em I didn't know. They can't prove I'm lying, so that looked like the efficient thing to do." Now he laughed at King Swemmel's favorite term — but softly, lest anyone but his wife hear.

Slowly, Annore nodded. "I don't see any better choices," she said. "But not all inspectors are fools, even if they are bastards. They're liable to figure out that *I don't know* means *haven't seen 'em for years*. If they do . . ."

If they did, sergeants would teach a lot of young men from the village the arcane mysteries of marching and countermarching. Garivald knew he was liable — no, likely — to be one of them. He'd been too young the last time the impressers came through. He wouldn't be too young now. They'd give him a stick and tell him to blaze away for the glory of King Swemmel, which mattered to him not in the least. The Gyongyosians had sticks, too, and were in the habit of blazing back. He didn't want to go to the edge of the world to fight them. He didn't want to go anywhere. All he wanted was to stay with his family and bring in the harvest.

His daughter Leuba woke up and started to cry. Annore scooped her out of the cradle, then slid an arm out of her tunic, bared a breast, and put the baby on it. "You'll have to chop the sausage," she said above Leuba's avid gulping noises.

"All right," Garivald replied, and he did. He almost chopped off his finger a couple of times, too, because he paid as much attention to his wife's breast as to what he was supposed to be doing. Annore noticed, and stuck out her tongue at him. They both laughed. Leuba tried to laugh, too, but didn't want to stop nursing while she did it. She coughed and choked and sprayed milk out her nose.

When the smell of the vegetables and blood sausage made his stomach growl more fiercely than any inspector from Cottbus, Garivald went to the door and shouted for his son Syrivald to come in and eat supper. Syrivald came. He was covered in mud and dirt, and all the more cheerful because of it, as any five-year-old boy would have been. "I could eat a bear," he announced.

"We haven't got a bear," Annore told him. "You'll eat what we give you." And so Syrivald did, from a child-sized wooden bowl, a smaller copy of the one from which his parents spooned up supper. Annore gave Leuba little bits of barley and groats and sausage on the top of her spoon. The baby was just learning to eat things that weren't milk, and seemed intent on trying to get as messy as her big brother.

The sun went down about the time they finished supper. Annore did a little cleaning up by the light of a lamp that smelled of the lard it burned. Syrivald started yawning. He lay down on a bench against the wall and went to sleep. Annore nursed Leuba once more, then laid her in the cradle.

Before his wife could set her tunic to rights, Garivald cupped in his hand the breast at which the baby had been feeding. "Don't you think of anything else?" Annore asked.

"What should I think of, the impressers?" Garivald retorted. "This is better." He drew her to him. Presently, it was a great deal better. By the moans she tried to muffle, Annore thought so, too. She fell asleep very quickly. Garivald stayed awake longer. He did think of the impressers, whether he wanted to or not.

3.

Bembo had never seen so many stars in the sky above Tricarico. But, as the constable paced through the dark streets of his home town, he did not watch the heavens for the sake of diamonds and the occasional sapphire or ruby strewn across black velvet. He kept a wary eye peeled for the swift-moving shapes of Jelgavan dragons blotting out those jewels.

Tricarico lay not far below the foothills of the Bradano Mountains, whose peaks formed the border between Algarve and Jelgava. Every so often, Bembo could spy flashes of light – momentary stars – in the mountains on the eastern horizon: the soldiers of his kingdom and the Jelgavans blazing away at one another. The Jelgavans, so far, had not pushed their way through the foothills and down on to the southern Algarvian plain. Bembo was glad of that; he'd expected worse.

He'd also expected the Jelgavans to send more dragons over Tricarico than they had. He'd been a boy during the Six Years' War, and vividly remembered the terror dropped eggs had spawned. There hadn't been so many then, but even a few were plenty and to spare. Jelgava's dragon farms had bee anything but idle since.

A caravan hummed slowly past, sliding a couple of feet above the ground along its ley line. The lamps at the front of the coach had dark cloth wrapped around them so they gave out only a little light: with luck, too little to be spotted by Jelgavan dragonfliers high in the air.

The caravan steersman doffed his plumed hat to Bembo. Bembo swept off his own to return the compliment. He smiled a little as he set the hat back on his head. Even in wartime, the courtesies that made Algarvian life endured.

When he rounded a corner, the smile disappeared. A wineshop was not so securely shuttered as it might have been; light spilled out through the slats to puddle on the pavement. Bembo took the club off his belt and whacked the door with it. "Close up in there!" he called. A moment later, after a couple of startled exclamations, the shutters creaked as someone adjusted them. The betraying light disappeared. Nodding in satisfaction, Bembo walked on.

A Kaunian column of pale marble gleamed even by starlight. In ancient days, Tricarico, like a lot of northern Algarve, had belonged to the Kaunian Empire. Monuments lingered. So did occasional heads of blond hair among the red- and auburn- and sandy-haired majority. Bembo would just as soon have shipped blonds and monuments alike over the Bradano Mountains. The Jelgavans thought they gave a kingdom of Kaunian blood a claim to what Kaunians had once ruled.

A woman leaned against the column. Her legs gleamed like its marble; her kilt was very short, scarcely covering the swell of her buttocks. "Hello, sweetheart," she called, peering toward Bembo as he approached. "Feel like a good time tonight?"

"Hello, Fiametta," the constable said, lifting his hat. "Go peddle it somewhere else, or I'll have to notice you're here."

Fiametta cursed in disgust. "All this dark is terrible for business," she complained. "The men can't find me—"

"Oh, I bet they can," he said. He'd let her bribe him with her body a time or two, in the easy-going days before the war.

She snorted. "And when somebody does find me, who is it? A constable! Even if you want me, you won't pay for it."

"Not with money," Bembo allowed, "but you're out here on the job, not sitting in Reform sewing tunics or something."

"Reform would pay me better than this – and I'd meet more interesting people, too," Fiametta came over and kissed Bembo on the end of his long, straight nose. Then she flounced off, putting everything she had into it, and she had quite a lot. Over her shoulder, she called, "See? I'm going somewhere else."

Somewhere else was probably no farther than the other side of the column, but Bembo didn't follow her. She'd done what he'd told her, after all. One of these days, he might feel like telling her to do something different again.

He turned on to a side street, one with houses and apartment houses on it, not shops and offices. Once or twice every block, he had to rap on a window sill or a doorway and shout for people to let lamps die or cover their windows better. Everyone in Tricarico surely knew the new regulations, but every Algarvian was born thinking regulations applied to the other fellow, not to him. A rotund man, Bembo fumed when he had to trudge up to the fourth floor of an apartment house to get some fool to draw his curtains.

When he came out of the apartment house, someone disappeared down the dark street with remarkable haste. Bembo thought about running after the footpad or whatever he was, but not for long. With his belly, he wouldn't have had a prayer of catching him.

He came up to another house with a hand's breadth of open space between the edges of the curtains. He raised his club to whack the sill, then froze, as if suddenly turned to stone. Inside, a pretty young woman was getting out of her clothes and into a loose kilt and tunic for the night.

Bembo had never felt so torn. As a man, he wanted to say nothing and keep watching: the more he saw of her, the better she looked. As a constable, though, he had his duty. He waited till she was sliding the night tunic down over herself before he rapped the wall and called, "Darken this house!" The woman jumped and squeaked. The lamp died. Bembo strode on. Duty had triumphed – and he'd had a good peek.

He used the club several more times – though never so entertainingly – before emerging on to the Avenue of Duchess Matalista, a broad street full of fancy shops, barristers' offices, and the sort of dining establishments the nobility and rich commoners patronized. When he saw light leaking from places like those, he had to be more polite with his warnings. If a baron or a well-connected restaurateur complained about him, he'd end up on permanent night duty in the nasty part of town.

He had just asked – asked! it graveled a proud man – a jeweler to close his curtains tighter when a hiss in the air made him look up. He saw moving shadows against the stars. Before he could fill his lungs to shout, the egg he'd heard falling burst a couple of hundred yards behind him. Others crashed down all around Tricarico.

Bursts of light as their protective shells smashed sent shadows leaping crazily and chopped motion into herky-jerky bits. The bursts were shatteringly loud. Bembo clutched at his ears. Blasts of suddenly released energies knocked him off his feet. The pavement tore his bare knees.

Howling with pain, he scrambled up again and ran toward the nearest burst. The egg had come to earth on the Avenue of Duchess Matalista in front of an eatery where a supper for two cost about a week of Bembo's pay. It had blown a hole in the cobblestones and had blown in the front of the restaurant; he didn't know how the roof was staying up.

The egg had also blown in the front of the milliner's shop across the street, but Bembo didn't worry about that: the milliner's was closed and empty. Screaming, bleeding people came staggering out of the restaurant. A woman got down on her hands and knees and vomited an expensive meal into the gutter.

Fire was beginning to lick at the exposed roof timbers. Careless of that, Bembo dashed into the restaurant to help whoever hadn't managed to escape. Shards of glass crunched under his boots. That glass had been almost as deadly as the raw energy of the egg itself. The first person the flickering flames showed him had had his head almost sliced from his body by a great chunk that still glittered beside the corpse.

Someone farther in groaned. Bembo yanked up the table that pinned an old woman, stooped, got her arm around his shoulder, and half-dragged, half carried her out to the street. "You!" he snapped to the woman who'd thrown up. "Bandage this cut on her leg."

"With what?" she asked.

"Your kerchief, if you've got one. Your scarf there. Or cut cloth off her tunic or yours — you'll have a paring knife in your bag there, won't you?" Bembo turned to a couple of men who didn't look too badly hurt. "You and you — in there with me. She's not the only one left inside."

"What if the roof caves in?" one man asked.

"What if an egg falls on us?" the other added. More eggs *were* falling. Sticks bigger and heavier than a man could carry had been set up along some of Tricarico's ley lines. They blazed spears of light up into the sky at the Jelgavan dragons, but there weren't enough of them, not nearly enough.

That didn't matter, not to Bembo. "We'll be very unhappy," he answered. "Now come on, or I curse you for cowards."

"If you weren't a constable and immune, I'd call you out for that," growled the fellow who'd fretted about eggs.

"If you'd come without arguing, I wouldn't have had to say it,"
Bembo returned, and plunged back into the eatery without waiting
to see whether the two men would follow. They did; he heard them
kicking through the broken glass that covered the floor.

They worked manfully, once they got down to it. They and
Bembo dragged out customers and servitors and, from the kitchens,
a couple of cooks. As the flames began to take hold and the smoke
got thicker, Bembo had to make his last trip out crawling and
dragging a man after him. He couldn't breathe if he stood upright. He
could hardly breathe while he crawled; his lungs felt scorched and
filled with soot. The glass sliced the palms of his hands.

A horse-drawn pumper clattered up and began pouring water on
the flames. Hacking and spitting up lumps of thick black phlegm,
Bembo wished the crew could turn the hoses on the inside of his
chest.

They were fighting a losing battle here; the eatery was going to
burn. Before long, the crew realized as much. They began playing
water on the buildings to either side, neither of which had yet caught
fire. Maybe they wouldn't, now. Even if they didn't, though, the
water would damage whatever they held.

"I thank you, sir," the old woman Bembo had first rescued said
from the sidewalk.

He reached for his hat, only to discover he wasn't wearing it. It had
to be back in the eatery, which meant it was gone for good. Bembo
instead, he said, "Milady, it was my duty and" – another coughing
spasm cut off his words – "my duty and my honor."

"That's well said." The old woman – a noble, by her manners –
inclined her head to Bembo.

He bowed again. "Milady, I just hope we're giving the Jelgavans
worse than we're getting. The news sheets say we are. Every braggart
blabbing out of a crystal says we are, but how do we *know*? The
Jelgavans' news sheets are bound to be telling them they're beating
the stuffing out of us."

"How long have you been a constable, young fellow?" the woman
asked, a hint of amusement in her voice.

Bembo wondered what was funny. "Almost ten years, milady."

The old woman nodded. "That appears to be enough to have left
you a profoundly cynical man."

"Thank you," he said. She laughed out loud. For the life of him, he couldn't figure out why.

With the dawn, Talsu peered down from the Bratanu Mountains into Algarve. Smoke rose from the burning town of Tricarico. He smiled. His officers had assured him that Jelgava was doing far more damage to Algarve than the cowardly Algarvian air pirates were inflicting on his own kingdom.

His officers had also assured him that soon, very soon, Jelgava's ever-victorious forces would sweep out of the mountains and across the plains of Algarve. The Jelgavan army had visited fire and devastation on those plains in the last months of the Six Years' War. He saw no reason why Jelgava should not do the same thing again.

He saw no reason why Jelgava should not already have done it again, in fact. All of Algarve's neighbors hated her. All of them that mattered were at war against her. They were many. She was one, and beset from east and west and south. Why, then, were his countrymen not yet out of the mountains and racing to join hands with the Forthwegians? He scratched at his almost invisibly pale mustache, which he wore close-trimmed, not in any wild Algarvian style. It was a puzzlement.

A delicious smell distracted him. Turning his head, he saw Colonel Dzirnavu's servant carrying a covered silver tray toward the regimental commander's tent. "Ha, Vartu, what have you got there?" he asked.

"His lordship's breakfast – what else?" the servant answered.

Talsu made an exasperated noise. "I didn't think it was the chamber pot," he said. "What I meant was, what will the illustrious count enjoy for his breakfast?"

"Not much, if I'm any judge," Vartu said, rolling his eyes. "But if you mean, *What is he having for breakfast?* – I've got fresh-baked blueberry tarts here, and poached eggs and bacon on toasted bread with butter sauce poured over them, and some nice ripe cheese, and a muskmelon from by the seashore. And in the pot – not a chamber pot, mind you – is tea flavored with bergamot leaves."

"Stop!" Talsu held up a hand. "You're breaking my heart." His belly rumbled. "You're breaking my stomach, too," he added.

"See what you miss because the blood in your veins isn't blue enough?" Vartu said. "Red blood's good enough to spill for our dear Jelgava, so it is, but it won't get you a breakfast like this at the front, no indeed. And now I've got to get moving. If the hot stuff gets cold or the cold stuff warms up, the other thing his lordship will bite off is my head."

Neither soldier had spoken loudly; the colonel's tent lay only fifteen or twenty feet away. Vartu ducked inside. "Curse you, what took you so long?" Dzirnavu shouted. "Are you trying to starve me to death?"

"I humbly crave pardon, your lordship," Vartu answered, abject as a servant had to be in the face of a noble's wrath. Talsu jammed his own face against the brownish green sleeve of his uniform tunic so no one would hear him giggle. Dzirnavu was as round as a kickball. He looked as if he'd take years without food to starve to death.

With the regimental commander's breakfast attended to, the cooks could get around to feeding the rest of the soldiers. Talsu lined up with the other men in tunics and trousers of the same horse-dung color as his. When he finally got up to the kettles, he held out a tin plate and a wooden cup. One bored-looking cook plopped a ladleful of barley mush and a length of grayish sausage on the plate. Another poured sour beer into the cup.

"My favorites," Talsu said: "dead man's cock and what he pissed through it."

"Listen to the funny man," said one of the cooks, who'd probably heard the stale joke two or three times already. "Get out of here, funny man, before you end up wearing this pot."

"Your sweetheart's the one who knows about dead man's cock," the other cook put in.

"Your wife, you mean." Laughing, Talsu sat down on a rock, took the knife from his belt, and cut off a bite-sized chunk of sausage. It was greasy, and would have been flavorless except that it was heading toward stale. Along with the porridge, it filled his belly. That was the most he would say for it. He wondered if Colonel Dzirnavu had ever tasted what his men ate. He doubted it. If Dzirnavu tasted sausage like that, the Algarvians in Tricarico would hear him screaming.

Presently, the regimental commander deigned to emerge from the tent. With green-brown tunic and trousers stretched tight to cover his globular frame, with bejeweled medallions of nobility glittering on his chest, with rank badges shining from his shoulder straps, he resembled nothing so much as a heroic coconut. "My men!" he said, and the sagging flesh under his chin wobbled. "My men, you have not advanced far enough or fast enough to satisfy our most magnificent sovereign, his Radiant Splendor, King Donalitu V. Press ahead more bravely henceforward, that he may be more pleased with you."

One of Talsu's friends, a tall, skinny chap named Smilsu, murmured, "You don't suppose it's ever crossed the king's mind that one of the reasons we haven't gone farther and faster is that we've got Colonel Dzirnavu commanding, do you?"

"He's Count Dzirnavu, too, so what can you do?" Talsu answered. "The only thing that would happen if we moved fast against the Algarvians is that we'd leave him behind." He paused for a moment. "Might be the best thing that could happen to the regiment."

Smilsu snickered, hard enough to draw a glare from a sergeant. Talsu loathed sergeants and pitied them at the same time. They made themselves as hateful as possible to the men of their own estate under them, knowing all the while that the officers above them despised them for their low birth, and that, however heroically they might serve, they could not hope to become officers themselves.

Colonel Dzirnavu, perhaps exhausted at having addressed his soldiers, retreated behind canvas once more. Smilsu said, "You notice the king is displeased with us, not even with us and the colonel?"

"So it goes," Talsu said resignedly. "When we win the war, though, he'll be pleased with the colonel and then, if he happens to recollect, with us, too."

From inside the tent, Dzirnavu let out a bellow. Vartu hurried in to see what his master required. Then he hurried out again. When he returned, he was carrying a small, square bottle of dark green glass.

"What have you got there?" Talsu asked. He knew the answer, but wanted to see what Dzirnavu's servant would say.

Sure enough, Vartu had a word for it: "Restorative."

Talsu laughed. "Make sure he's good and restored, then. If he's back here snoring while the rest of us fight the Algarvians up ahead, we'll all be better off."

"No, no, no." Smilsu shook his head. "Just restore him enough to get him fighting mad, Vartu. I want to see him go charging between the rocks, straight at the Algarvians. They'll run like rabbits – like little fluffy bunnies they'll run. They won't have figured we'd be able to bring a behemoth through the mountains."

Vartu snickered. He almost dropped the dark green bottle, and had to make a desperate lunge for it. Fortunately for him, he caught it. Unfortunately for him, Colonel Dzirnavu chose that moment to bellow again: "Confound it, Vartu, you worthless turd, what are you doing out there, fiddling with yourself?"

"If you were fiddling with yourself, you'd be having more fun than you are now," Talsu told the servant. With a sigh, Vartu went off to deliver the therapeutic dose to his master.

"If he liked the illustrious count better, we couldn't talk to him the way we do," Smilsu said.

"If he liked the illustrious count better, we'd probably like the illustrious count better, too, and we wouldn't have to talk to him the way we do," Talsu said.

His friend chewed on that, then slowly nodded. "Some nobles do make good officers," Smilsu admitted. "If they didn't, we never would have won the Six Years' War, I don't suppose."

"I don't know about that," Talsu said. "I don't know about that at all. The Algarvians have noble officers, too."

"Heh." Smilsu shook a fist at Talsu. "Now look what you've gone and done, you lousy traitor."

"What are you talking about?" Talsu demanded.

"You've made me feel sorry for the stinking enemy, that's what." Smilsu paused, as if considering. "Not too sorry to blaze away at him and put him out of his misery, I guess. Maybe I won't have to report you after all."

Talsu started to say it would be softer back of the front than at it, but held his tongue. The dungeon cell waiting for anyone reported as a traitor would make the front feel like a palace. Worse things would happen to a traitor back there than to a soldier at the front, too.

By midafternoon, the regiment had taken possession of a little valley, in which nestled a village whose Algarvian inhabitants had fled, taking their sheep and goats and mules with them. Colonel Dzirnavu promptly established himself in the largest and most impressive house there.

His men, meanwhile, fanned out through the valley to make sure the Algarvians had not yielded it to set up an ambush. Talsu looked up at the higher ground to either side of the valley. "Hope they haven't got an egg-tosser or two stashed away up there," he remarked. "That sort of thing could ruin a night's sleep."

"That's not in our orders," one of his comrades said.

"Getting myself killed for no good reason isn't in my orders, either," Talsu retorted.

In the end, a couple of platoons did sweep the mountainside. Talsu made sure he got part of that duty, thinking, *If you want something done right, do it yourself.* But he soon discovered even the whole regiment couldn't have done the job right, not without working on it for a week. Near the valley floor, the mountainsides were covered with scrubby bushes. He might have walked past an Algarvian company and never known it. Farther up, tumbled rocks offered concealment almost equally good. The sweep found no one, but none of the Jelgavans – save possibly their captain, a pompous marquis – had any illusions about what that proved.

When Talsu got back to the village, he set out his bedroll as far from the handful of buildings as he could. He noted that Smilsu was doing the same thing not far away. The two men shared a wry look, shook their heads, and went on about the business of getting ready for the night.

Talsu woke up at every small noise, grabbing for his stick. No soldier who wanted to live to get old could afford to be a heavy sleeper. But he did not wake for the egg flying past till it slammed into the farming village. Three more followed in quick succession: not big, heavy, immensely potent ones, but the sort a crew might hurl with a light tosser a couple of men could break out and carry in and out with them on their backs.

They knocked down three houses and set several others afire. Talsu and his company went out into the fields to keep the Algarvians from getting close enough to blaze at their comrades, who labored to rescue the men trapped in the building the egg had wrecked. Looking back, Talsu saw the house Colonel Dzirnavu had taken as his own now burning merrily. He wondered whether or not he should hope the illustrious colonel had escaped.

Leofsig trudged east along a dirt road in northern Algarve, in the direction of the town of Gozzo. That was what his officers said, at any rate, and he was willing to take their word for it. The countryside looked much as it did back in Forthweg: ripening wheatfields, groves of almonds and olives and oranges and limes, villages full of houses built from whitewashed sun-dried brick with red tile roofs.

But the stench of war was in his nostrils, as it had not been around Gromheort. Smoke blew in little thin wisps, like dying fog: some of the wheatfields behind him were no longer worth admiring. And dead horses and cows and unicorns lay bloating by the roadside and scattered through the fields, adding their sickly-sweet reek to the sour sharpness of the smoke. Forthwegians and Algarvians lay bloating in the fields and by the roadside, too. Leofsig did his best not to think about that.

When he'd found himself included in King Penda's levy, he'd been proud, eager, to serve the king and the kingdom. Ealstan, his little brother, had been sick with jealousy at being too young to go off and smash the Algarvians himself. Having seen what went into smashing a foe – and how the foe could smash back – Leofsig would have been just as well pleased to return to Gromheort and help his father cast accounts the rest of his days.

What would please a soldier and what he got were not one and the same.

A trooper mounted on a brown-painted unicorn came trotting back toward the column of which Leofsig was a tiny part. He pointed over his shoulder, gesturing and shouting something Leofsig couldn't understand. The gestures were plain enough, though. Turning to the soldier on his left, Leofsig said, "Looks like the Algarvians are going to try to hold us in front of Gozzo."

"Aye, so it does," answered his squadmate, whose name was Beocca. Leofsig envied him his fine, thick beard. His own still had almost hairless patches on his cheeks and under his lower lip. When Beocca scratched his chin, as he did now, the hairs rustled under his fingers. "We've pushed 'em back before – otherwise, we wouldn't be here. We can do it again."

Before long, officers started shouting orders. The column deployed into skirmish lines. Along with his comrades, Leofsig tramped through the fields instead of between them. The grain went down under the feet of thousands of men almost as if cut by a reaper.

"One way or another, we'll make the redheads go hungry," Beocca said, stamping down the ripening grain with great relish. Leofsig, sweating in the hot sun, hadn't the energy to stamp. He just nodded and kept marching.

More shouts produced lanes between blocks of men. Unicorn and horse cavalry trotted forward to screen the footsoldiers who would do the bulk of the fighting. Forthwegian dragons flew overhead, some so high as to be only specks, others low enough to let Leofsig hear their shrill screeches.

"I hope they drop plenty of eggs on Gozzo," Beocca said.

"I hope they keep the Algarvians from dropping eggs on us," Leofsig added. After a moment, Beocca grunted agreement.

As the Forthwegians drew nearer to Gozzo, Leofsig kept cocking his head and looking up into the sky every so often. Even so, he was cautiously skirting a hedgerow when the Algarvian dragons came racing out of the east to challenge those of his kingdom.

The first he knew of the battle overhead was when a dragon fell out of the sky and smashed to earth a hundred yards or so in front of him. The great beast writhed in its death agony, throwing now its silvered belly, now its back – painted Forthwegian blue and white – uppermost. Its flier lay motionless, a small, crumpled heap, a few feet away. Flame spurted from the dragon's jaw, cremating the man who had taken it into action.

Leofsig looked up again: looked up and gasped in horror. He had seen very few Algarvian dragons till now. That had led him to believe the enemy had very few, or very few they could commit against the Forthwegians, at any rate. Since they were also fighting Jelgava and Valmiera and Sibiu, that made sense to him.

It might have made sense, but it proved untrue. Suddenly, two or three times the Forthwegians' numbers beset them. Dragons tumbled to earth, burned or even clawed by their foes. Most were marked in blue and white, not Algarvian green, red, and white. Other dragons, their fliers killed by an enemy's stick, either flew off at random or, mad with battle, struck out at friends and foes alike.

In what seemed the twinkling of an eye, the Forthwegian dragon-swarm was shattered. The remnant not sent spinning to their doom or flying wild without a man to guide them fled back toward Forthweg. They might fight another day. Against overwhelming odds, they would not fight above this field. Inside half an hour, Algarve, not Forthweg, ruled the skies.

Beocca made a rumbling noise, deep in his throat. "Now we're in for it," he said. Leofsig could only nod. The same thought, in the same words, had gone through his mind, too.

Most of the dragons that had driven off the Forthwegian swarm had flown without eggs, making them faster and more maneuverable in the air. Now still more flew in from the direction of Gozzo. Some of their fliers released their eggs from on high, as was the usual Forthwegian practice – the usual practice everywhere, so far as Leofsig knew.

But the enemy, with Algarvian panache, had also found a new way. Some of the Algarvian fliers made their dragons stoop on the Forthwegian forces below like a falcon stooping on a mouse. They loosed the eggs the dragons carried at what seemed hardly more than treetop height, then pulled out of their dives and flew away, no doubt laughing at their foes' discomfiture.

One of them, off to Leofsig's right, misjudged his dive and smashed into the ground. The egg he carried erupted, searing flier and dragon both in its burst of flame. "Serves you right!" Leofsig shouted, though the flier was far beyond hearing. But the Algarvian's swooping comrades kept on, placing their eggs far more precisely than did those who did not dive; they tore terrible holes in the Forthwegians' ranks.

"Forward!" an officer shouted. Leofsig heard him through stunned and battered ears. "We must go forward, for the honor of King Penda and of Forthweg!"

Forward Leofsig stumbled. Around him, men raised a cheer. After a moment, he joined it. Turning to Beocca, he said, "Once we close with the Algarvians, we'll crush them."

"Aye, belike," Beocca answered, "if there are any of us left to do the closing."

As if to underscore that, more eggs started falling among the advancing Forthwegians. Not all of them – not even most of them – came from the dragons overhead. The army had come into range of the egg-tossers outside Gozzo. Dragons carried larger eggs than the tossers flung, but could not carry nearly so many; Leofsig, head down and hunched forward as if walking into a windstorm, trudged past a broken-backed unicorn, one side of its body all over burns, that dragged itself along on its forelegs and screamed like a woman.

Forthwegian egg-tossers answered the rain of fire as best they could. But they'd had trouble keeping up with the rest of the army: horse-drawn wheeled tossers clogged roads and moved slowly going crosscountry, while the retreating Algarvians had sabotaged ley lines as they fell back. Forthwegian mages had reenergized some, but far from all. And, to make matters worse, the diving dragons paid special attention to the egg-tossers that were on the field.

Up ahead, Forthwegian cavalry was skirmishing with Algarvian troopers on horses and unicorns. Leofsig cheered when a Forthwegian officer's white unicorn gored an enemy horseman out of the saddle. He squatted down behind a bush and blazed at the Algarvian cavalry. The range was long, and he could not be sure his was the beam that did the job, but he thought he knocked a couple of redheads out of the saddle.

And then, when he blazed, no beam shot from the business end of the stick. He looked around for a supply cart, spied none, and then looked around for a casualty. On this field, casualties were all too easy to find. Leofsig scurried over to a Forthwegian who would never need his stick again. He snatched up the stick and dashed back to cover. An Algarvian beam drew a brown line in the grass ahead of him, but did not sear his flesh.

As more Forthwegian footsoldiers came forward to add their numbers to those of the cavalry, the Algarvian horsemen and unicorn riders began to fall back. Leofsig grunted in somber satisfaction as he advanced toward a large grove of orange trees. This skirmish, though bigger than most, fit the pattern of the fights that had followed Forthweg's invasion of Algarve. The Algarvians might have won the battle in the air, but they kept on yielding ground even so.

Under the shiny, dark green leaves of the orange trees, something stirred. Leofsig was too far away to blaze at the motion, too far away even to identify what caused it till a great force of behemoths came lumbering out of the grove. Their armor glittered in the sun. Each great beast bore several riders. Some behemoths had sticks larger and heavier and stronger than a man could carry strapped on to their backs. Others carried egg-tossers instead.

Forthweg used behemoths to help break into positions infantry could not take unaided, parceling the animals out along the whole broad fighting line. Leofsig had never seen so many all gathered together before. He did not like the look of them. He liked that look even less when they lowered their heads, pointing their great horns toward the Forthwegian force, and lumbered forward. They moved slowly at first, but soon built up speed.

They smashed through the Forthwegian cavalry as if it hadn't been there, trampling down horses and unicorns. As they charged, the crews of soldiers on their backs blazed and flung eggs, spreading havoc far and wide. The behemoths were hard to bring down. Their armor warded them against most blazes, and, while they were moving, the men on their backs – who, Leofsig saw, were also armored – were next to impossible to pick off.

The cavalry, or as much of it as could, fled before them, as the Forthwegian dragons had fled before those of Algarve. The Algarvian dragons now redoubled their attacks against the Forthwegians on the ground as the behemoths broke in among them. Leofsig blazed at the warriors aboard the closest one – blazed and missed. An egg burst close by him, knocking him off his feet and scraping his face against the dirt.

He scrambled up again. Algarvian footsoldiers were advancing now, rushing toward the great hole the behemoths had torn in the Forthwegian line. He saw an officer close by – not a man he knew, but an officer. "What do we do, sir?"

"What do we do?" the captain echoed. He looked and sounded stunned, bewildered. "We fall back – what else can we do? They've beaten us here, the bastards. We have to be able to try to fight them again, though how we're supposed to fight this—" Shaking his head, he stumbled off toward the west, toward Forthweg. Numbly, Leofsig followed.

Without false modesty, Marshal Rathar knew he was the second most powerful personage in Unkerlant. None of the dukes and barons and counts could come close to matching the authority of the man who headed King Swemmel's armies. None of the courtiers at Cottbus was his equal, either, and none of them had made the king believe Rathar a traitor, though many had tried.

Aye, below Swemmel he was supreme. Envy filled men's eyes as he marched through the fortresslike palace on the high ground at the heart of the capital. The green sash stretching diagonally across his rock-gray tunic proclaimed his rank to any who did not recognize his hard, stern features. Women the world called beautiful called those features handsome. He could have had many of them, including some whose courtier husbands sought to bring him down. Had he been able to judge with certainty which of them wanted him for himself, as opposed to for his rank, he might have enjoyed himself more.

Or he might not have. Enjoyment, as most men understood it, he did not find particularly enjoyable. And he knew a secret no one else did, though some of his own chief underlings and some of King Swemmel's other ministers might have suspected. He could have told the secret without danger. But he knew no one would believe him, and so kept silent. Silence suited his nature anyhow.

Before he went in to confer with his sovereign, he unbuckled his sword and set it in a rack in the anteroom outside the audience chamber. King Swemmel's guards then searched him, as thoroughly and intimately as if he'd been taken captive. Had he been a woman, matrons would have done the same.

He felt no humiliation. The guards were doing their duty. He would have been angry — and King Swemmel angrier — had they let him go through unchallenged. "Pass on, sir," one of them said at length.

Rathar spent another moment adjusting his tunic, then strode into the audience chamber. In the presence of the king of Unkerlant, his stern reserve crumbled. "Your Majesty!" he cried. "I rejoice to be allowed to come into your presence!" He cast himself down on his hands and knees, knocking his forehead against the strip of green carpet that led to the throne on which King Swemmel sat.

Any chair on which Swemmel sat was by definition a throne, since it contained the king's fundament. This one, while gilded, was far less spectacular than the bejeweled magnificence of the one of the Grand Hall of Kings (Rathar reckoned that one insufferably gaudy, another secret he held close).

"Rise, Marshal," Swemmel said. His voice was rather high and thin. Rathar got to his feet and honored the king yet again, this time with a low bow. Swemmel was in his late forties, a few years younger than his marshal. For an Unkerlanter's, his features were long and lean and angular; his hairline, which retreated toward the crown of his head, accentuated that impression.

What hair he had left was dark – these days, probably dyed to stay so. But for that, he looked more like an Algarvian than a typical Unkerlanter. The first kings in Unkerlant, down in what was now the Duchy of Grelz, had been of Algarvic blood. *Algarvic bandits, most likely*, the marshal thought. But those dynasties were long extinct, often at one another's hands. And Swemmel was an Unkerlanter through and through – he just didn't look like one.

Rathar shook his head, clearing away irrelevancies. He couldn't afford them, not dealing with his sovereign. "How may I serve you, your Majesty?" he asked.

Swemmel folded his arms across his chest. His robe was gorgeous with cloth-of-gold. Pearls and emeralds and rubies caught the light and winked at Rathar one after another as the king moved. "You know we have concluded a truce with Arpad of Gyongyos," Swemmel said. The *we* was purely royal – the king had done it on his own.

"Aye, your Majesty, I know that," Rathar said. Swemmel had fought a savage little war with the Gongs over territory that, in the marshal's view, wasn't worth having in the first place. He'd fought it with great determination, as if the rocks and ice in the far west, land only a mountain ape could love, were stuffed to bursting with rich farms and quicksilver mines. And then, after all the lives and treasure spent, he'd thrown over the war with no gains to speak of. Swemmel was a law unto himself.

He said, "We have found another employment for our soldiers, one that suits us better."

"And that is, your Majesty?" Rathar asked cautiously. It might have been anything from starting another war to helping with the harvest to gathering seashells by the shore. With Swemmel, there was no way to tell beforehand.

"Gyongyos is far from the only realm that wronged us during our recent difficulties," Swemmel said, adding with a scowl, "Had the nursemaids been efficient, Kyot would have known from birth *we* were the one destined for greatness. *His* destiny would have been the headsman's axe either way, but he would have spared the kingdom much turmoil had he recognized it sooner."

"Aye, your Majesty," Rathar said. He had no way of knowing whether Swemmel or Kyot was the elder of the twins born to their mother. He'd joined the one army rather than the other because Swemmel's impressers passed through his village before Kyot's could get to it. He'd been an officer within months, and a colonel by the time the Twinkings War ended.

What would he be now, had Kyot dragged him into the fight instead? Dead, most likely, in one unpleasant way or another.

Again, he cleared might-have-beens from his mind. Dealing with what was gave him trouble aplenty. "Is it now your will, your Majesty, to turn our might against Zuwayza? The provocations along the border they have offered" – he knew perfectly well that Unkerlant had offered them, but saying so was not done – "give us every reason for punishing them, and—"

Swemmel made a sharp, chopping gesture. Rathar fell silent and bowed his head. He had misread the king, always dangerous to do. Swemmel said, "We can punish the Zuwayzin whenever we like, as we can resume the war with Gyongyos whenever we like. More efficient to strike where the opportunity will not come round again so soon. We aim to lay Forthweg low."

"Ahh," Rathar said, and nodded. No one could tell what Swemmel would come up with next. A lot of people had guessed wrong over the years. Not many of them were still breathing. Most of those who did survive were refugees. Anywhere within Unkerlant, Swemmel could – and did – reach.

Not all the king's notions were good. That was Rathar's private opinion. He remained safe because it remained private. But when Swemmel's notions were good, they could be very good indeed.

Rathar's smile had a predatory edge to it, as it often did. "What pretext shall we offer for stabbing the Forthwegians in the back?"

"Do you really think we need one? We hadn't intended to bother," Swemmel said indifferently. "Forthweg, or most of Forthweg, is our domain by right, and stolen away by rebels and traitors."

Rathar said nothing. He raised an eyebrow and waited. Even such small disagreement with the king might mean his ruin. No one could tell what Swemmel would come up with – in anything.

In a testy voice, Swemmel said, "Oh, very well – if you like. You can dress up a couple of our men in Forthwegian frontier guards' uniforms and have them blaze a couple of soldiers or inspectors in a border town. We don't think it even remotely necessary, but if you will, you may."

"Thank you, your Majesty," Rathar said. "Advancing a reason for war is customary, and the one you've given will do the job splendidly." Rathar doubted he would have thought of anything so devious himself. Swemmel did have a gift for double-dealing. His marshal asked, "As we move forward against the Forthwegians" – Rathar had no doubt the Unkerlanters would move forward, not when they were hitting their new foes from behind and by surprise – "shall we move into land that belonged to Algarve before the Six Years' War?"

"No." Swemmel shook his head. "In no way do we intend to do that. We expect the Algarvians to take back their old dominions, and we do not wish to give them any excuse to attack our kingdom."

"Very well, your Majesty," Rathar said, not showing how relieved he was. This truly did look to be one of Swemmel's good days, when the king was taking everything into account. Having fought the Algarvians in the Six Years' War before his regiment had mutinied and he'd gone home, Rathar was less than eager to face the redheads again. He went on, "By the accounts of the battle outside Gozzo, the Algarvians are liable to be invading Forthweg any day themselves."

"Even so," King Swemmel said. "Nor do we judge that King Mezentio would halt his forces at the old frontier. Thus, if Unkerlant is to take back what is ours, we must move swiftly. King Mezentio, in our view, will not halt at anything, save where he is compelled."

"Even by ley-line caravan, transferring our forces from the far western frontier to the border with Gyongyos will take some little while, your Majesty," Rathar warned. He did not disagree with Swemmel about Mezentio – on the contrary – but did not believe his own sovereign knew where to stop, either: another opinion he held close. "Your Majesty's wide domains prove your might, but they also make movement slower than it would be otherwise."

"Waste not a moment." Anticipation filled Swemmel's laugh. "Curse us, but we wish we could be a mosquito in Penda's throne room in Eoforwic, to see his face when he hears Forthweg is invaded from the west. They will have to clean a stain off the throne under him."

"I obey, your Majesty." Rathar bowed. "Also, by your leave, I shall send some troops into the desert in the direction of Zuwayza, both to frighten the naked brown men and to mislead the Forthwegians."

"Aye, you may do that," King Swemmel said. "We shall be in closest touch with you, ensuring that all motions are carried out with the utmost celerity. In this matter, we shall brook no delay. Do you understand, Marshal?"

"Your Majesty, I do." Rathar bowed very low. "I obey."

"Of course you obey," Swemmel said. "Unfortunate things happen to people who disobey me. Even more unfortunate things happen to their families. Obedience, then, is efficient." He waved a hand, a brusque Unkerlanter gesture rather than an airy Algarvian one. "Go, and see to it."

Rathar went down on his hands and knees and knocked his head on the green carpet again. He could feel the fear-sweat on his skin as he did so. Swemmel commanded fear both by virtue of his office and by virtue of his person. Swemmel commanded fear – and fear obeyed.

After escaping the audience chamber, Rathar reclaimed his sword from the bowing attendants in the anteroom. His spirit strengthened with every step away from his sovereign he took.

His own aides bowed low and called him *lord* when he returned to his offices. They hurried to obey the orders he issued, and exclaimed in excitement as they worked. He took a quiet pride in his own competence. But all the while, the secret stayed in the back of his mind: being the second most powerful man in Unkerlant was exactly like being the next greatest whole number before *one*. Zero he was, and zero he would remain.

Cornelu stood on the pier in Tirgoviste harbor, listening to last-minute orders. Commodore Delfinu sounded serious, even somber: "Do as much damage to the wharves at Feltre as you can, Commander. Do as much as you can, but come home safe. Sibiu has not got so many men that we can afford to spend them lavishly."

"I understand." Cornelu bowed to Delfinu, who was not only commodore but also count. "I will do what needs doing, that's all. The mission is important, else you would not send me on it."

Delfinu returned the bow, then took Cornelu's face in his hands and kissed him on both cheeks. "The mission is important. That you return is also important – you will undertake more missions as the war goes on." Afternoon sun glittered from the six gold stripes on the sleeves of Delfinu's sea-green uniform tunic and from the gold trim on his kilt. Had Cornelu been in uniform, his tunic sleeves would have borne four stripes each. Instead, he wore a black rubber suit whose only marking was the impress of the five crowns of Sibiu above his heart. A rubber pack thumped on his back.

He walked awkwardly to the edge of the pier; his feet bore rubber paddles that let him swim more swiftly than he could have without them. Waiting in the water for him was a medium-sized dark gray leviathan: the beast was five or six times as long as he was tall, as opposed to the great ones, which might reach twice that size.

One of the leviathan's small black eyes turned toward him. "Hello, Eforiel," he said. The leviathan let out a grunting snort and opened a mouth full of long, sharp teeth. They were shaped for catching fish. If they closed on a man, though, she could swallow him in about two bites.

Cornelu slid into the water and grasped the harness wrapped around Eforiel's body and held in place by the leviathan's fins. He patted the beast's smooth skin, whose texture was not much different from that of his own rubber suit. It was not a pat that gave any order, merely one of greeting. He was fond of Eforiel. He'd named her after the first girl he'd bedded, but he was the only one who knew that.

Under Eforiel's belly, the harness supported several eggs in streamlined cases partly filled with air so as to make them no heavier than a corresponding volume of water. Cornelu bared his teeth in a fierce smile. Before long, he would deliver those eggs to Feltre. He hoped the Algarvians would be glad to have them.

Commodore Delfinu leaned out over the edge of the pier and waved. "Good fortune go with you."

"For this I thank you, sir," Cornelu said.

He tapped Eforiel, more firmly than before. The leviathan's muscles surged under him. With a flick of the tail, Eforiel left Tirgoviste harbor and the five chief islands of Sibiu behind and set out across more than fifty miles of sea for the Algarvian coast.

"Surprise," Cornelu muttered. He had trouble hearing himself; water kept slapping him in the face. Before he set out, Sibian wizards had set a spell on him that let him get air from water like a fish (actually, the savants insisted the spell worked differently from fishes' gills, but the effect was the same, and that was what mattered to Cornelu).

Algarvian ships no doubt patrolled the ley lines, to keep the Sibian navy and that of Valmiera from raiding Feltre, which had been by far the most important Algarvian port on the Narrow Sea till King Mezentio got his hands on Bari. The Duchy boasted a couple of excellent harbors. With them under Algarvian rule, containing Mezentio's fleet got a lot harder.

"But I'm not coming up a ley line," Cornelu said, and chuckled wetly. Unlike ships, Eforiel did not depend on the earth's energy matrix to take her from one place to another. She went under her own power, which meant she chose her own path. No one would be looking for her till she'd been there and gone.

That thought had hardly crossed Cornelu's mind before he got a nasty jolt: a spout rising from the sea a few hundred yards ahead of Eforiel. Had his path, by strangest chance, crossed that of an Algarvian leviathan rider intent on working mischief at Tirgoviste or one of Sibiu's other harbors?

Then the animal leapt out of the water. Cornelu sighed with relief to see it was only a whale. The leviathan's cousin was stocky, even chunky, and resembled nothing so much as an overgrown fish with an even more overgrown head. Eforiel and her kin were far slimmer and smaller-skulled, almost serpentlike except for their fins and tail flukes.

"Come on, sweetheart." He tapped the leviathan again. "Nothing for us to worry about – only one of your poor relations."

Eforiel snorted again, as if to say she too looked down her pointed nose at whales. Then she swam through a school of mackerel. Cornelu had a hard time keeping her on a straight course and not letting her swim every which way after the fish. She got plenty as things were, but seemed convinced she would have eaten many more if he'd let her go where she wanted.

She could have gone, disobeying his commands, and he would have been able to do nothing about it. She never realized that. She was a well-trained beast, raised from the time she was a calf to do as the small, weak creatures who rode her ordered.

Cornelu's greatest worry was not her going off in pursuit of mackerel but her diving deep after one. The spell would keep him breathing under water, but a leviathan could dive deeper than a man's body was designed for, and could rise from the depths so fast that the air in his blood would bubble. Leviathans were made for the sea in a whole host of ways men were not.

After a while, though, the mackerel thinned out, and Eforiel swam steadily on. Once, in the distance, Cornelu caught sight of a ship sliding along a ley line. He could not tell whether it came from Sibiu or Algarve. In the waters where he was then, it might have belonged to either kingdom.

Whosoever ship it was, no one aboard noticed him or Eforiel. The two of them did not disturb the ley lines in any way. Had the ancient Kaunians thought of something like this, they might have done it, though they'd known nothing of eggs and lacked the sorcery to keep a man from drowning underwater.

Some few in Sibiu would sooner have joined with Algarve than with the Kaunian-descended kingdoms. Cornelu's snort sounded very much like Eforiel's. Some few in Sibiu were fools, as far as he was concerned. A small kingdom joined a large one in much the same way as a leg of mutton joined a man dining off it. And after his repast, only the bones would be left.

No, Valmiera and Jelgava made better allies. If they sat down at the supper table with Sibiu, they thought of the island kingdom as a fellow guest, not as the main course. "If Sibiu sat off the Valmieran coast, things might be different," Cornelu told the leviathan. "But we don't. We are where we are, and we can't do anything about it."

Eforiel did not argue, a trait Cornelu wished were more common among the people with whom he dealt. He patted the leviathan's side in approval. And then, as if to prove him right even had Eforiel argued, he spied the southern coast of Algarve. He had to pause to get his bearings. He and Eforiel had come a little too far to the east. The leviathan swam along the coast till in the distance Cornelu spotted the lighthouse outside Feltre harbor.

He let Eforiel rest then. Daylight was fading from the sky. He intended to enter the harbor at night, to make the leviathan as hard to see as he could. She would have to spout every now and then, of course, but in the darkness she would be easy to mistake for a porpoise or dolphin. People had a way of seeing what they wanted to see, what they expected to see. Cornelu smiled. He intended to take full advantage of that.

No lamps began to glow as night fell over Feltre. The town got darker and darker along with the surrounding countryside. Cornelu's smile got broader. The locals were doing their best to protect Feltre against dragon raids from Sibiu and Valmiera. What helped there, though, would hurt against attack from the sea.

When the night had grown dark enough to suit Cornelu, he took a glass-fronted mask from the pack he wore and slid it on to his face. Then he tapped Eforiel, urging her ahead into the harbor. The leviathan's tail pumped up and down, up and down, propelling her and the man who rode her forward.

Cornelu slid off her back and clung to the harness from beside her. That way, he would be harder for the Algarvian patrol boats to notice. He knew they had swift little vessels sliding along the ley lines in the sheltered water inside the harbor. Every kingdom protected its ports the same way.

But he had to stick his head out of the water to see where the most valuable targets were berthed, and also to make certain he did not attach an egg to a trading ship from Lagoas or Kuusamo. He wanted to grind his teeth at the arrogance the folk on the great island displayed, assuming no one would dare stop them from trading with Algarve for fear of bringing them into the war on King Mezentio's side. The trouble was, they were right.

He wished he could spot unquestioned naval vessels, but, save for the flitting patrol boats, he saw none. He did see three large freighters with the rakish lines the Algarvians so loved. They would do: not the haul he'd hoped for, but one that would hurt the enemy. He guided Eforiel up to within a couple of hundred yards of them, then gave her the signal that meant *hold still*. She lay in the water as if dead, the top of her head awash so she could breathe.

She would be vulnerable if the Algarvian patrol boats spotted her. Cornelu's command would hold her in place while she should be fleeing. He knew he had to work as fast as he could. Slipping under the water, he detached the four eggs his leviathan had brought to Feltre harbor and swam toward the merchant vessels.

He had to lift his head above the surface a couple of times to get his bearings. Had the Algarvians on those freighters been keeping good watch, they might have spotted him. But they seemed confident nothing could harm them here inside Feltre harbor. Cornelu aimed to show them otherwise.

Everything went as smooth as a caravan down a ley line. He attached one egg to the first merchant ship, two to the second – the largest – and one to the third. The sorcery in the shells would make them burst four hours after they touched iron. By then, he would be long gone. He swam back to Eforiel.

They cleared the harbor even more easily than they had entered. None of the Algarvian patrol boats came near them. Not long after they reached the open sea, the moon rose, spilling pale light over the water. Along with the wheeling stars, it helped Cornelu guide the leviathan across the sea and back to Sibiu. They reached Tirgoviste harbor as the sun was rising once more.

Commodore Delfinu waited on the pier. As soon as the weary Cornelu climbed out of the water, his superior kissed him on both cheeks. "Magnificently done!" Delfinu exclaimed. "One of those ships was full of eggs itself, and wrecked a good stretch of the harbor when it went up. Our mages have picked up nothing but fury in the Algarvian crystal messages they steal. You are a hero, Cornelu!"

"Sir, I am a tired hero." Cornelu smothered a yawn.

"Better a tired hero than a dead one," Delfinu said. "We also sent leviathans to the Barian ports, and have no word of success from them. If they failed they probably did not survive, poor brave men."

"How strange," Cornelu said. "The Algarvians hardly kept any sort of watch over the approaches to Feltre. Why should they do any differently at the Barian ports?"

Men going off to war had a sort of glamour to them. So thought Vanai, at any rate. Forthwegians in uniform had seemed quite splendid to her as they tramped east through Oyngestun on their way toward Algarve. Had she seen them in their ordinary tunics, she would not have given them a second glance – unless to make sure they weren't seeking to molest her.

No such glamour attached itself to men retreating from war. Vanai quickly discovered that, too. Retreating, they did not move in neat columns, all their legs going back and forth together like the oars of a war galley from the Kaunian Empire. They weren't all nearly identical, with only the occasional blond Kaunian head among the dark Forthwegians distinguishing a few from the rest.

Retreating, men skulked along in small packs, as stray dogs did. Vanai feared they were liable to turn on her, as stray dogs might. They had that look, wild, half fierce, half fearful another rock or another blow from a club might knock them sprawling.

They didn't look identical any more, either. Their tunics were variously torn and tattered, with spots of dirt and grease and some-times bloodstains mottling the cloth. Some of them had bandages on arms or legs or head. They were almost uniformly filthy, filthier than the ancient Kaunians Vanai had viewed with Brivibas's archaeological sorcery. The nose-wrinkling odor that clung to them put her in mind of the farmyard.

Like the rest of the folk of Oyngestun, Forthwegians and Kaunians alike, Vanai did what she could for them, offering bread and sausage and water and, while it lasted, wine. "My thanks, lass," said a Forthwegian lance-corporal who was well-spoken enough but who hadn't bathed in a long, long time. He lowered his voice: "You folk here may want to get on the road to Eoforwic. Gromheort's not going to hold, and if it doesn't, this wide spot in the road won't, either."

He spoke to her as an equal, not looking down his curved nose at her because she was of Kaunian blood. She found even the casual assumption that he was as good as she on the offensive side, but not nearly so much as the leering superiority so many Forthwegians displayed. Because of that, she answered politely enough: "I don't think you could pry my grandfather out of Oyngestun with a team of mules."

"What about a team of behemoths?" the Forthwegian soldier demanded. For a moment, naked fear filled his face. "The Algarvians have more of the horrible things than you can shake a stick at, and they hit hard, too. What about a team of dragons? I've never imagined so many eggs could fall out of the sky on us." He gulped the mug of water Vanai had given him dry. She refilled it, and he gulped once more.

"He's very stubborn," Vanai said. The lance-corporal finished the second mug of water and shrugged, as if to say it wasn't his problem. He wiped his mouth on his sleeve, gave the mug back to Vanai with another word of thanks, and trudged off toward the west.

Brivibas came out of the house as Vanai was slicing more bread. "You were unduly familiar with that man, my granddaughter," he said severely. Reprimands sounded much harsher in Kaunian than in Forthwegian.

Vanai bowed her head. "I am sorry you think so, my grandfather, but he was giving me advice he thought good. I would have been rude to scorn him."

"Advice he thought good?" Brivibas snorted. "I daresay he was: advice on which haystack to meet him behind, I shouldn't wonder."

"No, nothing like that, my grandfather," Vanai said. "His view is that we might be wise to abandon Oyngestun."

"Why?" Her grandfather snorted again. "Because staying would mean we had Algarvians lording it over us instead of Forthwegians?" Brivibas set hands on hips, threw back his head, and laughed scornfully. "Why this should make a difference surpasses my poor understanding."

"But if the fighting goes through here, my grandfather, whoever holds Oyngestun will be lording it over the dead," Vanai answered.

"And if we flee, the Algarvian dragons will drop eggs on us from above. A house, at least, offers shelter," Brivibas said. "Besides, I have not yet finished my article refuting Frithstan, and could scarcely carry my research materials and references in a soldierly pack on my back."

Vanai was sure that was the biggest reason he refused even to think of leaving the village. She also knew argument was useless. If she fled Oyngestun, she would flee without Brivibas. She could not bear that. "Very well, my grandfather," she said, and bowed her head once more.

Another soldier came up. "Here, sweetheart, you have anything for a hungry man to eat?" he asked, adding, "My belly's rubbing my backbone." Wordlessly, Vanai cut him a length of sausage and a chunk of bread. He took them, blew her a kiss, and went on his way munching.

"Disgraceful," Brivibas said. "Nothing short of disgraceful."

"Oh, I don't know," Vanai said judiciously. "I've heard ten times worse from the Forthwegian boys in Oyngestun. Twenty times worse – he was just . . . friendly."

"Again, *unduly familiar* is the term you seek," Brivibas said with pedantic precision. "That the local louts are more disgusting does not make this trooper anything but disgusting himself. He is bad; they are worse."

Then a soldier of unmistakable Kaunian blood came by and asked for food and drink. He poured down a mug of water, tore off a big bite of sausage with strong white teeth, and nodded to Vanai. "I thank you, sweetheart," he said, and walked off toward the west. Vanai glanced over to Brivibas. Her grandfather seemed to be studying the stitching in his shoes.

Two soldiers came running into Oyngestun within a few seconds of each other, one from the north, the other from the south. They both shouted the same phrase: "Behemoths! Algarvian behemoths!" Each of them pointed back the way he had come and added, "They're over there!"

Shouts of alarm rose from the Forthwegian soldiers. Some dashed off to the north, others to the south, to force open the ring the Algarvians were closing around Gromheort and, incidentally, around Oyngestun. Others, despairing, fled westward, to escape before the ring closed.

Some of the folk of Oyngestun fled with them, bundling belongings and small children into wheelbarrows and handcarts and carriages and clogging the highway so soldiers had trouble moving. Rather more Forthwegians than folk of Kaunian blood ran off in the direction of Eoforwic. As Brivibas had said, Kaunians were under alien rule regardless of whether Forthwegian blue and white or Algarvian green, white, and red flew above Oyngestun.

"Should we not leave, my grandfather?" Vanai asked again. She trotted out the strongest argument she could think of: "How will you be able to go on with your studies in a village full of Algarvian soldiers?"

Brivibas hesitated, then firmly shook his head. "How will I be able to go on with my studies sleeping in the mud by the side of the road?" He stuck out his chin and looked stubborn. "No. It cannot be. Here I stay, come what may." He looked eastward in defiance.

But then, with a thunder of wings, Algarvian dragons flew by low overhead. A few Forthwegian soldiers blazed at them, but did not seem to bring any down. Flames spurted from the dragons' jaws as they swooped down on the roadway packed with soldiers and villagers. Screams rose, faint in the distance but hardly less horrifying for that. The breeze from out of the west wafted the stench of burning back into Oyngestun. Some of what burned smelled like wood. Some smelled like roasting meat. It might have made Vanai hungry, had she not known what it was. As things were, it almost made her sick.

More Algarvian dragons fell from the heavens like stones, dropping eggs on the road out of Oyngestun. The bursts smote Vanai's ears. She brought up her hands to cover them, but that did little good. Even though she could not see most of it, even if she muffled her hearing, she knew what was happening off to the west.

"It is for this that you waved at the Forthwegian dragonfliers when we went to examine the ancient power point, my granddaughter," Brivibas said. "This is what King Penda sought to visit upon the kingdom of Algarve. Now that he finds it visited upon his own kingdom instead, whom has he to blame?"

Vanai looked for such philosophical detachment inside herself: looked for it and found it not. "These are our neighbors who suffer, my grandfather, our neighbors and some of them folk of our blood."

"Had they but stayed here rather than foolishly fleeing, they would be safe now," Brivibas said. "Shall I then praise them for their foolishness, cherish them for their want of wisdom?"

Before Vanai could answer, the first eggs began falling inside Oyngestun. More screams rose, these close and urgent. Algarvian dragons ruled the sky above the village; none painted in Forthwegian colors came flying out of the west to challenge them. More and more eggs fell. "Get down, you lackwits!" a Forthwegian soldier shouted at Vanai and Brivibas.

Before Brivibas could move, a shard of glass or brickwork scored a bleeding line across the back of his hand. He stared at the little wound in astonishment. "Who is the fool now, my grandfather?" Vanai asked, speaking to him with more bitterness than she'd ever used before. "Who now wants wisdom?"

"Get down!" the soldier yelled again.

This time, Brivibas did, though still a beat behind his grand-daughter. Cradling the injured hand to his chest, he said, "Who would have imagined, after the Six Years' War, that folk would be eager for more such catastrophes?" His voice was plaintive and without understanding.

A Forthwegian officer called, "Build the rubble into barricades! If those redheaded whoresons want this place, they're going to have to pay for it."

"That's the spirit!" Vanai shouted in Forthwegian. The officer waved to her and went on directing his men.

In pungently sardonic Kaunian, Brivibas said, "Splendid! Encourage him to endanger our lives as well as his own." Still angry, Vanai ignored him.

The Forthwegian soldiers briskly went about turning Oyngestun into a strongpoint. They beat back the first Algarvian probe at the town that afternoon. Wounded Algarvians, Vanai discovered, screamed no differently from wounded Kaunians or Forthwegians. But then, toward sunset, the Forthwegian crystallomancer cried in fury and despair. "The Unkerlanters!" he yelled to his commander – and to anyone else who would hear. "The Unkerlanters are pouring over the western border, and there's no one to stop them!"

4.

"Now this," Leudast said as he tramped through western Forthweg, "this is what efficiency is all about."

Sergeant Magnulf nodded. "You had best believe it, soldier," he said. "Shows the Forthwegians need lessons. If you're stupid enough to start a war on one border when the kingdom on your other border can't stand you, seems to me you deserve whatever happens to you."

"I hadn't even thought about that," Leudast said. "I was just thinking we're going to have a lot easier time than we did against the Gyongyosians." He looked around. "A lot better country to fight in, too."

"Aye, so it is," Magnulf agreed.

"Reminds me of home, as a matter of fact." Leudast pointed westward. "My family's farm isn't that far on the other side of the border, and it looks a lot like this back there." He waved.

Most of the farm buildings hereabouts were of sun-dried brick brightened with whitewash or, less often, paint. Wheat ripened golden in the fields; plump, ripe olives made branches sag. The breeds of cattle and sheep the Forthwegians raised were similar to those with which Leudast had grown up back in Unkerlant.

Nor did the Forthwegians themselves look that different from Unkerlanters. They were, most of them, stocky and swarthy, with proud, hook-nosed faces. Save that the men wore beards, Leudast would have been hard pressed to prove he'd entered another kingdom.

Most of the beards he saw were grizzled or white; the young men were off in the east, fighting the Algarvians. Graybeards and women, those who had not fled, stared with terrible bitterness as the Unkerlanter soldiers marched past. Every so often, one of them would shout something Leudast almost understood; the Unkerlanter dialect he spoke wasn't that far removed from Forthwegian. It was close enough to make him certain the locals weren't paying compliments.

Every so often, Forthwegian border guards and the small garrisons King Penda had left behind in the west would try to make a stand against the Unkerlanters, defending a line of hills or a town or sending out cavalry to nip at the thick columns of men King Swemmel had flung into their kingdom.

They were brave. Leudast couldn't see that it did them much good. The Unkerlanters flowed around them, surrounded them, and attacked them from all sides at once. Behemoths trampled Forthwegian cavalry underfoot. Unkerlanter officers would go forward under flag of truce to urge surrenders, pointing out that the Forthwegians could not possibly hope to resist. Their foes sent them back and kept fighting as long as they could.

"Inefficient," Magnulf said as his squad encamped one evening after pushing another fifteen or so miles into Forthweg – a typical day's advance. "They aren't stopping us. They're hardly slowing us down. What's the point to throwing their lives away?"

"Stubborn fools," Leudast said. "They should see they're beaten and give up."

"I heard one of them shout, 'Better to die under King Penda than to live under King Swemmel!'" Magnulf said, mimicking the Forthwegian tongue as well as he could. The sergeant shrugged. "I think that's what he said, anyhow. And now he's dead, and it's not going to keep the Forthwegians from living under King Swemmel, not one little bit it's not. We'll be knocking on the door at Eoforwic in another few days."

Leudast looked east. "We don't quarrel with the Algarvians, though?"

"Not if they stay on their side of what used to be the border before the Six Years' War," Magnulf answered. "We won't cross it – we're just taking back what was ours, not stealing from anybody else."

That night, Forthwegian dragons dropped eggs on the Unkerlanters' forward positions. The noise from the bursts kept Leudast awake, but none of them came particularly close.

The next morning, the Unkerlanters approached Hwiterne, a city whose stone keep would have been a formidable defense in the days before eggs were flung for miles or fell from dragons. Again, King

Swemmel's officers went ahead to ask the town to surrender. Again, the Forthwegian garrison refused.

Before long, pillars of smoke rose into the sky from Hwiterne. Under cover of that barrage, Unkerlanter troops pushed through the patchily inhabited suburbs and into the town itself. Leudast discovered he had not only Forthwegian soldiers but also townsfolk blazing at him. He blazed back. He blazed at anyone he spied in Hwiterne who wasn't wearing Unkerlanter rock-gray. He suspected he might have wounded innocent bystanders. That was inefficient, but not nearly so inefficient as letting himself get killed.

He flopped down in the rubble that had been a house. A woman with a bandage on her head lay not far away from him. He didn't blaze her down; he could see she had no weapon. "Why?" she asked him. "Why did you cursed Unkerlanters come here? Why didn't you leave us alone?"

Leudast followed that well enough. "We came to take back what's ours," he answered.

She glared at him. "Can't you see we don't want you? Can't you see we" – a word he didn't know – "King Swemmel?" Whatever the word meant, he doubted it was praise.

"If you're not strong enough to stop us, what difference does that make?" Leudast asked in honest puzzlement.

She cursed him then, her voice full of bitter hopelessness. He could have killed her for it. No one would have been the wiser. No one who mattered to Leudast would have cared at all. She had to know as much. She cursed anyhow, as if defying him to do his worst.

He shrugged his broad shoulders. She cursed again, harder than ever. His indifference seemed more wounding to her than rage would have been. Shrugging once more, he said, "You didn't curse when King Penda invaded Algarve. What business have you got doing it now?"

She stared at him. "The Algarvians deserve everything that happens to them. We don't deserve any of this."

"That's not what King Swemmel thinks," Leudast said. "He's my king. I obey him." Dreadful things happened to Unkerlanters who didn't obey King Swemmel. Leudast preferred not to dwell on those.

A Forthwegian egg burst not far away. Chunks of wood and mud brick rained down on him and the woman with the bandaged head.

Dreadful things, he realized, could also happen to Unkerlanters who did obey King Swemmel. For a moment, he wondered why, in that case, he willingly put himself into danger.

He didn't have to search hard for the answer. Dreadful things might not happen to him if he fought the Gongs or the Forthwegians. Nothing too dreadful *had* happened to him yet. If, on the other hand, he set his own will against the king's . . . Swemmel had shown over the years that disaster surely befell anyone rash enough to do such a thing.

The Unkerlanters rained eggs on the center of Hwiterne, from which resistance was fiercest. Officers blew whistles. Sergeants shouted. Leudast scrambled to his feet and dashed forward. For a couple of heartbeats, he heard the Forthwegian woman cursing him yet again. Then her voice was lost in the greater din of battle.

He ran past the corpse of a behemoth, killed with most of its crew by a Forthwegian egg. A moment later, he dove for cover behind another dead behemoth. A strong stink of burnt meat rose from this one: the Forthwegians had concealed a stick heavy enough to blaze through the beast's armor in a building now wreckage. Leudast warily looked around for more such traps, though the Unkerlanters had driven the foe from this part of Hwiterne. Trying to use behemoths in the middle of a built-up area struck him as inefficient. He wondered if it would strike his officers the same way.

Hwiterne fell. So did the keep at its heart, smashed to ruins by the miracles of modern sorcery. Filthy, dejected Forthwegian captives shambled off into the west, a handful of Unkerlanters guarding them. A good many corpses wearing civilian-style tunics rather than those of the Forthwegian army lay in the streets, each dead man with a neat hole blazed in the center of his forehead. Someone had painted a sign in Unkerlanter and what Leudast presumed to be Forthwegian (the Forthwegians used an alphabet different from his): IF YOU ARE NOT A SOLDIER, THIS IS WHAT YOU GET FOR BLAZING AT KING SWEMMEL'S MEN.

Some few of the prisoners in Forthwegian uniform were tall, yellow-haired men, not short, swarthy ones. Pointing at them, a soldier in Leudast's company exclaimed, "Powers below! How did the cursed Gyongyosians get over here to the other side of the kingdom to help the Forthwegians?"

"Those aren't Gongs, Nantwin, you goose," Leudast answered. "They're just Kaunians. They've been here since dirt."

"What's a Kaunian?" Nantwin asked. He had a strong Grelzer accent, which meant he came from the far south of Unkerlant. No Kaunians in that part of the world, sure enough.

"They used to run a whole lot of the northeast," Leudast said, "back before the Algarvians and Forthwegians smashed up their empire."

"How come they look like Gongs?" Nantwin said.

"They don't, really," Leudast said. "Aye, they're blond, but that's about it." The differences seemed obvious to him; there were Kaunians not far from his farming village. Not only were they tall and skinny, but their hair lay flat on their heads, where the Gyongyosians' sprang out wildly in all directions. Kaunians' hair ran to silver gilt, too, while that of the Gongs was a tawny yellow.

Such subtleties were lost on Nantwin, who said, "Curse them, they look like Gyongyosians to me."

"Fine," Leudast said. "They look like Gongs to you." Life was too short for arguments over things that didn't matter. "Inefficient," he muttered.

A prisoner of Kaunian blood stared at him – through him. By the expression on the fellow's face, Leudast looked like scum to him. Leudast laughed. The Kaunian jerked as if he'd stepped on a thorn. Leudast couldn't have cared less about a worthless captive's opinion of him.

"Why are you wasting your time gaping at these miserable bastards?" Sergeant Magnulf demanded. "Odds are King Swemmel will put 'em to work mining brimstone and quicksilver, and they'll never come out from the holes again. They might as well be dead already. You get moving."

"Sorry, Sergeant," said Leudast, who knew he would be wasting his time if he tried to explain to Magnulf that he'd been trying to show Nantwin the Kaunians of Forthweg were different from Gyongyosians. Magnulf didn't want explanations. Obedience was all he craved.

He grunted now, satisfied that he'd got it. "Come on," he said. "We'll be breaking into Eoforwic in another few days." Leudast tramped after him. He would rather have been back on his farm. If he had to find himself in the middle of a war, though, he was just as well pleased to find himself in the middle of an easy one.

Colonel Sabrino ducked out of his tent. One of the tethered dragons at the temporary farm north of Gromheort flapped its wings and hissed at him. The Algarvian dragonflier stopped in his tracks, as if a human foe had insulted him. He sent the most obscene gesture he knew back at the dragon, which hissed again; it might have been insulted in turn. Laughing, Sabrino swaggered off toward the officers' club.

That too was housed in a tent. The tapman bowed when Sabrino came inside. "How may I please you, my lord?" he asked.

"If you'd turn into a beautiful woman, that would give you a head start on the job, no doubt about it," Sabrino answered. A couple of fliers from his wing who were sitting around with drinks in front of them laughed. So did the tapman, though he remained resolutely male and on the homely side. With a sigh, Sabrino said, "I suppose I'll have to content myself with a glass of port. Put it on my scot."

"Aye, my lord." The tapman pulled cork from bottle and poured. Sabrino sipped. The fortified wine was not of the best, but it would have to do. Wartime meant sacrifice.

"Join us, Colonel, if you would," Captain Domiziano said. He tapped the stool beside him. Senior Lieutenant Orosio, who shared the table with Domiziano, nodded to show the invitation came from him, too.

"Don't mind if I do." Sabrino perched on the stool and raised his glass. "Here's to a splendid little war."

"A splendid little war," Domiziano and Orosio echoed. They drank with their commanding officer. Orosio said, "As near as I can see, sir, we've got Forthweg in a box with a pretty ribbon around it."

"That's how things look to me, too," Sabrino said, nodding. "Pity we had to let them cross the border and do so much damage inside our kingdom, but we've paid them back and then some."

"So we have," Domiziano agreed. He had a bandage over one ear, which a Forthwegian beam had cooked. But he'd accounted for four Forthwegian dragons and torn up the enemy's countryside; the small wound hardly seemed to upset him. He went on, "We'd have done the same even if the Unkerlanters hadn't sneaked up behind King Penda and kicked him in the arse."

"No doubt about it," Sabrino repeated. "None at all. The Forthwegians are brave enough, but they haven't got enough behemoths and they haven't got enough dragons and they don't quite know what to do with the ones they have got. We'd have needed another couple of weeks to overrun the whole kingdom, but we'd have done it, all right."

Orosio scratched at the edge of his goatee. "Sir, what do we do if we meet Unkerlanter dragons in the air?"

"Pretend they don't exist," Sabrino said at once. "If the fliers blaze at you, evade. Not to put too fine a point on it, run away. King Mezentio does not want a war with Unkerlant. I'm told that's going to be the subject of a general order in the next day or two. We have enough on our plate now without worrying about King Swemmel, too."

"I don't think the Unkerlanters are any great worry," Domiziano said. "We taught them enough of a lesson in the Six Years' War that Swemmel isn't likely to want to tangle with us, either."

"Here's hoping," Sabrino said, and drank to the hope. His junior officers drank with him.

An orderly stuck his head into the officers' club. Spying Sabrino, he immediately looked relieved. "Ah, here you are, sir," he said. "A message on the crystal just came in: your wing is ordered to join in the attack on the town of Wihtgara." He pronounced the uncouth Forthwegian syllables as well as an Algarvian might be expected to do.

Sabrino drew a map from the vest pocket of his uniform tunic. He spread it out on the table so Domiziano and Orosio could study it, too. After a moment, Sabrino's forefinger stabbed out. "About fifty miles northwest of here," he said, and turned to the orderly once more. "Tell the crystallomancer to reply that we shall be flying within half an hour." He knocked back the rest of his port – it wasn't really good enough to linger over – and nodded to his companions. "Time to give the Forthwegians another dose, lads."

As usual, Sabrino had to pick his way among the tethered dragons to keep from fouling his boots with their noxious droppings. As usual, his own mount had forgotten he'd been flying it for years. As usual, it hissed and flapped and spluttered, doing its best to keep him from climbing aboard. It did refrain from trying to flame him down; that was beaten into war dragons from hatchlinghood. For small favors, Sabrino gave thanks.

He gave thanks again when the dragon's enormous batwings thundered behind him and the ground dropped away below. The view he got from on high was almost worth putting up with the stupidity and viciousness of dragons. The view of the rest of the dragons in his wing, bellies silvered, backs painted in red and white and green, was splendid, too.

"Come on," he said, and tapped his dragon with the goad to bring its course farther north of west. "We can do it."

The dragon, predictably, didn't want to. As far as it was concerned, it was up in the sky to hunt. Sabrino's purposes mattered little to it. It had been perfectly content to fly along in the direction it had chosen. When he tried to get it to change the small stubborn spot that passed for its mind, it twisted its head back along the length of its long, sinuous neck and did its best to pluck him off his perch with its teeth.

Even though it didn't flame him, its breath, full of the stinks of brimstone and old meat, was nearly enough to knock him over. "Son of a worm!" he shouted, and whacked it in the snout with the iron-shod goad. "Daughter of a vulture! I am your better! You shall obey me!"

Every once in a while, a dragon forgot the most fundamental part of its training – in which case, the dragonflier never got another chance to curse it. Sabrino refused to let that risk enter his mind. He whacked the dragon's scaly snout again. With an irate hiss, it straightened its neck once more. He gave it another tap, and this time, however sullenly, it swung its path more in the direction of Wihtgara.

Down below, Algarvian columns filed down roads and across fields. Here and there, scattered Forthwegian companies tried to withstand them. They had little luck. Sabrino shook his fist at them. "This is what you get for invading Algarve!" he cried, though only his dragon could hear him. "What you visited on us, we visit on you a hundredfold."

He'd been worried when the Forthwegians approached Gozzo. Had the city fallen, King Penda's soldiers could have spread across the plains of northern Algarve and done untold damage. But behemoths and dragons had turned the battle in front of Gozzo, and turned every fight since, too. However brave the Forthwegians were, they could not stand up against such force.

Here and there, the retreating Forthwegians had set fire in the fields and woods to slow the Algarvians' advance. Had they done that more systematically, they would have got more good from it. As things were, occasional whiffs of smoke rose to Sabrino's nostrils: hardly what the enemy could have hoped to accomplish.

More smoke rose above Wihtgara. Sabrino's countrymen had bypassed the town to the north and south and joined hands beyond it, as they'd done with Gromheort a few days before. The Forthwegians trapped inside the jaws of the pincers still battled to break free, but they had little chance. Unicorn cavalry, tiny as dots down below, charged a squadron of behemoths. The egg-tossers and heavy sticks the behemoths bore on their backs wrecked the charge before the Forthwegians got to close quarters.

Dragons wheeled above Wihtgara. Till Sabrino drew near, he thought them Algarvian beasts dropping eggs on the defenders below. Then he saw they were painted in blue and white: Forthwegian colors. There were only a dozen of them or so. Without hesitation – or without any more hesitation than balky dragons usually caused – they hurled themselves at his entire wing.

Sabrino waved to his dragonfliers. "If they want it, we'll give it to them!" he shouted, though he didn't think any of the other men could hear. That they would give it to the Forthwegians, he had no doubt. Even after losses in the fighting thus far, he still commanded four times as many dragons as the foe had.

Like the unicorn cavalry down on the ground, the Forthwegian dragonfliers cared nothing about the odds. On they came. Sabrino's dragon made a noise that reminded him of hot oil sizzling in a frying pan about the size of a small duchy: a challenge. Sabrino raised his stick and blazed at the nearest Forthwegian. If he didn't have to fight at close quarters, he didn't want to, no matter how eager his mount was to flame the Forthwegian dragon out of the sky.

But blazing straight wasn't easy, not with both him and the Forthwegian moving at high speed along courses that changed unpredictably as one dragon or the other took it into its ferocious, empty head to dodge a little. Fighting in the air wasn't just man against man. It was also dragon against dragon, and the beasts wanted nothing more than to burn each other and tear each other to shreds.

Here came the Forthwegian. He had some idea of what he was about, and a dragon that, by Forthwegian standards, was decently trained: the beast rose to give him a clear blaze at Sabrino instead of simply trying to close with the Algarvian's dragon. Sabrino flattened himself against his mount's neck to present a harder target as he goaded his dragon to climb, too.

And Forthwegian standards did not measure up to those practiced in King Mezentio's domain. Moreover, Sabrino's dragon was larger and stronger and swifter than his foe's. He outclimbed the Forthwegian and got round behind him, despite the enemy's best efforts to twist in the air. When Sabrino's dragon flamed, fire licked the other beast's back and left wing.

The Forthwegian dragon's hissing shriek of anguish was music to Sabrino's ears. Very likely, the Forthwegian dragonflier shrieked, too, but his cry, if he made one, was lost in the greater cry of his mount. The enemy dragon plummeted out of the sky, not just burnt but burning. Because of the brimstone and quicksilver that had helped fuel it, dragonfire clung and clung.

Sabrino's dragon bellowed its triumph and spurted more flame. He whacked it with the goad to make it stop. It might need that fire in future fights. His head swiveled as he tried to see which of his dragonfliers needed help. He spied none who did. Most of the Forthwegian dragons were falling in flames (so, he was sad to see, were a couple painted in Algarvian colors). A couple of the enemy flew west, off to the shrinking stretch of territory Forthweg still held. And one, its flier blazed off it, struck out at the dragons around it like the wild beast it was till it too tumbled out of the sky.

More dragons were flying in out of the east, these lower, and with eggs slung under their bellies. As the eggs began falling on Wihtgara, Sabrino smiled broadly. "A splendid little war!" he cried, exultation in his voice. "Splendid!"

Occupied. Ealstan had heard the word before the war, of course. He'd heard it, and thought he'd known what it meant. Now he was learning the bitter difference between knowledge and experience.

Occupation meant Algarvian troops swaggering along the streets of Gromheort. They all had sticks at the ready, and they all expected everybody to understand Algarvian. People who didn't understand the ugly, trilling speech – in Ealstan's ears, it sounded like magpies' chatter – fast enough to suit them were liable to get blazed for no better reason than that. No one could punish the Algarvians for doing such things. Their commanders probably praised them.

Occupation meant that Ealstan's mother and sister stayed inside their house and sent him or his father out when they needed errands run. The Algarvians hadn't perpetuated that many outrages, but they'd done enough to make decent Forthwegian women uninterested in taking chances.

Occupation meant that Sidroc and his family crowded the house to overflowing. An egg had turned their home to rubble. Ealstan knew it could have been his as easily as not. Sidroc and his father – Ealstan's father's brother – still shambled around as if stunned, for his mother and sister had been in the house when the egg burst.

Occupation meant broadsheets written in awkward Forthwegian going up on almost every wall that hadn't been knocked flat. THE KAUNIAN KINGDOMS YOU LED INTO THAT WAR, some of them said. Others asked, WHY DO FORTHWEGIANS FOR KAUNIANS DIE? Ealstan had never had any particular use for the Kaunians who lived within Forthweg's borders – except watching the blond women in their tight trousers. If the Algarvians wanted him to hate them, though, there had to be more to them than he'd thought.

Occupation meant having no idea what had happened to his brother, Leofsig. That was worst of all.

And yet, even with Count Brorda fled and an Algarvian officer ensconced in his castle, life had to go on. Ealstan's sister stuffed a chunk of garlicky sausage, some salted olives, a lump of hard white cheese, and some raisins into a cloth sack and thrust it at him. "Here," she said. "Don't dawdle. You'll be late for school."

"Thanks, Conberge," Ealstan said.

"Remember to stop at a baker's on the way home and bring us more bread," Conberge told him. "Or if the bakers are all out, get ten pounds of flour from a miller. Mother and I can do the baking perfectly well."

"All right." Ealstan paused. "What if the millers are out of flour, too?"

His sister looked a bit harried. "In that case, we all start going hungry. It wouldn't surprise me a bit." She raised her voice to a shout: "Sidroc! Aren't you ready yet? Your masters will beat you black and blue, and you'll deserve it."

Sidroc was still running a tortoiseshell comb through his dark, curly hair when he hurried into the kitchen to receive a lunch similar to Ealstan's. "Come on," Ealstan said. "Conberge's right – they'll break switches on our backs if we're late again."

"I suppose so," Sidroc said indifferently. Maybe he needed a thrashing to bring him out of his funk. Ealstan didn't, and didn't want to get one because his cousin remained in a daze. He grabbed Sidroc by the arm and hauled him out on to the street.

No Algarvians were strutting past his house, for which he was duly grateful. The mere sight of kilts set his teeth on edge. Being unable to taunt the Algarvians hurt, too, but he didn't care to take his life in his hands. Women were not the only ones the occupiers outraged.

Ealstan was sure Leofsig and his comrades had done no such things while on Algarvian soil. No: that Leofsig and his comrades could have done such things never entered his mind. And even if they had, the Algarvians would have deserved it.

When he turned the corner on to the main thoroughfare that led to his school, Ealstan could no longer pretend Gromheort remained a free Forthwegian city. For one thing, the Algarvians had checkpoints every few blocks. For another, signboards written in their script – so sinuous as to be hard to read, especially for someone like Ealstan, who was used to angular Forthwegian characters – sprouted everywhere. And, for a third, heading up the thoroughfare toward the school showed him what a battering Gromheort had taken before it finally fell.

The Algarvians had set gangs to work clearing the wreckage of ruined buildings. "Work, cursing you!" a kilted soldier shouted in bad Forthwegian. The Forthwegians and Kaunians the occupiers had rounded up were already working, throwing tiles and chunks of bricks and shattered timbers into wagons. A Kaunian woman bent to pick up a couple of bricks. An Algarvian soldier reached out and ran his hand along the curve of her buttocks.

She straightened with a squeak of outrage. The soldier and his companions laughed. "Work!" he said, and gestured with his stick. Her face a frozen mask, she bent once more. He fondled her again. This time, she went on working as if he did not exist.

Ealstan hustled past the work gang, lest the Algarvians make him join it. Sidroc followed, but kept looking back over his shoulder. His eyes were wide and staring as he watched the solider amuse himself. "Come on," Ealstan said impatiently.

"Powers above," Sidroc muttered, as much to himself as to his cousin. "Wouldn't you like to do that with a woman?"

"Sure I would, if she wanted me to," Ealstan answered, even though thinking a woman might one day want him to do such a thing required all the imagination he had. But despite that, he noted a distinction Sidroc had missed: "That soldier wasn't doing it with her — he was doing it to her. Did you see her face? If looks could kill, she'd have wiped out all those stinking redheads."

Sidroc tossed his head. "She was only a Kaunian."

"You think the Algarvian cared?" Ealstan asked, and shook his head to give the question his own answer. "He would have done it to" — he started to say *to your mother*, but checked himself; that hit harder than he wanted to — "to Conberge the same way. Everybody's fair game to Mezentio's men."

"They won," Sidroc said bitterly. "That's what you get when you win: you can do as you please."

"I suppose so," Ealstan said. "I never thought we could lose."

"We cursed well did," Sidroc said. "We might even be worse off, you know? Would you rather we were off in the west, and King Swemmel's Unkerlanters came stomping through Gromheort? If I had to chose between them and the Algarvians—"

"If I could make a choice, I'd choose to have all of them go far, far away." Ealstan sighed. "But magic doesn't work that way. I wish it did."

They got to the school just as the warning bell clanged, and then ran like madmen to their first class. In spite of his lethargy, Sidroc didn't want to have his back striped after all. "Why couldn't the Algarvians have dropped an egg here?" he muttered fretfully as he flung his bottom on to his stool.

But the master of classical Kaunian was not in the chamber to note

– and to punish – his tardiness and Ealstan's. After a heartfelt sigh of relief, Ealstan turned to the scholar next to him and whispered, "Did Master Bede have to visit the jakes?"

"Don't think so," the other youth answered. "I haven't seen him at all this morning. Maybe the Algarvians have him grubbing stones."

"He'd be on the other end of the switch if they do," Ealstan said. Seeing the Kaunian woman molested had bothered him. He could contemplate the master's being put to hard labor without batting an eye.

A man strode into the classroom. He was a Forthwegian, but he was not Master Bede, even if he did carry a switch in his left hand. "I am Master Agmund," he announced. "From this day forth, by order of the occupying authorities, all studies in classical Kaunian are suspended, the langauge being judged useless both because of its antiquated, outmoded nature and because folk of Kaunian blood have wickedly attempted to destroy the Kingdom of Algarve."

He spoke as if reading from a script. Ealstan gaped. Master Bede and earlier masters of Kaunian had drilled into him – often painfully – that anyone in eastern Derlavai with the slightest claim to culture had to be fluent in the language, regardless of his own blood. Had they been lying? Or did Algarve have its own purposes here?

Agmund answered that in a hurry, saying, "Instead, you shall be instructed in Algarvian, in which subject I am your new master. Attend me."

One of Ealstan's classmates, a youth named Odda, thrust his hand in the air. When Agmund recognized him, he said, "Master, can we not learn Algarvian from the soldiers in the city? Why, already I can say 'How much for your sister?' just from having heard them say it so much."

A vast silence fell on the classroom. Ealstan stared, admiring Odda's defiant bravado. Master Agmund's stare was of a different sort. He advanced on Odda and gave him the fiercest thrashing Ealstan had ever seen. Agmund said, "My clever little friend, if you were half as funny as you think you are, you would be twice as funny as you really are."

When the beating was over, the lessons began. Agmund proved himself a capable enough master, and was plainly fluent in Algarvian. Ealstan repeated the words and phrases the master set him. He had no desire to learn Algarvian, but he had no desire to be whipped, either.

He and Sidroc took turns telling the story around the supper table that evening. "The boy did a brave thing," Sidroc's father said.

"He certainly did, Uncle Hengist," Ealstan agreed.

"Brave, aye," his father said. Hestan looked from Ealstan to Sidroc to Hengist. "Brave, but foolish. The lad suffered for it, as you and your cousin said, and his suffering is not over yet, either, unless I miss my guess. And his family's suffering will barely have begun."

Hengist grunted, as if Hestan had hit him in the belly. "You are likely to be right," he said. "Of course this new master is an Algarvian lapdog. What he hears, the redheads will hear." He pointed to Sidroc. "We have suffered enough already. Whatever you think of this new language master, keep it locked in your head. Never let him suspect it, or we will all pay."

"I don't mind him so much," Sidroc said with a shrug. "And Algarvian looks to be a lot easier than classical Kaunian ever was."

That wasn't what Hengist had meant. Ealstan understood as much, even if Sidroc didn't. Understanding such things went with being occupied, too. If Sidroc didn't figure them out pretty soon, he would be sorry, and so would everyone around him.

Ealstan's mother understood. "Take care, all of you," Elfryth said, and that was also good advice.

The next morning, Odda was not in the Algarvian class. He was not in any of his classes that day. He did not return to school the next day, either. Ealstan and Sidroc never saw him again. Ealstan understood the lesson. He hoped his cousin did, too.

King Shazli nibbled at a cake rich with raisins and pistachios. He licked his fingers clean, then glanced at Hajjaj from lowered eyelids. "It would seem King Swemmel did not purpose attacking us after all," he said.

When his sovereign decided to talk business, Hajjaj could with propriety do the same, even if his cake lay on the tray before him only half eaten. "Say rather, your Majesty, that King Swemmel did not *yet* purpose attacking us," he replied.

"You say this even after Unkerlant and Algarve have split Forthweg between them, as a man will tear a peeled tangerine in half that he might share it with his friend?"

"Your Majesty, I do," the foreign minister said. "If King Swemmel intended to leave Zuwayza alone, we would not see these continual proddings along the border. Nor would we see his envoy in Bishah lyingly denying that any fault attaches to Unkerlant. When Swemmel is ready, he will do what he will do."

Shazli started to reach for his teacup. At the last moment, his hand swerved and seized the goblet that held wine. After drinking, he said, "I confess I am not sorry that King Penda chose to flee south instead of coming here." Hajjaj drank wine, too. Thinking of the King of Forthweg as an exile in Bishah was enough to make any Zuwayzi turn to wine, or perhaps to hashish. "We could not very well have turned him away, your Majesty, not if we cared to hold our heads up afterwards," he said, and then, before Shazli could speak, he went on, "We could not very well have kept him here, not if we cared to hold our heads on our shoulders."

"You speak nothing but the truth there." Shazli gulped the goblet dry. "Well, now he is Yanina's worry. I tell you frankly, I am more glad than I can say that King Tsavellas has to explain to Unkerlant how Penda came to go into exile in Patras. Better him than me. Better Yanina than Zuwayza, too."

"Indeed." Hajjaj tried to make his long, thin, lively face look wide and dour, as if he were an Unkerlanter. "First, King Swemmel will demand that Tsavellas turn King Penda over to him. Then, when Tsavellas tells him no, he'll start massing troops on the border with Yanina. After that" – the Zuwayzi foreign minister shrugged – "he'll probably invade."

"If I were Tsavellas, I'd put Penda on a ship or a dragon bound for Sibiu or Valmiera or Lagoas," Shazli said. "Swemmel might forgive him for harboring Penda just long enough to palm him off on someone else."

"Your Majesty, King Swemmel never forgives anyone for anything," Hajjaj said. "He proved that after the Twinkings War – and those were his own countrymen."

King Shazli grunted. "There, I judge, you speak nothing but the truth. Everything he has done since seating himself firmly on the throne of Unkerlant goes toward confirming it." He reached for his wine goblet again, so abruptly that a couple of his gold armlets clashed together. Discovering the goblet was empty, he called for a servant.

A woman came in with a jar and refilled the goblet. "Ah, thank you, my dear," Shazli said. He watched her sway out of the antechamber, then turned his attention back to Hajjaj: Zuwayzin saw too much flesh to let it unduly stir them. "If, as you seem to think, we are next on Swemmel's list, what can we do to forestall him?"

"Dropping an egg on his palace in Cottbus might have some effect," Hajjaj said dryly. "Past that, we are, as your Majesty must know, in something less than the best position."

"As I must know. Aye, so I must." Shazli's mouth twisted. "Finding allies would be easier if we were of the same blood as most of the other folk of Derlavai. If you were a tow-headed, fair-skinned Kaunian, Hajjaj—"

The foreign minister presumed to interrupt his sovereign (not much of a presumption, not with an easygoing king like Shazli): "If I were a Kaunian, your Majesty, I'd long since be dead in this climate of ours. It's no wonder the old Kaunian Empire traded with Zuwayza but never tried planting colonies here. Even more to the point, the only kingdom with whom we share a border is Unkerlant."

"Aye." Shazli looked at Hajjaj as if that were his fault – or perhaps Hajjaj was feeling the strain from continued Unkerlanter pressure, to imagine such a thing. "This also makes the search for allies more difficult than it might be otherwise."

"No one will ally with us against Unkerlant," Hajjaj said. "Forthweg might have, but Forthweg, as we have seen, as we have just discussed, is no more."

"And, as we have seen, Unkerlant and Algarve had divided the kingdom between them as smoothly as two butchers chopping up a camel's carcass," Shazli said discontentedly. "I had hoped for better – better from our point of view, worse from theirs."

"So had I," Hajjaj said. "Given half a chance, King Mezentio can be as headstrong as King Swemmel. But, with Algarve so sorely beset from so many sides at once, Mezentio almost has common sense forced upon him."

"What an unfortunate development." Shazli paused, looking thoughtful. "Of course, Mezentio no longer has to fret about his western frontier, which may leave him more room to maneuver."

"If I may correct your Majesty, King Mezentio no longer has a war on his western frontier," Hajjaj said. "With Unkerlant as his new neighbor, he would be a fool indeed did he not fret about it."

"You have the right of it there, Hajjaj, without a doubt," King Shazli admitted. "See how delighted *we* are, for instance, to have Unkerlant for a neighbor. And Unkerlant and Algarve are by no means enamored of each other. Have we any hope of exploiting that to our advantage?"

"As your Majesty will know, I have had certain conversations with the Algarvian minister here in Bishah," Hajjaj answered. "I fear, however, that Marquis Balastro has not been encouraging."

"What of Jelgava and Valmiera?" Shazli asked.

"They are sympathetic." Hajjaj raised an eyebrow. "Sympathy, however, is worth its weight in gold." King Shazli pondered that for a moment, then laughed. It was not a happy laugh. Hajjaj went on, "Also, the Kaunian kingdoms are not only warring against Algarve but very far away."

Shazli sighed and drained his second goblet of wine. "We are truly in a desperate predicament if King Mezentio offers our best hope of aid."

"It is not a good hope," Hajjaj said. "It is, if anything, a very faint hope. Balastro has made it clear Algarve will not anger Unkerlant while the war goes on in the east and south."

"A faint hope is better than no hope at all," Shazli said. "Why don't you pay another call on the good marquis today?" Seeing the foreign minister's martyred expression, the king laughed again, this time with something approaching real amusement. "Spending an afternoon in clothes will not be the death of you."

"I suppose not, your Majesty," Hajjaj replied in a tone that supposed anything but. King Shazli laughed again, and gently clapped his hands together to show the meeting with the foreign minister was over.

While Hajjaj's secretary spoke on the crystal with the Algarvian ministry to arrange a time for the appointment, Hajjaj himself went through his meager wardrobe. He did have some Algarvian-style tunics and kilts, just as he kept tunics and trousers – which he truly loathed – for consultations with envoys from Jelgava and Valmiera. After donning a blue cotton tunic and a pleated kilt, he examined himself in the mirror. He looked as he had in his student days. No –

his clothes looked as they had then. He'd grown old since. But Marquis Balastro would be pleased.

Hajjaj sighed. "What I do in the service of my kingdom," he muttered.

His secretary had set up the meeting with the Algarvian minister for midafternoon. Hajjaj was meticulously on time, though the Algarvian set less stock in perfect punctuality than did the folk of Unkerlant or the Kaunian kingdoms. Outside the ministry, clothed and sweating Algarvian guards stood watch, as their Unkerlanter counterparts did outside the residence of King Swemmel's envoy. The Algarvians, though, were anything but still and silent as they watched good-looking Zuwayzi women saunter by. They rocked their hips and called lewd suggestions in their own language and in what scraps of Zuwayzi they'd learned.

The women kept walking, pretending they hadn't heard. Such public admiration was anything but the style in Zuwayza. Hajjaj had been shocked the first time he'd heard it when he'd gone off to Algarve for college. It didn't start clan feuds there, though. Algarvian girls giggled and sometimes gave back as good as they got. That had shocked him, too.

He was harder to shock these days. And the Algarvian minister's secretary was a polished man by any kingdom's standards. Escorting Hajjaj past the guards and into the ministry, he murmured in fluent Zuwayzi: "I do beg your pardon, your Excellency, but you know how the soldiers are."

"Oh, aye," Hajjaj answered. "I have learned to make allowances for the foibles of others, and hope others will make allowances for mine."

"What an admirable way to look at things," the foreign minister exclaimed. He ducked into a doorway and returned to his own native tongue: "My lord, the Zuwayzi foreign minister."

"Send him in, send him in," Marquis Balastro said. He did not speak Zuwayzi, but, since Hajjaj knew Algarvian well, they had no trouble talking with each other. Balastro was in his early forties, and wore a little stripe of hair under his lower lip and mustaches waxed till they were as straight and sharply pointed as the horns of a gazelle. Such adornments aside, he had as little of the fop in him as any Algarvian, and was, for a diplomat, forthright.

He – or his secretary – also knew not to plunge too abruptly into business with a Zuwayzi. A tray of cakes and wine appeared as if by magic. Balastro made small talk, waiting for Hajjaj to open: another nice courtesy. At length, Hajjaj did begin, saying, "Your Excellency, it is surely destructive of good order among the kingdoms of the world when the large can with impunity bully and oppress the small for no better reason than that they *are* large."

"With Algarve so grievously beset, I could hardly fail to admit the principle," Balastro said. "Its application, though, will vary according to circumstances."

Algarve was hardly a small kingdom. Hajjaj refrained from saying as much. What he did say was, "As you will have heard from me before, King Swemmel of Unkerlant continues to make unreasonable demands on Zuwayza. Since Algarve, from its own experience, understands such extortion—"

Balastro held up a hand. "Your Excellency, let me be plain about this. Algarve is not at war with Unkerlant. King Mezentio does not now desire to make war on King Swemmel. This being so, Algarve cannot reasonably object to whatever King Swemmel chooses to do on frontiers distant from her. King Mezentio may privately deplore such deeds, but he will not – I repeat, will not – seek to hinder them. Do I make myself clear?"

"You do, unmistakably so." Hajjaj did his diplomatic best to hold disappointment from his voice. Balastro had not been encouraging before. Now he was blunt. Zuwayza would have no help from Algarve. Zuwayza, very probably, would have no help from anyone.

Krasta was angry. When she was angry, people around her suffered. That was not how she thought of it, of course. As far as she was concerned, she was making herself feel better. In any case, other people's feelings had never seemed quite real to her, any more than the idea that there could be numbers smaller than zero had. But the master who'd taught ciphering had been so marvelously handsome, she'd pretended to believe it harder than she would have otherwise.

Now, though, the noblewoman had no reason to dissemble. Waving a news sheet at Bauska, she cried, "Why do they feed us such lies? Why don't they tell us the truth?"

"I don't understand, milady," the servant said. She would not have presumed to read the news sheet before her mistress saw it. Had she so presumed, she would not have been rash enough to admit it.

Krasta waved the news sheet again; Bauska had to leap back hurriedly to keep from getting hit in the face. "They say only that we are advancing in Algarve and moving on the enemy's fortifications. We've been moving on them for weeks. We've been moving on them since this stupid war started. Why haven't we moved past them yet, in the name of the powers above?"

"Perhaps they are very strong, milady," Bauska replied.

"What are you saying now?" Krasta's eyes sparked furiously. "Are you saying that our brave soldiers – are you saying that my brother, the hero – cannot break through whatever defenses the barbarians throw up against us? Is that what you're saying?"

Bauska babbled denials. Krasta listened with only half an ear. Servants always lied. Krasta threw down the news sheet. As far as she was concerned, the war had gone on far too long already. It had grown boring.

"I am going into town," she announced. "I shall spend the day in the shops and the cafes. Perhaps – perhaps, mind you – I shall find something of interest there. Summon the coachmen at once."

"Aye, milady." Bauska bowed and hurried away. As she went, she muttered something under her breath. It could not possibly have been what it sounded like, which was, *Out of my hair for a while.* Krasta dismissed the possibility from her mind. Bauska would never have dared say such a thing, not where she could hear it. The servant knew what was liable to happen to her if Krasta found her even slightly disrespectful. All the servants at the estate knew.

With a low bow, the coachman handed Krasta up into the carriage. "Take me to the Avenue of Equestrians," she said, naming the street with the most shops – and the most expensive shops – in Priekule. "The corner of Little Hills Road will do. I shall expect to see you there again an hour before sunset."

"Aye, milady," the coachman said, as Bauska had done before. Some nobles let their servants speak to them in tones of familiarity. Krasta was not one to make that mistake. They were not her equals, they were her inferiors, and she intended that they remember it.

The carriage went swiftly through the streets. Not much traffic was on them. Many common folk, Krasta knew, had had their horses and donkeys impressed into the service of the kingdom. The public caravans that traveled the ley lines were also far from crowded. Most of the passengers aboard them were women, so many men having been summoned into King Gainibu's army.

Like the traffic on its thoroughfares, Priekule seemed a shadow of its former self. Many shops and taverns were shuttered. Some of those shutters no doubt meant the owners had gone off to war. And some shutters were up because owners wanted to save their expensive glass if Algarvian eggs burst in the capital of Valmiera. None had yet. Krasta was serenely confident none would.

Workmen were piling sandbags around the base of the Kaunian Column of Victory. Cloth sheathed the carved stone. Krasta giggled, thinking of lamb's-gut sheaths for other columns. A wizard walked around the ancient monument, incanting busily. Perhaps he was fireproofing the cloth or otherwise sorcerously strengthening it. Valmiera could afford to do that for its treasures. Few nobles and even fewer commoners could afford to do it for their private property.

Horses snorting, the carriage pulled to a stop. Krasta stepped out on to the Avenue of Equestrians. She did not look back, nor wonder even for a moment what the coachman would do till it was time to retrieve her. As far as she was concerned, he stopped existing when she no longer needed him. If he didn't start existing again the moment she required him, he would be sorry.

Shops on the Avenue of Equestrians remained open. Clerks fawned on Krasta as she strutted into a jeweler's, a milliner's, a fancy lampseller's. The clerk in a fine tailor's shop did not fawn enough to suit her. She had her revenge: she ran the young girl ragged, trying on every pair of silk and leather and linen trousers in the place.

"And which will milady choose for herself today?" the sweating clerk asked when Krasta redonned her own trousers at last.

"Oh, I do not care to buy today," Krasta answered sweetly. "I was just comparing your styles to the ones I saw the other day at the House of Spogi." Out she went, leaving the clerk, slump-shouldered with dejection, staring after her.

Setting the commoner in her place immensely improved Krasta's mood. She hurried across the street to the Bronze Woodcock, a cafe she'd always favored. An old waiter with a bushy mustache of almost Algarvian impressiveness was leading her to an empty table by the fire when a man a couple of tables away sprang to his feet and bowed. "Will you join me, Marchioness?"

The waiter paused, awaiting Krasta's decision. She smiled. "Of course I will, Viscount Valnu," she replied. With a tiny shrug, the waiter steered her to Valnu's table. The viscount bowed again, this time over her hand. He raised it to his lips, then let it fall. Krasta's smile got wider. "So good to see you, Viscount," she said as she sat down. "And since I hadn't seen you in a while, I thought you must have put on a uniform, as my brother has done."

Valnu took a pull at the flagon of porter in front of him. Firelight played off his cheekbones. Depending on how it struck his features, they were either beautifully sculpted or skeletal: sometimes both at once. His blood, Krasta thought, was very fine. With a wry smile of his own, he said, "I fear the rigors of the field are not for me. I am a creature of Priekule, and could flourish nowhere else. If King Gainibu grows so desperate as to need my martial services, Valmiera shall be in desperate peril indeed."

"Porter, milady?" the waiter asked Krasta. "Ale? Wine?"

"Ale," she said. "Ale and a poached trout on a bed of saffron rice."

"And I will have the smoked sausage with vinegared cabbage," Valnu declared. "Hearty peasant fare." He himself was neither peasantish nor hearty. As the waiter bowed, he went on, "You need not hurry the meals overmuch, my good fellow. The marchioness and I shall amuse ourselves in the meantime by talking about rank." The waiter bowed again and departed.

Krasta clapped her hands together. "That is well said!" she cried. "Truly you are a man of great nobility indeed."

"I do my best," Valnu said. "More than that, I cannot do. More than that, no man can do."

"So many of the superior class do not even try to come up to such standards," Krasta said. "And so many of the lower order these days are so grasping and vulgar and rude, they require lessons in the art of dealing with their better." She explained how she had dealt with the clerk in the clothier's establishment.

Valnu's delighted grin displayed very white, even teeth and made him look more like a skull than ever, save only for the glow of admiration in his bright blue eyes. "That is excellent," he said. "Excellent! You could hardly have done better without running her

through, and, had you done that, she would not have long
appreciated what you'd taught her."

"I suppose not," Krasta agreed regretfully, "though that might
have left a stronger impression on the rest of the vulgar herd."

Valnu clicked his tongue between his teeth several times, shaking
his head all the while. "People would talk, my dear. People would
talk. And now" – he sipped his porter – "shall we talk?"

Talk he and Krasta did: who was sleeping with whom, who was
feuding with whom (two topics often intimately related), whose
family was older than whose, who had been caught out while trying
to make his family seem older than it was. That was meat and drink
to Krasta. She leaned across the small table toward Valnu, so intent
and interested that she hardly noticed the waiter bringing them their
luncheons.

Valnu did not at once attack his sausage and sour cabbage, either.
In a sorrowful voice, he said, "And, I hear, Duke Kestu lost his only
son and heir in Algarve the other day. When I think of how the Six
Years' War cut down so many noble stems, when I think of how
likely this war is to do the same . . . I fear for the future of our kind,
milday."

"There will always be a nobility." Krasta spoke with automatic
confidence, as if she had said, *There will always be a sunrise in the
morning.* But her family's male line depended on her brother. And
Skarnu was fighting in Algarve, and he had no heir. She did not care
to think about that. To keep from thinking about it, she took a long
pull from her flagon of ale and began to eat the trout and rice on the
plate before her.

"I hope everything goes as well as it can for you and yours,
milady," Valnu said quietly. Krasta wished he had not said anything
at all. If he had to say something, that was more kindly and less
worrisome than most of the other things she could think of.

He dug into the pungent cabbage and sausage – peasant fare indeed
– and made them disappear at an astonishing rate. However
emaciated he appeared, it was not due to any failure of appetite.

Nor, very plainly, was anything wrong with any of his other
appetites, either. As Krasta ate, she was startled – but, given some of
the things she'd heard about Valnu, not surprised – when, under the
table, his hand came down on her leg, well above the knee. She

brushed it away as she might have brushed away a crawling insect. "My lord viscount, as you yourself said, people would talk."

His answering smile was hard and bright and predatory. "Of course they would, my dear. They always do." The hand returned. "Shall we, then, give them something interesting to talk about?"

She considered, letting his hand linger and even stray upwards while she did. He was well-born, and was attractive in a bony way. While he would certainly be unfaithful, he would never pretend to be anything else. In the end, though, she shook her head and took his hand away again. "Not this afternoon. Too many shops I haven't yet visited."

"Thrown over for shops! For shops!" Valnu clapped both hands over his heart, as if pierced by a beam from a stick. Then, in an instant, he went from melodrama to pragmatism: "Well, better that than being thrown over for another lover."

Krasta laughed. She almost changed her mind. But she still had gold in her handbag, and plenty of shops along the Avenue of Equestrians she hadn't seen. She paid for her luncheon and left the Bronze Woodcock. Valnu blew her a kiss.

Skarnu stared in grim dismay at the line of fortresses ahead. Having seen them, the Valmieran captain no longer wondered why his superiors hesitated before hurling their army at those works. The Algarvians had lavished both ingenuity and gold on them. Whoever tried to smash them down, whoever tried to break through them, would pay dearly.

"Come away, Captain," Sergeant Raunu urged. "Like as not, the stinking Algarvians'll put a hole through anybody who takes too long a look."

"Like as not, you're right," Skarnu said, and ducked back down into the barley that helped shield him from unfriendly eyes – and, east of where he crouched, there were no eyes of any other sort. East of where he crouched, too, were very few places to hide. Whatever else might happen to it, the Algarvians' defensive line would not fall to surprise attack.

"In the last war, we'd throw eggs at forts and then just charge right at 'em," Raunu said. "Maybe they've learned something since."

"If they'd learned anything since, we wouldn't be in a war now,"

Skarnu answered. The veteran sergeant blinked, then slowly nodded.

Off to the north, Valmieran egg-tossers started lobbing destruction at the line of forts. The burst resounded like distant thunder. Skarnu wondered how much damage they were doing. Not so much as he would have liked: he was certain of that. The Algarvians had used stone and earth and cement and iron and bronze to fashion a line of death that ran for many miles north and south and was most of a mile deep. How long would soldiers batter their heads against that line, as Raunu had said, in search of a breakthrough that might not be there at all? Forever?

Probably not. Even so, Skarnu sighed as he said, "They built that to dare us to try to go through it, to dare us to spend the men we'd need to get to the other side. They don't think we have the nerve to do it."

"I wouldn't be sorry if they were right, either," Raunu said.

"Would you rather fight inside Valmiera, the way we did for most of the Six Years' War?" Skarnu returned.

"Sir, it's like you said: if you ask me what I'd rather, I'd rather not fight at all," the sergeant said.

Skarnu clicked his tongue between his teeth. Sergeant Raunu had indeed used his own words to reply to him, which meant he could hardly take exception to what the veteran said. But he'd seen that a good many of the common soldiers had little stomach for the fight against Algarve in general, and even less for the assault on the forts. He said, "We should have pushed harder, so we would have been through this line before the Forthwegians collapsed."

"Aye, I see what you're saying, sir, but I don't know how much difference that would have made." Raunu pointed ahead. "Doesn't look like the cursed redheads have put any new men in their lines, even if they don't have to worry about their western front any more."

"They don't have to worry about Forthweg any more," Skarnu corrected. "Now they're face to face with Unkerlant. If they're not worried about that, they're fools."

"Of course they're fools. They're Algarvians." Raunu spoke with an automatic scorn Skarnu's sister Krasta might have envied. But then, as Krasta would never have done, he changed course slightly: "They're fools most ways, I mean. They make good soldiers, whatever else you say about 'em."

"I wish I could tell you you were wrong," Skarnu said. "Our lives would be easier." The Algarvians had resisted the Valmieran advance to the fortified line with only light forces, but they'd fought stubbornly. They'd also fought skillfully, perhaps more skillfully than the men he commanded. Had there been more of them, he wondered if his men would have been able to advance at all. Along with most of his other worries, he kept that one to himself.

A runner came up to him. "My lord marquis?" the fellow asked.

"Aye?" Skarnu said in some small surprise. Far more often these days, he was addressed by his military rank, not title. After a moment, a possible reason for this exception came to mind.

And, sure enough, the runner said, "My lord, his Grace the Duke of Klaipeda bids you sup with him and with some of the other leading officers of our triumphant army at his headquarters this evening. The supper shall begin an hour past sunset."

"Please tell his Grace I am honored, and of course I shall attend him," Skarnu answered. The runner bowed and hurried away.

Raunu eyed Skarnu. He'd understood Skarnu was a noble, of course. That was one thing. An invitation extended to a captain to sup with the commander of an army of tens of thousands was something else again. Almost defensively, Skarnu said, "I went to school with his Grace's son."

"Did you, sir?" the sergeant said. "Well, you'll get a good meal out of it, and that's the truth. I will say, though, sir, the men think well of you for eating out of the same pot they use."

"It's the best way I could think of to make sure they got decent food," Skarnu said. "Nobody cares when a common soldier fusses and complains. When a captain grumbles, though, people start to notice."

"Aye, sir," Raunu said, "especially when he's a captain who went to school with the Duke of Klaipeda's son." More than half to himself, he added, "It's a wonder you're just a captain and not a colonel."

Skarnu wished he hadn't had to mention his connection with the duke, whose son, while not the depraved little monster so beloved of romancers without much imagination, had been one of the most boring youths he'd ever met. He also wished the duke were paying more attention to the commanders who would lead great parts of the Valmieran army into battle and less to his son's social connections.

But, regardless of the duke's shortcomings, Skarnu spruced himself up and made his way back toward the village of Bonorva. The village was a good deal more battered than it had been when he'd first seen it from the woods that now lay on the far side from the front. The duke had taken up residence in one of the larger houses there. It still looked scarred and abused: no point cleaning it up and offering the Algarvians a target. Skarnu chuckled as he drew near. After he wrote to Krasta, she'd be sick with jealousy at the exalted company he was keeping.

When he went inside the unprepossessing building, Skarnu might have been transported to another world, the world in which the Valmieran nobility had idled away its time in Priekule and on estates out in the provinces. Lights blazed; dark cloth over the windows and behind the door kept it from leaking out and drawing the notice of Algarvian dragons overhead or the cunning snoops who kept trying to spy targets for the enemy's egg-tossers.

Marstalu, the Duke of Klaipeda, stood just inside the doorway greeting new arrivals. He was a portly man in his late fifties, his complexion very pink, his hair gone white as snow: he looked like everyone's favorite grandfather. His uniform put Skarnu in mind of those the Kaunian Emperors had won. So did the brilliant constellation of medals – some gold, some silver, some bejeweled, some with ribbons like comets' tails – spangling his chest.

Skarnu bowed low, murmuring, "Your Grace."

"Good to see you, lad. Good to see you," the duke said, beaming in a grandfatherly way. "Make yourself at home. Plenty of good things to eat and drink here – better than you'll find at the front, that's certain."

"No doubt, sir." Skarnu felt out of place here despite Marstalu's friendly words. Most of the other noble officers present glittered hardly less than their commanders. Skarnu's unadorned uniform made him look and feel like a servant. It also made him feel like a real soldier in amongst a flock of popinjays. Perhaps that was what made him ask, "Sir, when will the attack against the Algarvian works go in?"

"When all is in readiness," Marstalu answered easily. That might mean anything. It might mean nothing. Skarnu suspected it meant nothing here. The duke went on, "Perhaps we could be more zealous now had we reached this position before the Algarvians finished their dismantling of Forthweg."

Skarnu didn't know what to say to that. Marstalu was saying the same thing he had to Raunu. Raunu hadn't thought it would make a difference. Skarnu had to hope the sergeant was right and he and the commander of the army wrong. But, had the Duke of Klaipeda wanted to reach the fortified belt before Forthweg collapsed, he should have pushed harder. He could have. Of course, he couldn't have known Algarve's attack would shatter Forthweg, but everything Skarnu had ever soaked up about the military art suggested that wasting time was never a good idea.

Pushing Marstalu further would accomplish nothing but getting him on the commander's black list. He could see as much at a glance. That being so, what better choice than enjoying the choice viands and potables set out on the tables before him? He sat down between a pair of bemedaled colonels. One of them jabbed a serving fork into the large, savory bird lying on a tray in front of him. Juices spurted. "Have some, Captain," he said. "As you can see, we've finally gone and cooked Algarve's goose."

The colonel on the other side of Skarnu laughed so uproariously at that sally, Skarnu was convinced he'd already emptied the crystal goblet before him several times. Lifting his own wine goblet, Skarnu said, "May we serve the king as we have served the goose."

"Oh, well said, young fellow, well said," both colonels exclaimed in the same breath. They drank. So did Skarnu. He carved off a thick slice of goose, then spooned a good helping of parsnips seethed in cream and dotted with butter on to his plate. The salad was of fine lettuces and chopped scallions dressed with wine vinegar and walnut oil.

One of the colonels boasted about the speed of the fine horses he had liberated from an Algarvian noble's stables. The other boasted about the agility of the fine mistress he had liberated from an Algarvian noble's bedchamber. Skarnu tried to boast about the fighting qualities of the men in his company. Neither colonel seemed the least bit interested. They were fascinated with each other's brags, though. Sometimes it was hard to tell which one was talking about his new acquisition.

Gloom settled over Skarnu like a winter fog in Priekule. King Gainibu had been more interested in starting the war against Algarve than his officers were in fighting it. They'd taken what the Algarvians were willing to yield. Now that the Algarvians had yielded everything up to their long-established defensive line, they weren't going to be willing to yield any more. And going up against that line was, ever more plainly, the last thing any Valmieran commander wanted to do.

One of the boastful colonels upended his goblet once too often. He set his head down on the table and started to snore. Skarnu felt like getting that drunk, too. *Why not?* he thought. *Raunu runs the company just as well when I'm not there.*

In the end, though, he refrained. He started to make his way over to the Duke of Klaipeda to say his farewells, but Marstalu seemed far gone in wine himself. Skarnu slipped out into the cool, dark night and headed east toward his company. All things considered, he would rather not have been invited to the feast. He'd hoped for reassurance. What he'd got was more to worry about.

5.

Fernao strolled through the streets of Setubal, delighting in the life that brawled around him. The capital of Lagoas had long been the most cosmopolitan city in the world. Now, the mage thought sadly, it was, as near as made no difference, the only cosmopolitan city left in the world.

Lagoas was not at war with anyone. That made the island kingdom unique among the major powers. Oh, Unkerlant was not at war with anyone at the moment, but Fernao, along with everyone else, assumed that was only because King Swemmel, having helped himself to a large chunk of Forthweg, was looking around for his next neighbor to assault. Zuwayza affronted him merely by existing, as Forthweg had, but Yanina had taken in King Penda when he fled Eoforwic. One of them would go under soon. Maybe both of them would go under soon. Fernao guessed Yanina would go first.

But Lagoas, with any luck at all, could stay neutral through the whole mad war. Fernao hoped his kingdom could. Monuments in Setubal's many parks and at street corners warned of wars past: recent monuments to the fight against Algarve in the Six Years' War, older ones to war against Valmiera, older ones still to wars against Kuusamo and the pirates of Sibiu who were all the rage in Lagoan romances these days, even a couple of Kaunian columns from the days before the Empire brought its armies back home to the mainland of Derlavai.

What sort of monument might a kingdom erect to a war in which it hadn't fought? Fernao visualized a marble statue, three times life size, of a man swiping the back of his hand across his forehead in relief. After a moment, he realized the man he'd visualized looked a lot like him. He laughed at that. He'd known he was vain. Maybe he hadn't known how vain he was.

He turned into a tavern (*a good piece of magecraft, that*, he thought, now with a laugh that was more like a snort) and ordered a glass of

Jelgavan red wine. When the taverner gave it to him, he took it over to a small table by the wall and sipped in leisurely fashion. The taverner gave him a sour look, as he might have done with any man likely to occupy space without bringing in much business.

Plenty of other people were drinking more than Fernao: Lagoans, slant-eyed Kuusamans, Valmierans in trousers, Sibians, even a few Algarvians who'd managed to run their foes' blockade. The mage wondered what sort of shady deals they were cooking up. Since everyone could come to Setubal, anything was liable to happen here. He knew that very well.

Along with noting the conversation humming around him, he listened with a different part of his being to the power humming through Setubal. There were more power points in a smaller space here than anywhere else in the world; more ley lines converged on the Lagoan capital than on any other city. In a mage's veins, the song of that power sometimes seemed stronger than his pulse.

A man slid down on to the ladderbacked chair across the table from Fernao. "Mind if I join you?" he asked with a friendly smile.

"It's all right," Fernao answered. He would sooner have been alone with his thoughts, but the tavern was crowded. He lifted his wineglass. "Your good health."

"I thank you, sir. And yours." The stranger lifted his mug in return. Steam and a sweet, spicy smell rose from it: hot mulled cider in there, unless Fernao's nose had lost its cleverness. The stranger sipped, then nodded with the air of a connoisseur. "Powers above, that's good," he said.

Fernao nodded, politely but without intending to encourage further conversation. But, as he drank a little more wine, he could not help starting to size up the man across from him. And, once he'd started, he found he couldn't stop. The fellow spoke unaccented Lagoan, but he didn't look like a native of King Vitor's domain. Lagoans were more various in their appearance than the folk of many kingdoms – Fernao's slanted eyes said as much – but very few were dark and stocky and heavily bearded.

Even fewer wore trousers. That was a Kaunian fashion no kingdom sprung from Algarvic stock had ever adopted. Taken all in all, the stranger might have been put together out of pieces from three or four different puzzles.

He also noticed Fernao scrutinizing him, which he wasn't
supposed to do. He smiled again, a surprisingly charming smile from
a man less than handsome. After another sip at his hot cider, he said,
"Am I correct in understanding, sir, that you are more than a little
skilled at getting into and out of places where others might possibly
not want to go?"

A trip into Feltre despite the anger of the Sibian Navy qualified
Fernao to answer aye. He did nothing of the sort, instead saying,
"You are correct in understanding, sir, that my business is my
business – and no one else's unless I choose to make it so."

The fellow across the table from him laughed gaily, as if he'd said
something very funny. Fernao knocked back his wine – the taverner,
no doubt, would be pleased – and started to get to his feet. Where
nothing else had, that made the stranger lose his too-easy smile.
"Please, sir, don't go yet," he said in a voice that, despite its polite
tones, held iron underneath.

His right hand rested, broad palm down, on the tabletop. He might
have had some sort of weapon – a cut-down stick, perhaps a knife –
under it. But when he lifted it, taking care that Fernao and no one
else could see what he did, he revealed not a weapon but the sparkle
of gold.

Fernao sat back down. "You have engaged my attention, at least
for the time being. Say on, sir."

"I thought that might do the trick," the stranger said complacently.
"You Lagoans have the name of being a mercenary folk. That you
trade with both sides during the current unpleasantness does nothing
to detract from it."

"That we trade with both sides shows a certain common sense, in
my view," Fernao said. "That you sneer at my people does nothing
to attract me to you. And, if we are to continue this discussion, give
me a name to call you. I do not deal with nameless men." *Unless I
have no choice*, he thought but did not say aloud. Here, though, the
choice was his.

"Names have power," the man across the table from him observed.
"Names especially have power in the mouth of a mage. But you may
call me Shelomith, if you must stick a handle on me as if I were a hot
pot."

"If whatever notion you have in mind could not burn me, you

would have approached me in a different way," Fernao said. And *Shelomith* was not the name with which the stranger had been born. It sounded like one the barbarous Ice People used. Whatever blood ran in Shelomith's veins, it was not from that stock. Fernao went on, "You have shown me gold. I presume you have in mind paying me some. How do you expect me to earn it?"

"This for listening," Shelomith said, and shoved the coin he had concealed across to the mage. It showed the fuzzy-bearded king of Gyongyos, whose image was bordered by an inscription in demotic Gyongyosian script, which Fernao recognized but could not read. He did not think the coin's origin said anything about what Shelomith had in mind. Gold circulated freely all across the world, and a crafty man could use it to conceal rather than to reveal. As if to point in that same direction, Shelomith spoke again: "For listening – and for your discretion."

"Discretion goes only so far," Fernao said. "If you ask me to betray my king or my kingdom, I will do nothing of the sort. I will shout for a constable instead."

He wondered if Shelomith would find urgent business elsewhere on hearing that. The stranger only shrugged wide shoulders. "Nothing of the sort," he said in reassuring tones. Of course, he would have said the same thing had he been lying. He went on, "You may remain apart from the proposal I shall put to you, but it could not offend even the most delicate sensibility."

"Such a statement is all the better for proof," Fernao said. "Tell me plainly what you want from me. I will tell you if you may have it and, if so, at what price."

Shelomith looked pained. Fernao got the idea that asking him to speak plainly was like asking the Falls of Leixoes to flow uphill. At last, after another long pull at his cider, he said, as he had before, "You are, are you not, good at getting into and out of tight places?"

"This is where we began." The mage made as if to get up again, this time with the goldpiece in the pouch on his belt. "Good morning."

As he'd more than half expected, another goldpiece appeared under Shelomith's palm. Fernao kept rising. "Good my sir," Shelomith said plaintively. "Only sit, and be patient, and all will be made clear." Fernao sat. The stranger passed him the second goldpiece. He made it disappear: a good, profitable morning. Shelomith looked even more pained. "Are you always so difficult?"

"I make a point of it," Fernao said. "Are you always so obscure?"

Shelomith muttered under his breath. To Fernao's disappointment, he could not make out which language the stranger used when angry. He sat quietly and waited. Maybe Shelomith would feed him still more gold for doing nothing. Instead, with the air of a man yielding himself up to a dentist, Shelomith said, "Does it not wring your heart to see a crowned king trapped in exile far from his native land?"

"Ah," Fernao said. "Sits the wind so? Well, a question for a question: don't you think King Penda is a lot happier sitting in exile in Yanina than he would be had the Algarvians or Unkerlanters caught him in Forthweg?"

"You are as clever as I hoped," Shelomith said, slapping on the flattery with a broad brush. Fernao would have been naïve to fail to get his drift. "The answer to your question is aye, but only to a degree. He is not only in exile; he might as well be in prison. King Tsavellas holds him close, so he can yield him up to King Swemmel if the Unkerlanter's pressure grows too great."

"Ah," Fernao repeated. He fell into slow, sonorous Forthwegian: "And you want him taken beyond King Swemmel's reach."

"Even so," Shelomith answered in the same language. "Having a mage with us will make us more likely to succeed. Having a *Lagoan* mage with us will make it less likely that King Swemmel can take reprisal against him."

"A distinct point, from all I have heard of King Swemmel," Fernao said. "The next question is, what makes you think I am the Lagoan mage you want?"

"You have gone into Algarve in time of war, why should you not go into Yanina in time of peace? You are a mage of the first rank, so you will have the strength to do whatever may be needed. You speak Forthwegian, as you have shown. I would be lying if I said you were the only mage at whom we are looking, but you are the man we would like to have."

His friends were probably saying the same thing to the other candidates. As soon as someone was rash enough to say aye, they would lose interest in the others. Fernao wondered if he was rash enough to say aye. He'd never been to Yanina. Getting there would be easy enough, if King Swemmel didn't invade; the small kingdom between Algarve and Unkerlant remained nervously neutral. Getting out – especially getting out with King Penda – was liable to be something else again.

Of course, Shelomith was liable not to care whether Fernao got out or not, so long as Penda did. That might make life interesting in several unpleasant ways. A sensible man would pocket the two Gyongyosian goldpieces and go about his business.

"When do we sail?" Fernao asked.

Marshal Rathar endured the search to which King Swemmel's bodyguards subjected him with less aplomb than he usually showed. He had not conceived so high an opinion of himself as to think he was above searching. But he did begrudge the time he had to waste before being admitted to his sovereign's presence.

Once he'd got past the guards, he also begrudged the time he had to spend knocking his head against the carpet before the king. Ceremony was all very well in its place; it reminded people what a great and mighty sovereign ruled them. Rathar, though, already knew that well. Wasting time on ceremony, then, struck him as inefficient.

King Swemmel saw things otherwise. As always, how King Swemmel saw things prevailed in Unkerlant. Having at last been granted permission to rise, Rathar said, "May it please your Majesty, I am come at your command."

"It pleases us very little," Swemmel replied in his light, rather petulant voice. "We are beset by enemies on all sides. One by one, for Unkerlant's greater glory and for our own safety, we must be rid of them."

He quivered a little on his high seat. He was quite capable of deciding on the spur of the moment that Rathar was an enemy and ordering his head stricken from his body. A lot of officers, some of high rank, had died that way during the Twinkings War. A lot more had died that way since.

If he decided that, he would be wrong, but it would do Rathar no good. Showing fear would do Rathar no good, either. It might make Swemmel decide he had reason to be afraid. The marshal said, "Point me at your foes, your Majesty, and I will bring them down. I am your hawk."

"We have too many foes," Swemmel said. "Gyongyos in the far west—"

"We are, for the moment, at peace with Gyongyos," Rathar said.

Swemmel went on as if he had not spoken: "Algarve—"

Now Rathar interrupted with more than a little alarm, saying, "Your Majesty, King Mezentio's men have been most scrupulous in observing the border between their kingdom and ours that existed before the start of the Six Years' War. They are as happy to see Forthweg gone from the map again as we are. They want no trouble with us; they have their hands full in the east."

He needed a moment to decipher King Swemmel's expression. It was a curious blend of amusement and pity, the sort of expression Rathar might have used had his ten-year-old son come out with some very naïve view of the way the world worked. Swemmel said, "They will attack us. Sooner or later, they will surely attack us – if we give them the chance."

If King Swemmel wanted to go to war with one of his small, weak neighbors, that was one thing. If he wanted to go to war with Algarve, that was something else again. Urgently, Rathar said, "Your Majesty, our armies are not yet ready to fight King Mezentio's. The way the Algarvians used dragons and behemoths to open the path for their foot in Forthweg is something new on the face of the world. We need to learn to defend against it, if we can. We need to learn to imitate it, too. Until we do those things, which I have already set in motion, we should not engage Algarve."

He waited for King Swemmel to order him to hurl the armies of Unkerlant against King Mezentio in spite of what he had said, in which case he would do his best. He also waited for his sovereign to curse him for having failed to invent the new way of fighting himself. Swemmel did neither. He merely continued with his catalogue of grievances: "King Tsavellas casts defiance in our face, refusing to yield up to us the person of Penda, who pretended to be king of Forthweg."

Swemmel had recognized Penda as king of Forthweg until Algarvian and Unkerlanter armies made Penda flee his falling king- dom. That was not the point at the heart of the matter, though.

Rathar said, "If we invade Yanina, your Majesty, we collide with Algarve again. I would sooner use Yanina as a shield, to keep Algarve from colliding with us."

"We never forget insults. Never," Swemmel said. Rathar hoped he was talking about Tsavellas. After a moment, Swemmel went on, "And there is Zuwayza. The Zuwayzi provocations against us are intolerable."

Rathar knew perfectly well that Unkerlant was the kingdom doing the provoking. He wondered whether Swemmel knew it, too, or whether his sovereign truly believed himself the aggrieved party. You never could tell with Swemmel. Rathar said, "The Zuwayzin do indeed grow overbold." If he could steer the king away from launching an attack on Yanina, he would.

He could, which he reckoned hardly less a miracle than those a first-rank mage could sometimes produce. King Swemmel said, "The time has come to settle Zuwayza, so that Shazli may no longer threaten us." As he refused to accord Penda the royal title, so he also did with Shazli. He went on, "Ready the army to fall upon Zuwayza at my order."

"It is merely a matter of transporting troops and beasts and equipment to the frontier, your Majesty," Rathar said with relief. "We have planned this campaign for some time, and shall be able to unleash our warriors whenever you should command – provided," he added hastily, "that you give us time enough to deploy fully before commencing."

"You can do this and still leave a large enough force in reclaimed Forthweg to guard against Algarvian treachery?" Swemmel demanded.

"We can," Rathar said. Unkerlanter officers had been planning for war against Zuwayza since the day Swemmel drove Kyot's forces out of Cottbus. Some of those plans involved fighting Zuwayza while holding the line against Algarve in the east. It was just a matter of pulling the right sheet of orders from the file, adapting them to the precise circumstances, and issuing them.

"How soon can we begin to punish the desert-dwellers?" Swemmel asked.

Before answering, Rathar reviewed in his mind the man he was likeliest to use. "Not so many ley lines leading up toward Zuwayza as we would like, your Majesty," he said. "Not many through the desert leading toward Bishah, either. If we hadn't already established supply caches up there, we'd be a good while preparing. As things are . . . We can move in three weeks, I would say." In practice, it would take rather longer, as such things had a way of doing, but he was sure he would be able to keep King Swemmel from actually ordering the assault till everything was ready.

But, as he'd thought only a few minutes before, you never could tell with Swemmel. The king screwed up his face till he looked like an infant about to throw a tantrum. "We cannot wait that long!" he shouted. "We will not wait that long! We have been waiting for twenty years!"

Rathar spoke in what he thought to be the voice of reason: "If you have been waiting so long, your Majesty, would you not be wise in waiting just a little longer, to make sure everything goes forward as it should?"

"If you show yourself a disobedient servant, Marshal, we shall find another to wield the righteous sword of Unkerlant," Swemmel said in a deadly voice. "It is our will that our army redeem the land the Zuwayzin stole from us beginning no later than ten days hence."

If someone else suddenly became Marshal of Unkerlant, he would make a worse hash of the war against Zuwayza, and of any later wars, than Rathar would himself. Rathar knew the men likeliest to replace him if he fell, and knew without false modesty that he was abler than any of them. Not only that, but he had his hands on the reins and knew exactly how to guide the horse. Anyone else would need a while to figure out how to do whatever needed doing.

All that went through Rathar's mind before he worried about his own extinction. He was not sure his wife would miss him; they spent little time together these days. His oldest son was a junior officer. His fall would injure the lad's career – or Swemmel might decide to destroy the whole family, to make sure no trouble arose later.

Steadily, even stolidly, Rathar asked, "Would you throw away twenty years of waiting, your Majesty, because you cannot bear to wait twenty days?"

Swemmel's chin was hardly the more prepossessing Rathar had ever seen. Nonetheless, the king stuck it out. "We shall not wait even an instant longer. Will you or will you not launch the assault in ten days' time, Marshal?"

"If we strike too soon, without all our regiments in their proper places, the Zuwayzin will be far better able to resist," Rathar said.

King Swemmel's eyes bored into his. Rathar dropped his own eyes, staring down at the green carpet on which he stood. Nevertheless, he felt the king's gaze like a physical weight, a heavy, heavy weight. Swemmel said, "We would not have so much patience with many men, Marshal. Do you obey us?"

"Your Majesty, I obey you," Rathar said. Obeying Swemmel would cost lives. Odds were, it would cost lives by the thousands. Unkerlant had lives to spend. Zuwayza did not. It was as simple as that. And with Rathar in command, the king's willfulness would not cost so many lives as it would under some other commander. So he told himself, at any rate, salving his conscience as best he could.

When he looked up at Swemmel again, the king was relaxed, or as relaxed as his tightly wound spirit ever let him be. "Go, then," he said. "Go and ready the army, to hurl it against the Zuwayzin at our command. We shall publish to the world the indignities Shazli and his burnt-skinned, naked minions have committed against our kingdom. No one will lift a finger to aid them."

"I should think not," Rathar said. With the rest of the world embroiled in war, who would even grieve over one small, distant kingdom?

"Go, then," Swemmel repeated. "You have shown yourself to be a good leader of men, Marshal, and the armies you commanded did all we expected and all we had hoped in taking back Forthweg. Otherwise, your insolence here would not go unpunished. Next time, regardless of circumstances, it shall not go unpunished. Do you understand?"

"I am your servant, your Majesty," Rathar said, bowing low. "You have commanded; I shall obey. All I wanted was to be certain you fully grasped the choice you are making."

"Every man, woman, and child in Unkerlant is our servant," King Swemmel said indifferently. "A marshal's blade makes you no different from the rest. And we make our own choices for our own reasons. We need no one to confuse our mind, especially when we did not seek your views on this matter. Do you understand *that*?"

"Aye, your Majesty." Rathar's face showed nothing of what he thought. So far as he could, his face showed nothing at all. Around King Swemmel, that was safest.

"Then get out!" Swemmel shouted.

Rathar prostrated himself again. When he rose to retreat from the king's chamber, he did so without turning around, lest his back offend his sovereign. In the antechamber, he buckled on his ceremonial sword once more. A guard matter-of-factly got between him and the doorway through which he'd come, to make sure he could not attack the king. Sometimes the idea *was* tempting, though Rathar did not let his face show that, either.

He went off to do his best to get the army ready to invade Zuwayza at King Swemmel's impossible deadline. His aides exclaimed in dismay. Normally as calm a man as any ever born, Rathar screamed at them. After his audience with Swemmel, that made him feel a little better, but not much.

Tealdo liked being stationed in the Duchy of Bari just fine, even if, as a man from the north, he found oncoming autumn in this part of Algarve on the chilly side. The folk of the Duchy remained thrilled to be united with their countrymen, from whom old Duke Alardo had done his best to sunder them. And a gratifying number of girls in the Duchy remained thrilled to unite with Algarvian soldiers.

"Why shouldn't they?" Tealdo's friend Trasone said when he remarked on that. "It's their patriotic duty, isn't it?"

"If I ever told a wench it was her patriotic duty to lay me, she'd figure it was her patriotic duty to smack me in the head," Tealdo said, which made Trasone laugh. Tealdo went on, "The other thing I like about being here is that I'm not blazing away at the Valmierans or the Jelgavans – and they're not blazing away at me."

Trasone laughed again, a big bass rumble that suited his burly frame. "Well, I won't argue with that. Powers above, I can't argue with that. But sooner or later we'll have to do some blazing, and when we do it's liable to be worse than facing either one of the stinking Kaunian kingdoms."

"Sooner or later will take care of itself," Tealdo said. "For now, nobody's blazing at me, and that's just fine."

He strode out of the barracks, which were made of pine timber so new, they still smelled strongly of resinous sap. Off in the distance, waves from the Narrow Sea slapped against the stone breakwater that shielded the harbor of Imola from winter storms. Endless streams of birds flew past overhead, all of them going north. Already they were fleeing the brief summer of the land of the Ice People. Soon, very soon, they would be fleeing the Duchy of Bari, too, bound for warmer climes. Some would stop in northern Algarve and Jelgava; some would cross the Garelian Ocean and winter in tropic Siaulia, which hardly knew the meaning of the word.

Above the twittering flocks, dragons whirled in lazy – no, in lazy-looking – circles. Tealdo looked south, toward the sea and toward Sibiu. More dragons circled over the sea. Tealdo resented the dragonfliers less than he had when he was marching into the Duchy. They kept the Sibs from dropping eggs on his head. He heartily approved of that. They also kept the enemy's dragons from peering down on him and his comrades. He approved of that, too.

A trumpeter on the parade ground in front of the barracks blew a sprightly flourish: the call to assembly. Tealdo dashed for his place. Behind him, men poured from the barracks as if from a bawdy house the constables were raiding. He took his assigned place in the ranks of the regiment ahead of almost everyone else. That gave him half a minute to brush a few specks of dust from his kilt, to slide his boots along his socks, and to adjust his broad-brimmed hat to the proper jaunty angle before Sergeant Panfilo started prowling.

Prowl Panfilo did. He favored Tealdo with a glare sergeants surely had to practice in front of a reflecting glass. Tealdo looked back imperturbably. Panfilo reached out and slapped away some dust he'd missed – or perhaps slapped at nothing at all, to keep Tealdo from thinking he had the world by the tail. Sergeants did things like that.

"King Mezentio doesn't want slobs in his army," Panfilo growled.

"Told you so himself, did he?" Tealdo asked innocently.

But Panfilo got the last word: "That he did, in his regulations, and I'll thank you to remember it." He stalked off to make some other common soldier's life less joyous than it had been.

Colonel Ombruno swaggered out to the front of the regiment. "Well, my pirates, my cutthroats, my old-fashioned robbers and burglars," he called with a grin, "how wags your world today?"

"We are well, sir," Tealdo shouted along with the rest of the men.

"Diddling enough of the pretty girls around these parts?" Ombruno asked.

"Aye!" the men shouted, Tealdo again loud among them. He knew Ombruno chased – and caught – the Barian women as frequently as he had farther north in Algarve.

"That's good; that's good." The regimental commander rocked back on his heels, then forward once more. "No diddling for now, though, except that we're going to figure out how to diddle our enemies. Go load your packs, grab your sticks, and report back here in ten minutes. Dismissed!"

This time, Tealdo groaned. He knew what they would be doing for the rest of the day: the same thing they'd been doing most of the days since they'd established themselves by Imola. Unless it involved a pretty girl, he soon got sick of doing the same thing over and over. He realized that, when the time for fighting came, all this practice was liable to help keep him alive. That didn't, that couldn't, make him enjoy it while it was going on.

His pack sat at the foot of his cot, in precisely the prescribed place. His stick leaned against the wall at the left side of the bed, at precisely the prescribed angle. Panfilo hadn't been able to find a thing to complain about in the way he handled his gear, If Panfilo couldn't find it, it wasn't there.

Tealdo slung the pack over his shoulder, grunting at its weight. When he picked up the stick, his finger accidentally slid into the blazing hole. It didn't matter here, not directly: in training, well away from any fighting front, none of the weapons carried a sorcerous charge. But it was not a good habit to acquire.

He wasn't one of the first men back out to the parade ground. But he wasn't one of the last men out, either, the men at whom his superiors screamed. He enjoyed people screaming at him no more than he enjoyed endless practice. Practice he couldn't escape. He could keep people from screaming at him, could and did.

"Form by companies!" Colonel Ombruno shouted: a useless order, since the regiment always formed by companies. "Form by companies, and report to your designated practice locations."

The company commanders shepherded the men off to their own areas. Soon, when a new practice field combined all those areas, they would work together. In the meanwhile . . .

In the meanwhile, the company commanders got to puff out their chests and strut, like so many pigeons trying to impress mates. Captain Larbino's strut and his shouted orders did not impress Tealdo: he was no dimwitted female pigeon. But he had to obey, which a female pigeon did not.

Larbino led his company to a cramped underground chamber that had two stairways leading down into it, one broad, the other narrow. The men entered the chamber by the broad stairway. Only a few lanterns, stinking of fish oil, cast a dim, flickering glow there. "Powers above, it's like falling back through a thousand years of time," Tealdo muttered.

"Take your places!" Larbino's loud voice dinned in the small, crowded chamber. "Five minutes till the exercise begins! Take your places! No mercy on any man who's out of place when the whistle blows."

The soldiers were already taking their places. They had been doing this for three weeks. They knew, or were convinced they knew, at least as much about their part of the operation as did Larbino. They formed a single serpentine line that led to the bottom of the narrow stairway and kinked at each earthen wall. Seen from above, it would have looked like a long string of gut twisted to fit into the abdominal cavity.

Shrill and deafeningly loud, the brass whistle screeched. "I love running in full kit," Trasone said through the blast, and then, in a lower voice, "In a pig's arse I do." Tealdo chuckled. He felt the same way.

"Out! Out! Out!" Larbino was screaming. "They'll be blazing at you when you do this for real! Don't stand around playing with yourselves."

"I'd rather be playing with myself than doing this," Tealdo said. He didn't think anyone heard him. The line was uncoiling rapidly as soldier after soldier dashed up the narrow stairs. They'd had dreadful tangles the first few times they tried it. They'd got better with practice. Tealdo declined to admit that, even to himself.

His feet thudded on the timbers of the narrow stairway. Up he went. Anyone who tripped here was a cork in the bottle for everyone behind him. Panfilo had a more expressive term for it: as far as he was concerned, anyone who tripped on the narrow stairway was a dead man.

Tealdo emerged into daylight. Before long, they'd be running the exercise at night, which would make it even more delightful. He dashed to a broad plank that spanned a deep trench and raced across it. Two men from his company had fallen into the trench. One managed to escape without being hurt. The other broke his leg.

Cloth flags on stakes marked the narrow way he and his comrades had to take. He rushed along that narrow way till it suddenly widened out. Where it did, buildings – or rather, false fronts – defined streets through which they had to run. Soldiers with uncharged sticks "fought" from those false fronts, trying to impede the company's progress. Umpires with green ribbons tied to their tunic sleeves signaled theoretical casualties.

Tealdo "blazed" back at the defenders. One after another, the umpires ruled them deceased. But Tealdo's comrades were taken out of action, too. He rather hoped he would be, as had happened during a couple of practice runs. Then he could lie down and grab a breather, and no sergeant would be able to complain.

But, at the umpires' whim, he was allowed to survive. Panting, he raced left, right, and then left again before coming to the gateway for whose capture his company was responsible. More soldiers tried to keep the company from seizing the gate. The umpires ruled those soldiers failed and fell.

The egg one of Captain Larbino's soldiers set against the gateway was only a wooden simulacrum. An umpire's whistle blew, signaling a blast of energy. A couple of defenders, miraculously revived from their "deaths", opened the gate to let the "survivors" of the company inside.

More narrow ways lay beyond, some as twisted as the paths in a maze. Still more soldiers tried to keep Tealdo and his comrades from passing those ways to the end. Again, they failed. More whistles shrilled. Tealdo raised a weary cheer. He and enough of the other soldiers had reached the end of the practice area to have succeeded were this actual battle.

"King Mezentio and all of Algarve will have reason to be proud of you when you fight this well with your lives truly in the pans of the scale," Larbino declared. "I know you will. You need no lessons in courage, only in how best to use that courage. Those lessons will go on. Tomorrow, we will take the practice course in the dark."

Weary groans replaced the weary cheers. Tealdo turned and saw Trasone not far away. "Marching into Bari was a lot more fun," he said. "All this running around looks too much like work to me."

"It'll look even more like work when the bastards on the other side start blazing back for real," Trasone answered.

"Don't remind me," Tealdo said with a grimace. "Don't remind me."

Leofsig felt like a beast of burden, or perhaps an animal in a cage. He was not a Forthwegian soldier any more, the Forthwegian army having been crushed between those of Algarve and Unkerlant. Not a foot of Forthwegian soil remained under the control of men loyal to King Penda. From east and west, the enemies' forces had joined hands east of Eoforwic; joined hands over Forthweg's fallen corpse.

And so Leofsig languished with thousands of his comrades in a captives' camp somewhere between Gromheort and Eoforwic, not far from where his regiment, or what was left of it, had finally surrendered to the Algarvians. He scowled when he thought of the dapper Algarvian officer who'd inspected the dirty, worn, beaten Forthwegian soldiers still hale enough to line up for the surrender ceremony.

"You fought well. You fought bravely," the Algarvian officer had said, trilling the slow sounds of Forthwegian as if they belonged to his native tongue. Then he'd hopped into the air, kicking up his heels in an extravagant gesture of contempt. "And for all the good it did you, for all the good it did your kingdom, you might as well not have fought at all. Think on that. You will have a long time to think on that." He'd turned his back and strutted away.

Time Leofsig did indeed have. Inside these wooden fences, inside these towers manned by Algarvians who would sooner blaze a captive coming near than listen to him, time was very nearly the only thing he did have. He had the tunic and boots in which he'd surrendered, and he had a hard cot in a flimsy barracks.

He also had work. If the captives wanted wood for cooking and wood for heating – not so great a need in Forthweg as farther south in Derlavai, but not to be ignored as winter drew nearer, either – they had to cut it and haul it back. Work gangs under Algarvian guard went out every day. If they wanted latrines to keep the camp from being swamped by filth and disease, they had to dig them. The place stank anyway, putting Leofsig in mind of a barnyard once more.

If they wanted food, they had to depend on the Algarvians. Their captives doled out flour as if it were silver, salt pork as if it were gold. Like most Forthwegians, Leofsig was on the blocky side. The block that was he had been narrowing ever since he'd surrendered.

"They don't care," he said to his neighbor after yet another meager meal. "They don't care in the least."

"Why should they?" the fellow with the cot next to his replied. He was a blond Kaunian named Gutauskas, and already lean. "If we starve to death, they don't have to worry about feeding us any more."

That was so breathtakingly cynical, Leofsig could only stare. The fellow with the cot on the other side of his, though, a burly chap called Merwit, spat in disgust. "Why don't you shut up and die now, yellow-hair?" he said. "Weren't for you cursed Kaunians, we wouldn't have gotten sucked into this war in the first place."

Gutauskas raised a pale eyebrow. "Oh, indeed: no doubt," he said, speaking Forthwegian without perceptible accent but with the elegant precision more characteristic of his own language. "Both his name and his looks prove King Penda to be of pure Kaunian blood."

Leofsig snickered. Penda was stocky and swarthy like most Forthwegians, and bore a perfectly ordinary Forthwegian name. Merwit glared; he was the sort who fought with a verbal meat-axe, and wasn't used to getting pierced with a rapier of sarcasm. "He's got a bunch of Kaunian lickspittles around him," he said at last. "They clouded his mind, that's what they did, till he didn't know up from yesterday. Why should he care a fart what happens to Valmiera and Jelgava? Algarve can blaze 'em down, for all I care. I'll watch 'em burn and wave bye-bye."

"Aye, King Penda's lickspittles have done wonders for the Kaunians in Forthweg," Gutauskas said, sardonic still. "They've made us all rich. They've made all our neighbors love us. If there were ten of us for one of you, Merwit, you'd understand better." He paused. "No. You wouldn't. Some people never understand anything."

"I understand this." Merwit made a large, hard fist. "I understand I can beat the stuffing out of you." He started toward Gutauskas.

"No, curse it!" Leofsig grabbed him. "The redheads'll come down on all of us if we brawl."

Merwit surged in his grasp. "They won't care if we stomp these sneering blond scuts. They can't stand 'em, either."

"In the case of Mezentio's men, it is, I assure you, quite mutual," Gutauskas said.

When Leofsig didn't let go, Merwit slowly eased. "You just better watch your smart mouth, Kaunian," he told Gutauskas, "or one fine day all of you stinking bastards in this camp'll have your pretty yellow heads broken. You better pass the word, too, if you know what's good for you." He twisted free of Leofsig and stomped off.

Gutauskas watched him go, then turned back to Leofsig. "You may find your head broken for having taken our part." He studied him like a natural philosopher examining some new species of insect. "Why did you? Forthwegians seldom do." The Kaunian's mouth twisted. "Folk not of our blood seldom do."

Leofsig started to answer, then stopped with his mouth hanging foolishly open. He had no special love for Kaunians. His admiration for Kaunians was principally limited to their women in clinging trousers. He needed to think for a bit before he could figure out why he hadn't joined Merwit against Gutauskas. At last, he said, "The Algarvians have all of us in the palm of their hand. If we start squabbling in here, they'll laugh themselves sick."

"That is sensible," Gutauskas said after his own pause for thought. "You would be astonished at how seldom people are sensible."

"My father says the same thing," Leofsig answered.

"Does he?" Gutauskas's eyebrow rose again. "And what, pray, does your father do, that he has acquired such wisdom?"

Is he laughing at me? Leofsig wondered. He decided Gutauskas wasn't; it was merely the Kaunian's manner. "He keeps books in Gromheort."

"Ah." Gutauskas nodded. "Aye. I can see reckoning up that on which men spend their silver and gold would give a man vivid insight into the manifold follies of his fellow men."

"I suppose so," said Leofsig, who hadn't thought about it much.

He waited for Gutauskas to thank him for stopping the fight. The Kaunian did nothing of the sort. He acted as if Leofsig could hardly have acted differently. Kaunians never made it easy for their

neighbors to get alone with them. Had they made it easy for their
neighbors to get along with them, they wouldn't have been the
Kaunians he knew. He wondered what they would have been.

Before he could take that thought any further, a squad of Algarvian
guards tramped into the barracks. In bad Forthwegian, one of them
said. "We search. Maybe you try escape, eh? You go out." The others
supplemented the order with peremptory gestures with their sticks.

Out Leofsig went, Gutauskas trailing after him. Crashes and thuds
inside said the Algarvians were tearing the barracks to pieces. If
anyone in there was plotting an escape, Leofsig didn't know about it.
He did know what he'd find when the Algarvians let him and his
fellow captives return: chaos. The Algarvians were good at tearing
things to pieces. They didn't bother setting them to rights again. That
was the captives' problem.

He strolled toward the fence around the camp – carefully, because
the guards there would blaze without warning Forthwegians who
came too close. The fence itself wasn't particulary strong. Captives
could rush it . . . if most of the ones who tried didn't mind dying
before they got there. A few captives had escaped, the Algarvians
discovering it only when their counts came out wrong. Leofsig didn't
know how the escapees had done it. Had he known, he'd have done
it himself.

"You there, soldier!" a Forthwegian officer snapped at him. "If
you haven't got anything better to do than waddle around like a
drunken duck, draw a shovel and go fill in some slit trenches or dig
some new ones. We've got no room in this camp for idle hands, and
I'll thank you to remember it."

"Aye, sir," Leofsig said resignedly. Even as captives, officers maintained the right to give common soldiers orders. The only difference
was, even the brigadier who was the captives' commandant had to
obey the orders of the lowliest Algarvian trooper. Leofsig wondered
how the brigadier, who was also a belted earl and a proud and touchy
man, enjoyed being on the receiving end of commands. Maybe the
experience would teach him something about what a common
soldier's life was like. Somehow, Leofsig doubted it.

The shovels made a sadly mismatched collection. A few were
Forthwegian army issue; more, though, looked to have been looted
from the farm surrounding the captives' camp. The officer in charge

of the latrines, an intense young captain, had nonetheless arranged them in a neat rack he'd built from scrap lumber.

"Ah, good," he said as Leofsig made his slow approach. "It's nasty work, to be sure, but someone's got to do it. Choose your weapon, soldier." He pointed toward the rack of shovels.

"Aye, sir," Leofsig said again, and took as long as he could deciding among them. No one expected a captive to move fast; on what the Algarvians deigned to feed them, the captives couldn't move fast. Leofsig knew as much, and took advantage of it.

"Now get to it," said the captain, who probably hadn't been deceived. As Leofsig started off toward the noisome trenches, the officer spoke again, this time with curiosity in his voice: "What did you do to get sent over here? The redheads mostly give this duty to Kaunians."

"It wasn't one of the redheads," Leofsig said sheepishly. "It was one of our own officers. I don't suppose I looked busy enough to suit him."

"Seeing how you went about getting a shovel there, I can't say I'm surprised," the captain answered. He sounded more amused than angry; Leofsig hadn't done anything drastic enough to deserve more punishment than latrine duty in a captives' camp. After a moment, the captain went on, "Maybe it's just as well you got nabbed. Seeing you, the Kaunians won't think they're the only ones getting stuck with the shit detail."

"Just as well for you, maybe, sir," Leofsig said, "but I don't see how it's just as well for me."

"Go on," the Forthwegian officer said again. "You're not going to get me to waste any more of my time arguing with you."

Leofsig wouldn't have minded doing exactly that. Since he hadn't managed it, he went off to work. He wished he could hold his nose and dig at the same time. A couple of Kaunians in trousers were already working among the slit trenches. The captain in charge of the latrines had been right; they seemed surprised to have a Forthwegian for company. Leofsig started filling in a trench. Flies rose, resentful, in buzzing clouds. Seeing he was doing the same thing they were, the Kaunians went back to it themselves. Leofsig noted that with some small relief, then forgot about them. He was working as fast as he could now, to get the job over with. If the

Kaunians liked that, fine. If they didn't, he thought, too cursed bad.

"You've got the wrong man, I tell you!" the prisoner shouted as Bembo marched him up the stairs of the constabulary building in central Tricarico. Bembo had clapped manacles on him; they clanked with every step he climbed.

When the prisoner's complaints started to get on Bembo's nerves, he pulled the club off his belt and whacked it into the palm of his hand. "Do you want to see how loud you can yell with a mouthful of broken teeth?" he asked. The prisoner suddenly fell silent. Bembo smiled.

At the top of the stairs, Bembo gave him a shove that took him into the door face first. Clucking at the prisoner's clumsiness, Bembo opened the door and gave him another shove. This one sent him through the doorway.

The constabulary sergeant at the front desk was at least as portly as Bembo. "Well, well," he said. "What have we here?" Like a lot of questions Algarvians asked, that one was for rhetorical effect. The next one wasn't: "Why'd you haul in our dear friend Martusino this time, Bembo?"

"Loitering in front of a jeweler's, Sergeant," Bembo answered.

"Why, you lying sack of guts!" Martusino yelled. He addressed the sergeant: "I was just walking past the place, Pesaro – I swear on my mother's grave. That last stretch of Reform did the trick for me. I've gone straight, I have."

He wasn't so persuasive as he might have been; the manacles kept him from talking with his hands. Sergeant Pesaro looked dubious. Bembo snarled. "Oh, he's gone straight, all right – straight back to his old tricks. After I spotted him, I grabbed him and searched him. He had these in his belt pouch." Bembo reached into his own pouch and pulled out three golden rings. One was a plain band, one set with a polished, faceted piece of jet, and one with a fair-sized sapphire.

"I never saw them before," the prisoner said.

Pesaro inked a pen and started to write. "Suspicion of burglary," he said. "Suspicion of intent to commit burglary. Maybe they'll get sick of this and finally hang you, Martusino. It'd be about time, if anybody cares what *I* think."

"This fat son of a sow is framing an innocent man!" Martusino cried. "He planted those rings on me, the stinking lump of dung. Like I just said, I never saw 'em before in my life, and there's not a soul can prove I did."

Being a constable required Bembo to take more abuse than most Algarvians would tolerate, as it let him deal out abuse with more impunity than most Algarvians enjoyed. But he took only so much. *Sack of guts* had come up to the edge of the line and *fat son of a sow* went over it. He pulled out his club again and hit Martusino a good lick. The prisoner howled.

"Struck while resisting arrest," Pesaro noted, and scribbled another line on the form he was filling out. Martusino yelled louder than ever, partly from pain, partly from outrage. Pesaro shook his head. "Oh, shut up, why don't you? Take him for his pretty picture, Bembo, and then to the lockup, so I don't have to listen to him any more."

"I'll do that, Sergeant. He's giving me a headache, too." Bembo gestured with the club. "Go on, get moving, or I'll give you another taste."

Martusino got moving. Bembo escorted him to the recording section, to get the particulars on him down in permanent form. A pretty little sketch artist took his likeness. Bembo marveled at the way she could get a man's essence on to paper with a few deft strokes of pencil and charcoal stick. It wasn't sorcery, not in any conventional sense of the word, but it seemed miraculous all the same.

He also marveled at the way the sketch artist filled out her tunic. "Why won't you go out to supper with me, Saffa?" he asked, not quite whining but not far from it, either.

"Because I don't feel like wrestling," Saffa answered. "Why don't I just slap your face now? Then it'll be as if we'd gone to supper." She bent her head to her work.

Martusino was rash enough to laugh. Bembo trod on his foot, hard. The prisoner yelped. Bembo did his best to grind off a toe or two, but didn't quite succeed. Saffa kept right on sketching. Such things happened all the time in constabulary stations. Sometimes worse things happened. Everyone knew that. No one saw any need to make a fuss about it.

When she was done with Martusino's portrait, she told Bembo, "You'll have to take the manacles off him for a little while. He needs to sign the sketch, and we'll need fingermarks from him, too."

One of the constables in the recording section covered Martusino with a small stick while Bembo unlocked the manacles. Unwillingly, the prisoner scrawled his name below the picture of him Saffa had drawn. Even more unwillingly, he let her ink his fingertips and set the impressions of the marks on the paper beside the sketch.

"You're out of business for a while now, chum," Bembo said genially. "Walk off with anything else that doesn't belong to you, and our mages will lead us straight to your door." The manacles closed on Martusino's wrists again.

"I didn't take anything this time," the prisoner protested.

"Aye, and they get babies from out behind the fig trees," Bembo said. He and Martusino both knew a crooked wizard could break the link between a criminal and his sketch, signature, and fingermarks. Having signature and fingermarks to go with the image, though, made breaking the link harder and more expensive for the fellow who wanted it broken.

"We're done here," Saffa said.

Bembo took Martusino off to the lockup. Martusino knew the way; he'd been there before. As he and Bembo drew near, the bored-looking warder hastily closed a small book and shoved it into a desk drawer. Bembo caught just a glimpse of a bare female backside on the cover. "I've got a present for you, Frontino," he said, and gave the prisoner a shove.

"Just what I always wanted." Frontino's expression belied his words. He examined Martusino. "This isn't the first time I've seen this lug, but I'll be cursed if I can remember his name. Who are you, pal?"

Martusino hesitated for a split second. Before he could give a false name, Bembo hefted the club. Martusino abruptly decided playing the game by the rules would be a good idea. He answered the warder's questions without backtalk after that. Bembo had questions to answer, too, some of them duplicating the ones Pesaro had asked. When they were over, Frontino took a small stick out of the desk drawer – Bembo got another glimpse of that interesting book cover – and aimed it at Martusino. At his nod, Bembo undid the manacles. The constable also held his club at the ready.

"Strip off," the warder told Martusino. "Come on, come on – everything. You know the drill, so don't make me tell you anything twice."

Martusino shed shoes and stockings, then pulled off tunic, kilt, and finally drawers. "Skin and bones," Bembo said disdainfully. "Nothing but skin and bones." The prisoner gave him a dirty look, but seemed to think another comment would earn him another clout. He was right.

Frontino rose, gathered up the belongings, and stuffed them into a cloth bag. Then he threw Martusino a tunic, a kilt, and cloth slippers all striped in black and white — lockup garb. Sullenly, the prisoner put it on. It didn't fit very well. He knew better than to complain. "The judge decides you're innocent, you'll get your own junk back then," the warder said. He and Bembo both grinned; they knew how unlikely that was. He went on, "Otherwise, come see me when you get out of Reform. I may have some trouble remembering where I stashed it, but I expect I will if you ask me nice." *If you pay me off*, he meant.

Helpfully, Bembo said, "Pesaro thinks they may just up and hang him this time."

Martusino scowled. The warder shrugged. "Well, in that case he probably won't be coming back for it. It won't go to waste." Bembo nodded. In that case, Frontino would keep what he wanted and sell the rest. Warders rarely died poor.

"They won't hang me," Martusino said, though he sounded more hopeful than confident.

"Come on." Frontino unlocked the big iron lock on the outer door to the lockup. "Go on in." Martusino obeyed. Bembo and the warder watched him through the barred window. The inner door had a sorcerous lock. The warder mumbled the words to the releasing spell. The inner door flew open. Martusino went in among the rest of the prisoners awaiting their punishment. Frontino mumbled again. The door slammed shut.

"What would happen if a prisoner who knew some magecraft went to work on that inner door?" Bembo asked.

"It's supposed to be proof against anyone below a second-rank mage," the warder answered, "and fancy mages don't go into the ordinary lockup — you'd best believe they don't, Bembo my boy. We have special holes for them."

"I've heard fancy whores say things like that," Bembo remarked.

Frontino snorted and gave him a shot in the ribs with an elbow. "I didn't know you were such a funny fellow," he said.

"I don't want too many people to know," Bembo said. "If they did, I'd have to go up on the stage and get rich and famous, and I don't suppose I could stand that. I'd rather stay a simple constable."

"You're pretty simple, all right," Frontino agreed.

Bembo laughed, but not the way the warder thought he did: he'd expected Frontino to say something like that, and was amused to be right. Something else crossed his mind. "Say, what was that you were reading?" he asked. "It looked pretty interesting."

"Talk about your fancy whores," the warder said, and pulled the book out of the desk. When Bembo could tear his eyes away from that arresting cover illustration, he discovered the romance was called *Putinai: the Emperor's Lady.* Frontino gave it his most enthusiastic recommendation: "She does more screwing in a week than an army of cabinetmakers could in a year."

"Sounds good." Bembo read the fine print under the title: "Based on the exciting true history of the turbulent Kaunian Empire." He shook his head. "Kaunians have always been filthy people, I guess."

"I'd say so," the warder agreed. "Putinai does *everything*, and loves every bit of it, too. You can borrow the book after I'd done with it – *if* you promise to give it back."

"I will, I will," Bembo assured him, with something less than perfect sincerity.

Frontino must have recognized that, for he said, "Or you could spring for one yourself. Seems like every third romance these days is about how vile the Kaunian Empire was and how the bold, fierce Algarvian mercenaries finally overthrew it. Our ancestors were tough bastards, if half what you read is true."

"Aye," Bembo said. "Well, maybe I will buy one. A little extra cash in my pockets wouldn't hurt, though."

"Maybe we can take care of that." Frontino got out the bag in which he'd stored Martusino's clothes and effects, and took from it the burglar's belt pouch. He and Bembo divided up the silver and the couple of small goldpieces they found inside.

"I get the odd coin," Bembo said, scooping it up. "Pesaro's going to want his cut, too." Frontino nodded. That was how things worked in Tricarico.

Dragons spiraled high above Tirgoviste harbor – above all the harbors of Sibiu – keeping watch against Algarvian attack from the air or from the sea. They reassured Commander Cornelu whenever he looked up into the heavens. No doubt mages behind closed doors also probed for any disturbance in the ley lines that would mean an Algarvian fleet was setting forth against the island kingdom. But, because the mages were hidden away, Cornelu had to assume they were on the job. The dragons he could see.

Today, he couldn't see them so well as he would have liked: mist and low, thin clouds made them almost disappear. The weather, which would only worsen as autumn gave way to winter, would make it harder for the dragons to give early warning and would put a greater burden on the mages' shoulders.

Cornelu frowned. Magic was all very well, but he wanted the eyes in the sky to be as effective as they could, too. Seamen who took chances did not often live to take very many. That held equally true for fishermen in sailboats, sailors in cruisers skimming along the ley lines, and leviathan riders like himself.

Musing on the wisdom of taking few chances, Cornelu tripped on a cobblestone and almost rolled down the hill into the sea. Tirgoviste rose swiftly from the shore; some of the bright-painted shops set on hillsides showed noticeably more wall on the side nearer the Narrow Sea than on the other.

A wine merchant had a QUITTING BUSINESS banner stretched across his window. Cornelu ducked in to see what bargains he might pick up. Sibiu was a merchant kingdom; lying where it did, it could scarcely be anything else. The scent of a bargain fired Cornelu's blood hardly less than the scent of his wife's favorite perfume.

He found few bargains in the wine shop, only empty shelves. "Why did you put the banner up?" he asked the merchant.

"Where am I going to find any more stock?" the fellow answered bitterly. "Almost all I sold were Algarvian vintages, and the war's blazed our trade there right through the heart. Oh, I can get in a few bottles from Valmiera and Jelgava, but that's all I can get: a few. They're expensive as all getout, too – expensive for me to buy, and too expensive to sell very fast. Might as well pack it in and try another line of work. I couldn't do worse, believe me."

"King Mezentio would be lording it over us if we didn't do something about him," Cornelu said. "We almost waited too long in the Six Years' War. We don't dare take that chance again."

"You can talk like that – King Burebistu pays your bills." The wine
merchant's scowl was gloomier than the weather. "Who will pay
mine, when the war cuts me off from my source of supply? You
know as well as I do: nobody."

Cornelu left in a hurry. He wished he'd never gone into the shop.
He wanted to think of Sibiu as united in the effort against Algarve.
He knew that wasn't so, but thinking of it as being so helped him do
his job better. Getting his nose rubbed in the truth had the opposite
effect, one he didn't want.

He hurried down the hill to the harbor. Gulls scavenging garbage
from the gutters rose in mewing, squawking clouds as he strode past
them. He hoped none of them would avenge itself on his hat or the
sleeve of his tunic. As if to give that hope the lie, a dropping splashed
on to the cobbles only a yard or so from his shoe. He hurried on, and
reached Commodore Delfinu's office unbefouled.

After the two men exchanged salutes and kisses on the cheeks,
Cornelu asked, "Sir, have we had any better luck in getting leviathans
into the Barian ports?"

Glumly, Delfinu shook his head. "No, and we've lost more men
trying, too, as you will probably have heard." When Cornelu
nodded, the head of the Leviathan Service went on, "The Algarvians
have Imola and Lungri as tightly locked up as if they were virgin
daughters. They keep dragons in the air over them all the time, too,
so we can't learn from above what they're doing, either."

"Curse them," Cornelu said. Dragons above Tirgoviste were one
thing, dragons above the ports the enemy had taken for his own
something else again – something ominous. Cornelu took a deep
breath. "If you like, sir, Eforiel and I will cross the strait and see what
they're up to – and, if you like, put down some eggs to keep them
from doing it, whatever it is."

Delfinu shook his head again. "I am ordering no man across the
strait to Lungri and Imola. I have lost too many. The Algarvians are
not so skilled in using leviathans as we are" – pride rang in his voice
– "but they have become all too skilled at hunting them down." The
pride leaked away, to be replaced by chagrin.

"My lord, you need not order me." Cornelu drew himself up to
stiff attention. "I volunteer my leviathan and myself."

Delfinu bowed. "Commander, Sibiu is fortunate to have you in her service. But I will not take advantage of your courage in this way, as if I were a cold-blooded Unkerlanter or a calculating Kuusaman. The odds of success do not justify the risk . . . and your wife is with child, is it not so?"

"Sir, it is so," Cornelu said. "But I am not with child myself, and I took oath to serve King Burebistu and his kingdom as best I could. What the kingdom requires of me, that shall I do."

"This the kingdom does not require of you," Delfinu said. "I have no desire to make your wife grow old a widow, nor to make your child grow up not knowing its father. I will send you into danger: indeed, I will send you into danger without a qualm. But I will not send you to almost certain death when no good to king or kingdom is likely to come from it."

Cornelu bowed in turn. "My lord, I am lucky to have you as my superior. Unlike the no—" He stopped, unsure how Count Delfinu would take what he'd been on the point of saying.

Even though he hadn't said it, Delfinu figured out what it was. "Unlike the nobles in the Kaunian kingdoms, ours are supposed to know a little something before they put on their fancy uniforms? Is that what you had in mind, Commander?" To Cornelu's relief, he laughed.

"Well, aye, sir — something on that order, anyhow," Cornelu admitted.

"Kaunian blood is older than ours, which makes them take more pride in it than we do," Delfinu said. "If you ask my opinion, being older only makes it thinner, but no Kaunian has seen fit to ask my opinion. For my part, I confess to losing very little sleep over theirs. Personally, I feel more sympathy for Algarve, but I know my kingdom's needs come ahead of my personal sympathies."

"Myself, I have no great use for the Kaunian kingdoms," Cornelu said, "but I have no use at all for Algarve. Did King Mezentio get his hands on us, he would squeeze till our eyes popped out of our heads."

"Since I think you are right about that, I can hardly argue with you," Delfinu said. "But, for the time being, I cannot in good conscience send you forth against the Barian ports, either. Enjoy your time off duty, Commander, and keep in mind that it is not likely to last."

"Very well, my lord." Cornelu saluted again. "I think I'll draw a bucket from the rest crate and pay Eforiel a visit in her pen. She'll think I've forgotten her, poor thing. I don't want that."

"No, indeed." Count Delfinu returned the salute. "Very well, Commander, you are dismissed from my presence."

The chamber in which the large Leviathan Services rest crate sat had a strong fish smell. The smell would have been much stronger had the rest crate been other than what it was. Cornelu reached in and drew forth a big bucket full of mackerel and squid, all of them as fresh as when they'd been pulled from the sea. He lugged it down to the wire-enclosed pen where his leviathan slowly swam back and forth, back and forth.

Eforiel swam to the little wharf that jutted out into the pen. She stuck her head out of the water and examined Cornelu first with one small black eye, then with the other. "Aye, it's me," he said, and reached out to pat the end of her tapered snout. "It's me, all right, and I've brought you presents."

He tossed her a squid. Those enormous jaws came open. They closed on the squid with a wet smacking noise. When they opened again, the squid was gone. Eforiel emitted a soft, pleased grunt. Cornelu fed her a mackerel. She approved of that, too. He kept tossing her treats till the bucket was empty.

He had to show her it was empty. "Sorry – no more," he said. Now the noise she made, though like nothing that could come from a human throat, was full of disappointment. "Sorry," he repeated, and patted her again. She didn't take his hand off at the wrist – or his arm at the shoulder. She was a clever, well-trained beast.

Commodore Delfinu had as much as ordered Cornelu to have a good time while he wasn't assailing the Algarvians. After taking the empty bucket back for scrubbing, he headed away from the harbor, off to the quarters he shared with his wife. He could think of no one in whose company he would sooner be.

Costache was baking when he walked in; the spicy smell of cakes made the small, square rooms in which they lived seem anything but military. "I'm glad you're back," she said. "I didn't know whether Delfinu would send you out or not."

"He didn't," Cornelu said. That Delfinu had kept him in Tirgoviste because he judged going out to the Barian ports a suicide

mission was nothing his wife needed to know. He walked over to
Costache, took her in his arms, and gave her a kiss, leaning over the
swell of her belly to plant it on her mouth. With a grin, he told her,
"I'm glad I'm taller than you are. Otherwise, I'd have to sneak up on
you from behind instead of doing this the regular way."

"If you'd sneaked up on me from behind instead of doing it the
regular way, I wouldn't be expecting now," Costache retorted. Her
green eyes sparkled. Now that she wasn't throwing up every morning
any more, pregnancy agreed with her. Along with her belly, her
cheeks were rounder than they had been. To disguise that a bit, she
let her red-gold hair fall straight to her shoulders, where she had worn
it piled high on her head.

Cornelu did step behind her. He reached around and cupped her
breasts in his hands. They were fuller and rounder than they had
been, too. They were also more tender – he had to be careful not to
squeeze too hard. When he was careful, they were more sensitive
than they had been; Costache's breath sighed out.

"You see?" Cornelu murmured into her ear. "From behind isn't
so bad." Having murmured into that ear, he nibbled it.

Costache turned and put her arms around him. "And how are
things from in front?" she asked.

Things from in front were fine. In its generosity, the kingdom of
Sibiu had furnished them with two military cots, which they'd pushed
together. With Cornelu and Costache both eager, the cots might have
been a fine, soft bed at a fancy hostel. Before long, his wife gasped and
quivered beneath Cornelu. Her belly grew hard and firm as her womb
tightened during her spasm of pleasure. Cornelu spent himself a
moment later.

He didn't let his weight down on her, as he would have before she
was with child. "We won't be able to do it like that much longer,"
he said, and set a hand on her belly to show why. "Someone in there
is getting in the way." As if indignant, the baby kicked. Cornelu and
Costache both laughed, as content as any two people could be during
wartime.

6.

Pekka was working, and working hard, though no one could have proved it by looking at her. She sat at the desk in her office at Kajaani City College, staring out the window at the driving rain. Every once in a while, her eyes would slip down to the sheets of paper spread across the desk.

Once, as the rain kept drumming down, she reached out, inked a pen, and wrote a couple of lines below what was already on the last of the sheets. She didn't look at them again for several minutes. When she did, she blinked in surprise, as if someone else's hand, not her own, had done that writing.

Partly recalled to herself, Pekka wondered what the students in her theoretical sorcery class would think if they could see her now. They would probably laugh like loons. Comics had been making jokes about absent-minded mages since the days of the Kaunian Empire. Some of the Kaunian jokes had survived to the present day, and sounded remarkably like their modern equivalent. Some of them had doubtless been ancient in Kaunian times, too.

And then Pekka drifted away again, back into the haze of concentration that was the next thing to a trance. She noticed the rain only as background noise. Somewhere down at the root of things, the laws of similarity and contagion were connected. She was morally certain of it, though wizards had been treating them as separate entities for as long as men had been working magic. If she could link them together . . .

She had no idea what would happen if she could link them together. She would know something she hadn't known. She would know something no one in the world had ever known. That was enough. That was more than enough.

She scribbled another line. She wasn't close to an answer. She had no idea how long she would need to get close to an answer. She was getting closer to designing a sorcerous experiment that might tell her whether she was on the right track.

Someone knocked on the door. Pekka did her best not to hear. Her best was not good enough. She'd been about to write another line. Whatever she'd been on the point of setting down vanished from her mind.

Fury roared in to take its place. Kuusamans were as a rule easygoing, especially when set alongside the proud and touchy folk of the kingdoms of Algarvic stock. But every mage had to keep in mind the difference between the rule and the exception.

Springing to her feet, Pekka dashed to the door and flung it wide. "What are you doing interrupting me?" she screeched, even before it had opened all the way.

Her husband, fortunately, lived up to the Kuusaman reputation for calm. "I'm sorry, dear," Leino said. His narrow eyes didn't widen; no surprise showed on his broad, high-cheekboned face. He'd seen Pekka burst like a large egg before. "It is time to head home, though."

"Oh," Pekka said in a small voice. The real world returned with a rush. She wouldn't unify contagion and similarity this afternoon, nor even figure out how to take that one step closer to finding out whether unifying them was even possible. With the real world's embrace came acute embarrassment. Looking down at her shoes, she mumbled, "I'm sorry I shouted at you."

"It's all right." Leino's shrug made water drip from the brim of his hat and the hem of his heavy wool rain cape; his office was in a different building from Pekka's. "If I'd known you were thinking hard, I'd have stood out here a while longer. We're not in that big a hurry, not that I know of."

"No, no, no." Now Pekka turned briskly practical. She was that way most of the time: except when thinking hard, as her husband put it. She pulled on rubber overboots, took her cap from the peg on which it hung, and jammed her own broad-brimmed hat down over her straight black hair. "You're right – we'd better get back. My sister's been trying to corral Uto long enough – I'm sure she'd say so."

"She loves him," Leino said.

"I love him, too," Pekka said. "That doesn't mean he isn't a handful — or two handfuls, or three. Come on. We can catch the caravan at the edge of the campus. It'll take us most of the way there."

"Good enough." Amusement danced in Leino's eyes: watching Pekka go in the space of a few breaths from wooly-headed scholar to a planner who might have served on the Kuusaman General Staff never failed to tickle him.

Raindrops pelted down on Pekka as soon as she stepped outside. She hadn't gone ten paces before her hat and cape were as wet as Leino's. She ignored the rain in a different way from the one she'd used while off in the realm of theory back in her office. Any Kuusaman who couldn't ignore rain had had the misfortune of being born in the wrong land.

"How was your day?" she asked, squelching along beside her husband.

"Pretty good, actually," Leino answered. "I think we've made a breakthrough on strengthening behemoth armor against beams from heavy sticks."

"They've had you working on that for a while," Pekka said. "I haven't heard you talk about breakthroughs before."

"This is a whole new idea." Leino looked around to make sure no one was close enough to overhear before going on, "Ordinary armor's just iron, of course, or steel. It can reflect a beam if it's polished enough, or spread the heat around so the beam won't burn through if it doesn't stay right in the same spot long enough."

Pekka nodded. "That's how people have always done it, sure enough. You've found something different?" She cocked her head to one side and looked at her husband with approval, glad she wasn't the only one in the family straying off the beaten track.

"That's what we've done, all right." Leino also nodded, enthusiastically. "It turns out that, if you make a sort of sandwich of steel and then a special porcelain and then steel again, you get armor that's a lot stronger than what we're using now without weighing any more."

"You don't mean a sandwich with three separate layers, do you?" Pekka asked with a small frown. "I can't think of any kind of porcelain so special that it wouldn't be easy to break in large, thin sheets."

"You're absolutely right. I think that's why nobody's taken this approach before," Leino said. "The trick is sorcerously fusing the porcelain to the steel on either side of it, and doing it so we don't wreck the temper of the steel in the process." He grinned at her. "We've wrecked a lot of other tempers in the process, I'll tell you that. But now I think we're getting the hang of it."

"That will be good," Pekka said. "It will be especially good if we get drawn into the madness on the mainland of Derlavai."

"Aye, though I hope we don't," Leino said. "But you're right again – not much place for behemoths in the island–hopping kind of war we're fighting against Gyongyos."

"Oh!" Pekka muttered something worse than *Oh!* under her breath. "There goes the caravan. Now we'll have to wait a quarter of an hour for the next one."

"At least we'll be out of the rain," Leino said. Every caravan stop in Kajaani – so far as Pekka knew, every stop in Kuusamo – was roofed against rain and sleet and snow. The stops wouldn't have been worth having if they weren't.

A news–sheet vendor was taking advantage of the shelter when Pekka and Leino came in to get out of the wet. He waved a sheet at them, saying, "Want to read about the ultimatum Swemmel of Unkerlant has handed Zuwayza?"

"Something unfortunate should happen to Swemmel of Unkerlant," Leino said. That didn't keep him from handing the vendor a couple of square copper coins and taking a sheet. He sat down on a bench, Pekka beside him.

They read together. Pekka's eyebrows rose. "Swemmel doesn't ask for much, does he?" she said.

"Let's see." Leino ran his hand down the page. "All the border fortifications, all the power points halfway from the border to Bishah, the right to base a fleet at the harbor of Samawa – and to have the Zuwayzin pay for it. No, not much: not much he deserves, I mean."

"And all that on pain of war if Zuwayza refuses," Pekka said sadly. "If he were an ordinary man instead of a king, he'd be up before a panel of judges on extortion charges."

Leino had read a little more than she had. "Looks like another war, sure enough. Here, see a crystal report from Bishah quotes their foreign minister as saying that yielding to an unjust demand is worse than making one. If that doesn't sound like the Zuwayzin intend to fight, I don't know what does."

"I wish them well," Pekka said.

"So do I," her husband answered. "The only thing I'm sorry about is that, if they'd given in, Swemmel might have gone back to war with Gyongyos. As is, the Gongs are only fighting us, and that makes them tougher."

"If a few islands out in the Bothnian Ocean were in different places, if a few ley lines ran in different directions, we'd have no quarrel with Gyongyos," Pekka said.

"Gyongyos would probably have a quarrel with us, though," Leino answered. "The Gongs enjoy fighting, seems like."

"I wonder what they say about us," Pekka said in musing tones. Whatever it was, it did not appear in the *Kajaani Crier* or any other Kuusaman news sheet.

A caravan hummed up to the stop. The conductor opened the door. A couple of people in hats and capes got off. Pekka preceded Leino up the steps and into the car. They both plopped eight-copper silver bits in the fare box. Nodding, the conductor waved them back to the seats, as if it were only through his generosity that they had so many from which to choose.

As the caravan began to move, Pekka said, "My grandmother said that, when she was a little girl, *her* grandmother told her how frightened she was when *she* was a little girl, the first time she got up on the step to go into a ley-line caravan. There it was, floating on *nothing*, and she couldn't see why it didn't fall down or tip over."

"Can't expect a child to understand the way complex sorceries work," Leino answered. "For that matter, back in those days ley lines were a new thing in the world, and nobody understood them very well – though people thought they did."

"People always think they know more than they do," Pekka said. "It's one of the things that make them people."

They got off at the road that led up to their house. No butterflies flitted now. No birds sang. Rain fell. Rain dripped from trees. Wet branches slapped them in the face as they slogged uphill to pick up Uto from Pekka's sister.

When Elimaki came to the door, she looked harried. Uto, on the other hand, seemed the picture of innocence. Pekka did not need grounding in theoretical sorcery to know appearances could deceive. "What did you do?" she asked him.

"Nothing," he answered sweetly, as he always did.

Pekka glanced to her sister. Elimaki said, "He went climbing in the pantry. He knocked over a five-pound canister of flour, and then tried to tell me he hadn't. He might have gotten away with it, too, if he hadn't left a footprint right in the middle of the pile of flour on the pantry floor."

Leino started to laugh. So did Pekka, in spite of herself. She and her husband weren't the only ones in the family straying off the beaten track, either. Ruffling Uto's hair, she said, "You'll go a long way, son — if we decide to let you live."

Colonel Dzirnavu was not a happy man. So far as Talsu could tell, Dzirnavu was never a happy man. Like a lot of common people, the Jelgavan count took out his unhappiness on everyone around him. Since he was an officer and a noble, the soldiers in his regiment couldn't tell him to jump off a cliff, as they surely would have if he'd been a commoner like themselves.

"Vartu!" he shouted one morning — he shouted the way singers went through the scales, to warm up his voice. "Confound it, Vartu, where have you gone and hidden yourself? Get your whipworthy arse into my tent this instant!"

"Confound it, Vartu!" Talsu echoed as Dzirnavu's servant came by on the dead run. Vartu gave him a dirty look before ducking under the tentflap and facing his principal's wrath.

"How may I serve you, my lord?" he asked, his words clearly audible through the canvas.

"How may you serve me?" Dzirnavu bellowed. "How may you *serve* me? You may get me that rascally cook, that's how, and serve me his guts for tripe at my luncheon today. Will you look at this? Will you *look* at this, Vartu? The ham-fisted thumbfingered son of a whore had the gall to serve me a plate of runny scrambled eggs. How in the names of the powers above am I supposed to eat runny scrambled eggs?"

Talsu looked down at his own tin plate, which contained the usual breakfast scoop of mush and the equally usual length of cheap, stale sausage. He glanced over to his friend Smilsu, who was sitting on a rock close by. In a low voice, he asked, "How in the names of the powers above am I supposed to eat runny scrambled eggs?"

"With a spoon?" Smilsu suggested. His breakfast ration was no more prepossessing than Talsu's.

"I've got one of those, sure enough." Talsu held it up. "Now if I only had some eggs, I'd be in business."

Smilsu sadly shook his head. "If you're going to grouse and grumble about every least little thing, my boy, you'll never get to be a colonel like our illustrious regimental commander." He set a finger by the side of his nose. "Of course, if you don't grouse and grumble, you'll never get to be a colonel, either. You haven't got the bloodlines for it."

"Bloodlines are fine, if you're a horse." Talsu let his eyes slide toward Count Dzirnavu's tent. "Or even some particular part of a horse." Smilsu, who was in the middle of swallowing a mouthful of mush, almost choked to death on it. Talsu went on, "For picking soldiers, though . . ." Now he shook his head. "If we had real soldiers leading us, we'd be down in Tricarico this time, instead of still slogging our way through these cursed hills." He snapped his fingers. "I bet that's why the stinking Algarvians haven't really counter-attacked."

He'd got a jump ahead of Smilsu. "What's why?" his friend asked. "What are you talking about?"

Talsu dropped his voice to hardly more than a whisper, so only Smilsu would hear: "If the redheads hit us hard, they'd be bound to kill off a lot of officers. Sooner or later, we'd run out of nobles to take their places. Then we'd have to start using men who knew what they were doing instead. We'd be sure to lick Algarve after that, so they're just playing it safe and smart."

"I'd be sure you were right, if only I thought the Algarvians had that much upstairs." Without doing anything more than sitting a little straighter, Smilsu managed to convey the Algarvians' swaggering pomposity. As he slumped back down, he went on, "And you'd better not say anything like that around anybody you're not sure of, either, or you'll be sorry for a long time."

Vartu came out of Dzirnavu's tent just then. Talsu and Smilsu both fell silent. Talsu liked the colonel's servant, and trusted him fairly far, but not far enough to speak treason in front of him.

Mumbling under his breath, Vartu stalked past the two soldiers. A moment later, Talsu heard him yelling at a cook. The cook yelled back. Smilsu's snicker was amused and sympathetic at the same time. "Poor Vartu," he said. "He gets it from both sides at once."

"So do all of us," Talsu answered, "from our officers and from the Algarvians."

"Someone put vinegar in your beer this morning, that's plain," Smilsu said. "Why don't you go over there and scream at the cooks, too?"

"Because they'd stick a carving knife in me or hit me over the head with a pot," Talsu said. "I can't get away with things like that. I'm not a count, or even servant to a count."

"Aye, you're a no-account, all right," Smilsu said, whereupon Talsu felt like hitting him over the head with a pot.

After their less than magnificent breakfast, the Jelgavan soldiers cautiously advanced. Exhortations from King Donalitu to move faster kept coming forward. Colonel Dzirnavu would read them out whenever they did, and would blame the men for not living up to their sovereign's requests. Then he and his superiors would order another tiptoeing step ahead, and would seem surprised when King Donalitu found it necessary to exhort the troops again.

The Algarvians did their best to make life unpleasant for their foes, too. The country through which Talsu and his comrades moved was made for defense. One stubborn soldier with a stick who found a good hiding place could hold up a company. There were plenty of good hiding places to find, and plenty of stubborn Algarvians to fill them. Each redhead had to be flanked out and flushed from cover, which made what would have been a slow business slower.

And the Algarvians had taken to burying eggs in the ground, and attaching to them trips lines that would rupture their shells. A soldier who didn't watch where he put his feet was liable to go up in a great gout of sorcerous fire. That slowed the Jelgavans, too, till dowsers could find the eggs and mark paths past them.

Most of the redheads who lived in the mountain country had fled to lower ground farther west. A few people, though, were obstinate, as Jelgavan mountain folk also had a name for being. Talsu captured an old Algarvian with a bald head, a big white mustache, and knobby knees and hairy calves sticking out from under the hem of his kilt.

"Come on, gramps," he said, and gestured with his stick. "I'm going to take you back to our encampment so they can ask you some questions."

"A dog should futter you," the old man growled in accented Jelgavan. He added a couple of other choice oaths in Talsu's language, then fell back on Algarvian. Talsu didn't know any Algarvian, but he didn't think the captive was paying him compliments. All he did was gesture with the stick again. Cursing still, the old man got moving.

Back at the camp, a bored-looking lieutenant who spoke Algarvian started questioning Talsu's captive. The old man kept right on cursing, or so Talsu thought. The lieutenant stopped looking bored and started looking harassed. Talsu hid a smile. He didn't mind seeing an officer sweat, even if it was because of an Algarvian.

He was about to head off toward the front line again when a trooper from a different company brought in another cursing captive. Talsu stopped and stared. Everyone who heard those curses stopped and stared. The other soldier's captive (*you lucky bastard*, Talsu thought) was a good-looking – a very good-looking – woman of about twenty-five. Coppery hair flowed halfway down her back. Her knees were not knobby, nor her calves hairy. Talsu examined them carefully to make sure of those facts.

Her curses even drew from his tent Colonel Dzirnavu, who had been in there alone except, perhaps, for a bottle of what his servant called restorative. By the lurch in his stride, he was quite thoroughly restored. His eyes needed a moment before they lit on the captive. "Well, well," he said when they finally did. "What have we here?"

"That's what they call a woman," a soldier near Talsu muttered. "Haven't you ever seen one before?" Talsu coughed to keep from laughing out loud.

Dzirnavu advanced on her at a ponderous waddle. He looked her up and down, plainly imagining everything the tunic and kilt concealed. She looked him up and down, too. Her face also showed what she was thinking. Talsu would not have wanted anyone, let alone a good-looking woman, thinking such things about him.

"Where did you find her?" Dzirnavu asked the soldier who had brought her back to camp. "Spying on us, unless I miss my guess."

"Lord, she was going into a little cottage up ahead." The trooper pointed. "My thought is, she was trying to take away a few last things before she fled for good."

The Algarvian woman pointed at Dzirnavu. "Where did you find him?" she asked the soldier who had captured her. Her Jelgavan was accented but fluent. "I would say under a flat rock, but where would you find a flat rock big enough to hide him?"

Like most Jelgavans, Dzirnavu was quite fair. That let Talsu watch the flush mount from his beefy neck to his hairline. "She *is* a spy," he snapped. "She must be a spy. Take her to my tent." A murky light kindled in his bloodshot gray eyes. "I shall attend to her interrogation personally."

Talsu could think of only one thing that might mean. He knew a moment's pity for the Algarvian woman, even if he wouldn't have minded having her himself. Dzirnavu's "interrogation," though, was liable to crush her to death — and he wouldn't learn anything while he was doing it.

After a while, the soldier who'd captured the woman came out of the tent. His face bore a curious mixture of excitement and disgust. "He had me cover her while he tied her to the bed," he reported, and then, "He made her lie on her belly."

Along with his comrades, Talsu sadly shook his head. "Waste of a woman, especially one so pretty," he said. "If that's what he's got in mind, he could do it with a boy instead."

"Officers have all the fun," the other soldier said, "and they get to pick what kind of fun they have."

Since Talsu couldn't argue with that, he started back toward the front line. He hadn't gone far before the Algarvian woman screamed. It sounded more like outrage than anguish. Whatever it was, it was none of his business. He kept walking.

When he returned to the encampment at suppertime, no one had been into or out of the regimental commander's tent since he'd left. "You should have heard what he called me when I asked him if he needed anything an hour ago," Vartu said.

"Is the redhead still screaming in there?" Talsu asked. Dzirnavu's servant shook his head. Talsu sighed. Maybe she'd seen screaming did her no good. Maybe, too, she was in no shape to scream any more. From what he knew of Dzirnavu, he found that more likely. He stood in line for supper. If Dzirnavu was skipping a meal for the sake of his pleasure, it wouldn't hurt him a bit. No sound at all came from the tent. Eventually, Talsu rolled himself in his blanket and went to sleep.

Dzirnavu's tent was still quiet when Talsu woke up the next morning. When Vartu cautiously asked whether the count wanted breakfast, no one answered. Even more cautiously, the servant stuck his head in through the flap. He recoiled, clapping a hand to his mouth. He choked out one word: "Blood!"

Talsu dashed toward the tent. So did everyone else who'd heard Vartu. There lay the naked and unlovely Count Dzirnavu, half on the bed, half off, his throat cut from ear to ear. Blood soaked the sheets and the ground below. There was no sign of the Algarvian woman, no sign she'd ever been there but for the length of rope tied to each bedpost.

"An assassin!" Vartu gasped. "She was an assassin!"

No one argued with him, not out loud, but expressions were eloquent. Talsu's guess was that Dzirnavu had fallen asleep because of his exertions, the woman had managed to work a hand free, and then had found a tool to take her revenge. He did wonder how she'd managed to escape afterwards. Maybe she'd been able to sneak past the sentries. Or maybe, in exchange for silence, she'd given out some of what Dzirnavu had taken by force. Any which way, she was gone.

Smilsu had the last word. He saved it till he and Talsu were heading up to the front: "Powers above, the Algarvians wouldn't want to murder Dzirnavu. They must have hoped he'd live forever. Now we're liable to get a regimental commander who knows what he's doing." Talsu considered that, then solemnly nodded.

Garivald's worn leather boots squelched through mud. The fall rains in southern Unkerlant turned everything into a swamp. Spring, when a winter's worth of snow melted, was even worse – though the peasant did not think of it that way. The weather did what it did every year. For Garivald, it was simply part of life.

As a matter of fact, he was on the whole pleased with the way the year had gone. King Swemmel's inspectors had gone away and not come back, and no impressers had arrived in their wake. The villagers of Zossen had got in the harvest before the rains came. Waddo the obnoxious firstman had fallen off the roof while he was rethatching it, and had broken his ankle. He was still hobbling around on two sticks. No, not such a bad year after all.

The pigs approved of the year, too, or at least of the rain. The whole village might have been a wallow for them now. They approved of Garivald, too, when he threw them turnip tops from a wicker basket. The only trouble was, each seemed to think its neighbors had got a better selection of greens, which made for snortings and snappings and loud grunts and squeals.

Garivald had grain for the chickens, too. The chickens did not like rain, as their draggled feathers attested. A lot of them had taken shelter inside one peasant's house or another. Some of them were making a racket and a mess inside his house. If they annoyed his wife enough, Annore would avenge herself with hatchet and chopping block.

When the blizzards came, all the animals would crowd into the houses. If they didn't, they'd freeze to death. The warmth they gave off helped keep the villagers alive, too. After a while, the nose stopped noticing the stink. Garivald chuckled. Had those hoity-toity inspectors come in winter, they would have stuck their noses into any old house, taken one whiff, and fled back to Cottbus with their tails between their legs.

Syrivald was playing in the mud when Garivald got back to his family's house. "Does your mother know you're out here?" he demanded.

Syrivald nodded. "She sent me out. She said she was sick of the way I was driving the chickens crazy."

"Did she?" Garivald let out a grunt of laughter. "Well, I believe it. You drive your mother and me crazy sometimes, too." Syrivald grinned, mistaking that for a compliment.

Rolling his eyes, Garivald ducked inside. Even with Syrivald out getting filthy, the chickens remained in an uproar. Leuba was crawling around on the floor, doing her best to catch them and pull out their tail feathers. Garivald's little daughter thought that great sport; the chickens had a different opinion.

"You're going to get pecked," Annore warned Leuba.

Two years from now, Leuba might, on a good day, pay some attention to a warning. Now she didn't even understand it. Her mother's tone might have meant something, but not when she was intent on her game. "Ma-ma!" she said happily, and went right on after the closest chicken.

The chickens were a lot faster than she was, but she had a single-minded determination they lacked. Garivald was heading toward her to pick her up when she did manage to grab a hen by the tail. The hen let out a furious squawk. An instant later, Leuba started crying: Sure enough, it had pecked her.

"There, see what you get?" Garivald scooped her off the ground. Leuba, of course, saw nothing of the sort. As far as she was concerned, she'd been having a high old time, and then one of her toys unaccountably went and hurt her. Garivald examined the injury, which was minor. "I expect you'll live," he said. "You can stop making noises like a branded calf."

Eventually, she did settle down, not so much because he'd told her to as because he was holding her. When he set her down again, she started after the nearest chicken. This time, luckily for her and the fowl, it spied her and escaped.

"She's a stubborn thing," Garivald said.

Annore looked at him sidelong. "Where do you suppose she gets that?"

Garivald grunted. He didn't think of himself as stubborn, except insofar as a man had to work hard to scrape a living from the soil. "What's for dinner tonight?" he asked his wife.

"Bread," she answered. "What's left of last night's stew is still in the pot: peas and cabbage and beets and a little salt pork thrown in for flavor."

"Any honey for the bread?" he asked. Annore nodded. He grunted again, this time in satisfaction. "Well, that won't be too bad. And the stew was good last night, so it should be good again today." He sat down on a bench along the wall. "Get me some."

Annore had been stuffing guts with ground meat for sausages. She set aside what she was doing, got a bowl and a spoon, went over to the iron pot hanging above the fire, ladled the bowl full, and brought it to Garivald. Then she went back to the counter, tore off a chunk of black bread, and carried that and the honey pot over to him, too.

He broke the bread, dipped some in the honey, and ate it. Annore went back to work. Garivald spooned up some of the stew, then ate another piece of bread. "In the cities," he said, "they make fancy flour so they can have white bread, not just black or brown." His broad shoulders went up and down in a shrug. "I wonder why they bother. By what I hear from people who've eaten it, it's no better than any other kind."

"City people will do anything to be in fashion," Annore said, and Garivald nodded. People in the farming villages where most Unkerlanters lived were deeply suspicious of their urban cousins. Annore went on, "I'm glad we live in the same way our grandparents did. Why borrow trouble?"

Garivald nodded again. "That's right. I'm not sorry there aren't any ley lines close by, or that Waddo hasn't been able to put a crystal in his house. What can you hear on a crystal? Only bad news and orders from Cottbus."

"Orders from Cottbus *are* bad news," his wife said, and he nodded once more.

"Aye. If somebody there could tell Waddo what to do without coming here, Waddo would just up and do it, no matter how hard it was on the village," he said. "Waddo's one of those people who kicks every arse below him and kisses every arse above him."

He waited for Annore to answer. She didn't; she was peering through tiny gaps in the shutters drawn tight against the rain. After a moment, she opened them wide so she could see better. Surprise in her voice, she said, "Herpo the spice man's here. I wonder what possessed him to come in the middle of the rains."

"Some of those people just have itchy feet – they go when and where they choose," Garivald said. "Never could see the sense of it myself; I've always been happy to stay right where I am." But he finished eating in a hurry, while Annore was plopping Leuba in her crib and putting on her own rain cape and hat. They started to go out together to see Herpo. Leuba squalled angrily. Annore gave a martyred look and went back to pick up the baby.

Half the people in the village were out to see Herpo. Despite what Garivald had said about not wanting a crystal nearby and about being content where he was, he craved the news and gossip the spice seller had, and he was far from the only one.

And Herpo had news: "We're at war again," he said.

"Who is it now?" somebody asked. "Forthweg?"

"No, we already fought Forthweg," somebody else said, and then, doubtfully, "Didn't we?"

"Let Herpo speak his piece," Garivald said. "Then we'll know."

"Thank you, friend," the spice man said. "I will speak my piece, and then I'll hold my peace. We are at war with" — he paused dramatically — "the black people up in Zuwayza." He pointed north.

"Black people!" a granny said scornfully. "Save your lies for folks who believe them, Herpo. Next thing you know, you'll tell us we're at war with the blue people over there or the green people over *there*." Laughing at her own wit, she pointed first to the east and then to the west.

But a gray-haired man said, "Nay, Uote, these black men are real. There were a couple of 'em in my company in the Six Years' War. Brave enough, they were, but would you believe it, they had to learn to wear clothes. Their country is so hot, they said, that everybody there goes bare naked all the time, even the women." He smiled, as at the memory of something pleasant he hadn't thought of in a while.

Uote's face looked like curdled milk. "You shut up, Agen! The very idea!" she said. Garivald wasn't sure whether she disapproved of Agen's having the nerve to tell her she was wrong or of people — especially women — running around naked. *Probably both*, he thought.

Herpo said, "I don't know about this naked business myself, but I know we're fighting 'em. I expect we'll lick 'em pretty cursed quick, too, just like we did the Forthwegians." He looked at Uote out of the corner of his eye. "You going to tell me the Forthwegians ain't real, too?"

She looked as if she wished he weren't real. Instead of answering him, though, she showered more abuse on Agen. He was the one who'd embarrassed her in front of her fellow villagers. He bent his head and let her curses run off him like the rain. Under the wide brim of his hat, he was grinning.

"Along with the news," Herpo said, "I've got cinnamon, I've got cloves, I've got ginger, I've got dried pepper that'll make your tongue think it's on fire, and all for cheaper than you'd ever guess."

Garivald had tasted fire peppers a couple of times, and didn't fancy them. He bought a couple of quills of cinnamon and some powdered ginger and slogged back to his house. Herpo was still doing a brisk business when he left.

"Those will perk up the winter baking," Annore said when he showed her what he'd bought. Leuba had calmed down by then, and was after the hens again. His wife went on, "What was this great news? I was making the baby shut up, so I didn't get to hear it."

"Nothing very important." Garivald gave another shrug. "We're at war again, that's all."

Istvan walked along the beach on the island of Obuda. Scavengers had taken most of the meat from the skeleton of the Kuusaman dragon that had fallen. It skull stared at him out of empty eye sockets. He bared his teeth in a fierce grin; a Gyongyosian might feel fear, but he wasn't supposed to show it.

A lot of the dragon's fangs were missing. Some of Istvan's comrades wore one or more as souvenirs of having thrown back the Kuusamans. More, though, had sold them to the Obudans. Since the islanders did not know the art of dragonflying, they had an exaggerated notion of how much magic it required and how potent a talisman a dragon's tooth was.

Chuckling, Istvan scaled a flat stone into the sea. Anyone who'd ever shoveled dragon shit would know better. He had. He did. The Obudans, in their ignorance, didn't.

He wondered if he should have used the stone to knock out a couple of the remaining fangs for himself. After a moment, he shrugged and kept on walking down the beach. Money mattered little to him here on Obuda; he couldn't buy much with it. And the women, he'd heard, wouldn't put out for dragon's teeth: it was their menfolk who wanted them.

A wave ran farther up the gently sloping sand than most of its fellows. He had to skip aside to keep it from splashing his boots. It still wasn't very big. Out on the sea, Obudan fishing boats bobbed. Their sails were dyed in bright colors to make them visible from a long way off. Watching the wind push them along bemused Istvan. He'd never imagined such a thing, not while he was growing up in a mountain valley.

The Bothnian Ocean was calm now, but he'd never imagined what it could be like in a storm, either. Then the waves leapt like wild things and went down the beach only sullenly, as if they wanted to drag Obuda down under the water with them. They seemed to have teeth then, great white teeth of foam that sought to tear chunks out of the land.

He shook his head – he was getting as foolish as the Obudans. Their language had endless words to name and describe different kinds of waves. Gyongyosian, like any sensible speech, made do with one. Snow, now, Istvan thought, snow was something worth describing in detail. But the Obudans seldom saw snow.

A red and yellow and black shell caught Istvan's eye. He stooped and picked it up. Obuda boasted any number of colorful snail shells, all with different patterns. He didn't think he'd seen this one before. Back in his valley, snails had plain brown shells. The only good thing he had to say about those snails was that they made fine eating when fried with garlic and wild mushrooms.

Coming down from the barracks on the slopes of Mt. Sorong had been easy. Going back up took more work, even though the climb wasn't too steep. Leaving the beach and returning to the barracks also transformed Istvan from tourist back into soldier, a transformation he would just as soon not have made.

Sergeant Jokai descended on him like a mountain avalanche. "Good to have you back with us, your splendiferous magnificence," the veteran sergeant growled. "Now you can go fix your bunk the way the army taught you, not the way your mama taught you – if she was the one who taught you, and not some goat in a pen."

Istvan fought to keep his face expressionless. By main force of will, he succeeded. Gyongyosians did not keep goats, reckoning them unclean because of their eating habits and their lasciviousness. Had Jokai offered Istvan such an insult in civilian life, it would have started a brawl if not a clan feud. But the sergeant was Istvan's superior – thus his effective clan senior – and so he had to endure.

"I am very sorry, Sergeant," he said in a voice as empty as his features. "I thought I left everything in good order before I went on my morning's leave."

Jokai rolled his eyes. "Sorry doesn't get the cart out of the mud. Thinking doesn't get the cart out of the mud, either, especially when you're not good at it – and you're not. A week's labor policing up the dragon pens might do a better job of keeping your tiny little mind on what it's supposed to be doing. If it doesn't, we'll find something really interesting for you."

"Sergeant!" Istvan said piteously. Jokai had come down on him before, but never like this. Something else had to be irking the sergeant, Istvan thought. Whatever it was, Jokai was taking it out on him. He could, too, because he had the rank.

"You heard me," he said now. "A week, and thank the stars it isn't more. A mountain ape could have done a neater job here than you did."

Arguing more would only have got Istvan in deeper. With a sigh, he went into the barracks to inspect and repair the damage. None of his comrades wanted to look at him. He understood that. If they showed him any sympathy, Sergeant Jokai might land on them with both feet, too.

As Istvan had expected, pulling straight a tiny crease in his blanket took but an instant. Had Jokai been in a decent humor, he wouldn't even have noticed it. Maybe his emerods were bothering him. He was likely to have big emerods, because he was certainly a big . . .

Istvan sighed. He could think Sergeant Jokai as much of a billy goat as he liked, and it wouldn't change a thing. All that mattered was that Jokai was a sergeant and he wasn't.

Jokai inspected the repairs, then grudgingly nodded. "Now report to Turul. He'd better give you a good character at the end of the week, too, or you'll wish you'd never been born." Istvan was already inclining in that direction. Jokai added, "And I'll have my eye on you, too – don't think I won't. Do you understand what I'm telling you, soldier?"

"Aye, Sergeant." Istvan said the only thing he possibly could. Jokai stomped off. Istvan hoped he would find someone else with whom to be furious. Misery loved company. Besides, he might get stuck with less work that way.

Turul cackled like a laying hen when Istvan came slouching up to him. "I was waiting for Jokai to find somebody to give me a hand with the beasts," the old dragonkeeper said. "How'd he happen to choose you this time?"

"I was there," Istvan answered bitterly.

"That'll do, that'll do," Turul said. "Now you're here. The world won't end, even if it will stink for a while. And after you've been on this duty for a bit, you won't hardly even notice that."

"Maybe *you* don't," Istvan said, at which the dragonkeeper

laughed again. Istvan didn't think he'd been joking; after so much
time around quicksilver and brimstone, dragon fire and dragon dung,
how could Turul have any sense of smell left at all?

At the moment, Istvan's own sense of smell was working
altogether too well to suit him. He and Turul stood downwind of the
pens of the dragon farm. Along with the brimstone reek of their
fodder and droppings, he also inhaled the strong reptilian musk that
was their own distinctive scent.

Two of the beasts, both big males, began hissing and then shrieking
at each other. They reared up and spread their wings, each trying to
look as enormous and impressive as he could. The chains that secured
them to their iron tethering posts rattled and clanked.

Other dragons started hissing, too. Through the growing commotion, Istvan asked, "Can they break loose? Will they start
flaming?" He knew he sounded anxious. He couldn't help it. From
everything he could see, anxiety made perfect sense.

"They'd better not," Turul said indignantly. He picked up an iron-
shod goad, similar to the ones dragonfliers used but with a longer
handle, and advanced on the closer male. The dragon swiveled its
unlovely head on its snaky neck and stared at him out of cold golden
eyes. In spite of his protective clothing, it could have flamed him to
a cinder.

It did nothing of the sort. He shouted at it, a shout without words
but with strong overtones of the shrieks dragons aimed at one
another. The male hissed and flapped its wings; Istvan wondered why
the blast of wind from them didn't knock Turul over.

The old dragonkeeper shouted again. He whacked the dragon on
the end of its scaly nose with the goad. And, as a big fierce hound will
yield to a pampered lapdog that learned to dominate it when it was a
puppy, so the dragon, trained from hatchlinghood to obey puny men,
subsided now.

Istvan admired Turul's nerve without wanting to imitate it. The
dragonkeeper picked his way between pens and walloped the other
contentious dragon, too. A tiny puff of smoke burst from its mouth.
Turul hit it again, harder this time. "Don't you do that!" he yelled.
"Don't you even think of doing that! You do that when your flier
tells you, not any other time. Do you hear me?" *Whack!*

Evidently, the dragon did hear him. It crouched down, almost like

a puppy that knew it had made a mess in the house. Istvan watched
in fascination. Turul sent a few more yells at it, these wordless. Only
after he was sure he'd established his mastery did he stamp back
towards Istvan.

"I didn't think they were smart enough to obey like that," Istvan
said. "You really made them behave themselves."

"Smart hasn't got a whole lot to do with it," Turul answered.
"Dragon's *aren't* very smart. They never were. They never will be.
What these bastards are is *trained*. They're almost too stupid to be
trained, too. If they were, we couldn't fly 'em at all. We'd have to
hunt 'em down and kill 'em, same as we do with any other vermin.
Curse me if I don't sometimes think that'd be for the best."

"But you're one of the people who do train them," Istvan
exclaimed. "Would you want to be out of a job?"

"Sometimes," Turul said, surprising Istvan again. "You put in so
much work training dragons, and what do you get back? Shit and fire
and screeches, that's all. If you didn't train 'em so hard, the cursed
things'd eat you. Oh, I'm good at what I do, and I make no bones
about it. But when you get right down to it, lad, so what? Even a
horse, which isn't the smartest beast that ever came down the pike,
will make friends with you. A dragon? Never. Dragons know about
food and they know about the goad, and that's about it. It wears thin
now and again, that it does."

"What would you do if you weren't a dragonkeeper?" Istvan
asked.

Now Turul stared at him. "Been a while since I thought about
that. I don't rightly know, not now. I expect I'd have ended up a
potter or a carpenter or some such thing. I'd be settled down in some
little town with a fat wife getting old like me, and children, and
maybe – likely – grandchildren by now, too. Don't have any get I
know of, not unless my seed caught in one of the easy women I've
had down through the years."

Again, Istvan had got more answer than he'd bargained for. Turul
liked to talk, and didn't look to have had anyone to listen to him for
a while. Istvan asked another question: "Would that have been better
or worse than what you have now?"

"Blaze, how do I know?" the old dragonkeeper said. "It would
have been different, that's all I can tell you." The net of wrinkles

around his eyes shifted as they narrowed. "No, it's not all I can tell you. The other thing I can tell you is, there's lots and lots of dragon dung out there, and it won't go away by itself. Put on your leathers and get to it."

"Oh, aye," Istvan said. "I was just waiting for you to finish up here." That was close enough to true to keep Turul from calling him on it. With a stifled sigh, he went to work.

Hajjaj stood in front of the royal palace in Bishah, watching a parade of Unkerlanter captives shambling past. The Unkerlanters still wore their rock-gray tunics. They looked astonished that the Zuwayzin had captured them instead of the other way round. Being herded by naked Zuwayzi soldiers seemed as demoralizing to them as being jeered by naked Zuwayzi civilians.

Following the captives came Zuwayzi soldiers marching in neat ranks. The civilians cheered them, a great roar of noise in which Hajjaj delightedly joined. It picked him up and swept him along, as if it were the surf coming up the beach at Cape Hadh Faris, the northernmost spit of land in all Derlavai.

A woman turned to him and said, "They're pretty ugly, these Unkerlanters. Do they wear clothes because they're so ugly: to make sure no one can see?"

"No," the Zuwayzi foreign minister answered. "They wear clothes because it gets very cold in their kingdom." He knew the Unkerlanters and other folk of Derlavai had more reasons for wearing clothes than the weather, but, despite his study and his experience, those reasons made no sense to him, and surely would not to his countrywoman, either.

As things turned out, he might as well have not bothered speaking. The woman followed her own caravan of thought down its ley line: "And they're not just ugly, either. They're pretty puny fighters, too. Everyone was so afraid of them when this war started. I think we can beat them, that's what I think."

Plainly, she did not know to whom she was speaking. Hajjaj said only, "May the event prove you right, milady." He was glad – he was delighted – the Zuwayzin had won their first engagement against King Swemmel's forces. Unfortunately for him, he knew too much to have an easy time thinking one such victory would translate into a victorious war. Only a few times in his life had he wished to be more ignorant than he was. This was another of those rare occasions.

Another swarm of captives tramped glumly past the palace. People cursed them in Zuwayzi. The older men and women in the crowd, those who'd been to school while Zuwayza remained a province of Unkerlant, cursed the captured soldiers in rock-gray tunics in their own language. The old folks had had Unkerlanter rammed down their throats in the classroom, and plainly enjoyed using what they'd been made to learn.

More Zuwayzi troops followed, these mounted on camels. From the reports that had come into Bishah, the camel riders had played a major part in the victory over Unkerlant. Even in the somewhat cooler south, Zuwayza was a desert country. Camels could cross terrain that defeated horses and unicorns and behemoths. Appearing on the Unkerlanters' flank at the critical moment, the riders had thrown them first into confusion and then into panic.

Someone tapped Hajjaj on the shoulder. He turned and saw it was one of King Shazli's servants. Bowing, the man said, "May it please your Excellency, his Majesty would see you in his private reception chamber directly the parade is ended."

Hajjaj returned the bow. "His Majesty's wish is my pleasure," he replied, courteously if not altogether accurately. "I shall attend him at the time named." The servant nodded and hurried away.

As soon as the last captured egg-tosser had trundled past the palace, Hajjaj ducked inside and made his way through the relatively cool dimness to the chamber where he so often consulted with his sovereign. Shazli awaited him there. So, inevitably, did cakes and tea and wine. Hajjaj enjoyed the rituals and rhythms of his native land; to him, Unkerlanters and Algarvians always moved with unseemly haste. There were times, though, when haste was necessary even if unseemly.

Shazli felt the same way. The king broke off the polite small talk over refreshments as soon as he decently could. "How now, Hajjaj?" he said. "We have given King Swemmel a smart box on the ear. Whatever the Unkerlanters aim to extract from us, we have shown them they will have to pay dearly. We have shown the rest of the world the same thing. May we now hope the rest of the world has noticed?"

"Oh, aye, your Majesty, the rest of the world has noticed," Hajjaj replied. "I have received messages of congratulations from the ministers of several kingdoms. And each of those messages ends with the warning that it is but a personal note, and not meant to imply any change of policy on the part of the minister's sovereign."

"What must we do?" Shazli asked bitterly. "If we march on Cottbus and sack the place, will that get us the aid we need?"

Hajjaj's voice was dry: "If we march on Cottbus and sack the place, the Unkerlanters will be the ones needing aid. But I do not expect that to happen. I did not expect such good news as we have already had."

"You are a professional diplomat, and so a professional pessimist," Shazli said. Hajjaj inclined his head, acknowledging the truth in that. His sovereign went on, "Our officers tell me the Unkerlanters attack with less force than they expected. Maybe they were trying to catch us by surprise. Wherever the truth lies there, they failed, and have paid dearly for failing."

"Swemmel has a way of striking before he is fully ready," Hajjaj replied. "It cost him in the war against his twin brother, it made him start the pointless war against Gyongyos, and now it hurts him again."

"Only against Forthweg did striking soon serve him well," Shazli said.

"Algarve did most of the hard work against Forthweg," Hajjaj said. "All Swemmel did there was jump on the carcass and tear off some meat. This is, of course, also what he seeks to do against us."

"He has paid blood," Shazli said, sounding fierce as any warrior prince in Zuwayza's brigand-filled history. "He has paid blood, but has no meat to show for it."

"Not yet," Hajjaj said. "As you say, we have blooded one Unkerlanter army. Swemmel will send others after it. We cannot gather so many men together, try as we will."

"You do not believe we can win?" The king of Zuwayza looked wounded.

"Win?" Hajjaj shook his graying head. "Not if the Unkerlanters persist. If any of your officers should tell you otherwise, tell him in return that he has smoked too much hashish. My hope, your Majesty, is that we can hurt the Unkerlanters enough to keep more of what is ours than they demand, and not to let them gobble us down, as they did before. Even that, I judge, will not be easy, for has not King Swemmel shouted he aims to rule in Bishah?"

"The generals do indeed speak of victory," Shazli said.

Hajjaj bowed in his seat. "You are the king. You are the ruler. You are the one to decide whom to believe. If my record over the years has caused you to lose faith in me, you have but to say the word. At my age, I shall be glad to lay down the burdens of my office and retire to my home, my wives, my children, and my grandchildren. My fate is in your hands, as is the kingdom's."

No matter what he said, he did not want to retire. But he did not want King Shazli carried away by dreams of glory, either. Threatening to resign was the best way Hajjaj knew to gain his attention. If the ploy failed – then it failed, that was all. Shazli was a young man. Dreams of glory took root in him more readily than in his foreign minister. To Hajjaj's way of thinking, that was why the kingdom had a foreign minister. Of course, Shazli might think otherwise.

"Stay by my side," Shazli said, and Hajjaj inclined his head in obedience – and to keep from showing the relief he felt. The king went on, "I shall hope my generals are right, and shall bid them fight as fiercely and cleverly as they can. If the time comes when they can fight no more, I shall rely on you to make the best terms with Unkerlant you may. Does that suit you?"

"Your Majesty, it does," Hajjaj said. "And I, for my part, shall hope the officers are right and I wrong. I am not so rash as to reckon myself infallible. If the Unkerlanters make enough mistakes, we may indeed emerge victorious."

"May it be so," King Shazli said, and gently clapped his hands in the Zuwayzi gesture of dismissal. Hajjaj rose, bowed, and left the palace. When he was sure no one could see him, he let out a long sigh. The king still had confidence in him. Without that, he was nothing – or nothing more than the retired diplomat he had said he might want to become. He shook his head. Whom else could King Shazli find to do such a good job of lying for the kingdom?

One of the privileges the foreign minister enjoyed was a carried at his beck and call. Hajjaj availed himself of that privilege now. "Be so good as to take me home," he told the driver, who doffed his broad-brimmed hat in token of obedience.

Hajjaj's home lay on the side of a hill, to catch the cooling breezes. Bishah had few cooling breezes to catch, but they did blow in spring and fall. Like many houses in the capital, his was built of golden sandstone. Its wings rambled over a good stretch of the hillside, with gardens among them. Most of the plants were native to Zuwayza, and not extravagant of water.

The majordomo bowed when Hajjaj went inside. Tewfik had been a family retainer longer than Hajjaj had been alive; he was well up into his eighties, bent and wrinkled and slow, but with wits and tongue still unimpaired. "Everyone's still going mad with celebrating, eh, lad?" he croaked.

He was the only man alive who called Hajjaj *lad*. "Even so," the foreign minister said. "We have won a victory, after all."

Tewfik grunted. "It won't last. Nothing ever lasts." If anything refuted that, it was himself. He went on, "You'll want to see the lady Kolthoum, then." It was not a question. Tewfik did not need to make it a question. He knew his master.

And Hajjaj nodded. "Aye," he said, and followed the majordomo. Kolthoum was his first wife, the only person in the world who knew him better than Tewfik. He'd wed Hassila twenty years later, to cement a clan tie. Lalla was a recent amusement. One day before too long, he'd have to decide whether she'd grown too expensive to be amusing any more.

For now, though, Kolthoum. She was embroidering with one of Hassila's daughters when Tewfik led Hajjaj into the room. One look at her husband's face and she told the girl, "Run along, Jamila. I'll show you more about that stitch later. Right now, your father needs to talk with me. Tewfik—"

"I shall fetch refreshments directly, senior wife," the majordomo said.

"Thank you, Tewfik." Kolthoum had never been a great beauty, and had put on flesh as she aged. But men paid attention to her because of her voice, and also because she made it very plain that she paid attention to them. As soon as Tewfik shuffled away, she said, "It's not as good as the crystal makes it sound, is it?"

"When is anything ever as good as the crystal makes it sound?" Hajjaj returned. His senior wife laughed. He went on, "You aren't the only one who thinks it is, though, and you have friends in high places." He told her about his conversation with King Shazli, and about what he'd had to do; when speaking with his wife, he did not need to wait through the ritual of tea and wine and cakes.

"A good thing he didn't take you up on it!" Kolthoum said indignantly. "What would you do, underfoot here all day? And what would we do, with you underfoot here all day?"

Hajjaj laughed and kissed her on the cheek. "Powers above be praised that I have a wife who truly understands me."

"Well, of course," Kolthoum said.

Fernao had visited Yanina a couple of times before what news sheets in Setubal were calling the Derlavaian War broke out. Unless his memory had slipped, Patras, the capital, hadn't been so frantic then. Yaninans *were* frantic – or, at least, they looked that way to foreigners – but they'd seemed less on edge then.

Of course, he thought, being a small kingdom sandwiched between Algarve and Unkerlant went a long way toward helping to make a folk frantic. Having King Penda of Forthweg cooped up somewhere in the royal palace couldn't have helped matters, either, not with King Swemmel breathing down King Tsavellas's neck to get his hands on Penda.

And so broadsheets sprouted on every wall. Fernao couldn't read them; the Yaninans used a script all their own – as much to be difficult as for any other reason, as far as the Lagoan mage was concerned. But they were full of pictures of soldiers and dragons and red ink and the punctuation marks for excitement and urgency that a lot of scripts shared. If they didn't mean something like LOOK OUT! WE'RE GOING TO BE IN A WAR! – if they didn't mean something like that, Fernao understood nothing of symbols.

Two Yaninans were quarreling on the plank sidewalk in front of the doorway to the shop Fernao wanted to enter. They were going at it hammer and tongs, getting madder by the minute. In Fernao's ears, Yaninan sounded like wine pouring out of a jug too fast, glug, glug, glug. He knew only a handful of phrases of it; it wasn't a tongue closely related to any other.

A crowd gathered. Arguing and watching arguments seemed to be the Yaninan national sports. Men in tunics with puffy sleeves and tights and women with kerchiefs on their heads egged on the two combatants. At last, one of the skinny, swarthy men grabbed the other's bushy side whiskers and yanked. With a shriek, the second man hit the first in the belly. They grabbed each other and rolled into the street, clawing and gouging and cursing. The crowd surged after them.

With a sigh of relief, Fernao slid through the now vacant doorway of the gourmet-foods shop. Varvakis supplied King Tsavellas with delicacies; selling him a shipment of smoked Lagoan trout gave Fernao an innocuous reason for coming to Yanina. The foodseller spoke fluent Algarvian, for which Fernao gave thanks. "Just another day," the mage remarked, pointing to the commotion outside.

"Oh, indeed," Varvakis answered. He was a short, bald man with a big black mustache and the hairiest ears Fernao had ever seen. Fernao's irony went past him; as far as he was concerned, it *was* just another day. Patras was like that.

Fernao glanced around the shop. Varvakis did business with the whole world. Jars of Algarvian liver paste stood beside hams and sausages from Valmiera, Jelgavan wines next to Unkerlanter apricot brandy, Kuusaman lobsters and oysters by chewy strips of dried conch from Zuwayza, mild red peppers from Gyongyos alongside fiery ones out of tropic Siaulia. The mage pointed to some large brown dried leaves he didn't recognize. "What are those?"

"I just got them in, as a matter of fact," Varvakis answered. "They're from one of the islands of the north, I forget which one. The natives crumble them in a pipe and smoke them like hashish. But they speed you up instead of slowing you down, if you know what I mean."

"That might be interesting," Fernao said. "But now—" Before he could get down to business, a plump woman with a distinct mustache walked in. Varvakis fawned on her. They walked over to a bin of prunes and had a long discussion of which Fernao followed not a word. The woman finally condescended to buy a few ounces' worth. Varvakis gave her a couple of coppers in change with the air of a man conferring a kingdom-saving loan upon his sovereign. Fernao let out a muffled snort. Even more than Algarvians, Yaninans overacted.

"But now—" Varvakis said when the plump woman had left. Yaninans also had – and needed – a gift for picking up the threads of interrupted conversation. "But now, my friend, I have, or think I have, good news for you. A steward of my acquaintance tells me that—" He bowed himself double when a man came in and went over to examine the lobsters. At the prices he was charging for them, only a rich customer could have afforded any. Fernao quietly fumed till the transaction was done.

"A steward of your acquaintance tells you what?" the mage asked when Varvakis remembered he was there – he was learning to handle multiple interrupted conversations, too, although not to enjoy them. In some exasperation, he added, "*Could* you let a clerk handle people till we're done here?"

"Oh, very well." The fancy grocer sounded testy. "But customers want to see *me*. They come to deal with *me*." He puffed out his chest with pride – and with air, which he used to shout, "Gyzis!" The clerk emerged from the back room, wearing a leather apron over a Yaninan-style puffy-sleeved tunic. Grudgingly, Varvakis put him in charge of the front of the shop and took Fernao into the back room.

More delicacies lined the shelves there, some in jars, others kept fresh in rest crates. "About this steward—" Fernao prompted.

"Aye, aye, of course." Varvakis's eyes flashed. "Do you take me for a halfwit? For a price, he says, he can get you in to see King Penda – maybe Penda can moan that he's pining for smoked trout. What you do once you see Penda, I know nothing about. I wish to know nothing about it." He held an arm in front of his head, so that his sleeve drooped down and covered his eyes.

"I understand that," Fernao said patiently. "Money shouldn't be any trouble." By all the signs, Shelomith had money coming out of his ears. He'd given Fernao a goodly sum, and he'd given Varvakis a goodly sum, too: Varvakis did not strike the mage as a man who would be very cooperative without a well-greased palm.

He proved that again, saying, "What I give to Cossos does not come from my fee. It will be redeemed."

"I agree," Fernao said at once. Why not? He wasn't spending his own money. "Set up the meeting. Pay whatever you have to pay. We will reimburse you."

Varvakis dipped his head in agreement. "Go, then. Take yourself out of here. We should not be seen together. When the meeting is arranged, you will hear from me. You will also hear how much you owe. You will pay before you see Cossos."

Was that the edge of a threat? Probably. Varvakis could pocket the money and let Fernao walk into a trap. For that matter, he could pocket it and set up a trap for Fernao. The unpleasant possibilities were almost endless.

Back at the nondescript – indeed, dingy – hostel where he and Fernao were staying, Shelomith waxed enthusiastic. "This is just the chance we need!" he said, clapping Fernao on the back. "I knew that, sooner or later, one of my contacts would survey a ley line to his Majesty for us."

Fernao mentally substituted *I hoped* for *I knew*. Aloud, he said, "Whatever this Cossos wants, he won't work cheap." Shelomith only shrugged. They were staying at a hostel less than of the finest to keep from drawing notice to themselves. Shelomith had plenty of gold – just how much, Fernao didn't know. Plenty for all ordinary and most extraordinary purposes, that was certain.

And so, with Varvakis along as a go-between, Fernao approached King Tsavellas's palace a couple of days later. Yaninan architecture ran to tall, thin watchtowers and to onion domes, all very exotic to a practical Lagoan. The guards at the entrance wore tights with red and white stripes and red pompoms on their shoes, but looked tough and determined despite the absurd costume. Recognizing Varvakis, they bowed in greeting, and accepted Fernao because he accompanied the purveyor of fancy foods.

Paintings on the walls showed Yaninan kings with odd domed crowns; long somber faces; and robes so thick with gold and silver threads, they had to be almost too heavy to wear. Other paintings celebrated the triumphs of Yaninan arms. Judging by those paintings, Yanina had never lost a battle, let alone a war. Judging by the map, those paintings didn't tell the whole story.

"We can talk here," Cossos said, escorting Fernao and Varvakis into a small chamber. Like Varvakis, he spoke good Algarvian. The Yaninans had learned a great deal from their eastern neighbors. Not all the lessons had been pleasant.

Varvakis said, "The two of you talk. What you talk about, I don't want to hear. If I don't hear it, I don't have to tell lies about it." He bowed first to Fernao, then to Cossos, and departed before either of them could say a word.

"No stones to that man," Cossos remarked, tossing his head in a

Yaninan gesture of scorn. He was about forty-five, wiry, shrewd-looking, with a nose like a swordblade. "Now, my friend, what can I do for you?"

"I doubt I am your friend," Fernao said. "If all goes well, I may be your benefactor, though."

"That will do well enough," Cossos said briskly. "I ask you once again: what can I do for you?"

Fernao hesitated. Here was where the jaws of the trap might close on him. If someone besides Cossos was listening . . . If that was so, Fernao might find out more about the dark places of Yanina than he ever wanted to know. He could not sense anyone listening, but he could not gauge whether Yaninan wizards were masking a spy from his powers, either.

But he had not come here to be cautious. Taking a deep breath, he said, "I would like half an hour alone with Penda of Forthweg, with no one to know I have come to see him. I also require your studied forgetfulness that you ever arranged such an appointment for me."

"Studied forgetfulness, eh?" Cossos bared his teeth in what was almost, but not quite, a smile of genuine amusement. "Aye, I can see how you would. Well, I can manage that. In fact, I'd better, or my head would answer it, after the other. But it'll cost you." He named a sum in Yaninan lepta.

After Fernao converted it into Lagoan sceptres, he whistled softly. Cossos did not think small. But Shelomith had gold aplenty. "Agreed," the mage said, and Cossos blinked, evidently having expected him to haggle. Fernao added, "I will take any oath you like that I mean Penda no harm."

Cossos shrugged. "It'd cost you less if you did mean him harm," he said. "King Tsavellas would just as soon see him dead. Then he wouldn't have to worry about him any more. Bring me the money and—"

"I'll bring you the first half," Fernao broke in. "The other half comes afterwards, in case you'd just as soon see me dead." Cossos bared his teeth. Fernao stood firm against all his complaints, saying, "You need a reason not to betray me." In the end, grumbling, the steward gave in.

Well pleased with himself, Fernao headed back to the hostel. Shelomith would pay without blinking; he was sure of that. He was less sure he could walk out of the palace with Penda and with no one the wiser, but he thought so. Lagoan mages knew more than those in this benighted corner of the world. He'd already had a couple of good ideas, and more would come to him.

He rounded the last corner and stopped dead. Green-uniformed constables surrounded the hostel like ants at an outdoor feast. A couple of them carried a body out on a litter. Fernao knew it would be Shelomith's before he got close enough to recognize it, and it was. The constables were laughing and joking, as if they'd found treasure. They probably had found treasure − Shelomith's treasure. Fernao gulped. Now all he had was the money in his own pouch, and he was alone and friendless in a foreign town.

7.

Dragons swooped low over Trapani. Marching in the triumphal procession through the streets of the Algarvian capital, Colonel Sabrino hoped none of the miserable beasts would choose the moment in which it flew over him to void. Long and intimate experience informed his mistrust of dragons.

No sooner had that thought crossed his mind than he had to step smartly to keep from putting his foot down on a pile of behemoth dung. Squadrons of the great beasts were interspersed among the marching troops, to give the swarms of civilians who packed the sidewalks something extra at which to cheer.

Sabrino marched with his shoulders back, his head up, his chin thrust forward. He wanted everyone who saw him to know he was a fierce fighting man, one who would never take a step back from the foe. Algarvians made much of appearances. *And why not?* Sabrino thought. *Have the mages not proved that appearances help shape reality?*

He also wanted people, especially pretty women, to notice. He was happy with his wife, he was happy with his mistress, but he would not have been broken-hearted had some sweet young thing adoringly cast herself at his feet. No, he would not have been broken-hearted at all.

Whether he would find himself so lucky after the end of the parade, he did not know. He was pretty sure a good many soldiers would, though. Women kept running out to kiss them as they tramped past. A lot of the cheers that washed over them weren't the sort of cheers soldiers usually got. They sounded more like the ones excited followers usually gave popular balladeers or actors.

Behind Sabrino, Captain Domiziano must have been thinking along similar lines, for he said, "If a man can't get laid today, sir, it's only because he's not trying very hard."

"You're right about that," Sabrino answered. "You are indeed." He kept eyeing women, though he told himself that was foolish: the ones he passed here would be long gone by the time the parade ended. But his eyes were less disciplined than his mind – or, to put it another way, he enjoyed watching regardless of whether or not he could do anything but watch.

People held up signs saying things like GOODBYE, FORTHWEG! and ONE DOWN, THREE TO GO! and ALGARVE THE INVINCIBLE! It hadn't been like that in the Six Years' War, Sabrino remembered. The kingdom had fought only reluctantly then. Now, with her neighbors declaring war on her after she had done no more than retrieve what was rightfully hers, Algarve was united behind King Mezentio – and behind the army that had won this triumph.

The parade ended at the royal palace, men and behemoths tramping by under the balcony from which King Mezentio had announced that Algarve was at war with Forthweg and Sibiu, Jelgava and Valmiera. Mezentio stood there now, reviewing the troops who had won such a smashing victory. Sabrino doffed his hat and waved it in the direction of his sovereign. "Mezentio!" he shouted at the top of his lungs, his cry one of hundreds, thousands, aimed at the king.

Around the palace to the far side, the side opposite the Royal Square and also out of sight of the crowd, the triumphal procession disintegrated. Behemoth riders took their beasts off through alleys so narrow, they had to go in single file. Martinets led their companies and regiments back toward their barracks. Officers with more heart gave their men liberty. The released soldiers hurried back toward the Royal Square to see what arrangements they could make for themselves.

Sabrino had just turned his men loose, and was about to follow them back toward the square and try his luck when someone tapped him on the shoulder. He spun, to find himself facing a man in the green, red, and white livery of a palace servant. "You are the Count Sabrino?" the servitor asked.

"I am," Sabrino admitted. "What do you desire of me?"

Before answering, the servant made a mark on the list, probably checking off his name. Then he said, "I have the honor, my lord, of inviting you to a reception in an hour's time in the Salon of King

Aquilante V, wherein his Majesty shall express his gratitude to the nobility for supporting him and Algarve during our present crisis."

"I am honored," Sabrino said, bowing. "You may tell his Majesty that I shall certainly attend him."

He wondered if the servant even heard; the fellow had already turned away to look for the next man on his list. He must have assumed Sabrino would accept the invitation. And why not? Who in his right mind would refuse a summons from his sovereign? Sabrino hurried toward the nearest palace entrance.

Guards there unsmilingly examined his uniform, his dragonflier's badge, and his badge of nobility. They ticked off his name as the servitor who'd tendered him the invitation had done. Irritated, Sabrino snapped, "I am not a Sibian spy, gentlemen, nor a Valmieran assassin, either."

"We believe you, my lord," one of the guards said. "*Now* we believe you. Pass on, and enjoy the pleasures of the palace."

Sabrino knew his way to the Salon of King Aquilante V; he had attended several other gatherings there. Nonetheless, he did not object when a serving woman stepped forward to guide him. He would have liked it even better had she guided him to her bed-chamber, but walking along flirting with her was pleasant enough.

"Count Sabrino!" a herald cried in a great voice when he entered the salon. To his disappointment, the pretty serving girl went off to escort someone else. *Faithless hussy*, he thought, and laughed at himself.

Tables piled high with refreshments stood against one wall. He took a glass of white wine and a slice from a round of flatbread piled high with melted cheeses, salt fish, eggplant slices, and olives. Thus equipped, he sallied forth on to the social battlefield.

Naturally, he did his best to put himself in the way of King Mezentio, who circulated through the reception hall. Being a resourceful man, he soon succeeded in drawing the king's notice. "Your Majesty!" he cried, and bowed low enough to gladden a protocol officer's heart without spilling a drop of wine or losing a single olive from his flatbread.

"Powers above, straighten up!" Mezentio said irritably. "Do you think I'm King Swemmel, to need all that head-knocking nonsense? He thinks it makes people afraid of him, but what does an

Unkerlanter know? Nothing to speak of – Unkerlanters grow like onions, with their heads in the ground."

"Even so, your Majesty," Sabrino said, nodding. "If only there weren't so many of them."

"By the hamhanded way he's fighting that war against Zuwayza, Swemmel is doing his best to make them fewer," the king answered. "And my congratulations, by the way, on how well you and your wing fought above Wihtgara. I was very pleased by the reports I read of your exploits."

"I shall pass on your praise to my dragonfliers," Sabrino said with another bow. "They, after all, are the ones who earned it for me."

"Spoken as a good officer should speak," Mezentio said. "Tell me, Count, in your fighting above Forthweg, did you find many of Kaunian blood opposing you on dragons painted in Forthwegian colors?"

"Speaking solely from my own experience, your Majesty, that's hard to say," Sabrino replied. "One often doesn't get close enough to the foe to see exactly who he is. When the dragons fly high, going up there's a chilly business, too, so the men who fly them are often bundled against the cold. I'm given to understand, though, that the Forthwegians set a good many obstacles in the way of Kaunians who seek to fly dragons, the same as they do against Kaunian officers of any sort."

"I know for a fact that last is true." Mezentio frowned. "Curious how the Forthwegians look down their beaky noses at the Kaunians inside their own borders, but follow like lapdogs when the Kaunians in the east seek to savage us."

"They've paid for their folly," Sabrino said.

"Everyone who harms Algarve shall pay for his folly," Mezentio declared. "Everyone who has ever harmed Algarve shall pay for his folly. We lost the Six Years' War. This time, come what may, we shall win."

"Certainly we shall, your Majesty," Sabrino said. "The whole world is jealous of Algarve, of what we are and of the way we've pulled ourselves up by the bootstraps even after everyone piled on to us in the Six Years' War."

"Aye, the whole world is jealous – the whole world, and especially the Kaunian kingdoms," Mezentio said. "You mark my words,

Count: those yellow-haired folk still hate us for destroying their cozy little empire more than a thousand years ago. If they could kill us all, they would. Since they can't, they seek to crush us so we may never rise again."

"It won't happen." Sabrino spoke with great sincerity.

"Of course it won't," Mezentio said. "Are we as stupid as Unkerlanters, to let them scheme and plot to destroy us without making plans of our own?" The king laughed. "And the Unkerlanters are stupid indeed, with Swemmel always bellowing 'Efficiency!' at the top of his lungs and then blundering into one idiotic war after another." He turned away from Sabrino toward a noble who stood waiting to be recognized. "And how are you, your Grace?"

Sabrino went back for another goblet of wine. That was more time than he'd enjoyed with the king in any other meeting. And Mezentio not only knew who he was – which he'd expected – but also where his wing had served – which he hadn't. He didn't fight to gain royal notice, but he wouldn't turn down royal notice if it came his way.

He drifted through the room, greeting men he knew, flirting with serving women and the companions of nobles who happened to live in Trapani, and keeping his ears open for gossip. There was plenty; the only trouble was, he didn't always know to what it referred. When one white-goateed general said to another, "We have only to kick in the door and the whole rotten structure will come crashing down," what door was he talking about? Whoever was standing behind it wouldn't care to have it kicked in on him. Of that Sabrino was certain.

A commodore in naval black spoke to a colleague: "Well, this ought to set the history of warfare on the sea back about a thousand years."

Laughing, his friend answered, "They pay off on what you do. They don't pay off on how you do it." Then he noticed Sabrino was listening. Whatever he said after that was in a voice too low for the dragonflier to hear. Annoyed at having been caught, Sabrino took himself elsewhere.

A woman put a hand on his arm. She wasn't a servant; the green of her silk tunic was darker than that of the national banner, and she wore more gold and emeralds than a servant could even have dreamt of. As Algarvian women sometimes did, she came straight to the point: "My friend's drunk himself asleep, and I don't want to go back to my flat alone."

He looked her up and down. "Your friend, my dear, is a fool. Tell me your name. I want to know whose fool he is."

"I am Ippalca," she answered, "and you are the famous Count Sabrino, the man in all the news sheets."

"My sweet, I was famous long before the news sheets ever heard of me," Sabrino said. "When we get back to your flat, I will show you why." Ippalca laughed. Her eyes glowed. Sabrino slid an arm around her waist. Together, they left the Salon of King Aquilante V.

"Efficiency." Leudast made the word into a curse. It had already doomed a lot of Unkerlanter soldiers. He looked around. After the homelike fields of western Forthweg, this Zuwayzi waste of sunbaked rock and blowing sand seemed a particularly cruel joke.

He checked his water bottle. It was full. He'd filled it at the last water hole, only half a mile or so south of where he was now. The Zuwayzin hadn't poisoned that one. He'd seen men drink from it, and they'd taken no harm. The naked black savages hadn't missed many water holes. They weren't perfectly efficient themselves – just far too close for comfort.

Sergeant Magnulf trudged by. His boots scuffed through sand. His shoulders slumped, ever so slightly. Even his iron determination, which had never faltered during the war against Gyongyos, was wearing thin here. "Tell me again, Sergeant," Leudast called to him. "Remind me why King Swemmel wants this land bad enough to take it away from anybody. Remind me why anybody who's got it isn't happy to give it to the first fool who wants it."

Magnulf looked at him. "You need to be more efficient with your mouth, soldier," he said tonelessly. "I know you didn't mean to call King Swemmel a fool, but somebody else who was listening might get the idea you did. You wouldn't want that to happen, would you?"

Leudast considered. If they arrested him for disloyalty to King Swemmel, they'd take him out of this Zuwayzi wilderness. He wouldn't have to worry about black men who wanted to blaze him – or, as army rumor had it, to cut his throat and drink his blood. On the other hand, he would have to worry about Swemmel's interrogators. He might escape the Zuwayzin. The interrogators . . . no.

"Thank you, Sergeant," he replied at last. "I'll watch what I say."

"You'd better." Magnulf wiped his forehead on the sleeve of his tunic. The Unkerlanters called the tunic's color rock gray, but it didn't match any of the rocks hereabouts, which were various ugly shades of yellow. That also struck Leudast as inefficient, but he kept his mouth shut about it. Magnulf went on, "I'll even answer your question. The king wants this land back because it used to belong to Unkerlant, and so it ought to again. And the Zuwayzin don't want us to have it on account of it blocks our path toward better country farther north."

"*Is* there better country farther north?" Leudast asked, again speaking more freely than he should have. "Or does this miserable desert go on forever?"

"There's supposed to be better country," Magnulf said. "I suppose there must be better country – otherwise, the Zuwayzin couldn't raise so many soldiers against us."

That made sense. Along with the rest of the men in his company, Leudast slogged north. Thornbushes grew here and there among the rocks. Very little else did. Very little lived here, either – snakes and scorpions and a few little pale foxes with enormous ears. Scavenger birds circled overhead, their wings looking as wide as those of dragons. They thought the Unkerlanter army would come to grief in the desert. Leudast remained far from sure they were wrong.

He tramped past a dead behemoth. The big beast hadn't been blazed; its corpse bore no mark he could see. Maybe it had just keeled over from trying to haul the weight of its armor and weapons and riders through the desert. Since he felt like keeling over himself, Leudast knew a certain amount of sympathy for the poor brute. The army had its own scavengers; they'd already taken away the ironmongery the behemoth had carried on its back.

Magnulf pointed. "There's the line," he said: Unkerlanters crouching and sprawling behind stones, blazing away at the Zuwayzin who blocked their path. As Leudast got down behind a rock himself so he could crawl forward, one of his countrymen shrieked and clutched at his shoulder. This terrain was made for defense. A handful of men could hold up an army here – and had.

"Come on, you reinforcements, take your places," an officer shouted. "We'll get those black bastards out of there soon enough – see if we don't." He ordered some of the soldiers already in line forward to flank out the Zuwayzin who'd stalled the advance.

Leudast blazed away at the rocks behind which the enemy sheltered. He had no idea whether his beams hit anyone. At the least, they made the Zuwayzin keep their heads down while his comrades slid around by the right flank.

But more Zuwayzin waited on the right. They hadn't been blazing, perhaps hoping to draw the very attack the officer had commanded. They broke it. After a few minutes, Unkerlanters came streaming back to the main line, some of them helping wounded comrades escape the enemy's beams.

When the Zuwayzin attacked in turn, the Unkerlanters threw them back. That cheered Leudast – till he heard an officer say, "We're the ones who are supposed to be moving forward, curse it, not the black men."

"Tell it to the Zuwayzin – maybe they haven't heard," somebody not far from Leudast muttered. That struck him as dangerously inefficient speech, but he wasn't inclined to report it. For the moment, he was content to be able to hold his position and not have to retreat.

He swigged from his water bottle. That wouldn't last indefinitely, and, except for the known water holes, the dowsers hadn't had any luck finding new supplies. Leudast found himself unsurprised: if no water was out there to find, the best dowsers in the world couldn't find it. That meant the army had to depend on the familiar holes and on what ley-line caravans and animals could bring forward. By the knots of mages Leudast had seen working along the ley lines, the Zuwayzin had done their best to make them impassable. That did nothing to add to his peace of mind.

And then he stopped worrying about such minor details as perhaps dying of thirst in a few days. Off to the left, the west, eggs smashed against stone. Leudast automatically hugged the ground. Hard on the heels of those roars came exultant cries in a language he did not know and despairing ones in a language he did: "The Zuwayzin! The Zuwayzin are on our flank!"

"Camels!" Sergeant Magnulf used the word as vilely as Leudast had used *efficiency* before. "Bastards snuck around our cavalry again." He bit out a few curses of a more conventional sort, then gathered himself. "Well, no help for it." He looked westward to gauge how close the attackers were. "Fall back!" he shouted. "Fall back – form a line so we're not enfiladed any more. Whatever happens, we have to hang on to that water hole back there."

He was thinking about water, too, though in a more immediate sense than Leudast had been. In this sun-baked country, not thinking about water was impossible. No doubt the Zuwayzin were also thinking about it, and making for that water hole themselves. At least Magnulf *was* thinking, which seemed to be more than any of the Unkerlanter officers could say.

Leudast scrambled back toward a stone that offered good shelter against attack from the west. As happened whenever a force found itself outflanked, some soldiers panicked and fled toward the rear. As often happened when they did, they paid the price for panic: Zuwayzi beams cut them down.

Howling with triumph, the Zuwayzin stormed forward. Leudast blazed a black man who showed too much of himself. Several other Zuwayzin also went down, dead or shrieking in pain. Then the enemy started flitting from rock to rock again, having learned a good many Unkerlanters still held fight.

More eggs crashed down around Leudast. The Zuwayzin must have taken apart some light tossers and carried them on camelback. Sand and shattered rock pelted him. He wanted to claw a hole in the ground, jump in, and pull the hole shut over him. He couldn't. And, if he stayed curled up behind this rock, the Zuwayzin could move forward and blaze him at their leisure.

Understanding that was easy. Making himself get up on one knee and blaze at the enemy was much harder, but he did it. He thought he wounded another Zuwayzi, too. But he could not stay where he was any more, for the Zuwayzin were still advancing. He slipped away to another stone, and then to another.

"We have to save the water hole!" an officer shouted, realizing only now what Magnulf had seen at once. "If we lose that water hole, we lose our grip on this whole stretch of desert." He shouted orders pulling more men from what had been the advance and shifting them to the turned flank.

It wasn't going to be enough. Leudast could see it wasn't going to be enough. The Zuwayzin could see it wasn't going to be enough, too. They knew what forcing the men of Unkerlant away from the water hole would mean. They were more clever than the Gongs, probably more clever than the Forthwegians, too. When they struck, they struck hard, and straight for the heart.

Leudast wondered if he had enough water to make it back to the next clean hole. It was, he knew, a long way to the south – a dreadfully long way, if a man was retreating with the enemy nipping at his heels. Maybe he could fill up the bottle before the black men reached this water hole.

More eggs fell – but these fell on the Zuwayzin. Dragons overhead had made the scavenger birds fly off. As the dragons wheeled, he saw their upper bodies were painted rock-gray: the color Unkerlant used. Now he shouted in triumph and the Zuwayzin in dismay. Unkerlanter egg-tossers well back of the line began adding their gifts to the ones the dragons were delivering.

A man in a rock-gray tunic took shelter behind the rock next to Leudast's. "How's it look, soldier?" he asked, an officer's sharp snap in his voice.

"Not too bad, sir – not now," Leudast answered, glancing over at the newcomer. That tunic was one a common soldier might have worn, but the collar bore a large star. Leudast's eyes widened. Only one man in Unkerlant was entitled to wear that emblem. "Not too bad, my lord Marshal," he corrected himself, wondering what a man like Rathar was doing at the front.

Rathar answered that question without his asking it: "Can't find out what's going on if I don't see for myself."

"Uh, aye, sir," Leudast said. The marshal hadn't just come to see. He'd come to fight, and carried a stick like any other footsoldier's. He used it, too, popping up to blaze at the Zuwayzin. Of course, he'd fought in the Six Years' War and the Twinkings War, which meant he'd been around combat longer than Leudast had been alive. His happy grunt had to mean he'd got a beam home.

Looking around, Leudast saw Rathar had also brought his crystallomancer with him. The marshal barked out a stream of orders, which the mage relayed to his colleagues back with the reserves. Those orders sent men and egg-tossers and dragons up toward the battle. Anyone who disobeyed them or delayed by even a heartbeat speedily regretted it.

For the first time since plunging into the Zuwayzin desert, Leudast began to feel hope. Up till now, the Unkerlanters' campaign had been bungled. Listening to Rathar's crisp commands, he didn't think the bungling would go on much longer.

It was Count Brorda's birthday, a holiday in Gromheort. An Algarvian dwelt in Brorda's castle these days, but he hadn't bothered canceling the holiday. Maybe he hadn't wanted to antagonize the Forthwegians over whom he sat in judgment, although Ealstan had a hard time imagining an Algarvian who cared a fig about what the folk of Gromheort thought. More likely, the occupiers were just too lazy to bother changing what they'd found when they overran the city.

Whatever the cause, Ealstan was glad to escape school. He'd grown as sick of Algarvian irregular verbs as he had been of their classical Kaunian equivalents. And besides, the first fall rains had brought out the mushrooms.

Forthwegians were mad for mushrooms – not surprising, when so many good ones grew in their kingdom. They ate them fresh, they ate them dried, they ate them pickled, they ate them in salads, they ate them with olives: they ate them with any excuse, or none.

Markets were always full of mushrooms, but Ealstan, like most Forthwegians, was convinced the ones he picked himself were better than any he could buy. Like most Forthwegians, he knew the differences between the edible varieties and the ones that were poisonous; like his schoolmasters, his father had operated on the principle that a warmed backside made blood flow more freely to the brain. And so, armed with a cloth sack, he sallied forth with his cousin Sidroc to see what he could find.

"It will be good to get out of the city," Sidroc said. Lowering his voice, he went on, "It will be good to get away from the cursed redheads, too."

"I won't say you're wrong, because I think you're right," Ealstan said. "I just hope they let us out. All their checkpoints are still up."

But the Algarvian soldiers at the checkpoint on the west side of town, seeing the sacks they carried, waved them through. "Mushrooms?" a soldier asked. Ealstan and Sidroc nodded. The

Algarvian stuck out his tongue and made a horrible face to show what he thought of them. He spoke in his own language. His comrades laughed and nodded. They didn't fancy mushrooms, either.

"More for us," Ealstan said as soon as he was out of earshot of the guard who spoke Forthwegian. Sidroc nodded again.

Before long, the two cousins split up. That way, they would bring a wider assortment of mushrooms back to the house they still shared. That way, too, they wouldn't quarrel if they both spotted a fine one at the same time. They'd quarreled over mushrooms before, more than once. Now they knew better.

Every so often, Ealstan would see someone else digging in a field or at the base of a tree. He didn't offer to go and help any of these people. Some folks loved to chat and share. Rather more, though, were inclined to be surly, to say nothing of greedy. He learned that way himself. If a pretty girl came along and wanted to give him a hand, he might let her. He laughed at himself. He liked the idea, but knew better than to find it likely.

He worked his way north, getting his shoes soggy and his knees dirty. One of the reasons he enjoyed hunting mushrooms – aside from the pleasure of eating them later – was that he never knew ahead of time what he'd find. He tossed a few meadow mushrooms into his sack, just to make sure he didn't come home empty-handed. They were good enough, but no better than good enough.

Chanterelles were better than good enough. He picked some egg-yellow ones because of their fine flavor, and some vermilion ones because his father enjoyed them, even if he himself found them acrid. Then, in some open woods he found a clump of orange Kaunian Imperial mushrooms. He studied them with care before plucking them from the ground; they were related to death caps and destroyers, both deadly poisonous. Only after he made sure they were safe did they go into the sack. They would be delicious.

And he felt like cheering when he stumbled upon an indigo milky mushroom. It wasn't one of his favorites as far as flavor went, but his mother always clapped her hands when he came home with one because the exotic color made any dish in which she used it more interesting.

Then he came to a stand of trees with oyster mushrooms and ear mushrooms growing on their trunks, especially on the southern sides where sunlight did not reach them. The oyster mushrooms were particularly fine: fresh and grayish white, not old and tough and yellow. He went from tree to tree picking all he could; some grew higher than he could reach, even by jumping. He wondered what Sidroc would bring home – probably a mix altogether different from his.

He was so intent on harvesting those mushrooms, he didn't notice anyone else was picking from the same stand of trees till they came round from opposite sides of the same big oak and almost bumped into each other. Nearly dropping his sack of mushrooms, Ealstan jumped back in surprise.

So did the other gatherer, a Kaunian girl not far from his own age. They both laughed shakily. "You startled me," they both said at the same time, with identical pointing forefingers. That made them laugh again.

"There are plenty for both of us," Ealstan said, and the girl nodded. She might have been a year or so older than he was. Doing his best not to be too obvious about it, he eyed her figure, which her Kaunian-style tight tunic and trousers revealed in more detail than the long, loose tunics Forthwegian women wore. The knees of those trousers were dirty; she'd come out for the same reason he had, all right.

"Aye, there are." She nodded again. She was looking at his dirty knees, too. Then, suddenly, she pointed to the sack he carried. "What have you got in there? Maybe we can trade a little, so we each have more different kinds."

Kaunians in Forthweg were no less fond of mushrooms than any other Forthwegians. "All right," Ealstan said. He grinned at her and dug out some of the orange mushrooms he'd found. "What will you give me for those Kaunian Imperials here? They ought to suit you."

She studied him before answering, her blue eyes hooded. Kaunians, he knew, got touchy if you said what they thought was the wrong thing, or even the right thing in the wrong tone of voice. He must have passed the test, for she nodded and showed him some dull brown mushrooms from her sack. "I found these horns of plenty under dead leaves, if you'd like some of them."

"All right," he said again, and they made the trade. He went on, "You must have had sharp eyes to spot them. Sometimes you can walk through a big patch and never even know it, because they're the same color as the leaves."

"That's true. I've done it." The Kaunian amended her words with the precision of her people: "I've done it a couple of times and then seen them, I mean. Who knows how many times I've done it without even noticing?"

After that, they started talking about mushrooms and, almost coincidentally, about themselves. He found her name was Vanai, and that she lived in Oyngestun; she'd come east to hunt mushrooms, while he'd gone west from Gromheort. "How are things there?" he asked. "Are the redheads any better than they are in the city?"

"I doubt it," Vanai answered bleakly. She added a word in Kaunian, a word Ealstan knew: "Barbarians." Kaunians sometimes applied that word to Forthwegians. Hearing it slapped on the Algarvians made Ealstan chuckle and clap his hands together. Vanai looked sharply at him. "How much Kaunian do you speak?" she asked in that language.

"What I have learned in school," he said, also in Kaunian. It was the first time he'd ever been glad he'd paid attention to his lessons. Only a couple of hours before, he'd laughed at himself for imagining he might meet a pretty girl while out picking mushrooms. Now he'd gone and done it, even if she was a Kaunian.

"You speak well," she said, falling back into Forthwegian. "Not quickly, as you would your birthspeech, but well."

Ealstan appreciated the praise all the more because she measured it so carefully. "Thank you," he said. Then he remembered the Algarvian soldier taking obscene liberties with the Kaunian woman in the rubble-clearing gang back in Gromheort. It suddenly occurred to him, almost with the force of getting spellstruck, that being a pretty girl could carry disadvantages. He picked his words with care, too: "I hope they haven't . . . insulted you."

Vanai needed only a moment to understand what he meant. "Nothing too bad," she said. "Shouts, jeers, leers – nothing I haven't known from Forthwegians." She turned red; with her fair skin, the blush was easy to see. "I don't mean you. You've been perfectly polite."

"Kaunians are people, too," Ealstan said, repeating a phrase his father was fond of using. Ealstan sometimes wondered if that was why his father used it. Kaunians had dwelt in Forthweg since the days of their ancient Empire, even if Forthwegians greatly outnumbered them these days. His own distant ancestors had known nothing of stone keeps and theaters and aqueducts when they entered this country. He wondered if one of the reasons they despised Kaunians was that, somewhere down deep, Kaunians made them wonder if they were people themselves.

"Well, of course," Vanai said. But it wasn't *of course*, and they both knew it. A lot of Forthwegians didn't think of Kaunians as people, and a lot of Kaunians returned the favor. Vanai changed the subject: "Your brother, you said, is a captive? That must be hard for your family. Is he well?"

"He says he is well," Ealstan replied. "The Algarvians only let their captives write once a month, so we've not heard much. But he is alive, powers above be praised." He didn't know what he would have done had he learned Leofsig was dead.

He was about to add something more when, from not far away, a man called out in Kaunian: "Where are you, Vanai? Look! I've found a—" Whatever he'd found, it wasn't a word Ealstan knew. Ealstan wondered if he'd found trouble himself. Was that Vanai's father? Her brother? Maybe even her husband? He didn't think she was old enough to wed, but he might have been wrong, disastrously wrong.

Then Vanai answered, "Here I am, my grandfather," and Ealstan's worry eased: a grandfather seemed unlikely to be dangerous. Nor did the man who came up a minute later look dangerous. He carried a fat puffball in his left hand; *puffball*, no doubt, was the Kaunian word Ealstan hadn't understood. In Kaunian, Vanai said, "My grandfather, this is Ealstan of Jekabpils" – the classical name for Gromheort. "We have traded mushrooms." She shifted to Forthwegian: "Ealstan, here is my grandfather, Brivibas."

Brivibas looked at Ealstan as if he were a stinkhorn or a poisonous leopard mushroom. "I hope he has not troubled you," he said to Vanai in Kaunian. He was, Ealstan saw at a glance, one of those Kaunians who automatically thought the worst of Forthwegians.

"I have not troubled her," Ealstan said in the best Kaunian he had. It was not good enough; Brivibas corrected his pronunciation. Vanai looked mortified. Making a point of speaking Forthwegian, she said, "He has not troubled me at all. He speaks well of our people."

Her grandfather looked Ealstan up and down, then looked her up and down, too. "He has his reasons," Brivibas said. "Come along with me. We must wend homeward."

"I will come," Vanai said obediently. But then she turned back. "Goodbye, Ealstan. The talk was pleasant, and the trade was good."

"I also thought so," Ealstan said in Kaunian. "I am glad I met you – and you, sir," he added for Brivibas's benefit. That last was a lie, but one of the sort his father called a useful lie: it would show up the older Kaunian's rudeness. Vanai would see it. Even Brivibas might.

He didn't. He stomped off toward the west, toward Oyngestun. Vanai followed. Ealstan watched till trees hid her from sight. Then he started back in the direction of Gromheort. He laughed to himself. The day had ended up a lot more interesting than it would have been had he spent it hunting mushrooms with Sidroc.

"Well, this is more like it," Talsu said to whomever would listen as the Jelgavan forces pushed through the eastern foothills of the Bratanu mountains. Before long, he thought, he and his comrades really would get past the foothills and down into the plains of southern Algarve. If things kept going well, they'd be able to start tossing eggs into Tricarico.

He wished the Forthwegians had put up a better fight against the redheads. Then their army would have joined the one of which he was a tiny part and cut Algarve in half. That had been the plan – well, the hope – when Jelgava went to war. Now King Donalitu and his allies would have to settle for less.

Smilsu banged Talsu in the ribs with his elbow. "Which do you mean is more like it? Having a colonel who knows what he's doing or moving forward instead of standing around all the time?"

"You don't think there's a connection?" Talsu returned.

"I'm not the one to ask," his friend said. "Why don't you find out what Vartu over there thinks about it?"

"I'm still here," Vartu said, grinning a leathery grin. After Colonel Dzirnavu's untimely and embarrassing demise, his servant might have gone back to the family estate to tend to the needs of Dzirnavu's heir. He'd chosen to stay on as a common soldier instead. What that said about the character of Dzirnavu's son was a point on which Talsu preferred not to dwell: how unfortunate that the new count should take after the old. Vartu went on, "There's one of the reasons I'm still here, too." He pointed to one side with his chin.

"Come on, men, keep moving," Colonel Adomu called cheerily. He was a marquis himself, but wore the title more lightly than most Jelgavan nobles. He was just in his early forties, and not only kept up with the soldiers in his regiment but urged them to a better clip. "Keep moving – and spread out. We don't want the cursed redheads to hit us when we're all bunched together."

Even marching in loose order, Talsu was nervous. The Algarvians had harvested these fields before their soldiers retreated through them, and the low stubble left behind offered little concealment for a prone man, let alone one up and walking. Algarvian civilians had fled along with the soldiers, and taken their livestock with them. But for the sound of boots crunching through dry grass and stubble and the occasional rustle of leaves in the breeze, the day was eerily quiet.

Colonel Adomu pointed to a pear orchard half a mile away. "That's where they'll be waiting for us, the sons of a thousand fathers. We'll have to see if we can find a way to flank them out – going straight at them will be too expensive."

Talsu dug a finger in his ear to make sure he'd heard right. Dzirnavu would have sent his men lumbering straight at the redheads. They'd have paid for it, too, but that wouldn't have bothered Dzirnavu. Well, now he'd paid for it himself.

Adomu sent the company to which Talsu belonged off to the right, to find a way around the pear orchard. "Come on, step it up," Talsu called to Smilsu as they trotted along. "The faster we move, the harder we are to hit."

"We're hard to hit anyway, at this range," Smilsu answered. "You have to be lucky to blaze a man with a footsoldier's stick out past a couple-three furlongs. You have to be even luckier to hurt him very bad if you do hit him."

As if to make him out a liar, one of his comrades fell, clutching at his leg and cursing. But most of the Algarvians' beams went wide or had dispersed too widely to be damaging. A couple of them started fires in the grass. That made Talsu want to cheer: Smoke weakened beams, too.

But then, with a roar and a blast of fire, an egg buried in the ground burst under a Jelgavan soldier. He had time for only the beginning of a shriek before the energies consumed him. The rest of the Jelgavans skidded to a halt. Talsu dug in his heels and stood panting where he was. "They don't hide those things by ones and twos," he said. "They put 'em down by the score, by the hundred." All the ground on which he was not standing at the moment suddenly seemed dangerous. Had he just trotted past an egg? If he took one step back or to either side, would he suddenly go up in a sheet of fire?

He didn't want to find out. He didn't want to stay where he was, either. If he kept standing here, the redheads in the pear orchard would blaze him sooner or later. He threw himself down on the ground, and didn't touch off an egg doing it. Slowly and carefully, he crawled forward, examining every stretch of ground before he trusted his weight to it. If it looked disturbed in any way, he crawled around it.

Colonel Adomu didn't take long to notice his flanking maneuver had slowed. Colonel Dzirnavu, had he bothered making a flanking maneuver — in itself unlikely — wouldn't have kept such close ley of it once it got going. But the energetic Adomu not only saw the slowing but realized what had caused it. He sent an egg-dowser forward to find a clear way through the stretch of ground filled with hidden peril.

Talsu watched the dowser — a tall, skinny man who managed to look disheveled despite uniform tunic and trousers — with the fascination any man gives to someone who can do something he cannot. The fellow held his forked rod out before him as if it were a pike. Dowsing was an ever more specialized business these days. Talsu's ancestors had found water with it in the days of the Kaunian Empire. Now people all over Derlavai dowsed for water with it in the days of the Kaunian Empire. Now people all over Derlavai dowsed for water, for metals, for coal, for rock oil (not that the latter had much use), for things missing, and everywhere and always for things desired.

And soldiers dowsed for dragons in the air and for eggs hidden under the ground. "How did you learn to find buried eggs?" Talsu called to the dowser.

"Carefully." The fellow's lips skinned back from his teeth in a humorless grin. "Now don't jog my elbow any more, or I'm liable not to be careful enough. I wouldn't like that: in my line of work, your first mistake is usually your last one." His rod dipped sharply downward. With a grunt of satisfaction, he took from his belt a sharp stake with a bright streamer of cloth at the unpointed end. He plunged it into the ground to show where the egg lay. The soldiers in the company followed him in as near single file as made no difference as he marked out a path of safety.

Smilsu said, "I wonder what happens when the Algarvians come up with a new kind of egg, or with a new way to mask the eggs they have already." He kept his voice down so the dowser wouldn't hear him.

Also quietly, Talsu answered, "That's when they start teaching a new dowser how to do the job." His friend nodded.

Had the Algarvians been present in large numbers, sergeants would have needed to start teaching a lot of new Jelgavan soldiers how to do the job. But the redheads could not take advantage of the way they had stalled their opponents. Before long, the dowser stopped finding eggs to mark. The company started moving faster again. The dowser went along in case the men ran into – literally and metaphorically – another troublesome belt of land.

But they didn't, and soon began blazing into the pear orchard from the side. The Algarvians had been protecting themselves behind trees against an attack from the front. And, as soon as Colonel Adomu realized his flanking force finally was doing what he'd intended it to do, in went that attack from the front.

That made the Algarvians stop paying so much attention to Talsu and his friends. Vartu let out a whoop, then howled, "Now we've got 'em!"

Talsu hoped Colonel Dzirnavu's former servant was right. If he was wrong, a lot of Jelgavans would end up dead, Talsu all too probably among them. He howled, too, as much to hold fear at bay as for any other reason.

Then he and the rest of the Jelgavans got in among the pear trees themselves, flushing out the Algarvians like so many partridges. Some of the redheads, their positions overrun, threw down their sticks and threw up their hands in token of surrender. They were no more anxious to die than their Jelgavan counterparts.

Smilsu cursed. "My beam's run dry!" he shouted angrily. A moment later, nothing happened when Talsu thrust his finger into the touch-hole of his own stick. Like Smilsu, he'd used up all the power in it while reaching the pear orchard. Now, when he needed it most, he did not have it.

"Where's that cursed dowser?" he called. "He can give us a hand. We haven't sent all the captives to the rear yet, have we?"

"No," Vartu said from behind him. "We've still got a few of them left with us." He raised his voice to a furious bellow, a good imitation of that of the late, unlamented (at least by Talsu) Colonel Dzirnavu: "Stake 'em out! Tie 'em down! Let's get *some* good out of 'em, anyway, the filthy redheads."

Some of the Algarvian captives understood Jelgavan, either because they came from near the border or because they'd studied classical Kaunian in school and could get the drift of the daughter language. They howled fearful protests. The Jelgavans ignored those, flinging a couple of redheaded soldiers down on to their backs and tying their arms and legs to stakes and tree trunks.

"You'd do the same to us if your sticks were running low," a Jelgavan soldier said, not without some sympathy. "You know it cursed well, too."

"Where's that dowser?" Talsu called again. The fellow shambled up just then, still looking very much like an unmade bed. Seeing the spreadeagled Algarvians, he nodded. He was no first-rank mage, but he didn't need to be, not for the sorcery the Jelgavan soldiers had in mind.

"Set your dead sticks on them," he said, and Talsu and the others who could not blaze obeyed. The dowser drew a knife from his belt and stooped beside the nearer Algarvian captive. He yanked up the Algarvian's chin by the coppery whiskers that grew there, then cut his throat as if butchering a hog. Blood fountained forth. The dowser chanted in classical Kaunian. When he was through – and when the Algarvian soldier he'd sacrificed had quit writhing – some of the Jelgavans snatched up their sticks from the dead man's chest.

Talsu's stick lay on the second Algarvian. The dowser sacrificed him, too. Such rough magic in the field wasted a good deal of the captives' life energy. Talsu cared not at all. What mattered to him was that enough of the energy had flowed into his stick to recharge it fully. As soon as the dowser nodded, he grabbed the stick and hurried forward to do more fighting. It blazed just as it should have.

Before long, the two-pronged Jelgavan attack drove the Algarvians from the pear orchard. But, just as victory became assured, a cry rose from the men who'd made the assault on the front of the orchard: "The colonel's down! The stinking redheads blazed Colonel Adomu!"

"Powers above!" Talsu groaned. "What sort of overbred fool will they foist on us now?" He didn't know. He couldn't know, not yet. He was afraid of finding out.

Brivibas gave Vanai a severe look, as he'd been doing for the past couple of weeks. "My granddaughter, I must tell you yet again that you were too forward, much too forward, with that barbarian boy you met in the woods."

Vanai rolled her eyes. Brivibas had trained her to dutiful obedience, but his carping was wearing thin. No: by now, his carping had worn thin. "All we did was swap a few mushrooms, my grandfather. We were polite while we did it, aye. You have taught me to be polite to everyone, have you not?"

"And would he have stayed polite to you, had I not happened to come up when I did?" Brivibas demanded.

"I think so," Vanai answered with a toss of her head. "He seemed perfectly well behaved – better than some of the Kaunian boys here on Oyngestun."

That distracted her grandfather, as she'd hoped it would. "What?" he said, his eyes going wide. "What have they done to you? What have they tried to do to you?" He looked furious. Was he, could he possibly have been, remembering some of the things he'd tried to do to girls before he met Vanai's grandmother? That was hard to imagine. Even harder was imagining him doing things like that *with* her grandmother.

"They've tried more than that Ealstan ever did," she said. "They couldn't have tried less, because he didn't try anything at all. He spent a lot of time talking about his brother, who's an Algarvian captive."

"I do pity even a Forthwegian in Algarvian hands," Brivibas said. By his tone, he pitied Kaunians in Algarvian hands far more. But, again, he found himself distracted, this time by a historical parallel: "The Algarvians have always been harsh on their captives. Recall how, under their chieftain Ziliante, they so cruelly sacked and ravaged the city of Adutiskis." He spoke as if the sack had happened the week before rather than in the waning days of the Kaunian Empire.

"Well, then!" Vanai tossed her head again. "You see, you don't need to worry about Ealstan after all."

She'd made a mistake. She knew it as soon as the words were out of her mouth. And, sure enough, Brivibas pounced on it: "I would worry far less had you forgotten the young barbarian's name."

Had he stopped nagging her about Ealstan, she probably would have forgotten the Forthwegian's name in short order. As things were, he looked more attractive every time her grandfather made a rude comment about him. If such a thing had happened to Brivibas during his long-ago youth, it had fallen from his memory in the years since.

"He was very nice," Vanai said. *Even handsome, in the dark, blocky Forthwegian way,* she thought. Having made one mistake, she did not compound it by letting her grandfather learn of that thought.

He did not need to learn of it to keep on carping. After a while, Vanai got tired of listening to him and went out to the courtyard around which the house was built. She didn't stay as long as she'd thought she would. For one thing, a raw breeze made her shiver. The sun ducked in and out from behind gray, nasty-looking clouds. And the courtyard, no longer bright with flowers as it had been through spring and summer, seemed a far less pleasant refuge than it would have been then. The alabaster bowl into which the fountain splashed was a genuine Kaunian antiquity, but it too failed to delight her. Her lip curled. Living with her grandfather was living with an antiquity. She needed no more examples.

She wished she could have gone out on to the streets of Oyngestun. These days, though, with Algarvian soldiers patrolling the village, she went out as seldom as she could. The Algarvians had committed relatively few outrages: fewer, certainly, than she'd expected when they occupied the place. But she knew they could. She might speak well of a Forthwegian, but of a redhead? About Algarvians, she completely agreed with Brivibas.

Why not? Indeed, how could she have done otherwise? He'd taught her. But that thought never crossed her mind, no more than the thought of water disturbed a swimming fish.

"My granddaughter?" Brivibas called from his study, where they'd been quarreling. Far more slowly than he should have, he realized he'd really irked her. *If only some ancient Kaunian had written a treatise on how to bring up a granddaughter!* Vanai thought. *He'd do a better job.*

She didn't want to answer him. She didn't want to have anything to do with him, not just then. Instead of returning to the study, she went into the parlor through a different door. Brivibas had set his mark there, too, as he had through the whole of the house. Bookshelves almost overwhelmed the spare, classical – and none too comfortable – furniture. All the ornaments were Kaunian antiquities or copies of Kaunian antiquities: statuettes, painted pottery, a little glass vial gone milky from lying underground for upwards of a thousand years. She'd known them her whole life; they were as familiar to her as the shapes of her own fingernails. Now, suddenly, she felt like smashing them.

On the wall hung a print of an old painting of the Kaunian Column of Victory in faraway Priekule. Vanai sighed. Thinking of Kaunians victorious didn't come easy now. Neither did thinking of a kingdom nearly all Kaunian, as Valmiera was. What would living in a land where everyone looked more or less the way she did be like? *Luxurious* was the word that sprang to mind. The Kaunians of Forthweg, remnants left behind when the tide of ancient empire receded, enjoyed no such luxury.

She went into the kitchen. A terra-cotta low relief of a fat little demon with a big mouth and a bigger belly hung on the wall there. Her imperial ancestors had fancied the demon of appetite looked like that. Sorcerous investigation had long since proved there was no such thing as the demon of appetite. Vanai didn't care what sorcerous investigation had proved. She liked the relief. Had there been a demon of appetite, he would have looked like that.

Had there been a demon of appetite, he would have turned up his nose at what he saw in that kitchen. Cheese, a little bread, mushrooms, strings of garlic and onions and leeks, an ever-shrinking length of sausage . . . not much to keep a spirit dwelling in a body.

Brivibas hardly cared what he ate, or sometimes even if he ate. His mind ruled; his body did strictly as it was told. Vanai sometimes wished she were the same way. Her grandfather assumed she was, though he would have been angry at others who judged people using themselves as a touchstone. But Vanai enjoyed good food. That was why, as soon as she grew big enough, she'd taken over the kitchen. Till the war came, she'd done as well as she could without much money.

Now . . . Now there wasn't much food of any sort to be had. Ley-line caravans carried what the Algarvians told them to carry, not what the towns and villages of Forthweg needed. The redheads plundered what they would. Fighting had wrecked many farms and left many farmers dead or captive.

Vanai wondered where it would end. Forthweg hadn't known famine during her lifetime, but she'd read of it. If this went on . . .

The wood bin and the coal scuttle weren't so full as they should have been, either. Coal, especially, was hard to come by. She might reach the point where she had food but no fuel with which to cook it.

With such gloomy reflections filling her, she didn't hear Brivibas come into the kitchen. "Ah, here you are, my granddaughter," he said.

"Here I am," Vanai agreed resignedly.

"I try my best to do what is right for you," her grandfather said. "I may not always be correct, but I do have your interest at heart." With no small surprise, she realized he was, in his fusty way, trying to apologize.

"Very well, my grandfather," Vanai said; arguing with Brivibas was more trouble than it was worth. In any case, she would see Ealstan again only by accident. Sooner or later, Brivibas would realize that for himself, and then, with luck, he would stop bothering her. Hoping to get his mind off the subject of the Forthwegian, she asked, "Can I cut you some bread and cheese?"

"No, never mind. I have no great appetite," Brivibas said. Vanai nodded; that was true most of the time. Then, to her surprise, her grandfather brightened. "Did I tell you the news I had yesterday?"

"No, my grandfather," Vanai answered. "What news is this? So little gets into Oyngestun these days, I'd be glad to hear any."

"Well, I had a note from the *Journal of Kaunian Studies* in Jekabpils," her grandfather said, using the classical Kaunian name for Gromheort. "They tell me the Algarvian occupying authorities will allow them to resume publication before long, which means I shall have an outlet for my scholarship."

"That *is* good news," Vanai said. If he could not publish his articles, Brivibas would grow even more peevish than usual. He would also have more leisure in which to try to oversee every facet of her life, which was nothing she wanted.

"On the whole, it is good news," he said, donning an indignant expression. "The drawback is, all submissions must henceforth appear in either Forthwegian or Algarvian. Those offered in classical Kaunian, *the* language of learning, must be rejected unread, by order of the occupiers."

Vanai shivered, though the kitchen was warm enough. "What right have the redheads to say our language is not to be used?" she asked.

"The conqueror's right: the right they understand best," Brivibas answered bleakly. He sighed. "I have not attempted serious composition in Forthwegian for many years. Who would, with Kaunian to use instead? I suppose I must make the effort, though, if I am to continue setting my researches before any part of the scholarly community." Not setting his researches before the scholarly community plainly never occurred to him.

Before Vanai could reply, shouts and the sound of running feet came from outside. She peered through the kitchen window, a narrow slit intended to give a little fresh air, not any great view: for views, all folk of Forthweg, regardless of their blood, far preferred their courtyards to the streets. She got a glimpse of a yellow-haired man running as if his life depended on his feet. And so it might have, for a couple of Algarvian soldiers pounded after him, sticks in hand.

They shouted again, first in their langauge, then in Forthwegian: "Halt!" One of them dropped to a knee to take dead aim at the fleeing Kaunian. The fellow must have ducked around a corner before he could blaze, though, for he sprang to his feet once more with what sounded like a curse. "Halt!" his comrade yelled again. They both pounded after the fugitive.

"I wonder what he did," Vanai said. "I wonder if he did anything."

"Probably not." Her grandfather's voice was weary and bitter. "Having done something is by no means a requirement for punishment, not where the Algarvians are concerned." Vanai nodded. She'd already seen as much for herself.

★

Bembo tramped up and down the meadow outside Tricarico's municipal stadium. Though the day was on the chilly side, sweat ran down his face and threatened to leave his mustache as limp as if he'd forgotten to wax it. The constable, a pudgy man, hadn't done much in the way of marching for a good many years.

Not that the drill sergeant cared. "Powers below eat all of you!" he screamed, in a temper extravagant even by Algarvian standards. "I bite my thumb at you! I bite my thumb at your fathers, if you know who they are!" From a civilian, that would have provoked a flock of challenges. But a soldier in the service of King Mezentio enjoyed even broader immunity from having to defend his honor than did a constable.

The sergeant waved the shambling column to a halt. Bembo had all he could do not to collapse on the grass. His legs felt like overcooked noodles. He could smell himself. Beneath their perfumes, he could smell the men around him.

"We'll try it again," the drill sergeant grunted. "I know you're stupid, but try and work at remembering which is your left foot and which is your right. If those stinking towheads from Jelgava break out of the mountains, *you* get to go into line to throw 'em back. Maybe you'll be able to fool them into thinking you're soldiers, at least for a little while. I doubt it, but maybe. Now . . . forward, *march!*"

Along with the rest of the men of Tricarico dragooned into this makeshift militia, Bembo started marching. The Jelgavans hadn't broken out of the Bradano Mountains yet, though they'd come close a couple of times. Bembo hoped the regulars could hold them. If they couldn't, if Algarve had to rely on the likes of him to fight, the kingdom was in a lot of trouble.

"Left!" the drill sergeant roared. "Left! . . . Left-right-left! Sound off!"

"One! Two!" Bembo called, as he'd learned to do.

"Sound off!"

"Three! Four!"

"Left-right-left!" The sergeant gathered himself for the next order: "To the rear, *march!*" Raggedly, the militiamen obeyed. The drill sergeant clapped a hand to his forehead. "You don't execute commands better than that, you'll all get fornicating executed if you have to go up to the line. Aye, the Jelgavans are a pack of trouser-wearing scum, but they know what they're doing, and you, you milk-fed virgins, you haven't got a clue. To the left flank, *march!*"

The fellow puffing along beside Bembo wheezed, "I'd like to see that loudmouthed oaf try to make pastries with no training, that's all I have to say."

"That's your line of work?" Bembo asked, and the pastry chef nodded. With a calculating smile, the constable found another question: "Whereabouts in the city is your shop at?"

Before his comrade could answer, the drill sergeant screamed, "Silence in the ranks! Next man who squeaks out of turn will squeak soprano for the rest of his days, do you hear me?" Bembo was convinced the whole town of Tricarico heard him. The Jelgavans in the western foothills of the Bradano Mountains probably heard him, too. And the pastry chef certainly heard him, for he shut up with a snap.

Bembo sighed. A constable who strolled into a pastry shop would surely come away with dainties full of almond paste and sweet cream and raisins and cherries, and he wouldn't have to set a copper on the counter to get them, either. And now he wouldn't be able to find out into which shop he should stroll. Life was full of small tragedies.

At last, after what seemed like forever but couldn't have been longer than half that, the drill sergeant released his captives. "I'll see you again day after tomorrow, though," he threatened, "or maybe sooner, if the enemy does break through. You'd better hope he doesn't, on account of they haven't dug enough burial plots to hold all of you lugs yet."

"Cheerful bugger, isn't he?" Bembo said, but the pastry chef had already turned away. Bembo sighed again. He'd have to stay ignorant of where the fellow labored, at least till two days hence. With another sigh, he started back toward the constabulary station. He didn't get time off for the militia drill; it was piled on to everything else he had to do. That struck him as monstrously unfair, but no one had asked his view of the matter. He'd received orders to report to that bellowing fiend in human shape, and he'd had to obey.

A street vendor waved a news sheet. "Black men throw Unkerlanters back again!" he shouted. "Read all about it!"

"Has King Swemmel started killing some of his generals yet, to persuade the rest to fight harder?" Bembo asked. He approved of killing Unkerlanter generals – *on general principles*, he thought with a grin at his own cleverness. For that matter, he approved of executions on general principles. He had trouble imagining a constable who didn't.

"Buy my sheet here, and see for yourself," the vendor answered. Bembo didn't feel like buying a news sheet. He felt like having the fellow tell him what he wanted to know. He and the vendor traded insults, more good-natured than otherwise, till he rounded a corner.

A couple of men on the next street corner, one of them fair enough to have a good share of Kaunian blood, saw him coming and made themselves scarce. He wasn't wearing his uniform tunic and kilt. Maybe one of them recognized his face. Maybe, too, both of them smelled him out as a constable even without seeing his uniform, even without recognizing his face. It wasn't quite sorcery on the part of the bad eggs, but it wasn't far removed, either.

When he walked up the stairs and into the station, Sergeant Pesaro greeted him with, "Ah, here is another one of our heroes!" No one had thrown Pesaro into the militia. He might have been able to march. On the other hand, he might as readily have fallen over dead from an apoplexy.

"A worn-out hero," Bembo said mournfully. "If I have to do too much more of this, I'll be a shadow of my former self." He looked down at his belly. It wasn't the size of Pesaro's, but he still made a pretty substantial shadow.

"You complain so much, you might as well already be in the army, not the constabulary," Pesaro said.

"Oh, and you've never grumbled in all your born days," Bembo retorted, wagging a forefinger at the fat man behind the desk. Pesaro coughed a couple of times and turned red, perhaps from embarrassment, perhaps just because he was a fat man who sat behind a desk all day: even coughing was an exertion for him. Bembo went on, "I see in the news sheet that Zuwayza's giving Unkerlant another clout in the head."

"Efficiency," Pesaro said with a laugh. "Don't know how long those naked burnt-skins can keep doing what they're doing, but it's pretty funny while it's going on."

"So it is." Bembo hid his disappointment. He'd hoped Pesaro would tell him more than he'd heard from the news-sheet vendor.

Maybe the sergeant hadn't felt like springing for a sheet today, either.

Then Pesaro said, "Only trouble is, I heard on the crystal this morning that we're not the only ones who think so. Jelgava and Valmiera have sent messages to the Zuwayzi king, whatever his cursed name is, congratulating him on giving King Swemmel a hard time."

"Can't say I'm surprised," Bembo answered. "When Swemmel jumped on Forthweg's back, that meant we wouldn't have to worry about our western front any more – or not about the Forthwegians there, anyway."

"Oh, aye," Pesaro said. "Not that Unkerlant's any great neighbor to have. We've fought more wars with those bastards than anybody likes to remember, and it wouldn't surprise me one bit if they were thinking about another one."

"That wouldn't surprise me, either," Bembo said. "Everybody's always plotting against Algarve. It's been like that since the days of the Kaunian Empire."

"A lot you know about the Kaunian Empire," Pesaro said. Before Bembo could make an irate reply to that, the sergeant went on, "Talk about inefficiency – we might as well be Unkerlanters ourselves, the way we're using constables for militiamen."

"Make up your mind," Bembo said. "You just called me a hero not five minutes ago."

"I remembered something else I heard on the crystal," Pesaro answered placidly. "A dozen captives broke out of a camp in Forthweg, and they're on the loose in the countryside. What do soldiers know about keeping captives? About as much as constables know about fighting campaigns, that's what. If they're going to use constables to help the war along, they ought to use us to take captives and guard them, not to blaze away on the front line. That'd be proper efficiency."

"Not a bad idea at all," Bembo said. Pesaro preened as if he were a writer of romances suddenly receiving critical acclaim. With a sly chuckle, Bembo added, "I never would have expected it from you."

"Funny," Pesaro said. "Funny like a man walking with two canes, that's what it is." He could take ribbing, could Pesaro, but only so much. Bembo, evidently, had gone over the line. "Here's another idea that isn't bad at all," Pesaro growled: "you getting into your uniform and doing some real work instead of hanging around and banging your gums with me."

"All right, Sergeant. All right." Bembo raised a placating hand. "I'm going, I'm going." As he went, he muttered under his breath: "Fat old fraud wouldn't know anything about real work if it paraded past him naked."

After donning the regulation tunic and kilt, he paused in the recording section, where Saffa was sketching a portrait of a haggard-looking miscreant. Bembo thought of the little artist parading past him naked, definitely a more attractive prospect than real work. What he was thinking must have shown, too, for Saffa snapped, "Drag your mind out of the latrine, if you please."

Bembo's ears heated. He glared over toward the wretch whose image Saffa had been committing to paper. Had the fellow said a word – had he even smiled – Bembo would have taken out his rage on him. But the captive, wiser than Martusino, kept his mouth shut and his expression blank. Doubly baulked, Bembo walked fuming to his desk.

Plenty of forms and reports awaited him there, as was true for most constables most of the time. Bembo ignored them. He worked diligently enough when he felt like it, but not when work was forced upon him. As most Algarvians would have done, he avenged himself by disobeying. He pulled a historical romance out of his desk and started reading. "I'll show you what I know about the Kaunian Empire," he mumbled in Pesaro's direction, though not loud enough for the desk sergeant – or anyone else – to hear.

Mercenaries' Revolt, the cover screamed in lurid red letters, with a smaller subhead reading, *Mighty Ziliante sets an empire afire!* The book showed a stalwart Algarvian, his coppery hair washed with lime to give him a leonine mane, brandishing a sword. Clinging to him was a Kaunian doxy wearing no more clothes than she'd been born with. Her hand was poised, as if about to reach under his kilt and caress what she found there. The text lived up to, or down to, the cover. Bembo couldn't remember a romance he'd enjoyed more.

The Kaunian Emperor had just ordered Ziliante made into a eunuch. Bembo was sure that wouldn't happen; the virile hero had already got too many blond noblewomen's drawers down. Which of them would rescue him, and how? Bembo read on to find out.

8.

Krasta sipped cherry brandy laced with wormwood. A band thumped away in the background: tuba and accordion, bagpipes and thudding kettledrum. On the dance floor, Valmieran nobles swayed and spun to the loud, insistent beat.

"This is the place to be," Valnu said, leering across the table at her. "Even if the Algarvians drop eggs on Priekule, they can't knock the Cellar down. We're already underground." He giggled as if he'd said something very funny.

"This is the place to be because it's the place to be," Krasta replied with a shrug. Had the Cellar been built atop the Kaunian Column of Victory, she still would have frequented the nightspot. Anyone who was, or who had pretensions of being, someone came here. People who weren't someone looked on from a distance and envied. That was the way the world worked.

Valnu lifted his mug of porter. "So good to find you thinking as clearly as ever." Malice flavored the affection in his voice as the wormwood embittered Krasta's sweet brandy. "I hope your brother is still safe, there in the west."

"He was well, last letter I had from him." Krasta tossed her head, sending pale gold curls flying: old imperial styles had suddenly become the rage. "But this is too much talk about the war. I don't want to think about the war." The truth of the matter was, she didn't want to think at all.

"Very well." Valnu's smile turned him into the most charming skull Krasta had ever known. "Let's dance, then." He got to his feet.

"All right, why not?" Krasta said carelessly. The room spun a little as she rose: that spiked brandy was potent stuff. She laughed as Valnu slid an arm around her waist and guided her out on to the floor.

Valnu was a thoroughgoing predator. His principal virtue was that he never pretended to be anything else. As he and Krasta danced, his hand slid from the small of her back to close on the smooth curve of her left buttock. He pressed her tight against him, so tight that she could not possibly doubt he had more than dancing on his mind.

She might have loosened some of his white, pointed teeth for him because of the liberties he took with her noble person. She contemplated it, in fact, as well as she could contemplate anything in her rather fuddled state. But his mocking smile said he was waiting for her to do just that. Except when making sure commoners stayed in their place, she hated doing anything someone else expected of her. And, she realized, she was feeling randy herself. She'd decide later how far she intended to let him go. For the moment, she simply enjoyed herself.

And it wasn't as if she were the only woman in the Cellar whose companion was feeling her up on the dance floor. It was not a place to which women who minded being rumpled in public commonly came. *I can always blame it on the brandy*, she thought. But she didn't really need to blame it on anything. She did as she pleased. No one could make her do anything else.

The music stopped. Krasta set her hand on the back of Valnu's head and pulled his face down to hers. She kissed him, open-mouthed. He tasted of porter: bitter, but not so bitter as the wormwood in her brandy. Halfway through the kiss, she opened her eyes. Valnu was staring at her. He was so close, his features blurred, but she thought he looked astonished. She laughed, down deep in her throat.

He broke the kiss and twisted away. Now she had no trouble reading his expression. He was angry. Krasta laughed again. He must have realized he'd gone from predator to prey, realized it and not cared for it at all. "You're a fire-breather, aren't you?" he said, his voice rougher than usual.

"What if I am?" Krasta tossed her head again, as she had back at the table. She pointed toward the musicians. "They're going to start again in a minute. Do you want to dance some more, or have we already done everything we can do standing up?"

Valnu did his best to rally. "Not quite everything," he answered, more self-collected now. Bold as brass, he reached out and cupped her breast through the fabric of her tunic. His thumb and forefinger unerringly found her nipple. He teased it for a few seconds, then let her go.

Maybe he hadn't understood how hot and reckless Krasta was feeling. Maybe she hadn't realized it herself, not till those knowing fingers further inflamed her. She reached out, too, at a lower level.

Had he pulled off his trousers and lain down on the floor, she might have mounted him then and there. Such things were said to happen at the Cellar now and again, though Krasta had never seen them there. But Valnu, after shaking himself like a wet hound, went back to the table in four or five long strides. Krasta followed him. Her cheeks burned. Her heart raced. She breathed quickly, as if she'd just run a long way.

Valnu gulped the porter left in his mug. He was looking at Krasta as if he'd never seen her before. "Brimstone and quicksilver," he muttered, more to himself than to her. "Dragon-bitch."

After what she'd drunk, she took it as a compliment: indeed, she never thought to wonder whether it might be anything else. Her own goblet, smaller than the earthenware mug from which he'd drunk, held brandy yet. She poured it down. An egg might have burst in her belly. But warmth flowed out of it: to her face, to her breasts, to her loins.

With a rumbling blast from the tuba player and a thunder of drumbeats, the band started up again. The rhythm seemed to be inside her, filling her to the brim; the laced brandy kicked like a wild ass. As if from very far away, Valnu asked, "Do you want to go out on the floor again?"

"No." Krasta shook her head. The room seemed to keep moving after she stopped. "Let's ride around the town in my carriage – or even out into the country."

"In your carriage?" Valnu frowned. "What will the coachman think?"

"Who cares?" Krasta said gaily. "Powers above! He's only a coachman."

Valnu silently clapped his hands. "Spoken like the true woman of nobility you are," he exclaimed, and got to his feet. So did Krasta, hoping the process looked smoother to him than it felt to her. They retrieved their cloaks from the little antechamber just outside the main room – the night had its full share of autumn chill – then went upstairs and out into the darkness.

That darkness was well-nigh absolute. Though no Algarvian war dragons had yet appeared over Priekule, the city encaped itself in black. A good many carriages waited outside the Cellar while their noble owners reveled the night away. Krasta had to call several times before she could sort out which one was hers.

"Where to, milady?" her driver asked when she and Valnu climbed up into the seat behind him. "Back to the mansion?"

"No, no," Krasta said. "Just drive about for a while. If you happen to come on a road that leads out of the city – well, so much the better."

The coachman stayed quiet longer than he should have. When at last he spoke, all he said was, "Aye, milady. It shall be as you command." He clucked to the horses and flicked the reins. The carriage began to move.

Krasta hardly noticed his words. Of course it would be as she commanded. How could it be otherwise, when she was dealing with her own servitors? She turned to Valnu, a vague shape in the darkness beside her. She reached out for him as he was reaching out for her. The coachman paid no attention. He knew better than to pay attention . . . or, at least, to be seen paying attention.

Under the cover of their cloaks, Valnu's hand found the bone toggles that held her tunic closed. He undid a couple of them and reached inside the tunic to fondle her bare breast. Careless of the coachman, Krasta moaned. When her mouth met Valnu's this time, the kiss was so fierce, she tasted blood: his or hers, she could not tell.

His hand slid out of her tunic. He rubbed at the crotch of her trousers. She thought *she* would burst like an egg then. Valnu chuckled. His hand dived under her waistband. His fingers, long and slim and clever, knew exactly where to go and exactly what to do when they got there. Krasta gasped and shuddered, for a moment blind with pleasure. Valnu chuckled again, as pleased with himself as he was with having pleased her. The horses plodded on, hooves clopping on cobbles. Stolid as the animals he drove, the coachman minded the reins.

Krasta thought of ordering Valnu out of the carriage now that he'd given her what she wanted. But, sated and tipsy, she felt more generous than usual. She rubbed him through the wool of his trousers. After an abrupt inhalation, he murmured, "I do hope you won't make me explain myself to my laundryman."

She laughed and rubbed harder. Nothing could have made her more inclined to do just that than his hoping she wouldn't. After a moment, though, still in that uncommonly kindly mood, she unbuttoned his fly and drew him forth. She stroked him some more.

"Ahhh," he said softly.

Had Krasta gone on for another minute or two, she would have made Valnu explain himself to his laundryman: of that she had no doubt. Instead, she lowered her head, saying, "Here. I will give you a treat you could have only from a noblewoman." She took him in her mouth. His flesh was hot and smooth.

His fingers tangled in her hair. Above her busy lips and tongue, he laughed. "You are quite a lot of woman, my sweet," he said, "but what you're doing there hasn't been a secret of the nobility for a long, long time, if it ever was. Why, only last week this pretty little shopgirl—"

In spite of his hands, she raised up so suddenly that the back of her head caught him in the chin. "What?" she hissed as he yelped in pain. Fury filled her as quickly and completely as lubriciousness had. Before he could even start to set himself to rights, she pushed him with all her strength. He had time for only a startled squawk before he tumbled out on to the cobbles.

"Milady, what on earth –?" he began.

"Shut up!" Krasta snarled. Careless of her left breast peeping out from the undone tunic, she leaned forward and tapped the driver on the shoulder. "Take me home this instant. Make your stupid beasts move or you'll be sorry for it, do you hear me?"

"Aye, milady," the coachman answered: not a word more, which was wise of him. He flicked the reins. After what sounded like surprised snorts, the horses moved up into a trot. Krasta looked back over her shoulder. Valnu took a couple of steps in pursuit of the carriage, then gave up. He vanished in the darkness behind her.

Absently, Krasta did up the toggles he had opened. She wiped her mouth on her sleeve, again and again. Disgust filled her, so much that she almost had to lean out of the carriage and vomit it forth into the roadway. It wasn't what she'd been doing; she'd done that before, and always been amused how such a small thing could make a man behave as if treacle filled his veins.

But that her mouth had gone where a commoner's – *a pretty little*

shopgirl's, Valnu had said – mouth went before . . . She could imagine
nothing more revolting. She felt ritually unclean, like a man of the
Ice People who had accidentally slain his fetish animal.

After she got back to the mansion, she routed Bauska out of bed
and had the servant fetch her a bottle of brandy. She rinsed her mouth
several times, then imperiously thrust the bottle back. Bauska took it
away without a word. Like the coachman, she'd learned better than
to ask questions of her mistress.

With his comrades, Tealdo tramped along the wooden quay in the
harbor of Imola toward the *Ambuscade*, from whose flagpole fluttered
the Algarvian banner. All the army that had spent so long training was
now filing aboard the ships that filled the harbor in the former Duchy
of Bari.

Tealdo marveled to see the men all together. He marveled even
more to see the ships all together. "We haven't put together a fleet
like this for a cursed long time," he said over his shoulder to Trasone,
who marched along behind him.

"Not for a thousand years, the officers say," his friend agreed.

"Silence in the ranks there!" Sergeant Panfilo bellowed. Someone
– fortunately, someone well away from Tealdo – made a noise that
probably came from his mouth but sounded as if it had a different
origin. Panfilo stormed off to see if he could catch and terrorize the
miscreant.

Up the gangplank Tealdo went. His feet thudded on the timbers
of the deck. The sailors scurrying around there and the men who
traveled the lines of the rigging like outsized spiders did not strike him
as an ordinary naval crew. That was only fair – they weren't an
ordinary naval crew, nor anything close to it. Every one of them was
a highly trained yachtsman, adept at the otherwise obsolete art of
sailing.

But that art was no longer obsolete, thanks to the ingenuity of
Algarve's generals and admirals. Tealdo wished he would be able to
watch the great sails fill with wind as the fleet weighed anchor.
Instead, he went down to a poorly lit compartment with whose
cramped dimensions he was all too familiar. There he and his
company would stay till their journey ended . . . or till something
went wrong.

Maybe Captain Larbino had something similar on his mind, for he said, "Men, what we do here tonight will go a long way toward winning the war for Algarve. The Sibians shouldn't realize we're coming till we shop up on their doorstep – we'll catch them with their kilts down. Nobody has gone to war with a fleet of sailing ships for hundreds of years. They'll never expect it, and their mages likely won't be able to give 'em much warning, either. If we sail over a ley line . . . so what? We don't draw any energy from it, so they won't notice us. We'll be as safe as we would on dry land till we get into Tirgoviste harbor. Make yourselves comfortable and enjoy the trip."

Tealdo made himself as comfortable as he could, which wasn't very. He listened to more soldiers tramping into their assigned compartments, and to sailors running around and shouting things the thick oak timbers that surrounding him kept him from understanding. But tone carried, even if words didn't. "They sound like they're having a mighty good time, don't they?" he said to Trasone.

"Why shouldn't they?" Trasone answered. "Once they get us to Sibiu, their job is done. They can sit back and drink wine. We're the ones who get to pay the bill after that."

He wasn't quite being fair. If the Sibs got the chance, they'd blaze at ships as well as soldiers. Before Tealdo could point that out, the motion of the *Ambuscade* changed. The pitching from bow to stern became more emphatic, and the ship began to roll from side to side as well. "We're off," Tealdo said.

His stomach took the ship's motion in stride. Before long, though, he discovered that, as painstaking as the company's combat rehearsals had been, they hadn't covered everything. Several soldiers started puking. The compartment did have buckets to cope with such emergencies, but the emergency often arrived before the bucket did. In spite of everyone's best efforts, the compartment became a very unpleasant place.

The amused contempt the yachtsmen showed as they carried buckets away did not endear them to their passengers. "If I could move, I'd kill those bastards," a sufferer groaned.

Nobody could move much. The compartment held too many men for that. Tealdo hoped no one would heave up dinner on to his shoes. Past that, he squatted and chatted with the men around him and took breaths as shallow as he could.

Time dragged on. He supposed it had grown dark outside. He couldn't have proved it, not down here. Every so often, someone fed the lantern oil. Those flickering flames were all the light he and his comrades had. For all he knew, they were below the waterline, which would have made portholes a bad idea.

He wished he were a horse or a unicorn, so he could sleep while he wasn't lying down. A couple of soldiers did start to snore. He envied them. Because he envied them, he laughed all the louder when a roll bigger than usual made them topple over.

After what seemed like forever, the *Ambuscade* heeled sharply. Sailors shouted in excitement. "Get ready, boys," Sergeant Panfilo said. "I think the shop is about to open for business."

While Captain Larbino was saying the same thing in more elegant words, the *Ambuscade* proved him right by thudding against a quay – Tealdo hoped that was what had happened, at any rate, and that the ship hadn't struck a rock instead. The door to the compartment flew open. "Out! Out! Out!" a yachtsman screamed.

Out the company went, and up the narrow stairway that led to the deck. "Nobody falls!" Panfilo bellowed. "Nobody falls, or he answers to me." And nobody did fall. The men had rehearsed going up stairs like these so many times, they might have been stairs to the houses in which they'd grown up.

Cold, fresh air smelling of sea salt and smoke slapped Tealdo in the face. Not far away, another Algarvian ship burned brightly, lighting up the darkened harbor of Tirgoviste. Tealdo hoped the soldiers had been able to get off the ship. Every man counted in this assault. If the Algarvians did not conquer Sibiu, they would not be going home again.

After that, he stopped worrying about anything except what he was supposed to do. He followed the man in front of him over the gangplank and on to the quay. That too went off as it should have done. No one fell into the water. Had anybody done so, the weight of his kit would quickly have dragged him under.

"Move!" Captain Larbino shouted. "We have to move fast! Don't stand there gaping. We've still got the headquarters building to take."

No one was standing around gaping, either. That would have been handing the Sibians an invitation to blaze the men. Nobody with sticks had set up at the landward end of the quay, and Tealdo and his comrades didn't propose to wait till someone did. "Easier than practice, so far," he said.

"So far, maybe," Trasone answered. "But nobody who got killed in practice stayed dead. Won't be like that here."

Sure enough, the Sibians began to wake up. They started blazing at the invaders from buildings by the port. But it was too late then, with Algarvians flooding into Tirgoviste from all their ships. Tealdo wondered how things were going at the other Sibian ports. Well, he hoped. Hope was all he could do.

Shouts rose, up ahead. He could understand most of them. Sibian was very close to the southern dialects of Algarvian, and not tremendously far removed from his own more northerly accent. The Sibs were yelling about stopping his pals and him. "Good luck," he snarled, a carnivorous grin on his face.

He hadn't realized how meticulously his superiors had reproduced the environs of Tirgoviste harbor at the rehearsal sites near Imola. When Sibians popped up to blaze at his comrades and him, they did so in the places from which Algarvian "defenders" had fought during those long, tedious practice runs. Tealdo knew where they would be almost before they got there. He knew where to take cover, and where to aim his stick. He didn't have to think. He just had to do, and to go on doing.

"Keep moving!" Larbino yelled. "Don't let them gather themselves. Don't let them make a stand. If we press them hard now, they'll break. We have to keep them back on their heels!"

"Listen to the captain!" Sergeant Panfilo bellowed, almost in Tealdo's ear. "He knows what he's talking about." Panfilo shook his head and spoke again, this time in a much lower voice: "Never thought I'd say that about an officer."

The strongpoint Larbino's company had been trained to capture turned out to be the naval offices at Tirgoviste. Till he flopped down behind some rubble not far away, Tealdo hadn't known what the target was, nor cared much, either. His superiors told him what to do, and he went out and did it. The arrangement struck him as equitable.

"Covering blazes!" Larbino roared, and Tealdo aimed his stick at a second-story window from which a Sibian was liable to do some blazing of his own. No sooner had he done so than he saw, or thought he saw, motion behind that window. His stick sent a beam into the offices. No Sibian blazed at the Algarvians from that spot, so Tealdo concluded he hadn't been imagining things after all.

Under the protection of the storm of blazes, a couple of men ran forward and set an egg against the iron door of the naval offices. One of them fell as he dashed away from the doors. His comrade stopped and picked him up and started to carry him toward something more like safety. Then he too went down.

Tealdo cursed to see such courage wasted. He hoped somebody would try to get him away if he got hurt. He hoped whoever it was would have better luck than the fellow from the egg crew, too.

The egg burst then. Tealdo blinked frantically, trying to clear away the fuzzy, glowing green-purple spot in the center of his field of vision. When he could see straight ahead again, he whooped: the doors had not been able to withstand the energies unleashed against them. One leaned drunkenly on its hinges, while the other had been hurled into the building, with luck smashing a good many Sibians in the corridor behind it.

"Forward!" Larbino and Panfilo cried the order at the same time. Larbino added "Follow me!" and dashed toward the opening torn in the naval offices. Tealdo scrambled to his feet and did follow the captain. An officer who led from the front could pull his men after him: that was a lesson as old as war. An officer who led from the front was also horribly likely to die before his time: that was a lesson driven home during the Six Years' War.

It held here, too. Larbino got through the riven doorway, but no more than a couple of strides farther. Then he crumpled bonelessly, blazed through the head. But the soldiers on his heels killed the Sibian who'd blazed him. Howling like wolves and calling Larbino's name along with King Mezentio's, the Algarvians fought their way into and through the naval offices.

"Hold it right there!" Tealdo screamed as a Sibian hurried toward a window to escape. Firelight coming in through the window showed a lot of gold braid on the fellow's sleeves: an officer, but one intent on leaving the front, not leading from it.

For a moment, Tealdo thought he would try to jump out the window. That would have been a mistake, a particularly fatal mistake. The Sibian officer must have realized it. He raised his hands. "I am Count Delfinu; my rank is commodore," he said in slow, clear

Algarvian. "I expect to be used with all the dignity due my rank and station."

"That's nice," Tealdo said. He might have to act polite around his own nobles. He didn't care a fig for the fancy titles foreigners carried, though. Gesturing with the stick, he went on, "You come along with me, pal. Somebody'll figure out what to do with you." A captive commodore was an excuse plenty good enough to let him leave the fighting for a little while. And if the rest of the fight was going as smoothly as this . . . Tealdo laughed. "Come on, pal," he repeated. "Tirgoviste's ours. Way it looks to me, your whole cursed kingdom's ours."

Cornelu cursed. He and Eforiel had been out on a routine patrol, finding nothing much. When the leviathan brought him back toward Tirgoviste harbor, though . . . He cursed again, cursed and wept, mingling his salty tears with the salt sea. "The harbor is theirs," he groaned. "The city is theirs."

Fires burning up in Tirgoviste silhouetted the masts and spars of the Algarvian invasion fleet. Cornelu did not need long to figure out what King Mezentio's men had done. In an abstract way, he admired their nerve. Had a couple of Sibian ley-line cruisers happened on that fleet of sailing ships, they could have worked a ghastly slaughter. But they hadn't. The galleons, or whatever the old-fashioned name for them was, had ghosted across the ley lines with no one the wiser. The rest of the Algarvian navy, no doubt, would follow now.

"Costache," Cornelu said: another groan. All he could do was hope his wife remained safe, and the child to whom she would soon give birth. He didn't think the Algarvians would deliberately outrage her – were they not civilized men? – but anything could happen during a battle.

Eforiel rolled a little in the water, so she could look up at him from one large, dark eye. The leviathan let out what sounded like a puzzled grunt. Cornelu understood why: he wasn't behaving as he usually did when the two of them returned to their home port. Eforiel didn't understand that, if she blithely swam into Tirgoviste harbor now, Cornelu would get blazed and she would either have eggs tossed at her or would be captured and pressed into the service of King Mezentio's men.

Instead of having her go into the harbor, Cornelu started to guide her toward a little beach just outside Tirgoviste. There he could slip off her back, gain the shore, and . . . *And what?* he asked himself. What would he do then? Go into town, rescue his wife, bring her back to Eforiel, and flee? The hero of an adventure romance might have managed that, pausing somewhere in there to make love to her, too. In real life, unfortunately, Cornelu had no notion how to bring off such a coup.

If he couldn't rescue Costache, could he head inland and join whatever resistance to the Algarvian invaders might be brewing there? He wondered how strong that resistance could be. Algarve was a much bigger kingdom than Sibiu, and boasted a much, much bigger army. Sibiu had relied upon her ships to keep her safe, and Mezentio had found a way to hoodwink them.

Besides, as a soldier Cornelu was nothing out of the ordinary. He was far more useful to King Burebistu as part of a team with Eforiel than by himself. He wished the leviathan had several eggs in the harness under her belly. Were that so, he might have done the invaders some real damage.

Eforiel grunted again, sensing his indecision: unlike dragons, leviathans liked men and understood them pretty well. "I need to know more," Cornelu said, almost as if he were talking to Costache. "That's what I need more than anything else. For all I know – powers above grant it be so – the invasion has failed on the other four islands. If it has, I can help reconquer Tirgoviste."

He patted the leviathan, steering her west toward Facaceni, the island closest to his own. Eforiel obeyed, but more slowly than she might have. Had she been able to speak, she might have said something like, *Are you sure this is what you want me to do?* She was even more skeptical of anything that smacked of innovation than the briniest old salt in the Sibian navy.

Cornelu wished with all his heart that some better course lay before him. He could see none, though. With no chance to be useful around Tirgoviste, he had to hope the island and port of Facaceni remained in Sibian hands. If they did, well and good. If not . . . He would not let himself worry about that now.

Dawn broke while Eforiel was still swimming west. Dragons flew high overhead – far too high for him to tell whether they bore Sibian colors or those of Algarve. None of them swooped down to drop an egg on the leviathan. For that, at least, Cornelu was grateful.

It was the first thing he'd found for which he might be grateful since discovering his kingdom invaded. Before long, he became convinced it was the last thing for which he might be grateful for some time to come. Before he saw the hills at the center of Facaceni rise over the horizon, he spotted a great cloud of smoke towering higher than those hills. Unless Facaceni had suffered a natural disaster, it had suffered disaster at the hands of the Algarvians.

Cornelu had never wished so hard for an earthquake. But wishes, no matter how fervent, were sorcerous nullities. Cornelu had no skill in magecraft, any more than a mage was likely to have skill in riding leviathans. Learning to do one thing well was hard enough in this world; learning to do more than one thing well often pressed the limits of the possible.

Not that even magecraft could annul what had already happened. As Eforicl drew Cornelu ever nearer the harbor of Facaceni, he saw for himself that King Mezentio's men were there before him. Sailing ships had emptied soldiers out on to the quays, as they had at Tirgoviste – as they had, probably, at every Sibian port.

And, just as Cornelu had guessed, the rest of the Algarvian navy had followed the invasion fleet south. Algarvian and Sibian ships were tossing eggs at each other outside the harbor, and blazing with powerful sticks. Every time a beam went low, a great cloud of steam rose from the ocean.

Eforiel shuddered beneath Cornelu. She paid no attention to the beams, but eggs bursting in the water frightened her. She had reason to fear, too; a burst too near might kill her. Cornelu dared approach Facaceni no closer.

A puff of steam rising only a couple of hundred yards away warned that he might already have come too close. It came not from a stick but from another leviathan spouting. A moment later, leviathan and rider broke the surface. "Who are you?" the rider called to Cornelu.

Was he speaking Algarvian or Sibian? With only three words to go on, Cornelu had trouble being sure. "Who are *you*?" he called back. "Give me the signal." He did not know what the signal was, but hoped to learn more by the way the other leviathan rider responded.

Learn he did, for the fellow said, "Mezentio!"

"Mezentio!" Cornelu answered, as if he too were an Algarvian, and delighted to find another one in this part of the world. But, while his mouth spoke the name with every sign of gladness, his hand delivered a different message to Eforiel: *attack!*

The leviathan's muscles surged smoothly beneath him as she arrowed through the water toward the other rider and his mount. Calling Mezentio's name must have lulled the Algarvian, for he let Cornelu and Eforiel approach without taking any precautions against them.

He learned his mistake too late. Eforiel's pointed snout rammed his leviathan's side, not far behind the creature's left flipper. The impact almost pitched Cornelu off Eforiel's back, though he was as well strapped and braced as he could have been. The Algarvian leviathan twisted and jerked in startled agony, much as a man might have done if unexpectedly hit in the pit of the stomach.

After delivering that first blow with her jaws closed, Eforiel opened them and bit the other leviathan several times. Blood turned seawater crimson. Cornelu laughed to see the Algarvian rider splashing in the ocean, separated from his mount. Eforiel did the Algarvian no harm. She had not been trained to hunt men in the water – too much likelihood of her turning on her own rider, should some mischance have separated the two of them.

Had circumstances differed, Cornelu might have captured the other rider. But he doubted he had any place on Sibiu to which he could bring the Algarvian for interrogation. And he spied other spouts not far away. He had to assume they came from Algarvian leviathans.

When he ordered Eforiel to break off the attack, he thought for a moment she would refuse to obey him. But training triumphed over instinct. She allowed the leviathan she'd wounded to flee into the depths of the sea. Cornelu did not think a Sibian-trained animal would have abandoned its rider like that – but the Algarvians, as he'd seen to his sorrow, had tricks of their own up their sleeves.

And they had these leviathans. "Mezentio!" their riders called, hurrying toward the commotion at least one of them had spotted.

Cornelu did not think he could fool them as he had the first Algarvian he'd encountered; few tricks worked twice. Nor, being outnumbered, was he ashamed to flee. He hoped to escape them and then go on looking for Sibians still resisting the invaders.

In war, though, what one hopes and what one gets are often far removed from each other. The Algarvians pursuing Eforiel were better riders than most of their countrymen, and mounted on sturdier leviathans. They chased Cornelu far to the south of Facaceni, and seemed intent on driving him from Sibian waters altogether.

To make matters worse, a dragon flew high over Eforiel, helping the Algarvians and their leviathans keep track of her. The dragonflier was sure to be speaking into a crystal. If one of the riders was likewise equipped . . . If that was so, the Algarvians had devoted a great deal of effort to tying their forces together in ways no one had thought of before.

Another dragon came flapping up behind the first. This one carried a couple of eggs slung under its belly, and did its best to drop them on Eforiel. The flier's aim, though, was not so good as it might have been. Both eggs fell well short of their intended target; one, in fact, came closer to hitting the Algarvian leviathan riders than it did to Cornelu.

He hoped that would make the enemy lose him, but it didn't. Cursing the Algarvians, he kept Eforiel headed southeast, the only direction in which they permitted him to travel. He shook his fist at them. "Force me to Lagoas, will you?" he shouted.

Lagoas was neutral. If he came ashore there, he would be interned, and out of the fighting till the war was over: a better fate than surrendering, but not much. He cursed the Lagoans even more bitterly than he did the Algarvians. In the Six Years' War, Lagoas had fought alongside Sibiu, but this time around her merchants had loved their profits too well to feel like shedding any blood.

And then, as if thinking of Lagoans had conjured them up, a patrol boat came speeding along a ley line from out of the south. He could have escaped it. The ocean was wide, and the ship could not leave the line of energy from which it drew its power. But, if he was going to be interned, sooner struck him as being as good as later. This way, as opposed to his coming ashore on their soil, the Lagoans might heed his wishes about Eforiel. And so he waved and had the leviathan rear in the water and generally made himself as conspicuous as he could.

The Algarvian leviathan riders turned and headed back toward Sibiu. Cornelu shook his fist at them again, then waited for the

Lagoan warship to approach. "Who might you be?" an officer called from the deck in what might have been intended for either Sibian or Algarvian.

Cornelu gave his name, his rank, and his kingdom. To his surprise, the Lagoans burst into cheers. "Well met, friend!" several of them said.

"Friend?" he echoed in surprise.

"Friend, aye," the officer answered in his accented Sibian. "Lagoas wars with Algarve now. Had you no heard? When Mezentio your country invaded, King Vitor declares war. We all friends together now, aye?"

"Aye," Cornelu said wearily.

Skarnu stood up before his company and said the words that had to be said: "Men, the redheads have gone and invaded Sibiu. You'll have heard that already, I suppose." He waited for nods, and got them. "You ask me," he went on, "they were fools. Lagoas is a bigger danger to them than Sibiu ever could have been. But if the Algarvians weren't fools, they wouldn't be Algarvians, eh?"

He got more nods, and even a couple of smiles. He would have been gladder of those smiles had they come from the best soldiers in the company, not the happy-go-lucky handful who in the morning refused to worry about the afternoon, let alone tomorrow.

"We can't swim over to Sibiu to help the islanders," he said, "so we have to do the next best thing. King Mezentio must have pulled a lot of his soldiers out of the line here when he invaded Sibiu. That means there won't be enough men left in the redheads' works to hold us back when we hit them. We are going to break through, and we are going to go rampaging right into the Algarvian rear."

Some of the men who'd smiled before clapped their hands and cheered. So did a few others – youngsters, mostly. Most of the soldiers just stood silently. Skarnu had studied the Algarvian fortifications himself, studied them till he knew the ones in front of him like the lines on his palm. As long as they held any men at all, they would be hard to break through. He knew it. Most of the men knew it, too. But he had his orders about what to tell them.

He also had his pride. He said, "Remember, men, you won't be going anywhere I haven't gone myself, because I'll be out in front of you every step of the way. We'll do all we can for our king and kingdom." He raised his voice to a shout: "King Gainibu and victory!"

"King Gainibu!" the men echoed. "Victory!" They cheered enthusiastically. Why not? Cheering cost them nothing and exposed them to no danger.

Seeing that Skarnu had finished, Sergeant Raunu strode out in front of the company. He glanced at Skarnu for permission to speak. Skarnu nodded. The company would have got on fine without him, but he couldn't have run it without Raunu. The veteran underofficer affected not to know that. Skarnu understood perfectly well that the pose was an affectation. He wondered how many company officers really believed their sergeants thought them indispensable. Too many, odds were.

Raunu said, "Boys, we're lucky. You know it, and I know it. A lot of officers would send us forward but stay in a hole themselves. If we won, they'd take the credit. If we lost, we'd get the blame – only we'd be dead and they'd try again with another company. The captain's not like that. We've all seen as much. Let's give him a cheer now, and let's fight like madmen for him tomorrow."

"Captain Skarnu!" the men shouted. Skarnu waved to them, feeling foolish. He was used to accepting the deference of commoners because of his blood. Like his sister Krasta, he'd taken it for granted. The deference he got here in the field was different. He'd earned it. It made him proud and embarrassed at the same time.

"Whatever we can do, sir, we'll do tomorrow," Raunu said.

"I'm sure of it," Skarnu said. That was a polite commonplace. He started to add something to it, then stopped. Sometimes Raunu, if given the chance to talk, came out with things he wouldn't have otherwise, things an officer would have had trouble learning any other way.

This proved to be one of those times. "Do you really think we'll break the Algarvian line tomorrow, sir?" the sergeant said.

"We've been ordered to do it," Skarnu said. "I hope we can do it." He went no further than that.

"Mm." Raunu's wrinkles refolded themselves into an expression less forbidding than the one he usually wore. "Sir, I hope we can do it, too. But if there's not much chance . . . Sir, I saw a lot of officers with a lot of courage get themselves killed for nothing during the Six Years' War. It'd be a shame if that happened to you before you figured out what was what."

"I see." Skarnu nodded brightly. "After I figure out what's what, it will be all right for me to get myself killed for nothing."

"No, sir." Raunu shook his head. "After you know what's what, you'll know better than to go rushing ahead and get yourself killed for nothing."

Skarnu quoted doctrine: "The only way to make an attack succeed is to go into it confident of success."

"Aye, sir." Raunu frowned again. "The only trouble is, sometimes that doesn't help, either."

Skarnu shrugged. Raunu looked at him, shook his head, and walked off. Skarnu understood what the veteran was trying to tell him. Understanding didn't matter. He had his orders. His company would break through the Algarvian line ahead or die trying.

All through the night, egg-tossers hurled destruction at the Algarvian positions. Dragons flew overhead, dropping more eggs on the redheads. Skarnu had mixed feelings about all that. On the one hand, slain enemy soldiers and wrecked enemy works would make the attack easier. On the other, the Valmierans couldn't have done a better job of announcing where that attack would go in if they'd hung out a sign.

The Algarvians made little reply to the eggs raining down. *Maybe they're all dead*, Skarnu thought hopefully. He couldn't make himself believe it, try as he would.

He led his men to the ends of the approach trenches they'd dug over the previous couple of days. That new digging might also have warned the Algarvians an attack was coming. But Skarnu and his men would not have to cross so much open ground to close with the enemy when the assault began, and so he reluctantly decided it was likely to be worthwhile.

"This is how we did it in the Six Years' War," Raunu said as the soldiers huddled in the trenches, waiting for the whistles that would order them forward. "We licked the redheads then, so we know we can do it again, right?"

Some of the youngsters under Skarnu's command grinned and nodded at the veteran sergeant. They were too young to know about the gruesome casualties Valmiera had endured in that victory. Raunu deliberately didn't mention those. The men hadn't suffered badly in this war, not yet, not least because their leaders did remember the slaughters of the Six Years' War and had avoided repeating them. Now the risk seemed acceptable . . . to men who weren't facing it themselves.

Off in the west, behind Skarnu, the sky went from black to gray to pink. Peering over the dirt heaped up in front of the approach trenches, he saw the enemy's field fortifications had taken a fearful battering. He dared hope that no Algarvian position during the Six Years' War had been so thoroughly smashed up.

He said as much to Raunu, who also stuck his head up to examine the ground ahead. The sergeant answered, "Just where it looks like there couldn't be even one of the bastards left alive, that's where you'll find whole caravans full of 'em, and they'll all be doing their best to blaze you down."

Raunu had been loud and enthusiastic while heartening the common soldiers in the company. He spoke quietly to his superior, not wanting to dilute the effect he'd had on the men.

More eggs and still more eggs fell on the Algarvian entrenchments and forts. And then, without warning, they stopped falling. Skarnu pulled a brass whistle from his trouser pocket and blew a long, echoing blast, one of hundreds ringing out along several miles of battle line. "For Valmiera!" he cried. "For King Gainibu!" He scrambled out of the approach trench and trotted toward the Algarvians' works.

"Valmiera!" his men shouted, and followed him out into the open. "Gainibu!" He looked to either side. Thousands of Valmierans, thousands upon thousands, stormed west. It was a sight to make any soldier proud of his countrymen.

Only a few hundred more yards, Skarnu thought. *Then we'll be in among the redheads, and then they'll be ours*. But already flashes ahead warned that some Algarvians had survived the pounding the Valmierans had given them. More and more enemy soldiers began blazing at Skarnu and his comrades. Men started falling, some without a sound, others shrieking as they were wounded.

The Algarvians had endured all the eggs the Valmierans tossed at them without responding – till this moment, when the men attacking them were most vulnerable. And now they rained eggs down on the Valmierans. Skarnu found himself on the ground without any clear memory of how he'd got there. One moment, he'd been upright. The next –

He scrambled to his feet. His trousers were torn. His tunic was out at the elbow. He wasn't bleeding, or didn't think he was. *Lucky*, he thought.

He waved to show his men he was all right, and looked back over his shoulder to see how they were doing. Even as he did so, a couple of them went down. They hadn't come very far – surely not halfway – but he'd lost a lot of them. If he kept losing them at that rate, he wouldn't have any men left by the time he got to the forwardmost Algarvian trenches. He probably wouldn't live to get to those trenches himself, an unpleasant afterthought to have.

The headlong charge was simply too expensive to be borne. "By squads!" he shouted. "Blaze and move by squads!"

Half his men – half the men he had left – dove into such cover as they could find – mostly the holes burst eggs had dug in the ground. The rest raced by them. Then they flattened out and blazed at the Algarvians while the others rose and dashed past. Little by little, they worked their way toward the trenches from which the redheads were blazing at them.

Skarnu took shelter in a hole himself, waiting for his next chance to advance. He looked around, hoping the order he'd had to give hadn't slowed his company too badly. What he saw left him wide-eyed with dismay. As many Valmierans were running back toward their own lines as were still going forward against the enemy. Of the ones still advancing, most paid no attention to tactics that might have cut their losses. They kept moving up till they went down. When they could bear no more, they broke and fled.

"You see, sir?" Raunu shouted from a hole not far away. "This is how I feared it would be."

"What can we do?" Skarnu asked.

"We aren't going to break through their lines," Raunu answered. "We aren't even going to get into their lines – or if we do, we won't come out again. Best we can do now is hang tight here, hurt 'em a bit, and get back to where we started from after nightfall. If you order me forward, though, sir, I'll go."

"No," Skarnu said. "What point to that but getting us killed to no purpose?" He assumed that, if he ordered Raunu forward, he would have to try to advance, too. "This is what you warned me about before the attack began, isn't it?"

"Aye, sir. Good to see you can recognize it," Raunu said. "I only wish our commanders could." Skarnu started to reproach the sergeant for speaking too freely. He stopped with the words unspoken. How could Raunu have spoken too freely when all he did was tell the truth?

Leofsig still retained the tin mess kit he'd been issued when mustered into King Penda's levy. As captives went, that made him relatively lucky. Forthwegian soldiers who'd lost their kits had to make do with bowls that held less. The Algarvians might have issued their own kits to men who lacked them, but that didn't seem to have entered their minds.

What had crossed their minds was carefully counting the captives in each barracks in the encampment before those captives got anything in their mess kits or bowls. Leofsig would not have bet that the Algarvian guards could count to ten, even using their fingers. The endless recounts to which the captives had to submit argued against it, at any rate.

Every so often, a captive or two really did turn up missing. That meant the redheads tore the encampment apart till they found out how the men had disappeared. It also meant a week of half rations for the escapees' barracksmates. No one got fat on full rations. Half rations were slow starvation. Half rations were also an argument for betraying anyone thinking of getting away.

This morning, everything seemed to add up. "Powers above be praised," Leofsig muttered. He was cold and tired and hungry; standing in formation in front of the barracks was not his idea of a good time. Standing in line and waiting for the meager breakfast the cooks would dole out didn't strike him as delightful, either. Eventually, though, he'd get food in his belly, which came close to making the wait worthwhile.

Plop! The sound of a large ladle of mush landing in his mess kit was about as appetizing as the stuff itself. The mush was mostly wheat porridge, with cabbage and occasional bits of salt fish or pork mixed in. The captives ate it breakfast, dinner, and supper. It was never very good. This morning, it smelled worse than usual.

Leofsig ate it anyhow. If it made him sick – and it did make people sick every so often – he'd go to the infirmary. And if anybody claimed he was malingering, he'd throw up in the wretch's lap.

The handful of Kaunians in his barracks ate in a small knot by themselves, as they usually did. He would sometimes join them. So would a few of his fellow Forthwegians. Most, though, wanted nothing to do with the blonds. And a few, like Merwit, still stirred up trouble every chance they got.

"Hey, you!" Merwit said now. Leofsig looked up from his mush. Sure enough, Merwit was staring his way with a smile that made him look neither friendly nor attractive. "Aye, you, yellow-hair lover," the burly captain went on. "You going on latrine duty after breakfast? That'd give you the chance to hang around with your pals?"

"You ought to try it yourself, Merwit," Leofsig answered. "There's nobody else I know who's half so full of shit."

Merwit's eyes went big and wide. He and Leofsig had quarreled before, but Leofsig hadn't given back insult for insult till this moment. Carefully, Merwit set down his own mess kit. "You're going to pay for that," he said in matter-of-fact tones. He charged forward like a behemoth.

Leofsig kicked him in the belly. It was like kicking a plank. Merwit grunted, but he slammed one fist into Leofsig's ribs and the other into the top of Leofsig's head. He'd meant to hit him in the face, but Leofsig ducked. Merwit howled then. With any luck at all, he'd broken a knuckle or two.

Being smaller and lighter, Leofsig knew he'd need all the help of that sort he could get. He tried to end the fight in a hurry by kneeing Merwit in the crotch, but Merwit twisted away and took the knee on the hip. He seized Leofsig in a bearhug. Leofsig knocked his feet out from under him. They went down together, each doing the other as much damage with fists and elbows and knees as he could.

"Halting! You halting!" somebody shouted in accented Forthwegian. Leofsig did nothing of the kind, having a well-founded suspicion that Merwit wouldn't. "You halting!" This time, the command had teeth: "You halting, or we blazing!"

That must have convinced Merwit, because he stopped trying to work mayhem on Leofsig. Leofsig gave him one more inconspicuous elbow, then pushed him away and got to his feet. His nose was bleeding. A couple of his front teeth felt loose, but they were all there. None was even broken – pure luck, and he knew it.

He looked over at Merwit. Merwit looked as if he'd been in a fight: one of his eyes was swollen shut, and he had a big bruise on the other cheek. Leofsig felt as if he'd been pummeled with boulders. He hoped Merwit did, too.

The Algarvian guards who'd stopped the brawl were shaking their heads. "Stupid, stupid Forthwegians," one of them said, more in sorrow than in anger. He gestured with his stick. "You coming, stupid Forthwegians. Now you seeing just how stupid you being. Come!" Glumly, Leofsig and Merwit came.

Sometimes, the Algarvians chose not to notice captives fighting among themselves. Sometimes, without rhyme or reason Leofsig could see, they chose to make examples of them. He eased a little when he saw they were taking him and Merwit to Brigadier Cynfrid, the senior Forthwegian officer in camp, rather than to their own commandant. Cynfrid had far less power to punish than did the Algarvian authorities.

"What have we here?" the brigadier asked, looking up from some paperwork. With his gray hair and snowy mustache and beard, he seemed more a kindly grandfather than a soldier. Had he been a better soldier – had a lot of Forthwegian commanders been better soldiers – he might not have ended up in a captives' camp, but might instead have kept the war going.

"These two, they fighting," one of the Algarvian guards said.

"Oh, aye, I can see that," Cynfrid said. "The question is, why were they fighting?" The guard gave back an extravagant Algarvian shrug, one that declared he not only didn't know but found beneath him the idea of wondering why Forthwegians did anything. The brigadier sighed, evidently having encountered that attitude before. He examined Leofsig and Merwit. "What have you men got to say for yourselves?"

"Sir, this stinking Kaunian-lover called me a filthy name," Merwit said, his voice dripping with righteous innocence and indignation. "I got sick of it, so when he started the fight, I did my best to give him what-for."

"I didn't start the fight," Leofsig exclaimed. "He did! And he's been calling me names since we got here — you just heard him do it again now. I finally called him one back. He didn't like that so much. Most bullies are better at giving it out than taking it."

"Conflicting stories," Cynfrid said with another sigh. He glanced over toward the guards. "I don't suppose you gentlemen know who did start the fight?" The redheads laughed, not so much at the idea that they should know, but at the notion that they might care. The Forthwegian brigadier sighed yet again. "Any chance of witnesses?"

Now Leofsig had all he could do not to start laughing himself. His fellow captives wanted as little to do with the guards as they could. They would make themselves scarce and deny seeing anything . . . or would all of them? Slowly, he said, "Sir, I think the Kaunians in my barracks would tell the truth about what went on."

"They'd lick your arse for you, you mean, like you lick theirs," Merwit snarled, his eyes blazing.

Leofsig had succeeded in gaining the guards' attention. He wasn't nearly sure he wanted it. To Cynfrid, one of the Algarvians said, "The Kaunians, they is no to being trusted, eh?"

"No, probably not," the Forthwegian brigadier said, "although they haven't done nearly so much to Forthweg as you Algarvians, wouldn't you think?"

If the Algarvians thought any such thing, their faces didn't show it. With a dismissive gesture, the one who did most of the talking said, "You no can trusting nothing no yellowheads telling you."

"That's right," Merwit said. "That's just right, sir."

"Is it?" Cynfrid didn't sound convinced. "You seem none too trustworthy yourself there, soldier." But he failed to follow through, just as Forthwegian officers had failed to follow through on their early victories over Algarve. "Well, if we've got no trustworthy witnesses, these two chaps will have to share and share alike. A week's latrine duty each ought to teach them to keep their hands to themselves."

Merwit jerked a thumb toward Leofsig. "*He* likes latrine duty. He gets to hang around with his Kaunian chums."

"They're better company than you are," Leofsig retorted. "They smell better than you do, too."

Only the presence of the Algarvian guards kept the fight from flaring again. "That will be quite enough, both of you," Brigadier

Cynfrid said sternly. "The order holds – a week's latrine duty for each of you. Any further incidents between you two, and we shall see what sort of view the Algarvian authorities take of such business."

"Aye, sir," Merwit and Leofsig said together. Leofsig did not want to go before the redheads, not after he'd got a name for sticking up for Kaunians. The Algarvians lorded it over his own people, aye, but their feud with folk of Kaunian blood went back into the ancient days of the world.

He hoped Merwit wouldn't be clever enough to see that. Merwit, fortunately, had never struck him as very clever. Merwit had struck him, though – struck him with fists like rocks. He knew no small pride at having come close to holding his own against the other captive.

"You hearing the brigadier," the talky Algarvian guard said. "Now you coming, you do your deservings. You do the shovelings of shits, aye?" He and his comrades both gestured with their sticks. Leofsig and Merwit left. Looking back over his shoulder, Leofsig saw Brigadier Cynfrid return to the paperwork he'd had interrupted.

Merwit did as little as he could on latrine duty, or perhaps a bit less. Leofsig had expected nothing else; he'd already seen that Merwit was a shirker even by the lax standards of the captives' camp. He did his own work, not as if he were in a race but steadily nonetheless.

Late that afternoon, a shout made his head whip around. Somehow, Merwit had contrived to fall into a slit trench about due to be covered over. When he scrambled out again, he was as magnificently filthy a man as Leofsig had ever seen. He glared at Leofsig, but Leofsig hadn't been anywhere near him.

At the moment, none of the Kaunians who did most of the latrine work was anywhere near him, either. Leofsig hadn't noticed any of them hurrying away. Maybe Merwit had been clumsy. Maybe some Kaunian had been sneaky. By the way Merwit stared wildly around him, he thought some Kaunian had been sneaky.

The Kaunians ignored him. They didn't even suggest that he pour a bucket of water over himself because he stank. If they looked pleased with themselves – well, Kaunians often looked pleased with themselves, that being one of the characteristics that failed to endear them to their neighbors. If they'd been sneaky enough to dump Merwit into the slit trench without getting caught: if they'd been that sneaky, Leofsig wondered how sneaky they might be in other ways.

That might be worth finding out one of these days, if he could figure out how.

Down in the farming villages of the Duchy of Grelz, fall gave way to winter early. Most of Unkerlant had a harsh climate; that in the south was far worse than the rest. Animals that hibernated went into their burrows sooner there than anywhere else in the kingdom.

People in those farming villages went into their burrows sooner than anywhere else in the kingdom, too. Like dormice and badgers and bears, Garivald and his fellow farmers had stuffed themselves and filled their larders. Now, with the harvest gathered, they had little to do but keep themselves and their livestock alive till spring eventually returned.

Garivald had mixed feelings about the long winters. On the one hand, he didn't have to work so hard as he did when the weather was better. If he felt like pulling out a jug of raw spirits and spending a day – or a couple of days, or more than a couple of days – drunk, he could. It wouldn't mean starvation because he hadn't done something that vitally needed doing. The worst it would mean was a disastrously thick head when he stopped drinking. He was used to those, and sometimes even took a certain melancholy pleasure in them. They were one more way of helping time go by in winter.

As far as he was concerned, making time go by was the biggest trouble winter offered. Unlike a dormouse or a badger or a bear, he couldn't sleep away the whole season. Except when very drunk, he remained aware: aware he was cooped up in a none-too-big farmhouse with his wife and son and daughter and with a lot of livestock that would otherwise have starved or frozen.

Annore, his wife, liked it even less than he did. "Can't you keep anything clean?" she shouted when he threw the shell of a hardboiled egg on the floor after scooping out white and yolk with a horn spoon.

"I don't know what you're fretting about," he answered in what he thought were reasonable tones. "There's cow shit over there" – he pointed – "and pig shit over there" – he pointed again – "and the hens shit all over everywhere, so why are you shouting at me over an eggshell?" Trying to be helpful, he ground it into the dirt floor with the sole of his boot.

Annore put her hands on her hips and rolled her eyes, so maybe he hadn't been so helpful after all. "Can I make the cows do their business where I tell them to? Can I do that for the pigs? Can I do that for the miserable, stinking chickens? They won't listen to me. Maybe you will."

Garivald didn't feel like listening. He'd been drunk up until the day before, and was still feeling the effects. He'd beaten Annore only a couple of times, which made him a prodigy, as husbands in the village of Zossen went. That was only partly because he had a milder temper than most of the other village men. The other side of the coin was that Annore had a fiercer temper than most of the other village women. If he beat her too hard or too often, she was liable to cut his throat or break his head while he lay in a drunken stupor. Almost every winter, someone in Zossen met an untimely demise.

Garivald's son Syrivald grunted like a pig. He was looking at Garivald as he did it, mischief on his face. Garivald grunted, too, and got to his feet. The mischief vanished from Syrivald's face; alarm replaced it. Garivald caught him and thumped him a couple of times. "Don't call me a hog – have you got that?" he demanded.

"Aye, Father," Syrivald blubbered. Had he been rash enough to say anything else, his father would have made him regret it.

As things were, Garivald found a different way to make him regret getting out of line: "Since you haven't got anything better to do with yourself, you can clean up after the animals. And while you're at it, you can pick up my eggshell, too."

Syrivald got to work, not with any enormous enthusiasm but with a very plain sense that he'd be sorry if he didn't go at it fast enough to suit his father. In that, he was absolutely right. Garivald kept a sharp eye on him till he was almost done, then turned to Annore and said, "There. Are you happier now?"

"I'd be really happy if this house didn't turn into a sty every winter," she said. She wasn't looking at the pigs. She was looking at Garivald.

Her words could have held any of several meanings. Having been married to her a good many years, Garivald knew which one was likeliest. He also knew he would be foolish to acknowledge that one. He said, "Only way I can think of to keep a house clean through winter is by magic."

"I believe *that*," Annore said, a reply not calculated to warm his heart. Before she could elaborate on it, Leuba woke from her nap and started to cry. Annore took care of the baby, whose soiled linen added to the winter atmosphere of the farmhouse. But, after Annore put her daughter to her breast, she resumed: "How much magic can anyone work here?"

"I don't know," Garivald answered grouchily. "Enough, maybe."

Annore shook her head. Leuba, following the motion, found it very funny. "Not likely," Annore said. "This far from a power point, this far from a ley line, you'd need a first-rank mage. Where would we get the silver to pay a first-rank mage?" Her bitter laugh said she knew that question had no answer even as she asked it.

Garivald said, "I like living without much magic fine, thanks. If we had power points and ley lines coming out of our ears, this place would be just like Cottbus, you know that? We'd have inspectors and impressers peering at us every minute we weren't squatting on the pot, and half the time we were, too."

Syrivald wrinkled up his nose at that idea. So did Garivald. In a couple of sentences, he'd summed up everything he knew about the capital of Unkerlant: that it was full of magic and full of people who spied on other people for King Swemmel. He had no notion that that wasn't a full and complete portrait of Cottbus. How could he? He'd never seen a city, and had been to the market town nearest his village only a couple of times. That didn't make his opinions any less certain – on the contrary.

"Hurry up there, Syrivald," he snapped, also having definite opinions on how much work his son ought to be doing. Syrivald's occasional failure to meet his standards made him add, "Of course, if we offer a sacrifice, we don't need a power point, let alone a first-rank mage."

"Stop that!" Annore said at Syrivald's horrified stare. Garivald laughed; he'd succeeded in getting his son's attention. "It isn't funny," his wife told him.

"Oh, I think it is," Garivald said. "Look – I've worked a magic of my own, and the farmhouse is getting clean. If you think you can get better sorcery around these parts, you'd better to talk to Waddo or to Herka."

"I don't want to talk to the firstman or his wife, thank you,"

Annore said tartly. "They wouldn't be able to help me, anyhow. If they knew anything about getting real magic out here, don't you think they'd have a crystal in their own house?"

"Maybe they don't want one." But Garivald shook his head before Annore could correct him. "No, you're right; never mind. Waddo and Herka always want things. If they didn't, would they have built that second floor on to their house?" He chuckled. "I bet Waddo has fun getting up there these days, on his bad ankle."

But that second floor let the firstman and his family live above the livestock during the winter, not with it, as everyone else in the village did. Building a second floor on to his own home would have let Garivald satisfy Annore's longing for a clean house, or at least part of a clean house, without magic and without threatening to make Syrivald a blood sacrifice. But he and Annore both thought Waddo's addition a piece of big-city pretentiousness. Doing anything like it had never crossed his mind, nor his wife's, either.

Annore sighed and said, "It's no use. I know it's no use. But I couldn't help wishing sometimes . . ." She sighed again. "I might as well wish you were a baron."

"That would be something, wouldn't it?" Garivald got off the stool on which he was sitting and puffed out his chest. "Baron Garivald the Splendid," he boomed in a deep voice bearing little resemblance to the one he usually used.

Syrivald snickered. Annore laughed out loud. Leuba didn't understand why her mother was laughing, but she laughed, too. So did Garivald. The idea of him as a baron was even funnier than the idea of a farmhouse that stayed clean through the winter. It would need a stronger magic, too.

"Maybe I'd better be happy with things the way they are now," Annore said.

Garivald snorted. "You think I'd make a lousy baron." He scratched. He was probably lousy now. People got that way when winter closed down on the land. Nobody bathed often enough to hold the nasty little pests at bay. Sitting in the steam bath till you couldn't stand being baked any more and then running out and rolling in the snow felt wonderful – once a week, or once every other week. More often than that, it felt like death. And that often wasn't enough to kill lice and nits. Garivald scratched some more. *Can't be helped*, he thought.

Annore didn't answer him, which might have been just as well. Instead, she put Leuba on her shoulder till the baby rewarded her with a belch. "There's a good girl," Annore said. "Don't you feel better now that that's out?" She seemed to feel better now that she'd got her complaints out, too.

"Winter," Garivald said, more to himself than to anyone else. Here he was, in the house with his family and his livestock, and he wouldn't be going anywhere – or nowhere far, and not for long – for quite a while. Neither would Annore. No wonder she felt like complaining sometimes.

One of the cows dropped more dung on the floor. The only thing Annore said was, "Clean that up, Syrivald."

She still held Leuba. Syrivald knew better than to think that meant she wouldn't get up and wallop him if he didn't hop to it. He'd made that mistake a couple of times. He wouldn't make it any more.

"Just as well Waddo and Herka don't have a crystal," Garivald said. "We'd get endless yattering about the war against the black people up in the north, and how we'd won *another* smashing battle." He snorted again. "Don't they know we know the war would be over by now if it were really going well? And besides" – he added the clincher – "if they had a crystal, the inspector and impressers would be able to give them orders without bothering to come out here."

"Powers above!" Annore exclaimed. "We wouldn't want *that*. I think I am happier with things the way they are now."

"I think I am, too." Garivald knew perfectly well he was happier with things as they were. He couldn't imagine a peasant in Unkerlant who wasn't happier with things as they were. The only thing change and fancy magic got Unkerlanter city folk was going right under King Swemmel's thumb. Nobody could want that. He was sure of it.

9.

Marshal Rathar peered north across the Zuwayzi desert. Had King Swemmel let him use the plan his aides had long since developed, he might well have been in Bishah by now. So he reminded the king in every despatch he sent him. Maybe King Swemmel would pay attention and not start his next war too soon. Rathar sighed. Maybe dragons would stand up and start giving speeches, too, but he wasn't going to hold his breath waiting for that, either.

And Rathar might well not have been in Bishah by now. He'd been forcibly made aware of that, though not a hint of it got into the letters he sent Swemmel. The Zuwayzin had had plans of their own, and they might have made them work even against the full weight of the Unkerlanter army.

Unkerlant had not had to fight a desert campaign since bringing Zuwayza under the rule of Cottbus. No one was left alive from those days, and the art of war had changed a good deal since. The Unkerlanter officer corps had not figured out how best to apply all the changes: the plan with which Unkerlant had gone to war involved nothing more complicated than hammering at Zuwayza till she broke.

"The black men know us better than we know them," Rathar muttered discontentedly. That the Zuwayzin should have a good notion of what Unkerlant intended made all too much sense. Unkerlanters had been overlords in Zuwayza for more than a hundred years. Their resentful subjects had had to learn to know them well. The reverse, unfortunately, did not apply. All the Unkerlanters had done in Zuwayza was give orders. That hadn't encouraged them to try to understand the dusky people on the other end of those orders.

A messenger came up and stood to attention, awaiting Rathar's notice. At last, Rathar nodded to him. The fellow said, "My lord, I have the honor to report that General Werpin's force is ready for the attack over the Wadi Uqeiqa." His tongue stumbled over the unfamiliar syllables, so different from those of Unkerlanter.

"Good," Rathar said, nodding. "I shall order the attack tomorrow morning, as planned. Go back to the crystals and tell General Werpin to keep a tight watch for camels on his flank."

"Camels on his flank," the messenger repeated. "Aye, my lord; just as you say." He saluted and hurried away.

"Camels," Rathar said, mostly to himself. "Who would have imagined camels could cause so much trouble?"

For more than a generation, the emphasis in most armies – all armies that could afford them – had been on great herds of behemoths. Behemoths could carry men and weapons and armor enough to make them invulnerable to a footsoldier's stick. That made them the nearest terrestrial equivalent to warships. In the hands of the Algarvians, they'd smashed the Forthwegian army to bits. Rathar and his underlings were still studying how the redheads had done that.

Zuwayza, though, was proving less than ideal country for behemoths. They ate a lot. They drank even more. That wasn't good, not in a landscape with many more wadis – dry riverbeds – than rivers. Even in winter, the allegedly wet season hereabouts, the wadis stayed dry. Winter was also allegedly the cool season hereabouts. That didn't keep behemoths from falling over dead, cooked inside their own armor.

Till King Swemmel ordered him to strike at Zuwayza, Rathar hadn't paid much attention to camels. Unicorns, aye. Behemoths, aye. Horses, aye. Camels? For the life of him, he hadn't seen much use to camels.

Now he did. In terrain where wadis outnumbered rivers, where poisoning wells was a useful stratagem, camels looked a lot less ugly than they did anywhere else. Zuwayzi camel dragoons kept appearing out of nowhere, almost as if by magecraft. They would strike stinging blows to the Unkerlanters' flanks, ravage supply columns, and then vanish as swiftly and unexpectedly as they'd struck. It was maddening.

For quite a while, Rathar had been too busy responding to Zuwayzi raids – some of which reached a startling distance back into Unkerlant – to carry on his own campaign in anything like proper fashion. He hoped he was turning the corner there. Any minute now, he'd find out.

When, after half an hour, he still hadn't heard from General Droctulf, who commanded the eastern prong of the army, he went over to the crystallomancers' tent to find out what was going on with that part of the force and whether it would be ready to move at the time he had appointed. "I will call his headquarters, my lord," said the young specialist to whom he gave his requirements. "I remind you also to speak with care. The Zuwayzin are liable to be listening in spite of all our spells to keep these talks secret."

"I understand," Rathar said. "I have reason to understand; they've hurt us more than once with what they've stolen. Somehow, we haven't had the same luck with them."

"No, lord," the crystallomancer agreed. "They tell so many lies, it's hard for us to sort out the truth. And their masking magic is very good, very sneaky. I wish ours were half so effective."

Rathar sighed. If he had a copper for every time he'd heard someone wish Unkerlant did something or other as well as its neighbors, he wouldn't have needed the salary King Swemmel paid him. "We just have to learn to be more efficient," he said, and the crystallomancer nodded.

The man did his job well enough; before long, Rathar saw the face of one of Droctulf's crystallomancers staring out of the globe in front of him. "My superior needs to speak to your superior," Rathar's crystallomancer said. If the Zuwayzin were listening, they would have trouble sorting out who was who.

Droctulf's crystal man had trouble sorting out who was who. "Who is your superior?" he demanded in haughty tones. Some of that toploftiness vanished when Rathar bent low and made his image appear beside his crystallomancer's. Gulping, the other crystal man stammered, "I – I – shall fetch my superior."

"Next time, do it without any backtalk," Rathar growled. But Droctulf's crystallomancer had already disappeared. By the last expression Rathar had seen on his face, he'd wished he could vanish permanently.

In a gratifyingly short time, Droctulf's own image filled the crystal in front of Rathar. Droctulf's appearance, however, did not gratify the marshal. The general looked like a peasant who'd been whiling away the winter with a jug of something potent. "A good day to you, my lord," he said in what, even though a crystal, Rathar recognized as a careful voice: one Droctulf didn't want to make too loud for fear of hurting his own head.

"Will your men be ready to push across their present line at the appointed hour?" Rathar snapped without preamble.

"I think they will," Droctulf answered. "They ought to be able to." He stared owlishly at Rathar's image.

"General, I relieve you," Rathar said crisply. "You will report here for reassignment. Let me speak to General Gurmun, your second-in-command."

"My lord!" Droctulf exclaimed. "Have mercy, my lord! When word reaches the king that I was not so efficient as I might have been, what will he do to me?"

"I suggest you should have thought of that before you got drunk," Rathar replied. "If our attack fails because of your inefficiency, what will the king have to say of me? You *are* relieved, General. Get me Gurmun."

Droctulf disappeared from the crystal. Rathar wondered if he would have to send soldiers to enforce his subordinate's relief. If he did, he thought Droctulf's head would answer for it. King Swemmel did not tolerate anything that smacked of rebellion. The marshal sighed again. He and Droctulf had fought for Swemmel during the Twinkings War. Droctulf had liked his drink then, too. Now, though, this war had already gone on too long. Swemmel would not stomach any more delay. Rathar could not stomach any more, either.

General Gurmun appeared in the crystal. "How may I serve you, my lord?" He was younger than either Droctulf or Rathar, younger and, in some indefinable way, harder. No, not indefinable after all: he looked as if he really believed in King Swemmel's efficiency campaign rather than giving it polite lip service.

"You are familiar with the plan of attack?" Rathar asked. Gurmun nodded, a single up-and-down motion. "You can be certain your half of it goes in at the proper time and at full strength?" Gurmun nodded again. So did Rathar. "Very well, General. That half of the army is yours. Unkerlant expects nothing but victory from us, and has already been disappointed too often."

"I shall serve the kingdom as efficiently as I may," Gurmun said.

Rathar nodded to his crystallomancer, who broke the link with the eastern army. Here in the field, away from King Swemmel, Rathar was supreme. Everyone yielded to his will, even a veteran campaigner like Droctulf. Droctulf had survived all of Swemmel's massacres during and after the Twinkings War. But he could not survive his own inefficiency.

The next morning, precisely on schedule, both wings of the Unkerlanter army attacked. The racket from the thump of bursting eggs reached back to Rathar's headquarters. He had a swarm of dragons in the air, both to drop still more eggs on the Zuwayzin and to keep an eye out for yet another of their assaults against his flanks. On camelback or afoot, they ranged through the desert like ghosts.

Despite the pummeling his egg-tossers gave the enemy, Zuwayzi resistance remained fierce. He had expected nothing less. Both Werpin and Gurmun started screaming for reinforcements. Rathar had expected nothing less there, either. He had the reinforcements ready and waiting – his logistics had finally caught up with King Swemmel's impetuosity – and fed them into the fight.

The Zuwayzin did everything they could to hold the line of the Wadi Uqeiqa. Rathar had been sure they would; if he could secure a lodgement north of the dry riverbed, that would set him up to take a long step toward the valley in which Bishah lay. As he'd looked for the black men to do, they sent out a flanking column of camel riders to hit his reinforcements before the Unkerlanters could reach the front.

Dragons rose with a thunder of wings. For once, the Zuwayzin weren't going to catch him with his drawers down in this desert country. He didn't have so many crystals with the troops as he would have liked; with more, he could have done a better job of coordinating his attacks. The Algarvians had shown themselves dangerously good at that.

This time, though, he had enough. One of the dragonfliers reported raking the Zuwayzin with eggs and with the dragons' own fire. The blacks pressed the attack anyhow, those who were left. His reinforcing column, forewarned, gave them a savage mauling and pressed on toward the Wadi Uqeiqa.

And, while the Zuwayzin threw everything they had into stopping Werpin's army, they didn't have enough to stop Gurmun's force at the same time. Getting them to that point had taken longer and cost much more than Rathar expected, but now it was done. He ordered Gurmun to swing his advance to the west and come in behind the Zuwayzin who still stalled Werpin. Droctulf might have done brilliantly – or he might have botched things altogether. Gurmun handled everything with matter-of-fact competence, which, under the circumstances Rathar had worked so hard to create, proved more than adequate.

Studying the maps, Rathar smiled a rare smile. "We've broken them," he said.

Ignoring the weight of the heavy pack on his back, Istvan watched in fascination as the dowser prowled the west-facing beach on the island of Obuda. The dowser, whose name was Borsos, aimed his forked branch out toward the sea. "I thought dowsers found water," Istvan said. "Why did they bring you out here, into the middle of all the water in the world?"

Borsos threw back his head and laughed; his tawny yellow curls bounced in rhythm to his mirth. "A man from the days when the Thököly Dynasty ruled Gyongyos might have asked the same question," he said, where a man from the far east of Derlavai would have spoken of the days of the Kaunian Empire. "Dowsers are much more than water-sniffers nowadays, believe you me."

"Well, sir, I do understand *that*," Istvan replied, a trifle testily. "Even in my little valley up in the mountains, we had dowsers who'd look for lost trinkets, and others who'd point herders after a lost sheep. But if things went missing in water or near it, they wouldn't find them: the water kept them from sensing anything else. Why doesn't that happen to you?"

"A different question altogether," Borsos said. "A better one, too, if you don't mind my saying so. You can understand I can't give you all the details, not unless you promise to take off your head and throw it away after I'm done. Military sorcery has even more secrets than any other kind."

"Aye, that's plain enough," Istvan said. "Tell me what you can, if you'd be so kind. It'll be more than I know now, that's sure." He hadn't been so curious before coming to Obuda. But there wasn't much to do here, and his underofficers didn't give him much time to do what he could. Without quite intending to, he'd picked up a lot of dragon lore. Learning about dowsing might be interesting, too.

Borsos said, "Ever since the early days, the days of stone and bronze, dowsing has stood apart from the rest of magecraft. Dowsers have done what they could do, and no one thought much about how they did it. That isn't so any more. The past few generations, people have started applying the laws of sorcery to dowsing, the same as they have to other kinds of magic."

Istvan scratched his head. "How? If a magic works, aren't you likely to ruin it by looking at it too close?"

Borsos laughed again. "You *do* come from back in the mountains, don't you, soldier? That's old doctrine, outmoded, disproved. It's all in the *way* you look at things, not in the act of looking. And, by turning the law of similarity on its head, modern magecraft lets a dowser look for anything in water but the water itself, if you take my meaning."

"Maybe," Istvan said. "None of the dowsers in my valley knew anything about that, though. Water stymied them."

"It doesn't stymie me," the dowser said. "All of this chatter, though, this is liable to be another story."

He wore the three silver stars of a captain on each side of his collar, which meant he could have been much ruder than that. Knowing as much, Istvan shut up. Borsos went about his business. He aimed his dowsing rod – the straight length wrapped with copper wire, one fork with silver, the other with gold – at an Obudan fishing boat out near the edge of visibility. The rod quivered in his hand. He grunted, presumably in satisfaction.

"Seems to be performing as it should," he said. "I got rushed out here in a hurry, you know, after Algarve jumped on Sibiu with sailing ships. Nobody wanted anyone pulling the same trick on us. The ordinary mages are good enough to spot ships coming down the ley lines, but those galleons slid right past them. They won't get past me."

"That's good," Istvan answered easily. "Of course, I don't expect a lot of Algarvian warships out here in the Bothnian Ocean."

Borsos wheeled on him and started to scorch him for an idiot. Then the dowser caught the gleam in his eyes. "Heh," Borsos said. "Heh, heh. You're a funny fellow, aren't you? I'll bet all your friends think you're the funniest fellow around. What does your sergeant think when you get funny?"

"Last time it happened, sir, he put me to shoveling dragon shit for a week," Istvan answered, doing his best not to gulp. He really did have to remember to keep his mouth shut. Borsos wasn't merely a sergeant. If he so desired, he could make Istvan's life most unpleasant indeed.

But all he did was grunt again. "Sounds about like what you would have deserved," he said. "Were you as clever then as you were with me just now?"

"I'm afraid so, sir," Istvan admitted, his voice mournful. One way to duck punishment was to sound as if you'd already figured out you'd been a cursed fool.

It didn't always work. This time, it did. Borsos turned away from him and aimed the forked staff at another Obudan fishing boat. It quivered again. As far as Istvan was concerned, the rod acted the same way for the second boat as it had for the first. That was why Borsos was a dowser and he wasn't. The newcomer to Obuda pulled out a pen and tablet and scribbled some notes.

"What are you writing, sir?" Istvan reckoned it safe to remind Borsos of his existence. And he truly was curious. Unlike a lot of the young men from his valley, he could read and write, provided no one expected anything too hard along those lines from him.

"I'm beginning to compile a distance and bearing table," the dowser replied. "I have to do that every place I go, for the waters are always different, and I get a different feel in the rod, depending on the waters." He raised an eyebrow. "And if you crack wise about the feel your rod gives you, soldier, I'll kick your arse off this beach and into the ocean. Have you got that?"

"Aye, sir." Istvan made himself into the picture of innocence – no easy feat. "I didn't say a thing, sir. I wasn't going to say a thing, sir, and you can't prove I was."

"And a good thing for you I can't, too." Borsos pointed to the pack on Istvan's back. "Turn around, if you please. I want to get something out of there."

"Aye, sir," Istvan repeated, and turned his back on the dowser. He suspected Sergeant Jokai had assigned him as Borsos's beast of burden to make his life miserable. There, for once, the sergeant had

miscalculated. Istvan enjoyed being able to shoot the breeze with the
dowser, even being able to pick his brain a little, more than the
ordinary routine of soldiering. Lugging Borsos's equipment about
was the price he paid for the privilege.

Borsos rummaged through the pack till he found whatever he was
looking for. After the dowser closed up the oiled-leather pack, Istvan
turned back around to see what he'd taken. Borsos was stripping the
bright copper wire from most of its length of his dowsing rod. He
replaced it with wire with a green patina.

Seeing Istvan's eye upon him, he condescended to explain: "I
think the greened wire here will give me better accuracy for a couple
of reasons. For one, its color, like that of the sea, enhances the effects
– both positive and negative – of the law of similarity. And, for
another, it got that color by being soaked in seawater. That also gives
it a greater affinity for the ocean here."

"I see," Istvan said, which was more or less true. "If all that's so,
though, sir, why didn't you have the sea-soaked wire on the rod from
the start?"

Borsos's eyes were green as the wire he'd wrapped around the rod.
They widened slightly now. "You're *not* a fool, are you?" the dowser
said in some surprise. "I didn't have that wire on the rod because I've
been doing lake work, and because, as I said before, they rushed me
out here in a tearing hurry. I didn't have the chance to adjust
everything perfectly."

*And, unless I miss my guess, you were hoping the regular wire would do
well enough.* But Istvan didn't say that out loud. He'd already tried
Borsos's patience once. He might not get by with it twice.

The dowser aimed the forked staff at the Obudan fishing boats
once more. He nodded, as if he'd proved himself right. Then he
scrawled more notes on the pad. "I did think so," he said, more to
himself than to Istvan. "The correction factor makes enough
difference to be worth taking into account."

"I'm glad you did it, then, sir," Istvan said.

His speaking recalled him to the dowser's mind. "Magecraft isn't
like carpentry, soldier," Borsos said. "If you don't vary your methods
depending on where you are, you won't get the results you should.
My own view is, the laws of magecraft change a little, too, from one
place to another."

"How could that be?" Istvan asked. "A law is a law, isn't it?"

Borsos was aiming the dowsing rod at yet another little fishing boat, and didn't answer right away. At last, he said, "Carpentry just deals with things. Magecraft deals with forces, and some forces have minds of their own. If you don't keep that in your own mind, you may start out to be a mage, but you won't last long in the craft. Everyone will tell your widow and your clan head how sad it was you had an accident."

"I see," Istvan said again. What he thought he saw was the mage making his work out to be harder and more dangerous than it really was. A carpenter might do something like that, or a blacksmith. Soldiers would do it, too, especially when they were bragging in front of civilians. Istvan knew how deadly dull most of a soldier's life really was.

Farmers, now, farmers never made their work out to be harder than it was. Istvan understood why, too, having grown up on a farm. No matter what a farmer said about his work, he couldn't make it seem harder than it was.

Borsos pointed the rod due west. Seeing no fishing boats in that direction, Istvan asked, "Are you searching out past the horizon, sir?"

"That's right." The dowser's head bobbed up and down, very much as his rod was doing in his hand. "I can feel boats out there – out farther than I can see, I mean – but they all move like the fishing boats I can see, so I don't have to worry about them much. If I felt them heading straight toward this island from out of the west, I'd be shouting my head off."

Istvan pointed to a dragon wheeling high overhead. "They're on watch up there, too," he remarked. His stints with dragons had given him a certain sympathy with – and for – the men who flew them. He wondered whether Borsos had been sent out to Obuda because he was valuable or because some officer back on the mainland had had a brainstorm.

"They're watching up there, too," the dowser agreed. "They have their uses, but I also have mine. They can't see at night, but I can still sense danger then. When winter weather closes down, they won't be able to see so well by daylight, either. I don't need good weather."

"Ah," Istvan said, one syllable that meant, *Maybe he'll be worth having here after all.* Borsos laughed out loud, which embarrassed

Istvan, for he hadn't wanted the translation of that one syllable to be so obvious. Trying to make amends, he remarked, "There's a place up in Sorong – the village, I mean, not the mountain – where the girls are friendly. I'll take you there, if you like."

"Duty first," Borsos said, stern as if he were a true Gyongyosian warrior and not a dowser wearing the stars of rank to give him authority over ordinary soldiers like Istvan. "Duty first. But then . . ."

Pekka scribbled a calculation. With the inexorable logic of mathematics, the next step was plain before she wrote it down. She didn't write it down, not then. Instead, she looked out the window at the snow dancing in the wind. In her mind's eye, she saw not the next step, but where the whole sequence was leading.

"It *does* all fit together," she breathed. "When you get to the bottom of it, the very very bottom of it, all of magic everywhere has the same essence."

She couldn't prove that, not yet. She didn't know if she would ever be able to prove it. Seeing where the mathematics led and getting there were two different things. Even if she did get there, she didn't know for certain what she might do with the knowledge. Leino's magecraft was concrete, definite, practical; if her husband and his colleagues discovered something new, they could quickly apply it.

But Pekka couldn't escape the feeling that, if she ever got down to the bottom of her theoretical sorcery, the yield would be a lot bigger than improved armor for behemoths. Her mouth twisted wryly. She couldn't prove that, either, and everything about it depended on proof.

She abruptly realized her teeth were chattering. That proved something, all right: it proved she was a fool. She'd been so far off in the world of theory, she hadn't noticed she was starting to freeze. She got up, scooped coal out of the scuttle, and fed the stove in the corner of her office.

The room was just getting back to tolerable warmth when someone knocked on the door. Pekka thumped her forehead with the heel of her hand, again recalled to the real world. "Leino's going to clout me!" she said as she leaped to her feet.

Sure enough, it was her husband standing there in the hall. He didn't clout her; that sort of behavior was for Unkerlanters and

Algarvians (though Algarvians were likely to slip on a glove before hitting a woman). He did give her a severe look, which, among Kuusamans, more than sufficed. "Have you forgotten the reception at your sister's tonight?" he demanded.

"I had, aye," Pekka answered, hoping she sounded as embarrassed as she felt. "I hate acting out a cliche: the absent-minded mage. But since you remembered, I'm sure we'll be there in good time. Here, let me get my cloak."

Mollified, Leino grumbled only a little more as they crossed the Kajaani City College campus and took the ley-line caravan to the stop nearest their house. Not enough snow lay on the ground to give the caravan any trouble. The real storms hadn't started roaring in out of the south. Drifts sometimes got as high as the top of a floating caravan car, not the base.

Slogging up the hill to take Uto back from Elimaki, Pekka didn't want to think about snowdrifts. "Powers above be praised, you're here!" Elimaki exclaimed when she and Leino got to the door.

Leino laughed. "I don't need to be a mage to divine that you felt like stuffing our son and heir into the rest crate today, do I?"

"Well, no," Pekka's sister said, adding defensively, "It *is* hard to clean house with a small boy underfoot."

"It's not hard – it's impossible," Pekka said. "Come on, Uto. Let's get you out of here." Elimaki let out a small, involuntary sigh of relief. Pekka rounded on her son. "What *have* you been doing today?"

"Nothing." Uto, as usual, was the picture of innocence. Pekka, as usual, found him unconvincing. So did Leino, but his obvious amusement didn't help instill discipline in the boy.

They took Uto next door, fed him salty venison sausage – one of his favorites – and put him to bed. When he did sleep, he slept like a log. He was a risk to do a great many appalling things, but getting up in the middle of the night and making trouble wasn't one of them. With sorcerous wards in and around the house – commercial ones, Leino's, and her own – and with her husband and herself only a door away, Pekka didn't feel nervous about leaving Uto asleep by himself. If anything went wrong, she and Leino would know, and would be back in seconds. But she didn't expect anything to go wrong. Kuusamans were, on the whole, an orderly, law-abiding folk.

Pekka changed out of the long, drab wool tunic she'd worn to Kajaani City College while Leino was taking off his own shorter tunic and trousers. Being of neither Algarvic nor Kaunian stock, Kuusamans wore what they pleased and what pleased them, and did not turn tunics and kilts and trousers into politics. Pekka put on a long skirt of sueded deerhide and a high-necked white wool tunic heavily embroidered with bright, colorful fantastic animals: a costume out of Kuusamo's past. Leino's nearly matched it, save that his skirt was knee-length and he wore woolen leggings beneath it. They both wore sensible modern boots.

"Let's go," Leino said. Pekka nodded. They wouldn't even be late, or not very. And no one with any social graces showed up on time for a reception.

Elimaki's husband was a short, burly fellow named Olavin. Being one of Kajaani's leading bankers, he earned more by himself than Pekka and Leino did together. He never tried to rub their noses in his gold, though, for which Pekka was duly grateful.

After handclasps and embraces, Olavin said, "I'm very glad you could come tonight."

"We wouldn't miss it," Pekka said loyally.

"It's not as if we have far to come, either," Leino added with a smile.

"No, indeed." Olavin laughed. "But I am particularly glad you could come tonight. I am not certain, you understand, but I have hopes that Prince Joroinen may join us. You should be here for that, if it happens."

"Husband of my sister, you are right." Pekka's eyes sparkled. "And you are truly coming up in the world if you expect one of the Seven Princes to visit your home. No wonder Elimaki wanted to wallop Uto."

"I don't expect it. I hope for it." In some ways, Olavin was as precise as a theoretical sorcerer. "I learned at the bank that he would be in Kajaani for a few days, and took the chance of tendering the invitation. We have met before, he and I, and done some business together, so there is some reasonable chance he will accept."

"I *would* like to meet him," Pekka said.

Leino nodded agreement, adding, "I would like to find out which way Kuusamo is likely to go now that Lagoas has joined the war against Algarve." His chuckle was wry. "Husband of my wife's sister, you need not look alarmed. I don't look for an answer on the spot. If the Seven Princes argue about where they should meet, they will argue about higher things as well."

"Even so." Olavin laughed again. He worked hard at being jolly, perhaps because bankers had a name for being anything but. "As I say, he may be here and he may not. Either way, we will have interesting people here – besides the two of you, I mean – and there is plenty to eat and drink."

"I am not shy," Pekka declared. "I am not the most outgoing person in the world, but I am not shy."

As if to prove it, she marched past her brother-in-law into the parlor of the house he shared with Elimaki. Leino followed in her wake. Pekka got herself a mug of hot spiced ale – Kuusamo was not a land where cold drinks flourished – and a plate of mushrooms stuffed with crab meat. Her husband chose mulled Algarvian wine and seaweed-wrapped boiled shrimp in a mustard sauce.

Some of the people at the reception were kin to Pekka and Elimaki, others to Olavin; some were neighbors; some were bankers; some were merchants and artisans who dealt with the banking firm Olavin served. Talk ranged from raising children to importing wine (Kuusamo's climate did not encourage fine vintages, or even rough ones) to the war with Gyongyos.

"If anyone wants to know what I think," one of Olavin's cousins said, obviously sure everyone wanted to know what he thought, "I think we ought to cut our losses against the Gongs and get ready to pitch into the fight on the mainland of Derlavai."

"On which side?" somebody asked. Pekka thought that a good question. With Lagoas in the war, Kuusamo could jump on her island neighbor's back and regain land lost centuries before. If she did, though, Algarve would likely win the war on the mainland and dominate eastern Derlavai. No one had done that since the days of the Kaunian Empire. Pekka wondered if anyone should.

Olavin's cousin had no doubts. Olavin's cousin, apparently, had no doubts about anything, including his own wisdom. "Why, King Mezentio's, of course," he said. "A man like that doesn't come along every day. We could use someone with that kind of energy, with that kind of vision, right here at home."

Pekka thought of King Swemmel, and of what he had done with – and to – Unkerlant. But before she could mention the efficient monarch, Olavin gave his cousin an even more efficient come-uppance, saying, "I have the great honor to announce the presence of Prince Joroinen, not least among the Seven of Kuusamo." None of the Seven was least, nor most. The arrangement, like Kuusamo itself, endured.

Men bowed from the waist. Like the other women, Pekka went to one knee for a moment. That gesture of respect had an earthy history behind it. Pekka didn't let it offend her. The meaning had changed over the centuries. No one knew better than a theoretical sorcerer that symbols were only what people made of them.

Joroinen said, "Let the thought be taken for the deed for the rest of the evening," which made him sound like a theoretical sorcerer himself. He went on, "One of the longstanding traditions of Kuusamo is that we pay attention to the longstanding traditions of Kuusamo only when it suits us." Pekka blinked, then grinned. Maybe the prince wasn't a theoretical sorcerer. Maybe he was an oracle instead.

Unlike Swemmel or Mezentio or Gainibu, Joroinen did not bother with the outward trappings of royalty. He wore an outfit of warm wool and leather much like Leino's, if rather finer. He mingled with the crowd as if he were a banker or merchant himself. After a couple of minutes, everyone took his presence for granted.

He got hot ale and smoked salmon on flatbread from the refreshments table, then made Pekka's acquaintance by stepping on her foot. "I beg your pardon," he said, as if he were a commoner.

"No harm done, sir," she said, and introduced herself and Leino.

Joroinen's gaze sharpened. He was in his mid-forties, his black hair marked by the first few silver threads. "Ah, Elimaki's sister and her husband," he said, impressing Pekka. "The mages at the city college," he added, impressing her more. Then, instead of impressing her, he astonished her: "I was hoping to meet the two of you here tonight. You're one – or rather, two – of the reasons I accepted Olavin's kind invitation."

"Sir?" Pekka and Leino said together. Leino sounded as surprised as she was.

"Aye." Prince Joroinen nodded. To Leino, he said, "Everyone is pleased and excited at your research. Very good things will come of it, I think, and soon. You have served Kuusamo well; we of the Seven shall not be ungrateful."

"I thank you, sir," Leino said, sounding as if he'd had several mugs of spiced wine, not just one. Pekka set a hand on his arm, proud of what he'd achieved.

Joroinen turned to her, saying, "I also know somewhat of your present work, if less than I might like. I bear you a message from others who know more than I, some of them examining related areas." Pekka raised an eyebrow, waiting. The prince leaned close to her and spoke in a low voice: "For the sake of the safety of the realm, it is strongly suggested that you seek to publish no further findings."

Pekka's other eyebrow flew upwards. "Why ever not?" she demanded. A scholar who could not publish was like a singer forced into a vow of silence.

"For the safety of the realm, I said," Prince Joroinen answered. "I shall say no more, not here, not now. But of this please let me assure you: I do not speak lightly."

Fernao felt trapped in Patras. Fernao *was* trapped in Patras. With Lagoas and Algarve now at war, he would have had trouble leaving Yanina even without King Penda. Yanina inclined strongly toward Algarve. The only other possible course for King Tsavellas would have been to incline strongly toward Unkerlant. He preferred his eastern neighbors to those to the west. Fernao was glad he didn't have to make such an unpleasant choice himself.

He had very little else about which to be glad. Since Shelomith's untimely demise, he'd lived with an eye on every copper. No doubt Shelomith had had friends in Patras who were helping him get Penda out of the palace. But Fernao had met only a couple of them, and Varvakis and Cossos were about as eager to aid him as they would have been to wash a leper's sores.

That didn't mean they weren't aiding him. Varvakis fed him delicacies from his gourmet emporium, not least because Fernao had hinted he would sing a song to Tsavellas's men if the fancy grocer didn't feed him. Blackmail was a language Yaninans understood.

These days, Fernao wore clothes he'd got from Varvakis, too. He consoled himself with the notion that tights were more nearly hose than trousers, but found the Yaninan tunics with their puffy sleeves almost laughably absurd. Local costume didn't go far as disguise, either. His height, his red hair, and his narrow, slanted eyes all made him stand out from the Yaninans, who were generally small, swarthy, and big-nosed.

Nor did he need to be the first-rank mage he was to divine that Varvakis was a great deal less than delighted to see him when he walked into the fellow's shop. "Good day," Fernao said in Yaninan, of which he'd picked up a fair smattering since getting stuck in these parts.

"And to you, good day," Varvakis answered grudgingly. Most places, from what Fernao had seen, learning the local language made the locals like you better. His learning Yaninan hadn't ingratiated him to Varvakis, who growled, "The day would be even better if you weren't here."

"Aye," Fernao said. He dropped back into Algarvian, which he still needed to get complex ideas across: "If you take me to see Cossos one more time, maybe I won't be here much longer after that."

Varvakis glared at him. "Too much to hope for. Better I should take you to see King Tsavellas's bodyguards instead."

Better I should betray you, he meant. Fernao smiled. "Let's go. I'll see them, all right. They'll talk with me. I'll talk with them, too." *Betray me and I betray you.* "Mages can be very hard to kill outright, you know." *I'll make a point of betraying you.*

Could looks have killed, Varvakis would have sorely tested his assertion. Had the fancy grocer kept a stick in his shop, he might have tested it another way. As things were, he snapped, "Ah, very well – once more." He waved a sausagelike finger in Fernao's face. "But only once more, you understand me?"

"I understand you," Fernao said. Varvakis was a great many things, but never unclear.

"You had better," he said now. "Come back tomorrow night. Either I take you to him then, or I tell you when I can take you to him."

"It is good," Fernao said in Yaninan. He wasn't sure whether it was good or not. Varvakis might be setting up an ambush. But Varvakis could have done that several different times, could have and hadn't. And, by now, Fernao had acquired by one means or another some specialized sorcerous gear. He'd lost what he'd brought from Lagoas when Shelimoth got killed. Replacing all of it would have been impossible. Replacing even a small part of it would have been impossible had the Yaninans who sold him this and that realized they were selling him sorcerous paraphernalia. But the art had traveled different roads in Lagoas and Yanina, and the Lagoans had traveled rather farther along theirs.

When Fernao returned to the fancy grocery the next evening, then, he was ready for trouble. But Varvakis, despite mutterings and mumblings his mustache muffled, led him to the palace. By then, Fernao had given up on expecting any Yaninan to do anything without grumbling. As soon as Varvakis saw Fernao and Cossos clasp hands, he departed. "I do not know what you do here," he said. "I do not wish to know what you do here."

Cossos studied Fernao with no great friendliness. "I do not know that we will do anything here," the palace steward said. "I cannot get you in to see Penda: my own head would answer for it. Things have tightened up. And with your kingdom at war with Algarve . . ." He shook his head. "Why don't you just go away?"

"But if I went away, think of all the bribes you would lose," Fernao answered mildly. Cossos scowled. Bribery was a way of life in Yanina. Talking about it, though, was very bad form.

Fernao did not care. Now he mumbled to himself, at the same time clutching a dried dormouse's tail he carried in a tunic pocket. Cossos might have taken the mumble for Lagoan. It wasn't. It was classical Kaunian, a tongue less widely studied in Yanina than in many other kingdoms. The spell was ancient, too: the primitive ancestor of the ones on which rest crates and much of modern medicine depended.

As a dormouse falls asleep for the winter, so Cossos fell asleep now. But it was not a natural sleep. He did not breathe. His heart barely beat. Had he been battling a soldier of the Kaunian Empire, he would have been killed without knowing he was dead. As things were, he merely toppled over. Fernao left the chamber where they'd been talking and hurried toward the wing of the palace in which King Penda was imprisoned.

He walked quickly, confidently. He had reason for his confidence. The servitors and nobles he passed saw him, aye. One or two, those of uncommon cleverness and strong will, even turned to look after him, perhaps to start to speak. Then they, like the rest, forgot about him and went on with their business. He smiled a small, slow smile. Among the Yaninans, as among most peoples, wormwood was a flavoring, and easy enough to obtain. The Valmierans brewed a nasty brandy with it; Varvakis stocked the stuff. But the Yaninans did not use it in sorcery. Lagoans did, not least for spells of temporary oblivion.

Had Fernao passed a mage, the spell would not have sufficed. He assumed Penda's quarters were sorcerously as well as physically watched and warded. He touched the dormouse tail again. This was a different spell, one only a first-rank Lagoan mage was likely to use (although Fernao did hope Tsavellas relied on native Yaninan wizards; an expert from Algarve might have recognized and countered the sorcery).

People around him slowed down, as if they were dormice settling in for a long winter's nap. That was an illusion, an inversion of the law of similarity. In fact, he had sped up. It was not a magic to use without great need; under it, he aged twice as fast as usual. But he passed out of the ken of those around him.

He started casting about for Penda like a hound seeking a fox's scent. The trail was obscure, even though he moved above and beyond, so to speak, the ordinary plane of reality. Maybe Yaninan mages weren't quite the bunglers he had come to reckon them.

But Penda's trace was harder to hide than an ordinary man's would have been. Fernao set his thumb on the obverse of a Forthwegian silver bit he carried with his other specialized sorcerous gear. The coin bore Penda's tough, blunt profile. Both the law of similarity and, at several removes, the law of contagion linked it to the Forthwegian king.

Fernao found him in a bedchamber. He lay asleep beside a Yaninan woman; his captivity, evidently, was not of the most onerous. Fernao tapped him on the shoulder. At the tap, the Forthwegian king not only woke but also sped to Fernao's level of living. He had less time to spare than the mage; gray filled his beard. No help for it, though, not now.

"Your Majesty, I have come to get you away from here," Fernao said in Forthwegian.

"Whither shall we go?" Penda did not seem to care what the answer was, for he sprang naked from the bed and threw on the first clothes he found. "So long as it be not Cottbus or Trapani, I am with you."

"By no means," Fernao said. "I aim to bring you to Setubal."

"It is good." Now the king of Forthweg did hesitate. "Or rather, it may be good. How do I know I can trust you? I expected to be rescued ere this. Whence came the long delay?"

"How do you know you can trust me? You don't," Fernao replied. "If you would rather, I will remove this spell from you and you can go back to bed. And you might have been rescued sooner, your Majesty, had the fellow with whom I came from Lagoas not got himself slightly murdered. He had the connections in Patras. I've had to make mine. And so – will you come, or will you not come?"

"I am answered," Penda said. "I am answered, and I shall come." He eyed Fernao from under lowered lids. "And I would have known you for a Lagoan not by your looks, not by your accent, but by your studied lack of respect for those set above you."

"Your Majesty, you are not set above me; you are set above Forthweg," Fernao answered evenly, refraining from pointing out that, at the moment, Algarve and Unkerlant were set above Forthweg. "And if you will come, you had better come. This spell requires much sorcerous energy. Were we not so close to a power point, I could not use it. Even now, it will not hold long, not for two."

Penda, for a wonder, argued no further. He followed Fernao out of the bedchamber without a glance back at the woman with whom he'd been sleeping. That told Fernao something he hadn't known but had suspected about royalty. It made him a little sad. He wondered if the woman would be sad when she woke, sad or just relieved. He knew what he would guess.

As soon as King Penda and he were out of the wing of the palace in which Penda had been held, he relaxed the spell that seemed to slow the rest of the world to the pace of a sleepy dormouse. He sighed with relief of his own; had he not let go of that spell, it would soon have let go of him, with results likely to be unpleasant. The forget-fulness spell with the wormwood he retained. It cost him much less wear and tear than the other – and, had he dropped it, he and Penda would have been captured at once. He was opposed to that.

More Yaninans looked back over their shoulders at Penda and him than had turned back when he walked the corridors alone; spread to cover two men, the magic was a little less effective. But it held. The palace servitors scratched their heads, shrugged shrugs even the melodramatic Algarvians might have envied, and went back to whatever they were doing.

Once out of the palace, Penda peered this way and that, then nodded in slow wonder. "I had almost forgotten there were wider vistas than rooms and hallways," he remarked.

"Well, your Majesty, if you want to keep on enjoying them, you'd better get moving," Fernao said, setting a brisk pace away from the palace and into Patras.

King Penda matched him stride for stride. "Tell me now, sir mage," the fugitive Forthwegian monarch said, "how you purpose spiriting me out of Yanina and into Lagoas, where I may hope to breathe free even if in exile.

Fernao wished Penda had not picked this moment to ask that question. He gave it the only answer he could: "Your Majesty, right now I haven't the faintest idea."

Behind a Zuwayzi soldier carrying a spear point downward in token of the truce now in force between his army and that of Unkerlant, Hajjaj advanced across battered, broken ground toward the Unkerlanter lines. Both the soldier and he wore wide-brimmed hats and long mantles, not just to salve Unkerlanter sensibilities but also to ward off the rain that leaked from a dirty-gray sky.

An Unkerlanter soldier in rock-gray hooded cape and tunic came forward to meet them. He too carried a spear with its point aimed at the ground. To Hajjaj's surprise, the fellow spoke Zuwayzi: "Your Excellency, you come with me," he said, his speech slow but clear. "I take you to Marshal Rathar."

He seemed stuck in the present indicative. Hajjaj didn't mind. Hearing his own language from the Unkerlanter was more courtesy than his kingdom had got from King Swemmel's since the war began. "I will come with you," Hajjaj said.

Rathar waited less than a blaze behind the forwardmost Unkerlanter positions. As his reputation said he would, he looked solid and steady. After bows and what were, by Unkerlanter standards, polite, leisurely greetings, he spoke in his own tongue: "I am sorry, but I do not know Zuwayzi. Do you speak Unkerlanter?"

"Only a few words," Hajjaj answered in that language. He shifted speeches: "I know Algarvian well enough, and I have heard you also do. Is this so?"

"Aye, it is," Rathar answered in Algarvian. He was indeed fluent in that speech, continuing, "I wish to congratulate you on the brave resistance you Zuwayzin have offered to the armies under my command."

"It was not enough." Hajjaj had been sure from the beginning of the war that it would not be enough, though the Unkerlanters' blunders had raised even his almost unraisable hopes once or twice. "Now, Marshal, I have come at the bidding of King Shazli to inquire of you what Unkerlant's terms will be for converting this truce into a peace."

Rathar looked astonished. "Your Excellency, I have no authority to treat with you in this matter. It took all the authority I had to create the present truce, and even then I had to confirm it with my sovereign. If you seek peace, I must send you to Cottbus, for only there will you obtain it."

Hajjaj sighed. He had hoped for better, but had not expected it. "If it must be so, so it must be," he said. "Let me go back to my side of the truce line, that I may use a crystal there to let King Shazli know what you require. I shall return here, I hope, within an hour's time."

"Very well," Rathar said. "A cart will be waiting to take you south to the closest functioning caravan. Efficiency. In aid of which, my compliments to your soldiers on the highly professional way in which they sabotaged the local ley lines. They made our campaign much more difficult than we expected."

"It was not enough," the Zuwayzi foreign minister repeated. Rathar struck him as being as efficient as King Swemmel wanted to make everyone in his kingdom. Hajjaj found efficient Unkerlanters even more alarming than the usual sort.

On returning to his own side of the truce line, he had a crystallomancer link him to his sovereign up in Bishah. Shazli's image, tiny and perfect and unhappy, stared at him out of the crystal. "Go where you must go. Do what you must do. Save what you can," the king said. "If war resumes, we can still hurt the Unkerlanters, but, my generals warn me, we cannot be certain even of holding them out of Bishah. Therefore, war must not resume."

"Even so, your Majesty," Hajjaj said. He remembered the days when Zuwayza was an Unkerlanter province. Shazli, who'd been a child then, really didn't. He thought an Unkerlanter conquest would be dreadful. Hajjaj knew it would.

As Rathar had promised, a carriage was waiting. It fought its way along a muddy track and over a wooden bridge laid across the roaring torrent now filling the Wadi Uqeiqa. Even with the rain beating down, the stench of death was everywhere. Hajjaj recalled it from the Six Years' War and the chaos afterwards. He would have been just as well pleased – better than just as well pleased – not to have his memory jogged. The Zuwayzin had indeed fought hard. Would they end up any better off than if they had not fought at all?

At last, after what seemed forever, the carriage reached the ley-line caravan, and Hajjaj seemed to return from the distant past to the present – or, at least, to the not too distant past, for the caravan cars had plainly seen better decades. An Unkerlanter in the lead car spoke to Hajjaj in Algarvian: "I am Zaban, from our foreign ministry. You will be in my charge until you return to Bishah." He did not say *to* *Zuwayza*; Zuwayza might not be a kingdom on Hajjaj's return. Zaban went on, "I see you are wearing nothing warm. Fortunately, I can supply your needs. Efficiency."

"I thank you, Zaban." Hajjaj spoke crisply, not with the flowery politeness that would have been automatic were he speaking Zuwayzi. In their arrogance, Unkerlanters took that politeness as weakness and a sign of submission. He was weak and would have to submit, but he did not have to advertise it.

He climbed up into the wagon. The caravan sat where it was for most of another hour before starting to move. "Efficiency," Hajjaj remarked to Zaban. The official from the foreign ministry gave him a dirty look, but said nothing. That suited Hajjaj fine.

As he traveled south, he found himself moving into winter. The caravan wagon boasted a coal-fired stove. It had been burning even down in Zuwayza, which struck Hajjaj as a typical piece of Unkerlanter "efficiency." By the middle of the night, though, he was glad of the warmth. Snow had started to dapple the ground before darkness fell. By the time day returned, white blanketed the rolling Unkerlanter prairie. The caravan stirred up the snow as it glided above the ground, making an icy wake that had Hajjaj thinking wistfully of ships on the warm ocean.

He had traveled down to Cottbus before, but not in a good many years and never in winter. Somehow, the snow only made the plains of Unkerlant seem more immense than they did in good weather. Looking out the dirty windows of his caravan car, Hajjaj thought he could see to the edge of the world, or even a little over the edge.

Every so often, the caravan would glide past or through a village or town. However big the place might be, it seemed tiny when set against the vastness of the plain. And when it was gone, it was gone as if it had never been, as if the flatlands had swallowed it up when Hajjaj turned his head for a moment. Even the woods that grew more frequent as the caravan got farther south felt like interlopers on the endless plain.

The caravan reached Cottbus in the late afternoon, a little more than a day after leaving Unkerlanter-occupied southern Zuwayza. The Unkerlanter capital sat at the junction of Cottbus and Isartal Rivers. Both had ice floating on them, which chilled Hajjaj's blood. Zaban took it in stride, saying, "The season is early yet. They haven't frozen over from bank to bank." The Zuwayzi foreign minister shivered at the mere idea.

He had something like a revelation as a carriage took him from the caravan station to his lodging. He needed it, too, for cold struck at his nose and ears – almost all the flesh he exposed to it – like a viper. "You built your roofs so steep here to let the snow slide off them!" he exclaimed.

"Well, of course," Zaban replied, giving him an odd look. But it wasn't *of course* to Hajjaj, any more than making sure you drank plenty of water was *of course* to Unkerlanters in Bishah.

King Swemmel chose to put Hajjaj up in a hostel near his palace. The rooms were large enough to suit him, though by Zuwayzi standards very indifferently clean. The bed boasted heavy wool blankets and fur coverlets; a stove sat in a corner of the bedroom. Hajjaj heartily approved of all that, and of the enormous hot bowl of beef-and-barley soup the servants fetched him. He thought – he hoped – he wouldn't freeze to death before morning after all.

Nor did he. Another servant brought in an enormous omelette – eggs and ham and sausage and onions and cheese – for his breakfast.

Eating such a thing down in Bishah, he might have keeled over on the spot. In Cottbus's ghastly climate, he gobbled up every crumb and wished for more.

As soon as he'd finished eating and robed and caped himself against winter, Zaban took him downstairs for the journey to the palace. He traveled in an enclosed carriage, for which he was thankful. He peered out through foggy windows at Unkerlanters taking the cold in stride. Some of them paused to look back at him, and at his carriage. Most went about their business. People didn't stop to greet one another and chat, as they would have on the streets of Bishah. That had nothing to do with the cold, as at first he thought it might. Unkerlanters simply seemed less outgoing than his own folk.

It was decently warm inside the palace. Before he could go in to meet with Swemmel, the bodyguards began to feel him up as if he were a ripe maiden, not a skinny old man. "Tell them to wait," he said to Zaban, who was enduring the same sort of search. Hajjaj got out of his clothes and stood unconcernedly naked while the guards, when they weren't gaping at him, went through the garments till they were satisfied. Then he dressed again and accompanied Zaban into King Swemmel's audience chamber.

Zaban prostrated himself before his sovereign. Hajjaj bowed low, as he would have done with King Shazli. King Swemmel spoke in Unkerlanter. Hajjaj followed fairly well, but waited to respond till Zaban translated his words into Algarvian: "You are insolent. All Zuwayzin are insolent, we think."

"We have our own opinion of Unkerlanters," Hajjaj replied. He intended to yield as little as he could, here or anywhere else. "Our opinion is lower now that Unkerlant has broken the Treaty of Bludenz."

"Kyot made that treaty," Swemmel said. His eyes bored into Hajjaj. "Kyot is dead, slowly dead, horribly dead. Less than he deserved. And Zuwayza is beaten. Would you be here, were Zuwayza less than beaten?"

He might well have been mad. Mad or not, he was right. Hajjaj did his best not to acknowledge it, saying, "We have hurt you. If you press us too hard, we can hurt you more, much more. Your ultimatum was too harsh. If your demands now are too harsh, we will go on fighting. You may, perhaps, eventually gain all of what you want, but you will pay an enormous price for it. Would you not rather settle for a bit less, knowing you do not have to pay so much?"

That was sensible, rational, reasonable. Glancing at King Swemmel, Hajjaj realized with a shiver that none of those words was apt to apply to him. Swemmel's eyes seemed made of obsidian, with the thinnest layer of glittering Unkerlanter ice above. The king said. "We do not care what we pay. We want what is ours."

I will not give way to despair, Hajjaj thought, and then wondered why. He started to form another polite, diplomatic reply. He rejected the words before they passed his lips. Whatever Swemmel responded to, it was not polite diplomacy. Hajjaj tried a different tack: "Your Majesty, it is even so with us of Zuwayza. Were it not, why would we have risen against Unkerlant so often, even with little hope of victory?"

He watched Swemmel carefully. The king's eyes narrowed, then widened. The ice, or some of it, melted. The hard, shiny stone beneath remained. But Hajjaj had got through to him, at least to some degree, for he said, "Aye, you are a stubborn folk," and said it in the tones of a man doling out a grudging compliment. He stabbed out a forefinger at Hajjaj. "You may be stubborn, but you *are* beaten. Else you yourself would not be here."

"We are beaten." The Zuwayzi foreign minister conceded what he could hardly deny. "We are beaten badly enough to have to yield you some of what you demand of us. We are not beaten so badly as to have to yield it all."

"Shall we treat Shazli the pretender as we treated Kyot the usurper?" Swemmel asked.

"Zuwayzi lords know how to die," Hajjaj said, as steadily as he could. Again, he gave the king the directness Swemmel did not look to get from his own subjects: "Unkerlant has given them much practice in the art."

Zaban looked at him with a face the color of whey. No, no one in Cottbus spoke to King Swemmel so. Hajjaj gestured harshly. The man from the Unkerlanter foreign ministry did translate accurately; Hajjaj knew enough of his language to be sure of that. He waited on Swemmel. The Unkerlanter king might want to find out how well *he* died. That violated every law of diplomacy, but King Swemmel was a law unto himself.

Swemmel hunched forward on his high seat, like a hawk about to spring into the air from a falconer's wrist. In a voice harsh as a hawk's, he said, "We shall dicker." Hajjaj breathed again, but tried not to let the king of Unkerlant see him do it.

Krasta was angry. Krasta was frequently angry, but most often at people she knew, not at whole kingdoms. Now her outrage stretched far enough to encompass all of Valmiera.

"Will you look at this, Bauska?" She waved the news sheet in the serving woman's face. "Will you *look* at it?"

"I see it, milady." Bauska kept as much of herself from her voice as she could, leaving Krasta next to nothing to seize on.

But Krasta needed next to nothing. "Unkerlant has won another war," she snarled. "The western barbarians have won two wars now, against Forthweg and against this Zuwayza place, wherever it may be. The Unkerlanters have won two wars. Has Valmiera won even one war? *Has* it, Bauska?"

"No, milady," the servant answered. But then, no doubt rashly, she added, "Unkerlant hasn't fought the Algarvians, though."

Krasta tossed her head. A golden curl escaped the pins Bauska had put in her hair earlier in the morning and slid under her nose, as if she'd suddenly grown a mustache. Sniffing, she brushed it aside. Sniffing in a different way, she said, "The Algarvians are barbarians, too. They should have stayed in their forests a long time ago, and not come out to bother civilized people." By that, of course, she meant people of Kaunian blood, her notion of civilization extending no further.

"No doubt, milady," Bauska said. Having got away with one additional comment, she tried another: "They may be barbarians, but they're monstrously good at war."

"We've beaten them before," Krasta said. "They didn't win the Six Years' War, did they? Of course they didn't. Valmiera won the Six Years' War. Oh, we had a little help from Jelgava, but *we* won it." Jelgavans were of Kaunian stock, too; she acknowledged their existence. Sibian? Lagoans? Unkerlanters? They'd fought side by side with Valmiera, too. As far as she was concerned, they might as well have stayed out of the war. How it would have ended had they stayed out never entered her mind.

"Powers above grant we win this war, too, milady," Bauska said. "And powers above grant that your brother comes home safe from it."

"Aye," Krasta said; the serving woman had hit on a way of mollifying her, at least for the moment. "As of his last letter, Skarnu was well." She paused. She might have let it go there, but she still held the news sheet. Seeing it rekindled her anger. "Skarnu is well, but we have not broken through into Algarve. How can we hope to win this miserable, inconvenient war if we can't break through?" Her voice rose to a shout once more.

"Milady, I know not. How can I know? I am a maidservant, not a warrior." Bauska bowed her head. In a barely audible voice, she asked, "Have I your leave to go, milady?"

"Oh, very well," Krasta said in some annoyance; she usually got more sport out of baiting her servant. Bauska retreated much faster than the Algarvian army had fallen back before Valmiera's foes. But she did not retreat fast enough. Krasta snapped her fingers. "No. Wait."

"Milady?" Bauska froze near the doorway. Her voice might have been a fragment of winter wind let loose within the mansion.

"Come here. I have a question for you," Krasta said. The serving woman came much more slowly than she had gone. Krasta went on, "I've been meaning to ask you this for some little while now, but it keeps slipping my mind."

"What is it, milady?" Bauska still looked alarmed, which was good, and also curious, which was acceptable.

"When you are with your sweetheart, do you ever pleasure him by taking his member in your mouth?" Krasta asked her question as matter-of-factly as she would have asked a farmer about stock-breeding. In her mind, the differences between livestock and servants were not large.

Bauska's fair skin flushed bright red. She coughed and turned away, but she did not dare flee the chamber again, not unless Krasta told her she might. When at last she spoke, it was in a prim near-whisper: "Milady, I have not got a sweetheart, so I do not know what to say to you."

Krasta laughed in her face, knowing a servant's evasions when she heard them. "Curse it, have you ever pleasured a man so?" she demanded.

Bauska got even redder. Her eyes down on the floor, she said, "Aye." Krasta had to watch the way her lips shaped the word, for she could not hear it. Then, more loudly, the servant repeated, "Have I your leave to go?"

"No, not yet." Krasta's voice was sharp. Valnu, curse him – curse him horribly – had not lied to her after all. She wanted to go clean her teeth yet again. Instead, probing the depths of commoners' iniquity, she asked, "And your friends – I suppose servants have friends – do they do likewise?"

"Aye, milady, or I know of some who do, or who have," Bauska answered, still looking down at the intricate pattern of birds and flowers on the thick, handwoven carpet beneath her feet.

Krasta made an angry noise, back deep in her throat. Like most of her class, she'd always assumed commoners just fornicated, as animals did, and that other, related, delights were beyond them. Discovering she'd been wrong disgusted her. She wanted to share as little with those below her as she could.

Something else occurred to her. "And your sweethearts – when you have them – do they pleasure your secret places with their tongues?"

"Aye, milady," Bauska answered in a resigned whisper. But then, in what seemed a sudden access of spirit, she added, "Not likely we'd do for them if they didn't do for us, is it? Fair's fair."

Fairness was something about which Krasta rarely had to worry, especially when dealing with servants. Her elegantly sculpted nostrils flared in exasperation. "Go on, get out of here," she said. "What *are* you doing, hanging about like this?"

Bauska left. Bauska, in fact, all but flew. Krasta hardly noticed; having dismissed the serving woman, she forgot about her till she might need her again. She thought about going into Priekule for a tour of the shops, but in the end decided not to. Instead, she had her coachman drive her to the royal palace. If she was going to complain about the way the war against Algarve was going, venting her spleen at a servant would do no good. She wanted to talk to a soldier.

Finding the war ministry took her a while. She couldn't simply bark demands in the palace, as she could on her estate; too many of the people going through the corridors were nobles, and they were often hard to tell from servitors in fancy dress. To avoid giving offense, Krasta had to ask polite questions, an art for which she had little inclination and scant practice.

At last, she found herself standing in front of a desk behind which sat a rather handsome officer; a placard identified him as Erglyu. "Please sit, milady," he said, waving her to a chair. "Will you drink tea? I regret that I am not permitted to offer you anything stronger."

She let him pour her a cup; she would let anyone serve her at any time, reckoning it no less than her due. As she sipped, she asked, "And what is your rank?"

"I am a captain, milady." Some of Erglyu's smiling urbanity slipped. "You may read as much on the placard there."

"No, no, no," Krasta said impatiently, wondering whether the war ministry wasn't doing a better job against Algarve because it hired idiots. "What is your *rank*, Captain?"

"Ah." Erglyu's face cleared. *Maybe he's not an idiot*, Krasta thought with what passed for charity from her. *Maybe he's only a moron.* The captain went on, "I have the honor to be a marquis, milady."

"Then we are well met, for I am a marchioness." Krasta smiled. Erglyu might be a moron, but he was of her class. She would give him the same courtesy she granted any member of her circle, courtesy a commoner, no matter how clever, would never know. With a vivacious gesture, she said, "I want to tell you, we are going about this war altogether wrong."

Captain Erglyu leaned forward, his face the picture of polite, even fascinated, interest. "Oh, milady, I do so wish you would show me how!" he exclaimed. "All our best generals have been wracking their brains over it for weeks and months, and the results have not been perfectly satisfactory."

"I should say they have not," Krasta said. "What we need to do is strike the redheaded barbarians such a blow, they will flee before us as they did in the ancient days. I can't imagine why we haven't done it yet."

"Neither can I, not when you put it so clearly." Erglyu reached into his desk and pulled out several sheets of paper, a pen, and a squat bottle of ink. "If you would but give the kingdom the benefit of your insight, I am certain all Valmiera will soon hail you as its benefactress and savior." He pointed to a table and chair – both of severely plain make – set against a side wall of his office. "Perhaps you would be kind enough to set forth your strategic plan in as detailed a form as you can, that I may share it with my superiors."

"I will do that." Krasta took the writing tools and went over to the table. Once there, though, she stared down at the first blank leaf with the same angry despair she'd always known in the women's finishing academy. After gnawing on the end of the pen, she wrote, *We need to hit the Algarvians as hard as we can. We need to do it where they do not expect it.*

She started to add something more, then savagely scratched it out. More pen gnawing followed. She sprang to her feet and slapped the piece of paper on to Captain Erglyu's desk. He glanced down at it, then said, "I am certain King Gainibu himself will be grateful to you for what you have done here today."

"Why can't anyone else in the kingdom think clearly?" Krasta demanded. Without waiting for an answer, she headed out toward her carriage. She noticed she'd got ink on one finger. With a snort of annoyance, she rubbed it off.

10.

Leofsig was becoming, if not thrilled about latrine duty, at least resigned to it. It was nasty, smelly work, but no harder than chopping wood or any number of other assignments in the captives' camp. Both his Algarvian captors and his Forthwegian superiors seemed content to make him the token Forthwegian on the largely Kaunian latrine crew.

He made the best of it, or tried. His own Kaunian had grown rusty since his escape from school. When he'd first tried speaking it again, the lean blonds had smiled among themselves and, more often than not, replied in Forthwegian. But he'd persisted. He'd never be mistaken for a Kaunian when he opened his mouth, but these days he was even getting a good notion of how to use the optative mood, which had always baffled him even when his masters drilled it into him with a switch.

Having his cot next to Gutauskas in the barracks helped in getting the Kaunian captives on the latrine crew to accept him. So did his continued enmity with Merwit. If Merwit called him a Kaunian-lover, he wore what was meant for an insult as a badge of pride.

One day, as he was covering over a stinking slit trench, Gutauskas came up to him with a gleam in his blue-gray eyes. "You know, stale piss is a good bleach," the Kaunian said in his own language. Leofsig had not learned the Kaunian word for *piss* in school; latrine duty was educational in all sorts of ways. Gutauskas went on, "Maybe we should dye your hair blond. Do you think you would look like one of us if we did?"

"Oh, indeed – without a doubt," Leofsig answered. He pointed to the stinking slit into which he was shoveling dirt. "And shit" – another word he hadn't picked up in school – "will turn your hair brown. Do you think you would look like a Forthwegian if I flung you in there?"

"It could be," Gutauskas said imperturbably. "We have been known to call Forthwegians dungheels, just as Forthwegians have their own pleasant names for us." He cocked his head to one side, waiting to see how Leofsig would take that.

With a shrug of his broad shoulders, Leofsig said, "Everyone calls his neighbors names. Why, I would bet even the Unkerlanters aren't too efficient" – he had to drop into Forthwegian for that, being unable to come up with the Kaunian word – "to call their neighbors names." He rolled his eyes to show he intended sarcasm.

Gutauskas nodded. "I would bet you are right: you prove it with your own speech, in fact. So tell me, would you sooner dwell in that part of Forthweg occupied by the Algarvian barbarians or the portion occupied by the Unkerlanter barbarians?"

"I would sooner no one occupied Forthweg," Leofsig answered.

"That was not one of the choices offered," Gutauskas said in the quietly mocking way that so often set Forthwegians' teeth on edge.

By then, though, Leofsig had grown used to it. He gave the question serious thought; it was more interesting than what he had been doing. At last, he said, "It is likely easier for your people under the Unkerlanters, for my people under the Algarvians."

"Aye, I think you are right," the Kaunian agreed, "for the Algarvians have us to despise, which keeps them from despising you quite so much." He waited while Leofsig threw a couple of shovels' worth of dirt into the slit trench, then went on, "Perhaps around midnight tonight, you will need to make a call of nature, as I shall."

"Will I?" Leofsig scratched his head. "I knew you Kaunians were an orderly, regular folk, but I didn't realize you were as regular as all that." Gutauskas said nothing, but kept looking at him with head cocked slightly to one side. Leofsig scratched his own head again. In a romance about the Six Years' War, he would have figured out right away what the Kaunian was trying to tell him. At least he'd figured out Gutauskas was trying to tell him something. He said, "Well, who knows? Maybe I will."

Gutauskas still didn't say anything. He went off and started digging a new slit trench. Leofsig went back to covering over the one at which he'd been working. He didn't move any faster than he had to. The Algarvians didn't feed him enough to make him want to move

very fast — and latrine duty wasn't the sort of work that fired a man's
enthusiasm anyhow.

At last, as sunset drew near, he stowed his shovel in the rack and
lined up for the meager supper that made a perfect accompaniment
to his meager breakfast and meager dinner. He got a small slab of
brown bread and a bowl of cabbage-and-turnip soup with a few small
floating bits of salt pork so fatty it might as well have been lard. He
also got a small cup of what the Algarvians insisted was beer. By the
way it tasted, it might have come straight from the latrine trenches.

He drank it anyway. He ate and drank almost anything he even
vaguely suspected of containing nourishment. He'd seen men pop their
own lice into their mouths. He hadn't fallen that far himself, but he
knew he might. All too often, his belly ached like a rotting tooth. He
cherished the hour or so after each meal, when that ache drew back and
waited for a while.

After supper, the captives formed up in front of their barracks hall
for the day's final roll call and count. For a wonder, the Algarvian
guards managed to get the same number twice running, which
satisfied them. Their leader spoke in bad Forthwegian: "You going
in now. You no coming out till morning roll call unless you pissing,
you shitting. You trying any other come-outings . . ." He drew a
finger across his throat. Leofsig wished that finger were the sharp edge
of a knife.

Along with the rest of the men from his barracks, he went inside.
Some of them clumped into little groups to talk. Others diced for
money or, more often, for food. A few wrote letters or read the
handful they'd been allowed to receive. By far the largest number lay
down on their cots to rest or sleep away as much time as their captors
allowed them.

Merwit glared at Leofsig in the dim lanternlight. Leofsig glared
back. They were both too hungry and tired to do anything more than
glare — and neither was eager to go up before the Algarvian
authorities. That would mean half rations for sure, and whatever
other punishments the redheads chose to add. Such delights made
good behavior seem sensible even to Merwit.

The bruiser eventually rolled over and started to snore. Leofsig
wanted to go to sleep, too; every fiber of his being cried out for it. If
he did doze off, he'd miss whatever Gutauskas had in mind for

midnight. If he didn't, he'd be a wreck tomorrow. Which had the greater weight? Not nearly sure he was doing the right thing, he feigned sleep instead of falling headlong into it.

Gutauskas came back to his own cot. He'd been talking in a low voice with the few other Kaunians in the hall, as he usually did before the guards came in and blew out the lanterns. His breathing soon grew slow and regular. Had *he* fallen asleep?

Leofsig watched him out of half-closed eyes that kept wanting to slide all the way shut. No strip of moonlight shone on the barracks floor to let Leofsig gauge the hour even roughly; the moon, nearing new, would not rise till a little before the sun did. *How*, Leofsig wondered resentfully, *is Gutauskas supposed to know when it's midnight, anyway?*

He got angry enough at the Kaunian captive to keep himself a little less sleepy than he might otherwise have been. And at last, at an hour that might have been midnight or might not, Gutauskas rose from his cot and walked toward the barracks door, which was always open – and which, at the moment, let a chilly breeze into the hall.

Heart pounding, Leofsig got to his feet and walked out into the night after Gutauskas. If anyone challenged him, he intended to curse the Kaunian for waking him and making him get up in the middle of the night. But no one did. Yawning, he stumbled toward the latrines.

The one advantage of the cold was that the slit trenches did not stink quite so badly – or maybe it simply numbed Leofsig's prominent nose. That dim shape ahead had to be Gutauskas. Leofsig yawned again, wishing he were back on his hard cot under his thin blanket: a strange wish, when most of the time he would have given anything to get away from the barracks.

Someone – a Forthwegian – came back from the latrine, tugging at his tunic. He grunted at Leofsig as they passed each other in the darkness.

Several men straddled slit trenches. All, by their silhouettes, were Kaunians. A couple exchanged soft comments in their own language: "They're here." "Aye. The last of them."

Gutauskas set a hand on Leofsig's arm. "Come. Come quickly. Come quietly. Ask no questions, not now. Soon enough, you will know."

Naturally, questions flooded into Leofsig's head. When he started to ask the first one, Gutauskas's hand closed tight enough to hurt. Leofsig's mouth stayed closed, too. Gutauskas jerked his chin toward the small knot of Kaunians ahead. Leofsig followed him over to them without another word.

As he came up, one of the Kaunians spoke in quiet Forthwegian: "An advantage to digging trenches is that there is digging, and then there is digging."

A light shone in Leofsig's dark, sleepy mind, bright as if an egg had burst in front of his face. Gutauskas said, "Come. It will be noisome. We could not keep everyone from using this trench. But will you set filth on your feet against the chance for freedom?"

"By the powers above, no!" Leofsig said in the best classical Kaunian he could muster.

"Hmm. As well we do take him, Gutauskas," said the Kaunian who'd spoken a moment before. "Some of them, in truth, can be decent." By *them*, Leofsig realized, he meant *Forthwegians*. He himself was the only non-Kaunian here.

Gutauskas said, "We can all be caught if we stand around here much longer."

By way of answer, the other Kaunian scrambled down into the stinking trench. He yanked at the side – and pulled up a tiny square door covered with dirt and muck. "Go, my friends. Crawl as fast as you may. Crawl on one another's heels. Never stop. There *is* an opening at the other end. Go to it."

One by one, the six or eight men slid down into the trench and into the mouth of the tunnel. Gutauskas gave Leofsig a tiny shove. "Go before me," he murmured. Leofsig got into the slit trench as quietly as he could. The muck at the bottom tried to suck the sandals off his feet. He scrambled through the doorway. It was barely wide enough for his broad Forthwegian shoulders.

Outside, it had been dark. In the tunnel – shored up here and there with boards that caught Leofsig in the head when he raised up too far, but mostly dirt, like a grave – it was black beyond black. The air felt dead. He crawled on, crawled for his life. A tiny thump came from behind him as the last Kaunian let the door fall. With luck, it would be filthy enough to keep the Algarvians from noticing it for a while.

Leofsig crawled. Sometimes he touched the feet of the man in front of him. Sometimes Gutauskas bumped his. How far had he come? How far to go? He had no idea. He kept crawling. He aimed to keep crawling till he came out, even if that were in Gyongyos or Lagoas. Blackness and dirt and shoving one knee past the other.

Fresh air, live air, ahead. He smelled it, as a hound would. The tunnel rose a little under his shins. A Kaunian pulled him out. The night looked like a hazy day to his light-starved eyes. Gutauskas came up behind him, and then the last man. "Now," Gutauskas said in quiet but businesslike tones, "we all piss."

"Why?" Leofsig asked — at last, a question he could put.

One of the other Kaunians answered, mirth in his voice: "To put running water between us and the Algarvians' searching sorceries."

Hot piss splashed out of them, there near the mouth of the tunnel, hidden from the captives' camp by a grove of olive trees. Leofsig laughed, silently but with great joy, as he shook himself. He was filthy and stinking and liable to be recaptured or blazed on sight, but not one bit of that mattered, not now. Now — for the moment — he was free.

Bembo strolled along the streets of Tricarico, swinging his club and doing his best to make people notice him. Like most Algarvian towns, Tricarico was, among other things, a center of display. Even the most outrageously swaggering constable got less notice than he craved.

Still, Bembo would rather have been swaggering along the street than marching and countermarching in the park. He didn't care for the weight of the dummy stick on his shoulder, and he especially didn't care for the way that monster of a sergeant screamed at him and at everybody else in the makeshift militia. If any screaming went on, he wanted to give it, not to be on the receiving end.

He glanced nervously toward the east. The real army, or such part of it as Algarve could spare on this part of the frontier, was still holding the Jelgavans in the foothills of the Bradano Mountains. Bembo couldn't quite figure out how the army was holding them there. The news sheets made it sound like strong sorcery, but no sorcery was *that* strong. He just hoped the regulars could keep doing it. If they couldn't, he would have to try. He relished that notion not at all.

A couple of people started yelling at each other down a side street.

At first, Bembo was inclined to keep on walking. People shouting at one another was nothing out of the ordinary in any Algarvian city. But then he thought that, since he'd had a quiet shift, he ought to find out what was going on there. He could bring the story back to the stationhouse, which would keep Sergeant Pesaro from calling him a lazy son of a whore.

He turned the corner. A crowd had already started to gather around the quarreling pair. "What's going on here?" Bembo said loudly. Several people in the crowd looked his way, saw what he was, and discovered urgent business elsewhere. He chuckled. He'd expected nothing different.

One of the people who'd been doing the yelling was a redheaded woman heading hard toward middle age. Her clothes and her wary eyes didn't say *whore*, not quite, but they did say *slattern*. Facing her was a rather younger man who wore tunic and kilt and spiky waxed mustaches of unimpeachably Algarvian style. But those mustaches and his hair were pale gold, not red or auburn or chestnut.

Uh-oh, Bembo thought. Aloud, he repeated, "What's going on here?"

"This stinking Kaunian was trying to rob me," the slatternly woman shouted. "I bet he's a Jelgavan spy. He looks like a spy to me."

A couple of men behind Bembo growled. The constable's head started to ache, as if he'd poured down too much red wine. The man standing there looking affronted and innocent was undoubtedly of Kaunian blood, as Jelgavans were. That might mean anything, or nothing. His ancestors could have been living in Tricarico for centuries before there were any Algarvians within a couple of hundred miles. But even if they had been, that didn't prove anything, either. Some folk of Kaunian blood were perfectly loyal to King Mezentio. Some still dreamt of the days of the ancient Kaunian Empire.

"What have you got to say for yourself?" Bembo demanded of the blond man. His voice was rough with suspicion, partly because he was a constable, and so was suspicious on general principles, and partly because he'd been reading a lot of the torrid historical romances that had been coming out lately, and so was more suspicious of Kaunians than he had been.

"Why would I try to rob her?" the man asked. "Does she look like she's got anything worth having?" He spoke Algarvian with the accent of someone who'd grown up in the northeastern part of the kingdom – the same accent as Bembo's. *But a spy would be smooth*, the constable thought.

The blond man looked the woman up and down, then rolled his eyes, as any Algarvian who found a woman unattractive and wanted her to know it would have done. She screeched at him. Bembo looked her up and down. She didn't have anything he particularly wanted, though he probably wouldn't have said no if she offered it free of charge.

Wearily, Bembo hauled out his notebook. "Give me your names," he growled. "Don't get cute with 'em, either. We'll have a mage checking. We don't like people who lie to the constabulary." The woman called herself Gabrina. The man said his name was Balozio.

"A likely story," Gabrina sneered. "Probably started out as Balozhu." She twisted it from an Algarvian-sounding name to one that sprang from Jelgava or Valmiera.

"Your father never knew what your name was," Balozio told her: an insult as Algarvian as the day was long.

Gabrina screeched again. Balozio shouted at her. "Shut up!" Bembo yelled, hating them both. He pointed to the woman. "What did he try to rob you of? How did he do it?"

"My belt pouch," she answered, sticking out the hip on which she wore it. She remained unalluring to Bembo.

"Why, you lying slut!" Balozio shouted. She bit her thumb at the blond man. Turning to Bembo, he went on, "All I was trying to do was pat her on the bum."

For a moment, Bembo accepted that. He'd felt up a good many women strolling along the street. But then he stopped thinking like a man and started thinking like a constable. "Now just you wait," he said. "A minute ago, you were telling me this broad didn't have anything you wanted."

"Don't you call me a broad, you tun of lard!" Gabrina yelled at him.

Bembo brandished his club. "For that, you can come along to the station, too. We'll sort it out there."

Balozio and Gabrina both looked appalled. If one ran one way and one the other, Bembo didn't know what he'd do. Calling on people to help was about as likely to get them to help the fugitives as to help him: he knew his countrymen and how they felt about constables only too well. If they'd felt differently, Algarve wouldn't have needed so many constables.

But then the man and woman didn't run. Bembo smacked the club into the palm of his left hand. "Come on," he growled. They came. They came sullenly, but they came.

Before one of them could decide to make a break, Bembo spotted another constable and waved him over. "What's going on?" asked the newcomer, a burly fellow named Oraste.

"Curse me if I know," Bembo told him. "He says he was just letting his hand get happy, you know what I mean? She says he tried to steal her pouch."

Oraste eyed Gabrina. He rocked his hips forward and back; he must have liked what he saw. Gabrina noticed, too, and let her tongue slide along the edge of her lower lip. When Oraste inspected Balozio, he might have been looking at a pile of dog turds on the street. "I've never seen a blondie yet who wouldn't steal whenever he got the chance," he declared.

Balozio turned pale. Since he was already very fair, he ended up looking downright ghostly. "Now see here," he said. "I'm an honest man. I've always been an honest man, and I've always been a loyal man." He was trying to bluster, and not doing a good job of it – he sounded more frightened than arrogant. After a moment, he added, "I can't help the way I look. It's how I was born."

Gabrina contrived to brush against Oraste. "I still say he looks like a Jelgavan spy," she murmured in tones that shouldn't have been heard outside a bedchamber.

Balozio was too upset to notice the byplay. He snarled, "I say you look like a case of the clap on the hoof."

"Shut up, Kaunian," Oraste said in a deadly voice. He might have modeled himself after an Algarvian warrior chief in one of those popular historical romances; Bembo thought he read them, too.

Oraste looked about to lay into Balozio with his club. "Have a care," Bembo muttered behind his hand. "He might be a rich Kaunian." It didn't seem likely, not from the blond man's clothes, but stranger things had happened. Oraste scowled, but desisted.

When they went upstairs and into the station, Sergeant Pesaro set down the plum tart he'd been eating; a couple of flaky crumbs clung to the tuft of hair under his lower lip. "What's all this?" he rumbled.

Everyone started speaking . . . shouting . . . screaming at once, with increasingly frantic gesticulations to accompany the increasingly loud talk. Quite suddenly, Balozio ended up on the floor. Bembo didn't see how it happened; he'd been nose to nose with Gabrina, exchanging uncompliments.

Like most Algarvians, Pesaro was adept at following several different threads at once. "Enough," he said after watching and listening to the show for a while. "Bembo, you take this lug" – he pointed at Balozio – "down to the recording section. If he's tried stealing before, we'll drop him in a cell and charge him. If he hasn't, I guess he can go. Oraste, you handle the wench. Same deal: you find out she tries getting customers in trouble, we jug her. Otherwise, kick her tail back out on the street."

Bembo thought Gabrina would start screeching at Pesaro for implying she had customers. But she was shrewder than that: she sent another smile of invitation toward Oraste, who looked as if he'd like handling her just fine. Bembo got the idea her records wouldn't be searched so closely as, in a little while, her person would.

Resignedly, Bembo turned to Balozio, who had a bruise on his cheek the constable didn't remember. "Come on, pal, let's find out about you," Bembo said.

Balozio seemed to know his way to the recording station, which Bembo found interesting in a man who'd loudly proclaimed his honesty. The constable leered at Saffa. The sketch artist bit the thumb at him, as Gabrina had at Balozio, but then she winked. Was she teasing him to encourage him, or to drive him mad? Probably to drive him mad.

A bored-looking clerk took Balozio's name and his thumbprint. He mumbled a charm. One of the many file drawers in back of him came open. He nodded to Bembo. "There's a thumbprint in there similar to his, all right." Still bored, he went back and got the file with the thumbprint in it. When he opened it, Bembo recognized one of Saffa's sketches. "Let's see," the clerk said, flipping sheets. "Fine for cheating a courtesan of her fee, petty theft, petty theft again, charged with stealing a pouch, but that wasn't proved."

"Of course it wasn't proved," Balozio exclaimed. "I didn't do it." He spread his hands in despairing appeal. "I'm a blond, and they still couldn't convict me. I must have been innocent, right?"

"It's close enough," Bembo said to the clerk. "Thanks. We'll pack him away for a while. Getting a Kaunian off the streets sounds good to me."

"I don't even *speak* Kaunian!" Balozio said.

The clerk ignored him, except to put his file back in its proper drawer. Bembo took Balozio by the arm. "Come on, pal. Come quiet, and you'll just get packed away. If you don't—" Head hanging miserably, Balozio went with him.

Cornelu drank the bitter wine of exile. He ate the hard bread of the man cast from his home. The metaphor, he knew, was only a metaphor. The bread the Lagoans fed him was no harder than what he'd been used to eating in Sibiu. Now that Lagoas was at war with Algarve, wine had grown hard to come by, but he found nothing wrong with Lagoan ales and lagers, stouts and porters.

However well they fed him, though, an exile he remained. The Algarvian banner, green and white and red, flew above Tirgoviste and the other cities of Sibiu. King Burebistu was a captive, seized in his own palace before he could flee. And Costache, Cornelu's wife, was a captive, too. By now, he might well have a son or daughter. He did not know. He could not know. He did know Algarvians. They'd be sniffing around Costache like dogs around a bitch in heat.

His hands folded into fists as he sat on his hard cot in one of the barracks halls the Lagoans had given to the forlorn few soldiers and sailors who'd got out of Sibiu: the only free Sibians left. He cursed the Algarvians who occupied his kingdom. He cursed them twice, for being there and for being clever enough to figure out a way to get there that no one in the island kingdom had foreseen.

A Lagoan officer came into the barracks. Cornelu and his fellow exiles looked up from whatever dullnesses occupied them. Cornelu had never been enormously fond of Lagoans. As far as he was concerned, the only reason they'd ever got ahead of Sibiu in trade and war was that they had a larger kingdom.

And now that larger kingdom remained free, while Sibiu lay captive and Algarvian soldiers – or so he feared, at any rate – accosted his wife. That gave him another reason to resent Lagoans: they did not understand what he was going through. Oh, they'd taken him in, they'd fed him, they'd housed him, they'd even promised to use his leviathan and him in the fight against Algarve they now – belatedly – joined. But they did not understand. With gloomy Sibian pride, he was sure of it.

The officer, who wore the grayish green of the Lagoan navy, came toward Cornelu. His stride was easy, loose, confident: the stride of a man whose own king ruled his kingdom and was likely to keep on ruling it. That stride and the thoughtlessly cheerful smile on his face made Cornelu dislike him on sight.

"Good day, Commander, and how are you?" the Lagoan asked in what he no doubt fondly imagined to be Cornelu's language. To Cornelu, it sounded more like Algarvian, and bad Algarvian at that. Blithely oblivious, the fellow went on, "I am Lieutenant Ramalho. I hope you are not busy now?"

Slowly, Cornelu got to his feet. He was glad to find himself a couple of inches taller than Ramalho. "I do not know," he said. "There are, after all, so many important things for me to do right now."

Ramalho laughed a gay laugh, as if Cornelu had been jocular rather than icily sardonic. Maybe the Lagoan gave him the benefit of the doubt, which was a mistake. Maybe, too, Ramalho couldn't tell the difference. Still chuckling, the fellow said, "If you are not too busy, will you come with me?"

"Why? Where will we go?" Cornelu kept his words slow and simple, as if speaking to an idiot child. Even Lagoans who thought they spoke his language made heavy going of it. As for him, he despised their tongue, with its nasal vowels and sneezy consonants, with its hordes of words pillaged from Kaunian, Kuusaman, and every other language under the sun. How even people born speaking it figured out what they were going to say was beyond him.

"Well, you'll know more about that when we get there, won't you?" Ramalho said, cheerful still. "Come along." He turned away, certain Cornelu would follow – as indeed he did. He and his fellow Sibian exiles were tools in the Lagoans' hands – useful tools, to be employed with some care, but tools nonetheless.

He blinked against watery sunshine when he went outside. He also winced at the racket; whatever else the naval half of Setubal harbor was, it was a noisy place. Iron and steel clanged against each other. Sailors and stevedores and teamsters and mages shouted in their incomprehensible language. Every now and then, Cornelu caught a word close enough to its Sibian equivalent for him to recognize it. Those few words made him lonelier than ever; it was as if they were exiles, too.

"Do we go to the leviathan pens?" Cornelu asked. "I should see Eforiel." He did not want the leviathan to think he'd abandoned her. He counted her a friend – almost the only friend he had here – and did not want to worry her or make her sad.

"Not far from them," Ramalho answered. He pointed toward a couple of low, white-painted buildings set a little way back from the pens. "We go there."

"And what do we do there?" Cornelu inquired. All Ramalho did was laugh again, as if at another joke. Cornelu gritted his teeth. He wondered if he should have surrendered to the Algarvians. He'd be with Costache now – if Mezentio's men didn't fling him in a captives' camp. He sighed. He'd done this. He had to live with it.

Gulls, some with white heads, some with dark, rose in angry, skrawking clouds as he and Ramalho drew near. "Miserable beggars," Ramalho said, his tone halfway between annoyance and affection. "If we fed them, they would love us instead of making such a fuss."

Cornelu shrugged. The Lagoans fed him. In their offhand way, they tried to be kind to him. He recognized as much. Even so, he could not love them. Ramalho chattered on. If he had any notion what his companion was thinking, he gave no sign of it.

"Well, here we are," the Lagoan lieutenant said gaily as he led Cornelu up a short wooden staircase and opened the door at the top, standing aside so Cornelu could precede him. Cornelu's shoulders went back and then forward in a silent sigh. He wondered how, if Lagoas had men like this, Sibiu had ever come out on the short end of their naval wars in centuries past.

When he got a look at the men who stood to greet him, he reluctantly stopped wondering. Here, by all appearances, were Lagoan naval officers who might have stepped from the pages of a Sibian romance: arrogant, aye, but with solid ability underlying the arrogance. "Commander Cornelu," one of them said, and then went on in his own language: "You speak Lagoan?"

Cornelu understood the question, and could answer "No" in Lagoan – one of the few polite expressions out of the handful of words and phrases he'd picked up.

"Right." The Lagoan officer spoke good Algarvian, and didn't try to turn it into Sibian, as Ramalho ineptly kept doing. "We can get along in this tongue, I expect." He waited for Cornelu to nod, then continued, "I am Commodore Ribeiro; my colleague here is Captain Ebastiao." After handclasps, the commodore suddenly seemed to remember Ramalho was there. "Run along, Lieutenant," he said, and Ramalho disappeared.

Ebastiao also handled himself well in Algarvian, saying, "That's a fine leviathan you rode here. You Sibs have always been good at getting the most out of those beasts."

"For this I thank you." Cornelu stiffly inclined his head. "And this is why I have been summoned here, this matter of leviathans?" He realized he was speaking Sibian himself, and started to translate into the language the Lagoan officers had shown they knew.

Commodore Ribeiro made a chopping gesture. "Don't bother," he said. "I expect Ebastiao and I can follow your jargon well enough, even if we wouldn't care to try wrapping our tongues around it." He poked the other Lagoan officer in the ribs with an elbow. "Eh, Ebastiao?"

"I expect so, sir," Ebastiao said, nodding. "And if we don't know what the commander is talking about, maybe he doesn't know what he's talking about, either, eh?" He had narrow, slanted eyes; they would have been perfect Kuusaman eyes had they been dark rather than gray. The lid to one of them dipped in an unmistakable wink aimed Cornelu's way.

Cornelu didn't know how to respond to that. The Sibian navy enforced almost as much distance between ranks as did those of Valmiera and Jelgava. Cornelu tried to imagine Commodore Delfinu winking at him. He shook his head. Inconceivable. He stood still, waiting to see what the Lagoans would do next. You couldn't tell ahead of time with Lagoans. That was part of what made them dangerous.

Ebastiao said, "What we have in mind for you, Commander, is working with our leviathan riders, teaching them some of your tricks

– bringing them up to speed generally, you might say – and then commencing patrols out from our shores and as close to Sibiu as proves practicable."

"That's right." Ribeiro nodded. "We don't relish the notion of being taken by surprise, as your kingdom was. We shall have leviathans patrolling as far forward as possible, as Ebastiao told you – we shall do our best to equip the riders with crystals, that they may expeditiously report what they see. We shall have the navy moving along the ley lines. We shall also put yachts to see, to peer in between the lines, so to speak."

"I doubt you will need them," Cornelu said bitterly. "Some tricks work only once. This one worked on us."

"Better to have and not need than to need and not have," Ribeiro replied. "And we shall have long-distance dowsers out along the coasts – as your kingdom should have done, if I may speak frankly without giving offense."

"Looking back, you are right," Cornelu said. "But who could have thought ahead of time that even Algarvians would be mad enough to try such a stunt? Had it failed—" He scowled. It had not failed.

"Let's go back to your place in this," Ebastiao said. Commodore Ribeiro looked at the broad picture. His subordinate dealt with details. In that, the Lagoan navy operated like its Sibian counterpart – no, as its Sibian counterpart had done. Ebastiao went on, "You will train our men up to your standards. You will, as circumstances permit, draft a manual of training techniques so others may use them. And you will – you most assuredly will – patrol and, again as circumstances permit, take the war to the foe in and around Sibian waters. Will that put enough on your plate to keep you hopping?"

"Aye," Cornelu said hastily. He was indeed a tool to the Lagoans. But, at last, they were seeing he could be a sharp one.

Ealstan and Sidroc had a day free from school. They and some of their classmates were kicking a ball around in a park not far from Ealstan's home, along with a few boys – some older, some younger – they'd met there. It wasn't really a game – how could it be, with no goals, no nets, no properly marked pitch? They were just running and shouting and having as good a time as they could in occupied Gromheort.

It had rained the night before. Mud splashed up from under
Ealstan's shoes as he sprinted toward the beat-up old ball. He and his
cousin would come home filthy. His mother would shout at them.
He knew that, somewhere in the back of his mind, and was vaguely
sorry about it – but not enough to stop running.

Here came Sidroc, too, so intent on the ball that he didn't notice
Ealstan. Joy burst through Ealstan like the sun bursting out from
behind clouds. He lowered his shoulder and knocked his cousin
sprawling. Sidroc went rolling through the muck. With a wild shout
of triumph, Ealstan booted the ball toward a little grove of carob
trees. The pack of boys dashed after it.

"Curse you, Ealstan!" Sidroc shouted, spitting mud out of his
mouth. He scrambled to his feet.

"Powers below eat you!" Ealstan called back over his shoulder. "I
got you fair and square."

Three strides later, somebody – he never saw who – got him fair
and square. He was briefly airborne, like a dragon taking wing.
Unlike a dragon taking wing, he didn't stay airborne. He landed on
his belly and skidded along the muddy ground for a good ten feet. His
mother would yell, all right – the front of his tunic, he discovered as
he got up, was nothing but brown and green. It had started out
grayish blue.

He charged after the ball, which had gone its own merry way while
he was down. As he ran, he brushed mud from his tunic – and from
his arms. He was as grimy as some of the ragged men who stood
around watching the boys at their sport.

Before the war, Gromheort had been a quietly prosperous town.
Oh, it had some derelicts; Ealstan's father said there was no place in
the world that didn't have some derelicts, which made sense to
Ealstan. Now, though, with so many homes and shops destroyed,
with so many former soldiers around whom the occupying
authorities hadn't bothered formally capturing, Gromheort seemed
full of men – and some women, too – living as they could, cadging
what they could, sleeping where they could.

One of them, a scrawny fellow with an unkempt beard who wore
a tunic much too small, started to wave when Ealstan ran past. Ealstan
saw him only from the corner of his eye. The ragged men often
begged for coins. If he happened to have any, he sometimes gave

them out. When he did, he thought of Leofsig, who, in the captives' camp, couldn't get even that much help. Today, though, Ealstan had left his belt pouch at home; kicking a ball around was as good a way to lose a pouch as any he could think of offhand.

Then the beggar who'd waved called his name.

Ealstan stopped dead. Sidroc, who'd been about to hit him from the side, skidded past and nearly went down in the mud again. Ealstan didn't even notice his cousin had almost clipped him. He trotted out of the game, staring at the man he'd taken for a derelict.

"Leof—" he began.

"Don't say it," his brother cautioned. He coughed a couple of times before continuing. "I'm not exactly here on official business, you know."

He hadn't been released, then, as Ealstan had guessed. He'd escaped. The pride Ealstan felt for his brother swelled enormously. "How did you —?"

Leofsig cut him off again. "Don't ask stupid questions. And speaking of stupid questions—" He pointed with his chin. Sidroc was coming up.

"Found your own level?" Ealstan's cousin asked with a hard, sour laugh. "Beggars now? It'll probably be Kaunians next."

"I should have wrung your neck years ago," Leofsig said evenly. "Are you trying to show me it's not too late?"

Sidroc started to get angry. Then, far more slowly than Ealstan had, he recognized Leofsig. "I thought you were in a camp," he blurted.

"So did the fornicating redheads," Leofsig said. "And don't talk about Kaunians like that. You drip ignorance."

Sidroc rolled his eyes. "You sound like Ealstan."

"Do I?" Leofsig glanced at his younger brother. "Are you growing up? Maybe you are. Here's hoping, anyhow."

"We've got to get you home," Ealstan said.

"I didn't want to go straight there – didn't know how risky it was." Leofsig's face took on a look of bleak, cold calculation: the look of the hunted. "The Algarvians haven't been paying you any special attention?" He waited for both Ealstan and Sidroc to shake their heads before going on. "All right, we'll try it. Ealstan, you run ahead. Let them know I'm on the way. Sidroc, you come along with me. Keep me company. It's been a while."

Ealstan ran like the wind. He'd never run so hard after a ball, not in all his born days. A couple of Algarvian soldiers gave him fishy looks, but he was young enough to look like someone running for the fun of it, not someone running because he'd just done something nasty to one of their pals. One of the Algarvians shrugged, the other made a mildly disparaging gesture, and they walked on.

He kept running. He pounded on the front door to his house. When his sister unbarred it, alarm filled her face. "Ealstan! You're filthy!" she exclaimed. "And have you gone crazy? Mother and I thought you were a squad of redheads, come to tear the place apart or worse."

"They'd better not," Ealstan panted. All at once, how hard he'd run caught up with him. He pushed past Conberge into the short front hall, closed the door behind him, and barred it again. When his sister began to give him more of a hard time about the way he looked, he said, "Shut up." That made her start to shout; he wasn't supposed to speak to her so. He knew how to make her stop, though: "Leofsig is on the way home. He's coming with Sidroc. He'll be here in about five minutes."

Conberge went on for another couple of words before she really heard that. Then she hugged him, regardless of how grubby he was. "Did the Algarvians let him go?" she asked. "Why didn't they tell us if they let him go?"

"Because they're Algarvians," Ealstan answered. "And because they didn't let him go. But he'll be here any minute, all the same."

His sister understood at once what he was saying. "He'll have to hide, won't he?" Without waiting for an answer, she went on, "You'd better tell Mother. She'll know what to do."

"Of course she will." Ealstan was just young enough to say that without sounding sardonic. "Is she in the kitchen?" Conberge nodded. She stayed by the door, ready to slam it shut the instant Leofsig crossed the threshold.

When Ealstan burst into the kitchen, his mother looked up from the garlic cloves she was mincing. Her look was much more ominous than the one the Algarvian soldiers had turned on him. "What happened to you?" Elfryth demanded in tones that said he had no possible answer.

He found one anyhow: "Leofsig's right behind me. He's coming with Sidroc."

"Powers above!" his mother said softly. Unlike Conberge, she didn't think for an instant that the Algarvians had released Leofsig. In tones suddenly brisk and practical, she went on, "You had better go tell your father. He's casting accounts for Womer – you know, the linen merchant on the Street of the Green Unicorn. Go tell him right now. No – change your tunic first. Then go. You'll look like a proper human being, so you won't frighten Womer half to death."

"Why do I care about frightening Womer?" Ealstan rather liked the idea.

Elfryth looked at him as if he were five years old and none too bright. "We don't want to draw anyone's notice to us, not now, not for anything," she said. "Now go get your father. He'll know which redheads' palms we'll have to grease to stay out of trouble."

By the time Ealstan had on a clean tunic, Conberge was embracing Leofsig in the front hall. She even hugged Sidroc, and her dealings with her cousin were edgy at best. Ealstan squeezed past them all and out the door. As he started away, he was glad to hear someone bar it behind him.

The Street of the Green Unicorn wasn't far from Count Broda's battered keep. Most of Ealstan's father's clients came from the upper crust of Gromheort. Hestan was best at what he did; no wonder he dealt with folk who were best at what they did.

Womer's secretary was a big, scarred man who looked as if he hated everything and everybody. But when Ealstan said whose son he was and added, "My mother's been taken ill, sir," the secretary led him back to the large ledgers his father was poring over with the linen merchant.

Hestan looked up from the books. "Ealstan!" he said. "What are you doing here?"

"Mother's sick, sir," Ealstan said, as he had to Womer's secretary. "She wants you to come home."

What his father's face showed was terror. Ealstan, fortunately, didn't quite recognize it. Hestan sprang to his feet. "Your pardon, sir, I pray you," he said to Womer. "I'll be back as soon as I may."

"Go on, go on." Womer made as if to shove him out the door. "I hope everything turns out well for you."

Once they were on the street, Ealstan said, "Mother's not really ill, sir." Hestan seized his arm. He thought he was about to get a very public thrashing. But, again, he knew the charm to get himself out of it: "My brother's come home."

His father let him go as quickly and abruptly as he'd grabbed him. Hestan whistled softly, then ruffled Ealstan's sweaty hair, something he hadn't done since Ealstan was much smaller. "You did well not to say that in Womer's hearing," he admitted. "How is he?"

"Thin. Hungry. Dirty the way you are when you haven't washed for weeks," Ealstan said, and then, "But he's *here*."

"Aye." Hestan's gaze went far away. "And now I have to figure out how he can stay here without hiding under the bed for the rest of his days." He plucked at his beard. "It shouldn't be too hard. Algarvians are fond of cash. The records will have to read that he's been here with us since before Mezentio's men took the city. I know which redhead sergeant handles those lists."

Pride filled Ealstan's voice: "Mother said you'd be able to handle it." He was proud of both his parents – of his father for knowing what he knew and of his mother for knowing his father would know it.

Hestan set a hand on his shoulder. "If it has to do with money and papers, I can handle it." The hand tightened. "The trick is to use money and papers well enough to keep Algarvian soldiers with sticks from coming after us. I can't do anything about redheads with sticks." He sighed. "The way it worked out, no one in Forthweg could do anything about redheads with sticks."

Pekka enjoyed the ley-line caravan journey up to Yliharma, the capital of Kuusamo. She felt a little guilty about saddling Leino with Uto while she was gone, but he'd made craft-related trips before – and Elimaki was next door to lend a hand with the chaos elemental inadequately disguised as a small boy.

A steward came into the car with a tray of pickled herring, smoked salmon, and meat-stuffed rolls. On Kuusaman caravans, unlike those of, say, mercenary Lagoas, meals came with the fare. Pekka took a roll and some herring. Another steward followed the first with a tray of drinks. Pekka chose hot ale, though a stove at each end of the car kept it comfortably warm.

Outside, snow blanketed the Vaattojarvi Hills, the low range that ran across most of Kuusamo from east to west. North of those hills, the climate was less rugged. When Kajaani had blizzards, Yliharma had snowstorms. When Kajaani had snowstorms, Yliharma had flurries, or else freezing rain. When Kajaani had freezing rain, the rain around Yliharma didn't freeze. When Kajaani had ordinary rain, Yliharma had sunshine . . . every once in a while.

Some of the trees in the forests north of the Vaattojarvi Hills were oaks and maples, bare-branched in winter. The rest were the pines and firs and spruces that dominated the woods farther south. Once, Pekka thought she saw a red fox trotting over the crusted snow, but the caravan swept past before she could be sure.

She got into Yliharma around lamplighting time – an hour that varied through the year and that, in winter, came later in the capital than down in Kajaani, though it did not come very late in any part of Kuusamo. Steep-roofed buildings stood black against the sky. Steep roofs were Kuusamo and Unkerlant's contribution to the world's architecture, as surely as columns were the Kaunian contribution and extravagant detailing the Algarvian.

When the caravan sighed to a stop in the station – which also had a steep roof – Pekka threw on her heavy cloak and a rabbit-fur hat with earflaps. She pulled a pair of carpetbags from the rack above the seats and, thus burdened, walked up the aisle to the door near the forward stove. A square stone block not much different from the ones riders had used to mount horses in the days before stirrups helped her dismount from the car now.

"Mistress Pekka!" Among the folk waiting on the platform to meet and greet arrivals was a man calling her name. She had expected to be met and greeted. But when she saw who was waving to her, her eyes widened. She hadn't expected this man to do the job himself.

"Master Siuntio!" she called. She couldn't wave, not burdened as she was. She couldn't bow, either, which was what she really wanted to do. Siuntio had headed the theoretical-sorcery faculty at the Princely University of Yliharma for more than twenty years. Calling him a first-rank mage was an understatement on the order of calling the heart of the sun warm. Had scholars won prizes like athletes, he would have had a roomful. And he had come to meet her at the station? "Master, you honor me beyond my worth," she said as she came up to him.

"Pekka, I'm going to tell you a sorcerous secret: a lot of the really good ones haven't the faintest notion of what they're worth," Siuntio answered. He was a stooped, graying man only a couple of inches taller than Pekka, who was herself short even by Kuusaman standards. He looked like an apothecary on the point of retirement. Looks deceived, as they often did. He reached out. "Here, give me one of those bags."

Pekka did, the lighter one. She would have felt less strange, less constrained, with one of the Seven Princes carrying her carpetbag. They hadn't earned their rank; they'd just been born into it. Siuntio came honestly by every speck of the acclaim he'd gained through the years.

He seemed an ordinary enough man on the platform, though, using her bag to fend off other people and, once or twice, to help clear a path through them. He cursed when someone trod on his toes, and got cursed when he trod on someone else's. Pekka would have reckoned getting her toes stepped on by the greatest theoretical sorcerer of his generation a privilege, but not everybody shared her knowledge or her point of view.

"Here we are," he said when they reached his carriage. "I'll take you over to the Principality. We've got you booked there. I hope that's all right?" He cocked his head to one side and gave her an anxious look.

"I – think so," Pekka said faintly. When kings and their ministers visited Yliharma, they stayed at the Principality. Kuusamo did not have another hostel to compare to it; every third romance set a banquet scene there – and a spicy scene in one of the famous bedchambers.

"Well, fine, then." Siuntio put the bag he was carrying into the carriage, then took the other one from Pekka and set it alongside. He handed her up on to the seat, unhitched the horse, went around to the other side of the carriage, took up the reins, and began to drive. He could readily have afforded a coachman, but didn't bother. As the carriage started to roll, he said, "You won't be the only one at the Principality, you know. Several others have come in from the provinces. It should be an interesting gathering in the Ahvenanmaa Room tomorrow midmorning, don't you think?"

"Should it?" Pekka plucked up her courage and said, "Master Siuntio, I'm not precisely sure why I was asked up to Yliharma."

"Is that a fact?" Siuntio chuckled, as if she'd said something funny.

Had most people done that, she would have got angry. Siuntio she granted the benefit of the doubt. He went on, "It has to do with the business Prince Joroinen asked you not to put in the journals any more. From the bits and pieces you have published, you may be closer to the bottom of things than any of us."

"That?" Pekka gaped. "I've been doing that for my own amusement, nothing more. I don't know if it will ever have any use."

"As a matter of fact, neither do I," Siuntio said. "But it may, Mistress Pekka; it may. You have seen deeper into it than most, as I told you. Others, though, may have had a wider vision." Before Pekka could say anything to that, Siuntio pulled back on the reins and the horse stopped. "Here we are. You see, it wasn't far. Go right on in. Shall I carry that bag for you?"

"Please don't bother. I can manage." Pekka jumped down and took both carpetbags.

Siuntio beamed. "I'll see you at midmorning, then. The Ahvenanmaa Room, remember." He clucked to the horse and flicked the reins. The carriage rattled off, leaving narrow wheel tracks in the slush on the street.

Still dazed, Pekka went into the Principality. By the way the staff fawned on her, she might have been Swemmel of Unkerlant, with the power and the will to take their heads if they displeased her in the slightest. The chambers to which they led her could not have displeased Swemmel or anyone else; they were about the size of her house, and ever so much more luxuriously appointed. She ordered mutton and kale and parsnip fritters from the menu by the enormous bed. The supper came up by dumbwaiter with almost magical speed. It was almost magically good, too.

And the bed, besides being enormous, was almost magically soft. When Pekka lay down on it, she knew a moment's regret that Leino couldn't have come along to enjoy it with her and help her enjoy it more. But it was only a moment's regret. Though she'd dozed a little on the journey up from Kajaani, travel remained wearing. She yawned once, twice, and then slept soundly till morning.

Her suite had an attached steam room and cold plunge. She was still toweling her hair dry when she sent down a breakfast order. The fat smoked herrings and mashed turnips came up almost before she could blink. By the time she'd got outside them and some hot tea, she felt ready to go looking for the Ahvenanmaa Room.

When she got down to the lobby, she almost bumped into Siuntio. He was talking with another theoretical sorcerer, a man of her own generation named Piilis. After the greetings, Piilis said, "Everyone who's anyone in our business is here today. I just left Master Alkio and Mistress Raahe in the hostel's cafe."

"Master Ilmarinen will be here, too," Siuntio said, "or I'll know the reason why. And that should be the lot of us."

Pekka felt like a herring – not like a smoked one, but like a live one swimming in the company of a pod of leviathans. For some unfathomable reason, they seemed to think her a leviathan, too. Piilis pointed and said, "There go Raahe and Alkio. They must know where our room is."

When Pekka and the other theoretical sorcerers walked into the room, they found Ilmarinen already there. He had close to Siuntio's years, and stood second only to Siuntio in reputation – first, if you listened to him. Raahe and Alkio were both comfortably middle-aged; Raahe, Pekka thought, would have been a beauty in her younger days.

"Let us begin," Siuntio said, and then, "Before the Kaunians came, we of Kuusamo were here. Before the Lagoans came . . ." The age-old ritual soothed Pekka, as it always did. When it was over, Siuntio went on, "All of us, in one way or another, have been seeking a unity below the Two Laws."

Everyone nodded. Gruffly, Ilmarinen said, "Aye, we've been seeking it, all right. And if we find it, we're all liable to end up wishing we hadn't."

Siuntio inclined his head in grave agreement. Raahe said, "But if someone else finds it, we shall all wish we had sought harder." Siuntio also inclined his head to her. So did Ilmarinen, but his agreement seemed sour, not grave.

"All of you, I think, know more of this than I do," Pekka said. "My approach has been purely theoretical, with no thought to consequences."

"Which is, I daresay, why you have made such progress," Siuntio said.

Ilmarinen snorted. "Who could have dreamt such innocence survived in this day and age?" he said. Piilis's laugh was small and dry.

Alkio turned to Pekka. "Consider, Mistress," he said. "The more we've learned of how the world works, the more effective our sorcery has become. If One is the foundation of the Two, will we not be able to attempt things never imagined before?"

"I suppose that may be so," Pekka said. "I had not thought much about it, but I suppose it may be so."

"If we can handle sorcerous energies at a level below the Two," Ilmarinen said roughly, "don't you think we'll be able to make the biggest eggs look like glowworms alongside lightning bolts? I do, curse it, and I wish I didn't."

Pekka had not thought along those lines at all. She wished no one else had, either. But Ilmarinen was right. She saw that at once. Understanding the laws of sorcery did give control over them. And the theoretical sorcerer had been right before that, too. Pekka said, "I hope none of the kingdoms fighting the Derlavaian War is working on this."

"So do we all, my dear," Siuntio said slowly. "We hope Gyongyos is not working on it, either. We hope – but we do not know. That something is absent from the journals does not prove no one is examining it. And, before the war began, there were hints in the literature from Lagoas, from Algarve, and from Gyongyos. How seriously the sorcerers in those lands are following where those hints lead – again, we do not know." His smile was sweet and sad. "I wish we did."

"They must not get ahead of us!" Pekka exclaimed.

"That is why we are met here today," Alkio said. "That is why we will go on meeting. That is why we will go on working, and sharing with one another what we know – eventually sharing it with more mages, I suppose, as we progress, if we progress. But, for now, we are racing blindly. Lagoas and the others may be ahead of us, or they may not have started at all. We just have to keep running."

Heads bobbed up and down around the table in the posh Ahvenanmaa Room. Pekka's agreement was no less emphatic than anyone else's.

Talsu and his regiment were back to slogging. He'd enjoyed Colonel Adomu's brief tenure as regimental commander. The dashing young marquis had gained more ground during that brief tenure than the late Colonel Dzirnavu had managed in a much longer time. But Adomu's dash had cost him, too; he was as dead as Dzirnavu.

Colonel Balozhu, the count who'd replaced Adomu, was not actively vile, as Dzirnavu had been. But he wasn't aggressive, either, as Adomu had been. So far as Talsu could tell, Balozhu wasn't much of anything. He would have made a perfect clerk, keeping track of boots and belts, tunics and trousers. As a regimental commander, he was hardly there at all.

"We are ordered to advance two miles today," he would say at morning parade. "I am sure all of you will do your duty to King Donalitu and to the kingdom." He didn't sound sure. What he sounded was bored. And then he would return to his tent, and it would be up to the captains and sergeants to see to it that the regiment gained the required two miles. And sometimes it would, and sometimes it wouldn't. The Algarvians had officers telling them what to do, too.

One evening, with both of them leaning back against tree trunks and gnawing on bread and smoked beef, Talsu said to Smilsu, "You ever get the feeling that the cursed redheads' officers don't give them as much trouble as ours give us?"

Smilsu looked around to see who else might be listening. Talsu had already done that, and hadn't seen anyone. Maybe Smilsu thought he did, or maybe he felt cautious, for he answered, "I haven't seen Colonel Balozhu giving us any trouble. Powers above, you hardly know he's around."

"*Powers above* is right. That's trouble all by itself, isn't it?" Talsu burst out. Maybe the beer he was drinking with his supper had gone to his head. "He's supposed to be leading us against the enemy, not pretending he's invisible."

"Colonel Adomu led us against the enemy," Smilsu said, still either cautious or contrary. "Are you going to complain about him, too?"

"Not a bit of it," Talsu answered. "I wish we had more officers like him. I think the Algarvians do have more officers like him."

Smilsu took a pull at his own beer. "Well, maybe they do. Vartu would say so, anyhow." He chuckled. "Of course, Vartu was Colonel Dzirnavu's body servant, so he's not in the mood to be fair. But no matter what the redheads have, pal, we're still the ones doing the advancing."

"So we are, but we ought to be doing more of it," Talsu said. "You can see the Algarvians don't have anything more than skeleton forces facing us. We should be in front of Tricarico by now." He shook his head. "That's not right – we should be *in* Tricarico by now, and past it, too."

"I'm so sorry, General Grand Duke Talsu, sir, my lord," Smilsu said with a snort. "I didn't know King Donalitu had set you in command of the fight against Algarve."

"Oh, shut up." Talsu's voice was as sour as the beer he was drinking. "Maybe I will go looking for Vartu. You're no cursed good, not when it comes to making sense you're not." He started to get to his feet.

"Sit tight, sit tight," Smilsu said. "One thing you've got to know is that the redheads have some men who are really good with a stick lurking around here somewhere, waiting to see if they can put a beam through a fellow's ear. You want to give them a clean blaze at you?"

"No, but I don't want to hang around with a fool, either. It might be catching." Despite his harsh words, Talsu didn't get up.

And Smilsu didn't get angry. He spat out a piece of gristle, then said, "And what if you're right? What are we supposed to do then? There's nothing we can do. If the Algarvians don't get us, the dungeons back of the line will. We're stuck in the middle. All we can do is hope we win in spite of ourselves."

"We can hope the Algarvians kill *all* our nobles," Talsu said savagely. "Then we'd be better off."

"We've been round that barn before – and you want to be careful with what you say, and you want to be careful who you say it to." Smilsu kept his own voice very low indeed. "Otherwise, *you* won't be better off, no matter what happens to the rest of us. Do you hear what I'm telling you, my friend?"

"I hear you." Talsu remained furious at the world in general and at the hidebound Jelgavan nobility in particular.

Because Smilsu kept his mouth shut, the Jelgavan nobility did not take their revenge. The world was another matter. Not ten minutes later, a cold, nasty rain started falling. A couple of weeks earlier in the season or a little higher in the foothills and it would have been snow.

Even though Talsu had to make a wet, miserable bed, he didn't loathe the rain so much as he might have. Like dust and smoke, it cut down the range at which beams were effective. He hoped all those clever Algarvian stick men came down with chest fever from staying out in the bad weather. He wouldn't grieve a bit.

The Algarvians, unfortunately, found other ways to be troublesome than with sneaky stick men struggling not to sneeze. They started lobbing eggs in the direction of the Jelgavan encampment. They didn't know exactly where King Donalitu's men were resting, but they had a fair notion – fair enough to get Talsu and the other Jelgavan soldiers out of their blankets and digging holes in the rocky, muddy soil.

He cursed with every shovelful of dirt he flung aside. "Stinking redheads," he muttered. "Won't even let a man get a decent night's sleep." An egg burst close by. The flash illuminated the camp for a moment, as a lightning bolt would have done. The suddenly released energy also picked up earth and stones and flung them about. A good-sized rock hissed past, only a foot or two from Talsu's head. He cursed again and dug harder.

Every so often through the long night, someone would shriek as he was wounded. The redheads weren't tossing eggs in enormous numbers – this wasn't anything like the enormous cataclysms of the Six Years' War, where battlefields became scorched, cratered wastelands. But the eggs the Algarvians tossed did serve their purpose: they hurt a few Jelgavans and kept the rest from getting the sleep they needed. Had Talsu commanded the Algarvian forces, he would have pinned gold stars on the men tossing them.

At last, sullenly, the darkness lifted, though rain kept pouring down. It had put out all the cookfires during the night. Talsu breakfasted on cold, soggy porridge, on cold, greasy – almost slimy – sausage, and on beer that even insistent rain had trouble making any more watery than it already was. He enjoyed it about as much as he'd enjoyed trying to sleep in the wet hole he'd dug for himself.

Colonel Dzirnavu would have thrown a tantrum because the rain interfered with cooking his fancy breakfast. Colonel Adomu would have eaten what his men did and then led them in an attack on the egg-tossers that had harassed them in the night. Talsu didn't know what Colonel Balozhu ate. Balozhu did appear at an hour earlier than

Dzirnavu would have stirred abroad. He carried an umbrella and looked more like a schoolmaster than a noble who commanded a regiment.

"No point trying to move forward in this," Balozhu said after peering in all directions. "You couldn't hope to blaze a man till you got close enough to hit him over the head with your stick. We'll keep scouts out ahead of us, maybe send forward a patrol, but as for the rest, I think we'll sit tight till this finally decides to blow over."

Talsu couldn't argue with any of that, not even to himself – had he proposed to argue with the colonel and count, jumping off a cliff would have put him out of his misery faster and less messily. But, as he squelched off to stand against a tree, he remained vaguely dissatisfied. *Maybe I'm tired*, he thought, unbuttoning his fly. No doubt he was tired. Was he tired enough for his wits to be wandering? If he was, how could he tell?

He put the question to Smilsu when relieving his friend on sentry-go: "Isn't the idea behind this war to stamp the cursed redheads into the dirt?"

"You've got that look in your eye again – or maybe it's the rain." Smilsu thought for a little while, then shrugged. "You really *want* to advance in this stuff?"

"It might catch the Algarvians by surprise," Talsu said. He added what he thought the final convincer. "Colonel Adomu would have done it."

Unconvinced, Smilsu said, "Aye, and look what it got him, too. Dead men don't have a whole lot of fun."

"We advanced more under Adomu than under Dzirnavu and Balozhu put together," Talsu said.

Smilsu sent him a quizzical look. "You're the one who wants the nobles dead, right? So why are you so cursed eager to fight their fight for 'em?"

Talsu hadn't looked at it that way. It was his turn to stop and think. At last, he said, "Just because I can't stand the nobles doesn't mean I love the Algarvians. No good Kaunian should do that."

"Tell it to Dzirnavu – but he got his, didn't he?" Smilsu chuckled, then sobered. "The redheads don't love us, either, not even a little they don't."

"Cursed robbers, cursed thieves, cursed bandits – as if what they love should matter to us." Talsu grimaced. If Algarvians and what they loved and didn't love hadn't mattered to Jelgava, he wouldn't have been out here in the foothills of the Bratanu Mountains with chilly rain dripping down the back of his neck.

Smilsu put it a slightly different way: "If one of those whoresons points his stick your way and blazes you down, it'll matter a lot that he doesn't love you."

"Aye, aye, aye." Talsu waved, yielding the point. "I still wish we were giving the redheads a good kick in the balls." Smilsu started to say something; Talsu shook his head to show he wasn't finished. "If we don't, sooner or later they'll give us one, and you can take that to the bank and turn it into goldpieces."

"They're busy," Smilsu said. "They've got the Sibs and Forthwegians to hold down, they're in a sea fight with Lagoas, and the Valmierans are trying to smash through their lines down south. With all that in their mess kit, they aren't going to be bothering us any time soon."

"There – you've gone and proved my point," Talsu said. "If they can't bother us, what better time to bother them?"

"Ahh, you bother me, so I'm going back to camp." Off Smilsu went, dripping. Talsu stood in the warm glow surrounding any man who has won an argument. Then he wondered, *What good did it do me?* The glow faded.

11.

When Vanai heard the knock on the door, her first thought was that it meant trouble. She'd grown quite good at telling Kaunians from Forthwegians simply by the way they knocked. Kaunians did it as softly as they could to make themselves heard inside, almost as if they were apologizing for causing a disturbance. The Forthwegians of Oyngestun came less often to the house she shared with her grandfather. When they did, they forthrightly announced themselves.

This knock – it came again as Vanai hurried toward the door – did not seem to fall into either the apologetic or the forthright school. What it said was, *Open up or suffer the consequences*, or, perhaps, *Open up and suffer the consequences anyway*.

"What is that dreadful racket?" Brivibas called from his study. "Vanai, do something about it, if you please."

"Aye, my grandfather," Vanai said. Brivibas sensed something out of the ordinary, too, which worried her. He paid as little heed as he could to such mundanities as knocks on the door. No ancient Kaunian author Vanai knew and no modern journal of things anciently Kaunian mentioned them; thus, they might as well not have existed for him.

She opened the door, telling herself she was imagining things and a Forthwegian tradesman would be standing there irritably wondering what took her so long. But the man standing there was no Forthwegian. He was tall and lanky, with a red chin beard and mustaches waxed to needle points. On his head, cocked at a jaunty angle, sat a broad-brimmed hat with a bright pheasant feather sticking up from the band. He wore a short tunic above a pleated kilt, and boots and knee socks. He was, in short, an Algarvian, as Vanai had feared from the first.

She thought about slamming the door in his face, but didn't have the nerve. Besides, she doubted that would do any good. Trying to keep a quaver from her voice, she asked, "What – what do you want?"

He surprised her by sweeping off his hat and bowing almost double, then astonished her by replying in Kaunian rather than the Forthwegian she'd used: "Is this the home of the famous scholar Brivibas?"

Was it a trap? If it was, what could she do about it? The occupiers had to know where Brivibas lived. They didn't need to waste time on politeness, either. Had they wanted her grandfather for dark reasons of their own, they could have broken down the door and sent soldiers storming in. Despite the obvious truth in all that, she couldn't bring herself to say anything more than, "Who wishes to learn?" She kept on speaking Forthwegian.

The Algarvian bowed again. "I have the honor to be Major Spinello. Will you do me the courtesy of announcing me to your – grandfather, is that correct? I wish to seek his wisdom in matters having to do with antiquities in this area." He kept using Kaunian. He spoke it very well, and even used participles correctly. Only his trilled "r"s declared his native language.

Vanai gave up. "Please step into the front hall," she said in her own tongue. "I will tell him you wish to see him."

Spinello rewarded her with another bow. "You are very kind, and very lovely as well." That made her retreat faster than the Forthwegian army ever had. The redhead did keep his hands to himself, but she didn't let him get close enough to do anything else.

Brivibas looked up in some annoyance when she poked her head into the study. "Whoever that was at the door, I hope you sent him away with a flea in his ear," he said. "Drafting an article in Forthwegian is quite difficult enough without distractions."

"My grandfather" – Vanai took a deep breath, and also took a certain amount of pleasure in dropping an egg on Brivibas's head – "my grandfather, an Algarvian major named Spinello would speak with you concerning antiquities around Oyngestun."

Brivibas opened his mouth, then closed it again. He tried once more: "An – Algarvian major?" Each word seemed to require a separate effort. "What am I to do?" he muttered, apparently to himself. But the answer to that, even for a scholar, was only too obvious. He rose from his chair. "I had better see him, hadn't I?"

He followed Vanai back to the hall that led to the street door. Spinello was examining a terra-cotta relief of a cobbler at work hanging there. After bowing to Brivibas and yet again to Vanai, he said, "This is a splendid copy. I've seen the original in the museum at Trapani."

That he should recognize such an obscure piece and recall where the original was displayed flabbergasted Vanai. Her grandfather said only, "A shame it was carried away from its original site."

Spinello wagged a finger at him, like an actor playing an Algarvian on the stage. "The original site for this one was in Unkerlant, if I recall," he said in his excellent Kaunian. "The local barbarians probably would have smashed it when they were drunk."

"Hmm," Brivibas said. Vanai watched him weighing one dislike against another. At last, brusquely, he nodded. "It could be so. And now, if you will, tell me why a major of the occupying army seeks me out."

Spinello bowed again. Watching him made Vanai dizzy. He said, "I am a major, true: I serve my king, and serve him loyally. But I am also an antiquarian and, being an antiquarian, I seek to learn at the feet of the great scholar whose home, I discover, is in the otherwise unimpressive village where I find myself stationed."

Vanai thought he laid it on with a trowel. She looked for her grandfather to send him away, probably with his ears ringing. But Brivibas proved no more immune to flattery than most men. After coughing a couple of times, he said, "In my own small way, I do what I can."

"You are too modest!" Spinello cried. However well he spoke Kaunian, he did so with Algarvian theatricality. "Your studies on late imperial pottery in the Western Kaunian Empire? First-rank! Better than first-rank!" He kissed his fingertips. "And the monograph on the bronze coinage of the usurper Melbardis? Again, a work scholars will use a hundred years from now. Could I ignore the opportunity to seek wisdom from such a man?"

"Ahem!" Brivibas ran a finger inside the neck of his tunic, as if it had suddenly become too tight for comfort. He turned pink. Vanai couldn't remember the last time he'd flushed. He coughed again, then said, "Perhaps we should discuss this in the parlor, rather than standing here in the hall. My granddaughter, would you be good enough to pour wine for the major and me – and for yourself, of course, if you would care for some?"

"Aye, my grandfather," Vanai said tonelessly. She was glad to escape to the kitchen, even though the goblet of wine the Algarvian major would drink meant one goblet fewer that she and Brivibas could share.

When she went back to the parlor, Spinello was knowledgeably praising the ornaments in the chamber. He took his goblet and beamed at Vanai. "And here is the finest ornament of them all!" he said, lifting the wine cup in salute to her.

She was glad she hadn't taken any wine. She had nothing that made her linger in the parlor. As soon as she gave her grandfather his goblet, she could – and did – leave. Her ears felt on fire.

She stayed in the kitchen, soaking peas and beans and chopping an onion for the meager stew that would be supper. She didn't have enough of anything. Since the war ended, she'd given up on the idea of having enough of anything. That she and Brivibas weren't starving she reckoned no small accomplishment.

Her grandfather's voice and Spinello's drifted across the courtyard to her. She could not make out much of what they said, but tone was a different matter. Spinello sounded animated. Spinello, though, was an Algarvian – how else would he sound? She hadn't heard her grandfather so lively in . . . She tried to recall if she'd ever heard him so lively. She had trouble being sure.

After what seemed like forever, Brivibas escorted Spinello out to the street once more. Then her grandfather came to the kitchen. His eyes were wide with wonder. "A civilized Algarvian!" he said. "Who would have imagined such a thing?"

"Who would have imagined such a thing?" Vanai echoed coldly.

Brivibas had the grace to look flustered, but said, "Well, he was, however strange you may find that. He discoursed most learnedly on a great many aspects of classical Kaunian history and literature. He is, as it happens, particularly interested in the history of sorcery, and sought my assistance in pinpointing for him some of the power points the ancient Kaunians utilized in this area. You will perceive at once how closely this marches with my own researches."

"My grandfather, he is an Algarvian." Vanai set the peas and beans and onions over the fire to start cooking.

"My granddaughter, he is a scholar." Brivibas coughed on a note different from the one he'd used when Spinello praised him; no doubt he was remembering the unkind things he'd said about non-Kaunian scholars in the past. "He has shown himself to be really quite an excellent scholar. I have a great deal to teach him." Vanai busied herself with supper. After a while, Brivibas gave up justifying himself and went away. He came back to eat, but the meal passed in gloomy silence.

That, however, did not solve the problem of Major Spinello. The Algarvian returned a couple of days later. He did not come empty-handed, either: he carried a bottle of wine, another bottle full of salted olives, and greasy paper enclosing a couple of pounds of ham cut so thin, each slice was almost transparent.

"I know times are not easy for you," he said. "I hope I can in some small way be of assistance." He laughed. "Call it my tuition fee."

The food was very welcome. Neither Brivibas nor Vanai said how welcome it was. Spinello likely knew. He never showed up without some sort of present after that: dried fruit, a couple of dressed squab, fine olive oil, sugar. Vanai's belly grew quieter than it had been in a long time. Her spirit . . .

She did not go out on to the streets of Oyngestun that often. When she did, though, she discovered she had more to fear from her own folk than from the Algarvian soldiers. Small boys threw mud at her. Kaunian youths her own age spat on her shadow. Blond girls turned their backs on her. Adults simply pretended she did not exist.

In the night, someone painted ALGARVIANS' WHORE on the front of the house she shared with Brivibas. She found a bucket of whitewash and covered over the big red letters the best she could. Her grandfather clucked sadly. "Disgraceful," he said. "That our own folk should not understand the call of scholarship . . ." He shook his head. If the villagers harassed him, too, he'd never spoken a word of it.

"They understand that they're hungry and we're not," Vanai said. "They understand we have an Algarvian visitor every few days and they don't."

"Shall we throw the food away?" Brivibas asked, more than usually tart. Vanai bit her lip, for she had no good answer to that.

And so Major Spinello kept visiting. The rest of the Kaunians of Oyngestun – and some of the Forgiathwens, too – kept ostracizing

Vanai and Brivibas. Brivibas cared more for antiquities than for his
neighbors' opinions. Vanai tried to match his detachment, but found
it hard.

When the weather was fine, as it was more often as winter waned,
Brivibas led Spinello out of Oyngestun to show him some of the
ancient sites nearby. Vanai stayed home as often as she could, but she
couldn't always. Sometimes Spinello asked her to come along. He
always chatted gaily when she did. Sometimes Brivibas did a little
digging at one site or another, and used her as a beast of burden.

Once, east of Oyngestun, he held up a Kaunian potsherd as if he'd
invented it rather than pulling it from between the roots of a weed.
Spinello applauded. Vanai sighed, wishing she were elsewhere. She'd
seen too many sherds to let one more impress her.

Bushes rustled. Vanai turned to look. Neither Brivibas nor Spinello,
lost in antiquarian ecstasies, noticed. Through burgeoning new leaves,
Vanai saw a Forthwegian peering out at her – and at the others. After
a moment, she recognized Ealstan. He'd already recognized her . . .
and Spinello. He pursed his lips, shook his head, and slipped away.

Vanai burst into tears. Her grandfather and the Algarvian major
were most perplexed.

Leudast wore one thin black stripe on each sleeve of his rock-gray
tunic. He had his reward for living through the desert war against
Zuwayza: promotion to corporal. That was the reward the Unkerlanter
military authorities thought they'd conferred on him, at any rate.

In his own view, being transferred back to occupation duty in
western Forthweg counted for far more. He'd seen enough naked
shouting black men to last him the rest of his days. If he missed the
chance to see some naked black women – well, that was a privation
he'd have to endure.

Discussing such matters with Sergeant Magnulf, he said, "The
burnt-skinned wenches are probably ugly, anyway."

Magnulf nodded. "Wouldn't surprise me a bit. Besides, far as I'm
concerned, any woman who'd sooner spit in my eye than smile at me
is ugly, and I don't care whether she'd naked or not."

"That's so, I expect," Leudast said after a little thought. "More
efficient to go after the ones who do smile."

"Of course it is." Magnulf had no doubts. Why should he? He was a sergeant. "And if you have to lay out a little cash to make 'em smile, so what? What else were you going to spend it on?" He changed the subject: "Go see that the men have gathered plenty of firewood."

"Aye, Sergeant." One of the things Leudast liked about being a corporal was that it freed him from duties like gathering wood and hauling water.

He'd never seen such a pack of lazy bastards as the common soldiers to whom he delivered Magnulf's order, either. "Come on, you shirkers," he growled. "Shake a leg, or you'll eat your supper raw." Had he been so useless when he was just a common soldier? He looked back across the immense distance of a few weeks – looked back and started to laugh. No wonder the underofficers in charge of him had spent so much time screaming.

The next morning, Colonel Roflanz, the regimental commander, assembled the entire regiment, something he hadn't done since they came back to Forthweg. In addition to a colonel's three stars grouped in a triangle on his shoulder, Roflanz also wore the silver belt of an earl. He was a good-sized man; a lot of silver had gone into that belt.

He said, "Enough of rest, men. Enough of relaxation. A little is efficient. Too much, and the rot begins. We start exercises today. We need to be ready. We always need to be ready. Anything can happen. Whatever happens, we will be ready."

Leudast wondered if he talked that way because he was stupid or because he was convinced his men were stupid. Then he wondered if both those things might not be true at once. It probably didn't matter, anyhow. A stupid commander would get a lot of his men killed. A commander who thought his men were stupid wouldn't care how many of them he got killed.

The exercise was against cavalry, but the horses had been tricked out with gray blankets. "For this drill, you are to make believe those animals are behemoths," Sergeant Magnulf said solemnly.

"Shall we make believe we're dragons?" somebody asked – somebody well back of the first rank, who had sense enough to disguise his voice.

"Silence!" Magnulf shouted, and Leudast surprised himself by echoing the sergeant. The horsemen advanced at a lazy trot. Magnulf glowered at his squad. "Here come the behemoths. What are you going to do about it?"

INTO THE DARKNESS 311

Had they been real behemoths, Leudast's thoughts would have
gone back and forth between *Run like blazes* and *Die on the spot*.
Because it was only an exercise, he could look on things in a more
detached way. "We'd better scatter," he said, "so they can't take out
all of us with one egg or one long blaze from a heavy stick."

Magnulf beamed at him, not something he was used to from a
sergeant. "Maybe we should have promoted you a while ago,"
Magnulf said. "Scattering is the efficient thing to do, all right. And
then what?"

Leudast knew the answer to that, too, but he'd already spoken up
once. Somebody else deserved a chance. A trooper named Trudulf
said, "Then we try and blaze the bastards up on the behemoths."

Each horse was carrying only one rider. All the horses looked as if
they'd fall over dead if asked to carry more than one rider. Even so, it
was the right answer, for real behemoths bore sizable crews. "Good,"
Magnulf said. "Now we'd better do it, before they trample us into the
dust."

The soldiers dove into the bushes. The riders on the horses made as
if to bombard them. Leudast and his comrades pretended they were
picking off the riders. Every so often, someone would pretend to be
slain and thrash about or dramatically fall off a horse. It was not a very
realistic exercise.

Even so, Leudast wondered why Colonel Roflanz's superiors had
ordered this particular drill now. All Leudast wanted to do was go on
peacefully occupying Forthweg. He didn't think the Forthwegians
were going to come after him with thundering herds of behemoths.
What Forthweg had had along those lines, she'd thrown at Algarve –
and then got thrown back.

After picking himself up and brushing dry grass off the front of his
tunic, Leudast peered east. Unkerlanter occupation of Forthweg
stopped not far east of Eoforwic, which had been the capital. The
redheads held the rest of the kingdom. Leudast's father and one of his
grandfathers had fought the Algarvians during the Six Years' War. If
a quarter of the stories they'd told were true, only a madman would
look forward to facing the armies of Algarve.

Leudast looked from east to west, toward Cottbus. Some of the
things people whispered about King Swemmel . . . Who could guess
if those things were true? Leudast hoped they weren't, for

Unkerlant's sake. But Zuwayza hadn't had many behemoths – the black men, curse them, had gone in for camels instead. The Gongs might have had herds of the great beasts – truth about Gyongyos was as hard to come by as truth about King Swemmel – but couldn't use many of them against Unkerlant, not in the mountains that marked the far western frontier.

Which left . . . Algarve. "Hey, Sergeant!" Leudast called. Magnulf looked a question his way; he didn't want to ask what was in his mind so everyone could hear. He almost whispered it, in fact, when the veteran came over: "Are King Mezentio's men going to jump us?"

Magnulf also glanced around to see who might be listening. When he'd satisfied himself no one was too close, he answered, "Not that I've heard. How come? Do you know something I don't?"

"I don't *know* anything," Leudast said. A spark glowed in Magnulf's eyes, but he didn't make the obvious joke. Leudast went on, "If we're not worried about Algarve, though, why drill against behemoths?"

"Ah." Magnulf thought about that, then nodded. "I see what you're saying," he continued, also speaking quietly. "It makes sense, I suppose, but no, from all I've heard, the border is quiet."

"Good." Leudast started to turn away, but something else occurred to him: "Are we going to jump the Algarvians?"

Just for a moment, Magnulf's eyes went very wide. Then he caught himself and answered, "No, of course not. What a daft notion."

He was lying. Leudast was as sure of that as of his own name. He wished he'd kept his mouth shut. He wished the idea had chosen a different time to pop into his head. He could have told himself it was so much moonshine, so much hogwash. Now he knew different. He sighed. The impressers hadn't asked him if he wanted to join the army. They'd told him what would happen if he didn't. It had seemed horrifying at the time. Next to what he'd seen since, it didn't look so bad.

Magnulf flipped him a coin. "Get the squad billeted, then go over to the tavern and buy yourself some ale or some wine or whatever suits you."

Leudast stared at the silver bit. King Penda's image stared back at him – it was a Forthwegian coin. Then Leudast stared at Magnulf. The sergeant had never tossed him money before. Maybe Magnulf did it because he was a corporal now, not a common soldier. Maybe, on the other hand, Magnulf did it so he would forget about the question he'd asked.

"Go on, get moving," Magnulf said. Some sergeantly snap returned to his voice, but only some – or was Leudast letting his imagination run away with him?

He didn't want to find out the hard way. "Aye, Sergeant," he said. "Thanks." He put the silver bit in his own belt pouch, then followed orders. No Unkerlanter who did exactly as his superior told him could go far wrong. King Swemmel's reign had changed a good many things, but not that. Never that.

As he strode through the village toward the tavern, the Forthwegians sent him resentful stares. His uniform tunic and his clean-shaven face marked him as an Unkerlanter, a foreigner, an occupier. But the Forthwegians didn't say anything where he could hear them. They'd learned the hard way that Unkerlanters could follow enough of their language to recognize insults.

A couple of soldiers were already inside the tavern when Leudast came through the door. Maybe they weren't supposed to be there, for they got up in alarm. They weren't from his company, so he didn't care what they did. He waved them back to their stools and went up to the tavernkeeper. "Plain spirits," he said, speaking slowly and distinctly so the Forthwegian couldn't misunderstand him.

"Aye, plain spirits," the fellow said, but he moved like a sleep-walker till Leudast set the silver bit Magnulf had given him on the counter. After that, Leudast got his drink very fast.

He sat down and sipped from the glass. The tavernkeeper had given him what he'd asked for, but even plain Forthwegian spirits tasted a little different from those brewed in Unkerlant. The Forthwegians also drank spirits they'd stored inside charred wooden casks, sometimes for years. Leudast had tried those, too – once. One taste was plenty to put him off them forever.

A Forthwegian paused in the doorway, saw three Unkerlanter soldiers inside the tavern, and decided to come back another time. The tavernkeeper sighed and swiped a wet rag over the counter with more force than the job needed.

One of the common soldiers laughed. He said to his friend, "The old boy's mad he's lost a customer. He ought to be cursed glad we pay him anything at all."

"Aye." His friend laughed, too. "Better than he deserves, you ask me."

The tavernkeeper polished the counter harder than ever. Just as Unkerlanters could understand some Forthwegian, Forthwegians could follow some Unkerlanter. This old boy probably wished he couldn't.

Leudast looked down into his glass of spirits. All at once, he knocked it back with a flick of the wrist. The spirits might have been plain, but they weren't smooth; he felt as if a dragon had breathed fire down his throat. Even so, he got up, bought another glass, and poured it down. He didn't feel any better after he'd drunk it, nor did he dare have a third; Magnulf hadn't given him leave to get drunk. But two glasses of spirits weren't nearly enough to make him feel easy about the prospect of going forward against the Algarvians.

Marshal Rathar was fighting a campaign he could not possibly win: memoranda and reports piled up on his desk faster than he was able to deal with them. He might have had a better chance to catch up had King Swemmel taken a couple of week's holiday at the spas west of Cottbus or at the royal hunting lodge in the woods to the south.

But, as Rathar had seen, Swemmel did not take holidays. For one thing, the king did not care to leave the capital, lest a usurper seize the reins of government while he was away. For another, Swemmel had no passions — indeed, so far as Rathar knew, had no interests — save ruling.

The marshal studied a map of what had been Forthweg and was now divided between Unkerlant and Algarve, as it had been before the Six Years' War. He studied the blue arrows that showed Unkerlanter forces slashing into eastern Forthweg and taking it away from King Mezentio's men. He noted only one flaw in the plan, which had King Swemmel's enthusiastic support: it required that the Algarvians not do anything out of the ordinary — *like resisting*, he thought with a snort.

When he looked up from that alarmingly optimistic map, he discovered a young lieutenant from the crystallomancy section standing in the doorway waiting to be noticed. "What is it?" Rathar asked, gruffness covering embarrassment — how long had the poor fellow been gathering dust there while he stayed in his brown study?

"My lord Marshal, his Majesty requires your presence in his audience chamber in an hour's time," the lieutenant replied. He touched his right hand to his forehead and bowed in salute, then turned on his heel and hurried away.

Well, that answered that: with a message from King Swemmel, the fellow had not been waiting long. Had Rathar not looked up almost at once, the lieutenant would have interrupted him. Swemmel's commands took precedence over everything else in Unkerlant.

For the sake of the kingdom, he endured stripping off his marshal's sword and hanging it in the anteroom to the audience chamber. For the sake of his kingdom, he endured the bodyguards' intimate attentions. "You should have seen that crazy old Zuwayzi, my lord," one of the guards said, patting the insides of his thighs. "He took off his clothes so we could search 'em. Have you ever heard the like?"

"Hajjaj?" Rathar asked, and the bodyguard nodded. The marshal went on, "He's not crazy – he's a very clever, very able man. And if you don't have a little care with your hand there, I may do the same thing the next time the king summons me."

That scandalized the guards, but not enough to make the search any less thorough. When they were finally satisfied Rathar carried no lethal implements, they suffered him to enter the audience chamber. He went through the prescribed prostrations and acclamations before King Swemmel, then received the king's permission to rise.

"How may I serve your Majesty?" he asked – always the question with Swemmel. That was what the king was for: to be served.

"In the matter concerning the war to come against Algarve," Swemmel answered.

Rathar had hoped his sovereign would say that – hoped for it and dreaded it at the same time. With Swemmel, nothing was ever simple. "I am yours to command, your Majesty," he said. *I am also going to talk you out of anything excessively foolish*, he thought. *I am going to do that, if you give me half a chance. Even if you give me a quarter of a chance, I am going to do it.*

He hid such thoughts away. Having them was dangerous. Showing them was fatal. And Swemmel, who stared down at him from his high seat like a bird of prey, had a bloodhound's nose for them. The king's genius ran in twisted channels, but ran strong where it did run.

Rathar's stolidity was not the least of the assets that had helped him rise to his present rank.

Swemmel said, "Algarve wars in the east. King Mezentio pays Unkerlant no mind. The best time to strike a redhead is when his back is turned."

"All you say is true, your Majesty." For a sentence, Rathar could be fulsome and tell the truth at the same time, and he took full advantage of that. It let him go on, "But recall, I beg, that Algarve also warred in the west when we reclaimed western Forthweg. Then you were scrupulous not to molest Mezentio's men, and also scrupulous not to go beyond Unkerlant's boundaries before the Six Years' War."

"Mezentio would have been looking for us to strike him then," King Swemmel replied. "He is a devious man, Mezentio." Coming from Swemmel, that was no small praise – or perhaps simply a matter of like recognizing like. "But we did not strike. Now we have lulled him. Now he thinks we will not strike. He may even think – we hope he does think – we fear to strike against Algarve."

Rathar feared to strike against Algarve. He and his aides had spent a lot of time examining the way the Algarvians had pierced the Forthwegian army like a spear piercing flesh. In the privacy of his own mind, he set the redheads' performance against the way the Unkerlanter army had handled itself facing the Zuwayzin. He found the comparison so alarming, he kept it to himself. Had he admitted his fear, Swemmel would have named a new marshal on the instant.

No matter how the Unkerlanters' performance against Zuwayza dismayed Rathar, though, he could turn it to his own purposes. "Your Majesty, do you recall the chief difficulty your forces had in the campaign in the north?" he asked.

"Aye," Swemmel growled: "that we could not even smash through the ragtag and bobtail the black men threw against us. Camels!" He screwed up his face till he looked remarkably like a camel himself. "We assure you, Marshal, your reports on the subject of camels grew most tedious."

"For this, I can only beg your Majesty's pardon." Rathar took a deep breath. "The Zuwayzin did indeed fight harder and do more with the camels than we had expected. But that was not our chief difficulty in facing them."

King Swemmel leaned forward once more, trying to put Rathar in fear – and succeeding, though Rathar hoped the king did not realize that. "If you say bad generalship was the flaw, Marshal, you condemn yourself out of your own mouth," Swemmel warned.

"Our generals, but for Droctulf, did as well as they could have done," Rathar said. Droctulf was no longer a general; Rathar thought Droctulf was no longer among the living. The marshal refused to let irrelevancies distract him. He took another deep breath. "Our chief difficulty, your Majesty, was that we struck too soon."

"Say on," Swemmel told him, in the tones of a jurist listening to a man already obviously guilty further condemning himself.

"We struck too soon, before all the regiments called for in the plan against Zuwayza were in place," Rathar said. He did not point out that that had been at Swemmel's express command. "We struck before we were fully ready, and paid the price. If we strike too soon against Algarve, we shall pay a larger price."

"You need not fear that," Swemmel said. "We know the redheads are tougher than the Zuwayzin. You have our leave to collect such soldiery as you need, provided you attack when we give the order. There, do you see? We endeavor to be flexible."

The clenched fist in Rathar's gut eased a little. Swemmel was, for Swemmel, in a reasonable mood. That emboldened the marshal to say what needed saying: "Your Majesty, this is but half the loaf. Here is the other half: that I would hesitate to attack Algarve even with all our forces assembled. *Now* I would hesitate."

Swemmel stabbed a forefinger out at him. "Did you leave your ballocks behind, up there in the Zuwayzi desert?"

"No." Standing still and speaking calmly were harder than facing the Zuwayzin in the front line, as he'd done. "For consider: now Algarve fights on the defensive everywhere in the east, against Jelgava and Valmiera both. If we strike the redheads, they will have men to spare, with whom to strike back. But spring is here, or near enough. Soon the Algarvians will strike at their foes. For that, they will have to throw all the men they can spare into the fight. All will be as it was during the Six Years' War, army locked with army, neither side able to go forward or back. Then, your Majesty, *then* we strike, and strike hard."

He waited. He could not judge which way King Swemmel would

go. Swemmel was a law of his own. The king would decide what he decided, and Rathar would obey, or, if not Rathar, someone else.

"Ahh," Swemmel said: more an exhalation than a real word. Whatever it was, though, Rathar knew he'd won his case. Swemmel's dark eyes glowed; had they been green like an Algarvian's, he would have looked a happy cat. "That is indeed subtle, Marshal." By the way he said it, he could have offered no higher praise.

Rathar inclined his head. "I serve your Majesty. I serve the kingdom." *And now I will go on serving a while longer.*

"Of course you do." Swemmel spoke as if no doubt were possible. Everyone in Unkerlant served him . . . and he destroyed without warning or mercy any servant who, in his sole judgment, had ambitions beyond serving him. For now, though, his suspicions were a banked fire. He took the bait Rathar dangled before him. "Aye, aye, and aye. Let them murder each other by the tens of thousands, by the hundreds of thousands, as they did for six years straight. This time, the Algarvians shall not slaughter the men of Unkerlant in the same way, as they did during our father's reign."

"Even so, your Majesty." Rathar hid relief as carefully as he had hidden worry.

"But you must be ready," King Swemmel warned him. "When the moment comes, when the hosts of Algarve bog down in the east of their kingdom or in western Valmiera or Jelgava – wherever they strike first – you must be prepared to smash through whatever garrisons they have left behind in Forthweg. We shall give the order, and you shall obey it."

"As you say, your Majesty, so shall it be," Rathar said. If Swemmel picked a time he judged wrong, he would try to talk the king out of it. If he was lucky, as he had been today, he might even succeed.

Something new seemed to occur to Swemmel. "In your plans for attacking Algarve, Marshal, you will assuredly have one wherein our armies strike through Yanina as well as through Forthweg."

"Aye, your Majesty. More than one, in fact." Rathar told the truth there without hesitation, even if he did not fully grasp why that mattered to the king.

"Make your dispositions according to whichever of those plans you reckon best, then," Swemmel said. For once, he condescended to explain: "Thus we shall punish King Tsavellas for letting Penda slip through his fingers instead of yielding him up to us, as we demanded."

"I serve your Majesty," Rathar repeated. That struck him as a weak reason for choosing one course over another, but such choices lay in Swemmel's hands, not his. And Yanina would likely be an enemy in any war against Algarve. Musingly, Rathar went on, "I do wonder where Penda is. King Mezentio has not got him – Tsavellas didn't yield him up to Algarve, either, as I might have guessed."

"Penda is not here. We ordered his person surrendered, and it was not." King Swemmel folded his arms across his chest. "Tsavellas shall pay for his disobedience."

Rathar had already got Swemmel to be reasonable once. Having won the larger battle, he yielded the smaller one, lest his victory come undone. "Aye, your Majesty," he said.

Istvan and Borsos the dowser walked through the dirt streets of Sorong. An Obudan man wearing a sort of kilt of woven straw, a Gyongyosian army tunic, and a big straw hat was spreading fresh thatching over the roof beams of a wooden house.

Borsos watched in fascination. "It's like coming to another world, isn't it?" he murmured.

"Aye, so it is," Istvan answered with a chuckle. "I expect you grew up in a solid stone house, same as I did – slates on the roof and everything?"

"Well, of course," Borsos said. "By the stars, in Gyongyos a man needs a house he can fight from. You never know when you'll be at feud with the clan in the next valley, or when a feud will break out in your own clan. A house like that" – he pointed – "wouldn't be much more than kindling for a bonfire."

Istvan chuckled. "That's the truth, sir, the truth and to spare. This whole place has gone up in smoke a couple of times since we and the accursed Kuusamans started swapping Obuda back and forth. Wooden houses with thatched roofs don't stand up to beams and eggs any too well."

Borsos clicked his tongue between his teeth. "They wouldn't, no indeed. But the Obudans didn't know about beams and eggs before ley-line ships started going through the Bothnian Ocean." He looked wistful, an expression so rarely seen on a Gyongyosian's face that

Istvan needed a moment to recognize it. "It must have been a quiet, peaceful sort of life."

"Begging your pardon, sir, but not likely," Istvan said. "They went right after each other with spears and bows and with these funny almost-swords they made by edging flat clubs with volcanic glass. I've seen those things. You could cursed near cut a man in half with one of 'em."

The dowser gave him a sour look. "You've just ruined one of my illusions, you know."

"Sorry, sir," Istvan said: the common soldier's last bastion. "Would you sooner have illusions, or would you sooner have what's so?"

"Always an interesting question." Now Borsos studied him in a speculative way. "I take it you've never been in love?"

"Sir?" Istvan stared in blank incomprehension.

"Never mind," Borsos said. "If you don't know what I'm talking about, all the explaining in the world won't tell you."

A couple of Obudans coming down the street nodded to Istvan and Borsos. They wore straw hats like that of the fellow repairing his roof. The man of the couple had on a tunic of coarse local wool over trousers from a Kuusaman uniform. The trousers left several inches of shin showing above the Obudan's sandals; his people were taller than Kuusamans. The woman's tunic matched his. Below it, she wore a brightly striped skirt that stopped at about the same place his trousers did.

As she and her companion drew near, they both held out their hands and spoke in Gyongyosian: "Money?"

Istvan made a face at them. "Go milk a goat," he growled: anything but a compliment in his language.

Borsos had a captain's pay to spend, not a common soldier's. He hadn't been on Obuda nearly so long as Istvan had, either. Pulling a couple of small silver coins out of his pocket, he gave one to each of them, saying, "Here. Take this, and then be off."

They showered loud praises on the dowser in Obudan, in broken Gyongyosian, and even in scraps of Kuusaman that proved they'd begged during the previous occupation, too. As they went on their way, they kept acclaiming him at the top of their lungs. He looked as pleased with himself as if he'd tossed a scrawny stray dog a bone with a lot of meat on it.

"Well, now you've gone and done it, sir." Istvan rolled his eyes. No doubt Borsos was a fine dowser, but didn't he have any sense? Istvan shook his head. Borsos had just proved he didn't.

And, sure enough, those loud praises from the Obudans to whom the captain had given money brought what seemed like half the people of Sorong out of their houses, all of them – men, women, and children – with hands outstretched. "Money?" they all cried. If they knew one word of Gyongyosian, that was it. Istvan fumed. The man and woman hadn't praised Borsos just to make him feel good. They'd done it to let their cousins and friends and neighbors know there was a Gyongyosian around from whom they could hope to get something.

Borsos doled out a few more coins, which Istvan thought was only compounding his foolishness. Then, far later than he should have, he too figured out what was going on. Instead of smiling, he began to frown, and then to scowl. Instead of saying, "Here," he began to say, "Go away," and then, in short order, "Go bugger a billy goat!"

The swarm of Obudans dispersed much more slowly than they'd gathered. The ones who hadn't got any money – the majority of them – went off disappointed and angry. They showered Borsos with abuse in Obudan, Gyongyosian, and Kuusaman, just as the first couple had showered him with praise. "A goat's horn up your arse!" a skinny little girl screeched at the dowser, and then, wisely, disappeared around a corner.

"By the stars!" Borsos said when he and Istvan were at last free of the crowd. He wiped his forehead with his sleeve. "It'll be a long time before I do that again."

"Aye, sir," Istvan said stolidly. "They don't much mind if you tell all of 'em to jump off a cliff. They're like beggars back home that way – they're used to *no*, and they hear it a lot more than *aye*. But if you give to some of them, they think you have to give to everybody."

Borsos still looked shaken. "Beggars back home are broken men, mostly, them and women too old and raddled to get by selling their bodies any more. Some of these folk were merchants and artisans and their kin: people able to live on their own well enough. Why should they shame themselves for silver when they already earn plenty?"

Istvan shrugged. "Who knows why foreigners do what they do? They're only foreigners. I'll tell you this, though, sir: the next

Obudan I meet with a proper warrior's pride, or even anything close to it, will be the first."

"Aye, I've seen that myself, though never like today," the dowser said. He looked thoughtful. "And why should they have a warrior's pride? Set against us, set even against the Kuusamans, they aren't proper warriors. They can't stand against sticks and eggs and war-dragons, not with spears and bows and clubs edged with volcanic glass. No wonder they're blind to shame."

"Well, isn't that interesting?" Istvan murmured, more to himself than to Borsos. Just when he'd reckoned his superior a perfect fool, the dowser came out with an idea he'd been thinking about for days.

And Borsos went on, "It's like that over big stretches of the world. The folk of Derlavai – aye, and the Lagoans and the accursed Kuusamans, too – know too much magic for anyone else to withstand them. Too much of the mechanic arts, too, though those count for less. There was a tribe on an island in the Great Northern Sea where, a couple of lifetimes ago, all the men slew themselves because the Jelgavans – I think it was the Jelgavans – trounced them every time they fought. They saw they couldn't win, and couldn't bear to lose any more."

"That, at least was bravely done," Istvan said. "The Obudans fawn and cringe instead."

"Nothing is ever simple," the dowser said. "The Obudans are still here to fawn and cringe. When those other islanders slew themselves, they slew their tribe as well. Other men took their women. Other men took their land. Other men took their goods. Their name is dead. It will never live again."

"It lives," Istvan insisted. "It lives even in the memory of their foes. If it didn't, sir, how would you have heard of it?"

"I am a scholar of sorts," Borsos answered. "I make it my business to learn of such strange things. The Jelgavans wrote down what these tribesmen did, and someone found it interesting enough to translate into our language so people like me could read of it. I doubt that the descendants of these men, if any still live, have the slightest notion of what they did. Are you answered?"

"Sir, I am answered," Istvan said. "If my great-great-grand-children forget the deeds of Gyongyos in this war, why do we bother fighting it?"

"Even so," Borsos said. He looked around. "Now that we've finally shaken free of that accursed swarm of beggars, where is this shop you were speaking of?"

"We go round this corner here, sir, and it's about halfway down the lane toward the woods." After rounding the corner, Istvan pointed. "That little building there, with the moldy green paint."

Borsos nodded. "I see it." He hurried on ahead of Istvan, opened the door, and then paused on the threshold, waiting for Istvan to join him. When Istvan stayed outside in the street, the dowser raised an eyebrow. "Come on in with me."

"It's all right, sir," Istvan said. "You get what you came for. I'll wait here."

"Short of silver?" Borsos asked. "Don't worry about that. You've been a lot of help to me since I got shipped out here. I'll spring for one, if you like."

Istvan bowed. "Very kind of you, sir," he said, and meant it – no regular officer, not even a sergeant, would have made such a generous offer. "But you go ahead. I haven't got anybody to send one to. And besides" – he coughed – "in the valley I come from, people would go on and on about newfangled city ways even if I did."

Borsos shrugged. "Fewer clan feuds get started this way. I don't know why the folk in the backwoods valleys can't see as much if even the Obudans can." Istvan only shrugged. So did the dowser, who said, "All right, have it as you'd have it." He went into the shop.

A little old woman hobbling by asked Istvan for money. He stared through her as if she didn't exist. She limped on down the narrow path. She wasn't angry. No one else had succeeded where she'd failed.

Presently, Borsos came out with what looked like a long, thick sausage covered in smooth, supple leather. "I got a good price," he said happily. "I'll send it to my wife on the next supply ship. Better Gergely should use it and think of me than go looking for some other man and cause all kinds of trouble, eh?"

"Whatever pleases you, sir," Istvan answered. Borsos started to laugh. So did Istvan, when he realized what he'd said. The toy wasn't for Borsos's pleasure, after all – only for his peace of mind.

Rain came down in sheets. Garivald supposed he should have been glad it wasn't snow. Annore was certainly glad. Now that the freezing weather had gone at last, she'd driven the livestock out of the house. With the beasts gone, she had less work than she'd had before.

Garivald wished he could say the same. He'd be plowing and planting as soon as the thaw let him. Except for the harvest, spring was the busiest time of year for him. And, before long, the roads would dry enough for inspectors to make their way along them. He looked forward to that as much as he would have to the arrival of any other locusts.

He pulled on his worn leather knee boots. "Where are you going?" Annore asked sharply.

"Out to throw some garbage to the hogs," he answered. "The sooner they put on fat, the sooner we can slaughter them. And besides" – he knew his wife well – "won't you be just as well pleased to have me out from underfoot for a while?"

"That depends," Annore said. "When you get drunk here, you mostly just go to sleep. When you get drunk in the tavern, you get into brawls, and then you come home with rips in your tunic or with bloodstains on it."

"Did I say anything about going to the tavern?" Garivald demanded. "I said I was going to slop the hogs. That's all I said."

Annore didn't answer, not with words. But the look she gave him was eloquent. His ears heated. His wife knew him well, too.

Getting out, then, felt like escaping. He squelched through the mud toward the hogs and flung them a bucketful of parsnip peelings and other such delicacies. The hogs weren't fussy. He could have thrown them soggy thatching, and they probably would have enjoyed that, too.

He set the wooden bucket by the door to his house, thought about going back inside, and then decided not to. Out here, all he had to worry about were rain and mud: such small things, when set against his wife's edged tongue.

He wasn't the only man out of doors despite the nasty weather, either. "As long as I'm out here," he muttered, "I may as well wander around a bit and say hello. Efficiency." He laughed. In a village like Zossen, to which inspectors came but seldom, Unkerlanters could laugh at King Swemmel's favorite word – provided no one knew they were doing it.

Rain beat down on his hat and his wool cape. The mud did its best to pull the boots right off his feet. It was thick and gluey, even deeper than in the fall. Each step took effort. He wondered if it would come up over his boot tops. That happened every so often, but usually later in the thaw.

When the first person Garivald spied through the curtain of rain was Waddo the firstman, he wished he'd gone indoors after all. Waddo saw him, too, which meant Garivald either had to ignore him, which was rude, or go over and talk with him, which he didn't want to do. Whether he wanted to or not, he went. Waddo had a long memory for slights.

"Good day to you, Garivald," the firstman said, his voice almost as slick and greasy as if he were speaking to an inspector.

"And to you," Garivald answered. He had less trouble sounding cheerful than he'd thought he would. The closer he got to Waddo, the more easily he could see how hard a time the firstman had making his way through the mud. After breaking his ankle, Waddo still walked with the help of a cane. Here in the spring thaw, the cane didn't help much. Instead of letting the firstman gain purchase, it sank deep into the mud.

"May the coming year be bountiful for you and yours," Waddo said. "May the harvest be abundant."

May you shut up and leave me at peace, Garivald thought. Aloud, he replied, "May all these things prove true for you as well." He was not even wishing falsely, or not altogether falsely. Anything that went wrong with Waddo's harvest – a blight, locusts, rain at the wrong time – was only too likely to go wrong with everyone's harvest, including his own.

Waddo inclined his head, which made water run off the front of his hat instead of the back for a moment. "You have always been a well-spoken man, Garivald," he said.

Only because you don't know what I say behind your back. But Garivald had always been careful to whom he said such things. Some of the people in the village were as much Waddo's inspectors as the men in rock-gray were King Swemmel's. Evidently, Garivald had been careful enough, for no one had betrayed him. "I thank you," he told the firstman, doing his best to match Waddo for hypocrisy.

It worked; under the wide brim of his hat, Waddo beamed. "Aye," he said, "it's thanks to folk like you that Zossen will be going places."

"Eh?" Garivald looked politely interested to conceal the stab of alarm he felt. He liked the village where and as it was just fine.

But the firstman repeated, "Going places." His eyelid rose and fell in an unmistakable wink. "We may — we just may, mind you — have a way to bring a crystal into Zossen after all. And if we bring a crystal into the village, we bring the whole world into the village." Under his cloak, he threw his arms wide with excitement, as if to say that would assuredly be a good thing.

Garivald was anything but assured. It hadn't been so long before that he and Annore had concluded Zossen was better off without a crystal. He saw no reason to change his mind. Being an Unkerlanter peasant like most Unkerlanter peasants, he seldom saw reason to change his mind. "How?" he asked, giving no sign of what he thought. "We have no power points close by. No ley line runs anywhere near us. As far as magic goes — well, magic might as well be gone, as far as we're concerned."

"Aye, and isn't it a pity?" Waddo said. "So much we could do if more sorcery worked around these parts. And it may. Before too long, it really may."

"How?" Garivald asked again. "You can't squeeze water out of a stone — there's no water to squeeze. You can't get magic out of a land with no power points, either."

"I don't know just how it's done," Waddo answered. "I'm no mage. But if it *is* done, wouldn't it be fine? We'd know what happened all over the world, and wouldn't have to wait till some trader came to Zossen with the news."

"That might not be so bad," Garivald said; coming right out and telling the firstman he hated the idea struck him as foolish. But he did give some hint of his own notions: "Of course, it's still news here whenever it gets to us."

"But that's not good enough!" Waddo exclaimed. "When traders and neighbors come to Zossen, I want us to be able to give them the news. I don't want to always be begging for it, the way old Faileuba has to beg for bread because her husband and her daughter are dead and her other daughter ran away with that tinker."

"Doesn't matter to me one way or the other," Garivald said. It mattered very much to him, but his hopes were opposite Waddo's.

With a shrug that flung drops of water from the shoulders of his cloak, he went on, "It's not like we're Cottbus, or anything of the sort."

"But wouldn't it be fine if we were?" the firstman said. "Zossen – the Cottbus of the south! Doesn't that have a fine sound to it?"

Garivald took a couple of shuffling steps to keep from sinking into the mud. He shrugged again, in lieu of roaring at Waddo that he didn't want his home village to be anything like Cottbus. That one crystal, even if it could be made to function here, wouldn't turn Zossen into a copy of the capital of Unkerlant occurred to him no more than it did to the firstman.

Waddo also shifted position. He almost fell while he was doing so. Had he gone down into the muck, Garivald would have been tempted to hold him there till he stopped struggling. If Waddo drowned, Zossen would stay as it had always been. To Garivald's disappointment, the firstman caught himself. "We'll see what we see, that's all," Waddo said. "Nothing's sure yet." He might have been firstman, but remained a peasant under the petty rank.

"Aye, nothing's ever sure," Garivald agreed. So would everyone else in the village. So would everyone else through vast stretches of Unkerlant.

"Well, then," Waddo said, as if everything were all settled.

He said it so convincingly, Garivald believed for a moment everything was all settled and started to go on his way. The firstman wasn't firstman for nothing. But then Garivald turned back. "This is the third time I've asked you, and you haven't told me yet: how would we make a crystal work here without a power point or a ley line anywhere close by?"

Waddo looked unhappy. Garivald thought that was because he had no answer, because the whole scheme lived in his head and nowhere else. But he discovered he was wrong, for Waddo said, "Power points and ley lines aren't the only ways to get sorcerous energy, you know. There is another source it would be more efficient to use here in Zossen."

"Oh, aye, I'll bet it would," Garivald said with a laugh. "Well, when you line people up to sacrifice 'em to make your precious crystal, you can start with my mother-in-law." He laughed again. All things considered, he got on pretty well with Annore's mother, her chief virtue being that she stayed out of his hair.

Then he watched Waddo's expression change. His own expression changed, too, to one of horror. He'd thought he was joking. He'd been sure he was joking. Just how badly did the firstman want a crystal here? What would he do — what would King Swemmel's inspectors, and maybe King Swemmel's soldiers, too, help him do — to get a crystal here?

"Powers above," Garivald whispered, thinking he *ought* to drown Waddo in the mud right this instant.

Waddo's arms fluttered under the cloak, as if he was making brushing-away motions. "No, no, no," he said. "No, no, no. We would never sacrifice anyone from Zossen to power the crystal. That would upset people" — which would do for an understatement till a bigger one came along — "and be inefficient. But there are plenty of criminals in the kingdom, especially in the cities, where people haven't got any morals at all. Who'd miss them if they had their throats cut? And they'd be doing something useful, wouldn't they? That's efficiency."

"Aye . . . so it is," Garivald said grudgingly. He didn't mind the idea of unpleasant strangers getting their throats slit — no doubt they had it coming. He did wish it would be for a better cause than bringing a cursed crystal to the village.

Waddo said, "Now do you see why I didn't want to come right out and talk about sacrifices and such? Everybody in the village would want to get rid of everybody else, or else be sure everybody else wanted to get rid of him. Things won't settle down till folks see it's only bad eggs from far away who get what they deserve."

"I suppose so," Garivald said. He knew whom people in Zossen would want to sacrifice. He was standing here talking with the fellow people in Zossen would want to sacrifice. He almost said as much, to see the look on Waddo's face. But the firstman would remember a crack like that. If something chanced to go wrong with the crystal — Garivald didn't know how he could arrange that, but figured it was worth a try — he didn't want Waddo thinking of him first. Come to that, he didn't want Waddo thinking of him at all.

Tealdo approved of Captain Galafrone, the late Captain Larbino's replacement as company commander. Galafrone was a thick-shoulderd veteran of the Six Years' War, his hair, mustaches, and side whiskers more gray than auburn. He was also a rarity in the Algarvian army – in those of Valmiera or Jelgava, he would have been an impossibility – an officer risen from the ranks.

"This one's for revenge, boys," he said as Tealdo and his comrades stood in the forwardmost trenches and waited for the trumpets to signal them into action. "The cursed Kaunians stole our land when I was a lad your age, near enough. Now we get to pay the stinking whoremasters back. It's that simple."

He couldn't have timed things better had he been a first-rank mage. No sooner had he finished speaking than eggs started falling on the Valmieran positions in front of Tealdo's company. Egg-tossers behind the line flung some of them. More fell from beneath the bellies of the swarms of dragons Tealdo could make out against the lightening sky.

Here and there along the line, Valmieran egg-tossers tried to answer, but the dragons, or so Tealdo had heard, were concentrating on them. In that duel, the Algarvians had the better of it.

Trumpets rang out. The notes were harsh and blaring, not the smooth tones of the royal hymn. "Follow me!" Captain Galafrone shouted. He was the first one out of the trench. If he'd done the same thing during the battles of the Six Years' War, Tealdo wondered why he remained among the living.

"Follow me!" Sergeant Panfilo echoed. "For King Mezentio!"

"Mezentio!" Tealdo cried, and awkwardly climbed the sandbag steps so he could expose his precious body to the Valmierans' beams and eggs. He wished he'd stayed on occupation duty in Sibiu instead of getting shipped back to southeastern Algarve to join in the assault against Valmiera. The powers that be back in Trapani had decided otherwise, though, and here he was.

"If Mezentio wants to lick the Valmierans so much, let him come fight them!" Trasone shouted. But he, like Tealdo, dashed toward the trenches the blond robbers had dug on Algarvian soil.

One or two men went down as beams smote them, but only one or two. The egg-tossers and dragons had done their work well. Behemoths advanced with the Algarvian infantry, to bring more egg-tossers and heavy sticks to the edge of the fighting. Other behemoths hauled supplies and bridging gear forward.

Tealdo sprang down into the forwardmost Valmieran trench. A

couple of blond men in trousers threw down their sticks and threw up their hands. "No fight!" one of them said in bad Algarvian.

"Send the captives back!" Captain Galafrone shouted, somewhere not far down the line. "Don't waste time going through their pockets, just send 'em on back. We've got plenty of plunder waiting ahead of us, lads – we won't go without. But the faster we move now, the sooner we kick the Kaunians out of our kingdom. Forward!"

Rather reluctantly, Tealdo didn't take the time to rob the Valmierans. No doubt Galafrone was right, in a strictly military sense. Still, Tealdo resented the certainty that the trousered Kaunians' money and trinkets would end up in the hands of behind-the-lines types who'd done nothing to earn them. ·

But with Galafrone already running on, Tealdo didn't see how he could do anything less. His comrades followed the veteran captain, too. The Valmierans fought back, but not so hard as he'd expected. The pelting they'd taken from egg-tossers and dragons seemed to have left a lot of them stunned. Others threw down their sticks the moment they first spied Algarvian soldiers.

"Our stinking nobles led us into a losing war," a blond man said bitterly as he went off into captivity. His Algarvian was already pretty good. He'd get the chance to improve it further in a camp.

Then Tealdo dove behind a pile of rubble as some Valmierans in a little stone keep showed themselves far from ready to quit. Their beams scorched the tender spring grass. Tealdo tried to sneak one of his own beams through their blazing slits. By the way they went on fighting, he knew he wasn't having much luck.

Galafrone and his crystallomancer sprawled in back of similarly makeshift shelter a few yards away. The company commander looked at a map, then yelled something – Tealdo couldn't make out what – to the man with the crystal. The fellow spoke urgently into his sorcerous apparatus; again, Tealdo caught tone without words.

Hardly more than a minute later, a couple of dragons with eggs under their bellies dove on the Valmieran strongpoint. Watching, Tealdo wondered if their fliers intended to take them straight into it. But they released the eggs at little more than treetop height, from which they had no chance of missing. The ground shook under Tealdo as the eggs burst. The Valmierans in that small stone fortress suddenly stopped blazing.

Galafrone jumped to his feet. "Come on, let's get moving!" he shouted. "Those bastards won't bother us any more."

He was right about that. Tealdo trotted past the ruins of the stone keep. The sharp stink of new-burst eggs still lingered; it always put him in mind of thunderstorms. Other odors lingered with it: burnt meat and the iron smell of blood.

Out ahead of the advancing footsoldiers, he spied a large band of behemoths. Like the dragons, they and their crews were busy smashing up the places from which the Valmierans fought hardest. By the time Tealdo and his comrades got to those places, they rarely needed to do more than mop up.

By the time that first day ended, Tealdo was more worn than he'd ever been in his life. He and his comrades had also come farther than he'd imagined they could. And, somehow, the field kitchens had kept up with them. The stew a cook with a dragon tattoo on his forearm ladled into his tin bowl wasn't anything over which a gourmet back in Trapani would have gone into ecstasies, but it was a lot better than anything he and his pals could have come up with by themselves.

Galafrone ate like a wolf. He looked dazed, and not from the hard marching and fighting he'd done. "I can't believe how fast we've moved," he said with his mouth full. He'd said that before, too. "We never advanced so fast in the Six Years' War, not even in the last push toward Priekule. Powers above, we've already taken back half of what the blondies stole from us up till now."

Around a yawn, Trasone said, "They don't seem so hot to fight now that we're pounding on them instead of them pounding on us."

Tealdo nodded. "I thought the same thing. One of them said he blamed their nobles for the war."

"I hope they all think that way," Galafrone exclaimed. "They fought like mad bastards the last time, you bet your arse they did. If their hearts aren't in it now, all the better for us."

The discussion around the fire would have gone on longer had the warriors not been so tired. Tealdo rolled himself into his blanket and slept like a dead man. He felt like a dead man when Sergeant Panfilo shook him awake before sunrise the next morning, too. Panfilo looked disgustingly fit and well rested. "Come on," he said. "You're not much, but if you're what we've got to hit the Valmierans another lick, you'll have to do."

"If I'm not much, why don't you leave me here and go on without me?" But Tealdo was already climbing to his feet. He smelled bread baking in the field kitchen's oven. He thought he smelled victory in the air, too.

And then, after washing down the bread with a few gulps of rough red wine, he tramped east again. Again, the behemoths had already done a lot of his work for him. Again, Algarvian dragons dove on the soldiers of Kaunian blood who kept on fighting after the behemoths had passed. A few eggs usually proved plenty to silence them. Hardly any Valmieran dragons attacked Mezentio's men. And, again, most Valmierans seemed not to have their hearts in the fight. They surrendered far more readily than the Sibians had.

"We took the Sibs by surprise, but they fought hard while they could," Tealdo said to Trasone after they sent another group of captives toward the rear. "These whoresons were supposed to be ready and waiting for us."

"Are you complaining?" his friend asked.

"Now that you mention it, no," Tealdo answered. Both soldiers laughed. They strode down the road leading east.

Tealdo did his best to stay close to Captain Galafrone and the crystallomancer. That wasn't easy; the veteran kept setting a blistering pace Tealdo had trouble matching. But he wanted to be among the first to learn if anything interesting happened: in that, he was a typical Algarvian. And, toward midafternoon, his curiosity and persistence paid off. The crystallomancer listened to his sorcerous apparatus, then spoke to Galafrone.

After hearing him out, Galafrone whooped. "What's up, sir?" Tealdo asked. Maybe the captain would tell him, maybe he wouldn't. Nothing ventured, nothing gained.

Galafrone wasn't just willing to talk. Had Tealdo not asked, the captain would have grabbed him and shouted the news: "The marquisate of Rivaroli has risen in revolt behind the Valmieran lines! Let's see those cursed Kaunians move men or supplies through there now!"

"Powers above," Tealdo said. Then he whooped, too. "That's what Valmiera gets for taking a marquisate full of good Algarvians away from us after the Six Years' War."

"That's just what Valmiera gets," Galafrone agreed. "And we're the fellows to give it to King Gainibu and his worthless nobles in their gilded trousers." Tealdo suspected Galafrone was imperfectly enamored of his own kingdom's nobility. Galafrone couldn't say that, so he took out his anger on the nobles next door.

He wasn't the only one, either. Tealdo said, "Talking with the blondies we've nabbed who speak a little Algarvian, a lot of them don't want to fight for their nobles, either."

Galafrone nodded and turned to the crystallomancer. "Send that on to Colonel Ombruno, and to the army headquarters, too. They'll probably have heard it already, but send it on the off chance they haven't. Maybe it'll help us find a way to make more Kaunians quit without fighting."

"Aye, Captain," the crystallomancer said. As soon as the message went out, Galafrone waved his men forward again.

By the end of the day, the company was inside the Marquisate of Rivaroli. Tealdo had no trouble telling when they crossed the border. All at once, Valmieran replaced Algarvian on every roadside sign – the retreating enemy had knocked down some of those, but not all – and in the first village through which the company passed. The people in the village remained Algarvian, even if their names were spelled Valmieran-style. Tealdo wondered what his own name would look like if he'd grown up here. Something like *Tealtu*, he supposed.

Most of the villagers greeted the Algarvian soldiers with wine and cakes and cheers. The women greeted them with hugs and kisses. The women might have greeted them with more, too, as they had when Tealdo helped reclaim the Duchy of Bari for Algarve, but Galafrone shouted, "Keep in line and keep moving, curse you all! The way this campaign's shaping up, you'll have plenty of chances to dip your wicks before long. The harder we press the Kaunians now, the sooner it'll be."

Tealdo saw a man and woman staring out through a shop window. *They* weren't Algarvians, not with hair yellow as butter. A good many Valmierans had moved into the Marquisate since the Treaty of Tortus. Tealdo wondered what they were thinking as they watched the Algarvian soldiers tramp past. "Nothing good," he muttered, "or I miss my guess."

"Keep moving!" Galafrone yelled again. Entering open country, his troopers spread out into a skirmish line. Maybe the Valmierans would be able to make a stand somewhere ahead. They hadn't done it yet, though.

12.

Skarnu felt like a man trying to fight back after getting hit in the head with a club. From everything the young captain could see, the whole Valmieran army might have been a man trying to fight back after getting hit in the head with a club. He couldn't see past his own tiny circle of the war, of course, but nothing inside it looked good.

His men had been coming up from rest and recuperation behind the line when the Algarvian blow fell. Had they gone into the line, no doubt they – or however many of them stayed alive – would be in an Algarvian captives' camp now. As things were, they'd been caught up in the headlong Valmieran retreat, fighting when they had to, traveling a lot by night so they could slip between the redheads' scouts. The Algarvians didn't always have great numbers. Wherever they were, though they had great strength. After a while, footsoldiers despaired of fighting behemoths, of having dragons plummet out of the sky to drop eggs on them.

Sergeant Raunu came up to Skarnu with a grim look on his face. "Sir, another three must have slipped away, on account of they sure as blazes aren't here." Pulling a map from his breast pocket, Skarnu spoke in musing tones: "I wonder where exactly *here* is." He had some idea – somewhere between their line of farthest advance and the border between Valmiera and Algarve – but couldn't pin it down within five miles, let alone to dot on the map. All he and his men had done was stumble backwards again and again.

"Sooner or later, we'll find a village," Raunu said. "Then we'll know." The veteran hesitated. At last, he went on, "By what I've heard, sir, desertion's a lot heavier in the other companies in the regiment than it is with us."

"Heard from whom?" Skarnu demanded. As far as he could tell, his company might have fallen off the edge of the world to his superiors. He hadn't had orders for a couple of days.

"People I run into in the woods," Raunu said with a shrug. He hesitated again. "Our men know you've been in there with 'em, sir. That means they aren't so likely to take off on their own or just sit on a stump and wait for the redheads to pick 'em up."

"People in the woods, eh?" Skarnu said. His sergeant shrugged again and nodded. He said nothing more. Skarnu had learned to gauge when not to push Raunu. This looked to be one of those times. He asked a different question instead: "Is it really as bad as that?"

"Aye, sir, it is," Raunu answered stolidly. "The companies, the regiments where the noble officers haven't pulled their weight, they're falling to pieces, sir." He hesitated even longer than he had in either of his earlier pauses, then added, "A lot of companies, a lot of regiments, in that boat, sir."

"Curse the soldiers for not defending the kingdom!" Skarnu burst out. Raunu stood mute. Skarnu thought for a while before making an addition of his own: "And curse the officers who didn't give them a better reason to defend the kingdom."

"Ah," Raunu murmured – or was it just an exhalation a little louder than usual? "Sir, you don't mind my saying so, it's because you're the kind of captain who'd come out with the first thing and the second both that so many men have stuck by you."

"Much good it's done them." Skarnu's voice was bitter. Then he sighed. "We can only do what we can do. Let's get moving."

"Aye, sir," Raunu said. "It could be worse, sir. At least we're moving through countryside that's pretty much empty – except for Algarvian soldiers, of course. Down in Rivaroli, we've got enemy soldiers and the locals hunting us."

Aye." Skarnu sighed once more. "And curse King Mezentio for stirring up rebellion against us down there. Only goes to show a generation isn't time enough to make Algarvians change their stripes."

He set off through the forest, walking as softly as he could. He knew Algarvian behemoths had already got ahead of his company. He knew redheaded footsoldiers couldn't be far behind. He kept scouts out ahead and to all sides of his main body of men. None of them reported anything untoward. He still wished he had eyes in the back of his head.

After about an hour, a man at the van came back and reported that the woods ended and, past some untended fields and vineyards, a village lay ahead. "Any sign of soldiers in it?" Skarnu asked.

"Redheads, you mean?" the scout asked, and Skarnu nodded. The soldier said, "No, sir, but I did see a couple of men in trousers on the street."

"Did you?" Skarnu made up his mind. "All right. We'll go forward and scoop them up. People can sort things out later. Right now, I want all the bodies I can get my hands on."

"Aye, that's sensible, sir," Raunu said. Skarnu would have gone on without the sergeant's approval, but was glad to have it.

The company cautiously moved out of the woods and toward the village. Skarnu supposed they were advancing on it, but could you advance during a retreat? That was a fine point of warfare with which he remained unacquainted.

Sure enough, trousered troopers did tramp along the village streets. One of them shouted when he spied the soldiers approaching in open order. In a twinkling, the men in the village took cover. "Be ready for anything," Skarnu called to his own men. "They may be Algarvians in our clothes, trying to lure us into a trap."

Inside the village, the soldiers seemed to have the same fear about Skarnu's company. They needed a good deal of wary calling back and forth before they decided they were all Valmierans. "Powers above be praised you're here," said a young lieutenant who came out to greet Skarnu.

Skarnu took out his map. "Where *is* here?" he asked.

"This miserable place is called Stornarella, sir," the lieutenant answered. When Skarnu found it, he whistled softly; the Algarvians had driven him even farther east than he'd thought. The lieutenant went on, "Now we have some sort of a decent guard force for Duke Marstalu."

"What?" Skarnu stared. "The army commander? Here?"

"Aye, sir." The lieutenant nodded. "We were falling back from the first Algarvian onslaught when their dragonfliers hit our column. I don't think they knew his Grace the Duke was part of it. We were just Valmierans on a road, and so they dropped eggs on us. They killed his Grace's unicorn. He broke his leg when the animal fell on him; we got him to the first shelter we could."

"Is he still in command?" Skarnu asked.

"As much as anyone is," the lieutenant said wearily, which summed up the plight of the army as well as anything. "We didn't think the redheads could do to us what they did to Forthweg last fall. We may have been wrong."

We may have been wrong. Such a bloodless sentence, to leave so much blood in its wake. Skarnu said, "Algarve didn't beat us during the Six Years' War. I expect we'll manage to halt the redheads again."

"I hope we do," the lieutenant said.

The difference between *hope* and *expect* spoke volumes. Skarnu did his best not to read them. He turned to Raunu. "Sergeant, have the men form a perimeter around this village. We'll want to be able to defend it and, if need be, to move out toward the east." He would not say *retreat.*

"Aye, sir," Raunu said, and began giving orders.

"If you will come with me, sir, I know Duke Marstalu will be glad to have your report," the lieutenant said. Skarnu knew nothing of the sort, but accompanied the other officer into Stornarella.

Close up, the village showed its abandonment. Only shards of glass remained in the windows. Leaves drifted against walls and fenceposts. Flowers and grass grew in rank, untended exuberance. The lieutenant led Skarnu to the biggest, fanciest house in Stornarella. Skarnu had expected nothing less. He hadn't thought having his expectations confirmed would leave him so sad.

When the lieutenant took Skarnu inside, Marstalu was lying on a sofa, a splint on his leg, giving a crystallomancer orders to relay: "Tell them to hold out as long as they can, curse it, and to counterattack if they see even the slightest chance. We *must* try to establish some kind of order at the front." He looked up. "Ah, Marquis Skarnu! So good to see you again." For a moment, he might have been in his drawing room at Klaipeda rather than a filthy village parlor with trash and leaves on the floor and pictures all askew on the wall.

Then the illusion shattered. Marstalu himself almost seemed to shatter. He'd always reminded Skarnu of a kindly grandfather. Now he reminded him of a kindly grandfather whose wife of many years had just died: Marstalu was suddenly a little old man cast adrift in a world he neither understood nor desired.

"Command me, your Grace!" Skarnu said, trying to put some

spirit back into the man who commanded not merely him but the entire Valmieran army struggling to resist the assault from Algarve.

It was no good. He could see it was no good before Marstalu spoke. "Your words prove you noble," the duke said with a sad, sweet smile. "But what good is nobility in these times? The commoners shun it, as do most even of our so-called nobles. We are beaten, Skarnu, beaten. All that remains is to learn how badly we are beaten."

"Surely we can yet rally," Skarnu said.

"Perhaps we can rally in the south – back of the Soretto," Marstalu said. "Defending true Valmierans may put the heart back in our soldiers. We do have to form a line here in the center. How and where we can do that, I am not so sure. In the north, I admit, things are rather better. The thick forests and rough country along the border there will leave the Algarvians with their work cut out for them."

"Then we ought to fall back to the Soretto in the south and use the men we save to help strengthen the center here," Skarnu said.

"What do you think I've been trying to do?" Marstalu showed temper for the first time. "But powers above, it's not been easy. The cursed folk of Rivaroli have raised a guerrilla against our soldiers there, and the Algarvian behemoth brigades smash through everything we can move against them, throwing us into disarray far behind what should be the line."

"Have we no behemoths of our own, your Grace?" Skarnu asked. In the retreat, he'd seen a handful of dead Valmieran beasts, but none in action.

"Aye, distributed along the line to support our foot," the Duke of Klaipeda answered. "That is the way sensible men have employed them as long as they have been utilized in warfare."

Skarnu was about to point out that the Algarvian way seemed to work better and therefore seemed more sensible when shouts came from the street. The young lieutenant dashed outside. When he came back a moment later, smiles wreathed his face. "Your Grace," he cried, "they have a carriage to take you to the rear."

"Oh, very good." Marstalu pointed to his splinted leg, then to Skarnu. "My lord Marquis, will you be so kind as to help my aide get me to the said carriage?"

With one of the duke's arms draped over each of them, Skarnu and the lieutenant did haul him to the carriage and heave him aboard. The lieutenant stuck his head into the carriage, spoke briefly with Marstalu, and then turned to Skarnu. "You and your company are to continue your stalwart defense, as before."

"Aye," Skarnu said in a hollow voice. The lieutenant mounted a unicorn. The carriage began to roll. Marstalu's followers rode off with it. They left Skarnu and his men behind, to salvage what they could.

Count Sabrino peered down at the ground from atop his dragon. Thick woods hid some of the roughness of the terrain, but could not conceal it all. For generations, generals on both sides had been convinced these uplands on the northern part of the border between Algarve and Valmiera were too rugged for any large operations. King Mezentio's men aimed to prove those generations of generals mistaken.

Had Sabrino swung his dragon so he could look more to the west, he would have seen the great columns of men and behemoths stretching back into Algarve. He didn't bother; he knew they were there. His task, and that of his wing, was twofold: to keep Valmieran dragonfliers from spying on them as they deployed and to support them when they come out into the open country east of the uplands.

He had not seen many enemy dragons. Maybe the Valmierans were using all they had in the south, against the Algarvian assault and against the rebellious men of the Marquisate of Rivaroli. Maybe they didn't have enough to cover all their frontier with Algarve. Maybe both those things were true. Sabrino hoped they were. If they were, Valmiera would soon get a nasty surprise.

"In fact," Sabrino breathed, "I think the cursed Kaunians may be getting a nasty surprise just about now." He patted the side of his dragon's scaly neck, a gesture of affection altogether out of keeping with his usual annoyance at the beast he rode.

Down below, the wooded uplands gradually gave way to the flatter farming country of most of western Valmiera. And now he spied emerging from the woods the heads of the columns whose tails stretched back into Algarve. Behemoths trotted across newly planted fields, marking fresh paths easily visible from the air.

Sabrino whooped. "The blonds will know they've been diddled, all right!"

The behemoth crews started tossing eggs into the first villages they reached and blazing at the buildings in them with the heavy sticks the great animals carried. Wooden houses and shops burst into flames. Smoke rose in thick clouds. Sabrino nodded approval. The Valmierans might not think Mezentio's men able to mount a major assault through the rough country lying between the two kingdoms, but they would have garrisons hereabouts.

And so they did. A behemoth went down, crushing some of the men who rode it. The rest perished when a Valmieran beam blazed through the metal-and-magic shell of an egg it carried. When that egg went up, it touched off the sorcerous energy stored in the others and in the heavy stick. The resulting blast of light made Sabrino close his eyes for a moment. When he opened them again, only a crater in the middle of the field showed where the behemoth and its crew had been.

But most of the others, and the mounted footsoldiers accompanying them, kept right on going forward. The dragoons entered the village. Before long, they came out the other side, rejoining the behemoths that had skirted the built-up area. The men who had held their horses brought them up so they could quickly move forward again. First tiny obstacles overcome, the advance rolled ahead like the oncoming tide.

Also like the tide, it left rubbish in its wake and pushed more along ahead of it. Not all the dots down there on the ground moved with military discipline and precision. Some were peasants and townsfolk, fleeing before King Mezentio's soldiers as the ancient Kaunians must have fled before the fierce Algarvian invaders of another day – and as Algarvians had assuredly fled when Valmieran troops pushed into eastern Algarve.

Sabrino was tempted to order his wing to swoop down on the Valmieran refugees, to rake them with dragonfire. A less experienced officer would have done it, and would have been raked over the coals for it afterwards. Sabrino knew the Valmierans would finally be discovering they'd worried more about one attack when another was more important. They'd be rushing all the men and behemoths and dragons they could to the north, to try to stanch the breach. He didn't want those dragons attacking his fliers with the advantage of altitude.

In any case, other, lower-flying, Algarvian dragons began dropping eggs on the roads and on the Valmierans clogging them. Sabrino nodded to himself. He'd been wise to resist temptation. The commanders were prepared for everything.

The first Valmieran dragons came winging their way out of the southeast less than half an hour later. Sabrino nodded again. Some Valmieran soldier in one of those little towns had had a crystal with him, and warned his comrades before he either died or ran away. The blonds had responded pretty quickly.

But they'd sent a boy to do a man's job. They couldn't have put more than a squadron of dragons in the air: more a reconnaissance force than one in any shape to fight hard. Sabrino laughed for joy as he signaled his wing to the attack. Even his dragon's hiss seemed to have a gloating anticipation to it. He knew that was a product of his own imagination; dragons barely had the brains to know they were alive at the moment, and couldn't possibly anticipate.

When the Valmierans realized how many Algarvian dragons they faced, some of them flew back the way they had come. The others soon wished they had. Sabrino and his men blazed some of the enemy fliers off their dragons' necks. Other Valmierans perished in the dragon-to-dragon fights that always broke out in spite of everything fliers could do. A couple of his own men perished, too, which made him curse.

Later that afternoon, the Algarvians on the ground bumped into the first defenders who weren't taken aback to find them there. The blonds held out in a small town and refused to yield. Sabrino laughed to watch the behemoths and mounted infantry simply go around the Valmieran strongpoint. If the enemy chose to come out from the town and fight, fine. If not, the strongpoint would soon wither on the vine. The Valmieran defenders, and the townsfolk with them, would get hungry in short order.

If everything had gone according to plan, ground troops would be laying out a dragon farm on this side of the uplands, so the wing wouldn't have to fly all the way back to Algarve to land. Soon, he would have to find out if everything had gone as planned. His dragon was soaring more now, flapping less; it would be hard pressed to hold off a rested Valmieran beast.

He began to fly in an expanding spiral, still alert for enemy war-dragons but also peering down to see if he could spy the promised dragon farm. When he did, he brought the dragon down to the ground. Handlers chained it to a stake. The rest of the fliers in his wing followed him down.

"We'll need some beasts in the air," Sabrino said worriedly to one of the handlers. "Some of my fliers should have mounts fresh enough to go back up." He wondered if he was telling the truth; his dragon was almost worn enough to be docile, a striking measure of its exhaustion.

"Don't worry about it, sir." The fellow in leather protective gear pointed to the sky. Sure enough, more Algarvian dragons were flying up out of the west to take the place of the worn wing. The handler grinned. "So far, everything's going just like it's supposed to."

"Isn't it, though?" Sabrino murmured. In the Six Years' War, nothing had gone as it was supposed to, either for Algarve or for her foes. They'd kept banging heads like a couple of rams till one side finally yielded. But the Algarvian army had had its own way in Forthweg, and everything here in Valmiera seemed to be working as the generals had drawn it on the map. Sabrino wondered how long that would last. He wondered how long it could last. For as long as it lasted, he – and Algarve – would enjoy it.

Another handler pushed up a cart full of chunks of meat thickly coated in red-orange powder: ground cinnabar, to give the dragons the quicksilver they needed. Along with the meat, the handler also set out a couple of lumps of yellow brimstone. Sabrino's dragon stretched out its long, scaly neck and began to eat. The flier nodded; he'd expected nothing less. A dragon that wouldn't eat wasn't merely exhausted; it was at death's door.

Sabrino fed himself, too. Supplies for the men had come forward along with those for their mounts, which proved everything was going according to plan. Gulping rough red wine and gnawing on a roll stuffed with ham and melon, Sabrino said, "I don't think the yellow-hairs know what's hit 'em yet."

"Here's hoping you're right, sir." Captain Domiziano lifted his tin cup to turn the words into a toast. "We've got 'em bending way forwards down south. Now we come around behind 'em and give it to 'em straight up the arse."

"You're a vulgarian, Domiziano," Sabrino said, "nothing but a cursed vulgarian."

"Why, thank you, sir," the squadron leader said. He and his wing commander laughed together. While they sat on enemy soil drinking wine, life looked monstrous good.

It looked even better the next morning. Dragons were blessed – some would say cursed, for it made them more difficult to handle – with enormous powers of recuperation. When Sabrino climbed aboard his mount in predawn twilight, the beast was as stupid and bad-tempered and ready to fight anything that moved – except possibly him – as ever.

He took his wing of dragonfliers into the heavens before sunup. They flew southeast, in the direction from which day would break. Sabrino scanned the brightening sky ahead. Enemy dragons would be silhouetted against the glow, and easy to see from a long distance. But he spied none.

Fighting on the ground had not waited for the sun to come up, either. Flashes from bursting eggs showed where the battle line lay. Sabrino whistled; the wind of his passage blew the sound away. King Mezentio's men had moved miles since the evening before.

And the Algarvians were still moving forward. Here and there, the behemoths and the fast-moving mounted infantry accompanying them found obstacles: Valmieran fortresses (although not many, for they'd penetrated well beyond the border), garrisoned villages, stubborn companies or occasionally even regiments of Valmierans.

As they'd done the day before, as they'd learned to do in the Forthwegian campaign, they flowed around as many obstacles as they could. Where they had to fight, the behemoths did the bulk of the work. They would stand off from the opposition and use their egg-tossers and heavy sticks to fight at ranges from which the Valmierans, who mostly had weapons individual soldiers could carry, had trouble replying.

Every so often, the Valmierans would keep on fighting in spite of everything the Algarvian warriors on the ground could do. Then the crystallomancers sent out the call for help from above. Dragons would dive out of the sky and drop heavier eggs on the enemy. Few indeed were the times when the dragons had to drop eggs twice on the same target.

Algarvian dragons also swooped on Valmieran egg-tossers that hurled sorcerous energies at King Mezentio's men. There were more of those as the day wore along, as the Kaunian kingdom slowly – too slowly – awoke to peril in the north. But the Algarvian advance rolled on, roughly paralleling the course of the middle reaches of the Soretto before that river bent from southeast to northeast but in any case well to the east of it: a spearthrust aimed straight at Valmiera's heart.

Watching it from above, helping to drive off the Valmieran dragons that tried to check it, Sabrino grew sure on the second day of what he'd believed on the first. "They can't stop us," he told his dragon, and the beast did not argue with him.

Tealdo looked east across the Soretto River, into land that had belonged to the Kingdom of Valmiera since time out of mind. On the far bank, Algarvian dragons dropped eggs on the enemy. Tealdo felt like cheering each flash of released sorcerous energy and each cloud of dust that rose from it.

Sergeant Panfilo had other things on his mind. "Curse the trousered swine for sending all the bridges into the river," he growled. "If they hadn't done that, we'd be halfway to Priekule by now."

"More than halfway," Tealdo said. "We went through Rivaroli like a dose of castor oil. The yellow-heads still don't know what landed on 'em."

Captain Galafrone was trotting by, as usual more energetic than troopers half his age. Hearing Panfilo and Tealdo, he stopped, threw back his head, and laughed. "Powers above, boys, we only got to the river a couple of hours ago. We'll be over it by this time tomorrow. *Then* we drive for Priekule." He paused, listening to what he'd just said. "We really *are* moving, aren't we? Things weren't like this during the Six Years' War, believe you me they weren't."

"I only hope those bastards coming down from the north don't beat us to King Gainibu's palace," Tealdo said.

Galafrone laughed again. "Those bastards coming down from the north are your fellow soldiers, you know. And they couldn't be doing what they're doing if we hadn't drawn the Valmierans' notice away from them."

"Doesn't seem fair, sir," Sergeant Panfilo said. "We're doing as much work – maybe even harder fighting – and they'll get all the glory. No, that doesn't seem fair at all."

He sounded like a little boy with a case of the sulks. Tealdo understood that. He felt much the same way, and chimed in, "That's right. What's the point of fighting if you can't swagger and boast afterwards? Those fellows will be able to, while we're nothing but afterthoughts."

"Well, anyone who listened to you would guess you're an Algarvian, all right," Galafrone said. "Here's the way I see it, though: if we lick the Kaunians, there's plenty of glory for the whole cursed kingdom. When we lost the last war, back when I was your age, there was plenty of shame to go around, I'll tell you that. But if you get to put on a *Conquest of Valmiera* ribbon, none of the pretty girls will care whether you fought in the northern army or the southern one."

Panfilo pointed back toward the west. "Here come the rafts, looks like."

Sure enough, soldiers aboard a couple of horse-drawn wagons started throwing what looked like large leather pancakes down on to the ground. They also threw down some pumps. Galafrone set his men to inflating the rafts.

"No paddles," Tealdo observed. "Do they expect us to get across by twiddling our fingers in the river?"

"Use your head, not your mouth," Panfilo suggested. Tealdo sent him an injured look. Panfilo ignored it. Never in the history of the world had a sergeant proved sensitive to an injured look.

About an hour later, a fellow wearing the insignia of a captain, a badge of the lesser nobility, and a mage's badge came up, looked over the soldiers at work, and shook his head. "This won't do," he said in fussy tones. "No, this won't do at all. You'll have to move upstream about a mile, and take these rafts with you."

"Why?" Galafrone growled. He might have gained captain's rank himself, but still thought like the common soldier he'd been for so many years. "What in blazes is wrong with where we're at?"

The mage sniffed at his grammar, and then again when he noted that Galafrone, though also an officer, sported no badge of nobility of any sort. But his answer was not only civil but also informative: "Because, my dear fellow, that's where the nearest ley line across the Soretto lies."

"Ah," Galafrone said, and light also dawned inside Tealdo. Galafrone went on, "No wonder they didn't issue us any paddles." He raised his voice: "Come on, boys, time to pack up and move. We have to get to the right doorway before we can pay the Valmierans a call." Now that he understood the reason for the mage's order, he complied without the least fuss.

The Valmierans knew that ley line crossed from the Marquisate of Rivaroli into their kingdom proper. They'd flung eggs across the Soretto to keep the Algarvians from concentrating near it till Algarvian dragons put their tossers out of action. More dragons kept working over the eastern bank of the river to make sure the Valmierans didn't cause any more trouble.

Colonel Ombruno's whole regiment and a couple of others were assembling near the ley line. So were a couple of companies of heavily armored behemoths. Tealdo smiled when he saw them. The big, ugly beasts pulled their weight and then some. He'd seen how they spread terror and confusion among the Valmierans. He favored fighting foes who were already afraid.

He waited with his comrades till darkness fell. A couple of Valmieran dragons got through the Algarvian squadrons in the air, but the eggs they dropped for the most part fell wide of the gathering force of Mezentio's men. And, as soon as they had dropped them, the Valmieran dragonfliers fled back to the east as fast as their mounts could carry them.

"Now we take the war to the enemy," Colonel Ombruno declared magniloquently. "Now we avenge their invasion of our soil, now we avenge their robberies after the Six Years' War, now we avenge the wicked plots by which they won that war. For King Mezentio!"

Tealdo shouted "Mezentio!" with the rest. So did his friend Trasone, who stood close by, but Trasone raised an eyebrow while he was shouting. Tealdo felt like raising an eyebrow, too. He cared more about living through the next few days than about the king of Algarve. He suspected most Algarvian soldiers felt the same way. Most Valmieran soldiers probably cared more about living through the next few days than about King Gainibu, too.

With any luck at all, a lot of the trousered Kaunians were going to be disappointed.

"Take to your rafts," Galafronc ordered the men of his company. "We want to hit the yellow-haired whoresons as hard as we can, drive 'em back from the river so we can set up proper bridges — meaning no disrespect to the mage here, of course."

"Of course," that worthy said in a voice like ice. He got into the leather raft with the company commander. After that, Tealdo didn't see him again for a while. He sat in his own raft, doing his best not to wonder what the Valmierans had waiting for him on the other side of the Soretto. All too soon, he'd find out. The rest of the soldiers in Sergeant Panfilo's squad — most veterans of the conquest of Sibiu, a couple of new men replacing casualties — also sat hunched and quiet. Whatever they were thinking, they kept it to themselves.

Tealdo heard the waves in the Soretto begin to slap at the sides of some other leather raft. Then his own began to move, pulled straight across the river by the energy the mage was drawing from the ley line.

He wondered what would happen if some Valmieran, alert or just lucky, blazed the mage in the middle of the stream. That was something he would sooner not discover for himself. He looked across the river, toward the side the Valmierans still held. Flashes showed where Algarvian dragons were dropping eggs on the enemy. "Paste 'em," Tealdo muttered under his breath. "Paste 'em hard."

Other, smaller flashes showed that not all the Valmierans were slain or cowering in their holes. A beam from a stick struck the water not far from Tealdo's raft. It raised a hiss and a brief cloud of steam.

Shouts from the eastern bank of the Soretto and more beams stabbing out announced the arrival of the first Algarvians. If the Valmierans could respond quickly, they'd give Tealdo's comrades a thin time of it. But the one thing the Valmierans hadn't yet shown they could do was respond quickly.

Gravel grated under the leather raft. It stopped so hard, it almost pitched Tealdo out on his face. "Come on!" Panfilo screamed. "Get moving, curse you! You want to sit around and wait for the Valmierans to blaze you for the pot?" Tealdo's boots splashed in shallow water. Then he was pounding through gravel-strewn mud, and then up on dry land.

"Mezentio!" he shouted, not so much to demonstrate his love for his sovereign as to keep any other Algarvians from blazing him in the dark. Speed and confusion had worked in the assault on Sibiu. They'd worked thus far in the fight against Valmiera. "Mezentio!" he shouted again. He didn't want them working against him, especially when he might have to pay with his neck.

He fell in the crater a bursting egg had dug, and then into a trench he hadn't seen in the dark. Picking himself up, he realized he could break his neck as well as paying with it any other way. A couple of dead Valmierans lay in the bottom of the trench. Had any live enemy soldiers been there with him, he would have stretched out cold and dead himself. But the Kaunians who hadn't perished had fled. "Mezentio!" Tealdo shouted once more, and stumbled forward.

Before long, he heard thunderous footsteps behind him. A behemoth pounded past, heading east, and then another and another. He cried out the king of Algarve's name again and again. The behemoth crews, not wanting their own men to blaze them in the night, were also yelling, "Mezentio!"

When dawn came, Tealdo found himself picking his way along the side of a gravel road. Valmierans, some of them soldiers but more civilians, had been retreating down it when Algarvian dragons hit them. The results weren't pretty: dead Valmierans, dead horses and unicorns that had been drawing carts, the carts themselves and all sorts of other worldly goods scattered and burned and wrecked.

Not all the Valmierans who'd been assailed on the road were dead yet, nor all the beasts of burden, either. Tealdo paused to give a moaning old woman who plainly wouldn't last much longer a swig of wine from his water bottle. She had trouble swallowing, but at last managed to choke some down. What she said in her own language sounded like thanks. He wondered if she knew he was an Algarvian soldier or took him for a fellow Kaunian.

"Keep moving!" someone called in Algarvian from behind him. "We've got to keep moving! If we push them now, maybe we can break them."

Tealdo shoved the cork back into his water bottle. His knees clicked as he rose from a squat. When he spied dragons flying west a moment later, he threw himself flat again. But the Valmieran dragons paid him no attention. They were streaking toward the Soretto, toward the river crossing the Algarvians had forced. If they could drop some eggs on the ley line, they could put it out of action for a while and trap the Algarvians on this side of the river.

"Keep moving!" someone else yelled – Captain Galafrone this
time. "They won't stop us. They can't stop us. Nothing Valmiera can
do will stop us now." Tealdo slogged east. He hoped his company
commander was right.

Sabrino was working harder these days than he had when the
Algarvian army broke through into northern Valmiera the week
before. King Gainibu's men had finally figured out that, if they didn't
halt the Algarvian thrust before it reached the Strait of Valmiera, it
would cut off their large force still in eastern Algarve and western
Valmiera – and would also keep more help from Lagoas from
reaching the mainland of Derlavai.

But the Lagoans, curse them, had already put dragons and
behemoths and footsoldiers into southern Valmiera. Lagoan
dragonfliers carried a reputation earned in the Six Years' War. From
everything Sabrino had seen, they still lived up to it, too. They were
certainly better in the air than their Valmieran counterparts, far better
than the Forthwegians Sabrino had fought as last summer passed into
autumn.

At the moment, Sabrino was wondering whether the Lagoan he
was fighting was better in the air than he was. The fellow put his red-
and-gold-painted dragon through maneuvers that should have tied it
in knots. He kept trying to get on Sabrino's tail at a range close
enough to let his dragon flame Sabrino's out of the sky. He kept
coming close to doing it, too.

He also had a way of leaning far over his dragon's neck to make
himself as small a target as he could. Sabrino wouldn't have cared to
lean over that far himself, not with so much empty, empty air
between him and the ground. He wondered whether the islander had
more balls than brains, or whether the Lagoans had come up with a
new kind of harness that made falling off harder.

However that was, the enemy dragonflier made a nasty foe.
Sabrino felt his own dragon begin to fade beneath him. The beasts
could put forth their greatest effort only in short spurts – although the
dragon the Lagoan flew seemed tireless. Sabrino blazed at the enemy
again, and missed again, too. He cursed, then threw his dragon into
a twisting dive to evade the Lagoan.

As he leveled off, the islander still pursuing him, one of the fliers from his wing dove at the Lagoan. The enemy had to break off his attack on Sabrino to defend himself. Algarvian doctrine stressed always keeping an eye on what was happening in back of you. Faster than the Lagoan must have imagined he could, Sabrino resumed the attack himself. His dragon roared to see the one painted in red and gold straight ahead of it.

Behind Sabrino, the dragon's powerful wings beat hard. Closer and closer it drew to the Lagoan's mount, which was part of a smaller force than the Algarvian count's. The embattled Lagoan could not fight two at once. Sabrino tapped the side of his dragon's neck. Flame burst from its mouth, enveloping the flank and right wing of the Lagoan dragon.

"That's my beauty!" Sabrino cried. For the moment, he didn't despise dragons at all. His, surely, was the best of the breed ever hatched.

The Lagoan flew a fine dragon, too. Even as it shrieked, horribly burned, even as it began to tumble out of the sky, it twisted its long, limber neck and sent a blast of flame back at Sabrino and his mount. He felt the heat against his cheek, but the fire fell short. Shrieking still, the Lagoan dragon fell.

Sabrino looked around for more foes. Seeing none close by, he waved to the Algarvian flier who'd fatally distracted his opponent. The dragonflier blew him a kiss, as if to say it was all part of the game.

Down plummeted the Lagoan dragon. Sabrino tried to mark just where it fell. If he got the chance, he wanted to look at the harness the enemy had used. If it turned out to be better than the ones he and his comrades had on their dragons, the saddlers' guild needed to know about it, and quickly.

There on the ground, Algarvian behemoths continued their push through Valmiera, southeast toward the sea. As they had throughout the campaign thus far, they did meet resistance here and there. The Valmierans were brave enough, even if some of their soldiers had no love for the noble officers who led them. And so were the Lagoan battalions fighting alongside them. But the onslaught of dragons, behemoths, and the dragons who kept right up with the behemoths had thrown the enemy into disarray, so that his units fought individually, not supporting one another so well as they might have done. Against the Algarvians, whose warriors and beasts on the ground and in the air worked together like the fingers on a single hand, that was a recipe for disaster.

A few enemy behemoths came out of a stand of trees. Sabrino could tell at a glance they were Valmieran: King Gainibu's men loaded them down with so much armor, it made them slow, so much armor that they couldn't carry as many crewmen or weapons as their Algarvian counterparts. And there were only a few of them. The Valmierans had parceled them out all along the line, while the Algarvians grouped their behemoths into large bands. No one had been sure which was the better way of using them.

"Now people know," Sabrino gloated.

The fight on the ground didn't last long. The Algarvians knocked a couple of Valmieran behemoths kicking with well-tossed eggs, and blazed down another despite the thick coat of mail it wore. After that, a Valmieran crew on a behemoth that hadn't been hurt threw up their hands and surrendered. The last couple of Valmieran behemoths fled back into the woods, pursued by the Algarvians. One Algarvian behemoth was down, too, but Sabrino could see the men who'd ridden it moving around on the ground. They'd come off lucky.

Sabrino flew on to the south. Beyond the front, Valmieran refugees clogged the roads. They fled the advancing Algarvians as if the Kaunian Empire were falling all over again. In their flight, they helped insure that Valmiera would fall, for soldiers could not use the roads they filled edge to edge. Here and there, Algarvian dragons had dropped eggs on them or swooped low to flame them. The havoc the dragons had wreaked only made travel tougher.

That would hurt Gainibu's soldiers. All the same, Sabrino was glad his wing hadn't been assigned to attacking civilians on the roads. War was a filthy enough business anyhow. Had he been ordered to drop eggs on women and children and old men, he would have done it. He had no doubt of that. But it would have left a bad taste in his mouth.

At a makeshift dragon farm near a small Valmieran town that evening, Sabrino assembled his squadron leaders and asked, "If you were King Gainibu, what would you do now?"

"Hop on a ley-line cruiser and scoot over to Lagoas while I still have the chance," Captain Orosio said. He'd inherited a squadron when its commander got badly burned. "If Gainibu doesn't, we'll nab him."

"You're like right about that," Sabrino said, "but it isn't quite what I meant. If the Valmierans and Lagoans are going to stop us before we get to the sea, how do they do it?"

"They'd have to strike back across our front lines from east and west at once," Captain Domiziano said: "with some of the force they sent into Algarve, and with whatever they can scrape up to the north and east. If they can open up a corridor and pull out most of their striking force, they might hold us out of Priekule, the way they did during the Six Years' War."

"That would be very bad," Orosio said.

"Aye, it would." Sabrino nodded. "Domiziano, I agree with you – that is their best hope. I don't think they can do it, though. Have you seen – have you seen anywhere – the kind of force they'd need to crack us off to the east? I haven't. They sent most of their best troops to the border against us, and they're under attack along the border, too. They won't be able to pull much without asking for disaster there."

"They're under attack behind the border, too," Orosio said. "The folk of Rivaroli still remember whose kingdom they rightly belong to."

"So they do," Sabrino said, "and the Kaunians are paying the price for greed. Well, our job is to make sure it's a big price."

"There's the truth, sir," Domiziano said. "We've waited a long time to have our revenge on them. Now that it looks like we finally do, they'll be paying plenty, they will." His eyes shone with anticipation. Algarvians savored vengeance almost as much as Gyongyosians did, and took it – or so Colonel Sabrino was convinced, at any rate – with far more panache.

"Oh, indeed," Sabrino said now. "We have to make sure they can't get back up on their hind legs and hit us again for a long time to come. They tried to do that to us a generation ago, but they couldn't quite bring it off. We will, though; King Mezentio won't make the mistake of being too mild."

Out at the edge of the dragon farm, a sentry called a challenge. A woman answered in Valmieran. Orosio started to laugh. The sentry asked, "What did she say, sir? I don't speak a word of their bloody language!"

"You must be a handsome fellow," Orosio answered, chuckling still. "If it means the same in Valmieran as it does in classical Kaunian, she just asked if you wanted to marry her."

"She's not too bad, sir, but no thanks all the same," the sentry said.

Sabrino also laughed. "That verb has changed meaning since the days of the Kaunian Empire," he said. "What she really asked was whether you wanted to screw her."

"Oh," the sentry said, suddenly thoughtful. "It's the best offer I've had tonight, anyway."

"You're on duty, soldier," Sabrino said. With women involved, his countrymen often needed reminding of such things. Sabrino went on, "You'd have to pay to get what you want, and she's liable to give you something you don't want along with it."

The woman let out an indignant screech; evidently she understood Algarvian even if she didn't speak it. "She's gone," the sentry said, his voice mournful.

"Just as well," Sabrino called to him. By the sentry's sniff, he had a different opinion. Well, even if he did, he couldn't do anything about it . . . tonight.

When Sabrino took his dragon into the air the next morning, he discovered that the Valmierans were trying to do what Domiziano had predicted: they mounted a fierce attack from the west against the Algarvian behemoths and dragoons blocking their line of retreat. They'd loaded eggs on to every dragon that could carry them, too, to drop on the Algarvians.

But egg-carrying dragons were slow because of the extra weight they bore, slow and awkward in the air. Sabrino's wing of wardragons flamed many of them out of the sky and blazed many of the fliers who controlled them. Only a few got through to add their weight to that of the attack on the ground.

That ground attack came only from the west. Sabrino grinned when he saw how little the Valmierans to the east of the Algarvians could do. If his countrymen could contain the Valmieran effort to break out now, they would swallow the rest of the Kaunian kingdom at their leisure.

Contain it the Algarvians did, over another couple of days of hard fighting. Reinforcements came up along the roads and by ley-line caravan. The retreating Valmierans had disrupted the ley-line network here and there, but only here and there: an effort of a piece with the way they'd fought most of the war. King Mezentio's men had little trouble working around the gaps.

By the end of the third day, it was plain the Valmierans would not, could not, break out. When Sabrino brought his dragon to the ground that evening, every part of him but his smile was exhausted. "Bring me wine!" he shouted to the first dragon handler who came up to him. "Wine, and quickly! We have them! They are ours!"

"They've beaten us," Skarnu said dully. He leaned back against the trunk of a chestnut tree. He was so worn, he couldn't have sat up straight without the tree behind him. "We're trapped between two blazes, and we can't get out."

"They move so cursed *fast*," Sergeant Raunu said. Though many years older than the Valmieran marquis who commanded him, he seemed fresher – not that that was saying much. "They're always there a day before you think they can be, and they always have twice as many men there as you expect. It wasn't like this during the Six Years' War." He'd said that before during this disastrous campaign, any number of times.

"More of our men are running off now, or just throwing down their sticks and surrendering to the first redhead they see," Skarnu said.

Raunu nodded. "Aye, they see there's not much hope, sir. After a while, you start asking why you should get killed when it won't do the kingdom any good. At that, we still have more men in the line and ready to fight than most companies. Powers above, we've got more men in the line and ready to fight than a lot of regiments. Some of the officers had given up, too, and the men know it."

"And some of the commoners don't want to fight for the nobility anyhow," Skarnu added.

"Sir, I wouldn't have said that," Raunu replied. "But, since you have gone and said it, I'm cursed if I can tell you you're wrong."

"Would they rather serve the Algarvians?" Skarnu knew his voice was bitter, but he couldn't help it. "If they think the redheads will treat them any better than their own rulers do, they'll be disappointed."

Raunu said nothing. He'd been a sergeant since the Six Years'

War. He would never rise above sergeant's rank in King Gainibu's army, not if he stayed in till he was a hundred years old. He might possibly have had a view different from Skarnu's, but that didn't occur to the young marquis till much later.

For the moment, his own immediate problem had more weight. "We can't break out, not as an army we can't," he said, and Raunu nodded again. Skarnu went on, "Since we can't break out, we're going to have to surrender or else get pounded to pieces right where we are."

"Aye, sir, I'd say that's so," Raunu responded.

"But there aren't Algarvians everywhere, especially to the east of us," Skarnu continued, as much to himself as to the veteran sergeant. "There are plenty of them where they really need to be, but their line has thin spots, too."

"That's so," Raunu said. "Wasn't like that in the last war, either. Then everything on both sides was sewn up right. But the Algarvians can move so much force so fast, they don't have to be strong everywhere at once — just where it counts, like you say."

"Which means that, if we slide through a few men at a time, we ought to have a decent chance of getting past them and into country they don't hold," Skarnu said. "Then we can go on fighting them."

"Worth a try, I suppose," Raunu said. "We can't do much more here; that's plain. Maybe, just maybe, they'll be able to put something together farther east. If the redheads spot us, they spot us, that's all. In that case, we either die fighting or we spend the rest of the war in a captives' camp."

Neither of those alternatives held any appeal for Skarnu. But they were the only ones he faced if he stayed here. If he kept moving, he had at least some chance of staying free and giving Algarve more trouble.

"Assemble the company, or what you can find of it," he told Raunu. "I'll put the choices to the men, too. I can't order anyone to come along with us, because I don't think our chances are very good."

"Better with you, sir, than with some other officers I can think of, and a lot of 'em carrying higher rank than yours," Raunu answered. "I'll round up the men."

Perhaps half the number of soldiers who'd been with the company

when the Algarvians launched their counterattack came together to
listen to Skarnu. Not all of them had started the campaign with his
company; some, cut adrift from their own units, had jointed his
because even during the worst of the retreat he'd kept giving orders
that made sense.

Now he set forth what he planned to do, finishing, "However you
choose, this is farewell. I won't be with you any more. I don't think
we move even by squads. It'll be every man for himself, or every
couple of men, if you choose to go. Powers above grant that you
come through safe to land where King Gainibu still rules."

Raunu added, "Night's coming soon. Probably the best time to
move, because the redheads will have the most trouble spotting us."

"Aye, that makes sense," Skarnu agreed. He turned to the men
he'd been leading. "You'll leave in separate groups, half an hour or
so apart. Keep in loose order, as I said. If you head northeast, you'll
cut across the land the redheads have grabbed at a right angle; that'll
be the shortest way. Good luck."

"What about you, sir?" one of the soldiers asked.

"Oh, I'm going to try it, never fear," Skarnu answered. "But I'll
wait till the last squad's out before I leave."

"You hear that, you lugs?" Sergeant Raunu growled. "Let's give a
cheer for the captain. If we had more officers like him, if we had
more nobles like him, we wouldn't be in this mess right now."

The cheer warmed Skarnu. That Raunu had proposed it warmed
him even more; the veteran hadn't had to do anything like that.

As twilight deepened, Skarnu sent soldiers out, group by group. At
last, only a dozen or so men remained. Some of them didn't bother
getting up when he formed a new group. "Might as well stay here,"
a trooper said. "War's as good as over, looks like to me."

Skarnu didn't bother arguing. He just said, "Everyone who cares
to, follow me." Four or five men did. The rest sprawled on the
ground and waited for Algarvians to come along and scoop them up.

He hadn't gone far when a man stepped out from behind a tree.
"Decided I'd come along with you, sir, but I figured you'd raise a fuss
if I stayed back there," Raunu said. "So I did it this way."

"You're insubordinate," Skarnu said, and the veteran sergeant
nodded. Skarnu laughed. "Curse me for a liar if I say I'm not glad to
see you. Let's get moving. The night won't last forever."

They stuck to the woods whenever they could, but the woods didn't last forever, either. When they had to travel open country, they spread out even wider than before and kept to the fields, avoiding roads even when they led in the right direction. That quickly proved wise: Algarvians on foot or on unicorns — which saw far better at night than horses — patrolled the roads in large numbers.

"I'd like to blaze some of them," Skarnu said as a patrol passed without spotting him or his comrades. "It would bring all the whoresons down on us, though. They carry a lot of crystals, curse them. We should do the same; it would help us move faster."

If he got through to the other side, he'd have some things to say about that. *One thing at a time,* he thought. *For now, worry about getting through.* Every so often, he had to cross roads running perpendicular to his direction. He and the other Valmierans would dash across, getting to cover as fast as they could.

Unlike the fields, which were mostly undamaged, many of the roads and roadsides showed the marks of war: ditches, egg craters, dead men and animals lying bloated and stinking under the starlight. The Algarvians had stormed along roads in their attack from out of the badlands. Why not? Roads let them move faster than they could cross-country. Skarnu's countrymen had fought them on and along the roads, too, fought them and been beaten.

More by the lingering stench of war than anything else, Skarnu realized he was still in Algarvian-held country when dawn began to paint the sky ahead of him with pink. He and Raunu and a couple of other men still with them lay up for the day in the thickest patch of woods they could find. They shared the biscuits and hard cheese and chunks of blood sausage they had. Skarnu took the first watch. Midway through the morning, he shook one of the soldiers awake and lay down himself.

Next thing he knew, his dream of an earthquake turned into Raunu's hand on his shoulder. "Sun's down, sir," the veteran reported. "Time to get moving again."

"Aye." Yawning, Skarnu wearily climbed to his feet. "If you hadn't got me up there, I could have slept another day around, I think."

Raunu's chuckle was dry. "Couldn't we all, sir? But we'd better not."

They went on as they had the night before. Once, they had to dive on to their bellies when a ley-line caravan full of Algarvian soldiers sped past, heading southeast. "They shouldn't be able to do that," Skarnu said angrily after the caravan had passed. "We should have done a better job of wrecking the grid."

"We should have done a better job of a lot of things, sir," Raunu said, and Skarnu could hardly have disagreed with him.

"How wide a sickle slice have they cut through us, sir?" one of the troopers asked, as the sickly-sweet smell of meat dead too long and the dangerous reality of Algarvian patrols went on and on and on.

"Too wide," Skarnu answered: a truth as obvious as Raunu's.

After another hour or so, he spotted yet one more patrol, this one, unusually, in a field rather than going down a road. He needed a moment to realize these soldiers wore trousers, not kilts. When he did, his heart leapt within him. Without coming out from behind the bush that concealed him, he called softly: "King Gainibu!"

The soldiers started. "Who goes there?" one of them rapped out – in Valmieran.

Skarnu's own language was sweet in his ears. He gave his name, adding, "My men and I have come across the Algarvian lines from the frontier force."

"You're lucky, then, because cursed few have made it," the soldier answered. Bleakly, he added, "Cursed few have tried, come to that. Show yourselves, so we know you aren't redhead raiders."

Skarnu emerged from cover ahead of his men. He did it ostentatiously, so the Valmierans wouldn't take alarm and blaze him. One of the soldiers came up, looked him over, talked with him, and called, "I think he's the real thing, Sergeant."

"All right," the fellow in charge of the patrol answered. "Lead his pals and him back to headquarters, then. We can use every man we find, and that's a fact."

Headquarters gave Skarnu hope. When he reached them, though, he discovered the senior officer there was an overage, overweight captain named Rudninku, whose command consisted of three understrength companies.

"Haven't got anything," he moaned. "Not enough men, not enough behemoths, not enough armor or weapons for half the ones we do have, not enough horses, no unicorns. I'm supposed to hold a couple of miles of front with this. I can't attack, not unless I want to kill myself. I can't stop the redheads if they turn on me, either."

"What *can* you do?" Skarnu demanded, hoping Rudninku would, if prodded, come up with something useful.

He didn't. All he said was, "Sit tight and wait to see what happens in the south. If we win, maybe I can pitch into the Algarvians' flank. If we lose — and things don't look good down there — I'll surrender. What else can I do?"

"Go on fighting," Skarnu said. Rudninku looked at him as if he'd lost his mind.

Some of the reports Hajjaj used to mark the progress of the Derlavaian War on the map in his office came from the Zuwayzi ministries in Trapani and Priekule. The two sets of reports didn't always gibe; the Algarvians had a way of announcing good news for their side days before the Valmierans admitted it was true.

And some of Hajjaj's reports came from the news sheets here in Bishah. Every once in a while, those were spectacularly wrong. More often than not, though, they got news from the far east faster and more accurately than either ministry there.

Hajjaj thrust a brass pin with a green glass head into the map east of the Valmieran town of Ventspils. Seeing just where Ventspils was made him whistle softly: it lay well to the east of Priekule, and was almost as far north. The Algarvians had reached the Strait of Valmiera and made the Lagoans pull their men and dragons out of King Gainibu's land or see them cut off and killed or captured. The Lagoans had had to slaughter a lot of their behemoths, too, to keep them from falling into Algarvian hands.

And the Algarvians, having knocked Lagoas out of the fight for the time being, having trapped and reduced to impotence the main Valmieran army, were now executing a grand wheeling movement to the north and east against . . . against not much, as far as Hajjaj could tell.

Shaddad, his secretary, came in and interrupted his contemplation. Shaddad, unusually for a Zuwayzi, was wearing a tunic and kilt that would have been stylish during Hajjaj's university days in Trapani before the Six Years' War. Bowing to Hajjaj, the secretary said,

"Your Excellency, I remind you that the Marquis Balastro will be here in less than half an hour."

"Meaning I had better shroud myself, eh?" Hajjaj said.

Shaddad nodded. "Even so, sir. It were better not to scandalize the Algarvian minister."

"Oh, Balastro wouldn't be scandalized," Hajjaj said as he walked toward the closet from which he sometimes had to pull out clothes. "He *is* an Algarvian: he enjoys leering at the women here whenever he has occasion to come out on business. I admit he wouldn't be so glad to stare at my scrawny old carcass, though, and so I shall deck myself out for him." He put on a tunic and kilt of somewhat more modern cut than Shaddad's.

Being of light, gauzy cotton, the clothing couldn't have made him much warmer than he was already. He imagined himself sweating more all the same. His body felt confined, clammy. Clucking sorrowfully, he endured.

Marquis Balastro strutted in at precisely the appointed hour. The strut said he was happy with the world. The gleam in his eye said he had indeed enjoyed the journey from the Algarvian ministry to King Shazli's palace. A serving woman dressed Zuwayzi-style – which is to say, in sandals and jewelry – brought tea and cakes and wine for him and Hajjaj. The gleam in his eye got brighter.

A cultivated man, Balastro accommodated himself to Zuwayzi rhythms. Only after the serving woman had taken away the tray – and after he'd finished ogling her while she did it – did he say, "I have news of moment, your Excellency."

"By all means, then, tell me what it is," Hajjaj said. To his annoyance, he'd spilled a drop of wine on his tunic. Another reason not to care for cloth – it was harder to clean than skin.

Balastro's eyes gleamed now in a different way. Leaning forward, away from the piled cushions against which he sat, he said, "Valmiera has asked for the terms on which we would consent to ending the war against her. She has, to put it another way, yielded."

King Mezentio's minister spoke of Gainibu's kingdom as if it were a woman. *Aye, very much an Algarvian*, Hajjaj thought. Valmiera had yielded – yielded to force. Aloud Hajjaj said, "This is a great day for Algarve."

"It is. It truly is." Balastro's smile held anticipation no Valmieran would have found pleasant. "We have plenty of scores to settle with the Kaunians, reaching back over many years. And settle them we shall."

"What terms will you impose?" Hajjaj asked. He knew more than he liked about imposed terms. Unkerlant had given him painful lessons on the subject.

"I am not privy to them all," Balastro replied. "I am not sure all have yet been set. Of a certainty, however, they shall not be light. Rivaroli will return to its rightful allegiance, that I know." He pointed to the map behind Hajjaj.

Hajjaj also turned to look at the map. The Zuwayzi foreign minister sighed as he faced Balastro once more. "Algarve is fortunate, to have a lost marquisate returned to her. We of Zuwayza, on the other hand, have had provinces torn away from their rightful sovereign."

"I know that. King Mezentio knows that," Balastro said gravely. "The injustice you suffered grieves him. It surely rankles the spirit of every Algarvian who loves honor and right dealing."

"If this be so" – Hajjaj was glad he recalled how to use the Algarvian subjunctive, for he wanted Balastro to know he thought the proposition contrary to fact – "if this be so, I say, King Mezentio might have done a great deal more to show his grief. Forgive me for sounding tart, I beg you, but expressions of sympathy, however gracious, win back no land."

"I know that, too, and so does my sovereign." Balastro spread his hands in an extravagant Algarvian gesture. "But what would you have had him do? When Unkerlant began bullying you, we were at war with Forthweg and Sibiu, with Valmiera and Jelgava. Should we have added King Swemmel to our list of foes?"

"You have knocked out three of your foes now, even if you added Lagoas to the list," Hajjaj said. "And Jelgava's fight against you, by all accounts, has been halfhearted at best."

"Kaunians fear us." Balastro sounded very fierce. "Kaunians have good reason to fear us. We have won our greatest triumph over them since the collapse of the Kaunian Empire." By the fierce triumph on his face, he might have overthrown the Valmieran army single-handed. Then he added, "Nor have we finished."

Hajjaj would never have been so indiscreet. If he passed those words on to the Jelgavan minister . . . *Well, what then?* he wondered. Maybe Balastro had told an open secret after all. If the Jelgavans couldn't figure out that Mezentio would try to deal with them next, they weren't very bright. Hajjaj didn't think the Jelgavan minister to Zuwayza *was* very bright, but that was Jelgava's problem far more than his.

He had more immediately urgent things to worry about, anyhow. "I also notice that, however grieved King Mezentio may be at what Zuwayza has suffered, he had no trouble sharing Forthweg with Swemmel of Unkerlant."

"Again, not sharing Forthweg would have led to war with Unkerlant, and Algarve could not afford that," Balastro answered.

Listening carefully to the way Algarvians said things had its reward. "You *could* not afford it," Hajjaj echoed. "Can you afford it now?"

"We are still at war in the east," the Algarvian minister replied. "Algarve fought in the east and west at the same time during the Six Years' War. The kingdom learned a lesson then: not to be so foolish twice."

"Ah," Hajjaj said, and then, "Suppose Algarve were not at war in the east? What might she do in that case?" He did not want to ask the question. It made him into a mendicant, hand out for alms. For his kingdom's sake, he asked it anyhow.

Balastro said, "For the time being we are at peace with Unkerlant. It would hardly be fitting for me to speak of an end to peace, which often proves so hard to come by. For that reason, I shall say nothing." He winked at the Zuwayzi foreign minister as if Hajjaj were a young, shapely, naked woman.

"I see," Hajjaj murmured. "Aye, that is the proper practice." Balastro nodded, rectitude personified. Hajjaj went on, "Perhaps, though, you might send your attaché here to the palace, on the off chance that he should have something of interest to say to certain of our officers."

"I find it very unlikely that he would," Balastro said, which disappointed Hajjaj – had he misread the Algarvian minister? Balastro continued, "I think they should meet at some quiet place – a tearoom or a café or maybe a jeweler's – so they can have something pleasant to do should it turn out that their conversation is not mutually interesting."

"It shall be as you say, of course," the Zuwayzi foreign minister replied, inclining his head. "You do realize, of course, that any meeting between one of your countrymen and one of mine will be hard to keep secret, however much we try."

"Oh? Why is that?" Balastro asked, so innocently that Hajjaj started to laugh. Balastro looked mystified, which made Hajjaj laugh harder. With coppery hair and skins ranging from pink to tawny, Algarvians stood out in Zuwayza even if they went naked. Every once in a while, one of them would, which made them unusual among the pale folk of Derlavai.

Hajjaj said, "A jeweler's might be a good place to meet, come to think of it. If your attaché happened to wear something other than a uniform, and if the officer with whom he spoke left off his ornaments of rank . . ."

"Oh, certainly," Balastro said, as if he already took that for granted. "Since they will not be meeting in an official capacity, they need not – indeed, they should not – be dressed, or not dressed, in any formal way."

"Nicely put," Hajjaj said.

"I thank you. I thank you very much." The Algarvian minister performed a seated bow. "All this is moonbeams and shadows and gossamer, of course. Algarve is at peace with Unkerlant. As a matter of fact, Zuwayza is at peace with Unkerlant."

"So we are." Now Hajjaj did not try to hide his bitterness. "Would that we had been at peace with Unkerlant this past winter as well."

"If you cannot live at peace with your neighbors, or if the peace forced upon you is unjust, what better to do than take your revenge?" Balastro asked.

"In this, you Algarvians are much like my folk," Hajjaj said, "though we are more likely to feud by clans than either as individuals, as you do, or as a united kingdom. But tell me, if you will, how Unkerlant has offended. King Swemmel, curse him, did not move a step over the border Unkerlant shared with Algarve before the Six Years' War."

"But he wickedly prevented King Mezentio from conquering all of Forthweg, which Algarve might easily have done after we smashed the armies King Penda sent into our northern provinces," Balastro replied.

That struck Hajjaj as a flimsy pretext. But a man looking for a fight needed no more than a flimsy pretext, if any at all. Unless Hajjaj altogether misread Balastro, the hot-blooded Algarvians were looking for a fight with Unkerlant, and looking for friends as well. Hajjaj did not know how friendly to Algarve Zuwayza ought to be. But Zuwayza was Unkerlant's enemy – he did know that. If Unkerlant had more enemies . . . *That will do*, he thought.

13.

Talsu dug like a man possessed. Beside him, his friend Smilsu also made the dirt fly. A few men over, Vartu, the late Colonel Dzirnavu's former servant, used his shovel with might and main. By the way they dug, all the men in the regiment might have suddenly imagined themselves turned into moles. All along the western foothills of the Bratanu Mountains, the Jelgavan army was digging in.

"So much for meeting Forthweg halfway across Algarve," Talsu said, flinging a spadeful of dirt over his shoulder. "So much for taking Tricarico." Another spadeful went. "So much for doing anything but waiting for the Algarvians to come and hit us." Another spadeful.

Smilsu looked around to make sure no officers were within earshot. Then he said, "Powers above know I think our nobles are a pack of fools. This time, though, they may be right. What if the stinking redheads come and hit us the way they hit Valmiera? We'd better be ready for them, don't you think?" Like Talsu, he kept digging as he spoke.

"How can they hit us the way they hit Valmiera?" Talsu demanded. He pointed back toward the east. "We've got the mountains to shield us, in case you didn't notice. I'd like to see the Algarvians try and go through them in a hurry."

Vartu put down his spade for a moment and rubbed his palms on his trousers. "That's what the Valmierans said about their rough country, too," he observed. "They were wrong. What makes you think you're right?"

"More to the Bratanus than 'rough country'," Talsu answered. "How are they going to move fast through those passes?"

"I don't know," Vartu said. "I'd bet a good deal that our generals don't know, either. What I wouldn't care to bet is that the Algarvians don't know."

"They aren't mages," Talsu said, and then amended that: "They aren't *all* mages, anyhow, any more than we are." Now he looked around. "Even with the stupid nobles we've got commanding us, we've pushed them back till now. Why should things change?"

Smilsu gnawed at the rough skin by one fingernail. "They can aim their whole cursed army at us now, near enough. They beat Forthweg. They beat Sibiu. They just got done beating Valmiera and chasing all the Lagoans off the mainland of Derlavai. That leaves them – and us."

"Hmm." Talsu hadn't looked at things from quite that angle. All at once, he started digging harder than ever. Smilsu laughed, took a swig of sour beer from the flask he wore on his hip, and also went back to digging.

If the Algarvians were about to fall on the Jelgavan army that had moved, however tentatively, into their territory, they gave no sign of it. Every now and then, a dragon would fly by from out of the west. No doubt the redhead aboard was looking down to see what the Jelgavans were up to. But no eggs fell on the trenches Talsu and his friends were digging. No kilted Algarvian troopers trilling out barbarous battle cries swarmed into the trenches, blazing or flinging little hand-tossed eggs or laying about them with knives. It was about as peaceful a war as Talsu could imagine.

Like any sensible soldier, he enjoyed that while it lasted. He still wondered how long it would last. That wasn't up to him. And, very plainly, his superiors had decided it wasn't up to them, either. That left it up to the Algarvians, a notion Talsu enjoyed rather less.

But the lull did have its advantages. Mail came up to the front line for the first time in weeks. Talsu got a package from his mother: socks and drawers she and his sister had knitted for him. He also got a letter from his father, urging him, in harsh, badly spelled sentences, to go forth and conquer Algarve singlehanded.

"What am I supposed to do with this?" he asked his friends. "My old man didn't fight in the last war. He doesn't know what things are like."

"I wouldn't lose any sleep over it if I were you," Smilsu said. "They tell all sorts of lies to the people back home. You can't blame the poor fools for believing some of them. During the last war, my mother told me, they were saying the Algarvians would slaughter everybody with blond hair if they won."

"That's pretty stupid, all right," Talsu agreed. "I wonder what the Algarvians have to say about us."

"Nothing good, that's for cursed sure," Smilsu said softly. "You ask me, though, it doesn't much matter to the likes of us which side wins the war, as long as we don't get blazed while it's going on."

Talsu looked around again, to make sure he was the only one who'd heard that. "And you say I'm careless about the way I talk," he murmured. "Do you want to find out how dungeons work from the inside?"

"Not so you'd notice," his friend answered. "But I don't think anybody would turn me in for the sake of licking some noble's backside." His mouth twisted into what looked like a smile. "Of course, I could be wrong. In that case, I'd probably have to try and kill the bastard before the nobles' watchdogs dragged me away."

"How would you know who it was?" Talsu asked.

"I'd have a pretty good notion," Smilsu said darkly. "Anyhow, I can think of a couple of people here who nobody would miss."

"Don't look at me like that," Talsu said, which made Smilsu laugh. Then Talsu looked back over his shoulder. He started whispering again, and urgently: "Here. Stuff one of the socks from my mother in it. An officer's coming."

Smilsu's mouth had been open to say more. He shut it with a snap and, alarm on his face, also turned to get a look at the newcomer. After a moment, he relaxed, at least to a degree. "It's not exactly an officer," he said. "It's only a mage."

"Ah, you're right," Talsu said. Mages serving in the Jelgavan army wore officer's uniform to show they had the authority to command ordinary soldiers, but did not wear officer's badges, which would have shown they enjoyed that authority by right of birth. Instead, they used smaller, plainer badges that put them midway between true – noble – officers and the common herd of soldiers. Their authority was not a birthright, but rather a privilege granted by King Donalitu.

Some sorcerers Talsu had seen enjoyed aping the arrogance of the nobility. Others realized they were just jumped-up commoners, and didn't take themselves so seriously. This mage seemed a chipper enough fellow. As he drew near, he said, "You get on with your work, fellows, and I'll do mine, and we'll all stay happy."

Even Smilsu couldn't find anything to complain about there. "Not so bad," he muttered out of the side of his mouth, and went back to digging.

Grinning, the mage went on, "Of course, we'd all be happier still if the war weren't on and we were sitting in a tavern drinking ale or wine laced with orange juice, but there's cursed little we can do about that, eh?"

"Powers above," Talsu whispered in astonishment. "He'd better be careful, or people will think he's a human being."

"What have they sent you up to the front for, sir?" Vartu asked the mage. By his tone, he wondered if the mage had been forced to come up as a punishment.

If the sorcerer noticed that, he gave no sign, answering, "I'm going to see what I can do to make it harder for the Algarvians to detect exactly where these forward positions are. Can't promise it'll do any enormous amount of good, because the redheads will have mages, too, and what one mage can do, another can undo, but it may help some. The generals back on the other side of the mountains think so, anyhow."

"Fat lot of good magecraft did Valmiera," Smilsu said, but the soldierly gripe came out sounding halfhearted: this was more, and friendlier, attention than the front-line soldiers had got up till now from the high nobles who led them.

And Talsu answered, "That's the point, I think. The king's got to be scared green that what happened to Valmiera will happen to us, too. If he can find anything that'll keep Algarve from riding rough-shod over us, looks like he's going to try it."

"Hitting the redheads harder from the start would have been nice, but you've been complaining about that for months," Smilsu said. He pointed at the mage with his short-handled spade. "What's he doing out there?"

"Working magic, I expect," Talsu said. "That's what they pay him for, anyhow." Smilsu snorted and flipped dirt on to his boots.

Out in front of the trench line, the mage paced back and forth. Had the Algarvians been in an aggressive mood, they would have had their line up close to that of the Jelgavans, and could easily have blazed the blond sorcerer. But, for the time being, King Mezentio's men were busy elsewhere, and seemed content to let the Jelgavans settle down in the foothills.

As the Jelgavan mage paced, he waved a large, fine opal that gleamed blue and green and red as the sun struck it at different angles. The charm he chanted was in a Kaunian dialect so archaic that Talsu, who had learned the classical tongue as part of what schooling he'd had, could make out only a few words. That impressed him: great virtue would surely fill such an ancient spell.

If it did, he couldn't discern it. When the mage stopped chanting and returned the jewel to a trouser pocket, nothing seemed to have changed. Talsu still saw the rolling hills ahead of him, and out beyond them the plains of northern Algarve, the plains the Jelgavan army hadn't quite reached.

He wasn't the only one who saw them, and saw they remained as they had been. A soldier farther down the trench line called, "Begging your pardon, sir, but what did you just do?"

"Eh?" The sorcerer seemed worn, as his kind commonly did after working some considerable magic. Then he brightened. "Ah. Of course – you can't see it from that side. Come out here and look at your position, those of you who care to."

Looking at the trenches was easier and more enjoyable than digging them. Talsu scrambled up on to level ground. So did a good many of his comrades. He walked backwards toward the mage, staring at the entrenchments. They kept right on looking like entrenchments. He wondered whether the wizard was as smart as he thought he was.

Then Talsu's backward peregrination carried him past the sorcerer. He and several other soldiers exclaimed, all more or less at the same time. He could still see the trenches he'd helped dig, but at the same time he also saw the ground undisturbed. He took another couple of steps away from the entrenchments, and they grew less distinct to his eye. He took a few more steps, and they almost vanished.

"There's a clever device – a Kuusaman discovery, actually – called a half-silvered mirror," the mage said. "If what's in front of it is brighter than what's in back, it reflects like any other mirror. But if what's in back of it is brighter than what's in front, it lets light through and turns into a window instead. This is sorcery on the same principle."

Talsu said, "Pity we didn't have something like this to protect us when we were moving forward against the Algarvians."

"No one's ever been able to make it a kinetic sorcery," the mage said. Seeing that Talsu didn't understand, he explained: "One that can move along with a party of soldiers. It's better suited to static defense. Even here, it's far from perfect. At too close an approach or at strong search sorcery, it fails. But it's better than nothing."

"Aye," Talsu said. He walked back toward the entrenchments, which returned to clear view as he stepped within the inner limit of the spell. It was indeed better than nothing. It was certainly better than any protection he and his comrades had had up till now. More than anything else, that told him how worried King Donalitu and his counselors were.

On the mainland of Derlavai, spring was giving way to summer. In the country of the Ice People, winter reluctantly admitted spring might be coming. Such chill, gloomy weather perfectly fit Fernao's mood. He'd managed to smuggle King Penda of Forthweg out of Yanina, but the only ship on which he'd been able to gain passage for them had been one sailing south across the Narrow Sea to Heshbon, the chief town – indeed, almost the only town – in the seaside stretch of the austral continent that Yanina controlled.

Here, Fernao was not Fernao. He styled himself Fernastro, and spoke Algarvian rather than Lagoan. Penda had shaved his beard and was going by the name of Olo, an Unkerlanter appellation. Forthwegian was close enough to the northeastern dialects of Unkerlanter to let him pass for one of King Swemmel's subjects. Fernao had also worked small sorceries on them, so neither looked quite as he had in Yanina.

Penda had not proved a good traveling companion. Used to palaces, he found distinctly less than appealing the grimy hostel in Heshbon where he and Fernao lodged. "Swemmel's dungeon would be more comfortable," he grumbled.

Fernao answered in Forthwegian: "I am sure it could be arranged."

The fugitive king shuddered. "Perhaps I was mistaken." His belly rumbled, loudly enough that he couldn't pretend Fernao hadn't heard it. Instead, he sighed and said, "We may as well go downstairs and eat something, if the kitchen can turn out anything worth eating."

"Or even if it can't," Fernao said.

The odds, he knew, were not much better than even money. Yaninans ran the hostel. They did their best to cook in the hearty style of their homeland, but what they had to work with was what the Ice People ate: camel meat, camel milk, camel blood, and tubers that tasted like paste. They came up with all manner of stews, but few of them, to Fernao's mind, were hearty.

He ate, anyway, spooning up meat and boiled tubers, drinking a spirit the folk of Heshbon distilled from the tubers. It also tasted like paste, but kicked like a unicorn. He found he enjoyed most meals more with his tongue numbed.

As quickly as they could, he and Penda left the hostel and headed for the market square. "Maybe today we shall find a caravan faring east," Penda said, as he did every day when they headed for the market square.

"Aye, maybe we shall," Fernao answered absently. For one thing, he was tired of hearing Penda say that. For another, he was looking south, toward the Barrier Mountains. Whenever he was on the streets of Heshbon, he looked toward the mountains. Tall and jagged, they serrated the southern skyline. Snow and ice covered them from their peaks more than halfway down to the lower ground that ran toward the sea. Adventurers had died climbing those peaks. Others had pushed past them into the frigid interior of the austral continent. Some had escaped the Ice People and mountain apes and other, lesser, dangers and written books about what they'd found.

About half the people on the street were short, swarthy Yaninans, most of them with wool cloaks over their big-sleeved tunics and tights. The rest, except for a scattering of aliens like Fernao and Penda, were Ice People. They wore hooded robes of fur or woven camel hair that covered them from head to foot. Their beards, which they never trimmed, grew up to their eyes; their hairlines started less than an inch above their eyebrows. The women, unlike those of other races, had faces no less hairy than those of the men.

They never bathed. The climate gave them some excuse, but not, to Fernao's mind, enough. Their stink filled the cold, crisp air, along with that of the camels they led. Those camels were as unlike those of Zuwayza as beasts sharing a name could be. They had two humps, not one, and thick coats of shaggy brown hair. Only their nasty tempers matched those of their desert cousins.

Ice People had nasty tempers, too. A woman cursed a camel in her own guttural language. Fernao had no idea what she was saying, but it sounded hot enough to melt half the ice on the Barrier Mountains. Penda stared at her. "Do you suppose they're that hairy all over?" Before Fernao could reply, he went on, "Who would want one of them enough to try to find out?"

"I think they are," Fernao told him. "And because they are, they're all the go for a certain kind of customer, shall we say, at the very fanciest brothels in Priekule and Trapani and, I have to admit, in Setubal, too."

Penda looked revolted. "I wish you had not told me that, sir mage." Fernao hid a smile. By his standards, Forthweg was a provincial land. Compared to this miserable stretch of semifrozen ground, though, Penda's kingdom suddenly looked a lot better.

Fernao sighed. "If it weren't for the cinnabar here, the Ice People would be welcome to the whole miserable continent."

"Were there no Derlavaians here, we should have had a much harder time escaping from Yanina," Penda said.

"That is so." Fernao admitted what he could scarcely deny. "Now, instead, we are having a hard time escaping from Heshbon."

They strode into the market square. It was something like the lively one in the center of Patras, the capital of Yanina, but only something. As in much of Heshbon, camels remained the dominant theme. Ice People and Yaninans bartered flesh, milk, cheese, hair, the beasts themselves, and what they brought into Heshbon on their backs: furs and cinnabar, which came packed in camel-leather sacks.

Yaninans and Ice People dickered in different ways. Yaninans were, as usual, even more excitable, or more sincerely excitable, than Algarvians. They clapped their hands to their foreheads, rolled their eyes, jumped up and down, and often seemed on the point of suffering fits of apoplexy.

"Call this cinnabar?" one of them roared, pointing to a sack full of the crushed orange-red mineral.

"Aye," answered the man of the Ice People with whom he was dealing. Every line of his body bespoke utter indifference to his opponent's fury.

That only made the Yaninan more furious. "This is the worst cinnabar in the history of cinnabar!" he cried. "A dragon would flame better if you fed him beans and lit his farts than if you gave him this stuff."

"Then don't trade for it," the man of the Ice People said.

"You are a thief! You are a robber!" the Yaninan shouted. The nomad in the long dirty robe just stood there, waiting for the allegedly civilized man from Derlavai to make his next offer. After the Yaninan calmed down enough to stop screeching for a moment, he did.

Penda said, "Most of the cinnabar the Yaninans buy here goes straight to Algarve."

"I know," Fernao said unhappily. Before the Six Years' War, Algarve had held trading towns along the coast of the austral continent, to the east of Heshbon. Now those towns were in the hands of Lagoas or Valmiera (although, with Valmiera fallen to King Mezentio's men, who could guess what would happen to the towns the Kaunian kingdom had controlled?). If Fernao and Penda could get to Mizpah, the closest Lagoan-ruled town, they would be safe.

If. The war on the mainland of Derlavai had disrupted caravan routes down here. Yanina remained formally at peace with Lagoas, but was so close to alliance with Algarve that she had all but cut off commerce with her larger neighbor's foe.

But there stood a man of the Ice People with laden camels he was not unloading in the market square. Fernao and Penda went up to him. "Do you speak this language?" Fernao asked him in Algarvian.

"Aye," the nomad answered. His dirty, hairy face was impossible to read.

"Do you travel?" Fernao asked, and the man of the Ice People nodded. "Do you travel east?" the Lagoan mage persisted. The nomad stood silent and motionless. Given the way things were in Heshbon these days, Fernao took that for affirmation. He said, "My king will pay well to see my friend and me installed in Mizpah."

He did not say who his king was. If the man of the Ice People assumed he followed Mezentio, he was willing to let the fellow do that. After a moment's thought, the fellow said, "The big talkers" – by which, Fernao realized, he meant the Yaninans – "will not make such a trip easy."

"Can you not befool them?" Fernao asked, as if inviting the man of the Ice People to share a joke. "And is profit ever easy to come by?"

A light kindled in the nomad's eyes. One of those questions, at least, had struck his fancy. He said, "I am Doeg, the son of Abishai, the son of Abiathar, the son of Chileab, the son of . . ." The genealogy continued for several more generations. Doeg finished, "My fetish animal is the ptarmigan. I do not slay it, I do not eat of it if slain by others, I do not allow those who travel with me to do it harm. If they do, I slay them to appease the bird's spirit."

Ignorant, superstitious savage, the mage thought. But that was beside the point now. He asked, "Do you tell me this because my friend and I are traveling with you?"

"If you wish it," Doeg answered with a shrug. "If you pay enough to satisfy me. If you are ready to move before the sun moves far."

They dickered for some time. Fernao did his best not to burst into Yaninan-style hysterics. That seemed to make a good impression on Doeg. Good impression or not, the nomad was an implacable bargainer. Fernao fretted; what the man of the Ice People wanted was about as much as he had, and Doeg seemed uninterested in promises of more gold and silver after reaching Mizpah. He saw only what lay right before him. "I am a mage," Fernao said at last, an admission he had not wanted to make. "Bring your price down by a quarter and I will work for you on that journey."

"You would anyway, if danger came," Doeg said shrewdly. "But you may have some use, so let it be as you say. But be warned, man of Algarve" – a misapprehension Fernao did not correct – "your sort of sorcery may not work so well in this country as it does in your own."

"It works here in Heshbon," Fernao said.

"Heshbon is in my country. Heshbon is no longer of my country," Doeg said. "So many Yaninans and other hairless folk" – his dark eyes swung to the clean-shaven Penda – "have come that its essence has changed. Away from the towns, the land is as it once was here. Sorcery is as it once was here. It does not look kindly on the ways of hairless ones."

Fernao didn't know how seriously to take that. It accorded with his own experience, but not with what some of the theoretical sorcerers of Lagoas and Kuusamo had been saying just before the war broke out. He shrugged. "I will do what I can, whatever it proves to be. And you will be seeking to evade the Yaninans, whose magic is not so different from mine."

"This is true. This is good." Doeg nodded. He thrust out his filthy hand. Fernao and, a moment later, Penda clasped it. The man of the Ice People nodded once more. "We have a bargain."

Krasta was going from one shop on the Avenue of Equestrians to the next when the Algarvian army staged its triumphal procession through Priekule. That the procession could have anything to do with her had not crossed her mind. She was glad she had so many of the shops to herself, but annoyed that about every third one was closed.

She had just bought an amber brooch from a shop girl obsequious enough to suit even her and was coming out on to the sidewalk with the new bauble pinned to her tunic when a blast of martial music made her turn her head. Here came the Algarvians, the band at the head of the procession blaring away for all it was worth. The sun gleamed off their trumpets and the metal facings of their drums. Like a jackdaw, Krasta was fascinated with bright, shiny things. She started to stare because of the reflections from the instruments. She kept staring because of the soldiers who carried those instruments.

When she thought of Algarvians, the word that echoed in her mind was *barbarians*. She was a typical enough Valmieran – a typical enough Kaunian – there. Maybe the troopers marching along the Avenue of Equestrians toward her were King Mezentio's finest. *Or maybe I was wrong all along*, she thought: a startling leap of imagination for her.

The Algarvian troopers – first the band, then a couple of companies of footsoldiers, then a squadron of unicorn cavalry, then warriors mounted on snorting, lumbering behemoths, then more footsoldiers, and on and on – impressed her much more favorably than she'd imagined they could, and also much more favorably than the Valmieran soldiers she'd seen coming through Priekule on the way to the war. It wasn't that these warriors were tall and straight and handsome: the same held true for many of her countrymen. It wasn't that their kilts displayed admirable calves; she knew all she needed to know about how men were made.

No, what struck her was partly their discipline – not something she was used to thinking about when she thought of Algarvians – and partly their attitude. They strode down the Avenue of Equestrians as if certain beyond the possibility of doubt that they deserved the victory they had won, deserved it because they were better men than the Valmierans they had beaten. The Valmieran soldiers she'd seen hadn't looked that way. They'd seemed sure they were heading for trouble – and they'd been right.

Having known that feeling of lordly superiority all her life, Krasta naturally responded to it in others. She even let Algarvians – surely commoners, almost to a man – stare at her as she stared at them without showing (indeed, without feeling) the furious resentment such lascivious looks from Valmieran commoners would have roused in her. But even these stares were well disciplined, especially by Algarvian standards: the soldiers' eyes turned toward her, but not their heads.

A handful of other Valmierans stood on the sidewalk watching the procession, but only a handful. Most of Priekule was doing its best to pretend the conquest had not happened and the conquerors did not exist. Krasta had intended to act the same way if and when she encountered any Algarvians, but this display of might and splendor caught her by surprise.

At last, though the procession was far from over, she tore herself away and went down the side street where her carriage waited. The driver was swigging from a flask he hastily put away when he saw his mistress. He descended from the carriage and handed her up into it. "Take me home," she said.

"Aye, milady." The driver hesitated, then volunteered speech, something he rarely did: "Was you watching the redheads pass by, milady?"

"Aye," Krasta answered. "Things may not be so dreadful as the doomsayers have been quacking."

"Not so dreadful?" the driver said as he got the horses going. "Well, here's hoping you're right, but nothing good comes of losing a war, I fear."

"Just drive!" Krasta snapped, and her servant fell silent.

The streets were almost deserted. Many of the men Krasta saw on them were more Algarvian soldiers, moving into place to take possession of Priekule. They were also well behaved. Unlike their parading comrades, they did turn their heads to look her over, but that was all they did. They didn't say anything, and they didn't come close to committing any outrages on her person. Frightened rumor in the city had credited King Mezentio's men with savagery to match their ancient ancestors'.

By the time Krasta neared her mansion, her mood was as good as it ever got. All right: Valmiera had lost the war (she did hope Skarnu was hale), but the Algarvians looked to be far more civilized victors than anyone had expected. After things settled down again, she expected she would be able to enjoy good times with her fellow nobles once more.

As the driver swung the carriage off the street and on to the path that led up to the mansion, that good mood blew out like a candle flame. She pointed angrily. "What are those horses and unicorns doing there?" she demanded, as if the driver not only knew how they'd arrived but could do something about it. He only shrugged; with Krasta, least said was usually wisest.

Then she saw the kilted Algarvian soldier standing by the animals. Before she could shout at him, he turned and went into the mansion. That only made her angrier – how dared he go in there without her leave?

"Bring me right up to the front entrance," Krasta told the driver. "I aim to get to the bottom of this, and right away, too. What business do these intruders have in my ancestral home?"

"I obey, milady," the driver answered, which was the best thing he could possibly have said.

He halted in front of the Algarvians' unicorns and horses. Krasta sprang from the carriage before he could come around and hand her down. She was storming toward the mansion when the door opened and a pair of Algarvians – officers, she realized by the badges on their tunics and hats – came toward her.

Before she could start screaming at them, they both bowed low. That surprised her enough to let the older of them speak before she did: "A splendid good day to you, Marchioness. I am delighted to have the honor to make your acquaintance." He spoke fluent Valmieran, with only a slight accent. Then, surprising her again, he shifted into classical Kaunian: "If you would rather, we can continue our conversation in this language."

"Valmieran will do," she said, hoping her haughty tone would keep him from realizing his grasp of the classical tongue was considerably better than hers. Anger welled up through surprise: "And now, I must require that you tell me the reason for this intrusion upon my estate."

Servants stared out from the windows on either side of the doorway, and from those of the second story as well. Krasta noticed them only peripherally; to her, they were as much a part of the mansion as the kitchen or the stairways. Her attention was and remained on the Algarvians.

"Allow me to introduce myself, milady," the older one said, bowing again. "I have the honor to be Count Lurcanio of Albenga; my military rank is colonel. My adjutant here, Captain Mosco, has the good fortune to be a marquis. By order of Grand Duke Ivone, commander of the Algarvian forces now occupying Valmiera, we and our staff are to be billeted in your lovely home."

Captain Mosco also bowed. "We shall do our best to keep from inconveniencing you," he said in Valmieran slightly less fluent than Colonel Lurcanio's.

Billeted was not a word Krasta often heard; she needed a moment to realize what it meant. When she did, she marveled that she didn't leap on the Algarvians with nails tearing like claws. "You mean you intend to *live* here?" she said. Lurcanio and Mosco nodded. Krasta threw back her head, a magnificent gesture of contempt. "By what right?"

"By order of the Grand Duke Ivone, as my superior told you," Captain Mosco replied. He was earnest and good-looking and patient, none of which, right this minute, mattered a jot to Krasta.

"By right of the laws of war," Colonel Lurcanio added, still polite but unyielding. "Valmierans billeted themselves on my estate after the Six Years' War. I would be lying if I told you I did not take a certain amount of pleasure in returning the favor. My adjutant had the right of it: we shall inconvenience you as little as we can. But we *shall* stay here. Whether *you* stay here depends on your getting used to that idea."

No one had ever spoken to Krasta like that in her entire life. No one had ever had the power to speak to her so. Her mouth opened, then closed. She shivered. The Algarvians weren't acting like barbarians in Priekule. But, as Lurcanio had just reminded her, they could act like barbarians if they chose, and like triumphant barbarians at that.

"Very well," she said coldly. "I shall accommodate you and your men, Colonel, in one wing. If you wish to inconvenience me as little as possible, as you claim, you and your men will have as little to do with me as possible."

Lurcanio bowed again. "As you say." He was willing to be gracious now that he'd got his way – in that, he was much like Krasta. "Perhaps, as time goes by, you will come to change your mind."

"I doubt it," Krasta said. "I never change my mind once I make it up."

Mosco said something in Algarvian, a language Krasta had never had the least interest in learning. Lurcanio laughed and nodded. He pointed to Krasta and said something else. *They're talking about me,* she realized with no small outrage. *They're talking about me, and I don't know what they're saying. How rude! They* are *barbarians after all.*

She stalked past them, back stiff, nose in the air. Out of the corner of her eye, she saw their heads swivel to watch her backside as she strode toward the door. That made her nose go higher than ever. It also gave her a small, sneaking satisfaction of a different sort. *Let them watch,* she thought. *It's the only thing they'll ever have the chance to do.* To inflame them, she put a little extra hip action in her walk.

When she got inside, the servants converged on her as if they were children and she their mother. "Milady! What shall we do, milady?" they cried.

"The Algarvians are going to quarter themselves here," she said. "I see nothing to be done about that. We shall put them in the west wing – first removing anything of value there. After that, as best we can, we shall ignore them. They will not be welcome in any other part of the mansion, which I shall make quite clear to their officers."

"What if they come anyhow, milady?" Bauska asked.

"Make them so unwelcome, they will not wish to come again," Krasta said. "They are nothing but Algarvians – not worth the notice of civilized people." She rounded on a couple of redheaded troopers who were looking at pictures and knickknacks. "Get out," she told them. "Go on, get out." She gestured to show what the words meant.

They left slowly, and laughing as they went, but they did leave. The servants looked gratified – all but one, whom a soldier patted on the bottom as he went by. And she didn't look so irate as she might have.

Krasta shook her head. What would she do if a servant let an Algarvian have his way with her? How could she stop it? If Bauska was any indication, commoners these days had no moral fiber whatever. Krasta clicked her tongue between her teeth. One way or another, she'd just have to manage.

Marshal Rathar threw himself down on his belly before King Swemmel. He made the usual protestations of loyalty with more than the usual fervor. He knew the king of Unkerlant was angry with him. He knew why, too. The king often got angry at his subjects for reasons no one but he could see. Not this time.

Swemmel let – made – Rathar stay on his belly, his head knocking against the carpet, far longer than usual. At last, evidently deciding Rathar was humiliated enough, the king spoke in a deadly voice: "Get up."

"Aye, your Majesty," the marshal of Unkerlant said, climbing to his feet. "I thank you, your Majesty."

"We do not thank you," Swemmel snarled, stabbing out a finger at Rathar as if his fingernail were the business end of a stick. Had it been, he would have blazed his marshal down. His voice, already high and thin, went higher and thinner as he mocked Rathar: "'Wait till the Algarvians are tied down against Valmiera,' you said. 'Wait till they're fully committed in the east. *Then* strike them, when they cannot easily move reinforcements against us.' Were those your words, Marshal?"

"Those were my words, your Majesty," Rathar said stolidly. "I judged that the most efficient course. It seems I was wrong."

"Aye, it seems you were." Swemmel returned to his normal tones. "Had we wanted a fool, a dunce, to lead the armies of Unkerlant, rest assured we could have found one. We hoped we had chosen a marshal who would know what might happen, not one who was *wrong*." He made the word a curse.

"Your Majesty, in my own defense, my only possible reply is that no one here, no one in the east, and, I daresay, no one in Algarve imagined the redheads' armies could overthrow Valmiera in the space of a month," Rathar answered. "Aye, I was wrong, but I am far from the only man who was."

He waited for Swemmel to sack him, to order him sent to dig coal or salt or brimstone, to order him killed on the spot. Swemmel was capable of any of those things. Swemmel was capable of things much worse than any of those. Anyone who served him lived on the edge of a precipice. Sooner or later, anyone who served him fell off. How the crows and vultures would gather to tear pieces from the fallen Rathar!

King Swemmel said, "Not that you deserve it, but we will give you a tiny chance to redeem yourself before meting out punishment. What will Mezentio do next? Will he strike Lagoas? Will he strike Jelgava? Will he strike our kingdom?"

Rathar's first thought was, *I had better be right.* Swemmel allowed few men the chance to be wrong twice. That he would allow anyone to be wrong three times struck Rathar as absurd. Picking his words with great care, he said, "I do not see how Algarve can attack Lagoas without control of the sea between them, which her navy does not have. The Lagoans will not be fooled as the Sibians were. And there are no signs in Forthweg that Mezentio is building to assault us."

"Jelgava, then," Swemmel said, and Rathar reluctantly nodded. Now he was pinned down. Swemmel could — Swemmel would — hold him to what he said here. The king went on, "And when Algarve fights Jelgava — what then?"

"Your Majesty, the war should be long and difficult," Rathar said. "But then, I said the same about the war against Valmiera, and the Algarvians surprised their foes with a thrust through rough country. I do not see how they can surprise the Jelgavans — there are only so many passes through the mountains between them. But that I do not see something does not have to mean Mezentio's generals are likewise blind."

"Your advice, then, is to wait for Algarve to become fully embroiled with Jelgava and then strike?" Swemmel asked.

"Aye, that is my advice," Rathar answered. He knew better than to say, *That is what I would do if I were king*, as some luckless courtier had done a few years before. Swemmel took that to mean the poor, clumsy-tongued fool was plotting against him. That poor fool was now shorter by a head, and no one had made his mistakes since.

Swemmel said, "And what if Algarve beats Jelgava as quickly and easily as she beat Valmiera? What then, Marshal?"

"Then, your Majesty, I will be surprised," Rathar said. "Algarvians have the arrogance to make good soldiers and good mages, but they are only men, as we are, as the Jelgavans are as well."

"Why not fling our armies at them the minute they start to fight with Jelgava, if this be so?" Swemmel said.

"Your Majesty, you are my sovereign. If you order this, I will do my best to carry out your orders," Rathar replied. "But I think King Mezentio's men will be ready and waiting for us if we try it."

"You think we will fail." Swemmel sounded like an inspector accusing a peasant in a law court.

What happened to peasants haled before such tribunals was usually anything but pleasant. Nevertheless, Rathar said, "The best plan in the world is useless at the wrong time. We struck too soon against the Zuwayzin, and paid a high price for that. We would pay more and suffer worse if we struck the Algarvians while they were ready and waiting for us."

"You have already complained that we struck too soon against Zuwayza," King Swemmel said. "We do not agree; our view is that we struck years too late. But never mind that. Because of your complaints, we delayed ordering our armies forward against Algarve, and the result has been worse than if we had attacked."

"Not necessarily," Rathar replied. "We might have been badly beaten. The Zuwayzin hurt us badly when that war began, but they were not strong enough to follow up on their early victories. That does not hold with Algarve, especially not after what the redheads showed first in Forthweg and then in Valmiera."

"A moment ago, you said the Algarvians were only men," Swemmel said. "Now you say you fear them. Are Unkerlanters, then, suddenly made into mountain apes in your mind?"

"By no means, your Majesty," Rathar said, although for hundreds of years Unkerlanters had felt the same blend of admiration and resentment for Algarvians that Algarvians felt for folk of Kaunian stock. Gathering himself, he went on, "When we attack, though – if we attack – I would want it to be at the moment I judge best."

"Will you ever judge any moment best?" Swemmel asked. "Or will you delay endlessly, like the old man in the fable who could never find the time to die?"

Rathar risked a smile. "He didn't have such a dreadful fate, did he? And the kingdom is at peace for now, which is also not such a dreadful fate. As a soldier who has seen much of war, I say peace is better."

"Peace is better, when those around you grant your due," Swemmel said. "But when we should have been raised to the throne, no one would recognize what was rightfully ours. We had to fight to gain the throne, we had to fight to hold the throne, and we have been fighting ever since. During our struggle with the usurper" — his usual name for his twin brother — "the kingdoms neighboring Unkerlant took advantage of her weakness. We have made Gyongyos respect us. We have humbled Forthweg. We have taught Zuwayza half a lesson, at any rate."

"All that you say is true, your Majesty," Rathar replied, "yet Algarve has done us no harm during your glorious reign." Like other courtiers, he'd had to learn the art of gently guiding the sovereign back from his memories — real or imaginary — of injustice and toward what needed doing in the here and now."

Sometimes King Swemmel refused to be guided. Sometimes he had his reasons for refusing to be guided. He said, "Algarve harmed us gravely during the Six Years' War. The kingdom requires vengeance, and the kingdom shall have it."

Algarve had indeed gravely harmed Unkerlant then. Had the redheads been fighting Unkerlant alone rather than all their neighbors, they might well have paraded through the streets of Cottbus in triumph, as they had just paraded through the streets of Priekule. If the Algarvians fought Unkerlant alone now, they might yet parade through the streets of Cottbus. Rathar understood the danger, which King Swemmel pretty plainly did not.

Again speaking with great care, the marshal said, "Taking vengeance is all the sweeter when it's certain."

"All our servants tell us reasons why we cannot do the things we must do, the things we want to do," Swemmel said testily.

"No doubt this is so: it is the way of courtiers," Rathar said. "But how many of your servants will dare to tell you there is a difference between what you want to do and what you must do?"

Swemmel looked at him from hooded eyes. Sometimes the king could stand more truth than most people thought. Sometimes, too, he would destroy anyone who tried to tell him anything that went against what he already believed. No one could be sure which way he would go without making the experiment. Few took the chance. Every once in a while, Rathar did.

"Do you defy us, Marshal?" the king asked in tones of genuine curiosity.

"In no way, your Majesty," Rathar replied. "I seek to serve you as well as I may. I also seek to serve the kingdom as well as I may."

"We *are* the kingdom," Swemmel declared.

"So you are, your Majesty. While you live – and may you live long – you *are* Unkerlant. But Unkerlant endured for centuries before you were born, and will endure for hundreds of years to come." Rathar was pleased he'd found a way to say that without mentioning Swemmel's death. He went on, "I seek to serve the Unkerlant that will be as well as the Unkerlant that is."

King Swemmel pointed to his own chest. "We are the only proper judge of what is best for the Unkerlant that will be."

When he put it like that, Rathar found no way to contradict him without also seeming to defy him. The marshal bowed his head. If Swemmel demanded anything too preposterous from him, he could either threaten to resign (although that was a threat best used sparingly) or pretend to obey and try to mitigate the effects of the king's orders through judicious insubordination (a tactic with obvious risks of its own).

Swemmel made an impatient gesture. "Go on, get you gone. We do not wish to see your face any more. We do not wish to hear your carping any more. When we judge the time ripe for attacking Algarve, we shall order the assault. And we shall be obeyed, if not by you, then by another."

"Choosing who commands the armies of Unkerlant is your Majesty's privilege," Rathar answered evenly. Swemmel glared at him. His calm acceptance of the king's superiority left Swemmel's anger nowhere to light – and left Swemmel angrier on account of it.

Rathar prostrated himself once more. Then he rose and bowed himself out of the audience chamber. He retrieved his ceremonial sword from Swemmel's guards, who stood between him and the door to the audience chamber while he belted it on. As he left the anteroom, he allowed himself a long sigh of relief. He'd survived again – or thought he had. But all the way back to the office where everyone else in Unkerlant imagined him to be so powerful, he kept waiting for a couple of King Swemmel's human bloodhounds to seize him and lead the way. And even after he got back there, he still shivered. That Swemmel's bloodhounds hadn't seized him didn't mean they couldn't, or wouldn't.

Whenever Leofsig went out on to the streets of Gromheort, he kept waiting for a couple of King Mezentio's human bloodhounds to seize him and lead him away. *I won't go back to the captives' camp without a fight*, he told himself fiercely, and carried a knife longer and stouter than the Algarvians' regulations allowed to Forthwegians in the area they occupied.

But the redheaded soldiers who patrolled his city paid no more attention to him than to any other Forthwegian man. Maybe that was because his father knew whom to bribe. No doubt it was, in part. A bigger part, though, was that the Algarvians seemed to have little interest in any Forthwegians save pretty girls, to whom they would call lewd invitations in their own language and in what bits of Forthwegian they'd learned.

That made the girls' lives harder, but it made Leofsig's easier. Before entering King Penda's levy, he had been training to cast accounts, as his father did. These days, Hestan barely had work enough for himself, and none for an assistant even of his own flesh and blood. When Leofsig worked – and he needed to work, for food and money were tight – he worked as a day laborer.

"Coming on! Doing better!" an Algarvian soldier bossing his crew shouted as they cobblestoned the road leading southwest from Gromheort. The fellow spoke Forthwegian in two-word bursts: "Coming on! You lazy! Like Kaunians! Working harder!" Several men in the gang were Kaunians. As far as Leofsig could see, they worked as hard as anybody else.

"Screwing you!" he muttered to Burgred, one of the other young men in the work gang, doing his best to imitate the redhead's way of speaking.

Burgred chuckled as he let a round stone thump into place. "You're a funny fellow," he said, also in a low voice. The laborers weren't supposed to talk with one another, but the Algarvian, a decent enough man, usually didn't give them a hard time about it.

"Oh, aye, I'm funny, all right." Leofsig also dropped a stone in the roadway. "Funny like a unicorn with a broken leg."

Burgred headed back toward a cart piled high with cobblestones and rubble. The animals that drew it were not unicorns but a couple of scrawny, utterly prosaic mules. Returning with a new stone, Burgred said, "It's all the cursed Kaunians' fault, anyway." He fitted the stone into place. "There we go. That whore's in good."

Leofsig grunted. He swiped at his sweaty forehead with a tunic sleeve. "I don't quite see that," he said. A moment later, he wished he'd kept quiet. Even so little might have been too much.

"Stands to reason, doesn't it?" Burgred said. "If it wasn't for the Kaunians, we wouldn't have gotten into the war in the first place. If we hadn't gotten into it, we couldn't very well have lost it, now could we?"

Broadsheets plastered all over Gromheort said the same thing in almost the same words. The Algarvians had put them up; a Forthwegian who presumed to put up a broadsheet in his own city was liable to be executed on the spot if the redheads caught him doing it. Leofsig wondered if Burgred even knew he was spitting back the pap the Algarvians fed him.

Burgred went on, "And a plague take the Kaunians, anyway. They may live here, but they aren't Forthwegians, not really. They keep their own language, they keep their own clothes – and their women don't come close to dressing decently – and they hate us. So why shouldn't we hate them? Powers above, I haven't had any use for Kaunians since I first knew they were different than regular people."

Leofsig sighed and didn't answer. He saw no point to it. Burgred, plainly, hadn't needed the redheads to shape his opinion of Kaunians. Like a lot of Forthwegians – maybe even most Forthwegians – he'd despised them long before the Algarvians overran Forthweg.

"You work!" the Algarvian straw boss yelled. "No standing! No talking! Talking – trouble!" He spoke Forthwegian with a horrible accent. He had no grammar and next to no vocabulary. No one ever had trouble understanding him, though.

As the day wound to an end, Leofsig queued up with the rest of the laborers to get his meager pay from an Algarvian sergeant who looked as pained at handing out the silver as if it came from his own belt pouch. At first, the Algarvians hadn't paid anyone even a copper to work for them. In tones of dry amusement, Hestan had said, "They didn't take long to discover people will work better if they have some reason to do it."

Wearily, Leofsig and the others in the gang trudged back toward Gromheort, the Kaunians (who earned only half as much as Forthwegians) a little apart from the rest. Most of the men walked by the side of the cobblestoned road, not on it. "Stupid redheads," Burgred remarked. "A road like this is harder on people's feet than a regular one made of dirt. Harder on horses' hooves, too, and on unicorns'."

"They can use it during the rain, though, when a regular road turns to mud," Leofsig said. With a certain sardonic relish, he added, "The Kaunian Empire had roads like these."

"And much good it did the cursed Kaunians, too," Burgred said, a better comeback than Leofsig had expected from him. "May it do the cursed Algarvians as much good as it did the blonds however long ago that was."

Inside Gromheort, the work gang scattered, each man heading off toward his own home – or toward a tavern, where he could drink up in an hour what he'd made in a day. Some of the men who did that were their families' sole support. Being very much his father's son, Leofsig looked on them with nothing but scorn.

Not that he would turn down a glass of wine – or a couple of glasses of wine – when he got home. But no one would go without food or firewood because he had some wine. He could even have afforded to spend a copper at the public baths beforehand. But the baths were always short of hot water these days. The Algarvians starved them for fuel – what did they care if Forthwegians stank? Leofsig didn't care so much as he would have before the war. He'd discovered in the field and in the captives' camp that no one stank when everyone stank.

Leofsig was almost home when a Kaunian youth in ragged trousers darted out of an alley and past him, plainly running for his life. Four or five Forthwegian boys pounded after him. One of them, Leofsig saw, was his cousin Sidroc.

Tired though he was, he started running after Sidroc before he quite realized what he was doing. At first, he thought he was mortified because he was Sidroc's close kin. After a few strides, he decided he was mortified because he was a Forthwegian. That hurt worse.

Because it hurt, he wanted to hurt Sidroc, too. And he did, bringing his cousin down with a tackle that would have got him thrown off any football pitch in Forthweg — or even in Unkerlant, where they played the game for blood. Sidroc squalled most satisfactorily.

"Shut up, you little turd," Leofsig said coldly. "What in blazes do you think you were doing, chasing that Kaunian like a mad dog foaming at the mouth?"

"What was I doing?" Sidroc squeaked. He was bleeding from both elbows and one knee, but didn't seem to notice. "What was I doing?"

"Has someone put a spell on you, so you have to say everything twice?" Leofsig demanded. "I ought to beat you so you can't even walk, let alone run. My father will be ashamed of you when I tell him what you've done. Powers above, I hope Uncle Hengist will, too."

He thought Sidroc would cringe. Instead, his cousin shouted, "You're crazy, do you know that? The little blond-headed snake cut the belt pouch right off me, curse him, and now I bet he's got away clean. Of course I was chasing him. Wouldn't you chase a thief? Or are you too high and mighty for that?"

"A thief?" Leofsig said in a small voice. So often, people chased Kaunians through the streets for no reason at all. That people might chase a Kaunian through the streets for a perfectly good reason had never crossed his mind. If Forthwegians could be thieves, Kaunians certainly could, too.

"Aye, a thief. You've heard the word?" Sidroc spoke with sarcasm Leofsig's father might have envied. He also realized he'd been hurt. "What were you trying to do, murder me? You almost did."

Since Leofsig had been trying for something not far short of murder, he didn't answer directly. He said, "I thought you were going after him for the sport of it."

"Not this time." Sidroc got to his feet and put hands on hips; blood trickled down his forearms. "You're worse than your brother, do you know that? He's a Kaunian-lover, too, but he doesn't kill people on account of it."

"Oh, shut up, or you'll make me decide I'm glad I flattened you after all," Leofsig said. "Let's go home."

When they got home and went into the kitchen, Leofsig's mother and sister both exclaimed over Sidroc's battered state. They exclaimed again when he told them he'd had his belt pouch stolen, and once more when he told them how he'd come to get battered. "Leofsig, you should ask questions before you hurt someone," Elfryth said.

"I'm sorry, Mother – there wasn't time," Leofsig said. He realized he hadn't apologized to Sidroc yet. That needed doing, however little he relished it. "I am sorry, cousin. Kaunians get the short end of the stick so often when they don't deserve it, I just thought this was once more."

"Well, I can understand that," Conberge said. Leofsig sent his sister a grateful glance. Sidroc sniffed loudly.

As she might have to one of her own sons, Elfryth said, "Come here, Sidroc. Let's get you cleaned up." She wet a rag and advanced on Sidroc. "This may sting, so stand still." Sidroc did, but yelped as she got to work.

Drawn by the yelps, Ealstan came in to find out what was going on. "Oh," was all he said when he found out why Sidroc was bleeding. "That's too bad."

Leofsig had expected more from him, and was obscurely disappointed not to get it. After supper, when the two of them went out to the courtyard together, Leofsig said, "I thought you'd figured out that Kaunians were people, too."

"They're people, all right." His younger brother did not try to hide his bitterness. "When they get the chance, some of them lick the Algarvians' boots the same way some of our people do."

Leofsig had already seen how some Forthwegians were perfectly content to do business with the occupying redheads. That disgusted him, but didn't especially surprise him. But Kaunians – "Where could you find an Algarvian who'd want a Kaunian to lick his boots?" He could think of some other possibilities along those lines, but forbore from mentioning them in case his brother couldn't.

"It happens." Ealstan spoke with great conviction. "I've seen it happen. I wish I hadn't, but I have."

"You've already said that much. Do you want to tell me about it?" Leofsig asked.

His younger brother surprised him again, this time by shaking his head. "No. It's not your affair. Not mine, either, really, but I know about it." Ealstan shrugged, a weary motion Hestan might have used.

Leofsig scratched his head. Some time after he'd gone into King Penda's levy, his little brother had indeed turned into a man, a man he was beginning to realize he barely knew.

"Come on." Hestan shook Ealstan out of bed. "Get moving, sleepyhead. If you don't go to school, what will you be?"

"Asleep?" Ealstan suggested, yawning.

His father snorted. "If you won't wake up for me, you will when the master for your first class brings the switch down on your back because you were tardy. The choice is yours, son: my way or the master's."

"Forthweg has a choice, too, these days: Algarve's way or Unkerlant's," Ealstan said as he got to his feet and stretched. "If they had a true choice, the Forthwegians would take neither the one nor the other. If I had a true choice, I would go back to bed."

"Forthweg has no true choice. Neither do you, however well you argue." Hestan no longer sounded amused. "You are the last one in the house up and moving. If you don't make up for it, you may get my way and the master's switch both."

Thus encouraged, Ealstan put on a clean tunic and his sandals and hurried to the kitchen. Conberge gave him porridge with almond slivers stirred through it and a cup of wine flavored with enough resin to put fur on his tongue, or so he thought. "If I can't speak Algarvian today, I'll blame it on this horrible stuff," he said.

"Better to blame it on not studying enough," Hestan said. "You should be learning Kaunian instead, but you *can* learn whatever your master sets before you." He turned to Ealstan's cousin. "The same applies to you, young man."

With his mouth full, Sidroc had an excuse for not answering. He took advantage of it. Ealstan's marks had always been higher than his. Lately, they'd been a good deal higher than his. Sidroc's father was imperfectly delighted with that.

Despite having sat down later than Sidroc, Ealstan finished his porridge and wine before his cousin did. He did not rub that in, which rubbed it in more effectively than anything else could have done. Hengist almost threw Sidroc out the door after him. They hurried off to school together.

They'd gone only a couple of blocks when they passed four or five

Algarvian soldiers half leading, half dragging a Kaunian woman into
an empty building. One of them held a hand over her mouth. Sidroc
chuckled. "They'll have a good time."

"She won't," Ealstan said. Sidroc only shrugged. Angry at his
cousin's indifference, Ealstan snapped, "Suppose it was your
mother."

"You keep my mother out of your mouth, or I'll put my fist in it,"
Sidroc said hotly. Ealstan thought he could lick his cousin, but this
wasn't the time or place to find out. He didn't know why he
bothered trying to make Sidroc see things as he did. Sidroc didn't and
wouldn't care about Kaunians.

Ealstan stopped caring about Kaunians for the time being the
moment he walked into Master Agmund's class. On the blackboard,
someone had written – in what looked to him like grammatically
impeccable Algarvian – KING MEZENTIO HAD NINE PIGLETS
BY THE ROYAL SOW. "Powers above!" he cried. "Get rid of that
before the master sees it and beats us all to death." He tried to figure
out whose script it was, but couldn't; whoever had written it had
done so as plainly as possible.

Echoing that thought, one of his classmates said, "It was up there
when we started coming in. Somebody must have snuck in during
the night and put it up."

Maybe that was true; maybe it wasn't. Either way, though . . . "It
doesn't matter who wrote it. Erase it!"

"You think we haven't tried?" Three boys said it at the same time.

"Haven't tried what?" Master Agmund strode into the classroom.
Nobody answered. Nobody needed to answer. When the master's
head turned, he naturally saw the message on the blackboard. Despite
his swarthy skin, he turned red. "Who wrote this seditious trash?"
he rumbled. His finger shot toward Ealstan. "Was it you, young
man?"

That meant he judged Ealstan did not love the Algarvian occupiers.
He was right, but Ealstan would sooner not have made such an
obvious target. He was lucky here; he had only to tell the truth: "No,
Master. My cousin and I just came in now, and saw it there as you
did. I said we ought to erase it."

Agmund's thick, dark eyebrows lowered like stormclouds, but
several of Ealstan's classmates spoke up in support of him. "Very well,

then," the master of Algarvian said. "Your suggestion was a good one. Those who came in earlier should have acted on it." He seized the eraser and rubbed vigorously.

But, however hard he rubbed, the message refused to disappear. If anything, the white letters got more distinct against their dark background. "Magecraft," someone said softly.

Agmund also spoke softly, but his quiet words held only danger. "Anyone daring to use magecraft against Algarve will pay dearly, for the occupiers reckon it an act of war. Someone — perhaps someone in this chamber now — will answer for it, and may answer with his head." He stalked out.

"Maybe we ought to run," somebody said.

"What good would it do us, unless we took to the hills?" Ealstan said. "Master Agmund knows who we are. He and the headmaster will know where we live."

"Besides, if anyone runs, Agmund will think he did it," Sidroc added. He had a gift for intrigue, if not for scholarship. Once he'd spoken, everyone could hear the likely truth in his words.

Footfalls in the hall warned that Agmund was returning. The students sprang to their feet, not wanting any show of disrespect to feed his suspicions. That proved wise, for with him came Swithulf, the headmaster of the academy. Agmund looked as if he disapproved of everything and everyone. So did Swithulf; as he'd practiced the expression for twenty or twenty-five more years, his gaze was downright reptilian.

He read the graffito aloud to himself. Had he been a student, Agmund would have corrected his pronunciation, probably with a switch. As things were, the master of Algarvian said only, "The students deny responsibility."

"Aye — they would," Swithulf grunted. As Agmund had, he tried to erase the rude words. As Agmund had, he failed.

"Because of the magecraft I mentioned and you have now seen for yourself, sir, I tend to believe them in this instance." Agmund sounded anything but happy at having to admit such a thing. That he admitted it anyhow made Ealstan, though equally reluctant, give him some small credit.

Swithulf spoke to the scholars for the first time: "No gossip about this, mind you." Ealstan and his classmates all nodded solemnly. He worked hard to keep his face straight. Swithulf might as well have ordered the boys not to breathe.

"What shall we do about this, sir?" Agmund asked. "I can hardly instruct with such a crude distraction behind me."

"I shall go get Ceolnoth, the magecraft master," Swithulf answered. "He is no first-rank mage, true, but he should be sorcerer enough to put paid to this. And he is discreet, and he will charge no fee." The headmaster departed as abruptly as he'd arrived.

Agmund made a good game try at teaching in spite of the comment about King Mezentio's taste in partners – or, perhaps, his taste in pork. With nine piglets in back of the master, though, verbs irregular in the imperfect sense did not sink deep into the students' memories.

Master Ceolnoth stuck his head into the chamber. "Well, well, what have we here?" he asked. "The headmaster didn't say much." Agmund pointed to the blackboard and explained. Ceolnoth came all the way inside so he could read the offending words. "Oh, dear," he said. "Aye, we need to be rid of that, don't we? I doubt anyone in Gromheort would be in a position to know any such thing, I do, I do."

Ealstan looked at Sidroc. That was a mistake. It meant he had even more trouble not snickering than he would have otherwise. Sidroc looked about ready to burst like an egg.

"That doesn't matter," said Agmund, whose sense of humor had been strangled at birth. "Just get the filth of my blackboard."

"Quite, quite." Ceolnoth started out the door.

"Where are you going?" Agmund demanded.

"Why, to get my tools, of course," Ceolnoth replied. "Can't work without 'em, no more than a carpenter can work without his. Swithulf just told me to come in here and look at what you had. Now I've looked at it. Now you've told me what the trouble is. Now I know I need to do something about it. So." Out he went.

"More comings and goings here than I've seen since the redheads ran the Forthwegian army out of town," Ealstan whispered to Sidroc.

His cousin nodded and whispered back: "I wonder if Ceolnoth worked that sorcery himself. He could look important that way, and say what he thought about the Algarvians at the same time."

Ealstan hadn't thought of that. He didn't get much chance to think of it, either, for the smack of Master Agmund's switch coming down on Sidroc's back made him jump. "Silence in the classroom," Agmund snapped. Sidroc glared at Ealstan, who'd spoken first but hadn't got caught. The glare grew more pained when Agmund went on, "Since you enjoy talking so much, conjugate for me the verb *to bear* in all tenses."

Sidroc floundered. Ealstan would have floundered, too; the verb was one of the most irregular in Algarvian, its principal parts seeming unrelated from one tense to another. Agmund kept after Sidroc till Ceolnoth returned. After that, he apparently decided Ealstan's cousin had an excuse for being distracted and left off grilling him.

"Let's see, let's see," Ceolnoth said cheerily. He produced a couple of stones, one pale green, the other a dull, grayish pebble. "Chrysolite to drive away fantasies and foolishness, and the stone called *adamas* in the classical tongue to overcome enemies, madness, and venom."

"*Adamas*," Agmund echoed. "What would that be in Algarvian?"

"I neither know nor care," Ceolnoth answered. "Not a very useful language, not for magecraft it isn't." Agmund looked furious. If the master of magecraft noticed, he didn't care. Ealstan snickered, but took care to snicker silently.

Ceolnoth rattled the two stones together and began to chant in classical Kaunian. That made Agmund look even angrier. The mage pointed to the offending graffito and cried out a word of command. The letters on the blackboard flared brightly. Ealstan thought they would disappear. Instead, they kept right on flaming, in the most literal sense of the word. Smoke began to pour from the blackboard, or from the timbers on which it was mounted.

Ceolnoth cried out again, in horror. So did Agmund, in rage. "You blundering idiot!" he bellowed.

"Not so," Ceolnoth said. "This was a spell set under a spell, so that quelling the first one set off the second."

They would have gone on arguing, but Sidroc shouted "Fire!" and dashed out of the room. That broke a different sort of spell. All his fellow scholars and the two masters followed him. Everyone was shouting "Fire!" by then, that and "Get outside!" As Ealstan ran, he got the idea that he wouldn't have to worry about the Algarvian imperfect tense for some time to come.

14.

Garivald hated inspectors on general principles. Any Unkerlanter peasant hated inspectors on general principles. Tales that went back to the days when the Duchy of Grelz was a kingdom in its own right had inspectors as their villains. If any tales had inspectors as their heroes, Garivald had never heard of them. As far as he was concerned, inspectors were nothing but thieves with the power of King Swemmel's army behind them.

He particularly hated the two inspectors who had come to Zossen to put a crystal in Waddo's house. For one thing, he did not want Waddo getting orders straight from Cottbus. For another, the inspectors were swine. They ate and drank enough for half a dozen men, and paid nothing. They leered at the village women, and even pawed at them.

"They might as well be Algarvians," Annore said after one of the inspectors shouted a lewd proposition at her while she was walking home from visiting a friend. Unkerlanters were convinced Algarve was a sink of degeneracy.

"If they touch you, I'll kill them," Garivald growled.

That frightened his wife. "If anyone in a village murders an inspector, the whole village dies," she warned. That wasn't legend; it was law and somber fact. Some kings of Unkerlant had been known to show mercy in applying it, but Swemmel was not one of them.

"They deserve it," Garivald said, but inside he was glad Annore had reminded him of the law. That gave him a chance to back away from his threat without sounding like a coward.

"I just wish they'd go away," Annore said.

"We all wish they'd go away," Garivald answered. "Waddo may even wish they'd go away by now. But they won't. Any day now, we're going to have to start making a cell to hold prisoners in till they get round to cutting the bastards' throats to make the crystal work."

"And that's another thing," his wife said. "What if these robbers or murderers or whatever they are get loose somehow and start robbing and murdering us? Will the inspectors care? Not likely!"

"I asked Waddo about that very thing the other day," Garivald said. "He told me they're going to bring in a couple of guards to make sure that doesn't happen."

"Oh," Annore said. "Well, that's a little better."

"No such thing!" Garivald exclaimed. "A crystal to tie us to Cottbus, guards here all the time . . . We couldn't breathe very free before. We won't be able to breathe free at all now."

Annore found another question: "Well, what can we do about it?"

"Not a cursed thing," Garivald said. "Not a single cursed thing. The only thing we could ever do about orders from Cottbus was pretend we never got them. Now we won't even be able to do that."

A couple of days later, he was one of the villagers the inspectors commandeered to build the cell to hold the condemned prisoners whose life energy would power the crystal. He couldn't work in the fields. He couldn't tend his garden or his livestock. The inspectors didn't care. "This has to be done, and it has to be done on time," one of them said. "Efficiency."

"Efficiency," Garivald agreed. Whenever anyone said that word, everyone who heard it had to agree with it. Dreadful things happened to those who failed to agree. Garivald worked on the cell with a will, sawing and hammering like a man beset by demons. So did the other peasants dragooned into building it. The sooner they got it done, the sooner they could get back to work that really needed doing, work that would keep them fed through the winter. That was the sort of efficiency Garivald understood.

After a couple of hours of offering suggestions that didn't help, the inspectors wandered off to find something to drink, and maybe something to eat, too. Garivald wouldn't have expected anything different; since the inspectors weren't devouring their own substance, they made free with the village's.

He said, "The really efficient thing to do would be to put the criminals in Waddo's house. He's the one who wants the crystal so much, so we ought to let him deal with what having it means."

"Aye," said one of the other peasants, a scar-faced fellow named Dagulf. He glanced over toward the firstman's home, which stood out from the others in Zossen, and then spat on the ground. "Would hardly put him out, even. After all, he built that cursed second story, didn't he? He could put the captives up there and slit their throats right by the cursed crystal."

"Now, *that* would be efficient," somebody else said.

"Who's going to be the one to tell Waddo to do it, though?" Garivald asked. Nobody answered. He hadn't expected anybody to answer. He went on, "He'd bawl like a just-gelded colt if anybody had the nerve to tell him he ought to do that. All that precious space is for his family, don't you know?"

"Like anybody needs that much space," Dagulf said, and spat again.

Everyone working on the cell grumbled and complained and called curses down on Waddo's head and the heads of the inspectors. But all the curses were so low-voiced, no one more than a few feet away could have heard them. And no one would have guessed the peasants were complaining from the way they worked.

Not even the inspectors could find anything to complain about over the speed with which the cell went up. "There, you see?" one of them said when it got done two days sooner than they'd demanded. "You can be efficient when you set your minds to it."

Neither Garivald nor his fellow carpenters chose to enlighten them. Annore had been doing much of Garivald's work along with her own. The work had to get done. Who did it mattered less. That was efficiency, too, efficiency as the peasants of Unkerlant understood it.

Once built in such a driving hurry, the jail cell stayed empty for three weeks. Every time Garivald walked past it, he snickered. That was efficiency as King Swemmel's men understood it: do something fast for the sake of nothing but speed, then wait endlessly to be able to do whatever came next.

At last, a column of guards marched up the road from the market town. There were a dozen of them to protect the villagers from four scrawny captives whose chains clanked and rattled with every step they took. Half the guards headed back toward the market town. The others prepared to settle down in Zossen. The first meal the villagers served them showed they were even more ravenous than the inspectors.

"Now all you need is the crystal and the mage to work the sacrifice and give it life, and you'll be connected with the rest of the world," one of the inspectors said, his tone somewhat elevated by strong drink. "Won't that be grand for you?"

Garivald thought it would be anything but grand. The inspectors, however, had long since made it plain they cared nothing for his opinion or that of anyone else in Zossen. He kept quiet.

Sharp-tongued old Uote, though, was moved to speak up: "You mean you haven't got a crystal here?"

"Of course we haven't," the inspector answered. "Do we look like mages?"

Uote rolled her eyes. "Call that efficiency?" she said. Maybe she'd had a good deal to drink herself, to dare to ask such a question.

Both inspectors and all six guards stared at her. A great silence fell over the village square. The inspector who'd spoken before snapped, "Efficiency is what we say it is, you ugly old sow."

"Sow, is it?" Uote said. "You're the pigs in the trough."

The silence got louder and more appalled. "Curb your tongue, old woman, or we shall assuredly curb it for you. When the crystal does come here, would you have King Swemmel learn your name?" The inspector's smile said he looked forward to informing on her.

Garivald had no use for Uote; even sober, she was a nag and a scold. But she was from his village. Hearing that gloating anticipation from the inspector — the king's man, the city man — made him feel like a piece of livestock, not a man. And Uote crumpled like a scrap of paper. She sneaked away from the gathering in the village square and stayed inside her house for several days afterwards. Garivald did not think it would do her any good, not unless the crystal came so late, the inspector found other villagers at whom to be angry in the meanwhile.

When the crystal did arrive a week or so later, it too was escorted by a squad of guards. So many strangers didn't come to Zossen in the course of an ordinary year. Along with the guards came a mage. His red nose and cheeks and red-tracked eyes said he had a fondness for spirits. So did the way he gulped from the flask at his belt.

Annore watched in distaste. "They've sent us a wreck, not a wizard."

"Must be all they think we deserve," Garivald answered. He shrugged. "It doesn't take much of a mage to sacrifice a man."

He never found out how they chose which condemned prisoner to sacrifice first. He'd done his best to pretend the prisoners and the guards and the mage weren't anywhere near the village. Some of the villagers had got friendly with the condemned men, bringing good food to the cell instead of just enough swill to keep them alive till they were used up. He thought that pointless; odds were the guards ate the meat and jam instead of giving them to the captives.

The guards staked the prisoner out in the middle of the village square. "I didn't do anything," he said over and over. "I really didn't do anything." No one paid any attention to his feeble protests. Garivald stood and watched along with a lot of other villagers. No one had been sacrificed in Zossen for a long time. What was strange was always interesting.

Up came the wizard, wobbling as he walked. He set the crystal on the condemned criminal's chest, then took a knife from his belt. Garivald wouldn't have wanted to handle a knife while that drunk. He would have been as likely to cut himself as what he was supposed to be cutting.

"I really didn't do—" The condemned man's words faded into a wet, choking gurgle. Blood spurted from his neck, just as it did from that of a butchered hog. The mage chanted, hiccuping in between the words. Garivald wondered if he was too drunk to get the spell right, but evidently not: through the blood that covered it, the crystal began to glow.

One of the inspectors picked it up and carried it over to a bucket of water to wash it off. The other inspectors pointed to the criminal's body, which was occasionally twitching. "Bury this carrion," he said, and pointed to several men. "You, you, you, and you."

Garivald was the second *you*. As he pulled up one of the stakes to which the condemned man had been tied, the inspector with the crystal said, "I've got Cottbus inside there." He sounded pleased. Garivald wasn't. That he wasn't pleased changed things not at all. He picked up the dead man's leg and helped carry him away.

Leudast tramped along the western bank of a small stream that marked some of the border between the part of Forthweg Unkerlant occupied and the part Algarve held. On the other side of the river, an Algarvian patrol mounted on unicorns drew near his squad.

One of the Algarvians waved to his squad. Not knowing whether to wave back, he glanced toward Sergeant Magnulf. Only when the squad leader raised a hand did he do the same. The Algarvians reined in. Their mounts were painted in splotches of dull brown and green. Unkerlant did the same thing, as had Forthweg when Forthweg had unicorns with which to fight. It made the beasts harder to see and to blaze. It also made them much uglier.

"Hail, Swemmel's men," an Algarvian called in what might have been either Forthwegian or Unkerlanter. "You understanding me?"

Again, Leudast looked toward Magnulf. He was a corporal, but Magnulf was the sergeant. Unkerlant and Algarve remained at peace. But they had been at war before, many times, and they might be again before long. All the drilling Leudast had been through lately made him think that likely. What if a military inspector found out he and his comrades had spoken with the almost-enemy?

"You understanding me?" the Algarvian called again when no one answered right away.

Magnulf must have been worrying about the same things as Leudast. The other side of the goldpiece was, what if the Algarvians had something important to say, something his superiors needed to know? "Aye, I understand you," the sergeant said at last. "What do you want?"

"You have burning water?" the cavalryman asked. He tipped back his head and put a fist to his mouth as if it were a flask.

"He means spirits, Sergeant," Leudast said.

"I know what he means," Magnulf said impatiently. He raised his voice: "What if we do?"

"Want to tread?" The Algarvian smacked his forehead with the heel of his hand. "No – want to *trade*?"

"What have you got?" Magnulf asked. In a low voice, he added to his comrades, "It had better be something good, if they want us to trade spirits for it."

"Aye," Leudast said, the same thought having crossed his mind. All he wanted to do with spirits was drink them himself.

The Algarvian who was doing the talking held up something that glittered in the warm northern sunlight. Squinting across the stream, Leudast saw it was a dagger. "Fancy knife," the redhead said, evidently not knowing how to say *dagger* in a language the

Unkerlanters could understand. "Taking from Forthwegians in war. Got plenty."

Magnulf rubbed his chin. Speaking to his fellow Unkerlanters, the sergeant said, "We ought to be able to trade fancy daggers for more spirits than we give the Algarvians to get 'em, eh?" The soldiers nodded. Magnulf started shouting again: "All right, come on across. We'll see what we can do." He waved to invite the Algarvians over to the west side of the river.

"Peace between us?" the redhead asked.

"Aye, peace between us," Magnulf answered. The Algarvians urged their unicorns into the river. Magnulf spoke to his own men: "Peace as long as they keep it. And don't let your cursed jaws flap, or the inspectors will pull out your tongues by the roots." Leudast shivered, knowing the sergeant wasn't likely to be either joking or exaggerating.

The river was shallow enough that the unicorns had to swim only a few yards in midstream. They came up on to the western bank, dripping and snorting and beautiful in spite of paint splashed over their hides. Their iron-shod horns looked very sharp. Some of the Algarvians dismounted; others stayed on the unicorns, alert and watchful. They were veterans, all right. Leudast, a veteran himself, wouldn't have taken anything for granted, either.

"Let's see these daggers close up," Magnulf said.

"Let us seeing—" The Algarvian spokesman made that drinking gesture again.

Magnulf nodded to the soldiers in his squad. Leudast let his pack slide off his shoulders. He opened it and took out a flask. He was unsurprised to see that every one of his squadmates had a similar little jug. Such flasks were against regulations, but keeping Unkerlanters and spirits apart was like keeping ham and eggs apart when the time to cook supper came.

Leudast held out his flask to an Algarvian. The redhead was several inches taller than he, but several inches narrower through the shoulders. Leudast had never seen anyone from Mezentio's kingdom before, not close up, and curiously studied the Algarvian. The fellow pulled the stopper from the flask, sniffed, and whistled respectfully. He took a couple of staggering steps, as if drunk from the fumes. Leudast chuckled. Maybe the Algarvians weren't so fearsome as people said they were.

This one put the stopper back in the flask, hefted it and shook it to see how much it held, and then took two knives off his belt. He pointed to one and then to the spirits before pointing to the other and the spirits. Leudast understood: the Algarvian was saying he could have one or the other but not both.

He examined the daggers. The blade on one was an inch or so longer than that on the other. The one with the shorter blade had a hilt decorated with what looked like jewels: red, blue, green. If they were jewels, that dagger was worth a lot. But if the dagger was worth a lot, the redhead wouldn't swap it for a flask of spirits. The other knife had a hilt of some dark wood, highly polished, with Forthweg's stag stamped into it and enameled in blue and white.

"I want this one," Leudast said, and took the less gaudy knife. He closely watched the Algarvian as he did so. The man from the east made a good game try at not looking surprised and disappointed, but not good enough. Leudast didn't smile, not on the outside of his face, but he was smiling inside. He handed the Algarvian the flask of spirits. That made the man in tunic and kilt look a little happier, but not much.

Leudast looked around to see how his comrades were making out in their bargains. Two or three of them had chosen the daggers with the colorful jewels. They were men he'd already tabbed as greedy. Now he did smile. Greed would get them what greed usually got. He had no doubt he'd done better.

Sergeant Magnulf, now, was not a man to be easily fooled. He and the Algarvian who had a smattering of Unkerlanter and Forthwegian were still dickering. At last, the redhead threw up his hands. "All right! All right! You winning!" he said, and gave Magnulf not only a knife Leudast thought quite fine but also a couple of Algarvian silver coins. He angrily snatched the flask of spirits from Magnulf's hands.

"If you don't want it, I'll give you back your stuff," Magnulf said.

"I wanting!" the Algarvian said. He seemed to get excited about everything, and clutched the flask to his bosom as if it were a beautiful woman. Then, relaxing a little, he asked, "We fighting war, you Unkerlanterians and we?"

Before Leudast could cough or otherwise warn Magnulf the question had teeth, the sergeant showed he'd figured that out for himself. He shrugged and answered, "How should I know? Am I a general? I hope not, is all I can tell you. Nobody who's seen a war can like one."

"Here you talking true," the Algarvian agreed. He turned to his men and spoke to them in their own language. The ones who were on foot swung up into the saddle. Again, they looked like soldiers who knew exactly what they were doing. In a real fight, though, the unicorns would suffer terribly before they could close with their foes.

The Algarvians forded the river once more and resumed their patrol on the eastern bank. The trooper who could make himself understood to the Unkerlanters turned to wave to Sergeant Magnulf's squad. Magnulf waved back. The Algarvians rode behind some bushes and disappeared.

"Not bad," Magnulf said to the men he led. "No, not bad at all. Since these are Forthwegian daggers, nobody needs to know we were trading with the Algarvians."

"What would happen if somebody found out?" one of his men asked.

"I'm not sure," the sergeant said. "I don't think trying to see would be the most efficient thing we could do, though." No one disagreed with him.

But after they'd walked on for another half a mile or so, Leudast went up to Magnulf and spoke in a low voice: "Sergeant, maybe we ought to let somebody know we did some talking with the redheads. That one Algarvian was spying on us, curse me if he was doing anything else. Don't you think our officers need to know the Algarvians are worried about us attacking them?"

Magnulf looked him up and down. "I thought you were a smart soldier. You came through the mountains in one piece. You came through the desert in one piece, and with a stripe on your sleeve. And now you want to stick your own sausage into the meat grinder? Why don't you just cut it off with your pretty new knife instead?"

Leudast's ears got hot. But his stubbornness was one of the reasons he'd come through the fighting he'd seen, and so he said, "Don't you think our officers would forgive us for trading with the Algarvians when they find out what we learned?"

"Maybe they would – maybe the line officers would, anyhow," Magnulf answered. "But this is intelligence information, and that means it would have to go through the inspectors. We couldn't very well tell them where we got it without telling them we broke regulations, could we? When have you ever heard of an inspector forgiving anybody for breaking regulations?"

"Not lately," Leudast admitted, "but—"

"No buts," Magnulf said firmly. "Besides, what makes you think we've been able to find out anything the inspectors don't already know? If ordinary soldiers are asking other ordinary soldiers about what's going to happen next, don't you think the spies on both sides are keeping busy, too?"

"Ah." Leudast nodded. That made sense to him. "You're likely right, Sergeant. That'd be the efficient thing for 'em to do, anyhow."

"Of course it would," Magnulf said. "And so, my most noble and magnificent corporal" – his expression was as jaundiced as that of a Zuwayzi camel – "is it all right with you that we keep our mouths shut?"

"Aye, Sergeant, it is," Leudast said, and Magnulf pantomimed enormous relief. Leudast went on, "Sergeant, do *you* think we'll be fighting the Algarvians next?"

That was not only a different question, it was a different sort of question. Magnulf walked on for several strides before saying, "Do you suppose we'd have done all that drilling against behemoths and such if we weren't going to fight them? Our generals aren't always as efficient as they might be, but they aren't that inefficient."

Leudast nodded. That also made sense to him: all too much sense. He said, "What's your guess? Will they hit us, or will we jump them first?"

Now Magnulf laughed out loud. "Answer me this one: when have you ever known King Swemmel to wait for anything or anybody?"

"Ah," Leudast said again. He looked east across the little river into Algarvian-occupied Forthweg. From a distance, the countryside over there looked no different from the chunk of Forthweg Unkerlant held. Leudast got the feeling he'd be seeing that distant countryside up close before too long.

Vanai had not enjoyed going out on to the streets of Oyngestun since the Algarvians occupied the village. (She hadn't much enjoyed going out on to the streets of Oyngestun before the war began, either, but chose not to dwell on that now.) But, with Major Spinello paying court to her grandfather these days, going out on to the streets of Oyngestun had become an impossible ordeal.

Before the war began, before the Algarvian major and scholar began calling at Brivibas's home, the Kaunians of Oyngestun had been well-inclined to her, even if the Forthwegians sneered at her because of her blood and leered at her because of her trousers. The Forthwegians still sneered and leered, as did the Algarvian troopers of Oyngestun's small garrison. Vanai could have dealt with that; she was used to it.

These days, though, her own people also rejected her, and that was like a knife in the heart. When she walked through the district in which most of Oyngestun's Kaunians lived, the politer folk turned their backs on her, pretending she did not exist. Others – mostly those closer to her own age – called her more filthy names than she'd found in the seamiest classical Kaunian texts.

"Look out!" The cry raced up the street ahead of her as she walked toward the apothecary's. "Here comes the redhead's dripholder!"

Laughter floated out through the small windows opening on to the street. Vanai held her head up and her back straight, however much she wanted to cry. If her own people pretended they could not see her, she would pretend she could not hear them.

The apothecary, a pale, middle-aged man named Tamulis, liked money too well to pretend Vanai did not exist. "What do you want?" he demanded when she came inside, as if anxious to get her out again as soon as he could.

"My grandfather suffers from headache, sir," Vanai answered in a low, polite voice. "I would like a jar of the willow-bark decoction, if you please."

Tamulis scowled. "You and Brivibas make all the Kaunians of Oyngestun suffer from headache," he said coldly. "Who else sucks up to the Algarvians as you do?"

"I do not!" Vanai said. She started to go on to defend her grandfather, but the words stuck in her throat. At last, she did find something she could truthfully say: "He has brought no harm to anyone else in the village. He has accused no one. He has denounced no one."

"Not yet," Tamulis said. "How long will it be before that comes, too?" But he bent and searched the shelves behind the high counter

until he found the decoction Vanai wanted. "Here. That will be one
and six. Take it and get out."

Biting her lip, she gave him two large silver coins. He returned half
a dozen small ones. She put them in her pocket. After a moment, she
put the jar of willow-bark decoction in another pocket. When she
walked down the street carrying something, boys had been known to
run by and strike it out of her hand. They thought that great sport.
Vanai didn't.

Tamulis spoke more kindly than he had before: "Have you
nowhere you might go, so your grandfather's disgrace does not stick
to you?"

"He is my grandfather," Vanai said. The apothecary scowled, but
then reluctantly nodded. Were Kaunian family ties not strong, no
recognizable Kaunians would have been left in Forthweg. Vanai
added, "Nor have I ever heard that pursuing knowledge brought
disgrace with it."

"Pursuing knowledge, no," Tamulis admitted. "Pursuing food
when others go hungry – that is a different matter. And you may tell
Brivibas I say so. I have said as much to his face."

"He has not pursued food," Vanai said. "By the powers above, he
has not!"

"Your loyalty does you credit: more credit than your grandfather
deserves," Tamulis said. "Tell me also that he has not accepted the
food the redheads give him to keep him sweet." When Vanai stood
mute, the apothecary grunted and gave another of those reluctant
nods. "You are honest, I think. You may discover, though, that being
honest does you less good than you might expect."

"You need not fear, sir." Vanai let her bitterness come out. "I have
already discovered that." She dipped her head in what looked very
much like respect, then left the apothecary's shop.

Going back to the house in which Brivibas had raised her, she ran
the gauntlet again. Some people ignored her, often ostentatiously.
Others shouted abuse at her or about her. Her strides grew longer and
more determined as she neared her house. If her fellow Kaunians
could not see that they'd hurt her, then in some the way they hadn't.

Her heart sank when she saw a bored-looking Algarvian trooper
standing in front of the house. That meant Major Spinello was inside,
and also meant her grandfather's reputation – and hers – would sink

even lower, if such a thing was possible. Blood started pounding at her temples and behind her eyes. Maybe she would take some of the willow-bark decoction herself.

The Algarvian soldier stopped looking bored the instant he spotted her. Instead, he looked like a hound that had just had a pork chop waved in front of it. He blew Vanai a loud, smacking kiss. "Hello, sweetheart!" he said in loud, bad, enthusiastic Forthwegian.

"I am sorry. I do not understand what you are saying," Vanai answered in Kaunian. The redhead did not seem the sort who would have studied the classical tongue in school. Sure enough, he looked blank. Before he could make up his mind whether she was lying, she walked rapidly past him and into the house. The door had been unbarred when she went out. She made sure she barred it behind her now.

Brivibas's voice, and Spinello's, too, came from the direction of her grandfather's study. As quietly as she could, Vanai went into the kitchen and set the jar of medicine on the counter there. Regardless of whether or not her grandfather had a headache, she did not want the Algarvian major with a passion for ancient history to know she was there. He'd never tried to do anything with her or to her, but, like all Algarvians, he watched her too hard.

"But, sir," he was saying now in his really excellent Kaunian, "you are a reasonable man. Surely you can see this would be in your own best interest and in that of your people here."

"Some people may well find lying to be in their best interest. I, however, am not any of those unfortunate individuals." When Brivibas sounded stuffiest, he was also stubbornest. "And how a lie can benefit my people is also beyond me."

Major Spinello's sigh was quite audible; from it, Vanai guessed he and her grandfather had been arguing for some time. The Algarvian said, "In my view, sir, I have asked you for no untruth."

"No, eh? The Algarvian occupation of Forthweg and Valmiera is in your view a positive good for Kaunianity?" Brivibas said. "If that be your view, Major, I can only suggest that you see an oculist, for your vision has suffered some severe derangement."

Vanai hugged herself for joy. She wished her grandfather had spoken thus to Spinello at his first visit. But Spinello hadn't talked of anything but antiquarian subjects then, and Brivibas enjoyed playing the master to a bright student, even a bright Algarvian student. It was, in a way, the role he played with Vanai.

"I think not," Spinello answered. "Tell me how wonderfully the Forthwegians treated you Kaunians when they ruled here. Were they not as barbarous as their Unkerlanter cousins?"

Brivibas didn't answer right away. That meant he was thinking it over, analyzing it. Vanai did not want him bogged down in an argument over details, where the main point would get lost. Hurrying into the study, she said, "That has nothing to do with the way the Algarvian army overran Valmiera."

"Why, so it doesn't, my dear child," Major Spinello said, which made Vanai see red that had nothing to do with his hair. "So good to see you again," he went on. "But had we not overrun Valmiera, King Gainibu's army would have overrun us, is it not so? Of course it is so, for that is what the Valmierans did during the Six Years' War. Now do please run along and let your elders discuss this business."

"There is nothing to discuss," Brivibas said, "and Vanai may stay if she so desires, this being her home, Major, and not yours."

Spinello bowed stiffly. "In this you are of course correct, sir. My apologies." He turned and bowed to Vanai as well, before giving his attention back to Brivibas. "But I continue to maintain that you are being unreasonable."

"And I continue to maintain that you have not the faintest notion of what you are talking about," Brivibas said. "If occupation by King Mezentio's soldiers be such a boon for us Kaunians, Major, why have you Algarvians ordered that we may no longer set our own language down in writing, but must use Forthwegian or Algarvian? This, mind you, when Kaunian has been the language of scholarship since the days of antiquity you say you love so well."

Major Spinello coughed and looked embarrassed. "I did not give this order, nor do I approve of it. It strikes me as overzealous. As you hear, I have no objections to your language: on the contrary."

"Whether it be your order does not matter," Brivibas said. "That it is an Algarvian order does. The Forthwegians never restricted us so: one more reason I fail to view the present order of things as beneficial to Kaunians."

"Oh, good for you, my grandfather!" Vanai exclaimed. At his best,

Brivibas aimed logic like the beam from a stick, and, she thought admiringly, with even more piercing effect.

"Your reasoning is elegant, as always," Spinello said. "I have, however, another question for you: do you view the present order of things as beneficial to yourself and your charming granddaughter, as compared to other Kaunians here in Forthweg? Think hard before you answer, sir."

Vanai sighed. So this was what Spinello had been after all along. She'd had a pretty good notion he was after something. Turning her grandfather into an Algarvian tool made excellent sense from his point of view. But Brivibas's integrity, while on the fusty side, was real – and Brivibas had never cared for redheads.

How much did he care for a full belly? Vanai wondered how much she cared for a full belly herself. She'd learned all she cared to about hunger before Major Spinello started paying court to her grandfather. Maybe it was just as well Spinello hadn't asked her.

Brivibas said, "Good day, sir. If you care to discuss the past, we may perhaps have something to say to each other. We do not appear to view the present in the same light, however."

"You will come to regret your decision, I fear," Spinello said. "You will regret it very soon, and very much."

"That is also part of life," Brivibas answered. "Good day." Spinello threw his hands in the air, then bowed and departed.

As the door to the street closed behind him, Vanai said, "My grandfather, I am proud of you. We are free again."

"We are free to starve again, my granddaughter," Brivibas said. "We are free to endure worse than hunger, too, I fear. I may have made a mistake that will cost us dear."

Vanai shook her head. "I'm proud of you," she repeated.

Her grandfather smiled a small, slow smile. "Though it may be unbecomingly immodest to say so, I am also rather proud of myself."

Cornelu wished the land ahead of him were one of the five islands of Sibiu. Had the Lagoans ordered him to strike a blow at the Algarvians occupying his own kingdom, he would have felt more useful. He tried to console himself with the thought that any blow against Algarve was a blow toward eventually freeing Sibiu. He had never before realized what a melancholy word *eventually* was.

He patted Eforiel, bring the leviathan to a halt a couple of hundred yards from the southern coast of Valmiera. If she came any closer to land, she ran the risk of beaching herself. That would have been a disaster past repair – not for the war, no doubt, but for Cornelu.

He turned and spoke in a low voice: "You go now." The words were in Lagoan, a command he had carefully memorized.

"Aye." That word was almost identical in Lagoan and Sibian and, for that matter, Algarvian, too. Half a dozen Lagoans with rubber flippers on their feet let go of the lines wrapped around Eforiel to which they had clung while the leviathan ferried them across the Valmieran Strait. Eforiel also carried some interesting containers under her belly. No one had told Cornelu what those held. That was sound doctrine; what he didn't know, he couldn't reveal if captured. The Lagoans undid the containers and swam with them toward the beach.

No shouts of alarm and anger rose from the land. Whatever the Lagoans were going to do, they could at least begin it without interference. In a way, that made Cornelu glad, as would anything that hurt the Algarvians. Still, he sighed as he urged Eforiel back out to sea. Had something gone wrong, it would have given him an excuse to ignore his orders to return to Setubal. He wanted an excuse to fight King Mezentio's men, and resented the Lagoans for making war out of what seemed no more than a sense of duty.

"Why should they care?" he asked Eforiel. "War has not come to their kingdom. I do not think war can or will come to their kingdom unless Kuusamo attacks them from the east. How Algarve would get an army across the Strait of Valmiera is beyond me."

Then he slapped the surface of the sea in his own alarm and anger. No one in Sibiu had imagined the Algarvians could get an army across the sea to overrun their islands. Algarvian imagination, Algarvian ingenuity, had proved more flexible, more capacious, than those of King Burebistu's generals and admirals. Could a like misfortune befall Lagoas?

"Powers above grant that it not be so," Cornelu muttered. Exile was bad. How bad exile was, he knew to the bottom of his soul. However bad it was, conquest would be worse. He knew that, too.

Beneath him, Eforiel's muscles surged as the leviathan swam south. Every now and then, the leviathan would twist away from the exact course back to Setubal to pursue a mackerel or squid. She'd fed well on the way up to Valmiera; had Cornelu wanted to keep her strictly to her work, he could have done so without harming her in the least. But he let her have her sport. If he returned to his cold, gray barracks an hour later than he might have otherwise, what of it?

One of those twists probably saved his life. He watched the sea for leviathans with Algarvian riders and for Algarvian ships sliding along the ley lines. He looked up at the sky, too, but only when he thought to do it, which was less often than it might have been. When he rode Eforiel, the water was his element. The air was not. Had he wanted to be a dragonflier, he would never have gone to sea.

Some Algarvian youth who had wanted to be a dragonflier released an egg from a great height. Had Eforiel not turned aside to go after squid, it would have burst on top of Cornelu and her, whereupon the small creatures of the sea would have feasted on them rather than the other way round.

As things were, they almost did. Even a near miss from an egg could kill, the outward pressure from the burst jellying a man – or a leviathan – the burst of energy itself did not reach. Cornelu did not quite know how close he and Eforiel came to being jellied, but he and the leviathan could not have escaped by much.

Eforiel gave a pained, startled, involuntary grunt when the egg burst, as a man might have done if suddenly and unexpectedly hit in the pit of the stomach. Cornelu felt as if he were being crushed in an olive press, but only for one brief, horrifying instant. Then, as she had been trained, Eforiel dove and swam away from the burst as fast as she could. Cornelu had only to hang on to the lines that moored him to the leviathan; Lagoan spells for breathing underwater were quite as effective as those Sibiu used.

Another egg burst, this one farther away. Eforiel swam harder – and deeper – than ever. Cornelu's guiding signals grew more urgent. Even with his sorcerous aids, the weight of the sea would crush him before it harmed the leviathan. If Eforiel gave way to panic and forgot that, the egg might as well have done its work, at least as far as he was concerned.

But the trainers at Tirgoviste had known their business, and Eforiel was a clever beast, little given to panic. After the first few frantic flaps from her flukes, she realized Cornelu was giving her signals, realized and obeyed. Her plunge to the depths of the sea slowed, then stopped. She angled up toward the surface once more.

Cornelu wished the Lagoan mages had used a spell to let the leviathan breathe underwater. So far as he knew, no such spell existed, though adapting the one the mages had used on him didn't strike him as likely to be difficult. Till this war, though, no one had seen the need, just as no one had seen the need to keep watch against sailing ships or to mass swarms of behemoths or . . .

When Eforiel spouted, Cornelu twisted his body to look up at the sky. He let out a startled grunt of his own, and ordered the leviathan to dive once more. That Algarvian dragon was stooping like a hawk, trying to get close enough to flame. He did not know whether dragonfire could kill a leviathan. He knew all too well that it could kill him.

He'd hoped the dragon would flame even though he and Eforiel had already submerged. If it ran out of flame, the leviathan and he would be safer. But no blast of flame boiled the sea above his head. He mumbled curses. The Algarvian up there, unfortunately, knew what he was about. And he would be able to watch for Eforiel to rise, where Cornelu would not, could not, know where he was until already exposed to danger.

Exposed or not, though, sooner or later Eforiel would have to breathe. Cornelu ordered her to swim north; going back the way he had come seemed likeliest to put distance between her and that cursed dragon. North and south, east and west, were all one to the leviathan. Cornelu sometimes thought his insistence on going this way or that way as opposed to any which way annoyed Eforiel. Sometimes, by the wiggle she gave when obeying his commands, he thought it amused her.

He let her swim as far as she could before surfacing. When she spouted, Cornelu looked around anxious for the dragon and the Algarvian flying it. He spotted the creature and its rider well off to the south, and nodded in no small satisfaction: he'd outguessed the dragonflier this time.

But his satisfaction did not last long. He'd wanted to give Eforiel a little while to rest, but the dragonflier spotted her almost as soon as Cornelu saw him. On came the great beast, the thunder of its wingbeats growing in Cornelu's ears above the plashing of the strait.

He sent Eforiel down below the surface well before the dragon got close enough to flame – and was glad he did, for a couple of sharp hisses above him said beams from the Algarvian's stick were boiling bits of ocean. They would have burned through him and the leviathan, too.

Cornelu sent Eforiel east this time, now worrying in earnest. Children in every kingdom played hiding games. When they lost them, though, the worst that happened was that they had to search next. If Cornelu lost this game, tiny fish would nibble the flesh from his bones.

After a long run under the protecting mantle of the sea, Eforiel came up to breathe once more. Cornelu looked around, trying to scan every direction at once. He spied the dragon off to the north. The Algarvian riding the stupid creature was anything but stupid himself. He hadn't stayed around and waited to see what Cornelu would do, and had nearly guessed right – Cornelu had thought hard about having Eforiel swim north again.

This time, the Sibian exile took the leviathan underwater as soon as she had breathed. He didn't know whether the dragonflier had spotted this surfacing or not. With a little luck, he would lose the Algarvian in the immensity of the sea.

Eforiel swam southeast; Cornelu wasn't yet ready to return to the straight course toward Setubal, the likeliest track on which the dragon would be hunting for him. So long as he reached the Lagoan coast anywhere, he could find his way back to the capital and its harbor.

But the dragonflier, realizing he'd been outfoxed, had gained altitude so he could survey a broad stretch of ocean. And, when he spotted Eforiel and Cornelu, he sent his mount winging after them.

Why doesn't he give up? Cornelu thought resentfully. *It's not as if I've done anything to him personally, the way he has to me, the way his kingdom has to mine.* Back in Tirgoviste, he had a son or daughter. He did not know which. He did not know how his wife was. Not knowing ate at him; it left an empty place where his heart should have been.

When Eforiel twisted and turned after fish, he let her. If he didn't know in which direction she was going, how could the dragonflier guess?

Logically speaking, that was perfect. Logical perfection didn't keep Cornelu and the leviathan from almost dying a few minutes later.

When Eforiel surfaced, her spout nearly soaked the dragon's tail. However he'd done it, that cursed Algarvian had gauged almost perfectly where the leviathan would rise.

Cornelu watched the dragon's head start to twist on its long, snaky neck, back under its body. He sent Eforiel diving, hard and fast as he could. The sea above them turned to a sheet of flame. That terrified the leviathan, which, a creature of water, knew nothing of fire. She swam farther and faster than Cornelu would have dreamt she could.

Her fear might have saved her, for the hunting dragon could not draw near enough to flame or for its rider to blaze when she surfaced again, and guessed wrong on the direction of her next run, so Cornelu was at last able to escape the stubborn dragonflier's pursuit.

"Routine," he said back in Setubal, when his Lagoan superiors asked how the swim to Valmiera had gone. "Nothing but routine." He did not think they were able to tell he was lying.

Bembo peered east, toward the Bradano Mountains, with nothing but relief. The Jelgavans didn't look like breaking out on to the plains after all, which meant the emergency militia wasn't drilling any more. Not marching under the eye of that fearsome sergeant warmed Bembo's heart. If Algarve needed a pudgy constable to help hold back her foes, the kingdom was in desperate straits indeed.

A broadsheet showed one blond in trousers running away from an Algarvian on a behemoth, with another blond cowering in a trench. The first trousered soldiers was labeled VALMIERA, the second JELGAVA. COWARDLY KAUNIANS, declared the legend below the picture.

Hardly knowing he was doing it, Bembo nodded as he swaggered by the broadsheet. Kaunians had always been cowards, even back in the ancient days. If they hadn't been, Tricarico would still be a city of the Kaunian Empire, and the Algarvians pinned back in the forests of the far south.

He kept an eye out for blonds who weren't on posters. Orders to take nothing for granted when it came to Kaunians had gone out to every constable in town – and, Bembo suspected, to every constable in the kingdom. Such orders made sense to him. It was, he supposed, possible for folk of Kaunian blood to be loyal to King Mezentio. Possible, aye – but how likely? Not very, in his judgment.

That Balozio, for instance, remained locked up. He hadn't been able to prove he wasn't a Jelgavan spy, and nobody felt like taking a chance on him. That also made sense to Bembo. How loyal would Balozio be after spending a while in a cell? Again, not very, not so far as the constable could see.

Bembo's eyes flicked back and forth, back and forth. He spied only a couple of blonds on the street: Kaunians weren't going out much these days. One was an old man hobbling along with the help of a cane, the other one of the ugliest, dumpiest women he'd ever seen in his life. He didn't bother either of them. The old man would have had trouble being dangerous to a snail, let alone a kingdom. As for the woman – had she been pretty, he probably would have found some questions to ask her. Since she was anything but, he pretended – and did his best to pretend to himself, too – he hadn't noticed her.

He marched past a hair-dressing salon, then stopped. He'd been in there not long before the war started, to investigate a burglary. He never had tracked down the thief, even though the man and woman who ran the place slipped him some cash to look extra hard. They were both blonds.

Whistling, he turned and walked back to the doorway. If they'd paid him back then to look for a burglar, they would likely pay him even more now to leave them alone. Constables never made enough money. Bembo didn't know a single colleague who would have disagreed with him. He opened the door and went inside.

The husband of the pair was trimming a customer's goatee while the wife curled a woman's hair. Another woman sat reading a news sheet, waiting to be served. They all raised their heads to stare at him.

He stared at them, too. The man and woman doing the work had red hair, as did all their customers. Had he come into the wrong place? He couldn't believe it. Maybe the Kaunians had sold the business. That made better sense to him.

Before he could apologize and leave – bothering ordinary Algarvians might land him in trouble – the man with the little scissors in his hand said, "Look, Evadne, it's Constable Bembo, who tried so hard to catch that miserable burglar." He bowed. "A good day to you, Constable."

Automatically, Bembo returned the bow. The woman – Evadne –

said, "Why, so it is, Falsirone." She dropped Bembo a curtsy. "A very good day to you, Constable."

Bembo bowed again. These were the people he'd seen about the burglary. They had ordinary Algarvian names and spoke Algarvian with an accent like his own. But they'd been blonds the last time he saw them. "You've dyed your hair!" he blurted as realization struck.

"Aye, we have." Falsirone nodded. "We got plumb sick and tired of people cursing us for dirty Kaunians whenever we struck our faces out the door. Now we fit in a mite better."

"That's right," Evadne said. "Life's been a lot simpler since we did it."

Their features still had a Kaunian cast, being rather sharper than those of most Algarvians. And their eyes were blue, not green or hazel. But those were details. The color of their hair wasn't. They could pass for ordinary Algarvians in the street, no questions about it.

Which meant . . . Bembo's jaw dropped when he thought about what it meant. "You, you, you!" he snapped to the other three people – the other three redheaded people – in the salon. "Are you Kaunians, too?"

He watched them all think about lying – as a constable, he had no trouble recognizing that expression. As he looked at them, he realized they *were* of Kaunian stock. They must have seen as much on his face, for, one by one, they nodded.

"It's like Falsirone told you," said the man in the chair in front of the barber. "All we want is for people to leave us alone. With our hair red, they mostly do."

"Powers above," Bembo said softly. He pointed to Falsirone. "How many Kaunians have you turned into redheads?"

"I couldn't begin to tell you, sir, not exactly," Falsirone answered. "A fair number, though, I'd say." Evadne nodded. Her husband continued, "All we want to do is get along, not make any trouble for anybody and not have anybody make any trouble for us. Nothing wrong with that, is there, sir? It's not against the law."

"No, I don't suppose it is," Bembo said abstractedly. The law hadn't considered that Kaunians who found trouble as blonds might reach for the henna bottle. The law could be pretty stupid.

"Are we in trouble, sir?" Evadne asked. "If we are, I do hope you'll give us the chance to make it right."

She meant she hoped Bembo would take another bribe. Like most Algarvian constables, he was seldom known to turn one down. This, though, looked to be one of those rare times. He thought he could get more from his superiors for telling what he'd learned than he could from the Kaunians for keeping quiet.

"I don't think there's any problem," he said, not wanting to give the game away. Evadne and Falsirone and their customers looked relieved. They looked even more relieved when Bembo left. Only after he headed back to the constabulary station did he realize he could have taken their money *and* that from his superiors. As constables went, he was relatively honest.

"What are you doing here, Bembo?" Sergeant Pesaro demanded when he came into the station. "You're supposed to be out there protecting our poor, endangered citizens from each other."

"Oh, bugger our poor, endangered citizens," Bembo said. "Bugger 'em with a pinecone, as a matter of fact. This is important."

"It had better be, after a buildup like that," the fat sergeant said. "Come on, give forth." He spread his hands in anticipation.

And Bembo gave forth. As he did, Sergeant Pesaro's expression changed. Bembo smiled to himself. Pesaro had been waiting for him to come out with something not worth interrupting his usual beat to deliver. Had he done so, the sergeant would have taken unholy glee in roasting him over a slow fire. But if what he had to say wasn't worth mentioning, he didn't know what would be.

"Why, those dirty, sneaking whoresons!" Pesaro burst out when he was through. "Going around hiding what they are, are they? We'll put paid to that, and bugger *me* with a pinecone if we don't."

"Right now, there's no law on the books against it," Bembo said. "I'm only too bloody sure of that. Used to be, the cursed Kaunians would flaunt what they were: wave their hair in our faces, you might say. They can't get away with that any more, so they're doing their best to turn into chameleons instead."

"They won't get away with it." Pesaro heaved his bulk out of the chair behind the front desk. "I'm going to have myself a talk with Captain Sasso. He'll know what we can do about the miserable yellow-hairs, law or no law."

"Aye, so he will." Bembo picked his next words with care: "Let me come along with you, Sergeant, if you'd be so kind. The captain will surely want to hear the details straight from the man who found them."

Pesaro glared at him as if he were half a worm in an apple. Bembo knew what that meant: the sergeant had been planning to grab all the credit himself. If he were a heartless enough bastard, he could still do it. For a moment, Bembo thought he would. But that would infuriate not just Bembo — which wouldn't have bothered Pesaro in the slightest — but all the other ordinary constables, too. Still looking sour, Pesaro nodded and jerked his head toward the stairs leading up to Captain Sasso's office. "Come on, then."

Sasso was a lean, middle-aged man with a startling streak of white in his cinnamon hair. He had a scar on his scalp from a knife fight in his youth, and the hair along it had been silver ever since. He looked up from paperwork as Pesaro and Bembo stood in the doorway waiting to be noticed. "All right, boys, come on in," he said. "What's going on?"

"Constable Bembo here noticed something I think you ought to know about, sir," Pesaro said: if he couldn't take all the credit, he'd take some. He nudged Bembo with an elbow. "Go on, tell the captain what the dirty Kaunians are up to."

"Kaunians, eh?" Sasso leaned forward, his form almost silhouetted against the window in front of which he sat. "Aye, do tell me."

Before Bembo could begin, shadows dappled the street outside. "A lot of dragons flying these days," he remarked. "Powers above be praised they're ours, and not the cursed Jelgavans'."

"Aye." Captain Sasso's smile displayed sharp teeth. By the way his eyes gleamed, Bembo got the notion he knew more than he was saying. Bembo got no chance to ask questions; Sasso gestured impatiently. "Out with it, Constable."

"Aye, sir." As Bembo had for Pesaro, he told Sasso how the Kaunians were dyeing their hair to become less conspicuous in Tricarico.

"Well, well," the constabulary captain said when he was through. "I heard a natural philosopher talk once about spiders that looked like flowers, so the bees and butterflies would come right up and get eaten. Sounds like what the Kaunians are doing, doesn't it? And if they're doing it in Tricarico, sure as sure they're doing it all over Algarve."

"I hadn't thought of that, sir," Bembo said, which was true. Officers got paid to worry about the whole puzzle; he had enough trouble trying to keep track of what was going on in his own little piece.

"We'll put a stop to it, though – curse me if we don't," Sasso said, his voice thoroughly grim. He nodded to Bembo and Pesaro. "And your name will be remembered, Constable, for ferreting this out, and yours, Sergeant, for bringing it to my notice. On that you both have my solemn word."

"Thank you, sir," the two men chorused. They beamed at each other. Bembo was willing to share the credit, so long as he got some. So was Pesaro, even if he had tried to steal it for himself. That made them both uncommonly generous for Algarvian constables.

Pekka had always maintained that a mage's most important tools were pen and paper: a fitting attitude for a theoretical sorcerer. Now she was in the laboratory rather than behind her desk. Instead of the abstracted expression she usually wore while practicing her craft, the look on her face at the moment was one of intense frustration.

She glowered at the acorn on the table in front of her. "Better you should have been fed to a pig," she told it. It lay there, mute, inert, unhelpful. It might also have reproached her for clumsy technique – and she was far more frustrated than she'd imagined, if she invested an acorn with the power to reproach.

She felt like reproaching the little brown nut far more loudly and stridently than she already had. Kuusaman restraint won out, but only barely. The foreign sailors whose loud foreign oaths sometimes spilled out of the harbor district of Kajaani never left any doubt of how they felt about things. Pekka envied the release they gained so easily.

"Let me learn the truth," she murmured. "That will release me."

If the acorn knew the truth, it wasn't talking. She'd thought she'd found a way to coax the truth from it, but hadn't managed that yet. She muttered again. She had no doubt Leino would have seen half a dozen ways to improve her experiment. Any mage with a practical bent would have. But she wasn't supposed to let her husband know about the work she was doing. She wasn't supposed to let anyone know but her colleagues – and they were theoretical sorcerers, too.

She gave the acorn another glare. For good measure, she walked across the laboratory and glared at the other acorn in the experiment. It sat on a white plate identical to that on which the first acorn rested. The two plates sat on identical tables. The two acorns themselves were tightly similar – Pekka had picked them and several more from one branch of an oak – and had been in contact not only through the tree but also in a single jar here in this chamber. She knew they'd touched. She'd made sure they touched.

And all her care had got her . . . nothing, so far. She strode back to the table that held the first acorn. Angry footsteps on the stone floor served her almost as well as angry curses served foreign sailors. She wanted to pick up the acorn and fling it out the window. With more than a little effort, she checked herself.

"It *should* have worked," she said, and then laughed in spite of her anger and frustration. That was the sort of thing Uto might have said. No one would have, no one could have, blamed a small boy for thinking that way. Pekka, however, was supposed to know better.

"But it should have," she protested, and laughed at herself again. Aye, she sounded very much like Uto.

Sounding like her son didn't necessarily mean she was wrong. If she wanted to get to the bottom of the relationship between the laws of similarity and contagion, till now reckoned the basic laws of sorcery, what better way to approach it than through acorns, the basic forms of oaks? She'd thought herself very clever to come up with that. It seemed the sort of notion a seasoned experimenter might devise.

Sometimes, of course, even seasoned experimenters failed. Up till now, Pekka certainly had. For all she'd learned, the laws of similarity and contagion might as well not have existed, let alone any relationship between them.

"And wouldn't that be grand?" she said with a small shiver. "Nothing but the mechanic arts forevermore?" She imagined disproving the laws of similarity and contagion and, as knowledge of the disproof spread, magecraft grinding to a halt. Then she shook her head, so violently that she had to brush her coarse black hair back from her face. It couldn't happen, and she was heartily glad it couldn't.

But what had gone wrong here? She still couldn't figure that out. When she'd done something to one acorn, nothing had happened to the other, even though they were similar and had been in contact. That made no sorcerous sense.

Pekka snapped her fingers. "I'll try something different," she said. "If that doesn't work . . . Powers below eat me, I don't know what I'll do if that doesn't work."

She carried a bucket and a trowel outside and scooped up some moist soil. Then she went back to the laboratory chamber and stirred the soil around as thoroughly as she could before dividing it into two equal piles. Using a tossed coin to make sure she chose the piles randomly, she buried one acorn in the first and the other in the second.

That done, she began to chant over one of the acorns. The chant sprang from one horticultural mages used to force fruits and flowers to flourish out of season, but she'd spent some time strengthening it so she could see results more quickly. One day, if she ever found the time – and if the chant proved useless to her present project, and so would not be reckoned a princely secret – she thought she might license out the improvements, which could well bring in enough money to make her brother-in-law smile.

Unlike some of the others she'd tried, this spell seemed to perform as it should have. An oak sapling sprouted up through the soil and stretched toward the ceiling, compressing several months' growth into half an hour. Satisfied, Pekka stopped the chant and looked over toward the other table, where the other acorn should have shown similar growth.

But it hadn't. Real fear ran through Pekka. If the other acorn hadn't grown, maybe the laws of similarity and contagion weren't so universal as she'd thought. Maybe nothing lay beneath them, and she'd reached through the fabric of belief to grasp it. Maybe magic really would start falling apart.

"Avert the omen," Pekka murmured. She hurried over to the other table, wondering what was wrong with the acorn on it.

There lay the white plate, with a mound of soil on it but with no sapling coming up. Pekka spread the soil aside to get at the acorn. Maybe, she thought hopefully, it was infertile. If it was, that would explain why her experiments kept going awry: it wouldn't be truly similar to the other. A very simple sorcerous test would tell her whether that was so.

"Where is the cursed acorn?" she said. She knew she'd buried it:

about a thumb's breadth from the top of the mound of soil. It wasn't there. She sifted through all the soil, spreading it out till it slopped off the plate and on to the table. Still no sign of the acorn.

Careless of the dirt on her fingers and palms, Pekka set hands on hips. She knew perfectly well that she'd set an acorn in the pile of soil. She couldn't have carried it over to the other pile and put it in there along with the other acorn – could she? She did that kind of thing around the house now and again. Everybody did. But she couldn't have been so careless in the laboratory . . . could she?

"Powers above," she said. "If I did that, Leino would never let me forget it. If I did that, nobody ought to let me forget it."

She walked back to the first table. If she had somehow – she couldn't imagine how – set both acorns in one pile of dirt, she should have got two saplings springing up toward the ceiling. If she'd made a major blunder *and* the other acorn was somehow infertile . . . She shook her head. How slim were the odds that two improbables had both gone wrong at the same time.

"But if they haven't, where's my acorn?" she demanded of the laboratory chamber. She got no answer. By then, she wouldn't have been too surprised had one of the tables up and spoken.

She sifted through all the dirt in the pile from which the sapling had sprouted. She did not find the missing acorn. She didn't know whether to be relieved or not. On the one hand, she hadn't done anything unpardonably stupid. On the other hand, if she hadn't done anything unpardonably stupid, the earlier question recurred: where had the bloody acorn gone?

"I know where it should be," Pekka said, and went back to the pile of dirt in which she had – she knew she had – planted the acorn now missing.

Could it have fallen off the table? Pekka couldn't see how, but she couldn't see how it had disappeared, either. She got down on hands and knees and, backside in the air, stuck her nose down to the stone floor and looked all around. She still couldn't find the acorn. It had been there. She was sure of that. It wasn't any more. She was becoming sure of that, too.

"Then where is it?" she asked herself and the world at large. "How am I supposed to write up my experimental diary if I don't know what to put in it?"

She started a list of all the places the acorn wasn't: in the soil, on the plate, on the table, on the other plate or table, anywhere on the floor – anywhere in the chamber, as far as she could tell. That was all good, solid information. It belonged in the diary, and she put it there.

It was, however, information of a negative sort. Where *was* the acorn? Positive information was a lot harder to come by. *The acorn,* she wrote, *was carried off by Gyongyosian spies.* Then she made sure that was too thoroughly scratched out to be legible, even though it made as much sense as anything else she'd thought of, and more sense than most of the things.

She tried again. *The parameters of the experiment were as follows,* she wrote, and set down everything she'd done, including the alterations she'd made to the horticultural magic that formed the basis for her spell. *The control acorn performed as expected in every way. The other acorn, although emplaced in a setting attuned to the first through both similarity and contagion, did not germinate as a result of the spell and, in fact, could not be located despite diligent search at the close of the experiment.*

There. That told the truth, even if in a bloodless way. She didn't know what it meant. Maybe one of her clever colleagues would be able to figure it out after seeing exactly what she'd done. Maybe, on the other hand, all her clever colleagues would laugh themselves silly at her clumsy technique.

"Suppose," she said to the air, "just suppose, mind you, that my technique wasn't clumsy. Suppose something *did* happen."

Imbued with fresh purpose, she nodded. Odds were, she had done something foolish. Repeating the experiment as exactly as she could would tell her, one way or the other.

To reduce the risk of magical contamination, she used different tables, different plants, and fresh soil for the new trial. Obviously, she used new acorns, too. This time, she took care to note where each of them went. She chanted over one. A sapling duly sprouted. No sapling grew at the other table. She went back there and sifted through the dirt. She found no acorn.

"It's real," she breathed. Then she started to laugh. It might have been real, but she had no idea what it meant.

15.

Sergeant Jokai clanged a gong that sounded like the end of the world. Gyongyosian soldiers tumbled out of the barracks, rubbing sleep from their eyes. Istvan clutched his stick, wondering what sort of new and fiendish drill his superiors had come up with this time.

"Come on, you lugs, down toward the beach," Jokai shouted. "The cursed Kuusamans are paying us another call."

Istvan looked around for Borsos. The dowser was nowhere to be seen. Maybe he was the one who'd raised the alarm. Whether he was or not, Istvan had no time to find him, not with Jokai and the officers set above Jokai screaming at the top of their lungs for every soldier to hurry down to the beaches and throw back the invaders. The Kuusaman attack had turned him into an ordinary warrior again. For that if for no other reason — and he had plenty of others — he cursed the Kuusamans as vilely as he could.

Along with his comrades, he stumbled down a path toward the sea. *Stumbled* was the operative word; the eastern sky behind him had gone gray with the beginnings of morning twilight, but dawn still lay most of an hour away. The Gyongyosians could hardly see where they were putting their feet. Every so often, someone would go down with a thump and a howl. As like as not, somebody else would trip over the luckless soldier before he made it to his feet again.

And then, before the Gyongyosians had got off the wooded slopes of Mt. Sorong, eggs began falling around them. "The stinking slanteyes have brought another dragon transport with them," somebody yelled.

When Istvan came out from under the trees for a moment, he looked up into the heavens. It was still too dark for him to see much, but he did spy a couple of spurts of fire. That meant Gyongyosian dragons had got into the air, too, and were contesting the sky above Obuda with the Kuusamans.

He came down on to the flatlands that led to the Bothnian Ocean. He knew exactly which trenches his company had to occupy. Serving Borsos had got him out of a lot of exercises, but not all of them. He discovered he still remembered such basics as taking cover and making sure no dirt fouled the business end of his stick.

"By the stars!" said one of his comrades, a burly youngster named Szonyi. "Will you look at all the ships!"

Istvan did look, and then cursed some more. "The Kuusamans brought everything they've got this time, didn't they?" he said. He couldn't begin to guess how many ships were silhouetted against the brightening sky, but he was certain of one thing: that fleet was larger than the one the Gyongyosians had in local waters.

"Don't despair!" an officer down the trench shouted. "Never despair! Are we not men? Are we not warriors?" In more practical tones, he went on, "Have we not got our great garrison on this island as well as our ships?"

That did help steady Istvan. He stopped feeling as if he were alone and facing the Kuusaman fleet without anyone to aid him. Egg-tossers on and near the beach began flinging their deadly cargo at the foe. Plumes of water mounting high in the air told of near misses. A burst of fire and a plume of smoke told of a hit. Istvan yelled himself hoarse.

But the Kuusamans had brought heavy warships east along the ley lines to Obuda. They carried egg-tossers that matched any the Gyongyosians had mounted on the island. Eggs came whistling in, some aimed at the tossers opposing the Kuusamans, others at the trenches where Istvan and his comrades crouched. He felt trapped in an earthquake that would not end. Not far away, wounded men wailed.

Like any others, Kuusaman cruisers also mounted sticks far heavier than a soldier or even a behemoth could bear. Where their mighty beams smote, smoke sprang skyward. A soldier caught in one of them burned like a moth flying through a torch flame. Istvan hoped the poor fellow hadn't had time to realize he was dead.

"Look!" Szonyi pointed. "Some of our dragons have broken through!"

Sure enough, several dragons were diving on the Kuusaman fleet. Szonyi wasn't the only one to have spotted them. But those great sticks could point to the sky as well as toward Obuda. Dragons could not withstand their beams, as they could the ones from the common soldiers' sticks. One after another, Gyongyosian dragons plunged burning into the sea.

Yet the dragons were fast and agile. Their fliers were fearless, they themselves too stupid to be afraid. Not all were struck before the fliers could release their eggs and even pass low above the warships' decks. The dragons flamed, enveloping Kuusaman sailors in fire, then flapped away.

"For all the good we're doing here, we might as well have stayed asleep in the barracks," Istvan said. "It was like that the last time the Kuusamans tried to take Obuda away from us, too."

"I don't think it will stay that way this time," Sergeant Jokai said. "I wish it would, but I don't think it will. Those sons of goats have brought a lot more ships and a lot more dragons than they did last time."

The offshore battle went on for most of the morning. The Gyongyosian admiral in command at Obuda threw in his ships a few at a time, which meant they were defeated a few at a time. Had he hurled the whole fleet at the Kuusamans, he might have accomplished more. As things were, the would-be invaders slowly beat down the Gyongyosian defenses.

Somewhere around noon, a new cry arose, one in which Istvan joined: "Here come the boats!"

Not all the Gyongyosian egg-tossers had been wrecked. Indeed, some had not taken part in the earlier fight against the Kuusaman naval expedition, and so had given the foe no clue about their position. Istvan shouted with glee as eggs fell among the boats carrying Kuusaman soldiers, wrecking some and overturning others.

Gyongyos painted her dragons in gaudy stripes of red and blue, black and yellow. They dove on the invaders. The small boats carried no sticks strong enough to slay them as they dove, and some of those boats began to burn.

But most kept on coming toward the beaches of Obuda. A few, the larger ones, glided swiftly along the ley lines whose convergence at the island made it a bone of contention between Gyongyos and Kuusamo. The rest advanced as they might have in the ancient days of the world, pushed by the wind or pulled by oars.

Small, stocky, dark-haired soldiers crowded the boats. "They don't look so tough," said Szonyi, who hadn't been on Obuda long enough to have seen Kuusamans before. "I could break one of them in half."

He was on the weedy side as Gyongyosians went, but that didn't mean he was wrong. It also didn't mean being right would do him any good, which he didn't seem to realize. Istvan made things as plain as he could: "As long as the slanteyes have sticks and know what to do with them – and they do, curse 'em, they do – you won't get close enough to break 'em in half."

"That's the truth." Sergeant Jokai sounded surprised to be agreeing with Istvan instead of harassing him, but he did. "Don't think for even a minute that those ugly little bastards can't fight, because they cursed well can. And don't think they can't take this stinking island away from us, because they've done that, too. The thing is, we'd better not let 'em do it again, not if we want to go on looking up at the stars."

The Kuusaman captives the Gyongyosians had taken when they last seized Obuda were slave laborers back on the mainland of Derlavai or on the other islands Ekrekek Arpad ruled. Something similarly unpleasant no doubt befell captured Gyongyosians in Kuusaman hands. An enslaved captive might still look up at the stars, but how much joy could he take in doing it?

Istvan hoped he would not have to find out. Kuusaman boats began beaching. Soldiers jumped out of them and ran for what cover they could find. Istvan and his comrades blazed away at them, and knocked down a good many. But not all the Kuusamans came ashore in front of positions that hadn't been too badly knocked about. Cries of alarm warned that some of the invaders were outflanking the Gyongyosian defenders.

"Fall back!" an officer shouted. "We'll make a stand on Mt. Sorong."

Retreat was galling to any troops, and more galling to the Gyongyosians, who fancied themselves a warrior race, than to most. If the choice was retreating or being attacked from the front and flanks at the same time, though, even the fiercest fighters saw where sense lay.

Eggs burst not far from Istvan and his comrades as they fell back. "Curse the Kuusamans all over again," Jokai snarled. "They've gone and fetched light tossers along with 'em."

"We did the same thing when we took Obuda back," Istvan said.

"Curse 'em anyway," his sergeant replied, a sentiment with which he could hardly disagree.

More eggs burst ahead of them, these large, throwing up great columns of riven earth. High in the sky, a dragon screeched harshly. Jokai had been right; the Kuusamans were indeed far better prepared for this attack than they had been for the one the year before.

Kuusaman eggs had already wrecked some of the defensive positions on the lower slopes of Mt. Sorong. As Istvan wearily stumbled into an undamaged trench, he asked the question surely uppermost in his comrades' minds as well: "Will we be able to hold out here?"

Whatever else Sergeant Jokai was, he was forthright. He answered, "It doesn't really depend on us. If the stinking slanteyes can hold the sea around this miserable island, they'll be able to bring in enough soldiers to swarm over us and enough dragons to flame all of ours out of the sky. If our ships drive theirs away, we'll be the ones who can reinforce and they'll be out of luck."

That made sense, even if Istvan didn't care for the notion that his fate rested in hands other than his own. Now that he wasn't on the move any more, he realized he was hungry. He had a couple of small rounds of flatbread in his belt pouch, and wolfed them down. His belly stopped growling. Some of his comrades had already eaten everything they'd brought from the barracks. No one from higher up on Mt. Sorong showed up with more in the way of supplies.

Istvan wondered if Borsos was safe, and if the dowser had given the Gyongyosians such warning as they'd had. Maybe Borsos was having to fight as a real captain would. Maybe, too, he was dead or captive by this time. Many Gyongyosians surely were.

"Nothing I can do about it now," Istvan muttered. It was getting dark. Where, he wondered, had the day gone? Unlike most on Obuda, it hadn't evaporated in boredom. He wrapped his blanket around himself and did his best to sleep.

By the way Skarnu swung a hoe, anyone who knew anything about farming and looked closely would have known he hadn't spent much time working in a field. Some of the Algarvian soldiers trudging along the dirt road surely came from farms themselves. But they didn't expect to see anything but farmers in the Valmieran fields, and so they didn't look closely.

After the soldiers had vanished behind some walnut trees, Skarnu leaned the hoe against his hip and looked at his hands. They too would have shown he was no farmer. The calluses on his palms weren't years old and yellowed and hard as horn; he still got blisters at their edges and sometimes even under them.

His back ached. So did his shoulders and the backs of his thighs. He sighed and spoke in a low voice: "Maybe we should have surrendered after all, Sergeant. It would have been easier."

Raunu spread his own hands. They were as raw as Skarnu's. He was a commoner and a longtime veteran, but he'd never done work like this, either. "Easier on the body – oh, aye, no doubt about it," he said. "But if it were easier on the spirit, we would have done it when most of the army gave up."

"I couldn't stomach it," Skarnu said, "so I suppose that proves your point."

His coarse wool tunic and trousers itched. Back when he was living the life of a marquis, he would never have let such rough cloth touch his skin. But he could not have kept up the fight against the Algarvians from a captives' camp, and they would never have let him out of one unless they were sure he had no fight left in him. He didn't think he could have fooled them into releasing him – and so here he was, pretending to be a peasant instead of pretending to be a collaborator.

In a matter-of-fact way, Raunu said, "If they catch us now, they'll blaze us, of course."

"I know. They did that in the parts of Valmiera they occupied during the Six Years' War," Skarnu said. "I learned about it in school."

"Aye, so they did," Raunu answered. "And afterwards, when we were holding some of the marquisates east of the Soretto, we paid 'em back in the same coin. Anybody even looked at us sideways, we figured the son of a whore was a soldier who hadn't had enough, and we gave it to him."

Skarnu hadn't learned about that in school. In his lessons, Valmiera had always had right and justice on her side. He'd believed that for a long time. He still wanted to believe it.

He stretched and twisted, trying to make his sore muscles relax. He hadn't learned farm work in school, though. Only a noble addled far past mere eccentricity would have thought learning to till the soil in the least worthwhile.

He swung the hoe again, and did manage to uproot weed rather than wheat. "Good to know there are some folk besides us who stay loyal to king and kingdom," he said, and knocked down another weed.

"Oh, aye, there are always some," Raunu said. "What's really lucky is that we found one. If we'd asked for help from half the peasants around these parts — more than half, I shouldn't wonder — they'd have turned us in to the redheads faster than you can spit."

"So it seems," Skarnu said grimly. "That's not the way it should be, you know."

Raunu grunted and went back to weeding for a while, attacking the dandelions and other plants that didn't belong in the field with the same concentrated ferocity he'd shown the Algarvians. At last, at the end of a row, he asked, "Sir — my lord — do I have your leave to speak what's in my mind?"

He hadn't called Skarnu *my lord* in a long time. The title, in his mouth, carried more reproach than respect. Skarnu said, "You'd better, Raunu. I don't suppose I'll last long if you don't."

"Longer than you think, maybe, but never mind that," Raunu said. "From everything I've been able to piece together, though, Count Enkuru, the local lord, is a right nasty piece of work."

"Aye, I think there's a deal of truth to that," Skarnu agreed. "But what has it got to do with —?" He broke off, feeling foolish. "The peasants would sooner have the Algarvians for overlords than Count Enkuru — is that what you're saying?"

Raunu nodded. "That's what I'm saying. Some of the nobles I've known, they never would have figured out what I meant." He took a deep breath. "And that's part of the trouble Valmiera's been having, too, don't you see?"

"Peasants should be loyal to the nobles, as nobles should be loyal to the king," Skarnu said.

"No doubt you're right, sir," Raunu said politely. "But the nobles should deserve loyalty, don't you think?"

Skarnu's sister would have said no in a heartbeat. Krasta would have thought – did think – her blood alone was plenty to command loyalty. She would have wanted Raunu flogged for presuming to think otherwise. Skarnu's attitude had differed only in degree, not in essence, till he took command of his company.

Slowly, he said, "That does make a difference, doesn't it? Men will go as far as their leaders take them, and not a step farther." He'd seen that throughout the recent disastrous campaign.

"Aye, sir." Raunu nodded. "And they'll go as far in the other direction if their leaders push 'em to it – which is why we've got our little game laid on for tonight. We have to show 'em what we're against along with what we're for."

Toward evening, the farmer who'd given them shelter came out to look over the work they'd done. Gedominu hobbled on a cane, and had ever since the Six Years' War. Maybe that was what made him dislike the Algarvians enough to keep working against them. Skarnu couldn't have proved it, though; Gedominu said little about himself.

He looked over the field now, rubbed his chin, and said, "Well, it's not *too* much worse than if you hadn't done anything at all." With that praise, such as it was, ringing in their ears, he led them back to the farmhouse.

His wife served up a supper of blood sausage and sauerkraut, bread and home-brewed ale. Merkela, a second wife, might have been half Gedominu's age, which put her not far from Skarnu's. Skarnu wondered how the half-lame farmer had wooed and won her. He also wondered certain other things, which he hoped he was gentleman enough to keep Gedominu from noticing.

After full darkness, Gedominu slowly climbed the stairs and as slowly came down again, his cane in his right hand a stick in his left. It wasn't so potent a weapon as the ones Skarnu and Raunu had brought to the farm, being intended more for blazing vermin and small game for the pot than for men. But a man who met that beam would go down, and might not get up again.

Gedominu tucked the stick under his arm to blow Merkela a kiss, then led Skarnu and Raunu out into the night. They got their own sticks from the barn. Gedominu moved well enough when he needed to, and took them along winding paths they couldn't have followed themselves at night. Skarnu doubted he could have done it in broad daylight.

At a crossroads, someone softly called out, "King Gainibu!"

"Valmiera!" Gedominu answered. Skarnu would have come up with a more imaginative challenge and countersign; those would the first ones to cross the Algarvians' minds. But that could wait for another time. Now, four or five men joined his comrades and him. Moving as quietly as they could, they hurried on toward the village of Pavilosta.

"Pity we can't pay this kind of call on Count Enkuru himself," Skarnu said. Seven or eight men were not enough to storm a noble's keep, not if his guards were alert – and Enkuru's, by all accounts, were.

"His factor will do well enough," one of the locals answered. "His factor will do better than well enough, as a matter of fact. He's the one who collects the taxes Enkuru screws out of us, and as much more besides to make him near as rich as the count. And you can hear for yourself that he's in bed with the redheads. Everybody for miles around'll be glad to see the bastard dead."

Before the war, such talk about a noble and his factor would have been treason. Technically, Skarnu supposed it still was. But it was also a chance to strike a blow at Algarve. That counted for more.

Gedominu underlined the point, saying, "Folks have got to learn they don't just go ahead and do whatever some turd in a kilt tells 'em to – not without they pay the price for doin' it."

"Let's be at it, then," Raunu said. He pointed to positions that covered the factor's house – much the largest and finest in the village – but remained in shadow. "There and there, and over there, too. Move!" The locals hurried to obey. Skarnu let his sergeant give orders. Raunu had proved he knew what he was doing. Nodding to Skarnu, he said, "Now we'll give 'em what-for." He pried a cobblestone out of the ground and flung it through one of those invitingly large windows.

Furious shouts followed the crash of broken glass. The door flew open. A man in velvet tunic and trousers – surely the factor – and a couple of Algarvians ran out on to the street, as ants might run out of their nest if a boy stirred it with a twig. They probably thought some brat was bothering them.

They soon discovered how wrong they were, but kept the knowledge only momentarily. The raiders blazed them down. They fell without a sound: so quickly and quietly, in fact, that no one else came out to investigate. Raunu solved that by pitching another stone through a different window.

Two more Algarvians and another cursing Valmieran hurried out. They stopped in the doorway when they saw their friends lying in the street. That was a little too late. Skarnu blazed one of them; a couple of his comrades knocked down the others.

"Might be more inside," Raunu remarked. "Shall we go look?" That was strategy, not tactics, so he asked his superior instead of leading.

After brief thought, Raunu shook his head. "We've done what we came to do. This isn't the sort of business where we want to take losses, I don't think."

"Aye — makes sense," Raunu said. "All right, let's disappear."

As silently as they'd entered Pavilosta, the raiders slipped out of the village. Behind them, more shouts and a woman's shrill scream said their handiwork had been discovered. "I think that other bugger in trousers might have been Enkuru his own self, come to visit the factor," Gedominu said. "Here's hoping it was."

"Aye, that'd be a good blow," Skarnu agreed. "Whatever we do next, we won't have such an easy time of it. They weren't wary this time. They will be."

"Let 'em be wary," Gedominu said. "We'll just go back to being peasants, that's all. Nobody ever pays peasants no mind. When the fuss dies down, we'll hit the redheads another lick." He looked over his shoulder. "Keep moving, there. I want to get home to Merkela tonight." Move Skarnu did. Gedominu could not have given him a more effective goad.

When Pekka went up to Yliharma this time, her colleagues didn't put her up at the Principality. Instead, Master Siuntio lodged her in his own home. That he would even think of doing such a thing left her limp with astonishment and awe. Staying in the Principality was a distinction. Staying with the greatest theoretical sorcerer of the age was a privilege.

"Oh, you think so, do you?" Siuntio said when Pekka couldn't hold that in after they walked into his parlor from the street. "And what of your husband, young Leino? Is he back in Kajaani, fretting that I, being a widower, would try and seduce you?"

"He would never imagine such a thing, Master!" Pekka exclaimed. "Never!"

"No?" Siuntio clicked his tongue between his teeth. "What a pity. I'm not so old as all that, you know."

Pekka's ears got hot. Trying to salvage something from the embarrassing exchange, she said, "He knows you are a man of honor."

"He's a clever young fellow, your husband," Siuntio said. "He'd have to be, to hold you to him. But is he clever enough to imagine what I was like when I was his age, or maybe even younger? I doubt it; the cleverness of the young seldom runs in such directions."

As an exercise, Pekka tried to imagine Siuntio as a man her own age. She filled in wrinkles, darkened hair, added vigor . . . and whistled softly. "Ah, Master, you must have cut a swath."

Siuntio smiled and nodded. His eyes sparkled. Just for a moment, Pekka thought he *might* try to seduce her – and, for that same moment, wondered if she might not let him. Then he smiled in a different way, and she relaxed (with, perhaps, the tiniest twinge of disappointment). "I would not seek the favors of a guest in my own house: that were unsporting," he said. "Next time, perhaps, you will stay at the Principality once more."

"Perhaps I will – or perhaps I will come back to stay with you, where I know I am safe," Pekka answered with a sassy grin.

She blessed Siuntio for letting it lie there. After a last chuckle, he said, "That might be for the best this time, too, as the lot of us will have a great deal to discuss when we assemble tomorrow."

"Aye," Pekka said. "I do not deny being surprised to learn that you duplicated my experimental results."

"Every one of us has done so," Siuntio replied. "Every one of us has done so repeatedly. If we repeated the experiment often enough, we might, I daresay, rid the world of a great many surplus acorns."

He still sounded easy, amused, very much as he had when he'd teased her. Under that, she thought, eagerness quivered, the eagerness of a hound on a scent. Pekka could hear it. She felt it herself. Like called to like, as surely as under the law of similarity. She asked, "What do you think is causing it, Master?"

"Mistress, I do not know," Siuntio said gravely. "You have found something new and unexpected. It is another reason, aside from purposes of lechery, that I wish I were younger: I would have more time to go down this track. For now, I know it is there, and that is all I know of it."

"I have tried my best to account for it, but it fits into no theoretical model with which I am familiar."

"All this means, my dear, is that we shall need some new theoretical models by and by," Siuntio said. "There are dull times, when the sages were sure they know everything there is to know. The days of the Kaunian Empire were such a time, though it would not do to say so in Valmiera or Jelgava. We had another one a couple of hundred years ago, all over eastern Derlavai and on our island as well. Then we discovered ley lines, and nothing has been the same since. Now things will be different again, different in a different way."

"Different in a different way," Pekka echoed. "I like that. When will the others gather here?"

"Midmorning, or perhaps a bit before," Siuntio answered carelessly. "Meanwhile, make yourself at home. It won't be the Principality, not for the bed and not for the food, either, but you may perhaps find something or other to read here that the Principality does not offer."

Pekka knew she'd been eyeing her host's bookshelves. "You'd better search my bags before you take me back to the caravan station," she said. "I am tempted to wreak havoc here, as the Sibian pirates used to do along our coast." Boldly, she pulled out a classical Kaunian text on growth spells and began looking through it. Maybe someone had found the answer to her riddle back in the days of the Empire Siuntio had just mocked.

He had to call her twice to supper; she'd got engrossed. The text did not have the answer – she hadn't really believed it would – but was interesting for its own sake. And Kaunian was such an elegantly precise language, even the most blatant nonsense sounded as if it ought to be true.

Supper turned out to be mutton chops and mashed parsnips with butter: closer to what she would have made at home than to the delicacies in which the Principality specialized, but far from bad. "You do me too much credit," Siuntio said when Pekka praised him for it. "I stick to simple things, where even a bungler like me has trouble going wrong."

"I don't give you too much credit," Pekka said. "You don't give yourself enough."

"Pah!" Siuntio waved that away, which annoyed her. Then he wouldn't let her help him clean up, which annoyed her even more. "You are my guest," he said. "You would not work for your supper at a hostel, and you will not work here." With an old man's mulishness, he got his way.

Next morning, she rose before he did (the bed wasn't all that comfortable, and she wasn't used to it) and had herrings grilling when he came into the kitchen. He glared at her. She smiled back sweetly. "Have some bread and honey," she said, pointing to the table. "That will make you look less sour."

It didn't. Pekka made a point of eating faster than he did, and then springing up while he had a mouthful so she could set the kitchen to rights. He started glaring again, but took a swig from his pot of beer and laughed instead. "If you *must* do things, go ahead and do them," he said. "I suspect it means your husband works you too hard, but it's his affair, and yours." Pekka refused to dignify that with even so much as a sniff.

Piilis came to Siuntio's house first, followed a couple of minutes later by Alkio and Raahe. All the theoretical sorcerers were full of praise for Pekka. "You've given us something we'll be arguing about for year," Raahe said with a smile so wide, she didn't seem capable of arguing about anything.

"Where is Ilmarinen?" Siuntio grumbled, pacing back and forth across his parlor. "If anyone can unravel a phenomenon too strange to be believed, he is the man. He thinks left-handed."

"If anyone can unravel this, Master, I think you are the one," Pekka said.

But Siuntio shook his head. "I think more widely than Ilmarinen. I think more deeply than Ilmarinen. Ilmarinen, though, Ilmarinen thinks more strangely than I do. Ilmarinen thinks more strangely than anyone does. Ilmarinen" – he sighed – "likely thinks it amusing to be late."

After most of an hour, the missing mage did arrive. He offered no apologies. Pekka thought he smelled of wine. If the others thought so, too, they said nothing.

"Well, here we are," Ilmarinen said loudly. "Theoretical sorcerers without any theories. Isn't that grand? And it's *your* fault." He leered at Pekka. "You turned the world upside down, and you didn't even know you were going to do it."

"If anyone knew he was about to turn the world upside down, he would not do it," Siuntio said. "I hope he would not do it."

"You're right," Alkio said. "When we look for things that extend what we know, we take small steps. It's only when we stumble and almost fall that we need long strides to help us get our balance."

"Very pretty," Ilmarinen said. "It would be all the better if it meant something, but very pretty just the same."

"Speaking of meaning," Piilis said with acid in his voice, "I suppose you're ready to tell us now what Mistress Pekka's experiment means."

"Of course I am," Ilmarinen said, which made everyone stare at him. Pekka wondered if Siuntio had known exactly what he was talking about. Ilmarinen went on, "It means we aren't so smart as we thought we were before she made it. I already told you that, but you weren't listening."

Piilis glowered. Ilmarinen grinned, no doubt having hoped to provoke him into glowering. Siuntio said, "In my opinion, we shall advance faster by discussing what we do know of this phenomenon than what we do not."

"Since we don't know anything about this cursed phenomenon, we haven't got anything to discuss," Ilmarinen pointed out. "In that case, this meeting has no point." He turned as if to go.

Raahe, Alkio, and Siuntio all exclaimed. When Ilmarinen turned back, he was grinning again. Pekka said, "Now that you've had your sport, Master, have we your leave to get on with things?"

"I suppose so," Ilmarinen answered, something like approval in his eyes. Now Pekka smiled. So Ilmarinen needed to be handled like Uto, did he? She knew how to take a firm line, whether with a crotchety four-year-old or an even more crotchety theoretical sorcerer.

"Unfortunately, Master Ilmarinen is too close to being right," Raahe said. "We know what happens in Mistress Pekka's fascinating experiment, but we do not know why, which is of the essence. Nothing in present theory indicates that one of those paired acorns should disappear."

"Nothing in the theory unifying similarity and contagion we have been struggling to develop indicates such an outcome, either," Piilis said.

Ilmarinen laughed. "Time to stand theory on its head, then, wouldn't you say? That's what you do when things like this happen."

"I should also point out that there is no proof similarity and contagion can be unified," Siuntio said. "If anything, Mistress Pekka's experiment seems to argue against unification."

"I fear I must agree with you," Pekka said sadly. "I thought the mathematics showed otherwise, but anyone who chooses mathematics over experiment is a fool. With no unity underlying the two laws, there seems little point even to these informal gatherings."

She waited for Ilmarinen's sardonic agreement. The sour mage said, "Anyone who chooses mathematics over experiment has done the mathematics wrong or the experiment wrong. The experiment is right. That means the mathematics have to be wrong. Sooner or later, somebody will find the right mathematics. The only reason I can see that it shouldn't be us is that we're too stupid."

"Maybe," Siuntio said, "just maybe, we aren't so stupid as all that. Whether we are or not might be worth finding out, don't you think?" *Maybe*, Pekka thought, *just maybe, what I feel is hope.*

Lagoans had a saying: *out of the pot and on to the stove.* That would have fit the way Fernao felt about Mizpah, save only that he did not believe in stretching metaphor far enough to compare the land of the Ice People with anything having to do with heat. Even if Mizpah did lie under Lagoan domination, it was even smaller and slower and duller than Heshbon, something the mage would have had a hard time imagining had he not seen it with his own eyes.

Where he was bored and restive, King Penda, having gone from exile to exile, seemed not far from snapping. "Will we have to spend the winter here?" he demanded.

He'd been demanding that since the day Doeg's caravan reached Mizpah. Fernao had expressed his own opinion of the caravan journey by buying a dressed ptarmigan carcass, roasting it, and devouring it, even if the flesh did taste of pine needles. By now, though, he was as sick of Penda's nagging as he had been of Doeg's swaggering savagery. He pointed to the harbor that was Mizpah's reason for being and said, "Jump right in, your Majesty. You shouldn't need more than a month to swim to Setubal, provided the Algarvians patrolling out of Sibiu don't catch you as you splash past."

Penda was slower on the uptake than he might have been; as king, he probably hadn't been exposed to much irony. He answered, "Lagoas should send out a ship to take us to Setubal instead of leaving us here to rot."

"It's cold enough that we're rotting very slowly," Fernao said.

"Enough – powers above, a surfeit – of your feeble jests and japes!" Penda cried.

That did nothing to endear him to Fernao. Nothing could have done much to endear him to Fernao, not when they'd had as much trouble putting up with each other as was the case. The mage snapped, "Your Majesty, Lagoas knows we are here. Getting a ship here is another matter. My kingdom is, I remind you, at war with Algarve. I also remind you – again, since you did not seem to hear me the first time – that Algarve holds Sibiu. Getting a ship into and out of Mizpah would be very difficult even in the best of times – and, as you point out, winter is coming, which will add drift ice to other difficulties."

Penda's shiver struck Fernao as overdramatic. But then, Forthweg was a northern kingdom with a mild northern climate. Contemplating ice in any liquid larger than a bowl of sherbet had to feel wrong to Penda. "What *is* winter like here?" the exiled king whispered.

"I do not know for a fact," Fernao said, "for I have never been here before. But I have heard it said that winter in this country makes an Unkerlanter winter balmy by comparison."

Was that a whimper, down there deep in King Penda's throat? If it was, he quickly choked it back. Fernao felt more sympathy for him than he was willing to show. In Forthweg, in Jelgava, in northern Algarve and Valmiera, summer lingered yet. Even in Sibiu, in Lagoas, in Kuusamo, the weather would still be mild, perhaps even warm.

Here at Mizpah, days remained above freezing and nights, as yet, seldom dropped far below it. A hearty Lagoan merchant, a few days before, had stripped to his drawers, gone swimming in the Narrow Sea, and emerged from the chilly water to find a crowd of Ice People, men and women both, gathered on the rocky beach staring at him. It wasn't so much that he was nearly naked in a land where the natives swaddled themselves: far more that he had plunged into the water and not come out a block of salty ice.

But Penda, as Fernao had already seen, was not interested in a dip in the Narrow Sea. He said, "You being a first-rank mage, can you not whisk us over the water to your homeland by sorcery?"

"If I could do that, so could many other mages," Fernao answered. "If many others could do it, all our wars would have seen soldiers popping out of midair in unexpected places. I work magic, not miracles."

He'd known Penda would scowl at him, and the king did. Like most laymen, Penda did not distinguish between the two. Some arrogant mages didn't, either. Because of those who refused to acknowledge the distinction, sorcery had advanced since the days of the Kaunian Empire. The vast majority of them, though, had failed, and a lot had paid for their arrogance with their lives.

Sulkily, Penda said, "What do you suggest that we do, then, sir mage?"

Fernao sighed. "When there's nothing we can do, your Majesty, we may as well make the best of doing nothing."

"Bah!" Penda said. "I had nothing to do in Patras, for I might as well have been a prisoner. I had nothing to do in Heshbon, for there was nothing to do in Heshbon. I have nothing to do here, for there is less than nothing to do here. In Setubal, I would still be an exile, aye, but there, at least, I could work toward the liberation of my kingdom. Do you wonder that I pine?"

Do you wonder that I tire of your pining? Fernao could not give the answer that first sprang to mind. Aloud, he said, "You cannot swim to Lagoas. You cannot hire a caravan to take you thither. Lagoas cannot send a ship hither, as I have already said. That leaves nothing I can think of. I assure you, I am also anxious to return."

Penda exhaled in exasperation; no doubt Fernao wore on his nerves, as he wore on Fernao's. "You are but a Lagoan," he said, as if to a backwards child. "I am not merely a Forthwegian: I am Forthweg. Do you now see the difference between us?"

What Fernao saw was that, if he had to spend another moment with Penda just then, he would smash a chamber pot over the exiled king's head. He said, "I am going down to the market square, to see what I might learn."

"You will learn that it is cold and bleak and nearly empty," Penda said, carping still. "Is that not something you already knew?" Perhaps fortunately, Fernao left instead of screaming at him or performing an earthenware coronation.

Unfortunately for Fernao, Penda had spoken the truth. Mizpah's market square *was* cold and bleak and nearly empty. Ships still put in at Heshbon, because they could trade with Yanina or Algarve or Unkerlant. Algarvian ships were not welcome here – although, had they not been busy in places more urgent to King Mezentio, they could have snapped up the little town easily enough. Heshbon was far closer to Yanina and Unkerlant. And so Mizpah's harbor remained as empty as a poor man's cupboard.

Without overseas trade, the overland trade that went through the market square also suffered. Doeg had taken one look around before shaking his shaggy head and faring back toward the west, and no caravan even close to the size of his had come in since. Fernao saw neither cinnabar nor furs on display, and cinnabar and furs were the only reasons Lagoans and men from Derlavai came to the land of the Ice People.

A tinker repaired a pot. A buyer and seller dickered over a two-humped camel, as a buyer and seller might have dickered over a mule in a Lagoan back-country village. A woman remarkable only for her hairy cheeks was selling eggs from a bowl that looked a lot like the chamber pot Fernao hadn't broken over King Penda's head. The market square would have seemed far less lonely had it not been six times as large as it needed to be for such humble trading.

Another woman of the Ice People sauntered past Fernao. She had drenched herself in enough cheap Lagoan perfume to mask the smell of her long-unwashed body; what she was selling seemed obvious enough. When Fernao showed no interest in buying, she screeched insults at him in her language and then in his. He bowed, as if at compliments of similar magnitude. That only made her more irate, which was what he'd had in mind.

Looking around the forsaken square, he wished he hadn't come. But when he thought about going back to the hostel and enduring more of King Penda's endless complaints, he realized he couldn't have done anything else – unless he wanted to head inland and climb the Barrier Mountains, that is.

And then, to his surprise, the square stopped being forsaken. The small force of garrison troops Lagoas maintained in Mizpah paraded across it in uniform tunics and kilts – with heavy wool leggings beneath the kilts as a concession to the climate. It did not look like an exercise; the men's faces were grimly intent, as if they were marching to war.

"What's toward?" Fernao called to the officer tramping along beside his men.

He watched the fellow working out what to say – and, indeed, whether to say anything at all. A shrug meant the Lagoan decided keeping the news to himself didn't matter. "The cursed Yaninans have come over the border between their claim and ours," he answered. "King Tsavellas has declared war on Lagoas, and may the powers below eat him for it. We're off to see how many of his men we can gobble down, to teach him treachery has a price."

"Can you hold the Yaninans back?" Fernao asked.

Now the officer didn't answer. Maybe he was too full of his own thoughts to reply. Maybe he didn't feel like telling the truth where his men could hear it but was too proud to lie. Whatever the reason, he just kept marching.

Yanina would have no trouble shipping troops by the hundreds – by the thousands – across the Narrow Sea. Fernao needed to be neither general nor admiral to see that at a glance. Lagoans would have endless trouble getting any troops into Mizpah. Even if the local garrison beat back the first Yaninan assault, what then?

What then? had another significance for Fernao, too. What would he and Penda do if the Yaninans triumphantly marched into Mizpah? All of a sudden, climbing the Barrier Mountains didn't seem like such a bad idea. King Tsavellas would not remember with joy and glad tidings the mage who had spirited Penda out of his palace and out of his kingdom. He probably would not be so glad to see Penda again, either.

Fernao did not give way to panic. Being a mage, he had more ways to disguise himself – *and King Penda, too,* he thought with a certain amount of reluctance – than the ordinary mortal. He'd already used some. He could use more. But disguises were of less use here in Mizpah than they would have been in crowded Patras or Setubal. Mizpah was woefully short on strangers. If he and Penda (or Fernastro

and Olo, as they still called themselves) disappeared and a couple of
other men with new appearances started strolling around the town,
people would notice. They might be encouraged to talk.

When Fernao looked south, he saw black clouds spilling over the
Barrier Mountains. Without the news he'd just got, the idea of a
storm blowing up out of the interior of the austral continent so early
in the year would have appalled him. As things were, he smiled
benevolently. King Tsavellas's troopers wouldn't be able to move east
very fast through driving rain, or more likely sleet and snow.

"Maybe I have time," he murmured. He'd have to speak by crystal
with Setubal. Maybe, now that Yanina and Lagoas were at war, King
Vitor would find King Penda – and, not quite incidentally, Fernao –
more worth rescuing. Fernao did wish he hadn't explained to Penda
in such exacting detail why rescue seemed so unlikely.

After a triumphal procession through the streets of Trapani and a
reception hosted by King Mezentio, after another triumphal procession through Priekule, capital of downfallen Valmiera – after those
high points to his soldierly career, Count Sabrino found Tricarico, a
provincial city with a long history of unimportance behind it,
distinctly uninteresting. The women were plain, the food was dull,
the wine . . . the wine, actually, was not bad at all. The dragonflier
wished he had the chance to drink more of it.

But he and the wing he commanded were in the air as often as their
mounts could stand it. When they weren't flying, other wings were.
Before long, no Jelgavan dragons could drop eggs on Tricarico or, for
that matter, on the Algarvian soldiers defending the kingdom east of
Tricarico.

"Easy work, this," Captain Domiziano said after another tour of
flying where not a single Jelgavan dragon had risen to challenge them.
"More Kaunian cowardice, that's what it is."

Sabrino shook his head and waggled a forefinger at the squadron
commander. "It's not so simple. I wish it were. The Valmierans were
brave enough, but they didn't figure out what we were doing till it
was too late for them. I don't see any reason to think the Jelgavans are
different."

"Why aren't they fighting us, then, Colonel?" Domiziano asked.
"They're like a turtle with its head and its legs pulled into its shell."

He shrugged his own head down as far as it would go and hunched up his shoulders, too.

Laughing, Sabrino said, "You should mount the stage, not a dragon. But consider, my dear fellow: together, Valmiera and Jelgava are almost as big as we are. During the Six Years' War, they stuck together and made us pay. This time, we knocked one of them out of the fight in a hurry. Do you wonder that the other kingdom is none too bold by its lonesome?"

Domiziano considered, then gave Sabrino a seated bow. "Put that way, sir, no, I don't suppose I do."

"They'll make us come to them," Sabrino said. "They'll make us pay the butcher's bill, the way the fellow who attacked did in the last war." He looked east toward the Bradano Mountains from the dragon farm, one of many that had sprouted around Tricarico over the past few weeks. He chuckled softly. "One day before too long, they may just find out they're not so clever as they think they are."

"Aye, sir." Domiziano's eyes glowed. "If this goes as it should, a thousand years from now they'll be writing romances about us, the same way everybody who can scribble nowadays is churning out stories about the Algarvian chieftains who overran the Kaunian Empire."

"Bad stories — or the ones I've seen are, anyhow." Sabrino's lip curled: he fancied himself a literary critic. He slapped his subordinate on the shoulder. "A thousand years from now, you'll be dead, and you won't know and you won't care what they're writing about you. The trick of it is, you don't want to be dead two weeks from now, not knowing or caring what they write about you."

"Aye — you're right again." Domiziano laughed the robust laugh of a healthy young man who was at the same time a healthy young animal. "I aim to die at the age of a hundred and five, blazed down by an outraged husband."

"And here's hoping you make it, my lad," Sabrino said. "Such ambition should not go unrewarded."

A sentry came trotting up. "Begging your pardon, Colonel, but Colonel Cilandro is here to see you."

"Well, good," Sabrino said. "Cilandro and I have a lot of things to talk about. We're going to be in each other's pouches for the next little while."

Colonel Cilandro walked with a limp. "The Valmierans gave me a present," he said when Sabrino remarked on it. "It's not blazed down to the bone, so it'll heal before too long. All it means is, I can't very well run away if we get into trouble. Since I wasn't going to run away anyhow, it doesn't matter."

Sabrino bowed. "A man after my own heart!"

The infantry colonel returned the bow. "And I have heard good things of you, my lord count. Let us hope we work well together. We haven't much time."

"We can't hope to hold anything like this secret for very long," Sabrino agreed, "and what point to going on with it if it's not secret?" He pointed back toward his tent, one of many that had sprouted on the meadow – a flock of sheep were probably annoyed at King Mezentio's forces. "I have some wine in there, and, as long as we're drinking, we can look at the maps."

"Well put," Cilandro said. "Oh, *well* put!" He bowed again. "To the wine, then, Colonel – and, while we're at it, the maps."

He took a glass of red. As Sabrino had expected – as Sabrino had certainly hoped – he contented himself with the one glass, nursing it to make it last. Sabrino pointed to the map he'd tacked down on a light folding table. "As I understand things, you'll be moving here." He pointed.

Cilandro bent over the map. "Aye, that's about right. If we can go in right there" – now he pointed – "everything will be perfect." He chuckled. "Last time I thought anything like that was when I was about to lose my cherry. But back to business, eh? This is the narrowest stretch, which means it'll be the easiest to hold, and it's also got a power point right there, so we'll be able to recharge our sticks and egg-tossers without cutting throats to do it."

"Aye." Sabrino put his finger down on the star that symbolized the power point. "You won't find a lot of Jelgavan throats to cut there. You'd better not find a lot of Jelgavan throats to cut there, or else you'll be cutting your own throats."

"And isn't that the sad and sorry truth, my dear Colonel?" Cilandro said. "No denying it's better to give a surprise than to get one, eh?" He tapped a fingernail against his wine glass. "The question that keeps eating at me is, can you get enough of my men into the right place fast enough to let us do what we're ordered to do?"

"We'll do our best," Sabrino said. "And we'll keep on doing our best as long as you have men on the ground there. We don't talk away from what we start – we aren't Unkerlanters, after all. But that's just if thing go wrong. I think they'll go right. King Mezentio has had all the answers so far."

Colonel Cilandro nodded. "That he has." He raised his glass. "Here's to a king who knows what he's doing. If we'd had one like that during the Six Years' War, we wouldn't be fighting this one now." He drained the last of the wine.

Sabrino emptied his goblet, too. "And that's also the truth. Well, day after tomorrow, if the weather holds, you'll bring your regiment on over here – and then we'll find out exactly how smart King Mezentio is."

"Aye and aye and aye again." Cilandro clasped Sabrino's hand, then swept him into an embrace. "Day after tomorrow, Colonel." He shook a fist at the sky – or Sabrino supposed it was at the sky, anyhow, rather than at the canvas roof of the tent. "And the weather had better hold."

It did. Cilandro's regiment tramped up to the dragon farm a little before dawn. At a good many places along the border between Algarve and Jelgava, regiments were marching up to wings of dragons. Along with its flier, a dragon could carry about half a ton of eggs to drop on the foe's head. If, instead of carrying eggs, each dragon carried five troopers . . .

"First three companies forward!" Colonel Cilandro commanded. The men of the dragons' ground crews had been frantically mounting harnesses on their charges' long scaly torsos. The dragons had liked that no better than they liked anything else. Cilandro gave Sabrino a cheery wave as he took his place just behind the dragonflier. "If we live through this, it will be jolly," the infantry colonel said. "And if we don't, we won't care. So let's be off."

"My crystal man is waiting for the signal," Sabrino answered, hoping he sounded calmer than he felt. "Everyone will move at the same time. We don't want the Jelgavans getting too many ideas beforehand."

Maybe Cilandro would have had something suitably impolite to say about the likelihood of Kaunians getting ideas. He never got the chance. A man came running up to Sabrino's dragon. He paused just out of range of the creature's long, scaly neck, raised to his lips the trumpet he was carrying, and blew a long, untuneful blast.

Sabrino whacked his dragon with the goad. The dragon let out a screech and began to flap its wings. It screeched again when it didn't take off quite so soon as it had expected; it was used to carrying only Sabrino's weight. But the great wings beat faster and faster, harder and harder. Dust flew up in choking clouds. And then, at last, the dragon flew up, too, still letting the world know it was indignant at having to work so hard. Behind Sabrino, Cilandro whooped.

As the dragon gained height, Sabrino also whooped, half with joy, half with awe. The whole wing was rising. All the other wings were rising. Almost all the dragons in Algarve, save for those flying against Lagoas and some patrolling the sky on the border with Unkerlant in the west, were rising. Sabrino knew he could not see them all. The ones he could see were by themselves more dragons than he'd ever seen gathered together before.

Seven main passes pierced the Bradano Mountains. Cut the Jelgavan army west of the mountains off from the kingdom that supported it . . . do that and, with any luck at all, the Algarvians would be able to roll it up and then parade through the rest of the kingdom. The plan was audacious enough to work. Whether it was good enough to work, his men and Cilandro's would soon find out.

Over the lines they flew, not so high as Sabrino might have liked. A squadron of Jelgavan dragons with only their own fliers aboard could have wreaked havoc among the heavily laden Algarvian beasts. Almost all of them were freighted with soldiers, leaving only a scant handful to serve as escorts.

One dragon did tumble out of the sky, blazed from below. But the rest of the men and mounts in Sabrino's flight kept going, up into the Bradano Mountains and through the pass Colonel Cilandro and his soldiers were charged with sealing. Sabrino's head swiveled back and forth as he gauged the landmarks. Even before Cilandro shouted at him, he was urging his dragon downward. The others in the flight followed. As soon as the dragon's claws touched the stone of the road through the narrowest part of the pass, Cilandro and his fellow soldiers sprang off. Other flights brought in the first companies of other regiments.

"We'll go back for your friends now," Sabrino shouted to Cilandro.

"Aye, do," Cilandro answered. "And we'll start plugging the pass here." He waved.

Waving back, Sabrino urged his dragon into the air once more. How swiftly, how effortlessly, he and his unburdened comrades flew back to the dragon farm outside Tricarico. Three more companies of infantry boarded them, to be leapfrogged over the Jelgavans and into the pass. Then they, almost all of them, returned yet again, and transported the rest of their assigned regiments.

Once the last contingent of footsoldiers was on the ground astride Jelgava's lifeline, Sabrino ordered his flight into the air once more. By now, the Jelgavans were beginning to wake up to what Algarve had done. Egg-carrying dragons came winging out of the east to attack the men the Algarvians had placed behind most of Jelgava's army. But they were, in Sabrino's judgment, far too few, and, being burdened with eggs, no swifter than the tired mounts he and his men were flying. Not more than a handful got to drop those eggs on the Algarvians.

Sabrino howled with glee and shook his fist. "The bottle is corked, curse you!" he shouted to the foe. "Aye, by the powers above, the bottle is corked!"

"Buggered!" Talsu said bitterly. "That's what's happened to us. We've been buggered."

"Aye." His friend Smilsu sounded every bit as bitter. "That's what happens when you keep looking straight ahead. Somebody sneaks around behind you and gives it to you right up the—"

"Pass," Talsu broke in. Smilsu laughed, not so much because it was funny as because it was either laugh or weep. Talsu went on, "We'd better do something about it pretty cursed quick, too, or this war goes straight into the chamber pot."

"You think it hasn't gone there already?" Smilsu demanded.

Talsu didn't answer right away. He did think it had gone there already. As long as the redheads held the passes – held all the passes, by what panicky rumor said – how were the Jelgavans to get food and other supplies and charges for their weapons up to the soldiers who needed them? The plain and simple answer was, they couldn't.

At last, Talsu said, "Maybe we should have pulled more men out of the front-line trenches to break through the Algarvian cork."

Smilsu gave him an ironic bow. "Oh, aye, General, that'd be splendid. Then they'd have pushed us back even farther than they already have."

Talsu waved his arms in exasperation. He stood behind a boulder big enough to make the gesture safe: no Algarvian could see him do it and blaze him for it. "Well, what did you expect? Of *course* the fornicating whoresons hit us from the front, too. They don't want to just cut us off – they want to bloody well massacre us." He lowered his voice. "And odds are we'd have done a lot better and gone a lot further in this stinking war if our own officers thought the same way."

"Only one I ever saw who even came close was Colonel Adomu," Smilsu answered, "and look what it got him."

He also spoke quietly, which was wise on his part, for Colonel Balozhu, who had taken over for the able, energetic, but unlucky Adomu, came walking by to look over their position. Talsu shook his head. *Walking* was probably too strong a word to describe what Balozhu was doing. *Wandering* came closer. Balozhu looked dazed, as if somebody had clouted him in the side of the head with a brick. Talsu had the nasty suspicion that most Jelgavan officers looked the same way these days. Algarve had clouted the whole kingdom in the side of the head with a brick.

Balozhu nodded to him and Smilsu. "Courage, men," he said, though he hadn't shown any enormous amount of it himself. "Before long, the Algarvians' attacks must surely lose their impetus."

"Aye, my lord count," Talsu answered, though Balozhu hadn't given any reason why the Algarvians should slow down. Talsu and Smilsu both bowed low; Balozhu might not have been a bold soldier, but he was a stickler for military punctilio. Satisfied, he went on his way, that mildly confused expression still spread across his bland features.

Very, very softly, Smilsu said, "Aye, *he'll* lead us to victory." In a different tone of voice, that might have been praise for Balozhu. As things were, Talsu looked around to make sure no one but him had heard his friend.

He too spoke in a whisper: "I don't know why we bother keeping up this fight when it's already lost."

"Another good question," Smilsu allowed. "Another question

you'd better not ask our dear, noble colonel. The only answer he'd come up with has a dungeon in it somewhere, you mark my words."

"I can do better than that for myself, thanks," Talsu said. "Staying alive comes to mind. You throw down your stick and throw up your hands in front of an Algarvian, it's not better than even money he lets you surrender. He's about as likely to blaze you down instead."

"Aye, the redheads are savages," Smilsu said. "They always have been. I expect they always will be." He spat in glum emphasis.

"That's the truth," Talsu said. But he recalled slitting Algarvian's throats when sticks needed charging. Not all the savagery lay on the Algarvian side.

And then he stopped caring where the savagery lay, for the Algarvians started tossing eggs at his regiment's position. Dragons appeared overhead, dropping more eggs and also swooping low to flame Jelgavans rash enough to be caught away from cover. Shouting like demons in their coarse, trilling tongue, the redheads swarmed forward.

They flitted from rock to rock like the mountain apes of the distant west. But mountain apes were not armed with sticks. Mountain apes did not bring heavy sticks and egg-tossers forward on the backs of armored behemoths. Mountain apes did not have dragons diving to their aid.

Along with the rest of the regiment, Talsu retreated. It was that or be outflanked, cut off, and altogether wrecked. Spotting Vartu not far away, a cut on his forehead sending blood dripping down the side of his face, Talsu called, "Don't you wish you'd gone home to serve Dzirnavu's relations?"

"Powers above, no!" the former regimental commander's servant answered. "There, they'd be paying me to let them abuse me. Here, if these stinking Algarvians want to do me a bad turn, I can blaze back at them." He dropped to one knee and did just that. Then he retreated again, falling back like the veteran he'd become.

Talsu was unhappily aware that his comrades and he couldn't retreat a great deal farther, not with the Algarvians still blocking the pass through which the main line of the retreat would have to go. He wondered what Colonel Balozhu and the men above him would have them do once they were well and thoroughly trapped. Whatever it was, it would probably be some half measure that didn't come close to solving the real problem, which was that the Algarvians had more imagination than they knew what to do with and the Jelgavans . . . the Jelgavans didn't have nearly enough.

More eggs rained down on the beleaguered regiment. More Algarvians pushed forward against its crumbling front, too. Talsu began to wonder whether the officers above Balozhu would have much chance to do anything with the regiment at all. It seemed to be breaking up right here. Maybe his chances of living through an attempted surrender were better than those of living through much more fighting after all.

Dragons stooped like falcons, flaming, flaming. Not far away from Talsu, a man turned into a torch. He kept running and shrieking and setting bushes ablaze till at last, mercifully, he fell. Talsu made up his mind to yield himself up to the first Algarvian who wasn't actively trying to kill him the instant they saw each other.

Then Smilsu shouted, "Over here! This way!" Talsu, just then, would have taken any way out of the trap in which the regiment found itself. The stink of his comrade's charred flesh in his nostrils, he ran toward the little path leading up into the mountains that Smilsu had found.

He wasn't the only one, either. Vartu and half a dozen others sprinted toward that path. None of them, Talsu was sure, had the least idea where it led, or if it led anywhere. None of them cared, either; he was equally sure of that. Wherever it went could not be worse than here.

That was what he thought till another dragon painted in white and green and red swooped toward his comrades and him. On that narrow track, they had nowhere to run, nowhere to hide. He threw his stick up to his shoulder and blazed away. He gave a sort of mental shrug even as he did so. If he was going to die, he'd die fighting. Given a chance, he would have far preferred not dying at all. Soldiers didn't always get choices like that.

Sometimes – not nearly often enough, especially not among Jelgavans these days – soldiers did get lucky. Talsu wasn't the only one blazing at the dragon, but he always insisted his was the beam that caught the great beast in the eye and blazed out its tiny, hate-filled brain. Instead of turning him into another human torch, the dragon and its flier slammed into the ground not twenty feet from him, cutting off the mouth of the path. The dragon's carcass began to burn then. The flier didn't move; the fall of his dragon must have killed him.

Talsu was not about to complain. He had his life back when he'd expected to lose it in the next instant. "Let's go!" he said. He still didn't know where he was going. He didn't care, either. He could go, and so he would.

"Blazed down a dragon!" Smilsu cried. "They'd give us a decoration for that, if only they knew about it."

"Bugger the decorations," Talsu said. He looked around. No, he had no officers, nor even any sergeants, to tell him what to do. He felt absurdly free, cut off not only from whatever was left of the rest of the regiment but also from the army and Jelgava as a whole. "Come on. Let's see if we can get away."

"We've already gotten away," Vartu said, which also held a great deal of truth. The ex-servant turned an eye to the sky, no doubt fearing another dragon might turn that truth into a lie.

But the Algarvians had more to worry about than a few fleeting footsoldiers. Their dragons rained death down on the Jelgavans still trying to push through their force plugging the pass. Talsu and his companions, out of the main fight, were quickly forgotten.

"Do you know," Smilsu said after they trudged east, or as close to east as they could, for a couple of miles, "I think this track is going to let us out into the foothills on the other side of the mountains."

"If you're right," Vartu said, "it sure as blazes doesn't look like anybody in a fancy uniform knows it's here. If the dukes and counts and what have you did know, they'd be moving men along it."

Smilsu nodded. "Aye. If we come out the other side, we could be heroes for letting the dukes know about it."

They walked on a while longer. Then Talsu said, "If I had my choice between being a hero and being out of the cursed war . . ." He took another couple of steps before realizing that might be exactly the choice he had. He spat. "What have the dukes and counts and what have you ever done for me? They've done plenty *to* me. They've done their cursed best to get me killed. Let them sweat." He kept going. None of the others said a word to contradict him.

16.

Tealdo and his company tramped down a road through fields fragrant with fennel. The Jelgavans used the spice to flavor sausage. Tealdo gnawed on a hard, grayish length of the stuff he'd taken from a farmhouse a few miles back. At first, he hadn't been sure he liked it; it gave the chopped and salted meat a slightly medicinal taste. Now that he'd grown used to it, though, it wasn't bad.

Here and there in the fields, Jelgavan farmers stood staring at the Algarvian soldiers advancing past them. Tealdo pointed to one of them, a thickset, stooped old man leaning on a hoe. "Wonder what's going through his head right now. He never expected to see us on this side of the Bradanos, I'll lay."

"I wouldn't mind getting laid myself," his friend Trasone answered. That wasn't what Tealdo had meant, but it didn't strike him as the worst idea in the world, either. Trasone went on, "I bet the Kaunian bastard is hoping he locked up his daughters well enough so we can't find 'em or maybe" – he took another look at the farmer – "maybe his granddaughters."

Sergeant Panfilo glared at both of them. "We don't have the time to waste for you cockproud whoresons to pull the pants off every Jelgavan slut we find. We finish this occupation, they'll set up brothels for us, set 'em up or more likely take over some that are already going. Till then, keep your pricks under your kilts."

In a low voice, Tealdo said, "Panfilo's an old man. Doesn't matter to him if he has to wait for his fun." Trasone laughed and nodded. Unfortunately for Tealdo, his voice hadn't been quite low enough. Panfilo spent the next mile and a half scorching his ears.

By the time the sergeant was through, Tealdo thought he could smell the organs in question sizzling. The only thing that kept him from being sure was the smoke already drifting in the air. Behemoths and dragons had gone ahead of the main force of footsoldiers, following the same pattern in Jelgava as they had farther south in Valmiera. Here, once they'd forced their way through the passes and down on to the plain, they'd met little resistance.

Four or five Jelgavans got out of the road to let the Algarvian soldiers march past them. The Jelgavans wore dirty, tattered uniforms, but none of them was carrying a weapon. "Sir, shouldn't we round them up and send them back to a captives' camp?" somebody asked Captain Galafrone.

"I don't see any point to bothering," replied the commoner who'd risen from the ranks. "The war's over for them. They're heading for home, no place else but. When they get there, they'll tell everybody who'll listen that we're too tough to lick. That's what we want the Jelgavans to hear."

He showed a hard common sense a lot of officers with bluer blood would have been better off having. Tealdo nodded approval. These Jelgavans weren't going to do any more fighting; they looked so tired and worn, they might have been some of the handful who'd made it back from the Algarvian side of the mountains. Indeed, why waste time and detail a man to escort them off into captivity?

One of them shook his fist toward the east. "Blaze our noblemen!" he said in accented Algarvian. Then he dropped back into Jelgavan to tell his pals what he'd said. Their blond heads bobbed up and down.

"Don't worry about it, chum," Trasone said. "We'll take care of it for you."

Tealdo couldn't tell whether the Jelgavans understood his friend or not. It mattered little, one way or the other. King Donalitu hadn't surrendered yet, but the war was as good as over even so. Some more Jelgavans would get blazed because their king was stubborn, and a few Algarvians, too, but that also mattered little, as far as Tealdo could see. Once the mountain shell was cracked, Jelgava had proved easy meat.

"Come on, you miserable, lazy bastards," Galafrone called to his own men. "Keep moving. The deeper we push the knife in, the less room the blonds will have to wriggle and the more they'll bleed." He did his best to drive his company forward with the force of his words and will, but Tealdo noted that he didn't sound so urgent as he had in the campaign against Valmiera. Even he thought the Algarvians were on the point of wrapping things up.

As if to prove as much, an hour or so later a few Algarvian guards led a great many more Jelgavans west toward captivity. The Jelgavans were not glum or downhearted. Instead, they smiled and laughed and joked with the men who guarded them. To them, a captives' camp looked good.

"Degenerate Kaunians," Trasone said scornfully.

"Well, maybe," Tealdo answered, "but maybe not, too. I don't think it's against the law to show you're glad to be alive."

"You could be right," Trasone said, but he didn't sound as if he believed it. "You're more generous than I am, though, I'll tell you that."

Tealdo only shrugged and kept plodding east. Jelgavans weren't worth arguing about. But he remained convinced he had it straight. If he'd been a Jelgavan soldier – especially a Jelgavan soldier east of the mountains, who wouldn't have expected to do much fighting till just before the fighting found him – he wouldn't have needed to be a degenerate to be happy he'd come through in one piece.

Toward evening that day, a couple of diehard Jelgavans blazed at Tealdo and his comrades from a brushy field. Galafrone turned his company loose, saying no more than, "You know what to do, boys. Hunt 'em down."

Methodically as if they were digging a trench, the Algarvians did. The trouser-wearing foes were fine soldiers, and made them work hard. But two against a company was not betting odds, even if the two did have good cover. One of the Jelgavan soldiers indeed died hard, blazed down from the flank as he in turn kept blazing away at the Algarvians in front of him. The other threw down his stick as the Algarvians closed in on him. He stood up with his hands high, smiling and speaking good Algarvian: "All right, boys, you've got me now."

He did not go west toward a captives' camp.

"Can't play that kind of game with us," Trasone rumbled as he picked his way through the bushes and back toward the road.

"Oh, you can play it," Tealdo answered, "but you're a fool if you expect to win. It's not like football or draughts – it's for keeps. You don't just up and quit when it's not going your way."

"Aye, by the powers above," Trasone said. "You blaze at me and my pals, you're going to pay."

"This whole kingdom is going to pay," Tealdo said. His friend nodded, then threw back his head and laughed, plainly enjoying the idea.

They camped by a village where the Jelgavans must have shown fight, for about half of it had burned. Eggs had smashed a good many houses, while others showed the scars of beams from the heavy sticks behemoths carried. Along with the sour stink of stale smoke, the sickly-sweet smell of death clogged Tealdo's nostrils.

A few Jelgavans still slunk around the village, their postures as wary and fright-filled as those of the dogs that kept them company. They weren't worth plundering; whatever they might have had before the first waves of Algarvians went through their village, they had nothing now. A couple of them, bolder than the rest, came up to the camp and begged for food. Some of the Algarvians fed them; others sent them away with curses.

Tealdo drew a midnight sentry turn. For one of the rare times since breaking into Jelgava, he felt like a soldier on hazardous duty. If some stubborn Kaunians like the ones the company had met that afternoon were sneaking up on him, they might give him a thin time of it. Shaken out of his blanket in the middle of the night, he should have been sleepy. He wasn't.

Every rustle of a mouse scurrying through the grass made him start and swing his stick in that direction, lest it prove something worse than a mouse. Every time an owl hooted, he jumped. Once, something in the wrecked Jelgavan village collapsed with a crash. Tealdo threw himself flat, as if a wing of wardragons were passing overhead.

He got to his feet again a moment later, feeling foolish. But he knew he'd flatten out again at any other sudden, untoward noise. *Better safe than sorry* made a good maxim for any soldier who wanted to see the end of the war.

A little later, a Jelgavan did approach him, but openly, hands held up so he could see they were empty. Even so, he barked out a sharp order: "Halt!" He had no reason to trust the folk of this kingdom, and every reason not to.

The Jelgavan did stop, and said something quiet and questioning in the local language. Only then did Tealdo realize it was a woman. He still kept his stick aimed at her. You never could tell.

She spoke again. "I don't know what you're saying," he answered. She spread her hands — she didn't understand him, either. Then she pointed to her mouth and rubbed her belly: she was hungry. He couldn't have missed that if he tried. When he only stood there, she pointed elsewhere and twitched her hips, after which she rubbed her belly again. He didn't need words for that, either: *if you feed me, you can have me.*

Afterwards, he wondered whether he might have responded differently had he not spent so much time marching and so little sleeping. Maybe – when he felt the urge, he satisfied it, even if he had to pay. But maybe not, too. Laying down silver was one thing. This was something else again. And he did feel worn down to a nub.

He took from his belt pouch a hard roll and a chunk of that fennel-flavored sausage and held them out to the woman. Nervously, she approached. Even more nervously, she took the food. Then, with the sigh of one completing an unpleasant but necessary bargain, she began to unbutton her tunic.

Tealdo shook his head. "You don't need to do that," he said. "Go on, get out of here. Go away and eat." He spoke Algarvian – it was the only language he knew. To leave her in no doubt of what he meant, he made as if to push her away. She got that. She bowed very low, as if he were a duke, perhaps even a king. Then she did up her tunic again, leaned close to kiss him on the cheek, and hurried away into the night.

He didn't tell his relief what had happened. He didn't tell any of his friends the next morning, either. They would have laughed at him for not taking everything he could get. He would have laughed at one of them the same way.

Not long after sunrise, the long slog east began again. But the company hadn't been marching long before a messenger from Colonel Ombruno, the regimental commander, rode up to Captain Galafrone. Galafrone listened, nodded, listened some more, and then threw up his hands to halt the men he led.

"We've licked 'em," he said. "King Donalitu has fled his palace, like Penda did in Forthweg when the Unkerlanters closed in on him. I hope we catch the son of a whore; if we don't, he'll end up in Lagoas, sure as sure. But whatever duke or minister he left in charge has yielded up the whole kingdom to us. Let's give a cheer for King Mezentio – aye, and for not having to fight any more, too."

"Mezentio!" Tealdo shouted, along with his happy comrades. Galafrone knew how an ordinary soldier thought, all right.

"Fool!" King Swemmel cried in a great voice. "Idiot! Jackanapes! Bungler! Get thee gone from our presence. Thou hast fallen under our displeasure, and the sight of thee is a stench in our nostrils. Begone!" The second-person familiar was almost extinct in Unkerlanter. Lovers sometimes used it. More rarely, so did people in the grip of other towering passions, as Swemmel was now.

Marshal Rathar got to his feet. "Your Majesty, I obey," he said crisply, as if the king had given him leave to rise some while before, rather than summoning him not to the audience chamber but to the throne room and humiliating him by forcing him to stay on his belly before the assembled courtiers of the kingdom for that concentrated blast of hate.

As if back at the royal military academy, Rathar did a smart about-turn and marched away from the king. Though he heard courtiers whispering behind their hands, he kept his face stolidly blank. He couldn't make out all the whispers, but he knew what the men in tunics covered with fancy embroidery would be saying: they'd be betting when King Swemmel would order his execution, and on what form the execution would take. Those questions were on Rathar's mind, too, but he was cursed if he would give anyone else the satisfaction of knowing it.

Eyes followed him as he strode out of the throne room. He wondered if the guards would seize him the moment he passed through the great brazen doors. When they didn't, he clicked his tongue between his teeth, a gesture of relief as remarkable in him as falling down in a faint would have been in some other man.

A hallway separated the throne room from the chamber in which the nobility of Unkerlant had to store their weapons before attending King Swemmel. Rathar stopped there and pointed to the blade that symbolized his rank. "Give it to me," he told the servitor who had no function but watching over all the gorgeous cutlery and looking gorgeous himself.

The fellow hesitated. "Uh, my lord Marshal—" he began.

Rathar cut him off with a sharp chopping gesture. Had he had the sword in his hand then, he might have used it, too. "Give it to me," he repeated. "I *am* the Marshal of Unkerlant, and the king did not demote me." Swemmel had done everything but that. He had, in a way, done worse than that. But Rathar was technically correct. He went on, "If his Majesty wants my sword, I will yield it to him or to his designee. You, sirrah, are not that man."

He spread his feet and leaned forward a little, plainly ready to lay into the servant if he did not get his way. Biting his lip, the man took the marshal's sword from the wall brackets that held it and handed it to Rathar.

"I thank you," Rathar said, as if he'd been obeyed without question. He slid the blade on to his belt and went off.

He created no small consternation as he tramped through the palace on his way back to his own chamber there. People stopped and stared and pointed at him: not only cooks and serving maids and other such light-minded folk but also guardsmen and nobles not important enough to have been invited to witness his excoriation. They might not have seen it, but they knew about it. Everyone in Cottbus doubtless knew about it. Peasants down in the Duchy of Grelz would hear about it no later than day after tomorrow.

He might have been a man who'd come down with a deadly disease but not yet perished of it. And so, in fact, he was, for the king's disfavour killed more surely and more painfully than many a phthisic against which mages and healers might struggle with some chance of success.

Even his own officers, once he was back among them, seemed at a loss over how to treat him. A few looked relieved that he had been allowed to return from the throne room. More looked astonished. Still more looked annoyed: now that he had been allowed to return, everyone else's advancement would necessarily have to wait till the axe fell.

He had trouble telling whether his adjutant, a major named Merovec, looked relieved or astonished. Merovec seldom showed expression of any sort; had he not chosen the army for his career (and had his blood not been high enough to ensure a commission), he would have made some noble house in Cottbus a splendid majordomo. All he said was, "Welcome back, my lord Marshal."

"For this I think you," Rathar answered. "You give me a warmer welcome than I had in the throne room, which is, I daresay, a truth you will already have heard."

That got even the impassive Merovec to raise an eyebrow. "My lord?" Around King Swemmel's court, such frankness was a commodity in short supply.

Every now and then, Rathar tired of dissembling. He'd survived such a dangerous eccentricity up till now. "Come with me," he said abruptly, and took Merovec by the arm to make sure his adjutant could do nothing else. Once they were inside Rathar's own sanctum, the marshal of Unkerlant closed and barred the door behind them.

"My lord?" Merovec said again.

"Are you wondering whether you'll have to pay for being too close to me, Major?" Rathar asked, and had the dour pleasure of watching Merovec flush beneath his swarthy skin. Rathar went on, "You may well have to, but it's too late in the game to fret over it, wouldn't you say?"

Merovec said nothing of the sort. Merovec, in fact, said nothing at all. He stood like a statue, revealing nothing of whatever went on behind his eyes.

Aye, a perfect majordomo, Rathar thought. As often as not, never saying much was a good way to get ahead. No one could think you disagreed with him if you acted that way. Such was certainly the key to survival at Swemmel's court — as far as anything was the key to survival at Swemmel's court. But Rathar, though as stolid a man as any ever born, had dared tell Swemmel to his face he thought the king was wrong. He would not keep silent now, either.

Sweeping out a hand toward the map on the wall behind his desk, he demanded of Merovec, "Do you know what my sin is in King Swemmel's eyes?"

"Aye, my lord Marshal: you were wrong." From Merovec, that was astounding frankness. After licking his lips, Rathar's adjutant added, "Even worse, my lord: you were wrong twice."

Few survived being wrong once around King Swemmel. Rathar knew as much. No courtier in Cottbus could help knowing as much. "And how was I wrong, Major?" he inquired, not altogether rhetorically.

Again, Merovec gave him a straight answer: "You underestimated Algarve. Twice, you underestimated Algarve."

"So I did." Rathar pointed to the map, to the new crosshatching showing that Algarve occupied Valmiera. "His Majesty wanted to assail King Mezentio while the redheads fought in the southeast, but they beat Valmiera faster than I thought they could, before we were ready. I advised waiting until they were fully embroiled with Jelgava." He pointed to the even newer crosshatching that showed Algarve occupied Jelgava. "Now they have beaten King Donalitu faster than I thought they could. And his Majesty is furious at me for having held him back, for having held Unkerlant back."

"Even so, my lord Marshal," Merovec replied. "In your own words, you have stated the king's grievance against you."

"So I have." Rathar nodded. "But consider this, Major: if Algarve was strong enough to overrun Valmiera faster than anyone could have imagined, if Algarve was strong enough to serve Jelgava the same way despite the mountains between them – if Algarve was strong enough to carry out those feats of arms, Major, *what would have happened to us had we in fact assailed King Mezentio's men?*"

Merovec's face went blank. Now, though, Rathar could see below the surface. Under that mask, his adjutant's wits were working. At last, carefully, Merovec said, "It could be, my lord, that the Algarvians would have been too heavily engaged in the east to stand against us."

"Oh, aye, it could be," Rathar agreed. "Would you care to bet the fate of the kingdom on its being so?"

"That is not my choice to make," Merovec answered. "That is the king's choice to make."

"So it is, and he made it, and he is furious at having made it, and furious at me for having kept him from rushing ahead into a war of uncertain outcome," Rathar said. "If I fall, I will console myself with the thought that I may well have kept the kingdom from falling instead."

"Aye, my lord," Merovec said. By his tone, he worried more about himself than about Unkerlant. Most men thought thus.

"I have not fallen yet," Rathar said. "His Majesty could have taken my head in the throne room. Blood has flowed there before when the king grew wrathy enough at a former favorite. I am still here. I still command."

"What you say is true, my lord," Merovec replied with another bow. That was a safe answer, safe and noncommittal. Rathar's adjutant went on, "And long may you continue to command me, my lord." That showed a little more spirit, but only a little, for Merovec's continued good fortune – indeed, quite possibly, Merovec's continued survival – depended on Rathar's.

"And, while I command, I do obey the king, even if he sometimes has trouble seeing as much," Rathar said. "I have never said we should not war against Algarve." *No matter how much I think so, I have never said so.* "That is not my place. My place is making sure we win the war once it begins." *If I can. If King Swemmel lets me.*

Merovec nodded. "The only one who could possibly disagree with you, my lord, is his Majesty." He paused to let that sink in. As it did, Rathar's mouth tightened. Merovec was, unfortunately, correct. If Swemmel took a different view of what Rathar's position should be – if, for instance, he took the view that Rathar's position should be kneeling, with his head on a block – that view would prevail.

"You have my leave to go," Rathar said sourly. His adjutant bowed and departed.

Rathar turned back to the map. Maps were simple, maps were straightforward, maps made good sense. This map said – all but shouted – that, come spring, he (or whoever was Marshal of Unkerlant by then) would have no excuses left for delaying the attack against Algarve. Rathar assumed he would still command then, for no better reason than that, if he turned out to be wrong, he would probably be dead.

The war would come. Rathar saw no way of avoiding it. If he could not avoid it, he would have to win it. At the moment, he saw no sure way of doing that, either. But the sun was swinging farther north every day. Fall was here. Winter was coming. He would not have to fight then. That gave him half a year to come up with answers.

In his desk sat a squat bottle of spirits. He took it out and looked at it. He wished he could stay drunk all winter instead, as so many Unkerlanter peasants did. With a sigh, he put the bottle back. For as long as King Swemmel let him, he had plenty of work to do.

Bauska bowed to Krasta. "Here is the morning's news sheet, milady," she said, handing it to her mistress.

Krasta snatched it away from her. Then, peevishly, she said, "I don't know why I bother. There's no proper scandal in here these days. It's all pap, the sort of pap you'd feed a sickly brat."

"Aye, milady," Bauska said. "That's how the Algarvians want it to be. If the news sheets are quiet, that helps keep us quiet, too."

Such a thought had never crossed Krasta's mind. To her, what showed up in the news sheets simply appeared on those pages. How it got there, why it got there, what else might have got there in its place — those were questions to trouble servants, or at most tradesmen: certainly not nobles.

And then Krasta's eye fell on a small item most of the way down the front page. It wasn't pap, at least not to her. She read it all the way through, in mounting horror and outrage. "They dare," she whispered. Had she not whispered, she would have shrieked. "They dare."

"Milady?" Bauska's face showed puzzlement. "I didn't notice anything that would—"

"Are you blind as well as stupid?" Krasta snapped. "*Look* at this!" She held the news sheet so close to Bauska's nose, the servant's eyes crossed as she tried to read it.

"Mistress," Bauska said in a hesitant voice, "the Algarvians won the war in the north, the same as they did here. King Donalitu fled from Jelgava. Of course the redheads would pick a new king in his—"

Krasta's hand lashed out and caught her serving woman across the cheek. With a hoarse cry, Bauska staggered back across the marchioness's bedchamber. "Fool!" Krasta hissed. "Aye, the redheads had the right to name a new king in Jelgava after Donalitu abandoned his palace. They had the right to name a king — from among his kin, or at most from among the high nobility of Jelgava. But this? Prince Mainardo? King Mezentio's younger brother? *An Algarvian?* It is an outrage, an insult, that cannot be borne. I shall complain to the Algarvians who have forced themselves upon my household." News sheet in hand, she swept toward the bedchamber door.

Bauska was rubbing at her cheek, already too late to have kept a red handprint from appearing. "Milady, you are still in your nightcl—" she began. Krasta slammed the door on the last part of the word.

Colonel Lurcanio, Captain Mosco, and their aides and guards and messengers were breakfasting in the wing of the mansion they had appropriated for their own. They stopped eating and drinking as suddenly as if turned to stone when Krasta burst in on them. Waving the news sheet, she cried, "What is the meaning of this?"

"I might ask the same question," Mosco murmured, "but I think I will be content to count myself lucky instead."

Krasta looked down at herself. She wore a simple tunic-and-trousers set of white silk – was she a commoner, to endure linen or wool when she slept? If her nipples thrust against the thin fabric, it was from outrage, not from any tender emotion. She knew no particular embarrassment at displaying herself before the Algarvians, as she knew none displaying herself before the servants – they were all equally beneath her notice.

What the Algarvians had done, though, was another matter altogether. She advanced on them, brandishing the news sheet like a cavalry saber. "How dare you set a barbarian on the ancient throne of Jelgava?" she shouted.

Colonel Lurcanio got to his feet. Bowing, he held out a hand. "If I may see this, milady?" he asked. Krasta jabbed the news sheet at him. He skimmed through the story then gave the sheet back to her. If his eyes lingered on her heaving bosom – heaving with indignation, of course – a little longer than they might have, she was too irate to notice. He said, "I trust you do not think I personally deposed King Donalitu or forced him to run away and installed Prince Mainardo in his place?"

"I don't care what you personally did," Krasta snapped. "That throne belongs to a Jelgavan noble, not to an Algarvian usurper. The royal family of Jelgava traces its line back to the days of the Kaunian Empire. You have no right to snuff out its claims like a stick of punk – none, do you hear me?"

"Milady, I admire your spirit," Captain Mosco said. By the way his eyes clung, her spirit wasn't all he admired. "I must tell you, however, that—"

"Wait," Lurcanio said. "*I* will deal with this." Mosco bowed in his seat, acknowledging his superior's prerogative. Turning back to Krasta, Lurcanio went on, "Milady, let us understand each other. I care not a fig whether or not the king – the former king, the fled king – of Jelgava traces his descent back to the days of the Kaunian Empire or, for that matter, back to the egg from which the world hatched. Algarvians overthrew the Kaunian Empire, and our chieftains became kings. Now we have overthrown Jelgava, and our prince becomes a king. We have the strength, so of course we have the right."

Krasta slapped him, just as she had slapped Bauska moments before. The reaction was completely automatic. He had displeased her, and therefore deserved whatever she chose to give him.

Her servants accepted that as a law of nature almost to the same degree she did. Lurcanio was cut from a different bolt of cloth. He hauled off and slapped Krasta in return, hard enough to send her staggering back several steps.

She stared at him in astonishment complete and absolute. Her parents had died when she was quite small. Since then, no one had presumed to lay a hand on her, or indeed to check her in any way. Bowing to her, Lurcanio said, "I assure you, milady, that I would never be so rude as to strike a woman unprovoked. But I also assure you that I do not suffer myself to be struck, either. You would do well – you would do very well – to remember as much from now on."

Slowly, Krasta raised a hand to her mouth. She tasted blood; one of her teeth had torn the inside of her cheek. "How dare you do that?" she whispered. The question held more simple curiosity than anger: so novel was receiving what she'd been in the habit of giving out.

Colonel Lurcanio bowed again, perhaps recognizing as much. When he replied, he might have been a schoolmaster: "It is as I said before, milady. I have the will and I have the strength, both in my own person and in my kingdom, to punish insults offered me. Having the strength gives me the right, and I am not ashamed to use it."

At first, he might have been speaking the horrid language of the Ice People for all the sense he made to Krasta. And then, suddenly, his words hit her with a force greater than that of his hand. *Valmiera had lost the war.* Krasta had already known that, of course. Up till now, though, it had been only an annoyance, an inconvenience. For the first time, what it meant crashed down on her. Up till now, she'd granted deference only to the tiny handful above her in the hierarchy: counts and countesses, dukes and duchesses, the royal family. But the Algarvians, by virtue of their victory, also outranked her in this strange new Valmiera. As Lurcanio had said – and had proved with his hard right hand – they had the power to do as they pleased here. That power had been hers and her ancestors' since time out of mind. It was no longer, unless the redheads chose to allow it.

Colonel Lurcanio might be a count in his own kingdom. Here in Valmiera, he counted for a prince or at least a duke, for he was King Mezentio's man. Krasta tried to imagine what would have become of her had she slapped a duke in King Gainibu's palace: a duke, that is, who had not tried to slide his hand inside her tunic or under the waistband of her trousers.

She would have been ruined. There was no other possible answer. Which meant she'd run the risk of ruin by slapping Lurcanio. He might have done far worse to her than he had. "I – I'm sorry," she said. The words came hard; she was not in the habit of apologizing.

She took a deep breath, preparatory to saying more. Colonel Lurcanio and Captain Mosco appreciatively watched her taking that deep breath. She saw them watching her, and looked down at herself once more. If they were her superiors in rank and she stood in dishabille before them . . . She let out a small, mortified squeak and fled the dining hall.

Back in the part of the mansion still hers, servitors gaped at her. Not till she passed a mirror did she understand why. Printed on her cheek was the mark of Colonel Lurcanio's hand. She examined her image with a fascination different from the one it usually held for her. She'd marked the servants often enough. Why not? They had no recourse against her. Now she was marked herself. And what recourse had she against Lurcanio, against Algarve.

None. None whatever. Lurcanio had made that plain with a scorn all the more chilling for being so polite. If he decided to ravish her and have all his aides line up behind him, the only person to whom he would answer was Grand Duke Ivone, his Algarvian superior. Nothing any Valmieran said or did would affect his fate in the least.

She shivered and brought her left hand up to touch the scarlet imprint of Lurcanio's palm and fingers. The flesh on that part of her cheek was hot, and tingled under the pressure of her fingers. She'd never been one to mix pain – not her own pain, anyhow – with lubricious pleasure. She still wasn't. She felt sure of that. What she felt now was . . .

Angrily, she shook her head. She didn't even have a word for it. *Respect* might have come close, but she was used to requiring that from others, not to granting it herself. *Awe* probably hit nearer still to the center of the target. Awe, after all, was what one gave to forces incomparably more powerful than oneself. Having dared lay a hand on her and having demonstrated he could do so with impunity, Colonel Lurcanio had proved himself just such a force.

Still shaking her head, Krasta went upstairs. Bauska awaited her at the top of the stairway. Servant and marchioness stared at the marks on each other's faces. In a voice empty of all feeling, Bauska said, "Milady, I have set out a daytime tunic and trousers for you. They await your pleasure."

"Very well," Krasta said. But instead of going in to change, she continued, "Have the butler convey to the Algarvians that from now on they are welcome to use every part of the mansion, not only the wing they have taken for themselves."

Bauska's eyes went even wider than they had when she saw her mistress with a mark on her cheek. "Milady?" she said, as if wondering whether she could possibly have heard right. "Why, milady?"

"Why?" Krasta's temper remained volatile. It would always remain volatile. Her voice rose to a shout not far from a scream: "Curse you, I'll tell you why, you stupid little twat! *Because they won the war, that's why!*" Bauska gaped, gulped, and incontinently fled.

Mushroom season again. Vanai relished the chance to escape Oyngestun from sunup to sundown. For one thing, most of the Kaunians and many of the Forthwegians in her village still thought her and Brivibas traitors to their people – or traitors to the Kingdom of Forthweg, depending – for their association with Major Spinello, even though that association had broken up in acrimony. For another, because that association had broken up in acrimony, she and Brivibas were once more as hungry as anyone else in Oyngestun. The mushrooms they gathered would help feed them through the winter.

Tramping with a basket under her arm through the stubbled fields, through groves of almonds and olives, through thickets of oak, took Vanai back to the happier days before the war. She found herself whistling a tune that had been all the rage the autumn before fighting broke out.

In fact, she didn't find herself doing it. She didn't consciously notice she was doing it till Brivibas said, "My granddaughter, I am compelled to tell you that your taste in music leaves a great deal to be desired."

"My —?" Vanai discovered her lips were puckering to whistle some more. Feeling foolish, she forced them to relax. "Oh. I'm sorry, my grandfather."

"No great harm done," Brivibas said, magnanimous in his dusty way. "I do not disapprove of high spirits, mind you, merely of the monotonous and irksome expression of same."

You think I'm monotonous and irksome, do you? went through Vanai's mind. *Have you seen yourself in a glass lately?* She did not say it. She saw no point to saying it. She had to live with Brivibas. If she made an armed camp of the house they shared, she would regret it as much as he.

What she did say was, "Why don't we split up for a while? We'll find more and different mushrooms separately than we would sticking together."

Brivibas frowned. "You must understand, I have a certain amount of concern about letting you wander the woods by yourself. Had I not been there to protect you from that Forthwegian lout last year—"

"He was not a lout, my grandfather," Vanai said with an exasperated sniff. "All we did was trade a few mushrooms back and forth." Had the Forthwegian — Ealstan; aye, that was his name — tried to do anything from which she needed protecting, she did not think Brivibas would have been much help. She also remembered her humiliation when Ealstan had seen her with her grandfather and Major Spinello. That made her defend him: "He spoke Kaunian very well, if you'll recall."

"He did no such thing," Brivibas said. "A typically barbarous accent."

Vanai shrugged. "I thought he spoke quite well." Out came her claws: "Maybe not so well as the redhead you reckoned such a splendid scholar for so long, but quite well even so."

"The Algarvian deceived me, deceitfully deceived me," Brivibas said, and then suffered a coughing fit. Once he recovered, he stopped arguing against their going separate ways. If anything, he looked glad to escape Vanai.

She knew she was glad to escape him. Thanks to Major Spinello, he had the taint of Algarve on him, too — and, even were that not so, she didn't care to be lectured while looking for mushrooms. She'd got to the point where she didn't care to be lectured at all: unfortunate, when the lecture was Brivibas's usual form of address.

Every so often, Vanai would see Forthwegians and Kaunians, sometimes in small groups, more frequently alone, plucking or digging up mushrooms or slicing them from tree trunks. She spied no Algarvians; the redheads did not care for mushrooms and could not understand why anyone else would. Not seeing Algarvians also helped give her the illusion of freedom. She would have enjoyed it even more had she not known it was an illusion.

As she walked farther east from Oyngestun, some of the mushroom hunters waved when she went by. She knew what that meant: they weren't from her home village and didn't know of Brivibas's cozying up to Spinello. That also gave her a feeling of freedom, and one rather less illusory than the other. Among strangers, she didn't have to be ashamed of what her grandfather had done.

She found some garlic mushrooms and then, not far away, a fairy ring in the grass. Like anyone with a modern education, she knew fairies had nothing to do with fairy rings, no matter what people — even scholars — might have thought back in the days of the Kaunian Empire. That didn't mean the mushrooms weren't good. She gathered a handful before going on.

When she got to an oak thicket on the other side of the field, she nodded to herself. This was where she'd met Ealstan the year before. No matter what her grandfather said about him, she found him pleasant enough — and how she wished he hadn't found her with Brivibas and Spinello!

The other thing she remembered about the grove was the oyster mushrooms she'd taken from him. Sure enough, more of them waited on the trunks of the trees. She cut them away with a paring knife and put them into her basket one after another. Some of them, older than the rest, were getting tough, but they'd do fine in slow-cooked stews.

She nibbled at a fresh young one. She'd never had real oysters; Oyngestun was too small a village to make any sort of market for such fancy, faraway foods. If they were as good as these mushrooms, though, she could understand why people thought so highly of them.

Her feet scuffed through fallen leaves while she went looking for more mushrooms. Abruptly, she realized hers weren't the only feet she heard scuffing through leaves. Her hand tightened on the handle of the paring knife. Most people, even strangers met gathering mushrooms, were harmless enough. In case she ran into one who wasn't . . .

But the Forthwegian who stepped out from between a couple of trees not far away wasn't a stranger, or not quite a stranger. "Vanai," he said, and then stopped, as if wondering where to go from there.

"Hello, Ealstan." Rather to Vanai's surprise, she answered in Kaunian. Was she putting him in his place? Or was she simply reminding him of who and what she was?

"I wondered if I would see you here," he said, also in Kaunian. "I thought of you when I came here to hunt mushrooms." His mouth tightened. "I did not know if I would see you here with an Algarvian."

Vanai winced. "No! Powers above, no! He wanted to persuade my grandfather to do something to serve Algarve's purposes. When my grandfather would not, he stopped bothering us."

"Ah?" It was a noncommittal noise, one almost altogether devoid of color. After a short pause, Ealstan went on, "He did not look as if he were bothering you or your grandfather." He used the subjunctive correctly. "He looked very friendly, in fact."

"He was very friendly," Vanai said. "He almost fooled my grand-father into being friendly in return. But he did not, and I am glad he did not."

"Ah," Ealstan said again. "And was he friendly to you, too?"

Vanai did not care for the emphasis he gave that word. "He might have liked to be friendly to me, but I was not friendly to him." Only after the words were out of her mouth did she realize Ealstan really had no business asking such an intimate question. She was relieved it didn't have an intimate answer.

Ealstan certainly seemed glad of the answer he'd got. He said, "Some Forthwegians are hand in glove with the redheads. I suppose some Kaunians could be, too, but I will say I was surprised at the time."

"*I* was surprised when Major Spinello knocked on our door," Vanai said. "I wish he'd never done it." That was true, no matter how well she and Brivibas had eaten for a while. Then she recognized that

Ealstan had admitted some of his own blood collaborated with the occupiers. That was more generous than he'd had to be.

He scratched his chin. The down there was darker than it had been the year before, closer to real whiskers. Slowly, he said, "Your grandfather must be a man of some importance, if the Algarvians wanted him to do something for them even though he is a Kaunian."

"He is a scholar," Vanai answered. "They thought his word had weight because of that."

Ealstan studied her: more nearly a grown man's sober consideration than the way he'd looked at her the last time they met. Then, of course, all he'd been trying to decide was whether he thought she was pretty or not. Now he was figuring out whether to believe her, which was rather more important. He evidently thought it was more important, too. That earned him a point in her book. If he didn't believe her, though, whether he earned a point in her book wouldn't matter.

She discovered that his believing her mattered quite a lot to her. If he didn't, then odds were he'd spoken her fair the autumn before for no better reason than that he'd thought she was a pretty girl – which would, in essence, prove her grandfather right about him. Brivibas was sometimes able to admit he'd made a mistake. When he turned out to be right, though, she found him insufferable.

Slowly, Ealstan said, "All right. That makes sense. I suppose the redheads are out to make themselves look good any way they can."

"They certainly are!" Vanai exclaimed. Ealstan never found out how close his comment came to getting him kissed; Vanai, just then, found anything like approval so seldom, she was doubly delighted when she did. But the moment never quite came to fruition. After a deep breath, all she ended up saying was, "Do you want to swap some mushrooms, the way we did last year?" That would let her score points off her grandfather, too.

His smile almost made her sorry she hadn't kissed him. "I was hoping you'd ask," he said. "Trading them can be about as much fun as finding them yourself." He handed her his basket. She gave him hers.

They stood close by each other, heads bent over the mushrooms, fingers sometimes brushing as they traded. It was at the same time innocent and anything but. Vanai didn't know about Ealstan, but she was noticing the *anything but* more and more when someone called out in Forthwegian from not far away: "Ealstan? Where in blazes have you gotten to, cousin?"

By the way Ealstan jumped back from Vanai, maybe he'd been noticing *anything but*, too. "I'm here, Sidroc," he called back, and then, in a lower voice, explained, "My cousin," as if Vanai couldn't figure that out for herself.

Sidroc came crunching through the dry leaves. He did share a family look with Ealstan. When he saw Vanai, his eyes widened. She didn't care for the gleam that came into them. "Hello!" he said. "I thought you were hunting mushrooms, cousin, not Kaunian popsies."

"She's not a popsy, so keep a civil tongue in your head," Ealstan snapped. "She's − a friend."

"Some friend." Sidroc's eyes traveled the length of Vanai, imagining her shape under her tunic and trousers. But then he checked himself and turned to Ealstan. "Bad enough to have Kaunian friends any old time, you ask me. Worse to have Kaunian friends now, with the redheads running things here."

"Oh, shut up," Ealstan said wearily; it sounded like an argument they'd had before.

"I'd better go," Vanai said, and did.

"I hope I'll see you again," Ealstan called after her. She didn't answer. The worst of it, by far the worst of it, was that his cousin − Sidroc − was so likely to be right. Vanai was out of the oak grove and halfway across the field before she realized she still had Ealstan's mushroom basket. She didn't turn back, but kept on walking west toward Oyngestun.

"I ought to pop you one," Ealstan growled as he and Sidroc tramped east toward Gromheort.

"Why?" His cousin leered. "Because I broke things up before you got her trousers down? I'm *so* sorry." He pressed his hands over his heart.

Ealstan shoved him hard − hard enough to send a couple of yellow horseman's mushrooms flying out of his basket. "No, because you say things like that," Ealstan told him. "And if you say any more of them, I will pop you one, and it'll curse well serve you right."

Sidroc picked up the mushrooms. He looked ready to fight, too, and Ealstan, despite his hot words, wasn't quite sure he'd come out on top if they did tangle. Then Sidroc pointed and started to laugh. "Go ahead, first-rank master of innocence, tell me that's the basket your mother gave you when you set out this morning."

Ealstan looked down. When he looked up again, he was glaring at his cousin. "She's got mine, I guess. That's because you couldn't have done a better job of driving her away if you'd hunted her with hounds."

Whatever Sidroc started to say in response to that, the look on Ealstan's face persuaded him it would not be a good idea. Side by side, they walked on in grim silence. The Algarvian soldiers at the gate looked at their baskets of mushrooms, made disgusted faces, and waved them into Gromheort.

Once they were out of earshot of the guards, Sidroc said, "Suppose I told them you got that basket from a Kaunian hussy? How do you think they'd like that?"

"Suppose I told your father what you just said?" Ealstan answered, looking at his cousin as if he'd found him under a flat rock. "How do you think he'd like that?" Sidroc didn't reply, but his expression was eloquent. They didn't say another word to each other till they got back to Ealstan's house. Silence seemed a better idea than anything they might have said.

"You're back sooner than I thought you would be," Conberge said when they brought their laden baskets into the kitchen. Neither Ealstan nor Sidroc said anything to that, either. Ealstan's sister glanced from one to the other. She looked as if she might be on the point of asking some sharp questions, but the only one that came out was, "Well, what have you got for me?"

Sidroc set his basket on the counter. "I did pretty well," he said.

"So did I," Ealstan said, and set his basket beside his cousin's. Only then did he remember that it wasn't his basket — it was Vanai's. Too late to do anything about that, too. He'd only look like a fool if he snatched the basket away now. He waited to see what would happen.

At first, Conberge noticed only the mushrooms. "I thought the two of you went out together. Except for some oyster mushrooms and a couple of others, it doesn't look like you were within miles of each other."

Sidroc didn't say anything. Ealstan didn't say anything, either. So much silence from them was out of the ordinary. Conberge eyed them both again, and let out a sniff before going back to her sorting.

Some things were almost too obvious to notice. She'd nearly finished the job before she stopped, a mushroom in her hand. "This isn't the basket Mother gave you, Ealstan." She set the mushrooms on the counter, frowning as she did so. "In fact, this isn't any of our baskets, is it?"

"No." Ealstan decided to put the best light on things he could: "I was trading mushrooms with a friend, and we ended up trading baskets, too. We didn't even know we'd done it till we'd both headed for home. Do you think Mother will be angry? It's as nice as any of our baskets."

His innocent tones wouldn't have passed muster even if Sidroc hadn't been standing there like an egg about to burst. "Trading mushrooms with a friend, were you?" his sister said, raising an eyebrow. "Was she pretty?"

Ealstan's mouth fell open. He felt himself flushing. Forthwegians were swarthy, but not, he was mournfully sure, swarthy enough to keep a blush like his from showing. Before he could say anything, Sidroc did it for him – or to him: "I saw her. She's pretty enough – for a Kaunian."

"Oh," Conberge said, and went back to sorting through the last few mushrooms.

Her other eyebrow had risen at Sidroc's announcement, but that wasn't a big enough reaction to suit him. "Didn't you hear me?" he said loudly. "She's a Kaunian. She wears her trousers *very* tight, too." He ran his tongue over his lips.

"She does not!" Ealstan exclaimed. He found himself explaining to his sister: "Her name's Vanai. She lives over in Oyngestun. We swapped mushrooms last year, too."

"She's a Kaunian," Sidroc repeated yet again.

"I heard you the first time," Conberge told him, an edge to her voice. "Do you know what you sound like? You sound like an Algarvian."

If that was supposed to quell Sidroc, it failed. "So what if I do?" he said, tossing his head. "Everybody in this house sounds like a

Kaunian-lover. You ask me, the redheads are going down the right ley line there."

"Nobody asked you," Ealstan growled. He was about to point out that Kaunians had helped his brother escape from the captives' camp. At the last instant, he didn't. His cousin had already spoken of something that sounded like blackmail. Ealstan didn't think Sidroc meant it seriously, but didn't see the need to give him more charges for his stick, either.

It was Sidroc's turn to go red. Whatever he might have said then, he didn't, because someone pounded on the front door. "That will be Leofsig," Ealstan said. "Why don't you go let him in?"

Sidroc went, looking glad to escape. Ealstan was glad to see him go before things started blazing again. By her sigh, so was Conberge. She said, "Powers above, but I wish Uncle Hengist would find someplace else to stay. He's not so bad – in fact, he's not bad at all, but Sidroc . . ." She rolled her eyes.

"They're family," Ealstan said.

"I know," Conberge said. "We could be staying with them as easily as the other way round. I know that, too." She sighed again. "But he is such a . . ." Her right hand folded into a fist. She'd been able to thump Ealstan right up to the day, a few years before, she'd decided it was unladylike. He didn't think she could now, but he wouldn't have cared to make the experiment.

"He knows everything," Ealstan said. "If you don't believe me, ask him."

"He *wants* to know everything." His sister's fist got harder and tighter. In a low, furious voice, she blurted, "I think he's tried to peek at me when I'm getting dressed." Ealstan whirled in the direction Sidroc had gone. Maybe he had murder, or something close to it, on his face, because Conberge caught him by the arm and held him back. "No, don't do anything. I don't know for sure. I can't prove it. I just think so."

"That's disgusting," Ealstan said, but he eased enough so that Conberge let him go. "Does Mother know?"

She shook her head. "No. I haven't told anybody. I wish I hadn't told you, but I was fed up with him."

"I don't blame you," Ealstan said. "If Father knew, though, he'd wallop him. Powers above, if Uncle Hengist knew, he'd wallop him, too." He didn't say what Leofsig might do. He was afraid to think about that – it might be lethal. He took death and dying much more seriously than he had before the start of the war.

"Hush," Conberge said now. "Here they come." Ealstan nodded; he heard the approaching footsteps, too.

In Leofsig's presence, Sidroc was more subdued than he was around Ealstan; Leofsig, visibly a man grown, intimidated him in ways Ealstan could not. At the moment, Leofsig was visibly a man grown tired. "Give me a cup of wine, Conberge," he said, "something to cut the dust in my throat before I go down to the baths and get clean. The water will be cold, but I don't care. Mother and Father won't want me around smelling the way I do – I'm sure of that."

As Conberge poured the wine, she said, "Mother and Father are glad to have you around no matter what – and so am I."

Being Leofsig's brother, Ealstan could say, "I'm not so sure I am," and wrinkle his nose. Leofsig didn't do anything but punch him in the upper arm, not too hard. But when Sidroc presumed to guffaw, both Ealstan and Leofsig gave him such stony stares, he took himself elsewhere in a hurry.

Leofsig drank down the rough red wine in three or four gulps. He wiped his mouth on the sleeve of his tunic. It was already so filthy, a little wine would do it no further harm. "That's good," he said. "The only trouble with it is, it makes me want to go to sleep, and I do need to bathe first."

"You're wearing yourself out, working as a laborer," Conberge said worriedly. "You know enough to be Father's assistant. I don't see why you wear yourself out with a pick and shovel instead."

"Aye, I know enough to be his assistant – and I know enough not to be, too," Leofsig answered. "For one thing, he doesn't really have so much work that he needs an assistant. For another, he's good at what he does; he even casts accounts for some of the Algarvians in Gromheort these days. Remember, a lot of people quietly know I'm home. I want to make sure it stays quiet. If he takes me along to help him in front of the Algarvian governor, say, it won't."

"Well, that's so," Conberge admitted with a sigh. "But I hate to watch you wasting away to a nub."

"Plenty of me left, never fear," Leofsig said. "Remember how I was when I first got out of the camp? Then I was a nub, not now.

Now all I do is stink, and I can take care of that." He kissed his sister on the cheek and headed out again.

Conberge sighed once more. "I wish he'd stay in more. No matter how well we've paid off the redheads, they *will* notice him if he makes them do it."

"That's what he just told you," Ealstan answered. Conberge made a face at him. He didn't feel too happy about it himself, because he knew his sister had a point. He said, "If he stayed in all the time, he'd feel like a bear in a cage at the zoological gardens."

"I'd rather have him be a live bear in a cage than a bearskin rug in front of some Algarvian's divan," Conberge said. Ealstan stood there looking unhappy; she'd turned his own figure against him too neatly for him to do anything else.

The metaphorical bear came back about half an hour later, clean but looking thoroughly grim. Before Ealstan or Conberge could ask him what was wrong, he told them: "The Algarvians have hanged a Kaunian in the market square in front of the baths. He was one of the fellows who escaped with me."

Leofsig reported to his labor gang the next morning wondering if he should be lying low instead. If the redheads had squeezed the Kaunian hard enough before they hanged him, or if the fellow had sung on his own, trying to save his own skin, the new masters of Gromheort would be able to scoop him up with the greatest of ease.

Had the escaped and recaptured captive sung, though, the Algarvians could have surrounded his house and dragged him away in irons the night before. He took that to mean the Kaunian had kept quiet, or maybe that the redheads hadn't known the right questions to ask.

No kilted soldiers shouted his name and pointed sticks at him. A couple of them, the friendlier ones, nodded as he came up to report. The one who bossed his group gave forth with another of his two-words bursts of Forthwegian: "Working good!"

"Aye," Leofsig said. He sounded unenthusiastic. The soldier laughed a laugh that said he wasn't slamming down cobblestones himself.

But Leofsig, unlike a lot of his comrades, honestly did not mind the work. Before he'd gone into King Penda's levy, he'd been a student and an apprentice bookkeeper: he'd worked with his head, not with his hands and back. In the Forthwegian army, though, he'd discovered, as some bright young men do, that work with the hands and back had satisfactions of its own. A job wasn't right or wrong, only done or undone, and getting it from undone to done required only time and effort, not thought. He could think about other things or, if he chose to, about nothing at all.

And, in the army and on the labor gang, he'd hardened in a way he'd never imagined. Only muscle lay between skin and bone, but more muscle than he'd dreamt of carrying. He'd been on the plump side before going into the army. His service there and in the gang would have taken care of that even without the intervening months in the captives' camp. He doubted he'd ever be plump again.

"All right!" the Algarvian straw boss shouted. "We go. Work hard. Plenty cobblestones." Sure enough, he sounded perfectly happy. A lot of people got even more satisfaction from watching others do hard physical labor than from doing it themselves.

Under his two-word bursts of what he thought was enthusiasm, the labor gang tramped down a road leading northwest till they got to the point where the cobbles stopped. They'd worked on the road leading southwest till they'd gone too far for them to march out from Gromheort, do a decent day's work, and then march back. Laborers – a lot of them probably Kaunian laborers – from towns and villages farther on down that road would be paving it now.

Mule-drawn wagons hauled the labor gang's tools and the stones with which they would be paving this stretch of road. The wagons' iron tires rattled and banged over the cobblestones already in the roadway. Leofsig's comrade Burgred winced at the racket. "Shouldn't have had so much wine last night," he said. "My head wants to fall off, and I bloody well wish it would."

"Wagons wouldn't make so much noise on a dirt road, sure enough," Leofsig said, showing more sympathy than he felt – nobody'd held a stick to Burgred's head and made him get drunk, and if this was the first hangover he'd ever had, then Leofsig was a slant-eyed Kaunian. He went on, "Of course, they'd go hub-deep in mud when it rained. The redheads don't want that."

"I wish I'd go hub-deep in mud about now," Burgred said – sure enough, he was much the worse for wear this morning.

Passing by some meadow mushrooms, Leofsig stepped out into the field in which they grew to pick them and store them in his belt pouch. "Meadow mushrooms are better than no mushrooms at all," he said to Burgred. He had to repeat himself, because the noise from the wagons was particularly fierce. Burgred looked as if the only mushrooms he would have wanted then were some of the lethal variety, to put him out of his misery.

Like most Algarvians, the straw boss had a low opinion of what Forthwegians and Kaunians reckoned delicacies. "Mushrooms bad," he said, sticking out his tongue and making a horrible face. "Mushrooms poisonous. Mushrooms disgusting." He spat on a cobblestone.

"Powers above," Leofsig said softly. "Even the yellow-hairs know better than that." Kaunians and local delicacies were both on his mind; he'd heard rather different versions from Sidroc and from his own brother about the Kaunian girl Ealstan had met in the woods while out hunting mushrooms. Sidroc had them all but betrothed, but Sidroc's mouth generally outran his wits.

Leofsig eyed Burgred. Mentioning Kaunians to him was a calculated jab. He responded to it, sure enough, but not in the way Leofsig had expected, saying, "Ought to hang all the stinking Kaunians, same as the redheads hanged that one bugger back in town. Serve 'em right."

"They're not that bad," Leofsig said, which was about as far as he could go without putting himself in danger. "What did they ever do to you?"

"They're Kaunians," Burgred said, which seemed to be the only answer he thought necessary. Several of the men in the labor gang were Kaunians, too, but Burgred didn't bother trying to keep his voice down. He took it for granted that the blonds would know what he thought of them. Maybe they took it for granted, too, because, while a couple of them must have heard him, they didn't get angry.

No. In the captives' camp, Leofsig had got to know Kaunians better than he had before. They got angry. They didn't show it. Had they dared show it in Forthweg, they would soon have become a tinier minority than they already were.

Before he could take that thought any further, they came to the end of the cobbled stretch of road. When the wagons stopped, Burgred let out a theatrical sigh of relief. The Algarvian soldier

pointed dramatically toward the northeast. "Moving on!" he cried.
Even in his bits of Forthwegian, he made the prospect of setting
stones in the roadbed more exciting than one of Leofsig's countrymen could do.

Not all the stones in the wagon were proper rounded cobblestones.
A lot of them came from the rubble left over from the fighting in
Gromheort. Whenever Leofsig picked up one of those, he tried to see
if he could figure out from what building it had come. He'd
succeeded a couple of times, but only a couple. Most of them were
just anonymous chunks of masonry.

He laughed at himself. He couldn't help thinking, even on a job as
mindless as roadbuilding. He watched Burgred carry a stone from the
wagon to the roadway, dig out the roadbed so his stone would lie
more or less level with its neighbors, and then slam it into place. Was
Burgred doing much in the way of thinking while he did that?
Leofsig had his doubts. Leofsig doubted Burgred did much in the way
of thinking any time.

Leofsig was carrying a stone – another anonymous bit of rubble –
of his own to what would be its place in the roadbed when the
Algarvian straw boss let out a furious shout. "Who doing?" he
demanded, pointing to a stone some ten or twenty feet away from the
present border between paving and dirt. "Who doing?" From his
point of view, he had a right to be exercised: the stone jaggedly
projected half a foot above its fellows.

No one in the labor gang said anything. No one had been close to
the stone when the Algarvian noticed it. Any one of four or five
differnet men might have set it there. Nobody'd paid any attention.

"Must have been one of the Kaunians," Burgred said. "Hang 'em
all."

"Sabotage bad," the straw boss said. *Sabotage* was a fancy word, but
one that tied in with his job. He shook his head. "Very bad. Killing
sabotagers."

"Oh, aye," Leofsig murmured. "That's clever, isn't it? Now
whoever did it is sure to admit it."

"Hang a couple of Kaunians," Burgred repeated loudly. "Nobody
will miss the whoresons, and then we can get on with the fornicating
road."

One of the blond men in the labor gang took a couple of steps toward him. "I have a wife," he said. "I have children. I have a mother. I have a father. I know who he is, too, which is more than you can say."

Burgred needed a bit to get that. For a couple of heartbeats, Leofsig thought he wouldn't, which would have been convenient. Probably because it would have been convenient, it didn't happen. "Call me a bastard, will you?" Burgred roared, and started toward the Kaunian.

Leofsig brought him down with a tackle as fierce and illegal as the one he'd used to level Sidroc. He'd regretted that one, because he should have let his cousin keep going. He wasn't the least bit sorry about knocking Burgred over. Burgred wasn't very happy about it, though. They rolled on the cobbles and then off the cobbles and on to the dirt, pummeling each other.

"You stopping!" the Algarvian yelled at them. They didn't stop. Had either of them stopped, the other would have gone right on doing damage. The straw boss turned to the laborers. "Stopping they!"

The men from the work gang pulled Leofsig and Burgred apart. Leofsig had a cut lip and a bruised cheek. Burgred, he saw, had a bloody nose and a black eye. Leofsig's ribs ached. He hoped Burgred's did, too.

"Kaunian-lover," Burgred snarled.

"Oh, shut up, you cursed fool," Leofsig answered wearily. "When you start talking about hanging people, you can't really be surprised if they insult you. Besides" — he spoke quietly so the Algarvian soldier wouldn't follow — "when we quarrel, who laughs? The redheads, that's who."

Had he just talked about Kaunians, he never would have got Burgred to pay him any attention. But Burgred did glance over at the straw boss. When he shrugged off the hands that restrained him, it wasn't so he could get at either Leofsig or the Kaunian. "A pestilence take 'em all," he muttered.

"No pay." The Algarvian pointed at Leofsig. "No pay." He pointed at Burgred. "No pay." He pointed at the Kaunian who'd questioned Burgred's legitimacy.

"I don't lose much," the Kaunian said.

Ignoring that, the Algarvian went on, "No treason. No sabotage." He'd learned the Forthwegian words he needed to know, all right.

He pointed back at the offending chunk of stone. "Fixing that. One more? Losing heads." This time, he pointed to everyone in the work gang in turn. By the expressions on the laborers' faces, none of them, Forthwegians or Kaunians, thought he was joking.

A tall, blond Kaunian and a couple of stocky, swarthy Forthwegians broke up the offending stone. They didn't quarrel about who did what. In the face of the straw boss's threat, that didn't matter. Getting the work done mattered, and they did it. Leofsig watched them with a certain sour satisfaction. Under the threat of death, they might have become brothers. Without it . . .? He sighed and went back to work.

17.

When he served the Sibian Navy, Cornelu had rarely ridden Eforiel to the south, toward the land of the Ice People. Sibiu had worried – and had had reason to worry – about Algarve. Almost all the time he'd spent aboard his leviathan had been in the channel between his island kingdom and the mainland of Derlavai to the north.

Now Lagoas had sent him and Eforiel down toward the austral continent. He wished the powers that be in Setubal had chosen to send him a couple of months earlier. Despite his rubber suit, despite the sorcery the Lagoan mages had added to the suit, he was chilly. Of course, the waters around the land of the Ice People weren't warm even in high summer, such as it was down near the bottom of the world. Now . . . the sea hadn't started freezing yet, but it wouldn't be long.

Cornelu's teeth might have felt like chattering, but Eforiel thought the Lagoans had sent her (and, incidentally, her rider) to a fine restaurant. For reasons mages had never been able to fathom, fish flourished in the frigid waters of the Narrow Sea. Eforiel put on more blubber with every mile she swam. It did a better job of keeping her warm than rubber and magecraft did for her master.

Thanks to the Lagoans, he'd taught her a new trick. At his tapped command, she stood on her tail, thrusting the front part of her body up out of the water. That let Cornelu, who clung not far back of her blowhole, see farther than he could have from a couple of feet above the surface of the sea.

He sighed. The Lagoans were clever, no doubt about it. They hadn't invaded his kingdom. They had taken him in as an exile. He wished he liked them better. He wished he liked them at all.

Whether he liked them or not, he preferred them to the Algarvians, whom he actively despised. Lagoas being the only kingdom still in the fight against Algarve, she perforce had his allegiance. He urged Eforiel up on her tail once more. Was that smoke he saw, there to the southwest?

"Aye, it is," he said, and urged the leviathan toward it.

Mizpah was falling. Had the Yaninans put their full effort into the attack on the Lagoan towns at the edge of the land of the Ice People, Mizpah would have fallen long since. But King Tsavellas kept most of his men at home, to watch the border with Unkerlant. Cornelu wasn't sure whether that made Tsavellas wise or foolish. King Swemmel *was* likely to go to war against Yanina. If he did, though, a few regiments wouldn't do much to slow him down. They might have been used to better purpose on the austral continent.

King Tsavellas had chosen otherwise, though. Because of that, the Lagoans and their nomad allies still had a grip on Mizpah, even if the Yaninans finally had fought their way into egg-tosser range, which meant the outpost would not hold much longer. But the Lagoans had the chance to salvage some of what they thought important from Mizpah before it fell.

"A fugitive king and a mage," Cornelu said to Eforiel. "I can see that. Both will be useful, and the Lagoans love what is useful. But I wager plenty of other people in Mizpah would sooner we were coming for them."

Eforiel's jaw closed on a good-sized squid that swam right in front of her. By the way she frisked under Cornelu, she would be delighted to visit these waters again. Cornelu gently patted the leviathan. By the time she took these men back to Lagoas, Mizpah would not be worth visiting, not for anyone with Lagoas's interests in mind. He couldn't explain that to the leviathan, and didn't bother trying.

"A little spit of land east of the harbor," Cornelu murmured. That was where the fugitives were supposed to be. He wondered if they could get there with the Yaninans investing Mizpah. He shrugged. If they weren't there, he couldn't very well pick them up.

He had Eforiel rear in the water again. If that wasn't the right spit of land, there a few hundred yards ahead, he didn't know what would be. He didn't see any people on it. He shrugged again. The Lagoan officers who sent him forth had thought the fugitives would be there.

"Oh, aye," one of them had said just before he and Eforiel left Setubal harbor. "The one of them has a name for getting out of scraps – and the mage isn't supposed to be bad at it, either." Cornelu remembered the fellow laughing uproariously at his own sally. Among Lagoans, it passed for wit.

Cornelu was harder to amuse. These days, nothing less than the prospect of King Mezentio's palace going up in flames, and all of Trapani with it, would have set him to laughing uproariously. He would have howled like a wolf for that, laughed like a loon. Even thinking about it with no likelihood of its happening was enough – more than enough – to make him smile.

He urged Eforiel closer to the end of the spit of land. Maybe the mage and the king hadn't got there yet. Maybe the mage would detect his arrival by some occult means and hurry out to meet him. Maybe, maybe, maybe . . .

He blinked. He would have taken oath . . . a proper oath, an oath on the name of King Burebistu – the spit was empty of people. Had he done so, he would have been forsworn. Suddenly, he saw two men there, one tall and lean and of Algarvic stock, the other shorter and stockier with, aye, a Forthwegian or Unkerlanter look. They saw him, too, or more likely the leviathan, and began to wave.

He had rubber suits along for men of their builds. If the mage knew his business, he'd be able to keep himself and his royal companion from freezing in this icy water. If he didn't – Cornelu shrugged one more time. He himself would do everything he could. What he couldn't do, he wouldn't worry about.

He brought Eforiel in toward the land as close as he dared. Having her beach herself wouldn't do, here and now even less than most other places and times. Cornelu slid off her back and swam toward the rocky, muddy land, pushing ahead of him a bladder that held the rubber suits.

When he came up on to the land, the mage greeted him with a slew of almost incomprehensible Lagoan. "Slow," Cornelu said. "I speak only a little." He pointed to the five crowns on the chest of his own rubber suit. "Cornelu. From Sibiu. Exile." That was one word of Lagoan he knew very well.

"I speak Sibian," the mage said, and he did, with a good accent – none of the variations on Algarvian that most Lagoans thought were Cornelu's native language. The fellow went on, "I am Fernao, and here before you you see King Penda of Forthweg."

"I speak Algarvian – not Sibian, I fear," Penda said.

Cornelu bowed. "I also speak Algarvian, your Majesty: better than I would like," he said. The king of Forthweg scowled at that, scowled and nodded.

"We are all speaking too much," the mage said in Sibian, and repeated himself in what Cornelu presumed to be Forthwegian. Whatever language he spoke, he made good sense. Turning back to Cornelu, he went on, "I presume those are suits to keep us from coming back to Setubal as if packed in ice?"

"Aye." Cornelu opened the bladder. "The suits, and whatever protective magic you can add to them. Warmth and breathing underwater would be useful, I expect."

The mage said, "Aye, I expected as much. I can do all that. Useful, you call the breathing spell? A good word for it, I would say. I will have to drop the magic that keeps people from noticing much about the spit. I tried not to project much of it out to sea; I'm glad you could find us."

"I can see how you might be," Cornelu agreed, his voice dry. "And we shall surely have much to discuss – at another time. Do now what you must do, that we may leave this place and eventually gain the leisure in which to hold such a discussion. For we have none here and now."

"There you speak the truth," Fernao said. He translated the truth into Forthwegian for Penda's benefit – though, if the king spoke Algarvian, he could probably follow some Sibian. Penda nodded and made an imperious gesture, as if to say, *Well, get on with it, then.*

Get on with it Fernao did. Cornelu knew the exact moment when the Lagoan mage abandoned the spell that drew eyes in Mizpah – and outside the Lagoan outpost – away from the spit of land. The Yaninan attackers, suddenly noticing people out there, began tossing eggs at them.

They were less than accomplished. Cornelu, accustomed to soldiers trained to higher standards, found their aim laughable and alarming at the same time. It was laughable because none of the eggs came very close to him. It was alarming because some of those eggs came down in the waters of the Narrow Sea – the waters where Eforiel waited. A spectacularly bad toss might prove as disastrous as a spectacularly good one. If, while missing Cornelu and the men he had come to take away, the Yaninans hit his leviathan, they would have done what they'd set out to do, though they might not know it.

"I suggest you make haste," Cornelu said to Fernao.

"I *am* making haste," the mage snarled through clenched teeth when he reached a point where he could pause in his incanting. Cornelu chuckled, recognizing the annoyance any good professional showed at having his elbow joggled. Cornelu understood and sympathized with that. Even so, he wished Fernao would make haste a little more quickly – or a lot more quickly.

After what seemed far too long – and after a couple of eggs had burst much closer than Cornelu would have liked – the mage declared, "I am ready." As if to prove as much, he pulled off his tunic and stepped out of his kilt, standing naked and shivering on the little spit of land. Penda imitated him. The king's body had more muscle and less fat than Cornelu would have guessed from seeing him clothed.

Both men rapidly donned the rubber suits Cornelu had brought, and the flippers that went with them. "And now," the Sibian exile said, "I suggest we delay no more. Eforiel awaits us in the direction from which I came up on to the land." He pointed, hoping with all his heart that Eforiel did still await them there. He didn't think the Yaninans had hit her, and didn't think they could frighten her away if they hadn't. He didn't want to discover he'd been disastrously wrong on either of those counts.

As he turned and started for the water, King Penda said, "Eforiel? A woman? Do I understand you?"

"No, or not exactly," Cornelu answered with a smile. "Eforiel – a leviathan."

"Ah," Penda said. "You in the south are much more given to training and riding them than we have ever been."

"Another discussion that will have to wait," said Fernao, who showed more sense than the fugitive king. Fernao splashed into the sea and struck out for Eforiel with a breast stroke that was determined if not very fast. Penda swam on his back, windmilling his arms over his head one after the other. He put Cornelu more in mind of a rickety rowboat than a porpoise, but he didn't look like sinking.

Cornelu shot past both of them, which was just as well. They would not have been glad to meet Eforiel without him there to let her know it was all right. As he drew near the leviathan, or to where he hoped she was, he slapped the water in a signal to which she had been trained to respond.

Respond she did, raising her toothy beak out of the water. Cornelu took his place on her back, then waited for his passengers. They were gasping when they reached the leviathan, but reach her they did. Cornelu slapped her smooth hide and sent her off toward the northeast, toward warmer water, toward warmer weather.

Hajjaj never relished a visit to the Unkerlanter ministry. He particularly did not relish it when Minister Ansovald summoned him as if he were a servant, a hireling. People kept insisting Unkerlanter arrogance had its limits. The Unkerlanters seemed intent on proving people wrong.

With autumn having come to Bishah, Hajjaj minded putting on clothes less than he did in summertime. And long, loose Unkerlanter tunics were less oppressive than the garments in which other peoples chose to encase themselves. Having to wear the clinging tunics and trousers of the Kaunian kingdoms was almost enough by itself to make the Zuwayzi foreign minister glad Algarve had conquered them and relieved him of the need.

As usual, Ansovald was blunt to the point of rudeness. No sooner had Hajjaj been escorted into his presence than he snapped, "I hear you have been holding discussions with the Algarvian minister."

"Your Excellency, I have indeed," Hajjaj replied.

Ansovald's eyes popped. "You admit it?"

"I could scarcely deny it," Hajjaj said. "Discussing things with the ministers of other kingdoms is, after all, the purpose for which my sovereign sees fit to employ me. In the past ten days, I have met with the minister of Algarve, as you said, and also with the ministers of Lagoas, Kuusamo, Gyongyos, Yanina, the mountain kingdom of Ortah, and, now, twice with your honorable self."

"You are plotting against Unkerlant, plotting against King Swemmel," Ansovald said, as if Hajjaj had not spoken.

"Your Excellency, that I must and do deny," the Zuwayzi foreign minister said evenly.

"I think you are lying," Ansovald said.

Hajjaj got to his feet and bowed. "That is, of course, your

privilege, your Excellency. But you have gone beyond the usages acceptable in diplomacy. I will see you another day, when you find yourself in better control of your judgment."

"Sit down," Ansovald growled. Hajjaj took no notice of him, but started toward the door. Behind him, the Unkerlanter minister let out a long, exasperated breath. "You had better sit down, your Excellency, or it will be the worse for your kingdom."

One hand on the latch, Hajjaj paused and spoke over his shoulder: "How could Unkerlant treat Zuwayza worse than she has already done?" His tone was acid; he wondered if Ansovald noticed.

"Do you really care to find out?" the Unkerlanter minister said. "Go through that door, and I daresay you will."

However much he wanted to, Hajjaj could not ignore such a threat. Reluctantly, he turned back toward Ansovald. "Very well, your Excellency, I listen. Under duress of that sort, what choice have I but to listen?"

"None," Ansovald said cheerfully. "That's what you get for not being strong. Now sit back down and hear me out." Hajjaj obeyed, though his back was stiff as an offended cat's. Ansovald paid no attention to his silent outrage. The Unkerlanter minister raised crude brutality almost to an art. He pointed a stubby finger at Hajjaj. "You are not to hold any more meetings with Count Balastro, on pain of war with my kingdom."

Hajjaj started to get up and walk out again. Ansovald's demand was one no representative of any kingdom had the right to make on the foreign minister of another kingdom. But Hajjaj knew King Swemmel only too well. If he openly defied the Unkerlanter minister here, Swemmel would conclude he had good reason to defy him, and would hurl an army of men in rock-gray tunics toward the north.

Swemmel might even be right, though his minister here would not know that. Ansovald leaned back in his chair, smugly delighted to see Hajjaj squirm. One reason he was good at bullying was that he enjoyed it so much. Hajjaj temporized: "Surely, your Excellency, you cannot expect me to refuse all intercourse with the minister from Algarve. Should he order me to do such a thing in regard to you, I would of course refuse."

Ansovald stopped leaning back and leaned forward instead, alarm and anger on his strong-featured face. "Has he ordered you to stop seeing me?" he demanded. "How dare he order you to do such a thing?"

What he did, he took for granted. That anyone else might presume to do the same thing was an outrage. Hajjaj might have laughed, had he not felt more like crying. "I assure you, it was but a hypothetical comment," the Zuwayzi foreign minister said, and spent the next little while smoothing Ansovald's ruffled feathers. When Hajjaj finally judged the Unkerlanter minister soothed enough, he resumed: "I can hardly avoid him at receptions and the like, you know."

"Oh, aye – that sort of business doesn't count," Ansovald said. Hajjaj had been far from sure he would prove even so reasonable. The Unkerlanter pointed at him again. "But when you and Balastro put your heads together for hours on end—" He shook his own head. "That won't do."

"And if he invites me to the Algarvian ministry, as you have invited me here?" Hajjaj asked, silently adding to himself, *He would be more polite about it, that's certain.*

"Refuse him," Ansovald said.

"He will ask me why. Shall I tell him?" Hajjaj inquired. Ansovald opened his mouth, then abruptly closed it again. Hajjaj said, "Your Excellency, I think you begin to see my difficulty. If I, the foreign minister of a sovereign kingdom, am forbidden to see the representative of another sovereign kingdom, would not that second kingdom reckon the kingdom that had forbidden me guilty of insult against it?"

With a certain malicious amusement, he watched the Unkerlanter minister's lips move as he worked his way through that. Ansovald was not swift, but he wasn't stupid, either. He took a bit, but got the right answer: *Algarve will think Unkerlant guilty of insult.* Considering what the Algarvians had done to every foe they'd faced in the Derlavaian War, Hajjaj would not have wanted them thinking him guilty of insult.

By the expression on Ansovald's face, he didn't want that, either. Hajjaj politely looked away while the Unkerlanter minister coughed and tugged at his ear and pulled loose a small flap of skin by his thumbnail. At last, Ansovald said, "Maybe I was a little hasty here."

From a Zuwayzi, that would have been a polite commonplace. From an Unkerlanter, and especially from King Swemmel's representative in Bishah, it was an astonishing admission. When Ansovald didn't seem inclined to come out with anything more, Hajjaj asked a gentle question: "In that case, your Excellency, what should my course be?"

Again, Ansovald didn't answer right away. Hajjaj understood why: the Unkerlanter minister had just realized that following instructions he'd got from Cottbus was likely to lead him into disaster. But not following any order he got from Cottbus was also likely to lead him into disaster. As Ansovald dithered, Hajjaj smiled benignly.

With a sigh, Ansovald said, "I spoke too soon. Unless I summon you again, you may ignore what has passed between us here."

Unless King Swemmel decides he doesn't mind insulting the Algarvians, was what that had to mean. Now Hajjaj had to fight to hide surprise. Might Swemmel think of taking such a chance? Hajjaj had often wondered whether the king of Unkerlant was crazy. Up till now, he'd never thought him stupid.

He wished the state of King Swemmel's wits didn't matter so much to Zuwayza. Far easier, far more reassuring, to think of it as Ansovald's problem and none of his own. He couldn't do that, worse luck. If Unkerlant caught cold, Zuwayza started sneezing – and Unkerlant went as Swemmel went.

Hajjaj also wished he could take Ansovald down a peg – down several pegs – for his insolence and arrogance. He couldn't do that, either, not when he'd just got what he wanted from the Unkerlanter. He said, "Let it be as you desire, your Excellency. I tell you truly, we have seen – all of Derlavai has seen – enough of war this past year and more. I wish with all my heart that we may have seen the end of it."

Ansovald only grunted in response to that. Hajjaj had trouble figuring out what the grunt meant. Was it skepticism, because Zuwayza had lost one war to Unkerlant and could be expected to want revenge? Or did Ansovald know Swemmel was indeed contemplating war against Algarve? For all Hajjaj's skill in diplomacy, he saw no way to ask without waking suspicions better left to slumber.

Rousing somewhat, Ansovald said, "I think we have done everything we can do today."

They'd alarmed each other. Ansovald had intended to harm Hajjaj. He hadn't intended to be alarmed in return. *Well,* Hajjaj thought, *life does not always turn out as you intend.* He got to his feet. "I think you are right, your Excellency. As always, a meeting with you is most instructive."

He left the Unkerlanter minister chewing on that and not nearly sure he liked the flavor. Getting out among his own people was a pleasure, going back to the palace a larger one, and pulling the tunic off over his head the greatest of all. Once comfortably naked, he went to report the conversation to King Shazli.

There he found himself balked. "Do you not recall, your Excellency?" one of Shazli's servitors said. "His Majesty is out hawking this afternoon."

Hajjaj thumped his forehead with the heel of his hand. "I'd forgotten," he admitted.

The servitor stared at him. He understood why: he wasn't supposed to forget anything, and came close enough to living up to that to make his lapses notable. He stared at her, too; she was worth staring at. Idly – well, a little more than idly – he wondered what sort of amusement she would make. Lalla really had grown too extravagant to justify the pleasure he got from her.

Resolutely, Hajjaj pushed such thoughts aside. He still craved the pleasures of the flesh, but not so often as he once had. Now he could recognize that other business might take precedence over such pleasure. With a last, slightly regretful, glance at the serving woman, he returned to his office.

He considered using the crystal there, but in the end decided against it. He did not think Unkerlanter mages could listen to what he said, but did not want to discover he was wrong. Paper and ink and a trusty messenger would do the job.

Your Excellency, he wrote, and then a summary of the relevant parts of his recent conversation with Ansovald. He had sanded the document dry when Shaddad appeared in the doorway. "How do you do that?" Hajjaj asked as he sealed the letter with ribbon and wax. "Come just when you're wanted, I mean?"

"I have no idea, your Excellency," his secretary replied. "I am pleased, however, that you find me useful."

"I find you rather more than useful, as you know perfectly well," Hajjaj said. "If you would be so kind as to put this in a plain pouch and deliver it . . ."

"Of course," Shaddad said. Only a slight flaring of his nostrils showed his opinion as he went on, "I suppose you will expect me to clothe myself, too."

"As a matter of fact, no," the Zuwayzi foreign minister said, and Shaddad smiled in glad surprise. Hajjaj continued, "You will be less conspicuous without mufflings, and there are times — and this is one of them — when discretion seems wisest. Just take this over to the Algarvian minister like the good fellow you are."

Shaddad's smile, now perhaps one of anticipation, grew broader. "Just as you say, your Excellency."

Garivald squelched through the mud to return a sharpening stone he'd borrowed from Dagulf. "Thanks," he said when the other peasant opened his door. "Did my sickle a deal of good when I needed it the most."

Dagulf's scar pulled the smile on his face into something like a leer. "Aye, you need sharp tools at harvest time," he said. "Bloody work's hard enough without you doing more than you need."

"Aye," Garivald said. "We did pretty well, we did, even if I do wish the rain would have held off for another couple of days."

"Don't we both? Don't we all?" Dagulf peered through drizzle toward the prison cell he and Garivald had helped to build. Lowering his voice, he went on, "Wouldn't be so bad if we didn't have to feed the captives and guards and that worthless, drunken mage through the winter."

"We'd get by easy then," Garivald agreed. Under his cape, his shoulders sagged as he sighed. "Would have been better if they — well, the guards, anyhow — would have helped with the harvest. Then they'd've earned their keep, you might say."

Dagulf's laughter was short, sharp, and bitter. "Don't hold your breath waiting for it, is all I've got to tell you."

"I wasn't," Garivald said. "Those miserable, lazy bastards just take. If you asked 'em to give, they'd fall over dead."

"But we've got a crystal connecting us to Cottbus." Dagulf seemed more disgusted than delighted.

"Oh, aye, so we do," Garivald said. If he was delighted, he concealed it so well, even he didn't know about it. "When Waddo gets a brainstorm nowadays, he tells us it's Cottbus's idea, so we have to go along with it. Isn't that grand?"

Dagulf spat. "You ask me, he doesn't talk on the crystal half as much as he says he does. He just tells us what to do and says it's an order from the capital. How can we prove any different? You have a crystal in *your* house so you can talk to King Swemmel and ask him what's going on?"

"Oh, of course I do," Garivald answered. "Two of 'em, matter of fact. The other one's attuned to Marshal Rathar, so he can send in the army when I tell him what a big liar Waddo is."

Both men laughed. Neither's laugh was altogether comfortable, though. Truth was, Waddo could talk to Cottbus and they couldn't. And if he wasn't talking to Cottbus, they had no way of knowing that, either. They'd always been powerless when measured against inspectors. Now they were powerless against their own firstman, too. Garivald shook his head. That wasn't how things were supposed to be.

He shook his head again. It wouldn't really matter till spring. Not even the most energetic firstman, which Waddo wasn't, would be able to accomplish much during winter in southern Unkerlant. The peasants would stay indoors as often as they could, stay warm as best they could, and drink as much as they could. Anyone who expected anything different was doomed to disappointment.

Interrupting Garivald's caravan of thought, Dagulf said, "I hear tell Marshal Rathar got on Swemmel's bad side some way or other. Don't know how much good your crystal attuned to him will do you."

"Now that I think on it, I heard that, too." Garivald threw his hands in the air. "Isn't that the way things turn out? You go to all the trouble to get the cursed crystal, and then it's not worth anything." He spoke with almost as much regret and resentment as if a crystal really did sit on the mantel above his fireplace.

Dagulf played along with him. "Ah, well, maybe you can attune it to the new marshal, whoever he turns out to be – and then to the one after him, too, when Swemmel decides he won't answer."

Garivald looked back toward the gaol again. No, the guards couldn't possibly have heard that. He didn't even think Dagulf's neighbors could have heard it. Still . . . "You want to be careful what you say," he told Dagulf. "Now word really can get back to Cottbus, and you won't be happy if it does."

"You're a good fellow to have around, Garivald," Dagulf said.

"You brought back my hone, and I didn't even have to come over and tell you I was going to burn down your house to get it. And you're right about this other nonsense, too. It's like having somebody peeking in your window all the time, is what it is."

"You're too ugly for anybody to want to peek in your window," Garivald said, not wanting an unfounded reputation as a paragon to get out of hand.

"My wife says the same thing, so maybe you've got something there," Dagulf answered. "But I still get some every now and then, so I must be doing something right."

Snorting, Garivald turned and headed back toward his own house. As he passed the cell he'd helped build, he paused in the drizzle to listen to one of the captives singing. It was a song about a boy falling in love with a girl – what else was there to write songs about, except a girl falling in love with a boy? – but not one Garivald had heard before. People had been singing most of the songs he knew for generations.

The captive had a fine, resonant baritone. Garivald didn't. He liked to sing anyway. He listened attentively, picking up tune and lyrics. Sure enough, it was a city song: it talked about paved streets and parks and the theater and other things he'd never know. It had an odd feeling to it, too, a feeling of impermanence, as if it didn't really matter whether he got the girl or not: if he didn't, he could always find another one. Things weren't like that in Zossen, or in any of the countless other villages dotting the broad plains and forests of Unkerlant.

"City song," Garivald muttered. He didn't walk away, though, even if he and Dagulf had just spent the last little while running down Cottbus and everything it stood for. He stood listening till the captive finished, and wasn't sorry when the fellow started over again. That gave him the chance to pick up the words to the first part of the first verse, which he'd missed while talking with Dagulf.

He was singing the song – not loudly, feeling his way through it – when he came in the door. His wife didn't need to hear more than a couple of lines before she said, "Where did you pick that up? It's new."

"One of the captives was singing it," Garivald answered. He groped for the next line and discovered he couldn't find it. "Ahh, curse it, you made me mess it up. Now I have to go back to the beginning."

"Well, do, then." Annore turned away from the dough she was kneading. Her arms were pale almost to the elbows with flour. "Been a while since we've had a new song. That one sounded good, even if you haven't got the best voice in the village."

"I thank you, dear," Garivald said, though he knew she was right. He thought for a moment — how *did* that first verse go? — then plunged back in. He wasn't so good a singer as the captive, but he remembered all the words and didn't do too much violence to the tune. Annore heard him out without a sound. Her lips moved a couple of times as she fixed phrases in her mind.

"That's a good song," she said when he was through, and then, thoughtfully, "Well, a pretty good song. It's . . . strange, isn't it? I bet it come out of Cottbus."

"I bet you're right," Garivald agreed. "If we hadn't got married for one reason or another, I'd still be a bachelor, and I'd be frantic about it. But the fellow in the song? 'Another boat at the dock, Another bird in the flock.'" After singing the lines, he shook his head. "Anybody wants to know, that's not the way people ought to think."

Annore nodded. "We have too many men chasing women who aren't their wives the way things are."

Garivald could think of only a couple of such cases in Zossen since he'd started paying attention to what men and women did. Maybe even a couple seemed too many to Annore. He could also think of a couple of women who'd gone after men not their husbands. If he brought them up, he was sure his wife would find something to say in their defense. Since he was sure, he didn't bother. They found enough things to quarrel about without looking for more.

He did say, "Even if the words are peculiar, I like the tune."

"So do I." Annore hummed it. Her voice was high and pure, a good deal better and more pliable than Garivald's. After a verse or so, she clicked her tongue between her teeth. "I do wish it had better words. Somebody should put better words to the tune."

"Who?" Garivald asked — a good question, since no one in Zossen had ever shown any signs of talent along those lines. "Waddo, maybe?" He rolled his eyes to make sure Annore knew he was joking.

"Oh, aye, he'd be the perfect one." His wife rolled her eyes, too.

"'Another story on his house,'" Garivald sang to the tune of the captive's song. "'A fancy crystal for the louse.'"

He and Annore both laughed. She looked thoughtfully at him. "Do you know, that's not bad," she said. "Maybe you could make a real song, not just a couple of lines poking fun at Waddo."

"I couldn't do that," Garivald exclaimed.

"Why not?" Annore asked. "You started to."

"But I'm not a person who makes songs," Garivald said. "People who make songs are—" He stopped. He had no idea what people who made songs were like, not really. Every so often, a traveling singer would come through Zossen. The only thing he knew about them was that they drank too much. Once, back before he was born, a traveling singer passing through Zossen had left with a peasant's daughter. People still gossiped about it; the girl seemed to get both younger and more beautiful every year.

"Well, if you don't want to . . ." Annore shrugged and went back to kneading dough. She also went back to humming the new song.

Garivald stood there rubbing his chin. Words crowded his head. Some of them were words from the song. The first verse was fine, and anybody could lose a girl he'd thought would be his for good. But what he did afterwards, what he thought afterwards, how he felt afterwards . . . Maybe someone up in Cottbus would do those things, would think and feel those things, but nobody in Zossen or any other peasant village would.

A line occurred to Garivald, and then a word that rhymed with it. He had to cast about for the rest of the line that would go with the word. He wished he could read and write. Being able to put things down so they didn't keep trying to change in his head would have helped. Waddo could do it. So could a couple of other men in the village. Garivald had never had time to learn.

But he had a capacious memory – partly because he couldn't read and write, though he didn't realize that. He kept playing with words, throwing away most of them, keeping a few. Leuba woke up from a nap. He hardly noticed Annore taking her out of the cradle: he was looking for a word that rhymed with *harvest*.

Half an hour later, he said, "Listen to this." Annore came in from the kitchen again. She cocked her head to one side, waiting. Garivald turned away, suddenly shy in front of her. But, even if he couldn't face her, he loosed his indifferent voice.

Only when he was through did he look back toward her. He tried to read the expression on her face. Surprise and . . . was she crying? He'd tried to make a sad song – it had to be a sad song – but . . . could she be crying? "That's good," she sniffed. "That's very good."

He stared, astonished. He'd never imagined he could do such a thing. Maybe a young swallow felt the same way the first time it scrambled out of its nest, leaped off a branch, and spread its wings. "Powers above," Garivald whispered. "I can fly."

Bembo lifted a long-stemmed wine glass. "Here's to you, pretty one," he said, beaming across the café table at Saffa.

The sketch artist raised her own glass. "Here's to your good notion, and to the bonus Captain Sasso gave you for it."

Since he was spending some of that bonus to take her out, Bembo drank to the toast. He hoped the bonus wasn't the only reason she'd finally let him take her to supper. If she was that mercenary . . . he didn't want to know about it right now. He took another sip of his own wine – better than he usually bought. "I'm a man on the way up, I am," he said.

Something glinted dangerous in Saffa's eyes. Whatever the egg of her thought was, though, she didn't drop it on his head, as she assuredly would have before. "Maybe you are," she said after no more than the slightest pause. "You didn't start pawing me the instant I came out of my flat. That's certainly an improvement."

"How do you know?" he said, and pressed a hand to his heart, the picture of affronted dignity. "You never let me meet you at your flat before."

"Do I look like a fool?" Saffa asked, which made Bembo go through another pantomime routine. Her laugh showed very sharp, white, even teeth. He wondered if she'd finally chosen to go out with him in hope of a good time (either vertical or horizontal) or in the expectation of sinking teeth and claws into him later on. That might mean a good time for her, but he didn't think he would enjoy it.

To keep from thinking about it, he said, "Good to see Tricarico lit up again at night."

"Aye, it is," Saffa agreed. "We're too far north for any dragon from

Lagoas to reach us here, and we've beaten our other enemies." Pride
rang in her voice. She glanced at Bembo with more warmth than he
was used to seeing from her. "And you helped, spotting those cursed
Kaunians with their dyed hair."

Before Bembo could go on for a while about what an alert, clever
fellow he was, the waiter brought supper, which might have been just
as well. Saffa had trout, Bembo strips of duck breast in a wine-based
sauce. He didn't usually eat such a splendid meal; he couldn't usually
afford such a splendid meal. Since he could tonight, he made the most
of it. He and Saffa emptied another bottle of wine during supper.

Afterwards, as they walked to the theater, she let him put an arm
around her shoulder. A few steps later, she let him slide it down to
her waist. But when, as if by accident, his hand brushed the bottom
of her breast, her heel came down hard on his big toe, also as if by
accident.

"I'm so sorry," she murmured in tones that couldn't have meant
anything but, *Don't push your luck.* With a good deal of wine in him,
Bembo promptly did push his luck, and as promptly got stepped on
again. After that, he concluded Saffa might have been dropping a
hint.

At the theater, the usher eyed Saffa appreciatively but gave what
passed for Bembo's best tunic and kilt a fishy stare. Still, Bembo had
tickets entitling him and Saffa to a pair of medium-good seats.
Whatever the usher's opinion of his wardrobe, the fellow had no
choice but to guide him down to where he belonged. "Enjoy the
production, sir – and you, milady," the young man said, bowing over
Saffa's hand.

Bembo tipped him, more to get rid of him than for any other
reason. Saffa let the constable slip an arm over her shoulder again.
This time, he had the sense not to go exploring further. The house
lights dimmed. Actors pranced out on stage, declaiming.

"I knew it would be another costume drama," Bembo whispered.

"They're all the rage these days," Saffa whispered back. Her breath
was warm and moist in his ear.

Up on the stage, actors and actresses in blond wigs played imperial
Kaunians, all of them plotting ways and means to keep the dauntless,
virile Algarvians out of the Empire – and the women falling into
clinches with the Algarvian chieftains every chance they got. The

story might have been taken straight from one of the historical
romances Bembo had been devouring lately. Along with the rest of
the audience, he whooped when a Kaunian noblewoman's tunic and
trousers came flying over the screen that hid her bed from the
spectators.

Afterwards, Saffa asked, "Do you suppose it was really like that?"

"Must have been," Bembo answered. "If it wasn't, how would we
ever have beaten the cursed Kaunians?"

"I don't know," the sketch artist admitted. She yawned, not too
theatrically. "You'd better take me home. We both have to work in
the morning."

"Did you have to remind me?" Bembo said, but he knew she was
right.

Outside her flat, she let him kiss her – actually, she kissed him.
When his hands wandered, she stretched and purred like a cat. Then
he tried to get one under her kilt, and she twisted away from him.
"Maybe one of these nights," she said. "Maybe – but not tonight."
She kissed him on the end of the nose, then slipped into her flat and
had the door barred before Bembo could make a move to follow her.

He wasn't so angry as he thought he should have been. Even if he
hadn't bedded her, he'd come closer than he'd expected he would –
and she hadn't clawed him too badly after all. Not a perfect evening
(had it been a perfect evening, she would have reached under his kilt),
but not bad, either.

He still looked happy the next morning, so much so that Sergeant
Pesaro leered. "What *were* you doing?" he said, in tones suggesting he
already knew the broad outlines but wanted the juicy details. He
made a formidable interrogator, whether grilling criminals or
constables.

Since Bembo had no juicy details to give him, and since Saffa
would kill him or make him wish she had if he invented some, all
he said was, "A gentleman goes out of his way to protect the
reputation of a lady."

"Since when are you a gentleman? For that matter, since when is
Saffa a lady?" Pesaro wasn't trying to get her to flip up her kilt, so he
could say what he pleased. Bembo just shrugged. Pesaro muttered
under his breath, then went on, "All right, if you won't talk, you
won't. I can't beat it out of you, the way I can with the ordinary lags.

Anyhow, there's a good job of work ahead for the force today."

Ah?" Bembo's ears came to attention. So, rather lackadaisically, did the rest of him. "What's toward, Sergeant?"

"We're going to round up all the cursed Kaunians in town." Pesaro spoke with considerable satisfaction. "Order came in just after midnight by crystal from Trapani, from the Ministry for Protection of the Realm. Everybody's been having kittens since you caught the blonds dyeing their hair. King Mezentio's decided we can't take the chance of letting 'em run around loose any more, so we won't. They'll be pulling 'em in all over Algarve."

"Well, that's pretty good," Bembo said. "I bet we got rid of a lot of spies that way. Probably should have done it back at the start of the war, if anybody wants to know what I think. If we had done it back at the start of the war, my guess is the stinking Jelgavans wouldn't have come half so close to taking Tricarico."

"Nobody cares what you guess," Pesaro said. But then he checked himself; after Bembo had discovered the Kaunians dyeing their hair, that might be less true now than a few weeks before. Grimacing at the absurdity of having to take Bembo seriously, the sergeant went on, "No matter when they should have done it, they are doing it now. We've got lists of known Kaunians, and we're going to send constables out in pairs to make sure they don't give us a tough time. Or if they try that, they'll be sorry." He folded a meaty hand into a fist.

Bembo nodded. Inside, he was laughing. Pesaro sounded tough, as if he'd be hauling in Kaunians himself instead of sending out ordinary constables like Bembo to do the job. The sergeant's comment sparked another thought, an important one: "Who are you pairing with me?"

"Have to check the roster." Sergeant Pesaro ran a fat finger down it. "I've got you with Oraste. Does that suit?"

"Aye," Bembo said. "He's not one to back away from trouble. And we've worked together before, in a manner of speaking — he helped me bring in that Balozio, remember?"

"I didn't, no, but I do now that you remind me of it," Pesaro said. The doors to the station house swung open. In came Oraste, as broad through the shoulders as a Forthwegian. "Just the man I'm looking for!" Pesaro exclaimed happily, and explained to Oraste what he'd just told Bembo.

Oraste listened, scratched his head, nodded, and said, "Give us the list, Sergeant, and we'll get at it. You ready, Bembo?"

"Aye." Bembo wasn't so ready as all that, but didn't see how he could say anything else. He was glad to have Oraste at his side precisely because Oraste never backed away from anyone or anything. Oraste didn't back away from duty, either.

The first Kaunians on the list were Falsirone and Evadne. "Those don't look like Kaunian names," Oraste said, but then he shrugged. "Doesn't matter what they call themselves. If they're Kaunians, they're gone."

Falsirone and Evadne stared in dismay when the constables strode into their tonsorial parlor. They stared in horror when Bembo told them why the constables had come. Pointing a finger at him, Evadne shrilled, "You told us we wouldn't get into trouble, you liar!"

"You're not in trouble for that," Bembo said, strangling the guilt that crept out from the dark places at the bottom of his mind. "This is only a precaution, till the war is safely won." He didn't know that – no one had said anything of the sort – but it seemed a reasonable guess.

Oraste smacked his club into the palm of his hand. "Get moving," he said flatly.

"But what about everything here?" Evadne wailed, waving an arm to show off the shop and everything in it.

Bembo glanced at Oraste. Oraste's face had not the slightest particle of give in it. Bembo decided he had better not show any give, either. "Hazard of war," he said. "Now come along. We haven't got all day here."

Still complaining loudly and bitterly – still acting very much as veritable Algarvians would have done – Evadne and Falsirone came. Bembo and Oraste led them to the park where Bembo had spent his unhappy hours as an emergency militiaman. More constables, and some soldiers as well, took charge of them there. "On to the next," Oraste said.

The next proved to be a prominent restaurateur. Bembo understood another reason why his superiors had sent constables out in pairs: it made them harder to bribe. With Oraste glaring at him as if looking for the smallest excuse to beat him bloody, the Kaunian didn't even try, but came along meek as a lamb heading for sacrifice.

Bembo let out a silent sigh. He would have been much more reasonable.

When he and Oraste got to the third establishment on their list, they found it empty. Oraste scowled. "Some other bastards beat us to it," he said.

"I don't think so," Bembo answered. "I think word's out on the street. A lot of blonds will be figuring they ought to disappear."

"We'll get 'em," Oraste said. "Sooner or later, we'll get 'em."

By nightfall, the constables had rounded up several hundred Kaunians. Almost an equal number, though, had not been there to round up. Despite that, Captain Sasso said, "Good job, men. The kingdom's long overdue for a cleanup, and we're the fellows who can take care of it. When we're done, when the war is won, Algarve will be a better place."

"That's right," Oraste said, and Bembo nodded, too.

Istvan longed for the days when the worst Sergeant Jokai could do to him was send him off to shovel dragon shit or to serve as a dowser's beast of burden. Jokai was dead these days, smashed to bits when a Kuusaman egg burst too close to him. For all practical purposes, Istvan was a sergeant himself, though no officer had formally conveyed the rank on him. He was a veteran on Obuda, and the soldiers he led new-come reinforcements. Having stayed alive gave him moral authority even without rank.

"Here," he said, pointing to a clump of bushes. "These fruits stay good even when they're dried out and wrinkled like that. Grab as many as you can; stars above only know when we'll see any proper meals again."

"What are these fruits called?" asked one of the new men, a thin, bespectacled fellow named Kun.

"Curse me if I know," Istvan answered. "The Obudans have a name for 'em, but I don't know what it is. Names don't matter, anyhow. What matters is, like I said, they're good to eat. With the supply system all buggered up the way it is, I think I'd eat a goat if one came strolling up the path."

Some of the men laughed and nodded. Some of them looked revolted. Despite profane bravado, Istvan wasn't sure if he would really eat goat. Only a starving Gyongyosian would even think of such a thing — a starving Gyongyosian or a depraved one. When he was a boy, four men in the next valley over from his had been caught at a ritual supper of goat stew after they'd murdered — and done worse things to — a pregnant woman. No clan feud had started when they were buried alive. Even their own families thought they deserved it, as much for the goat-eating as for their other crimes.

Kun cleared his throat a couple of times and said, "Names always matter. Names are part of the fabric from which reality is woven. If your name were different, you would not be the man you are, nor I, nor any of us. The same must surely hold true for these fruits."

He was, as he seldom let anyone forget, a mage's apprentice. He was also a bumbler, as tales said mages' apprentices often were. Istvan marveled that he still lived when better men had died around him. Sometimes pretending not to understand him was the best way to stop him from going on and on. Istvan tried it: "If these fruits had a different name, I think I'd still be the man I am."

"That is not what I meant," Kun said, giving him an indignant look over the top of those spectacles. "What I meant was—" He paused, looking foolish, as the possibility that Istvan might have been making a joke occurred to him. That took longer than it should have. Istvan was surprised it happened at all.

Before he could finish the job of putting Kun in his place, eggs started falling not far away. The men he led had been on Obuda and in action long enough to know what that meant. Istvan thought he was the first to throw himself flat, but none of the rest was more than a moment behind him.

The ground shuddered under him. Leaves and twigs fell on his back; someone close by cursed as a branch a good deal bigger than a twig came down on his leg. Through the din of bursting eggs and falling trees, Istvan shouted, "Now — is that us trying to kill the Kaunians or them trying to kill us?"

"If you like, I will undertake a divination to find out," Kun said.

"Never mind." Istvan shook his head, dislodging the end of a twig from his ear. "If one of those lands on us, we end up dead either way." Kun couldn't very well argue with that, and so, for a wonder, he didn't.

A dragon screeched, just above the treetops. It was, Istvan thought unhappily, more likely to be flown by a Kuusaman than by one of his own countrymen. The Kuusamans were able to bring dragons by the shipload from out of the east, where Gyongyos had to fly them from island to island to get them to Obuda. Because the Gyongyosian dragons inevitably arrived worn, the beasts from Kuusamo had the better of it in the air.

"I wish we could drive the Kuusaman fleet out of these waters," Istvan muttered, his face still in the dirt. He sighed. "I suppose the little slant-eyed sons of billy goats wish they could drive our fleet out of these waters."

Sometimes (mostly by night, for looking for a good view by day was asking a Kuusaman sniper to put a beam in one ear and out the other), he would look out at the warships tossing eggs and blazing at one another. Neither side, as yet, was able to keep the other from reinforcing its army on Obuda. A lot of ships had gone to wreckage and twisted metal trying, though. He wondered which side could go on throwing them into the fight longer than the other.

More screeches overhead, and then the noise, like a dozen men all being sick at once, of a dragon flaming. The sound that followed was not a screech but a shriek. More sounds came: the sounds of a large body crashing down through the canopy of leaves and branches above the Gyongyosians and then thrashing about on the ground only a stone's throw away.

Istvan scrambled to his feet. "Come on," he called to his men. "Let's get rid of that cursed thing before it flames half the forest afire. Let's see what we can do about the flier, too. He might not be dead – he didn't fall that far."

"If he's a Kuusaman, we'll take care of that," Szonyi said. He might not have done any fighting till the men from the far east invaded, but he was a veteran now.

"Aye," Istvan said. "Either we kill him or we send him back so our officers can squeeze him." Normally, Istvan would have done the latter. As things were, he'd been on his own for a couple of days, and wasn't sure where to send a captive if he got one.

Getting one, he realized, wouldn't be easy. That dragon might have been flamed out of the sky, but it was a long way from dead; branches must have done a better job than usual of cushioning its fall. It sounded as if it were trying to knock down every tree it could reach. It didn't flame, though, which argued it still had a flier on its back: an unrestrained dragon would have vented its fury every way it could.

Kun pointed ahead. "There it is," he said unnecessarily: that great scaly tail could not have belonged to any other beast. At the moment, it was doing duty for a flail, smashing bushes to bits.

"Surround it," Istvan said. "Blaze for the eyes or the mouth. Sooner or later we'll kill it. And watch out for the flier. He's liable to be blazing at you while you're blazing at the dragon."

"I find that highly unlikely," Kun said. But he did as Istvan told him, so Istvan couldn't come down on him for talking back. Istvan couldn't come down hard on him for talking back, anyhow – a disadvantage of lacking formal rank.

Spreading out to surround the dragon made the Gyongyosians cast their net widely indeed. The beast was still doing its best to level the woods. It couldn't knock over large trees. With that exception, its best was quite good; a stampeding behemoth would have been hard pressed to match it.

Istvan peered through the bushes toward it. Sure enough, it was a Kuusaman dragon, painted in sea green and sky blue. Its right wing and a stretch of the body behind the wing were charred and black. Without a doubt, a Gyongyosian dragon had won that duel in the air. But the Kuusaman still somehow astride it at the base of its neck seemed alert and not badly hurt. He had a stick in his hands and was looking now this way, now that, ready for anything that might happen to him.

For a moment, Istvan wondered why he didn't get off the dragon and make for the woods. Then he realized the dragon was liable to squash the flier if he dismounted. He raised his own stick to his shoulder and sighted along it. Before he could blaze, the Kuusaman did, but at someone off to the other side. A hoarse cry said the dragonflier hit what he'd blazed at, too.

When Istvan blazed at the Kuusaman, the fellow jerked as if stung. But, even if Istvan's beam bit, it didn't knock the foe out of the fight. The fellow used his own stick as a goad, and the dragon, hurt though it was, obeyed the command he gave it. Its head swung toward Istvan. He blazed at it, but it kept turning his way. Its jaws opened enormously, preposterously, wide. Flame shot from those jaws, straight at Istvan.

He thought he was a dead man. Though it was daylight, he looked up toward the heavens, toward the stars where he expected his spirit would go. But the sheet of flame fell short. Trees and bushes between the dragon and him began to burn. He threw his hands up in front of his face to protect himself from the blast of the heat, but the fire did not quite reach him. He stumbled backwards, his lungs feeling seared from the one breath of flame-heated air he'd drawn in.

Coughing, he staggered off to one side of the fire. It would spread, but not quickly; Obuda had had a lot of rain lately, so the plants were full of juice. The dragon was swinging its head away from Istvan now. It flamed again. A shriek of anguish announced that whoever it flamed at this time hadn't been far enough away to escape the fire.

Istvan blazed at the dragonflier again. His comrades were doing the same now. At last, after what seemed like forever, the Kuusaman slumped down on his dragon's neck, the stick slipping from his fingers. The dragon, with no one controlling it, began sending bursts of flame in all directions – until it had no flame left to send.

After that, disposing of the great beast was relatively easy, for the Gyongyosians could approach without fear. When it opened its mouth and tried to flame Szonyi, he sent a beam through the soft tissue inside that maw and into its brain. Its head flopped down. The body kept thrashing a while longer, too stupid to realize right away that it was dead.

Kun nodded to Istvan. Istvan nodded back, in some surprise; he thought the dragon had flamed the mage's apprentice. Kun looked surprised, too. Pointing to the dead Kuusaman flier, he said, "You were right. Those little demons really can fight bravely."

"Too right they can," Istvan answered. "If they couldn't, don't you think we'd have thrown 'em off this island long since?"

"We did throw 'em off this island once," Szonyi said. "The whoresons came back." He paused. "I suppose that says something about them."

"Aye," Istvan said. "They aren't Gyongyosians – they aren't warriors born – but they're men." He pulled a knife from his belt and advanced on the dragon's carcass. "I'm going to worry a tooth or two, by the stars. When I go back to my valley one of these days, I'll wear a dragon's fang on a chain around my neck. That should keep some of the local tough boys quiet." He smiled in anticipation.

He wasn't the only soldier who took a souvenir from the dragon, either. Kun cut several fangs from its mouth. "I ought to be able to get some sort of sorcerous use out of these," he said. "And, as Istvan says, one worn around the neck will be a potent charm against bullies."

"We earned them, sure enough." Szonyi's hands were bloody, as were Istvan's. They both kept rubbing them on the ground. Even a dragon's blood burned.

"Aye, we earned them," Istvan said. "Now we have to hope we drive the Kuusamans off this stinking island and that we get off it ourselves." A moment later, he wished he'd spoken as if that were assured. For better or worse, though, he'd seen too much fighting to fool himself for long.

Leudast squelched through mud. What the Forthwegians called roads were hardly better than their Unkerlanter equivalents: good enough when dry, boggy when wet. "Wait till the snow starts falling," Sergeant Magnulf said. "They'll harden up again then."

"Aye," Leudast said. "But winters are milder here than they are farther south, you know. It's not always one blizzard after another. Only sometimes."

"That's right – you're from not far from these parts, aren't you?" Magnulf said.

"Farther west, of course," Leudast answered. "Fifty, maybe a hundred miles west of what used to be the border between Forthweg and Unkerlant. Just about this far south, though, and the weather wasn't a whole lot different than the way it is here."

"I'm sorry for you," Magnulf said, which made Leudast and everybody else in the squad laugh. After he was done laughing, Leudast wondered why he'd done it. The weather in most of Unkerlant was worse than it was hereabouts, or in the part of the kingdom where he'd grown up.

"One good thing about the rain," a common soldier named Gernot said. "The cursed Algarvians aren't going to jump on our backs for a while."

"They'll drown in the muck if they try," Leudast said, at which his companions nodded. Some of them laughed, too, but only some. Most realized they would also drown in the muck if the Algarvians attacked.

Magnulf pointed ahead. "There's the village where we're supposed to billet ourselves. Miserable little hole in the ground, isn't it?"

Seen through spatters of rain, the village did look distinctly unappetizing. The thatch-roofed cottages weren't much different from the ones in the village where he'd lived till the impressers dragged him into King Swemmel's army. Two buildings were bigger than the rest. He knew what they'd be: a smithy and a tavern. The whole place, though, had a dispirited, rundown look to it. No one had bothered painting or whitewashing the houses for a long time. Sad clumps of dying grass stuck out of the ground here and there, like surviving bits of hair on the scalp of a man with a bad case of ringworm.

"Powers above," Gernot muttered. "Why would anyone want to live in a dump like this?" Unlike his comrades, he hadn't been dragged off a farm, but from the streets of Cottbus. He was vague about what he'd done on the streets of Cottbus, which naturally made Leudast figure he had good reason to be vague.

Magnulf said, "It'll be better than spending time under canvas, anyway."

"Aye, so it will," Leudast said, and wished he sounded more as if he believed it. *Maybe it's the rain*, he thought. With the sun shining, the place had to look better. It could hardly have looked worse.

A dog started barking as the Unkerlanter soldiers drew near the village, and then another and another, till they sounded like a pack of wolves in full cry. One of them, about as big and mean-looking as a wolf, stalked toward the soldiers stiff-legged and growling. They shouted and cursed at it. Somebody threw a glob of mud that caught it on the end of the nose. The dog let out a startled yip and sat back on its haunches.

"That was well done," Magnulf said. "We'd have had to blaze the cursed cur if it kept coming on."

None of the other dogs seemed quite so bold, for which Leudast was duly grateful. They kept on barking, though. Doors in the peasants' huts opened. Men and women came out – not far, staying under the protection of the overhanging eaves – to stare at the soldiers. Save only that the men let their whiskers grow, they might have been Unkerlanter peasants.

Leudast shook his head. Now that the Twinkings War was over, peasants would have looked at the soldiers with pity in their eyes, not the sullen hatred on the faces of these people.

Magnulf nudged him with an elbow. "You can make more sense of their language than the rest of us. Let 'em know what we're here for."

"Aye, Sergeant," Leudast said resignedly. More often than not, speaking a dialect of Unkerlanter close to Forthwegian came in handy. He had no trouble making taverners understand what he wanted. In the last village where the squad had been stationed, he'd talked a reasonably pretty girl into sleeping with him. But he sometimes got more work to do, too, as now. Turning to the villagers, he asked, "Who is the firstman here?"

No one said anything. No one moved. "Do they know what you're saying?" Magnulf asked.

"They know, Sergeant. They just don't want to give me the time of day," Leudast answered. "I can fix that." He spoke to the Forthwegians again: "We will stay here. Tell me who the firstman is. We will put more men in his house."

Magnulf chuckled. So did a couple of other men. Leudast had never known an Unkerlanter village where very many people loved their firstman. From what he'd seen, the Forthwegians weren't much different there.

And, sure enough, several of them looked toward a stern-faced fellow with an iron-gray beard. He glared at them and at the Unkerlanters in turn, as if trying to decide whom he hated more. His wife, who stood beside him, had no doubts. Could her eyes have blazed, she would have knocked down all her neighbors.

"You are the firstman?" Leudast asked.

"I am the firstman," the Forthwegian said. "I am called Arnulf." It might have been an Unkerlanter name. "What do you want with us?" Now that he had decided to speak, he spoke slowly and clearly, so Leudast could follow. He sounded like a man of some education, which was not what Leudast would have expected from anyone in a place like this.

"We are to stay here," Leudast answered. "Show us houses where we can stay." He said no more about billeting extra men on Arnulf.

"How long are you to stay here?" the firstman asked.

Leudast shrugged. "Until our officers order us to go."

Arnulf's wife wailed and turned that terrible scowl on the firstman. "It could be forever!" She tugged at Arnulf's sleeve. "Make them leave. Make them go away."

"And how am I to do that?" he demanded in loud, heavy exasperation. She spoke a couple of sentences in Forthwegian too quick and slangy for Leudast to follow. Her husband made a fist and made as if to thump her with it. She snarled at him. Several of the Unkerlanter soldiers behind Leudast laughed. They, or men in their villages, kept women in line the same way.

"Show us houses where we can stay," Leudast repeated. "Otherwise, we will pick the houses ourselves." Arnulf's face stayed blank. Leudast tried again, substituting *choose* for *pick*. The firstman got it then. He didn't like it, but he got it.

Scowling more darkly than ever, he asked, "How many houses?"

Leudast had to relay that to Magnulf, who answered, "Five houses," and held up his hand with the fingers spread. To Leudast, he said, "Two of our boys in each house and they won't get tempted to try anything cute."

"You will want food, too," Arnulf said, as if hoping Leudast would contradict him. Leudast didn't. Sighing, the firstman said, "The whole village will share in feeding you." He started pointing at villagers.

All five of the ones he picked shouted and cursed and stomped their feet, none of which did them any good. Arnulf's wife screeched something at them that Leudast, again, couldn't quite follow. The villagers did, though, and fell silent. They might not like the idea of having Unkerlanters quartered among them, but they didn't want to get on the wrong side of Arnulf's wife, either.

"This village will go hungry if we have to feed you through the winter," Arnulf said.

"Something worse will happen to you if you don't," Leudast told him. He got another vicious glare for that.

The villager whose hut he and Gernot went to take over had sons too young to have fought in the war. His wife was severely plain. However unhappy they looked, however hard they pretended not to understand Leudast's stabs at Forthwegian, they would have been more worried and surly still had they had daughters. Leudast was sure of that. Maybe Arnulf hadn't chosen only people he disliked.

Gernot complained about the porridge and cheese and black bread and almonds and salted olives they got to eat. "What's wrong with this stuff?" Leudast asked, puzzled. "Better than our rations, and that's the truth." He'd grown up eating just this sort of food.

"Boring." Gernot rolled his eyes. "Very boring." Leudast shrugged. His belly was full. He'd never found that boring.

After a few days, he might have been living back in his own village, except he didn't have to work so hard here. No one had to work so hard as a peasant, not even a soldier. The squad patrolled the surrounding countryside – they weren't far from Algarvian-occupied Forthweg – and returned to eat and rest and amuse themselves. The villagers didn't love them, but their loathing grew less overt.

Leudast liked that. Magnulf didn't. "It's like they're waiting for something to go wrong," the veteran sergeant said. "When it does . . ."

A couple of days later, it did. A Forthwegian girl stood in the village square, screaming that one of the Unkerlanter troops had forced her to lie with him. Rather to Leudast's surprise, she didn't accuse Gernot but a common soldier named Huk who'd always seemed too lazy to violate anyone. And Huk denied it now, saying she'd freely given herself to him and started screaming only when he wouldn't pay.

Knowing Huk, Magnulf ruled in his favor and did not punish him. Leudast waited for some outburst from the villagers. It didn't come. They looked to Arnulf. Arnulf stood by his doorway, dour but silent.

Two nights later, Leudast woke with cramps in his belly. So did Gernot, at just the same time. Their unwilling hosts stayed asleep, apparently well. "Are we poisoned?" Gernot whispered.

"I don't think so," Leudast whispered back. "I think we're magicked." He paused, then chuckled grimly as pieces fit together in his mind. "The firstman, or else his wife. But they'd have to be better mages than they are to break through the protections King Swemmel's soldiers get. They'll be sorry they tried, too. Come on."

The cramps pained him, but not so much that he couldn't move. He and Gernot stole out of the hut. He wasn't surprised to see other Unkerlanter soldiers coming out of the houses where they were billeted. When he saw Magnulf, he pointed toward the firstman's home. The sergeant nodded.

Behind the shutters there, a light was burning. Stick in one hand, Leudast tried the door with the other. It wasn't barred. If Arnulf and his wife were village wizards, who would dare steal from them? He threw the door wide.

Arnulf and his wife looked up in horror from where they crouched over an image – a cloth doll – in a rock-gray tunic. The firstman's wife still held a long, brass-headed pin in her hand. Her face twisted in a ghastly attempt at a smile. Arnulf knew smiles were wasted. Cursing, he threw himself at Leudast and the other Unkerlanters behind him.

Leudast blazed him down, then blazed his wife, too. He also blazed the doll, lest a stronger mage get hold of it. "That's good," Magnulf said. "That's very good."

"Aye," Leudast said. "We shouldn't have any more trouble here."

18.

Colonel Lurcanio came up to Krasta and gave her an extravagant Algarvian bow. "Milady, I am given to understand there is to be an entertainment laid on at the Viscount Valnu's this evening. Would you do me the honor of accompanying me there?"

She hesitated. However well Lurcanio spoke Valmieran, he remained one of the conquerors. She recalled all too well the feel of his hard hand against her cheek – scarcely a proper prelude to an invitation in her circle or any circle she knew. And, had any Algarvian sought to invite her, she would have preferred Captain Mosco, who was both younger and handsomer than his superior.

Still . . . Lurcanio was the more prominent of the two of them. If she turned him down, what would he do to her? *Whatever he likes* rang like a mournful bell in her mind, a bell with a nasty undertone of fear. The other side of the coin was that any entertainment at Valnu's was sure to be lavish and likely to be scandalous. She wanted to go, both to enjoy herself and to be able to hold her head up among her own set.

That decided her. With a smile the brighter for coming a beat or two late, she said, "Thank you, Colonel. I would be delighted."

Lurcanio's answering smile might have been pleased, might have been predatory, and was probably both at once. "Excellent!" he said, and bowed again. "Most excellent. Shall we meet at the front door at sunset? My driver will do the honors, the invitation being mine. He knows the way."

So Lurcanio had gone to Valnu's before, had he, and without her? Her back stiffened. She'd make sure he didn't want to do that again. She never went into anything halfheartedly. When she answered, "Till sunset, then, Colonel," her voice had a purr in it. She put a little extra in her walk as she went upstairs to primp and plan for the evening ahead. She didn't look back to see if the

Algarvian noble's eyes were following her. She knew they would be.

After bathing, after a hairdresser piled her hair into a mound of curls (an old-fashioned style suddenly popular again), she chose her outfit. The trousers of midnight velvet she put on were so tight, Bauska had to help lace them closed. "Easy, there," Kaunian wheezed. "I want to be able to breathe, a little.

"Aye, milady," Bauska said, and pulled them tighter yet. Her head was bent to the work, so Krasta did not see her smile. Krasta did admire the effect in the looking glass, which made her servant bite her lip.

The tunic Krasta chose was filmier than the nighttime one in which she had gone to upbraid Lurcanio and Mosco over the coronation of King Mezentio's brother as the new ruler of Jelgava. Then, though, the display had been inadvertent. Now it was intentional, even calculated. She wanted Lurcanio's eyes to pop.

She wanted to pick the time when they would pop, too, so she draped a short cape of glistening beaver fur over her shoulders to let her choose the moment and to protect her against the chill of the autumn evening. Snow hadn't started falling yet, but it wasn't more than a month away.

Rather knobby knees aside, Lurcanio looked dashing in dress tunic, kilt striped in his kingdom's colors, and a broad-brimmed plumed hat. He bowed over Krasta's hand, then raised it to his lips. "You are lovely this evening," he murmured. "You are, no doubt, lovely every evening, but you are particularly lovely this evening."

"I thank you," Krasta said in a smaller voice than she'd intended. The Algarvian officer could be charming when he chose. That he could also be anything but only made the charm more interesting.

Lurcanio's driver devoured Krasta with his eyes when the colonel handed her up into the carriage. Krasta expected Lurcanio to dress him down; he was impossibly forward. Instead, laughing, Lurcanio leaned forward to pat him on the shoulder and spoke to him in Algarvian. Krasta caught Valnu's name. The carriage rolled forward.

"That fellow's rude," Krasta complained.

"No." Lurcanio laughed again, and shook his head. "He is Algarvian. When it comes to pretty women, we do not hide what we think." He too looked Krasta up and down, slowly and lingeringly.

She decided she could have done without the cape, at least as far as concealment went. She was glad to have it, though; her breath smoked when she breathed out.

Valnu's house, not far from the center of Priekule, would have been classically elegant had he not painted columns and frieze in gaudy colors. He insisted that *was* good classical usage, and would wave learned articles to prove it. As far as Krasta was concerned, classical meant plain white marble, and that was that. Valnu, though, had never been one to keep his enthusiasms from running away with him.

He stood in the entrance hall, greeting guests as they arrived. When he saw Krasta, something simultaneously amused and malicious kindled in his eyes. He spoke to Colonel Lurcanio in Algarvian. Lurcanio raised an eyebrow. When he and Krasta had gone on into the main salon, he asked her, "Why did he say I should not be alone with you on a dark country road?"

"You'd better ask him that, hadn't you?" Krasta said with a toss of the head that set her curls flying. She spotted a servant watching wraps. When she shrugged off her cape, she discovered that Lurcanio hadn't imagined everything about her, not if the way his head swiveled was any sign.

Up on a platform at the back of the salon, a harpist and a couple of viol players performed one Algarvian tune after another. Used to the more emphatic rhythms of Valmieran music, Krasta wondered why anyone would bother listening to this. But Lurcanio smiled and bobbed his head in time to the songs that were so familiar to him, as did many of the other Algarvians who had come to Valnu's residence.

Looking around, Krasta saw that a lot of Algarvian officers and civilian functionaries had come to Valnu's. They outnumbered the Valmieran men there and, almost without exception, they had very pretty girls on their arms. Not all the girls, or even most of them, were of noble blood, either. Krasta knew who was. The rest . . . *Opportunists*, she thought scornfully.

They were hungry opportunists, too, converging like locusts on the buffet Valnu's servants had set out. Some of the dishes there were hearty Valmieran sausages and breaded chops and the like, others more delicate, more elaborate Algarvian-style creations. The Algarvian soldiers and civilians ate in moderation. Many of the

Valmierans gorged. Food, especially fine food like this, wasn't easy to come by in Priekule these days.

Krasta had no great interest in what the Algarvians ate, or in anything else new. Sausage and red cabbage suited her fine. After a couple of shots of sweet cherry brandy, everything Lurcanio said got wittier and funnier. When he slipped an arm around her waist in a proprietary way, she snuggled against him instead of flinging brandy in his face.

She was, by then, rather glad of that arm. It kept most of the Algarvians in the milling crowd from pinching her, patting her, and feeling her up. Not all of them, though: that she was a colonel's companion did nothing to intimidate a couple of brigadiers and more than a couple of the civilian dignitaries who ruled occupied Valmiera.

"Do your men always act this way?" she asked Lurcanio after snarling at a functionary who'd made too free with his hands and also contriving to step on his foot.

"Very often," he answered calmly. "But then, our women act much the same way. It is the custom in our kingdom – not better or worse than the customs here, simply different."

What Krasta had heard was that all Algarvian women were sluts. She started to say as much, but checked herself. She'd already seen that insulting the conquerors was not a good idea. And she'd also noted that Valnu's salon, at the moment, held a good many Valmieran sluts.

She kept looking around, spotting people she knew and seeing who among her set might have been there but was not. A lot of people, both Valmierans and Algarvians, kept looking around. Had people who weren't there simply not been invited – because they were dull, say? Or had they declined to come because they didn't care to be seen with the Algarvians? Much of the chatter was hard and brittle, a sort of crust over things better left unsaid.

A Valmieran band – thundering horns and thumping drums – replaced the musicians playing Algarvian songs. A little space cleared in the center of the large chamber. Couples began to dance. "Shall we?" Krasta asked, saucily glancing up at Lurcanio.

"And why not?" he said. He proved to dance very well, and knew the steps that went with the Valmieran music. When the time came to hold her close, he didn't try to consummate things out on the dance floor, as Valnu had in the cellar before the Algarvian invasion. Then again, Krasta wasn't egging him on, as she had with Valnu. Lurcanio acted as if he had nothing he needed to prove along those lines because everything was already decided. Krasta couldn't decide whether that miffed or excited her. Between dances, she drank more brandy. That helped make up her mind.

A lot of the Algarvians were with women who had already made up their minds. Krasta didn't see anything she hadn't seen before, but she'd seen a good deal. *They've decided who's won the war*, she thought. And if she had not, would she have been here on the arm of and in the arms of an Algarvian nobleman?

Presently, Lurcanio leaned forward and murmured in her ear: "Shall we return to your mansion? I fear I have a few too many years and a bit too much dignity to care to make a public exhibition of myself."

Krasta had drunk enough brandy to need a few seconds to realize what that meant. When she did, she hesitated, but not for long. Having gone this far, how could she stop? And she didn't want to stop, not now. She took Lurcanio's arm, reclaimed her cape, and made for the door.

Valnu stood just outside the doorway, arm in arm with a handsome young Algarvian officer. He smiled dazzlingly at Krasta and Lurcanio, then called after them: "Don't do anything I wouldn't enjoy!" As far as Krasta knew, that gave them free rein.

Lurcanio's driver smelled of brandy. He said something in Algarvian. He and Lurcanio both laughed. "He is jealous of me," Lurcanio said as he helped Krasta into the carriage. He laughed again. "He has reason to be jealous of me, I expect."

When they got back to the mansion, none of Krasta's servants was in sight. No one watched her and Lurcanio go up the stairs to her bedchamber together – or she saw no one watching, which in her mind amounted to the same thing.

In the bedchamber, Lurcanio took charge, as he had throughout the evening. He decided a lamp would remain burning. He undressed Krasta, kissing and caressing her breasts after he pulled her tunic off over her head, then unlacing her trousers and sliding them down her legs. She sighed, at least as much from relief as from desire.

But desire was there, too, and the Algarvian knew just how to fan it. Before long, Krasta was doing everything she could to inflame him, too. He was, she discovered, circumcised, which Valmieran men were not. "Rite of manhood," he said. "I was fourteen." He poised himself between her legs. "And now for another rite of manhood."

After the rite was accomplished – most enjoyably accomplished – they lay side by side. Even then, Lurcanio's hands roamed over her body. "You are generous to a soldier in a kingdom not his own," he said. "You will not be sorry."

Krasta rarely thought about being sorry. She'd never thought about it in the afterglow of lovemaking. She'd sometimes been angry then, which spoiled things, but never sorry. "Soon you Algarvians will rule the world, I think," she said, which was and was not an answer.

"And you have chosen the winning side?" Lurcanio ran his fingers through her bush. "You see? You are a practical woman after all. Good."

Even though Talsu sometimes wore his Jelgavan army uniform tunic and trousers on the streets of Skrunda, his home town, no Algarvian soldier who saw him had ever given him a rough time about it. He was glad. He did not have so many clothes as to make it easy for him to set any of them aside. Nor was he the only young man in Skrunda in pieces of uniform. That was true of most of the former soldiers the Algarvians hadn't scooped into their captives' camps.

Like his former comrades, he made money where he could, pushing a broom or carrying sacks of lentils or digging a foundation. One day, after lugging endless sacks of beans and clay jars of olive oil and sesame oil from wagons into a warehouse the Algarvians were using, he came home with half a dozen small silver coins stamped with the image of King Mezentio. They rang sweetly when he set them on the table at which his family ate.

"What have you got there?" his father demanded. Traku was a wide-shouldered man who looked as if he ought to be a tough but was in fact a tailor. His trade having left him shortsighted, he bent close to the coins to see what they were. Once he did, he growled a curse and swept them off the table and on to the floor. The cat chased one as it rolled.

"What did you go and do that for, Father?" Talsu crawled around on hands and knees till he'd found all the money. "Powers above, it's not like we're rich."

"I don't want that ugly whoreson's face in my house," his father said. "I don't want the fundament of that ugly whoreson's brother stinking up our throne, either. No redhead's got any business sitting on it. It's not their kingdom. It's ours, and they can't take it away from us."

"Silver is silver," Talsu said wearily. "Theirs spends as good as ours. Theirs spends better than ours, because they've buggered up the exchange rate so the redheaded soldiers can buy pretties for their mistresses on the cheap."

"They're thieves and robbers," Traku said. "They can keep their cursed money, and pile my curse on top of all the others that are already there."

In from the kitchen came Talsu's mother and younger sister. His mother, Laitsina, carried a bowl of stew. His sister, Ausra, had a fresh-baked loaf of bread on a tray. The bread was an unhealthy brownish-tan color, not because it hadn't been baked properly but because the flour wasn't all it might have been. Ground beans, ground peas — Talsu hoped there wasn't any sawdust mixed into it.

And the stew was more peas and beans and turnips and carrots, with only a few bits of meat here and there, more for flavor than for nourishment. Talsu wasn't all that sure he cared for the flavor it gave. "What is this stuff?" he asked, holding a bit out on his spoon.

"The butcher says it's rabbit," his mother answered. "He charges for it like it's rabbit, too."

"I haven't heard very many cats yowling on the roofs lately, though," Ausra said with a twinkle in her eye. She glanced over to the little gray tabby that had bounded after the Algarvian silverpiece. "You hear that, Dustbunny? Stick your nose outside and you're liable to be a bunny for true."

Talsu made sure his next spoonful of stew held no meat. After that, though, he ate it. If it wasn't all it might have been, the army had inured him to worse. And his mother had paid for it. With things as they were, the family couldn't afford to let anything go to waste.

His mother might have been thinking along with him, for she said, "Dear, it would be a shame not to use the silver Talsu worked so hard to get."

"It's Algarvian money," Traku said stubbornly. "I don't want Algarvian money. We should have beaten King Mezentio's men, not the other way around."

He looked at Talsu as if he thought Jelgava's defeat were his son's fault. He'd been just too young to fight in the Six Years' War, which if anything made him take its victory even more to heart than if he'd served, for he didn't know firsthand what the soldiers who'd won that victory had endured to do it.

"Well, we cursed well didn't," Talsu said — he knew what soldiering was like. "Maybe we would have, if our precious noble officers had known their brains from their backsides. I can't say one way or the other about that, because they didn't." He tore a chunk of bread off the loaf and took a big bite out of it.

Traku stared. "Those are the same lies you see on the Algarvian broadsheets all over town."

"They aren't lies," Talsu said. "I was there. I saw with my own eyes. I heard with my own ears. I'll tell you, Father, I've got no love for the redheads, and I don't think they've got any business putting a king of their own over us. If King Donalitu comes back, that'll be fine. But if the Algarvians hang every duke and count and marquis before he comes back, that'll be even better."

Close to a minute of silence followed. He hadn't tried to hide his bitterness toward the Jelgavan nobility since trudging back to Skrunda, but he hadn't been so blunt about it, either. At last, his father said, "That's treason."

"I don't care," Talsu said, which produced more silence. Into it, he went on, "And I don't think it is, not really, because the nobles don't run Jelgava any more. The Algarvians do, and I haven't said anything about them." He put the coins he'd earned back on the table. "You can have these if you want them. If you don't, I'll take them out and buy beer or wine and lemon juice."

His mother scooped up the Algarvian silver. "Laitsina!" his father said.

"It's money," his mother said. "I don't care whose face is on it. If our king comes home, I'll shout myself silly for joy. Until he comes home — and after he comes home, too — I'll spend whatever money people will take. And if you have any sense, so will you, and you'll take any money the redheads give you, too."

"That's trading with the enemy," Traku protested.

"That's making a living," Laitsina replied. "The Algarvians are here. Are we supposed to starve because they're here? That's foolishness. With the kind of food we can get nowadays, we're close enough to starving as is."

Ausra meowed, to remind Traku what sort of meat was liable to be in the stew. Her father gave her a dirty look. Talsu looked down into his bowl so Traku would not be able to see him laughing.

"Bah!" Traku said. "How can I say one thing when everyone else in my family says something else? But it's a sorry day for Jelgava – I will say that."

"That's so. It is a sorry day for Jelgava," Talsu said. "But we've had too many sorry days lately, and the Algarvians haven't given us all of them. If you don't believe me, Father, ask anybody else who was in the army and managed to come home again in one piece."

He expected the argument to boil up once more, but his father only looked disgusted. "If we'd done everything as we should have, we'd have won the war. Since we didn't win, we couldn't have done everything right." Traku settled down and ate his stew and bread and said not another word till they were gone. Even then, he talked about the coming of cooler weather and other innocuous things. Talsu concluded he'd won his point. He hadn't done that very often before going into the army.

Next morning, after bread and sesame oil and a cup of beer almost as bad as he'd had in King Donalitu's service, he went out to see what sort of work he could find for the day. During the night, the Algarvians had slapped a new set of broadsheets up on walls and fences all over Skrunda. They bore Mainardo's beaky profile – very much like his brother Mezentio's – and the legend, A KING FOR THE COMMON PEOPLE.

Seeing that slogan, Talsu slowly nodded. It wasn't the worst tack the redheads could have taken. Talsu knew how many commoners were disgusted with the Jelgavan nobility and the way the nobles, no doubt with Donalitu's approval, had governed the kingdom and botched the war.

A couple of women walking toward him along the street glanced at one of the broadsheets. She turned to her friend and said, "That might not be so bad, if only he weren't a redhead."

"Oh, aye, you're right," the other woman said. After casually passing judgment, they strode past Talsu, intent on their own affairs.

He turned the corner, heading for the market square. A crowd of half a dozen or so had gathered in front of another broadsheet. A man a little older than Talsu's father who leaned on a cane said, "If we cursed King Donalitu, we'd wind up in his dungeons. Anybody think that, if we curse this new stinking whoreson the redheads have foisted on us, we won't wind up in an Algarvian dungeon?"

Nobody told him he was crazy. A woman with a basket full of green and yellow squashes said, "I'll bet the Algarvians have even worse dungeons than we do, too." Nobody argued with her, either. Like everyone else who heard her, Talsu took it for granted that, however fierce King Donalitu's inquisitors were, those of the redheads would have no trouble outdoing them.

In the market square, a farmer was unloading big yellow wheels of cheese. "Give you a hand with those?" Talsu called: the fellow was taking them off a good-sized bullock cart.

"I suppose you'll want one for yourself if I say aye," the farmer answered, pausing with hands on hips.

"Either that or the price of one in coin," Talsu said. "Fair's fair. I'm not trying to steal from you, friend; I'm trying to work for you."

"You're a townman. What do you know about work?" The farmer tossed his head so that the flat leather cap he wore almost flew off. But then he shrugged. "You want to show me what you know about, come do it."

"I thank you," Talsu said, and sprang into action. He got the cheeses down from the wagon, stacked them on the burlap mat the farmer had already spread on the cobbles, and set a few of the best ones standing upright so customers could see how fine they were. That done, he told the farmer, "You ought to have a sign you could fasten to the side of the cart there, so people could see it all the way across the square."

"A sign?" The farmer shook his head now. "Don't much fancy such newfangled notions." But then he rubbed his chin. "It might draw folks, though, eh?"

"Like a bowl of honey draws flies," Talsu said solemnly.

"Maybe," the farmer said at last — no small concession from a man of his sort. "Well, pick yourself a cheese, townman. You earned it, I

will say." He dug in his pocket. "And here you are." He handed
Talsu a silver coin: a Jelgavan minting, not one with Mezentio's face
on it. "That for your idea. Fair's fair, like you said."

"I thank you," Talsu said again, and tucked it away. He knew just
which cheese he wanted, too – a fine round one, golden as the full
moon rising. He carried it back to his family's home.

When he returned to the market square, he discovered half a dozen
Algarvian soldiers making off with a large part of the farmer's stock in
trade. They were laughing and chattering in their own language as they
hauled away the cheeses. The farmer could only stand and stare, furious
but helpless. "Shame!" somebody called, but no one said or did
anything more.

Several copies of the broadsheet with King Mainardo's profile on
it looked out over the square. Maybe the Algarvian-imposed king
was for the common people, as the broadsheets claimed. The
Algarvian soldiers looked to be out for themselves and themselves
alone. Somehow, Talsu was not surprised.

Putting a crook in Skarnu's hands no more made him a shepherd
than putting a hoe in his hands had made him a proper cultivator.
Gedominu's sheep seemed to sense his inexperience, too. They
strayed much more for him than they did for the farmer. So he was
convinced, at any rate.

"Come back, curse you!" he growled at a yearling. When the
yearling didn't come back, he trotted after it and got the crook
around its neck. It bleated irately when brought up short. He didn't
care. He wanted it back with the rest of the small flock, and he got
what he wanted.

A couple of Algarvians rode unicorns down the road along the
edge of the meadow. One of them waved to Skarnu. He lifted the
crook in reply. The redheads kept on riding. They took Raunu and
him for granted these days. The two Valmieran soldiers – two farm
laborers, they were now – had been working for Gedominu as long
as the redheads had occupied this district. No one, yet, had bothered
letting the Algarvians know Skarnu and Raunu were as much
newcomers as they were themselves. With luck, no one would.

Gedominu came limping out towards Skarnu. He glanced at the
flock. "Well, you've not lost any of 'em," he said. "That's pretty fair."

"Aye, could be worse," Skarnu said, and the farmer nodded. Skarnu did his best, these days, to talk in understatements, to make himself fit in with the people among whom he was living. That did even more to make him seem to belong than imitating their rustic accent. When he'd first tried that, he'd laid it on too thick, so that he'd sounded more like a performer in a bad show than a true man of the countryside. As with spies, a little of the local dialect served better than a lot would have done.

"Come have a bite of supper," Gedominu said: understatement again. "Then we'll look for some more fun." That was also an understatement, of a slightly different sort.

Together, Skarnu and Gedominu chivvied the sheep back toward the pen where they would spend the night. Gedominu accomplished more without a crook than Skarnu with one. But neither had much trouble, for the animals went willingly enough. They knew grain would be waiting for them, to supplement what nourishment they got from the dwindling grass of the meadows.

Up on the barn roof, Raunu was hammering new shingles into places; rain a few days before had revealed some leaks. With carpenter's tools in his hands, the veteran sergeant looked far more at home than he did when he had to try to deal with crops or livestock.

"Come down," Gedominu called to him as Skarnu closed the gate to the pen after getting the last ewe inside. "Come down and eat a bite, and then we'll go play." He chuckled under his breath. "And we'll see how the redheads like the game."

"Not much, I hope," Raunu said as he descended from the roof. He took the hammer and nails into the barn. When he came out, he nodded to the farmer and to Skarnu. "I could eat a little something, I suppose." He hadn't needed long to master the art of understatement, either, though it was one for which a sergeant normally found but little use.

Inside the farmhouse, Merkela nodded to her husband and to Skarnu and Raunu. "Sit yourselves down," she said. "Won't be but a little bit."

Gedominu paused briefly to kiss her as he headed for the table. Skarnu looked away. He was jealous of the farmer, and did not want Gedominu to know it. Once, getting up from his bed of straw in the barn, he'd gone outside to make water just as a cry of delight from

Merkela came floating out of the upstairs bedroom she shared with her husband. So fiercely had Skarnu wished he'd been the one to make her cry out that way, he'd slept very little all the rest of the night.

Every once in a while, out of the corner of his eye, he caught her watching him, too. He hadn't done anything about it; that would have been a poor return for Gedominu, who could have handed him over to King Mezentio's soldiers and hadn't. But he could not – or maybe he simply didn't want to – get her out of his mind.

She brought in a tray from the kitchen. On it sat four wooden bowls of stew: beans and peas and onions and cabbage, simmered along with chunks of pork sausage she'd made herself. Farm work turned a man ravenous. Suppers like this one fought hunger the way fresh shingles on the roof fought rain.

Darkness fell early, and fell hard. Merkela got a twig burning at the fireplace and used it to light a couple of oil lamps. No power points, no ley lines close to the farm: no sorcerous light to hold night at bay. Farmers in the days of the Kaunian Empire had lit their homes like this. Skarnu had been used to better; Krasta, no doubt, still was. By now, he took lamps for granted.

After spooning up the last of his stew, Gedominu said, "Night's our time. Shall we be about it?"

"We'd better," Skarnu said. "If we don't, we aren't fighting the Algarvians, just knuckling under to them."

"Aye," Gedominu said. "They'd have been smarter if they hadn't popped Count Enkuru's son into his slot, for the brat's a nasty piece of work in his own right."

"Better for us this way," Raunu said. "If they'd put in somebody decent, fewer people would want to go on fighting them."

Gedominu nodded. "That's so, I reckon. But not a whole lot of folks in these parts love the redheads. Not like that in some of the bigger towns, the way the news sheets go on."

"And who says what goes into the news sheets?" Skarnu asked, though what Gedominu had said worried him, too. As if to force that worry behind him, he turned and started for the door.

"Come back safe, all of you," Merkela said. Skarnu hurried out into the night. To him, her voice was as sweet and intoxicating as a Jelgavan fortified wine. If he thought about what he was going to be doing out in the woods, he wouldn't think – so much – about what he wished he were doing up in her bedchamber.

He and Raunu and Gedominu got their sticks out from under the straw in the barn. The farmer looped a long coil of rope over his left shoulder and passed other coils to his comrades. "Let's go have ourselves some fun," he said, and chuckled. "Don't suppose the Algarvians will like it so well, though."

"Pox take 'em," Raunu said, at which Skarnu and Gedominu nodded.

Once they got off Gedominu's farm, the three men separated. Because he'd dwelt in these parts since the collapse of the Valmieran army, Skarnu had come to know the paths for several miles around the farm. Gedominu still knew them better, of course; to him, they were as familiar as the way upstairs in his own home. They weren't to Skarnu, and never would be. But he could make his way along them without the farmer, even in the darkness.

As he knew Gedominu and Raunu were doing, he made for the woods. Despite the stick he carried, he felt more like hunted than hunter. If an Algarvian patrol caught sight of him, he intended to run first and fight only if he had to. That wasn't heroic, but he hadn't come out here to be a hero. He'd come to be a nuisance, a role with a different set of requirements.

When he found a couple of trees near the edge of the path, he nodded to himself. He tied one end of the rope to the trunk of one tree, then ran it across the road to the other. He tied it to that one, too, cut off the length of rope, and went on his way looking for another spot to set a trip line.

If he was lucky, an Algarvian horse or unicorn would break a leg and have to be put out of its misery. If he was luckier, an Algarvian might break his leg or, if Skarnu was luckier still, his neck. At best, it would be a pinprick against King Mezentio's forces. If harassing the redheads was the best Skarnu could do right now, though, he would content himself with the knowledge that it *was* his best.

He chose where to place his trip lines with several different kinds of care. As many as possible went on land belonging to farmers friendly toward the Algarvians. If he got those farmers into trouble with the occupiers, so much the better: they wouldn't stay friendly toward them for long. And if the Algarvians blamed men who really were well inclined toward them, they wouldn't look so hard for people who weren't.

After Skarnu used the last of the rope, he made his way back toward Gedominu's farm. He was surprised at how confidently he moved in the dark. Once, not too far away, he heard some Algarvians on horseback. He slid off the path and into the bushes. The Algarvians hadn't heard him. On routine patrol, they chattered among themselves. Their noise faded and finally vanished.

A lamp was still burning downstairs when Skarnu got back to the farm. He glanced that way, sighed, and opened the barn door so he could roll himself in his blanket there. He must have made some noise, for the door to the farmhouse opened, too. Merkela stood silhouetted against the light within. Softly, she called, "Who is it?"

"Me," Skarnu answered, just loud enough to let her recognize his voice.

"You are the first one back," she said. "Come inside and drink a cup of hot spiced ale, if you care to."

"I thank you," he said, and had all he could do not to run to her side. When she gave him the ale, he held the big mug in both hands, warming them against the earthenware. He sat at the table where he'd eaten supper, sipping slowly. The ale was good. Watching Merkela was better. He didn't say anything. Had he said anything, the first words out of his mouth would have been too much.

In the dim light, her eyes were enormous. She kept watching him, too, and not saying anything. At last, she took a deep breath. "I think—" she began. The door opened. In came Gedominu, Raunu only a couple of paces behind him. "I think," Merkela went on smoothly, "I will pour some more ale." Whatever else she might have thought, she kept to herself. *Likely just as well,* Skarnu thought, and wished he could make himself believe it.

A few days later, two squads of Algarvian soldiers tramped up to the farm at first light. In fair Valmieran, the lieutenant leading them said. "We want the peasant Gedominu." He read the name from a list.

"I am Gedominu," the farmer said quietly. "Why do you want me?"

"As hostage," the lieutenant answered. "A warrior of King Mezentio's was killed by a trip line. We take ten for one, to keep this

foolishness from happening more. You come." His soldiers leveled
their sticks at Gedominu. "If the one who did this does not yield, we
kill you."

Skarnu stepped forward. "Take me instead." The words came out
of his mouth before he quite knew they would.

"You are brave," the Algarvian lieutenant said, and surprised him
by sweeping off his hat and bowing from the waist. "But his name is
on my paper. Your name is not. And so we take him. You and your
wife" – his eyes lingered on Merkela, as any man's might have; he did
not know the mistake he was making – "can keep this farm going
without two old men here. One will do." He waved toward Raunu
to show which old man he meant, then spoke to his men in their own
language.

A couple of them seized Gedominu and hustled him away. The
rest kept Skarnu and Raunu and Merkela so well covered that any try
at rescuing the farmer would have been suicide. Off the redheads
went, Gedominu limping along in their midst. Skarnu stared
helplessly after them. They had the right man and didn't even know
it. They didn't care, either. They would have been just as happy to
blaze him had he been the wrong man.

Count Sabrino had never imagined he could enjoy victory so
much. After Valmiera was vanquished, after Jelgava yielded, he'd
been ordered back to Trapani. All the civilians there were sure the
results of the Six Years' War had been overthrown forever, and that
peace would soon be at hand.

"How can Lagoas go on fighting us?" If Sabrino heard that once,
he heard it a hundred times. "Derlavai is ours."

Lagoan dragons still dropped eggs on southern Valmiera and
Algarve. Lagoan warships still raided the coasts of Valmiera and
Jelgava. It was still war, but it was war by fleabites. And Algarve could
inflict no more than fleabites on Lagoas, either. Sabrino knew that,
whether civilians did or not. He never tried to change their minds.
Much of what he knew, he could not speak about. Even if he could
have, he wouldn't. Pretty women were much likelier to throw
themselves at the feet of a man who had conquered than one in the
process of conquering.

One of the things Sabrino knew was that crushing the Kaunian kingdoms did not mean Derlavai belonged to Algarve. He could read a map. So could a great many civilians, of course. But he did it habitually, as part of his duties. More and more these days, he found himself looking west.

Invitations to the royal palace frequently came his way. He would have been insulted had it been otherwise. Not only was he a noble, he was also an officer who had distinguished himself in three of Algarve's four fights thus far. And so he would don his fanciest uniform tunic and kilt, put on every glittering decoration and badge of rank to which he was entitled, and swagger off to dance and drink and talk and display himself. He seldom came home alone.

He also went to the palace to listen to King Mezentio. Mezentio fascinated him, as the king fascinated most Algarvians. Unlike the vast majority of his countrymen, who could at most occasionally hear the king when he spoke by way of the crystal, Sabrino got to speak with him as well as listen. He took as much advantage of that as he could.

"It comes down to a matter of will," Mezentio declared one chilly evening. He waved a goblet of hot brandy punch to emphasize his point. "Algarve refused to admit herself defeated after the Six Years' War, and so, in the end, she was not defeated. She was split up, she was in part occupied, she was robbed – and she was forced to sign a treating declaring all this was good, all this was as it should have been. But defeated? Never! Not in her heart! Not in your hearts, my friends." He gestured again, this time in scorn of anyone who could think otherwise.

A marquis clapped his hands. A couple of young women dropped the king curtsies, hoping to make him notice them. He did notice them; Sabrino watched his eyes. But his mind was elsewhere – still on what he had caused his kingdom to do, not on what he might be doing himself.

"What next, your Majesty?" Sabrino asked. "Now that we have come this far, what next?"

He didn't know how much King Mezentio would say. He didn't know whether the king would say anything. One of Mezentio's advisers plucked at his sleeve. Mezentio shrugged the man off. Smiling at Sabrino, he replied, "When we commence, my lord count, the world will hold its breath and make no comment!"

"What does he mean?" one of the young women murmured to the

other. The second woman shrugged, a gesture worth watching. Sabrino watched it. So did King Mezentio. Their eyes met. They both smiled.

And then Mezentio's smile changed from the one any Algarvian man might give after watching a pretty girl to one of a different sort, one of complicity. He asked, "Are you answered, my lord count?"

Sabrino bowed. "Your Majesty, I am answered." He knew enough to draw his own conclusions from the little more the king gave him. Around him, those who knew less looked puzzled. Some of them looked resentful because Sabrino plainly could see things they could not.

"What did he mean?" one of the young women asked the dragonflier.

"I'm sorry, my sweet, but I can't tell you," he answered. She pouted. Sabrino still said nothing. She was plainly unused to not getting her way. When she realized she wouldn't this time, she poked him in the ribs with an elbow as she flounced away. He laughed, which only made her strides longer and angrier.

"You are a wicked man," Mezentio said.

"I must be," Sabrino agreed dryly.

"Oh, you are, never fear," Mezentio said with a chuckle. "A wicked, wicked man." Then the smile faded from his face like water flowing out of a copper tub. "But you are not so wicked as the Kaunians, who provoked this war in the first place and have now begun to pay the price for their arrogant folly."

"Begun? I should say so, your Majesty," Sabrino exclaimed. "King Gainibu doing whatever we tell him in Valmiera, King Donalitu fled and your own brother on the throne in Jelgava – oh, what a great wailing and gnashing of teeth that must cause the blonds. I don't know what higher price they could pay, as a matter of fact."

"They have only begun." Mezentio's voice went flat and harsh, the voice of a king who would brook no contradiction. "For a thousand years – for more than a thousand years – they have sneered at us, laughed behind their hands at us, looked down their noses at us. I say that will never happen again. From this war forth, from this day forth, whenever Kaunians think of Algarvians, they shall think of us with fear and trembling in their hearts."

He'd spoken louder and louder, until at the end he might almost have been addressing a crowd of thousands gathered in the Royal Square. All over the salon, other conversations fell silent. When Mezentio finished, people burst into applause. Sabrino clapped with everybody else. "We've owed the Kaunians for a long time," he said. "I'm glad we're paying them back."

"We have owed most of our neighbors for a long time, my lord count," King Mezentio said. "We shall pay them back, too." As Sabrino had done from time to time, he turned and looked toward the west.

"Can it be done, your Majesty?" Sabrino asked quietly.

"If you doubt it, sir, I invite you to return to your estate and leave the doing to those who have no doubts," Mezentio said, and Sabrino's ears burned. The king continued, "We have only to kick in the door and the whole rotten structure will come crashing down."

Sabrino stared. A couple of high-ranking officers had used those very words not long after Forthweg fell. Then, Sabrino had had no way of knowing what they were talking about. Now, a good many rotten structures already having come crashing down, he could see only one still standing. How long, he suddenly wondered, had Mezentio been preparing for the day when war would break out again? The Kaunian kingdoms had declared war on Algarve, but Algarve was the kingdom that had been ready to fight.

Sabrino raised his goblet high. "To his Majesty!" he exclaimed.

Everyone drank. Not to drink a toast to the king of Algarve would have been unthinkable. But Mezentio's hazel eyes glinted as he acknowledged the honor Sabrino and the salon full of notables had done him. He studied the dragonflier, then slowly nodded. Sabrino was convinced the king knew what he was thinking, and was telling him he was right. Asking any more would have been asking Mezentio to say too much. Mezentio might already have said too much, for those with ears to hear.

Not everyone had such ears. Sabrino had already insulted one pretty girl close to the king by not explaining what she thought she had the right to know. The other young woman there did not ask him to enlighten her. Instead, she chose an official from the ministry of finance. The fellow was plainly flattered to gain her attentions, but as plainly understood no more of what Mezentio had said and what he'd implied than she did.

Laughing a little to himself, Sabrino slipped off toward a sideboard and took another glass of wine. The pleasure that filled him, though, had little to do with what he'd drunk and what he was drinking. As Mezentio had done, he looked west. Slowly, he nodded. Algarve had been a long time finding her place in the sun. All her neighbors had tried to hold her down, hold her back. Once the Derlavaian War came to a proper end, though, they wouldn't be able to do that any more.

Never again, Sabrino thought, echoing Mezentio. He was old enough to remember the humiliation and the chaos that followed the loss of the Six Years' War. *Never again*, he thought once more. Victory was better. Whatever victory required, he wanted Algarve to do.

You can't make war halfheartedly, he thought. As if that needed proving, Valmiera and Jelgava had proved it to the hilt. And now, as King Mezentio had said, they were paying the price. Well, Algarve had paid. It was their turn.

Someone not far away shouted angrily. Sabrino turned his head. A Yaninan in shoes with decorative pompoms, tights, and a puffy-sleeved tunic was waving his finger in an Algarvian's face. "You are wrong, I tell you!" the Yaninan said. "I tell you, I was up by the Raffali River myself last week, and the weather was sunny – warm and sunny."

"You are mistaken, sir," the Algarvian said. "It rained. It rained nearly every day – quite spoiled the horseback ride I had planned."

"You call me a liar at your peril," the Yaninan said; his folk took slights even more seriously than Algarvians did.

"I do not call you a liar," the redheaded noble replied with a yawn. "A senile fool who cannot recall today what happened yesterday: that, most assuredly. But not a liar."

With a screech, the Yaninan flung his drink in the Algarvian's face. Among Algarvians, their friends would have made arrangements for them to meet again. The Yaninan was too impatient to wait. He hit his foe in the belly, and then a glancing blow off the side of his head.

The Algarvian grappled with him, pulled him down, and started pummeling him. The Yaninan didn't like that so well, as his foe was about half again as big as he was. By the time Sabrino and the other men pulled the Algarvian off him, he was more than a little worse for wear.

"You would be well advised to learn some manners," the Algarvian told him.

"You would be well advised to—" the Yaninan began as he climbed to his feet.

"Shall I give you another lesson on why you would be well advised to learn manners?" the Algarvian asked, as politely as if he were offering another glass of brandy punch rather than another punch in the eye. The Yaninan did not lack spirit, but he didn't altogether lack sense, either. Instead of starting up the fight again, he took himself elsewhere.

Sabrino bowed to the Algarvian victor, saying, "Well done, sir. Well done."

"You do me too much honor." His countryman returned the bow. "All these westerners – if you take a firm line with them, they are yours to command."

"Aye." Sabrino laughed. "That is the way of it, sure enough."

Marshal Rathar strolled through King Swemmel Square, which was said to be the largest paved-over open space in the world. He had no idea whether that was true, or whether everything associated with King Swemmel had to be the biggest or the most of whatever it was simply because of its association with the king. He wondered whether anyone had actually measured all the great plazas of the world and compared them one to another. Then he wondered why he worried his head about such unimportant things. It wasn't as if he had not important things about which to worry.

A wind howling up from the south blew little flurries of snow into his face. He pulled his cloak more tightly around him, and tugged the hood down low on his forehead. The cloak was the rock-gray of Unkerlanter army issue, but, unlike the long tunic beneath it, did not show his rank. Thus swaddled, he could have been anyone. He enjoyed his few minutes of anonymity. All too soon, he would have to return to the palace, return to his work, return to the knowledge that King Swemmel might order him dragged off to the headsman at any time.

Statues of past Unkerlanter kings, some in stone, some in bronze, marked the outer boundary of the square. One statue towered twice as tall as any of the others. Rathar did not need to glance at it to know it was made in King Swemmel's image. Swemmel's successor would no doubt knock it down. Maybe he would replace it with one to match the others in size. Maybe, having knocked it down, Swemmel's successor would not replace it at all.

Under the shielding hood, Rathar shook his head. He might have been a man bedeviled by gnats, but no gnats could withstand Cottbus's winter weather. No, he knew what he was: a man bedeviled by his own thoughts. Those were harder to shake off than gnats, and more dangerous, too.

He sighed. "I had better get back to it," he muttered. If he buried himself in work, he would not – he hoped he would not – have much time to think about King Swemmel the man even as he carried out the orders of King Swemmel the sovereign.

He turned back toward the palace. As he did so, a couple of other men in nondescript rock-gray cloaks who had also been walking through King Swemmel Square turned in the same direction. Not enough other people were abroad in the square to let them disguise their movements, try as they would.

Rathar laughed. The wind tore apart the puff of vapor that burst from his mouth. He'd been a fool to imagine he could stay anonymous even for a few minutes.

Inside the palace, he took off the cloak at once, draping it over his arm. As if to make up for the savage weather outside, Unkerlanters commonly heated their dwellings and workplaces beyond the comfortable.

Major Merovec saluted him when he came into the office. "My lord Marshal, a gentleman from the foreign ministry has been waiting to see you," his adjutant said. As usual, Merovec's voice and face revealed little.

"And what does he want?" Rathar asked.

"Sir, he says he will discuss that only with you." Merovec wasn't shy about letting the marshal know what he thought of that: it infuriated him.

"Then I'd better see him, hadn't I?" Rathar said mildly.

"I will get him, sir," Merovec said. "I did not wish to leave him alone in your private office." He'd probably found a broom closet for the foreign ministry official instead, if the gleam in his eye was any sign. That gleam still there, he hurried away.

When he returned, sure enough, he had an angry official with him. "Marshal, this man of yours has not granted me the deference due the deputy foreign minister of Unkerlant," the fellow snapped.

"My lord Ibert, I am sure he only sought to keep secrets from spreading," Rathar replied. "My aides can sometimes be more zealous on my behalf than I would be were I here in person."

Ibert kept on glaring at Merovec, who might have been carved from stone. The deputy foreign minister muttered under his breath, but then said, "Very well, my lord Marshal, I will let it go – this time. Now that you are here in person, shall we closet ourselves together to keep secrets from spreading?" He kept an eye on Merovec: he wanted his own back.

And Rathar could not refuse him. "As you wish, my lord," he said. "If you will do me the honor of accompanying me . . ." He led Ibert into his private office, closing the door behind them. The last he saw of the outside world was Merovec's face. He knew he would have to make things right with his adjutant, but that could wait. He nodded to the deputy foreign minister. "And for what reason have we closeted ourselves together here?"

Ibert pointed to the map behind Rathar's desk. "My lord Marshal, when we go to war against Algarve come spring, are we prepared to defend ourselves against a Zuwayzi attack from the north?"

Rathar turned to the map himself. Pins with colored heads showed concentrations of Unkerlanter soldiers and, somewhat less certainly, those of Algarve and Yanina. Almost all the gold-headed pins that represented Unkerlant's war-ready forces were near the kingdom's eastern border. The marshal clicked his tongue between his teeth. "Not so well as we might be, my lord," he answered. "If we are to beat the redheads, I have no doubt we shall need every man we can scrape up." He looked back to Ibert. "You are telling me we should prepare for such a misfortune, aren't you?"

"I am," Ibert said flatly. "Our spies and his Majesty's minister in Bishah report there can be no doubt that Zuwayza and Algarve are conspiring against us."

Sighing, Rathar tried to seem more surprised than he was. "That is too bad," he said, and marveled at how large an understatement he could pack into four short words. Another of King Swemmel's pigeons had come home to roost – and had shit on the windowsill as it flew in. Had Rathar been wearing King Shazli's shoes (all Shazli was in the habit of wearing), he would have thought about avenging himself on Unkerlant, too.

"What do you propose to do about this?" Ibert demanded, sounding almost as petulant as his sovereign.

However petulant he sounded, it was the right question. Rathar said, "Since you assure me we do need to ready ourselves to meet this danger, I shall consult with my officers and develop a plan to do so. My immediate response" – he glanced at the map again – "is not to worry a great deal."

"How not?" Ibert said. "The Zuwayzin were a thorn in our side during our last fight against them. Why should they prove any different now?"

Patiently, Rathar answered, "During the last war, they fought on the defensive. The going is usually harder when one attacks. And, even if the black men should win some early successes – if you will pardon my bluntness, my lord, so what?"

Ibert's eyes almost bugged out of his head. "'So what,' my lord Marshal? Is that all you care for the soil of Unkerlant, that you would let the naked savages of the north seize it for their own?"

"Seizing it is one thing," Rathar answered. "Keeping it is another. With the worst will in the world toward us, the Zuwayzin cannot go far beyond the borders they had before we forced them back a year ago. They have not the men, the behemoths, or the dragons to do more."

"That would be quite bad enough," Ibert said.

"Would it?" Rathar asked. "If we weaken the force with which we fight Algarve, we shall surely regret it, because it will mean we are less likely to beat the redheads. Once we have beaten the Algarvians, though, how can Zuwayza hope to stand alone against us?"

He studied Ibert. The man had held his post for some time, no mean achievement under King Swemmel. The easiest way to do so, though, was to do nothing but mirror the king's thoughts and desires. Rathar waited to discover whether the deputy foreign minister had any thoughts of his own.

Ibert licked his lips. "Suppose you take no troops from the

Algarvians, and they and the Zuwayzin defeat us anyhow?"

That was a very good question. Rathar wished Swemmel would ask such questions from time to time. So Ibert did have wits of his own: something worth knowing. The marshal said, "If that should happen – which the powers above prevent – it will be the redheads who beat us, not the black men. I would not wish to move soldiers away from the stronger foe to ward myself against the weaker."

"That strikes me as a reasonable reply, my lord Marshal," Ibert said. "I shall bear your words to his Majesty."

And if Swemmel threw a tantrum and ordered an all-out assault on Zuwayza instead of the attack on Algarve . . . Rathar would obey him, and would obey him with a small sigh of relief. He did not relish the prospect of assailing King Mezentio's men. He would have obeyed an order to attack Zuwayza with a large sigh of relief rather than a small one had he not begun to worry that the Algarvians were also contemplating an attack on Unkerlant.

But when he mentioned that to Ibert, the deputy foreign minister shook his head. "We've seen little evidence of it, aside from the attempted seduction of Zuwayza. Our ministries otherwise report unusually cordial relations with the redheads, in fact."

"We are not the only ones moving soldiers toward our common border," Rathar insisted.

"Neither the foreign ministry nor the king views these movements with alarm," Ibert said. "His Majesty is confident we shall enjoy the advantages of surprise when the blow falls in the east."

"Very well," Rathar said, somewhat reassured. Swemmel saw conspiracies all around him. If he did not think the Algarvians suspected anything here, then the chance that they truly did not seemed pretty good to the marshal of Unkerlant. Of course, Swemmel had made mistakes before – about Rathar himself, for instance – but the marshal chose not to dwell on those.

Besides, Rathar told himself, *then Swemmel was seeing danger where none existed. He wouldn't miss danger where it truly lurked . . . would he?*

Ibert said, "Submit to his Majesty a formal plan based on what you have discussed with me. I believe he will accept it."

Rathar hoped the deputy foreign minister was right. King Swemmel, though, had an enormous attachment to Unkerlanter territory. Would he be willing to yield any, even temporarily, to gain more? The marshal had his doubts. He wished he were free of them, but he wasn't. Still, he could only say, "He will have it before the week is out." What he did with it . . . Whatever he did with it, the sooner he did it, the more time Rathar would have to try to set things to rights again.

Ibert departed, looking pleased with himself. He looked even more pleased as he strutted past Merovec. Rathar's adjutant looked as if he wanted to see the deputy foreign minister shipped off to some distant village to keep a crystal going. As best he could, Rathar soothed Merovec's ruffled feathers. That was part of his job, too.

"Come on," Ealstan said to Sidroc. "New semester today. New masters. Maybe we'll get some decent ones, for a change."

"Fat chance," his cousin answered, as usual dawdling over his breakfast porridge. "Only difference will be new hands breaking switches on our backs."

"All right, then," Ealstan said. "Maybe we'll have a bunch of old men who can't hit very hard."

As he'd hoped it would, that made Sidroc smile, even if it didn't make him eat any faster. After a swig of watered wine, Sidroc said, "Curse me if I know why we bother with school, anyhow. Your brother had a ton of it, and what's he doing? Roadbuilding, that's what. You could train a mountain ape to put cobblestones in place."

Leofsig had already gone off to labor on the roads. "He would be helping my father, if it weren't for the war," Ealstan said. "Things can't stay crazy forever." Even as he said that, though, he wondered why not.

So did Sidroc. "Says who?" he replied, and Ealstan had no good answer. Sidroc got to his feet. "Well, come on. You're so eager, let's go."

They both threw cloaks over their tunics. Snow didn't fall in Gromheort more than about one winter in four, but mornings were chilly anyhow. So Ealstan thought, at any rate; maybe someone from the south of Unkerlant would have had a different opinion.

Ealstan was soon glad they had started out with time to spare, for they had to wait at a street corner while a regiment of Algarvian footsoldiers tramped by heading west. They weren't men from Gromheort's garrison; they kept looking around and exclaiming at the buildings – and at the good-looking women – they saw. Ealstan found he could understand quite a bit of their chatter. Master Agmund had a heavy hand with the switch, but he'd made his scholars learn.

At last, the redheads passed. Sidroc moved at a brisk clip after that. He didn't like getting beaten. The trouble was, most of the time he didn't like doing the things that kept him from getting beaten, either.

"We're here in good time." Ealstan knew he sounded surprised, but couldn't help himself.

"Aye, we are," his cousin answered, "and what does it get us? Not a cursed thing but the chance to queue up for the registrar."

He was right. A long line of boys already snaked out of the office. Ealstan said, "We'd be even farther back if we were later." Sidroc snorted. Ealstan's cheeks heated. It had been a weak comeback, and he knew it.

Little by little, the line advanced. More boys took their places behind Ealstan and Sidroc. Ealstan liked that. It didn't change how many boys were in front of him, but he wasn't a tailender any more.

As he got nearer to the registrar's office, he heard voices raised in anger. "What's going on?" he asked the fellow in front of him.

"I don't know," the youth said. "They're only letting in one at a time, and people aren't coming out this way." He shrugged. "We'll find out pretty soon, I guess."

"Something's going on." Sidroc spoke with authority. "This isn't how they did things last semester, and that means they're up to something. I wonder what." His nose quivered, as if he were one of the dogs some rich nobles trained to hunt truffles and other extra-fancy mushrooms.

Ealstan wouldn't have figured that out so quickly, but saw at once that his cousin was likely to be right. Sidroc had a gift for spotting the underhanded. Ealstan preferred not to wonder what else that said about him.

"It's an outrage, I tell you," the youth in the registrar's office shouted. Ealstan leaned forward, trying to hear what kind of reply the scholar got. Whatever it was, it was too soft for him to make out. He slammed a fist into the side of his thigh in frustration.

Before long, the fellow in front of him in the queue went inside. Now Ealstan could hear whatever happened. But nothing happened.

The scholar got his list of classes and didn't say a word about it. "Next!" the registrar called.

Ealstan was in front of Sidroc, so he went in. The registrar looked up at him over a pair of half glasses. Having gone through this twice a year for a good many years, Ealstan knew what was expected of him. "Master, I am Ealstan son of Hestan," he said. He didn't think anyone at the school shared his name, but ritual required that he give his father's name, too, and sticking to ritual was as important in registration as in sorcery. The registrar thought so, anyhow, and his was the only opinion that counted.

"Ealstan son of Hestan," he repeated, as if he'd never heard the name before. But his fingers belied that; they sorted through piles of paper with amazing speed and sureness. The registrar plucked out the couple of sheets that had to do with Ealstan. Glancing at one, he said, "Your fees were paid in full at the beginning of the year."

"Aye, Master," Ealstan answered with quiet pride. In spite of everything, his father did better than most in Gromheort.

"Here are your courses, then." The registrar thrust the other sheet of paper at Ealstan. Did he wince as he did so? For a moment, Ealstan thought he was imagining things. Then he remembered the shouts and arguments he'd heard. Maybe he wasn't.

He looked at the list. The Algarvian language, history of Algarve, something called nature of Kaunianity . . . "What's this?" he asked, pointing to it.

"New requirement," the registrar said, which was less informative than Ealstan would have liked. By the set of the man's chin, though, it was all he intended to say on the subject.

With a mental shrug, Ealstan glanced down the rest of the list: Forthwegian language and grammar, Forthwegian literature, and choral singing. "Where's the rest of it?" he asked. "Where's the stonelore? Where's the ciphering?"

"Those courses are no longer being offered," the registrar said, and braced himself, as if for a blow.

"What?" Ealstan stared. "Why not? What's the point of school, if not to learn things?" He sounded very much like his father, though he didn't fully realize it.

By the look on the registrar's face, he didn't want to answer. But he did, and in a way that relieved him of all responsibility: "Those courses are no longer offered, by order of the occupying authorities."

"They can't do that!" Ealstan exclaimed.

"They can. They have," the registrar said. "The headmaster has protested, but he can do no more than protest. And you, young sir, can do no more than go out that door yonder so I can deal with the next scholar in line."

Ealstan could have done more. He could have pitched a fit, as several of his schoolmates had done before him. But he was too shocked. Numbly, he went out through the door at which the registrar had jerked his thumb. He stood in the hallway, staring down at the class list in his hand. He wondered what his father would say on seeing it. Something colorful and memorable, he had no doubt.

Sidroc came through the door less than a minute later. Smiles wreathed his face. "By the powers above, it's going to be a pretty good semester," he said. "Only hard course they've stuck me with is Algarvian."

"Let's see your list," Ealstan said. His cousin handed him the paper. His eyes flicked down it. "It's the same as mine, all right."

"Isn't it fine?" Sidroc looked about to dance for joy. "For once in my life, I won't feel like my brains are trying to dribble out my ears when I do the work."

"We *should* be taking the harder courses, though," Ealstan said. "You know why we're not, don't you?" Sidroc shook his head. Ealstan muttered something his cousin fortunately did not hear. Aloud, he went on, "We're not taking them because the redheads won't let us take them, that's why."

"Huh?" Sidroc scratched his head. "Why should the Algarvians care whether we take stonelore or not? *I* care, on account of I know how hard it is, but what difference does it make to the Algarvians?"

"Have I told you lately you're a blockhead?" Ealstan asked. Sidroc wasn't, not in all ways, but he'd missed the boat here. Before he could get angry, Ealstan went on, "They want us to be stupid. They want us to be ignorant. They want us not to know things. You don't see Forthwegian history on this list, do you? If we don't know about the days of King Felgild, when Forthweg was the greatest kingdom in Derlavai, how can we want them to come back?"

"I don't care. I don't much care, either," Sidroc said. "All I know is, I'm not going to be measuring triangles this semester, either, and I'm cursed glad of it."

"But don't you see?" Ealstan said, rather desperately. "If the Algarvians don't let us learn anything, by the time our children grow up Forthwegians won't be anything but peasants grubbing in the dirt."

"I need to find a woman before I have children," Sidroc said. "As a matter of fact, I'd like to find a woman whether I have children or not." He glanced over at Ealstan. "And don't tell me you wouldn't. That blond wench in mushroom season—"

"Oh, shut up," Ealstan said fiercely. He might not have sounded so fierce had he found Vanai unattractive. He had no idea what she thought of him, or even if she thought of him. All they'd talked about were mushrooms and the Algarvians' multifarious iniquities.

Sidroc laughed at him, which made things worse. Then his cousin said, "If you're going to cast books like Uncle Hestan, I can see why you might want more ciphering lessons, I suppose, but what do you care about stonelore any which way? It's not like you're going to be a mage."

"My father always says the more you know, the more choices you have," Ealstan answered. "I'd say the Algarvians think he's right, wouldn't you? Except with them, it's the other way round – they don't want us to have any choices, and so they don't want us to know anything, either."

"*My* father always says it's not what you know, it's who you know," Sidroc said, which did indeed sound like Uncle Hengist. "As long as we can make connections, we'll get on all right."

That had more than a little truth in it. Ealstan's father had used his connections to make sure no one looked too closely at where Leofsig had been before he came back to Gromheort. In the short run, and for relatively small things, connections were indeed splendid. For setting the course of one's entire life? Ealstan didn't think so.

He started to say as much, then shook his head instead. He couldn't prove he was right. He wondered if he could even make a good case. Whether he did or not, Sidroc would laugh at him. He was sure of that.

Even though Ealstan kept his mouth shut, Sidroc started laughing anyhow, laughing and pointing at Ealstan. "What's so cursed funny?" Ealstan demanded.

"I'll tell you what's so cursed funny," his cousin replied. "If you can't get the courses your father thinks you ought to have here at school, what's he going to do? I'll tell you what: he'll make you study those things on your own. That's what's funny, by the powers above. Haw, haw, haw!"

"Oh, shut up," Ealstan said again, suddenly and horribly certain Sidroc was right.

19.

King Shazli beamed at Hajjaj. "We shall have vengeance!" he exclaimed. "King Swemmel, may demons tear out his entrails and dance with them, will wail and gnash his teeth when he thinks of the day he sent his armies over the border into Zuwayza."

"Even so, your Majesty," Hajjaj replied, inclining his head to the young king. "But the Unkerlanters are suspicious of us; Swemmel, being a treacherous sort himself, sees treachery all around him. As I have reported to you, my conversations with the Algarvian minister have not gone unnoticed."

By Shazli's expression, he started to make some flip comment in response to that. He checked himself, though, at which Hajjaj nodded somber approval. Shazli *could* think, even if he remained too young to do it all the time. "Do you doubt the wisdom of our course, then?"

"I doubt the wisdom of all courses," the foreign minister said. "I serve you best by doubting, and by admitting that I doubt."

"Ah, but if you doubt everything, how can I know how much weight to place on any particular doubt?" Shazli asked with a smile.

Hajjaj smiled, too. "There you have me, I must admit."

"Explain your doubts here, then, your Excellency, if you would be so kind," Shazli said. "That we want, that we are entitled to, revenge on Unkerlant cannot be doubted. What better way to get it than by making common cause with Algarve? The Algarvians have proved willing – nay, eager – to make common cause with us."

"Oh, indeed," Hajjaj said. "Count Balastro has been accommodating in every possible way. And why not? We serve his interests, as he serves ours."

"Well, then!" Shazli said, for all the world as if Hajjaj had just completed a geometric proof on the blackboard.

But Hajjaj knew all too well that kingdoms did not behave so neatly as circles and triangles and trapezoids. "Algarve is a great kingdom," he said, "but Unkerlant is also a great kingdom. Zuwayza is not a great kingdom, nor shall it ever be. If the small involve themselves in the quarrels of the great, they may be sorry afterwards."

"We are already sorry. Unkerlant has made us sorry," Shazli said. "Do you deny this? Can you deny it?"

"I do not. I cannot," Hajjaj said. "Indeed, I was glad to begin conversations with the Algarvians, as your Majesty surely knows."

"Well, then," Shazli said again. This time, he amplified it: "How can we go wrong here, Hajjaj? Algarve does not border us. She can make no demands upon us, as Unkerlant can and does. All she can do is help us get our own back, and get our own back we shall."

"She will be able to make demands afterwards, for we shall owe her a debt," Hajjaj replied. "She will remember. Great kingdoms always do."

"Here, I think, you start at shadows," the king said. "Perhaps she can make demands. How can she enforce them?"

"How many dragons did Algarve hurl against Valmiera?" Hajjaj asked. "How many against Jelgava? They could fly against us, too. How do you propose to stand against them, your Majesty, come the evil day?"

"If you would have us withdraw from the alliance we have made, say so now and say so plainly." Shazli spoke with a hint of anger in his voice.

"I would not," Hajjaj said with a sigh. "But neither am I certain all will go as well as we hope. I have lived a long time. I have seen that things rarely go as well as people hope they will."

"We shall take back the land Swemmel stole from us," Shazli said. "Perhaps we shall even take more besides. Past that, I am willing to let the future fend for itself."

It was a good answer. It was, at the same time, a young man's answer. Hajjaj, who would probably see far less of the future unfold than would his sovereign, worried about it far more. "Indeed, I think we shall take it," he said. "I only hope we shall keep it."

Shazli leaned forward, staring at him in surprise. "How can we fail? The only way I can imagine our failing would be for Unkerlant to defeat Algarve. How likely do you suppose that to be?" He threw back his head and laughed, which gave Hajjaj his view on the subject.

"Not very likely, else I would have warned you not to follow this course," the Zuwayzi foreign minister said. "But how likely would we have reckoned it that Algarve could overthrow Valmiera and Jelgava in bare weeks apiece?"

"All the more reason to think the redheads will give King Swemmel the thrashing he deserves," Shazli said, not quite taking Hajjaj's point. "Efficiency!" His lip curled. "Not in Unkerlant. Will you tell me otherwise?" He looked a challenge at Hajjaj.

"I will not. I cannot," Hajjaj said. Shazli nodded, an I-told-you-so look in his eye. Then he nodded again, in a different way. Hajjaj rose, knowing he had been dismissed. "We have only to wait for spring, to see what comes then. May it prove good for the kingdom, as I hope with all my heart it does."

When he got back to his own office, he found his secretary arguing with a fellow who wore several amulets and lockets that clanked together whenever he moved. "No," Shaddad was saying when Hajjaj walked in, "that is *not* acceptable. His Excellency would—" He turned. "Oh. Here you are, your Excellency. Powers above be praised! This bungler proposes to undertake sorcery in and around your office."

"I am not a bungler, or I hope I am not." The fellow with the amulets bowed, which produced more clinkings and clankings. "I am Mithqal, a second-rank mage, with the honor of serving in his Majesty's army. My orders, which your secretary now has, request and require me to do my best to learn whether any other mages have been sorcerously spying on you."

"Let me see these orders," Hajjaj said, and put on his spectacles to read them. When he was through, he looked over the tops of the spectacles at Shaddad. "Captain Mithqal appears to be within his rights."

"Bah!" his secretary said. "For all we know, he just wants to snoop about. Why, for all we know, he could be—"

"Do not say something you may regret." Hajjaj did not like to bring Shaddad up so sharply, but his secretary sometimes got an exaggerated notion of his own importance. And having a mage, especially a mage who was also a soldier, angry at Shaddad would not do the secretary any good. Hajjaj went on, "Use the crystal to consult with this man's superiors. If they have indeed sent him here, well and good. If not, then by all means raise the alarm."

"I tried to suggest this very course to him, but he would not hear me," Mithqal said.

Shaddad sniffed. "As if I should take seriously any mountebank who sets himself before me." He bowed to Hajjaj. "Very well, your Excellency. Since *you* require it of me—" He turned his back on Mithqal to use the crystal, bending low over it to speak in a quiet voice. After a moment, his shoulders slumped further. When he turned around again, he looked as embarrassed as Hajjaj had ever seen him. "My apologies, Captain Mithqal. I seem to have been mistaken."

"May I now proceed?" Mithqal asked, a sardonic edge to his voice. He was looking at Hajjaj, who nodded. Shaddad nodded, too, which the mage affected not to notice. Hajjaj bit the inside of his lip to keep from smiling.

Shaddad sidled up to the Zuwayzi foreign minister. "I must confess, I am mortified," he murmured.

"We are all foolish now and then," Hajjaj said. What he was thinking was, *Well you might be*, but that would only have flustered Shaddad further.

Mithqal said, "Your Excellency" – he kept right on ignoring Shaddad – "I aim to check two things: first, to learn whether anyone is spying on your office from a distance; and second, to learn whether anything has been secreted hereabouts to send word or your doings to whoever may be listening: a clandestine crystal, perhaps, though that is not the only way to achieve the effect."

"No one could have placed such a thing here," Shaddad said. "Had someone brought such an object during a meeting with his Excellency, it would have been noted, and we do have sorcerous wards in place to keep out unwelcome guests when his Excellency and I are not present."

"What one mage can do, another can undo," Mithqal said. "That is as basic a law of sorcery as those of similarity and contagion, though I own that many mages are loth to admit as much."

He took from the large pouch he wore on his belt a candle of black beeswax, which he set on Shaddad's desk, and used ordinary flint and steel to light it. The glow that came from it, though, was anything but ordinary. Hajjaj rubbed at his eyes. Not only could he see

Shaddad and Mithqal, but also, in an odd sort of way, into them and through them as well. He could also see into and through Shaddad's desk.

Mithqal took out a six-sided crystal. "The iris stone," he said, and held it up. Rainbows appeared on all the walls of the office. "Thus you note its chiefest property." He might have been delivering a lecture. "Should the rainbows be agitated, that will show the influence of some other magic."

He carried the iris stone all around the desk. The rainbows shifted and swirled, but he accepted that, so Hajjaj supposed he was seeking some larger derangement. And, sure enough, Mithqal put down the crystal with every sign of satisfaction. He blew out the candle, carried it into Hajjaj's chambers, and lighted it again, repeating the ritual he had used in the outer office.

Once more, the rainbows swirled on the walls as Mithqal carried the iris stone around the candle. Once more, that was the only thing that happened. The mage nodded to Hajjaj, "Your Excellency, as best I can tell, no one is spying on you from without."

"I am glad to hear it," Hajjaj said.

"I could have told you as much, your Excellency," Shaddad said. Hajjaj glanced at him. He coughed a couple of times. "Er – not with such certainty, perhaps."

"Indeed," Mithqal said, and mercifully let it go at that. "Now to see if anyone has been listening from within." He drew a couple of withered objects from his pouch, one small and looking rather like a bean, the other resembling a thick, curled brown leaf, but hairy on one side. "I have the heart of a weasel, with which to seek out treachery, and also the ear of an ass, to signify treachery in respect to hearing." As an aside, he remarked, "Perhaps I might have done without the latter." Shaddad suffered another coughing fit.

Holding the heart in one hand and the ass' ear in the other, Mithqal began to chant. The ear started writhing and twitching, as it would have done were it attached to a living animal. Shaddad jumped; he might never have seen magecraft before. Hajjaj watched in the fascination he gave any workman manifestly good at his craft. "Something?" he asked in a low voice, so as not to disturb the mage.

"Something, aye," Mithqal breathed. He stalked out to the outer office, in the direction toward which the ear pointed. Hajjaj followed. So did Shaddad, his eyes round and white and staring in his dark face. Guided by the ass' ear, Mithqal moved toward the secretary's desk.

Shaddad cried out in despair and fled.

Mithqal threw down his sorcerous implements and pursued. He was younger and lighter on his feet than Hajjaj's secretary. After a moment, Hajjaj heard more shouts, and then a thud. He sank to a cushion and buried his face in his hands. He had trusted Shaddad, and here was his trust repaid with treason. But anguish was only half of what he felt. The other half was fear. How long had Shaddad been suborned, and how much had he passed to Unkerlant?

The secretary cried out once more, this time in pain. Hajjaj winced. Those questions would have answers, and soon. Shaddad would not like giving them. That no longer mattered. He would give them whether he liked to or not.

"What one mage can do, another can undo." Pekka quoted the adage loud. She preferred talking to herself to listening to the icy winds from the south howling around her Kajaani City College office. The only trouble was, she was lying to herself. Her laugh came bitter. "What one mage can do, even the same mage can't undo – or figure out how she did it in the first place."

Her only consolation was that she wasn't the only baffled theoretical sorcerer in Kuusamo. Raahe and Alkio hadn't been able to discover where the missing acorn from the pair in her experiment had gone. Neither had Piilis. Neither had Master Siuntio, and neither had Ilmarinen, so far as she knew, though he was worse than any of her other colleagues at telling everyone what he was up to.

Pekka looked at her latest stab at an explanation. It wasn't going anywhere. She could feel it wouldn't go anywhere, and had to fight back the strong impulse to crumple up the sheet of paper and throw it away. She'd tried explanations based on the assumption that the laws of similarity and contagion had a direct relationship. They'd failed. She'd also tried explanations based on the assumption that the laws of similarity and contagion had no direct relationship. They'd failed, too.

That left . . . "Nothing," Pekka said. "Nothing, curse it, nothing, nothing, nothing."

Again, she resisted the urge to tear up her latest set of calculations. She wished she'd never got involved in theoretical sorcery in the first place. Her husband, a practical man if ever there was one, kept making progress in useful applications of magecraft that strengthened Kuusamo and delighted the Seven Princes.

"I didn't want to be practical," Pekka muttered. "I wanted to get down to the bottom of things and understand them, so that other people could be practical with them. And what happened? I've gotten down to the bottom of things, I don't understand them, and other people are doing just fine being practical without them."

Temptation, twice resisted, came back stronger than ever and won. She made a very small ball of her latest set of calculations and threw the ball toward the wastepaper basket. She missed. Shrugging, she got up and went over to retrieve the wadded-up sheets. She'd missed with the calculations. She supposed it made sense that she should miss in getting rid of them, too.

She'd just dropped the ball of paper into the wire basket – it had plenty of company there – when someone knocked on the door. She frowned. It was early for Leino to have finished his latest round of experiments. *Of course he works late*, Pekka thought. *His work is actually getting somewhere*. And that had to be the most peculiar knock she'd ever heard. It sounded more as if someone had kicked the door, but much too high up to make that likely, either.

Frowning still, she pulled the door open – and jumped back in alarm. Of all the things she'd expected to see in the hallway, a man standing on his head was the last. "Powers above!" she burst out, all the while thinking, *Well, that explains how he knocked on the door.*

"And a fine good day to you, Mistress Pekka," the man said with a grin his being upside down tried to transmogrify into a frown.

Only then did Pekka realize she knew him. "Master Ilmarinen!" she exclaimed. "What are you doing there?"

"Waiting for you to open the door," the elderly theoretical sorcerer replied. "Wondering if I was going to fall over before you did open the door." With a spryness that gave that the lie, he went from upside down to right side up. His face, which had been quite red, resumed its natural color.

"Master Ilmarinen . . ." Pekka repeated his name with such patience as she could muster. "Let me ask a different question,

Master: *why* were you standing on your head while you waited for me to open the door?"

"You are a true theoretical sorcerer, Mistress Pekka," Ilmarinen said, bowing. "No sooner do you observe an unexplained phenomenon than you seek the root cause behind it. Most commendable indeed."

That kind of mocking praise infuriated Pekka as nothing else could have done. "Master," she said tightly, "shall we see if the constabulary reckons your untimely demise an unexplained phenomenon? If you don't start talking sense, we can experimentally test the notion very soon."

Ilmarinen laughed, breathing spirit fumes into her face. She glared at him, really tempted to perform that experiment. Powers above, had he got drunk, hopped aboard a ley-line caravan coach, and traveled down to Kajaani in the middle of a Kuusaman winter for no better reason than to drive her mad? For anyone but Ilmarinen, the notion would have been absurd. Even for him, it should have been. The large rational part of her mind still insisted it was. But her large rational part also recognized that Ilmarinen's rational part wasn't anywhere near so large.

He kept on laughing for another couple of heartbeats. Pekka looked around for the blunt instrument nearest to hand. Maybe murder, or something like it, did show in her eyes, for Ilmarinen went from laugh to chuckle to a smile that only set her teeth on edge. Then he reached into a pocket. When he didn't find what he wanted, the smile fell off his face, too. He started going through his other pockets, and growing more and more frantic as whatever he was after remained elusive. Now Pekka laughed, in sardonic delight.

Ilmarinen looked harried. "However much it may amuse you, Mistress, it is not funny, I assure you."

"Oh, I don't know. It seems funny enough to me." Pekka pointed to a folded-up piece of paper behind the heel of Ilmarinen's left boot. "Is that by any chance what you seek?"

He turned, stared, and scooped it up. "Aye, it is," he answered, more sheepishly than she was used to hearing him speak. "It must have fallen out while I was standing on my head."

"You still have not explained *why* you were standing on your head," Pekka reminded him.

And Ilmarinen went right on not explaining, at least with words.

Instead, with a flourish, he presented Pekka the paper, as a sommelier in a fancy eatery up in Yliharma might have proffered an expensive bottle of Algarvian wine.

"You were standing on your head because of this piece of paper," she said in the now-tell-me-another-one tones she used after listening to Uto spin out some outrageous fabrication. Sure as sure, her son and Ilmarinen had the same imp indwelling in them.

But Ilmarinen, this time, seemed immune. "As a matter of fact, Mistress Pekka, I truly was standing on my head because of that piece of paper."

Pekka studied him. He was serious. He sounded serious. That only made her distrust him more than ever. But, after so much farce, what choice had she but to unfold the sheet and see what was on it? Only later did she wonder what Ilmarinen's expression would have been had she torn it up and thrown it in his face. There, in a nutshell – *not* an acorn – was the difference between the two of them. Ilmarinen would have had the thought at once, and might have acted on it.

Once opened, the sheet wasn't blank, as she'd half expected it to be. Calculations in Ilmarinen's sprawling script filled it. She glanced down at them for a moment. She started to look up at Ilmarinen again, but her eyes, of themselves, snapped back to the arcane symbols. Her mouth fell open. She held the paper in one hand and traced the logic, traced the symbolic path, with the forefinger of the other.

When, at last, she was finished, she bowed very low to Ilmarinen. "Master Siuntio had the right of it," she said, her voice a breathy whisper. "He told me that if anyone could find the meaning hidden in my experiment, you would be the mage, for you have the most original cast of mind. And he knew whereof he spoke. I would never in a thousand years have thought as you did."

Ilmarinen shrugged. "Siuntio is smarter than I am. Siuntio is smarter than anybody is, as a matter of fact. But he isn't crazy. You need to be a little bit crazy – or it doesn't hurt, anyhow." He eyed Pekka like a master eyeing a student who might have promise. "And now do you understand why I was standing on my head?"

"Inversion," Pekka answered, so absently that Ilmarinen clapped his hands together in delight.

"Just so!" He almost cackled with glee, sounding like a laying hen.

"I never would have thought of such a thing," Pekka said again. "Never. When I began to try to learn whether similarity and contagion were related, I always thought the relationship I found, if I found any at all, would be a direct one. When I failed to show a direct one, I thought that meant there was none at all — only that didn't work, either."

"If the experiment works and the mathematics don't, the mathematics are wrong," Ilmarinen said. "I told you — I told all of you — as much before, but you did not heed me. Now we have numbers that suggest why your cursed acorns acted as they did, and what happened to them as well."

That wasn't explicit in the sheet he'd given Pekka. She looked through the sprawling lines of symbols again. She had to look twice; even the implications were subtle. Once she found what Ilmarinen was driving at, though, she could work them out for herself. She looked up from the sheet to the theoretical sorcerer. "But that's impossible!"

"It's what happened." His voice was peculiarly flat. After a moment, she realized she'd angered him. She'd seen him play at anger before, when he ranted and blustered. This was different. This made her feel as if he'd caught her doing something vicious and rather nasty.

In a small voice, she said, "I suppose the classical Kaunians would have said the same thing if they saw the spells that went into making a ley-line caravan go."

"Not if they had any sense, they wouldn't," Ilmarinen said, but now in something close to his usual sardonic tones. He reached out and tapped the paper with a gnarled finger. "If you can show me an alternative explanation, then you may tell me this one is impossible. Till then, wouldn't it be more interesting to try to come up with more experiments to see whether we're crazy or not?" He shook his head and held up that finger again. "Of course we're crazy. Let's see if we're right or not."

"Aye." Ideas rose to the top of Pekka's mind from below like bubbles in a pot of water coming to a boil. "If this is right" — she shook the paper — "we have a lifetime's worth of experiments waiting ahead for us. Two lifetimes' worth, maybe."

"That's so, Mistress Pekka." Ilmarinen sighed.

He was old. He did not have a long lifetime ahead of him, let alone two. "I'm sorry, Master," Pekka said quietly. "I was tactless."

"What?" Ilmarinen stared, then laughed. "Oh, no, not that, you silly lass. I've known for a long time that I wouldn't be here forever, or even too much longer. No. I was thinking that, if things keep going as they have over there, over yonder" – he pointed north and west, toward the mainland of Derlavai – "we'd better pack those two lifetimes' worth of experiments into about half a year."

Pekka though about that and slowly nodded. "And if we can't?"

"We'd better do it anyway," Ilmarinen said.

Leofsig dipped his straight razor into the bowl of hot water he'd begged from his mother to get the soapsuds off it, then went back to trimming the lower edge of his beard. With his head tilted so far back, he had trouble seeing the mirror he'd propped on the chest of drawers in the room he now had to share with Ealstan.

Sidroc stuck his head in, perhaps to find out of Ealstan was there. When he saw what Leofsig was doing, he grinned unpleasantly. "Don't cut your throat, now," he said, almost as if he meant to be helpful.

In one smooth movement, Leofsig was off the stool he'd been using and halfway across the room. "You want to think about what you say to a man with a razor in his hand," he remarked pleasantly.

"Eep," Sidroc said, and disappeared faster than he would have had a first-rank mage enspelled him. Had a first-rank mage enspelled him, though, he would have stayed disappeared. That, Leofsig thought, was too much to hope for.

Laughing a little, he went back to the mirror and finished shaving. Then he put on his best tunic and his best cloak. A fussy grammarian would have called it his better cloak, for he had only two. He'd had more before the war started, but they were on Sidroc and Uncle Hengist's backs these days.

This one, of dark blue wool, would do well enough. His father had one very much like it, and so did Ealstan. "You can't go wrong with dark blue wool," Hestan had said, ordering all three of them at the same time. When the tailor delivered them, Ealstan had called them a proof of the law of similarity. Leofsig smiled, remembering.

"Let me see you," his mother said before he could get out the door.

Obediently, he stood still, Elfryth brushed away an almost-visible speck of lint, smoothed down the hair he'd just combed, and finally nodded. "You look very nice," she said. "If your young lady isn't swept off her feet, she ought to be." She'd been saying that as long as he'd been taking young ladies out. She added something newer: "Don't try sneaking in after curfew. It's not worth the risk."

"Aye," he said. His father would have told him exactly the same thing, and his father's advice, he knew, was nearly always good. Even so, he sounded at best dutiful, at worst resigned, rather than enthusiastic.

Elfryth stood on tiptoe to kiss him on the cheek. "Go on, then," she said. "If you must get home sooner than you'd like, you won't want to waste your time standing around chattering with the likes of me."

That being true, Leofsig nodded and left. He'd walked half a block before he realized he should have denied it for politeness' sake. *Too late now*, he thought, and kept going.

By then, he'd already pulled the cloak tight around him and fastened the polished brass button that closed it at the neck. A raw wind blew up from the southwest. There might be frost on the windows, maybe even on the grass, come morning. As Gromheort went, that made it a chilly evening.

A couple of Algarvian soldiers on patrol rode past him. They didn't look twice. To them, he was just another subject. Maybe they knew how much he hated them. If they did, they didn't care.

The sun was low in the northwest when he knocked on a door a few blocks from his own. A plump man a few years older than his own father opened it. "Good day, Master Elfsig," Leofsig said. "Is Felgilde ready?"

"She won't be but a moment," his companion's father said. "Step on in, Leofsig. You have time for a cup of wine, I think, but only a quick one."

"I thank you, sir," Leofsig said. Elfsig led him to the parlor and brought the wine himself. Felgilde's little brother, whose name Leofsig always forgot, made faces at him from the doorway – though only when Elfsig's back was turned. Leofsig ignored him. Ealstan had been only a bit too big to play such games when young men started coming to Hestan's house to take Conberge out.

Leofsig hadn't quite finished his wine when Felgilde came into the parlor. Elfsig said, "You'll want to bring her home before curfew, so we don't have trouble with the redheads." His eyes twinkled. "Maybe you won't want to do it – I recall what it's like being your age, believe it or not – but you will, for her sake."

"Aye, sir," Leofsig said, so mournfully that Elfsig laughed. He would cheerfully have disobeyed his own mother; evading the wishes of Felgilde's family was harder. Putting the best face on it he could, he turned to her. "Shall we be off?"

"Aye." She kissed Elfsig, who wore rather a bushy beard, on the end of his nose. Leofsig offered her his arm. She took it. Her maroon cloak went well with his blue one. She'd done up her black hair in a fancy pile of curls. She looked like her father, but in her Elfsig's rather doughy features were sharply carved. She said, "I hope the play is good."

"It's supposed to be very funny," Leofsig answered as they headed for the door. Most of the plays that ran in Gromheort these days were farces. Real life was grim enough to make serious drama less attractive than it would have been in better times.

People streamed toward the playhouse, which stood a couple of doors down from the public baths. Leofsig saw two or three couples come right out of the men's and women's wings of the baths, meet, and head for the theater. One such pair all but ran to get in line ahead of Felgilde and him. "I hope we'll have decent seats," Felgilde said.

If you'd been ready when I got there, we'd have a better chance. But Leofsig, like any other swain with an ounce of sense in his head, knew better than to say that out loud. He paid for two seats. He and Felgilde both held out their hands so a fellow could stamp them to prove they'd paid. Thus marked, they went inside.

Leofsig bought wine for both of them, and also bread and olives and roasted almonds and cheese. A stew of some sort bubbled in a pot, too, but he knew it wouldn't be much more than gruel. The playhouse had no easier time getting meat than anyone else in Gromheort. Spitting out olive pits as they walked, he and Felgilde headed for the benches in front of the stage.

At the entranceway, a sign that hadn't been there the last time he came to the theater announced, KAUNIANS IN REAR

BALCONY ONLY. "Oh, good!" Felgilde exclaimed. "More seats for the rest of us."

He looked at her. Most of what he wanted to say, he couldn't, not unless he also wanted to betray himself. Felgilde and her family didn't know he'd escaped from the Algarvian captives' camp, or how he'd escaped, or with whose help. Like most people, they thought the redheads had released him. The fewer folk who knew any different, the better.

He did say, "They're people, too."

"They're not Forthwegians, not truly," Felgilde said. "And the trousers their women wear – well, I mean really." She tossed her head.

As he'd grown toward manhood, Leofsig had eyed a good many trousered Kaunian women. He didn't know of a Forthwegian man who hadn't – including, he had no doubt whatever, Felgilde's father. Saying anything about that also struck him as unwise. He pointed. "There's a spot wide enough for two, I think," he said. "Come on – let's hurry."

The spot proved barely wide enough for two. That meant Felgilde had to squeeze in close behind him. He didn't mind. She leaned her head on his shoulder. He didn't mind that, either. She was wearing a floral scent that tickled his nose. When he slipped an arm around her, she snuggled closer. He should have been very happy. Most of him *was* very happy. Even the small part that wasn't very happy made excuses for Felgilde: if she didn't care for Kaunians, how was she different from most Forthwegians? She wasn't, and Leofsig knew it.

"Ah," she said as the lights dimmed and the curtains slid back from the stage. Leofsig leaned forward, too. He'd come here to forget his troubles and his kingdom's, not to dwell on them.

Out came an actor and actress dressed as Forthwegian peasants from a couple of centuries before: stock comic figures. "Sure is hard times," the actor said. He looked at the actress. "Twenty years ago, now, we had plenty to eat." He looked at her again. "Twenty years ago, I was married to a good-looking woman."

"Twenty years ago, I was married to a young man," she retorted.

He winced, as from a blow. "If I had red hair, I bet my belly'd be full."

"If you had red hair, you'd look like an idiot." The actress looked out at the audience, then shrugged. "Wouldn't change things much, would it?"

They took things from there, poking fun at the Algarvian occupiers, at themselves, and at anything else that happened to get in their way. The villain of the piece was a Kaunian woman – played by a short, squat, immensely fat Forthwegian actress in a blond wig; she looked all the more grotesque in tight-fitting trousers. Leofsig wondered what the real Kaunians in the rear of the balcony thought of her. Felgilde thought she was very funny. So did Leofsig, when he wasn't think about how laughing at her helped estrange Forthwegians and Kaunians.

In the end, she got what she deserved, being married off to a drunken swineherd, or perhaps to one of his pigs. The Algarvians in the paly went off to harass some other fictitious village: the sort of relief Gromheort wanted to see but never would. And the two peasants who'd opened the show stood at center stage. The man of the pair addressed the audience: "So you see, my friends, things *can* turn out all right."

"Oh, shut up, you old fool," said the actress who'd played his wife. The curtain slid out and hid them both, then parted so they and the rest of the company could take their bows and get their applause. The loudest cheers – and a lot of howls of counterfeit lust – went to the fat woman who'd played the Kaunian. She twitched her hips, which raised more howls.

"That was fun," Felgilde said as she and Leofsig filed out of the playhouse. "I enjoyed it. Thank you for taking me." She smiled up at him.

"You're welcome," he answered, more absently than he should have. He'd enjoyed the play, too, enjoyed it and at the same time been embarrassed at himself for enjoying it. He'd never known that peculiar mix of feelings before, and kept at them in his head, as a child will pick at a scab until it bleeds anew.

Out on the street, Felgilde said, "I'm cold," and shivered, as fine a dramatic performance as any back at the theater. Leofsig spread his cloak so it covered both of them, as he knew she wanted him to do. Under that concealment, they could be bolder than they would have dared without it. She put her arm around his waist, so they walked as close together as they had sat during the play. He caressed her breast through the fabric of her tunic. She hadn't let him do that before. Now she sighed and put her other hand on top of his, squeezing him against her soft, firm flesh.

Walking thus, they hardly walked at all, and got back to Felgilde's house only a few minutes before curfew. In front of the door, where her family might see, she let Leofsig chastely kiss her on the cheek. Then she hurried inside.

Leofsig hurried, too, back toward his own home. As he trotted through the dark streets of Gromheort, half of him wanted to ask her out again as soon as he could. *Maybe I'll get my hand* under *her tunic next time*, that half thought. The other half never wanted to see her again. On he ran, at war within himself.

Fernao reveled in the pleasure of a ley-line caravan. Traveling through Setubal in a snug, water-tight coach with a stove at the far end was infinitely preferable to a caravan across the land of the Ice People on camelback, to say nothing of his journey across the ocean on leviathanback. Fernao was perfectly willing to say nothing of that journey; he kept trying to forget it. Its sole virtue, as far as he was concerned, was that it had brought him back to Lagoas.

He stretched luxuriously — so luxuriously that he brushed against the man who shared the bench with him. "Your pardon, I crave," he murmured.

"It's all right," the fellow said, hardly raising his eyes from his news sheet.

To Fernao, that casual forbearance felt like a luxury, too. King Penda would have complained endlessly about being bumped. King Penda, as the mage knew to his sorrow, complained endlessly about everything. These days, King Vitor and his courtiers were nurse-maiding Penda; the fugitive King of Forthweg was no longer Fernao's worry.

Setubal seemed little changed from the way it had looked before Fernao set out for Yanina to pluck Penda from King Tsavellas's palace. Had he not already known, he would have been hard pressed to tell Lagoas was a kingdom at war. Or so he thought, till he saw one of his favorite restaurants and several other buildings on the same block reduced to charred rubble.

His exclamation must have held surprise as well as dismay, for his seatmate gave him a quizzical stare. "Where have you been, pal?" the man asked. "Mezentio's stinking dragons gave us that little present a couple months ago."

"Out of the kingdom," Fernao answered mournfully. He sighed. "The best fried prawns, the best smoked eel in Setubal – gone."

"You won't find eel any more smoked than it was the night those eggs fell, and that's a fact," the other man said before starting to read again.

He got out of the caravan coach a couple of stops later. No one took his place. Out here past Vinhaes Park, fewer people were traveling away from the center of the city. More would be going back when the caravan returned.

"University!" the conductor called. "All out for the university."

The mage hurried across the campus of Varzim University toward its beating heart: the library. Having finally put his own affairs in order after his long absence, he could begin to find out how his profession had changed, had grown, while he wasn't looking.

Students in their yellow tunics and light blue kilts eyed him curiously as he passed them. "What's that old man doing here?" one of them muttered to another, although Fernao was hardly old enough to have sired either of them.

"Maybe he's a lecturer," the other student said.

"Nah." The first one shook his head. "When did you ever see a lecturer move so fast?" That seemed an incontrovertible argument, or maybe Fernao had just hurried out of earshot before the second student replied.

In front of the library stood an excellent reproduction of a classical Kaunian marble statue of a philosopher. The original had been carved in a sunnier clime; in his light tunic and trousers, the philosopher looked miserably cold. The little icicle hanging off the end of his nose only added to the effect.

Two guards at the top of the stairs leading into the library looked miserably cold, too. If they'd had icicles on the ends of their noses, though, they'd knocked them off recently. Fernao started to stride past them, but one moved quickly to block his way. "Here, what's this?" he demanded, drawing himself up in indignation.

"A library is a weapon of war, sir," the guard said. "You'll need to show us what manner of man you are before you pass within."

"You don't suppose the Algarvians have libraries of their own?" Fernao asked, acid in his voice. But perhaps they did not have any one that matched Varzim University's. And worrying about knowledge as a weapon of war was, he supposed, better than ignoring it. From his belt pouch he took the small card certifying him as a first-rank member in good standing of the Lagoan Guild of Mages (he was glad he'd bought a life membership after making first rank; otherwise, his affiliation would have lapsed while he was on his journey, and he surely wouldn't have got round to renewing it yet). "Here. Does this satisfy you?"

Both guards solemnly studied the card. They looked at each other. The one who hadn't tried to block his way nodded. The one who had tried stepped aside, saying, "Aye, sir. Pass on."

Pass on Fernao did. Had he been an Algarvian spy, he might have forged or stolen his card. He did not mention that to the guard. Had he done so, odds were that no one would ever have been admitted into the library again.

He hurried upstairs to the third floor. When he got there, he was glad to discover the librarians hadn't gone through one of their periodic reshelving frenzies while he was far away. Otherwise, he would have had to hurry right back down again, to find out where the journals he wanted were hidden. Reshelving probably would have done as much as the guards did to keep Algarvians from ferreting information out of the library.

As things were, he found new numbers of such tomes as *The Royal Lagoan Journal of Pure and Applied Magecraft*, *Kaunian Sorcery* (the past year's last two fascicules were missing: either the fall of Priekule had prevented their publication or copies hadn't been able to make it across the Strait of Valmiera), and the *Annual Sorcerous Compendium of the Seven Princes of Kuusamo*. Having found them, he carried them to a battered old chair behind the shelves, a chair in which he'd done a lot of reading over the years.

There in Fernao's hideaway, he flipped rapidly through the journals, slowing down when he found an article that interested him. After he'd put aside the *Annual Sorcerous Compendium*, he noticed he'd hardly slowed down at all while going through it.

"That's odd," he murmured, and turned to the table of contents at the rear of the volume to see if he'd missed something. He hadn't, and scratched his head. Before he'd gone away, the Kuusamans had been doing some very interesting work at the deep theoretical level. Siuntio — who was world-famous, at least among mages — and younger theoreticians like Raahe and Pekka had asked some provocative questions. He'd hoped they might have come up with some answers by now, or at least some more new and interesting questions.

If they had, they weren't publishing them in the *Annual Sorcerous Compendium*. Its pages were full of articles on horticultural magecraft, ley-line engineering, and improvements in crystallomancy: interesting, significant, but not at the cutting edge of the field. With a shrug, he set the volume aside and went on to a Jelgavan journal, which also proved to cut off abruptly with the previous spring's fascicule.

He was three articles into the *Royal Lagoan Journal* when he suddenly sat up very straight and slammed the heavy volume closed. It made a loud, booming noise; someone somewhere else in the third floor exclaimed in surprise. Fernao sat still; to his relief, nobody came looking to see what had happened.

"If they've found any new answers, if they've found any new questions, they aren't publishing them," he muttered under his breath. He set his hand on the leather binding of the *Annual Sorcerous Compendium*. His first assumption was that the Kuusamans hadn't found anything, but how likely was that? Would all of their best theoretical sorcerers have fallen silent at once?

Maybe. He didn't know. He couldn't know. But maybe, too, maybe they'd found something interesting and important: so interesting and so important, they didn't care to tell anyone else about it.

"And maybe your head's full of moonbeams, too," Fernao told himself, his voice barely above a whisper.

But could he afford to take the chance? Kuusamo and Lagoas, once upon a time, had fought like cats and dogs. They hadn't fought in a couple of hundred years. He knew that didn't mean they couldn't fight again, though. If the Kuusamans ever decided to stop the halfhearted island war they were waging against Gyongyos, what would keep them from jumping on Lagoas's back? Nothing Fernao could see, the more so as his own kingdom couldn't give over the war against Algarve without becoming King Mezentio's vassals.

Reluctant as a lover having to leave his beloved too soon, he set the journals on their shelves and went downstairs. "The Guild may know more about this than I," he muttered under his breath, and then, "I hope the Guild knows more about this than I."

Both guards nodded to him as he hurried past them. Now that he was going away, they were content. He didn't laugh till they couldn't see his face. They might be better than nothing; he remained unconvinced they were a lot better than nothing.

He waited at the caravan stop for a car to take him back to Setubal. He had to change to a different ley line downtown, not far from the harbor. His second journey was shorter: less a mile. He got out of the caravan car across the street from the Grand Hall of the Lagoan Guild of Mages.

It *was* a grand hall, built of snowy marble in severe neoclassical style. The statuary group in front of it might have been snatched straight out of the heyday of the Kaunian Empire, too. The only thing that would have been odd to a veritable classical Kaunian was that the statues, like the hall, remained unpainted. Temporal sorcery had proved that the Kaunians, in the old days, slapped paint on everything that didn't move. But builders hadn't known that in the days when the guild hall went up. Most people still didn't realize it. And, by the time anyone at all knew it, pristine marble had become as much a neoclassical tradition as painted stone had been in Kaunian days.

Inside the hall, Fernao exchanged greetings with half a dozen mages. Some had heard he was back and were glad to see him; others hadn't, and were astonished to see him. Lagoans weren't inveterate gabbers like Algarvians or Yaninans, but he still needed longer than he'd wanted to make his way to the guild secretary's office.

"Ah, Master Fernao!" exclaimed that worthy, a plump, good-natured fellow named Brinco. "And how may I help you this, I fear, not so lovely day?"

"I should like to see Grandmaster Pinhiero for a few minutes, if such a thing be possible," Fernao answered.

Brinco's frown suggested that the mere thought he might have to tell Fernao no was enough to devastate him. "I cannot say with certainty whether it be possible or not, my lord," the secretary said. He got to his feet. "If your Excellency would have the generosity to wait?"

"Of course," Fernao answered. "How could I refuse you anything?"

"Easily, I doubt not," Brinco replied. "But bide a moment, and we shall see what we shall see." He vanished behind an elaborately carved oaken door. When he emerged, smiles filled his face. "Your desire shall be granted in every particular. The grandmaster says his greatest pleasure would lie in seeing you for as long as you desire."

Fernao had known Pinhiero a fair number of years. He doubted the grandmaster had said any such thing; a grumpy *Oh, all right* was much more likely. When it came to giving pleasure, Brinco liked to set his thumb on the scale. Sometimes that annoyed Fernao. Not today. Getting any of what he wanted suited him fine. "I thank you," he said, and went into the grandmaster's office.

Pinhiero was about sixty, his sandy hair and mustaches going gray. He peered up at Fernao through reading glasses that made his eyes look enormous. "Well," he growled, "what's so important?" In public ceremonies, he could be dignity, learning, and magnificence personified. Among his colleagues, he didn't bother with any such mask, and simply was what he was.

"Grandmaster, I've come across something interesting in the library – or rather, I've come across nothing interesting in the library, which is interesting in and of itself," Fernao said.

"Not to me, it isn't," Pinhiero said. "You get as old as I am, you don't have time for riddles any more. Spit it out or leave."

"Aye, Grandmaster," Fernao said, and explained what he'd found – and what he hadn't. Pinhiero listened with no change of expression. He was famous for that. Fernao finished, "I can't prove this means anything, Grandmaster, but if it does mean something, it means something important." He waited to see whether Pinhiero thought it meant anything.

"Kuusamans won't give you the time of day unless they feel like it," the grandmaster said at last. "Come to that, they won't give each other the time of day, either. Seven princes – cursed silly arrangement." He glared at Fernao. "You know how much trouble you can get into by trying to reason from something that isn't there?"

"Aye, Grandmaster," Fernao said, wondering if that was dismissal.

It wasn't. Pinhiero said, "Here. Wait." He pulled from a desk drawer an unfashionably large and heavy crystal. Staring down into it, he murmured a name: "Siuntio." Fernao's eyes widened. The grand-master went on, now in classical Kaunian: "By the brotherhood we share, I summon thee." Fernao's eyes got wider still.

The image of a white-haired, wrinkled Kuusaman formed in the crystal. "I am here, my bad-tempered brother," he said, also in Kaunian.

"You old fraud, we're on to you," Pinhiero growled.

"You dream," Siuntio said. "You dream, and imagine yourself awake." His image disappeared, leaving the crystal only a sphere of stone.

Pinhiero grunted. "It's big, all right. If it were smaller, he'd have done a better job of denying it. What *have* they gone and done – and will they do it to us next?" He scowled at Fernao. "How would you like to go to Kuusamo?"

"Not much," Fernao answered. The grandmaster ignored him. He was already making plans.

Bembo assumed a hurt expression. It was, he knew, a good hurt expression. Every once in a while, it even softened the heart of Sergeant Pesaro. Any hurt expression that could soften the heart of a constabulary sergeant had to be a good one.

But it did nothing to soften Saffa's heart. "No," the sketch artist said. "I don't want to take supper with you again, or go to the play-house with you, or go strolling in the park, or do anything with you. I really don't, Bembo. Enough was enough."

"But why not?" Bembo thought the question was, and sounded, perfectly reasonable. An impartial listener, of which there were none outside the constabulary station, would assuredly have called it whining.

"Why?" Saffa took a deep breath. "Because even though you had a good idea and Captain Sasso liked it, you still haven't been promoted. That's one reason: I don't want to waste my time with a man who isn't a winner. And the other is, you only want one thing from a girl, and you don't even bother hiding it."

"I am a man." Bembo struck an affronted pose. "Of course I want that."

"You aren't listening – and why am I not surprised?" Saffa said. "It's the only thing you really want from me. You wouldn't care about anything else I did, as long as I gave you that. And because you're like that, it's the one thing you'll never, ever get from me."

She turned away from him and headed for the stairs, putting a little something extra in her walk to give him a hint about what he might be missing. "How about next week?" Bembo called after her. "Suppose I ask you again next week?"

Saffa climbed the stairs. Bembo automatically tried to look up her kilt, but she kept her arms close to her sides to hold it down. She went into the station and closed the door. Then she opened it, looked out at him, smiled sweetly, and said, "No." Still smiling, she closed the door again.

"Bitch," Bembo muttered. "Miserable bitch." He trudged toward the stairway himself. *What I really need,* he thought, *is a Kaunian hussy like the ones in the romances I've been reading. They don't tell a man no. All they ever do is beg for more. They can't get enough of a strong Algarvian man.*

He scowled. All the Kaunians in Tricarico had gone into camps. He'd helped put them there, and he hadn't even had the chance to have any fun while he was doing it. Life wasn't fair, no doubt about it. Those Kaunian sluts were probably giving the camp guards all they wanted and then some, in exchange for whatever tiny favors they could get out of them.

When Bembo came into the station, Sergeant Pesaro laughed at him. He'd have bet the sergeant would. "She flamed you down like a dragon attacking from out of the sun, didn't she?" Pesaro said.

"Ahh, she's not as fancy as she thinks she is," Bembo growled. "Tell me one thing she's got that any other broad doesn't."

"You by the short hairs," Pesaro said, which was crude but unfortunately accurate. The sergeant went on, "Well, my boy, you can do your mooning over her on patrol today."

"I thought I could get caught up on my paperwork!" Bembo exclaimed in dismay. "If I don't get caught up on my paperwork cursed soon, Captain Sasso's going to have me for supper."

"Not as much fun as Saffa having you for supper, that's certain," Pesaro said, "but it can't be helped. I've got a couple of men down with the galloping pukes, and somebody's got to go out there and make certain none of our wonderful law-abiding citizens decides to walk off with the Kaunian Column in his belt pouch."

"Have a heart, Sergeant." Bembo gave Pesaro the famous wounded look.

It didn't work this time. "You're going out," the sergeant said implacably. "You're my first replacement in, though, so you do get to pick whether you want to head over to the west side or to Riversedge."

Bembo was almost indignant and glum enough to choose to patrol the thieves' nest down by the waterfront — almost, but not quite. "I'll take the west side," he said, and Pesaro nodded, unsurprised. Pointing to the city map on the wall behind the sergeant, Bembo asked, "Exactly which route am I stuck with?"

"You'll get stuck with Riversedge if you don't quit your griping," Pesaro said. He turned his swivel chair, which squeaked under him. "You get number seven." He pointed. "Plenty of fancy houses, and you shouldn't have too much to do unless you flush out a sneak thief."

"Could be worse," Bembo admitted. "Could be better, but could be worse, too." From him, that was no small concession. "Better than Riversedge, anyhow." And that, as he knew fair well, was no small understatement.

Pesaro wrote Bembo's name on a scrap of paper and pinned it to patrol route number seven. "Get moving," the sergeant told him. "That part of town, they want to know they've got a constable on the job all the time. If they don't, they get on the crystal and start breathing fire at us."

"I'm going, I'm going," Bembo said. In a way, he was glad to escape the station. If he sat at a desk and did paperwork, he'd keep watching Saffa and she'd keep sneering at him. But the paperwork really did need doing. If he didn't get caught up soon, Captain Sasso would have some pointed and pungent things to say to him. *Curse it, I was going to get it done — well, most of it, anyhow,* he thought. No help for that now.

His breath smoked when he went outside. Snow gleamed on the peaks of the Bradano Mountains to the east, but rarely got down to Tricarico. Before the war, rich people had gone up into the mountains for the privilege of playing in the snow. Now that Algarve ruled on both sides of the mountains, they could go up again. Folk from farther south would wonder why they bothered, though. As a matter of fact, Bembo wondered why they bothered. He'd seen just enough of snow to know he didn't want to see more.

Muttering at his unfortunate fate, he trudged west. A team of gardeners with long-handled shears trimmed the branches of the trees surrounding a home that probably cost as much as he would make in twenty years. He sighed. He lived in a flat even less prepossessing than Saffa's.

He started to walk by the tree trimmers, then stopped and took a second look at them. He whistled, a low note of surprise, and stepped off the sidewalk and on to the expanse of close-cropped grass that fronted the mansion. Swinging his club as he advanced on the gardeners, he did his best to put on a brave show.

They didn't need long to notice him; he wanted to be noticed. The boss of the crew came toward him. "Something wrong, Constable?" he asked. His shears, when you got down to it, made a more formidable weapon than Bembo's bludgeon.

"Wrong? I don't know about that, pal," Bembo answered. "But some of those people you've got working for you" – he pointed to the ones he meant – "they're women, aren't they? I've got pretty fair eyes, I do, and I know a woman when I see one. I know I've never seen one trimming trees till now, too."

"Well, maybe you haven't," the gardener allowed. "Half my workers have gone into the army. The work doesn't go away, even if the men do. And so—" He turned to the women he'd hired. "Dalinda, Alcina, Procla – knock off for a bit and come say good day to the constable here."

"Good day, Constable," they chorused, smiling at him.

"Good day, fair ladies," he answered, sweeping off his hat and bowing to each of them in turn. Dalinda wasn't particularly fair, and was brawnier than most of the men still working for the master gardener. Procla wasn't anything special, either. Alcina, now, Alcina was worth bowing to. Seeing her sweaty from pruning branches made Bembo wish he'd got her sweaty in a different way. Smiling back at all of them, but at her in particular, he asked, "And how do you like men's work?"

"Fine," they said, all together again, so much in unison that Bembo wondered if the gardener had hired them from a singing group that had fallen on hard times.

"Isn't that something?" the constable said, and gave the head gardener a poke in the ribs with his elbow. "Tell me, pal – does your wife know how you've managed to keep your crew going?"

"Now, Constable," the fellow answered with a nudge and a wink of his own, "do I look that foolish?"

"Not a bit of it, friend, not a bit of it," Bembo said, chuckling. "But, of course, the municipal business licensing bureau does know you've changed the conditions under which you're operating?"

Had the master gardener said aye, Bembo would have given up and gone on with his patrol. But the man only frowned a little and said, "I hadn't imagined that would be necessary."

Bembo clicked his tongue between his teeth and looked doleful. "Oh, that's too bad. That's really too bad. Those boys are sticklers, aye, they are. Why, if they were to find out what you were up to, if I were to tell them . . ." He looked up at the sky, as if he'd forgotten what he was saying.

"Perhaps we can come to an understanding," the master gardener said, hardly even sounding resigned. He knew how the game was played, and he'd given Bembo an opening. Taking the constable aside, he asked, "Would ten suit you?"

They haggled for a while before meeting at fifteen. Bembo said, "By the powers above, I'll settle for ten if that one wench – Alcina – feels like being friendly."

"I didn't hire her out of a brothel, so I'll have to ask her," the gardener said. "If she turns you down, I'll pay you the extra silver and you can buy what you want."

"That's fair," Bembo agreed.

The gardener went back to Alcina and spoke to her in a low voice. She looked back toward Bembo. "Him?" she said. "Ha!" She tossed her head in fine contempt.

"That costs you another five," Bembo growled at the gardener, his ears burning. The other man knew better than to argue with him. He paid out the silver without another word. Bembo took it and stalked off, pleased and angry at the same time. He'd made a profit, but if he'd been a little luckier, he could have had fun, too.

At last, as much by accident as any other way (or so it seemed to him), the Lagoans had given Cornelu an assignment he actually wanted to have. Looming out of the mist ahead of him and Eforiel was Tirgoviste harbor.

He thanked the powers above for the mist. Without it, he would have had a much harder time approaching his home island. The Algarvians patrolled much more alertly than the Sibian navy had – which was one huge reason why King Mezentio's men ruled in Sibiu these days.

Turning back to the Lagoans Eforiel carried, he asked, "All good?" He would never be truly fluent in their language, but he was beginning to be able to make himself understood.

"Aye," the three of them said, one after another. They slipped off the lines to which they'd clung while the leviathan brought them across the sea. Cornelu wondered if the toys under Eforiel's belly were of the same sort the riders going into Valmiera had used or something altogether different. He hadn't asked. It was none of his business.

"Here. Wait," he said as the Lagoan raiders got ready to swim off. Treading water, they looked back at him. From inside his rubber suit, he pulled out a thin tube of oiled leather, tightly sealed at both ends. He spoke Lagoan phrases he'd carefully memorized: "Envelope in here. Please put in post box. For my wife."

He had not fled Sibiu with any such envelopes – printed in advance to show the proper postage fee had been paid – in his possession. Neither had any of his fellow exiles from the island kingdom. But Lagoas had hobbyists who collected such things. He'd been able to buy what he wanted from a shop that catered to them, and hadn't paid above twice what he would have at his own post office.

One of the Lagoans took the waterproof tube. "Aye, Commander, we'll take care of it," he said in Algarvian. That was a two-edge sword; it would let him be understood by most Sibians, but might make him seem an occupier rather than someone fighting the occupiers.

Cornelu shrugged as he said, "I thank you." Few Lagoans really spoke his language. Most thought Algarvian was close enough, and most of the time, up till the war, they'd been right. Now, though, a man who used -o endings instead of u-endings and trilled his "r"s instead of gargling them showed he did not come from the unlucky islands King Burebistu had ruled.

With a last wave, the Lagoans swam toward the shore, pushing their canister full of trouble ahead of them. They vanished into the mist almost at once. Cornelu had everything he could do not to slip away from his leviathan and swim after them. To come so close to Tirgoviste and not be allowed to go ashore was cruel, cruel. And yet, if he disobeyed his orders and left Eforiel behind, how could he strike more blows against Algarve? If all he wanted was to stay home, he could have surrendered after King Mezentio's men seized Sibiu. He had not. He would not.

"Costache," he murmured. And, somewhere up there in Tirgoviste town, he had a son or daughter he'd never seen. That was hard, too.

Eforiel let out a questioning grunt. Leviathans were smarter than animals had any business being, and Eforiel and he had been together almost as long as he and Costache. She knew something was wrong, even if she couldn't quite fathom what.

Cornelu sighed and stroked her smooth, pliant skin. It wasn't the lover's caress he wanted to give his wife, but had satisfactions of its own. "I cannot abandon you, either, can I?" he said. Eforiel grunted again. She wanted to tell him something, but he was not clever enough to know what.

His orders were to make for Setubal once more as soon as he had dropped off the raiders or saboteurs or whatever they were. Obeying those orders exactly as he'd got them proved impossible. He was a warrior disciplined enough to keep from abandoning the fight and trying to sneak home to his wife. But not all the discipline in the world could have kept him from lingering for a while outside the harbor in the hope of at least getting a long, bittersweet look at the land he loved.

He knew the mist might lay on the sea all day; it often did, in wintertime. If it did today, he promised himself he would guide Eforiel southeast again when evening came. Till then, he would wait. The Lagoans could not complain about when he returned. As he reluctantly admitted to himself, they were seamen, too; they understood the sea was not always a neat, tidy, precise place.

He looked west, in the direction of distant Unkerlant. King Swemmel's commodores probably timed their leviathan-riders with water clocks, and docked their pay for every minute they were late coming into port. That was what they called efficiency. Cornelu called it madness, but the Unkerlanters cared no more for his opinion than he did for Swemmel's.

Eforiel lunged off to one side after a pilchard or a squid, almost jerking Cornelu out of his harness. He laughed; while he was thinking about Unkerlant, an unprofitable pleasure if ever there was one, the leviathan was worrying about keeping her belly full. "You have better sense than I," he said, and patted her again. She wriggled under his hand, as if to answer, *Well, of course.*

Little by little, the mist did lift. Cornelu peered into Tirgoviste harbor. The warships there were Algarvian now, save for a few captured Sibian vessels. Cornelu cursed in a low voice to see the sailing ships that had brought the Algarvian army to Tirgoviste still in port, their masts and yards as bare of canvas as trees were of leaves in this season of the year.

Tirgoviste rose steeply from the harbor. Cornelu tried to make out the house he shared with Costache. He knew where it would be, but it was just too far away for him to let himself pretend he could spy it. In his mind's eye, though, he saw it plain, and Costache in front of it holding their — son? daughter? The mental picture blurred and grew indistinct, like a watercolor left out in drizzle.

Fog and clouds still lingered on the slopes of Tirgoviste's central mountains. Not for the first time, Cornelu hoped remnants of the Sibian army still carried on the fight against the Algarvians. Someone had to be carrying on the fight, else the Lagoans would not have sent their men to lend a hand.

A couple of little ley-line patrol boats moved around inside the sheltered waters of the harbor. Cornelu didn't think anything much about that till the boats, both flying Algarve's banner of green, white, and red, emerged from the harbor and sped toward him and Eforiel at a clip the leviathan could not come close to matching. Then he cursed again, in good earnest this time: while he'd been eyeing Tirgoviste, King Mezentio's men on the island had spotted him, too.

Maybe they thought he was one of their leviathan-riders, coming in with news. He dared not take the chance. Besides, even if they did, he could not continue that masquerade for long, not in a rubber suit still stamped over the breast with Sibiu's five crowns. He urged Eforiel down into a dive.

He had played games with patrol boats before, during exercises against his own countrymen and during the war against the Algarvians. In exercises and in action, he'd always managed to evade them. That left him confident he could do it yet again. He was annoyed at himself for letting the Algarvians spy him, but he wasn't anything more than annoyed.

Eventually, Eforiel gave the wriggle that meant she needed to surface. Cornelu let her swim back up toward the air. He'd guided her as closely parallel to the shoreline as he could. Surface sailors had little imagination. They would assume he'd fled straight out to sea, terrified at the sight of them. Odds were they wouldn't even notice Eforiel when she spouted. If they did, one more underwater run and he'd shake free of them. That was how things worked.

Or so he thought, till Eforiel did come up to breathe. Then, to his horror, he discovered that the patrol boats had ridden down a ley line very close to the path the leviathan had taken. They'd overran her by a little, but they plainly had a good notion of how far and how fast she was likely to travel under the sea.

When she spouted, sailors at the sterns of the patrol boats cried out. They were close enough to let Cornelu hear those shouts, thin over the water. He forced Eforiel into another dive as fast as he could. He knew she hadn't fully refreshed her lungs, but he also knew the Algarvian boats were going to start flinging eggs any minute. He refused to give them a target they could not miss.

Fling eggs they did. He heard them splash into the sea. The Algarvian mages had come up with something new, too, for they did not burst as soon as they hit the water, but sank for a while before suddenly releasing their energy far below the surface.

The deep bursts terrified Eforiel, who swam faster and harder than ever, and barely under Cornelu's control. He knew she would have to surface sooner because of it, but he couldn't do anything about it. No – he could and did hope that, when she surfaced this time, she would have evaded the patrol boats.

And so she had. Oh, one of them was fairly close, but out of egg-tosser range. It did not turn and move toward her when she spouted. Maybe the boat couldn't. Maybe she'd come up for air in a stretch of ocean well away from any ley lines. Ships that pulled their energy from the world grid were swifter and surer than those that did not,

but they could travel only where the grid let them. Where it did not
. . . Cornelu thumbed his nose at the patrol boat. "Here, my dear, we
are safe," he told Eforiel. "Rest as you will."

He never saw the dragon that dropped the egg toward Eforiel. He
never saw the egg, either, though its splash drenched him. It sank
below the surface of the sea, as the ones the patrol boats tossed had
done, and then it burst.

Eforiel's great body shielded Cornelu from the worst of the
energies. The leviathan writhed in torment. Blood crimsoned the sea.
Cornelu knew – and the knowledge tore at him – he could not save
her; too much blood was pouring forth. He also knew it would draw
sharks.

That left him one choice. Cursing the Algarvians – and cursing
himself for not doing a better job of watching the air – he struck out
for Tirgoviste. He wasn't close to the town that bore the name, not
after Eforiel's desperate flight, but he could still reach land. Whether
the Lagoans liked it or not, he was coming home.

20.

When the hard knock came on the door, Vanai shivered. She thought – she feared – it had an Algarvian sound. Maybe, if she didn't answer, whoever was out there would go away. It was, of course, a forlorn hope. The knock sounded again, sharper and more insistent than ever.

"Powers above, Vanai! Go see who that is, before he breaks down the door," Brivibas called irritably. In a softer voice, he went on, "How *is* a person to think with distractions that never cease?"

"I am going, my grandfather," Vanai said, resignation in her own tone. Brivibas didn't deal with distractions. That was her job.

She unbarred the door and threw it wide. Then she shivered again – not only was the day about as chilly as weather ever got in Oyngestun, but there stood Major Spinello, a squad of Algarvian soldiers behind him. "Good day," he said in his fluent Kaunian, looking her up and down in a way she did not like. But, despite his eyes, he kept his voice businesslike: "I require to see your grandfather."

"I shall fetch him, sir," Vanai said, but she could not resist adding, "I still do not think he will aid you."

"Perhaps he will, perhaps he won't." Spinello sounded indifferent. Vanai did not believe he was, not for a moment. He went on, "I have, I admit, discovered a new inducement. Bring him here, that I may speak of it."

"Please wait." Vanai did not invite him into the house. If he came in uninvited, she could not do anything about that. Going into Brivibas's study, she said, "My grandfather, Major Spinello would have speech with you."

"Would he?" Brivibas said. "Well, I would not have speech with him." The expression on Vanai's face must have been eloquent, for, with a grimace, he set down his pen. "I gather the choice is not mine?" Vanai nodded. Brivibas sighed and rose. "Very well, my granddaughter. I shall accompany you."

"Ah, here you are," Spinello said when Brivibas appeared before him. "The next question is, why are you here?"

"Men have been looking to answer that question since long before the days of the Kaunian Empire, Major," Vanai's grandfather said coldly. "I fear that no satisfactory response has yet come to light, though philosophers do continue their work."

"I was not speaking of philosophy," the Algarvian officer said. "I was asking why you, Brivibas, are here, at this house. We have been recruiting laborers in this district for some time. Only an oversight can have kept you from being one of them. I have been ordered to correct the said oversight, and I shall. Come along with me, old man. There are roads that need building, bridges that need repairing, piles of rubble that need clearing. Your scrawny Kaunian carcass isn't worth much, but it will have to do. Come on. Now."

Brivibas looked down at his hands. They were pale and soft and smooth; the only callus he had was by the nail of his right middle finger: a writer's callus. He turned to Vanai. "Take care of my books, if you possibly can – and of yourself, of course." In character to the last, she thought – books first, then her. Before she could say anything, Brivibas nodded to Major Spinello. "I am ready."

Spinello and the soldiers led him away. He did not look back at Vanai, who stood in the doorway. The Algarvian major did look back. Just before he and Brivibas and the troopers turned a corner, he waved gaily to her. Then they were gone.

She stood there for another couple of minutes, letting heat leak out of the house through the open door, before she finally closed it. The chill around her heart made the weather hardly worth noticing. She didn't know exactly how old her grandfather was, but he had to be up past sixty. He'd never done a day's labor – not the kind of labor Spinello was talking about – in his life. How long would he, how long could he, last? Not long. She was sure of that.

There had been times – more than a few of them – when she wished he would go away and leave her alone and not bother her again. Now he was gone. The house they'd shared since she was tiny seemed much too big and much too empty without him. She wandered aimlessly from room to room.

Eventually, long after she took her midday meal most days, she realized she was hungry. She ate some bread and some dried figs, having no energy to make anything more ambitious. For supper, she started a thick soup with barley and what little sausage she found in the larder. She had no appetite, but her grandfather would be hungry.

Brivibas came home almost two hours later than she thought he would. She'd never seen him so filthy in all her life, nor half so worn. Most of his fingernails were broken; they all had black crescents ground under them. His palms were nothing but blisters and blood.

Vanai took one look at him and burst into tears. "There, there, my granddaughter," he said in what she heard for the first time as an old man's voice, brittle as dry grass. "Spinello thinks his logic keen, but it shall not persuade me."

"Eat," Vanai said, as he had so often said to her. Eat he did, and lustily, but he fell asleep a little more than halfway through the bowl of soup. Vanai shook him, but he would not wake. Had he not been breathing, she would have wondered if he was dead.

At last, she managed to rouse him and half carry him to the bedroom. "I must be up and away from here before sunrise tomorrow," he said, his voice distant but clear. Vanai violently shook her head. "Oh, but I must," Brivibas insisted. "I rely on you for it: if I am not, they will beat me and I shall have to labor anyhow. I rely on you, my granddaughter. You must not fail me."

Through tears, Vanai said, "I obey, my grandfather," and then, because she could not help herself, "Wouldn't it be easier to give Spinello, curse him, what he wants from you?"

"Easier? No doubt." Brivibas yawned enormously. "But it would be wrong." His head hit the pillow. His eyes closed. He began to snore.

Vanai felt like a murderer when she woke him the next morning. He thanked her, which only made things worse. She gave him the remains of the evening's soup for breakfast and bread and cheese and dried mushrooms – some from Ealstan's basket – to eat while he worked. And then he was off, and she was alone in a house where the wind rattling a shutter was enough to make her leap in the air like a startled cat.

He came back late again that night, and the next one, and the next. Every day of labor seemed to age him a month, and he had not so very many months to spare. "It gets easier as I grow accustomed to it," he would say, but it was a lie. Vanai knew it. Every day, the flesh thinned on his face, until she thought it was a staring skull that looked back at her out of bright blue eyes and spoke pedantic reassurances that did not reassure.

One morning after he staggered off, Vanai stood stock-still, as if a mage had suddenly made her into marble. *I know what I have to do.* The realization held an almost mystical clarity and certainty.

But it would be wrong. Brivibas's sleep-sodden voice sounded inside her head.

"I don't care," she said aloud, as if her grandfather were there to argue with her. It wasn't quite true. But she knew what was more important to her, and what less. If she could win the one, what did the other matter?

In that house, finding paper and pen was a matter of a moment. She knew what she wanted to say, and said it. The purity of the Kaunian she used would have brought a nod of approval from her grandfather, regardless of what he thought of certain other aspects of the note.

After she'd folded the paper on herself and sealed it with wax and her grandfather's seal, she threw on a cloak and carried the note to the Forthwegian barrister's home where the Algarvians made their headquarters in Oyngestun. She left it there, with a sergeant who leered at her and ran a red, red tongue over his lips. She fled.

"Still a whore for the redheads," a Kaunian woman hissed at her. She hung her head and hurried back to her home. There she waited, and waited, and waited. Nothing out of the ordinary happened the next day, or the day after that. Each morning, before first light, Brivibas shambled off to labor for the Algarvians. Each morning, he was more a crumbling ruin of the man he had been.

In the middle of the afternoon on the third day, the knock Vanai had been waiting for, the knock she recognized, came. She started, spilling some of the peas she'd been putting into water to soak. Even though she'd been waiting for that knock, she moved toward the door with the slow, reluctant steps she might have taken in a bad dream. *If I don't answer, he will think I am not at home, and go away,* went through her mind. But so did another thought; *if I don't answer, my grandfather will surely die.*

She opened the door. Major Spinello stood there, as she'd known he would. He bowed to her. "I greet you, my lady Vanai. May I come in?"

His formality surprised her. Had he got the note? He had. Oh, he had. She saw it in his eyes. "Aye," she whispered, and stood aside to let him.

He closed and barred the door. That done, he turned to her. "Did you know what you were saying when you said you would do anyhing to keep your worthless old grandfather from going off and doing what he should have been doing this past year and more?" he asked.

"Aye," Vanai whispered again, even lower this time. She looked at the floor to keep from looking at Spinello. Again to her surprise, he waited to see if she would say more. After a moment, she did: "He is all I have."

"Not all." The Algarvian shook his head. "Oh, no, my dear, not all." He stretched out a hand and undid the three wooden toggles that closed the neck of her tunic, then reached down to the hem and pulled it up over her head. Hating him, hating herself more, she raised her arms to help him. He looked at her for what felt like forever. "Brivibas is very far from all you have." He reached out again. This time, his hands stroked bare flesh.

He surprised her once more by not mauling her. His touch was knowing, assured. Had she freely chosen him, she might – she thought she would – have enjoyed it. As things were, she stood still and endured.

"To your bedchamber, then," he said after a while. Vanai nodded, thinking it would be easier there than on the floor, where she'd more than half expected him to drag her down. Pausing only to pick up her tunic, she took him where he wanted to go.

The bed would be narrow for two. The bed was none too wide for her alone. She waited beside it. If he wanted her out of her trousers, he would have to take her out of them. He did, and seemed to enjoy the doing. Then, amazingly fast, he undressed himself. She looked away. She knew how a man was made. She did not want to be reminded.

But even a brief glimpse reminded her that Algarvians were made rather differently – or made themselves rather differently. She'd known of their ritual mutilation, a custom that had persisted since ancient days. Till now, she'd never imagined it would matter to her.

"Lie down," Spinello said, and Vanai obeyed. He lay beside her. "It gives a man more pleasure if a woman takes pleasure, too," he remarked, and did his best with hands and mouth to give her some. When he told her to do something, she did it, and tried not to think about what she did. Otherwise, as she had in the hall, she endured.

When his tongue began to probe her secrets, she twisted away toward the wall. "Come back," he said. "If you will not kindle, you will not. But the wetter you are, the less it will hurt."

"A considerate ravisher," Vanai said through clenched teeth.

Spinello laughed. "But of course." Presently, he went into her. "Ah," he murmured a moment later, discovering no one had been there before him. "It *will* hurt, some." He pushed forward. It did hurt. Vanai bit down on the inside of her lip. She tasted blood: blood to match the blood the Algarvian was drawing down below. She closed her eyes and tried to ignore his weight on her.

He grunted and quivered and pulled out. That hurt, too. Vanai tolerated it, though, because it meant this was finally over. "My grandfather—" she began.

Major Spinello laughed again. "You know what you did this for, don't you?" he said. "Aye, a bargain: the wordy old bugger can come home and stay home – for as long as you keep giving me what I want, too. Do we understand each other, my dear?"

Vanai twisted toward the wall once more. "Aye," she said, huddling into a ball. Of course once would not be enough to suit him. She should have known that. She supposed she had known it, even if she'd hoped . . . But what good was hope? She listened to him dress. She listened to him leave. *Whore for the redheads*, the Kaunian woman had called her. It hadn't been true then. It was now. Vanai wept, not that weeping helped.

Winter on the island of Obuda brought endless driving rainstorms roaring off the Bothnian Ocean. Istvan hadn't cared for them when he could take shelter in his barracks. He honestly preferred blizzards. He knew how to get around on snow. Anyone who grew up in a Gyongyosian valley knew everything he needed to know about snow.

Rain was a different business. Bad enough in the barracks – far worse when the only shelter he had was a hole in the ground. His cape still shed some water. That meant he was only soaked, not drenched. He slept very little, and that badly. Being soaked was only part of it. The other part was a healthy fear that some sneaking Kuusaman would get through the lines and slit his throat so he'd die without ever waking. It wasn't an idle fear. Those little bastards could slip through cracks in the defenses a weasel couldn't use.

He peered down the side of Mt. Sorong toward the Kuusaman trenches and holes. He couldn't see very far through the trees and rain, but that didn't stop him from being wary. He kept his stick close by him every moment, awake or asleep. He also had a stout knife on his belt. In weather like this, the knife might do him more good than the stick. Beams couldn't carry far through driving rain.

Squelching noises behind him made him whirl – no telling from what direction a Kuusaman might come. But that big, tawny-bearded trooper was no Kaunian. "What now, Szonyi?" Istvan asked.

"Still here," Szonyi said.

"Oh, aye, still here," Istvan agreed. "The stars must hate us, don't you think? If they didn't, we'd be somewhere else. Of course" – he paused meditatively – "they might choose to send us somewhere worse."

"And how would they do that?" the younger soldier demanded. "I don't think there is a worse place than this."

"Put it that way and you may be right," Istvan said. "But you may be wrong, too." He wasn't sure how, but he'd seen enough bad to have a strong suspicion worse always waited around the corner. His stomach growled, reminding him bad was still bad. "What have you got in the way of food?" he asked Szonyi.

"Not much, I'm afraid," Szonyi answered, so regretfully that Istvan suspected he had more than he was admitting. The youngster was turning into a veteran, all right. But, short of searching his pockets and pack, Istvan couldn't make a liar of him. He wasn't desperate enough to do that, not yet. And maybe Szonyi wasn't lying, too, for he said, "Maybe we ought to raid the slanteyes again."

"Aye, maybe we should," Istvan said. "They aren't a proper warrior race, not even close – they think soldiers have to have full bellies to fight well. If we spent a quarter of the trouble on provisioning our men as they do, we'd be too fat to fight at all." Rain dripped from the hood of his cape down on to his nose. "Go ahead, tell me I'm wrong."

"Can't do it," Szonyi said. "Here's one, though: if they aren't a warrior race and we are, how come we haven't kicked 'em off Obuda once and for all?"

Istvan opened his mouth, then abruptly closed it again. That was a good question, such a good question that a man could break teeth on it if he was unwary enough to bite down hard. At last, Istvan said, "The stars know," which was undoubtedly true and which also undoubtedly did not come close to answering the question. He took the talk back in the direction it had gone before: "What do you say we slide down the hill and see if we can knock over a couple of Kuusamans? They'll have more food than we do – you can bet on that."

"Aye," Szonyi said. "They couldn't very well have less, could they?"

"I hope not, for their sake," Istvan said. "Come to think of it, I hope not for our sake, too." He slung his stick on his back and pulled his knife from its sheath. "Come on." *I am going to risk my life for no better reason than filling my belly*, he thought as he crawled out of his shelter and down the mountainside. Then he wondered if there could ever be any better reason than filling his belly.

He moved as silently as he could. The drumming rain helped muffle any sounds he did make. It also helped hide him from the Kuusamans' narrow eyes. At the same time, though, it muffled their noises and helped conceal them from him. He hadn't stayed alive as long as he had by being careless. Szonyi might have been a shadow behind him. If bad luck didn't kill the youngster, he would make a fine soldier.

The rain came down harder and harder, so that Istvan could see only a few yards in front of him. Spring wasn't that far away; before long, the storms would ease. Istvan had seen it happen before. He knew it would happen again. But it hadn't happened yet, and the storm didn't seem to think it ever would.

He crawled past the stinking, sodden corpse of a Gyongyosian trooper – no Kuusaman born had ever had hair that shade of yellow. The corpse warned him he was nearing the Kuusaman line. It also warned him he might not come back.

No sooner had that unpleasant thought crossed his mind than eggs started dropping out of the sky on and around the Kuusaman position. He looked up, but of course the low, thick gray clouds hid the dragons that carried the eggs. He hoped they were Gyongyosian, but they might almost as readily have had Kuusamans riding them. Gyongyosian dragons had dropped eggs on their own footsoldiers before; he did not think the enemy immune from such mischances.

He flattened himself out on the ground. Bursts of energy near him tried to pick him up and throw him away. He clung to the bushes for all he was worth.

A Kuusaman, either wild with panic or more likely caught away from shelter and running in search of some, tripped over one of his legs and crashed to the ground. That was the first either of them knew of the other's presence. They both cried out. Istvan's knife rose and fell. The Kuusaman cried out again, this time in anguish. Istvan drove the knife into his throat. His cries cut off. He thrashed for a couple of minutes, ever more weakly, they lay still.

Istvan let out a rasping sigh of relief and went through the fellow's pockets and pack. He found hard bread, smoked and salted salmon – a Kuusaman specialty – and dried apples and pears. The dead soldier's canteen proved to hold apple brandy, something else of which the Kuusamans were inordinately fond. Istvan took a nip. He sighed with pleasure as fire ran down his throat.

"Szonyi?" he called in a low voice. When he got no answer, he called again, louder this time. He could have shouted and not been heard far in the din of bursting eggs.

He peered around. The only company he had was the dead Kuusaman. He cursed under his breath. He couldn't go back up Mt. Sorong without knowing what had happened to his comrade. One warrior did not abandon another on the field. The stars would not shine for any man who did so base a thing as that.

"Szonyi?" Istvan called once more.

This time, he got an answer: "Aye?" Szonyi came through the curtain of rain toward him. The youngster had a smile on his face and a Kuusaman canteen in his hand. "I nailed one of the little whoresons," he said. "How about you?"

"This fellow here won't need his supper any more, so I may as well eat it for him," Istvan said, which drew a laugh from Szonyi. Istvan went on, "Now that we've got a little food, let's slide back up the side of the mountain."

"I suppose so." Szonyi didn't sound happy about it. "If we do, though, we'll have to share it with people who didn't get any of their own."

"And nobody has ever shared with you?" Istvan asked. Szonyi hung his head. Istvan slapped him on the shoulder. "Come on. We won't starve for a while longer, anyhow, even if we do have to share."

With eggs still falling almost at random, getting back up Mt. Sorong was easier than going down the sloping side of the low mountain had been. The Gyongyosian soldiers could make more noise, for with the bursting eggs it went largely unnoticed. But, just before they reached their own line, a sharp challenge rang out: "Halt! Who goes there?"

Istvan was glad to hear that challenge. If he couldn't sneak up on his comrades, maybe the Kuusamans couldn't, either. He gave his own name and Szonyi's, then added, "Is that you, Kun?"

"Aye." The mage's apprentice sounded reluctant to admit it. He returned to soldierly formality: "Advance and be recognized."

"Here we come," Istvan said. "Don't start blazing at us now, or we won't give you any of the Kuusaman treats we've brought back." Szonyi sent him a reproachful look. He pretended not to see it. With the rain, the pretense was easy enough.

Raindrops dappled the lenses of Kun's spectacles as he too showed himself. "Salmon?" he asked hopefully. When he had the chance, he ate like a dragon, and his scrawny carcass never put on an ounce. When he couldn't eat so much as he wanted, he got skinnier still.

"Aye, salmon, and bread and fruit, too. And that applejack the slanteyes brew," Istvan said. "Szonyi and I have put a dent in what we got of that, but you can have a slug or two, and some of the food to go with it."

What would have been plenty for two men wasn't quite enough for three, but even Szonyi didn't complain out loud. The two canteens held enough apple brandy to make complaint seem pointless to all three Gyongyosians. Presently, Szonyi landed back against the trunk of a tree and asked, "How did you spot us, Kun? You can't be able to see much in the rain with your spectacles, and I don't think

we made any noise. Even if we did, the racket down the hill should
have covered it."

"I have my methods," Kun said, and said no more.

His smile was so superior, Istvan wanted to kick him in the teeth.
"Some fifth-rank magical trick, I don't doubt," he growled. "Would
it have spotted Kuusamans, too? Tell me the truth, by the stars. Our
necks may ride on what you know and what you don't."

"Unless they're specially warded, it would," Kun answered. "It
spies men moving forward toward me."

It didn't spy men moving toward him from higher up Mt. Sorong,
as a crashing in the brush proved a moment later. Istvan stared in
astonishment at the apparition before him: an officer with the large
six-pointed star of a major on each side of the collar of a uniform
tunic surprisingly clean and fresh. He couldn't have been living in
that tunic for weeks, as Istvan had in his.

Istvan and Szonyi saluted without rising. Despite Kun's assurances,
Istvan didn't know the Kuusamans hadn't sneaked a sniper somewhere close. He noticed Kun didn't spring to his feet, either. The
major returned the salutes, then said, "Those goat-bearded lackwits
said Istvan's unit was somewhere around these parts. They had no
sure notion where. Do you know of it? Am I close to it?"

"Sir—" Now, cautiously, Istvan did rise. "Sir, I am Istvan."

"A common soldier?" The major's eyes got wide. "By the way
they spoke of you farther up the hill, I expected a captain." He
shrugged. "Well, no matter. Gather your warriors, Istvan, however
many they be, and accompany me to the shipping that awaits. In this
beastly weather, we need fear no Kuusaman dragons."

"Shipping, sir?" Now Istvan was the one taken by surprise.

"Aye," the major said impatiently. "We are transferring certain
units back to the mainland, for purposes I need not discuss. Yours is
among them; folk spoke highly of its fighting qualities. Now show
me they were right."

Numbly, Istvan obeyed. *I'm escaping Obuda*, he thought. *The stars
be praised. I'm escaping Obuda.*

The sun shone blindingly on the snow-covered fields surrounding
the village of Zossen. The glare did nothing to ease Garivald's
hangover. But he bore the pain more readily than he would have

during the tail end of most winters. He'd spent less time drunk this
season than in any winter since he'd started shaving.

He shook his head, even though it hurt. He'd spent less time drunk
on spirits this past winter than any since he'd become a man. The rest
of the time, though, he'd been drunk on words.

He glanced at the sun out of the corner of his eye. It climbed
higher in the north every day. Spring wasn't far away. The snow
would melt, the ground would turn to muck, and, when the muck
grew firm enough, it would be planting time. Most years, he'd
looked forward to that. Not now. He'd have to work hard for a
while. The more he worked, the less time he would have to make
songs.

I never knew I could, he thought, and then, automatically, made a
couplet of it: *I never knew it could be so good*. He felt like a middle-aged
man who'd never had a woman till he married a young, beautiful,
passionate bride: he was doing his best to make up for all the time
he'd gone without.

Already, the villagers of Zossen sang his version of the now
sacrificed captive's song in preference to the one the luckless convict
had known. They sang a couple of other songs of his, too, one his
own try at a love song and the other an effort at putting into words
what being cooped up through a longer winter in southern
Unkerlant was like.

He wondered if he could make a song about what being worked
to death most of the year felt like. No sooner had he wondered than
words started lining up in neat rows inside his head, as if they were
soldiers taking their formation at an officer's command. Even so, he
wondered if that song would be worth making. Everybody already
understood everything there was to understand about working too
much, understood it in the head and the heart and the small of the
back, too. Songs were better when they told you something you
didn't already know.

He took a couple of steps, his boots crunching on crusted snow.
Then he stopped again, a thoughtful expression on his face. He spoke
the idea aloud. That helped him hold it in his mind: "I wonder if I
could make a song that told people something they already know as
well as the taste of black bread but made them think of something
different, something they'd never thought of before."

That would be something special, he thought. *A song like that would last forever.* He kicked at the snow, sending little clumps of it flying. Now he would be thinking about that to the exclusion of everything else. He saw it was a thing that might be done, but had no idea how to go about it. He wished he knew more. He had no formal training in music or songmaking. He had no formal training in anything. He'd learned how to farm by watching his father, not by having a schoolmaster beat lessons into his back with a switch.

Standing out here at the edge of the village was peaceful. After so much time in the company of his wife and son and daughter and animals — in their company whether he wanted to be or not, for the most part — he savored as much peace as he could find.

He couldn't find much, even on the outskirts of Zossen. Here came Waddo, waving his arms and bearing down on him like a behemoth in rut. A rhyme flew out of Garivald's head, never to return. He glowered at the village firstman. "What is it now, Waddo? Whatever it is, couldn't it have waited?"

He was, perhaps, lucky. Waddo was so full of himself, he paid no attention to anything Garivald said. "Have you heard?" he demanded. "Powers above, have you heard?" Then he shook his head. "No, of course you haven't heard, and I'm an idiot. How could you have heard? I just got it off the crystal myself."

"Why don't you back up and start from the beginning?" Garivald asked. Whatever Waddo had heard had upset him beyond the mean.

"Aye, I'll do that," the firstman said, nodding. "What I heard is, the lousy, stinking Algarvians have gone and invaded Yanina, that's what I heard. King Swemmel is hopping mad about it, too. He's calling it a breach that will not stand, and he's moving soldiers to the border with Yanina."

"Why?" Garivald wondered. "From everything I've heard about Yanina" — he hadn't heard much, but had no intention of admitting it — "Algarve is welcome to the place. People with pompoms on their shoes?" He shook his head. "I don't know about you, but I don't want anything to do with 'em."

"You don't understand," Waddo said, which was likely to be true. "Yanina borders Algarve, right? And Yanina borders Unkerlant, too, right? If the redheads march into Yanina, what's the next thing they're going to do?"

"Catch the clap from all the loose Yaninan women," Garivald answered, "and maybe from the loose Yaninan men, too, if half the stories they tell about them are true."

Waddo exhaled in half scandalized exasperation. "That's not what I meant," he said, "and it's not what his Majesty meant, either." His chest swelled with self-importance; he'd heard King Swemmel with his own ears. "The next thing the Algarvians are going to do is keep right on marching, straight on into Unkerlant, and we aren't going to let that happen."

Impressers will be coming, Garivald thought. If Unkerlant got into a fight with Algarve, she'd need all the men she could find. The Six Years' War had written out that lesson in letters of blood. Aside from that, though . . . "Zossen's a long way from the border with Yanina," he said. "I don't see how it's going to matter to us, any more than the war with Zuwayza did. Just another loud noise in a room far away."

"It's an insult to the whole kingdom, that's what it is," Waddo said, no doubt echoing the angry voice he'd heard in the crystal. "We won't stand for it. We won't take it lying down."

"What will we do, then?" Garivald asked reasonably. "Sit on a bench? That's about the only thing left for us, wouldn't you say?"

"You're being absurd," the firstman said, though Garivald wasn't the one who'd used the figures of speech. "As soon as the ground is dry enough, we're going to have to drive the Algarvians out of there."

"Aye, that sounds efficient – if we can do it," Garivald said. "Can we do it, do you think?"

"His Majesty says we can. His Majesty says we will," Waddo said. "Who am I to argue with his Majesty? He knows more about the business than I do." He fixed Garivald with a sour stare. "And, before your mouth runs away with you again, he knows more about this business than you do, too."

"Well, that's likely so," Garivald admitted. "But talk with some of the older men here, Waddo. See how they like the idea of another war with the redheads."

"Maybe I will," said Waddo, who, like Garivald, was too young to have fought in the Six Years' War. The firstman went on, "But whether they like it or not doesn't matter. If King Swemmel says we're at war with Algarve, why then, by the powers above, we're at war with Algarve. And if we're at war with Algarve, we'd better lick the redheads, or else they'll lick us. Isn't that right?"

"Aye, it is," Garivald said. The only other choice was going to war against King Swemmel. Garivald was old enough to remember the Twinkings War. He didn't see how fighting Algarve could be worse than civil war in Unkerlant. After what Swemmel ended up doing to Kyot, he didn't see how any other challenger for the throne would dare try unseating the king, either.

"There you have it, then," Waddo said. "What his Majesty tells us to do, we'll do, and that's all there is to it."

Garivald couldn't argue with that, either. Something else occurred to him: "How did the Algarvians go marching into Yanina just like that? Yanina's down south, same as we are. The going can't be easy there. I'm not a king and I'm not a marshal, but I wouldn't want to go invading anybody at this time of year." He waved at the snowdrifts covering the fields.

"I don't know anything about that," said Waddo, who plainly hadn't thought about it, either. "King Swemmel didn't say how the cursed redheads did it. He just said that they did it. How doesn't matter. The king wouldn't lie to us."

Why not? Garivald wondered. He would have spoken that thought aloud with Annore. He might have spoken it aloud with Dagulf. Speaking to his wife or his trusted friend was one thing. Speaking to the firstman was something else again. Waddo was more Swemmel's man than a proper villager.

"I'm off to tell some others now," Waddo said. "You were the first man I saw, Garivald, so you were the first to get the news. But everyone in Zossen needs to hear." Off he went, kicking up snow from the path with each step he took.

Some men of Garivald's acquaintance would have gone with him, to spread the news farther and faster. Garivald liked his gossip as well as any man. Come to that, few old wives in Zossen liked gossip any better. But he did not follow Waddo. For one thing, this wasn't gossip, or not exactly gossip: it was too big. He couldn't think of anything much bigger than news of impending war. And, for another, he didn't like Waddo well enough to help him with anything he didn't have to.

Garivald stared east across the fields. He was glad a couple of hundred miles separated his village from Yanina's western border. The Algarvians hadn't come this far during the Six Years' War, nor anywhere close. That made it a good bet they wouldn't come so far this time, either.

Then he kicked up snow himself. That the war wouldn't come to Zossen didn't mean he wouldn't go to the war, wherever it ended up being fought. He looked back toward Waddo's two-story house and silently cursed the crystal the firstman had there. Evading the impressers would be much harder with that crystal here. They could report to Cottbus, get their orders for however many men the army required, and call for whatever help they needed, all right away.

He imagined an Unkerlanter dragon flying over the woods outside the village, dropping eggs on them to flush out the recalcitrants less than eager to fight in King Swemmel's army. Impressers would do that sort of thing in a heartbeat – assuming they had hearts, which struck Garivald as unlikely.

Several lines casting scorn on impressers, inspectors, and everyone from Cottbus sprang into his mind, all unbidden. The whole village would laugh if he started singing such a song: the whole village except Waddo and the guards who kept the captives in the gaol cell from escaping. Garivald did not think they would be the least bit amused.

Reluctantly, he pushed his thoughts away from that sort of song. He could make it, aye. He could do any number of things he would be better off not doing. Life in Zossen was sometimes hard. That didn't mean he had to go looking for ways to make it harder.

Behind him, he heard shouts of surprise. Those were the guards. Waddo must have given them the news. Garivald shook his head. He wouldn't have shared gossip of any sort with the guards. It wasn't as if they were villagers. Garivald shook his head again. Waddo had no sense of proportion.

"This is Patras," Captain Galafrone said as the ley-line caravan sighed to a stop. "From here on, boys, we don't ride any more. From here on, we march." He looked as if he relished the prospect. Tealdo, who was something less than half his captain's age, didn't.

Neither did Tealdo's friend Trasone. "I've already done enough marching to last me, thank you kindly," he whispered.

"It's not like we won't be doing more anyhow soon enough,"

Tealdo said. Like any soldier worth his pay, he was always ready to complain.

"What?" Trasone raised a gingery eyebrow. "You don't figure us being here will scare King Swemmel out of gobbling up Yanina, the way he was going to do? I figure one look at you would be enough to make every Unkerlanter in the world run off screaming for his mother."

"Come on, let's go," Galafrone said. "We want to impress Colonel Ombruno, right?" He pretended not to hear the jeers that rang through the car, continuing, "And some of the Yaninan women are supposed to be pretty cursed good-looking, too. I don't know about you boys, but I don't want 'em laughing at me on account of I can't remember which is my left foot and which is my right when I'm marching."

That put matters in a different light. Tealdo checked to make sure his tunic was perfectly straight and every pleat in his kilt knife-sharp. Trasone combed his mustache, not wanting a single hair out of place. Even Sergeant Panfilo set his hat on his head at a jauntier angle, and Tealdo would have sworn that only a blind woman, or one severely short of cash, could take the least interest in Panfilo.

"Get moving, you lousy lugs," Panfilo rumbled as he surged to his feet. "Let's show these foreign doxies what real men look like."

A raw breeze blew through the streets of Patras. Tealdo was glad of the long, thick wool socks he wore, and would have been gladder had they been thicker and longer. Not far from the platform on which he was debarking, a Yaninan band played a vaguely familiar tune. After a while, he recognized it as the Algarvian royal hymn. "I've never heard it with bagpipes before," he murmured to Trasone.

"I hope I never do again," his friend whispered back.

Yaninans lined the route along which the Algarvian soldiers marched. Some of them held up signs in badly spelled, ungrammatical Algarvian. One said, WELL COME LIBERATATORS! Another proclaimed, DEETH FOR UNKERLANT! More signs and placards were in Yaninan, whose very characters were strange to Tealdo. For all he knew, they might have been advertising sausage or patent medicine or wishing that he and his countrymen might come down with a social disease.

But the Yaninans cheered too lustily to let him believe that. Set against Algarvians, they were short and wiry. The men favored mustaches that were thick and bushy rather than waxed to spiked perfection, as was the Algarvian ideal. Some of the older women had fairly respectable mustaches, too, which was much less common in Tealdo's homeland.

He paid more attention to the young women. Like the men, they mostly had olive complexions and dark hair and eyes. Their features were sharply carved: wide foreheads; strong cheekbones and noses; narrow, pointed chins. They painted their lips red as blood.

"I've seen worse," he said to Trasone, in a tone another man might have used to judge horseflesh.

"Oh, aye," Trasone agreed. "And if we go into Unkerlant, you'll see worse again. Think of Forthwegian women, only more so."

Tealdo thought about it. He didn't like what he was thinking. "Best argument for peace I've heard yet," he said.

Trasone snickered, which brought Sergeant Panfilo's wrath down on his head. "Silence in the ranks, curse you!" Panfilo growled.

Along with the rest of the brigade, Colonel Ombruno's regiment assembled in front of King Tsavellas's palace, a sprawling edifice whose onion domes painted in swirling patterns and bright colors loudly proclaimed what a foreign land this was. Algarvian banners – red, white, and green – flew alongside those of Yanina, which were simply red on white.

Another band struck up something vaguely resembling a tune. Tealdo supposed it was the Yaninan royal hymn, for a man in a domed crown and robes of scarlet and ermine ascended to a rostrum while the locals lining the edge of the plaza chorused, "Tsavellas! Tsavellas!"

King Tsavellas raised a hand. Had King Mezentio used such a gesture, he would have got silence. Tsavellas got more noise: Yaninans were anything but an orderly folk. The king waited. Slowly, very slowly, quiet came. Into it, Tsavellas spoke in accented but understandable Algarvian: "I welcome you brave men from the east, who will help shield my small kingdom from the madness of my other neighbor." Then he said something – probably the same thing – in Yaninan. His subjects cheered. He waved to them and stepped down.

An Algarvian took his place. "That's probably our minister here,"

Tealdo said to Trasone, who nodded. Sure enough, the Algarvian spoke first not to the soldiers from his kingdom but to the assembled people of Patras in what sounded like fluent Yaninan. They cheered him with as much enthusiasm as they'd given their own sovereign.

Then he looked out over the ranks of Algarvian soldiers. "You are here for a reason, men," he told them. "King Tsavellas invited you, begged King Mezentio to allow you, to enter Yanina to prove to King Swemmel of Unkerlant that we are determined to defend the small against the large. Just as the Kaunian kingdoms oppressed us when we were weak, so Unkerlant sought to oppress Yanina. But we are not weak now, and we shall not let our neighbors be molested. Men of Algarve, do I speak the truth?"

"Aye!" the Algarvian soldiers shouted. Some of them waved their hats. Some scaled their hats through the air. Tealdo waved his. However tempted he might have been to throw it, he refrained. Sergeant Panfilo's comments would surely have been colorful, but might also have been imperfectly appreciative.

Two flagbearers went up on the rostrum. One held an Algarvian banner, the other a Yaninan. The flags blew in the breeze side by side. "About-*turn!*" Colonel Ombruno called to his regiment. Along with his comrades, Tealdo spun on his heel. The regiment led the brigade out of the square. After one wrong turn – fortunately, out of sight of King Tsavellas and the Algarvian minister – they made their way to the barracks where they would spend the night.

Surrounding the barracks like toadstools were tents full of Yaninan soldiers. "Uh-oh," Tealdo said. "I don't much like that. We're stealing their beds. They won't love us for it."

He liked it even less the next morning, when he woke up with bug bites. What the Yaninans served up for breakfast wasn't very good. Tealdo had expected as much. Captain Galafrone had warned the whole company to expect as much. "Boys, they're long on cabbage and they're long on bread. You'll be bored, but you won't be hungry."

Bored Tealdo certainly was, not that Algarvian army cooking was anything to send a noble connoisseur into flights of ecstasy. But Tealdo also ended up hungry, because the Yaninan cooks hadn't done up enough to fill the bellies of their new Algarvian allies. *Share and share alike* was the rule. A few bites of black bread and not enough cabbage-and-beet soup made Tealdo's stomach rumble and growl as if angry wild things dwelt there.

"I wonder what the Yaninans are eating," he said as he finished the meager meal – not that finishing it took long. "I wonder if the poor whoresons are eating anything."

"Aye. This isn't good." Trasone shook his head. Being a veteran, he knew how important questions of supply were. "If the Yaninans can't do a proper job of feeding troops in their own capital, how will they manage out in the field."

"We'll find out, won't we?" Tealdo said. "We'll pay the price of finding out, too."

But Sergeant Panfilo shook his head. "It won't be as bad as that," he said. "Our supply services come along with us. Once we're stationed, once the fighting starts – if the fighting starts – they'll take care of us. Those boys can find a six-course supper hiding under dead leaves."

"Well, that's true enough," Tealdo said, somewhat reassured. It wasn't quite so – Panfilo did exaggerate, but not by much. "Powers above pity the poor Yaninans, though. They haven't got much, and they don't know how to move what they do have."

"Come on, boys," Captain Galafrone called. "Lovely as this place is, we can't hang around here any more. We've got to go out and see the big, wide world – or at least the little, narrow chunk of it that belongs to Yanina."

Tealdo did more really hard marching that day than in any other he could remember. He'd marched farther a good many times, especially in the hectic fighting that led up to Valmiera's collapse. But Valmiera, like Algarve, had a decent network of paved roads. A man or a horse or a unicorn or a behemoth could tramp over the cobblestones or gravel or slabs of slate at any season of the year.

He'd come into Patras by ley-line caravan, and hadn't had to worry about what the roads were like. The streets of King Tsavellas's capital were paved as well as those of any Algarvian town. The highway that led toward the west, toward the border with Unkerlant, was also well paved . . . for the first few miles.

About an hour after leaving the barracks behind, Tealdo and his comrades also left the cobblestones behind. His feet plunged into cold mud. The first time he lifted one up out of the roadbed, a lot of the roadbed came with it. The second time he lifted one out, even more mud came along. He cursed in disgust.

He wasn't the only one cursing, either. A brimstone cloud might have surrounded the company, the regiment, the entire brigade. "These are our allies?" somebody not far away from Tealdo bellowed. "Powers below eat them, the Unkerlanters can have them and welcome!" He was more than usually exercised, but then, when he'd picked up a foot, his boot hadn't come out of the muck with it.

"Shut up!" Galafrone shouted. "You fools haven't got the faintest notion of what you're talking about. I fought against the Unkerlanters in the last war, along with your fathers — if you know who your fathers are. You think this is bad, Unkerlant makes this look like Mad Duke Morando's pleasure gardens outside of Cotigoro. You'll find out."

Algarvian soldiers obeyed orders. They kept marching, as best they could. That didn't mean they didn't speak their minds. The trooper who'd lost his boot spoke with great conviction: "I don't care how lousy Unkerlant is. That still doesn't make this stinking place any fornicating pleasure garden."

On the Algarvians slogged. They came to their assigned campsite long after nightfall. Tealdo was amazed they came to it at all. Ever since the cobbles stopped, he'd felt as if he were marching in place.

The Yaninan cooks also seemed astonished the Algarvians reached the campsite. Again, they had something less than adequate rations for the brigade. Having gulped down what he was given, Tealdo started toward the west, toward Unkerlant. King Swemmel was responsible for the dreadful day he'd put in, and for other dreadful days that no doubt lay ahead. As far as Tealdo was concerned, that meant Swemmel's subjects would pay. "Oh, how they'll pay," he muttered.

"Come on, curse you!" Leudast shouted to the ordinary troopers of his squad. He enjoyed being a corporal, sure enough. Being a corporal meant he got to do the shouting instead of having sergeants and corporals shout at him. "We have to move faster, curse it. You think the lousy redheads are going to stand around waiting for you to get your thumbs out of your arses?"

He left without the slightest twinge of regret the Forthwegian village in which his squad had been billeted. The locals hadn't given his comrades and him any more trouble since the Unkerlanters blazed down the firstman and his wife, but the Forthwegians didn't love his countrymen, and they never would.

Like rills and creeks and streams flowing together to form a great river, the Unkerlanter squads and companies that had been quartered on the countryside came together into regiments and brigades and divisions and flowed toward the east, toward the border with Algarvian-held Forthweg. Leudast smiled and nodded approval at every squadron of horsemen and unicorn-riders who kicked up dust on the newly dry roads. He felt like cheering at every section of behemoths he saw, and wished there were more of them to see.

In the fields between the roads, Forthwegian peasants plowed and planted as they had done for centuries since largely displacing the isolated Kaunians left behind when the Algarvians swept up from the south and wrecked the Kaunian Empire. The Forthwegian peasants did their best to ignore the Unkerlanter soldiers moving along the roads, just as, farther east, Forthwegian peasants were doubtless doing their best to ignore the Algarvian soldiers moving along the roads.

"They'll be planting back in my village about now, too," Leudast said to Sergeant Magnulf. He sniffed, then sighed. "Nothing like spring air, is there? It even *smells* green, you know what I mean? – like you ought to be able to grow crops from the smell without bothering with plowing and manuring and all that."

"Don't I wish!" Magnulf rolled his eyes. "Village I came out of is a lot farther south – matter of fact, it's only a couple of days' walk this side of the Gifhorn River, and on the other side of the Gifhorn they're Grelzers first and Unkerlanters only when they bother remembering the Union of Crowns. Liable to be snowing down there even now – and if it's not, people are still waiting for the mud to dry. Once it does, they'll work their arses off, too. None of this moonshine about growing things with the air."

"I didn't say you really could," Leudast protested. "I just said it smelled like you could."

Magnulf, like any sergeant worth his pay, was constitutionally unable to recognize a figure of speech. He could recognize a crude joke, though, and did, pointing to a band of Unkerlanter unicorns riding across a field a Forthwegian farmer had just finished plowing.

"Haw, haw, haw! Now that miserable whoreson'll have to do it all over again. Haw, haw!"

Leudast chuckled, too; a Forthwegian peasant's problems were none of his own. "I wish those unicorns were behemoths, is what I wish," he said.

"Aye, that'd be good," Magnulf agreed, laughing still. "Then he'd have bigger holes in the ground to worry about."

That wasn't why Leudast wished he saw more behemoths. All through Algarve's victory over Forthweg, and then in her smashing wins against Valmiera and Jelgava, her behemoths had done more than their share of the damage. Everyone said so. The summer and autumn before, he'd spent a lot of time training against horses tricked out as behemoths. The more of the great beasts he saw with Unkerlanter crews atop them, the happier he'd be.

He kept looking up into the sky, and cocking his head to one side to try to catch the harsh cries of dragons overhead. As with the behemoths, he saw and heard some, but not so many as he would have liked. When he remarked on that to Magnulf, the sergeant said, "Be thankful you don't see any flying out of the east. We're getting too bloody close to the border now. Here's hoping we've caught the redheads napping."

"Aye, here's hoping," Leudast said in what he hoped wasn't too hollow a voice. "Nobody else has managed to do that yet."

Magnulf spat in the dirt. "They put one arm in a tunic sleeve at a time, same as we do. Remember" – he planted an elbow in Leudast's ribs – "if they were as great as they think they are, they'd have won the Six Years' War. Am I right or am I wrong?"

"You're right, Sergeant. Can't argue with that." Leudast tramped on, feeling a little happier. His back ached. His feet ached. He wished King Swemmel's impressers had never found his village. He'd spent a lot of time wishing that. He didn't know why. It never did any good.

The regiment camped in the fields that night. That would give the Forthwegians who farmed them more work to do come morning – work likely to be undone when more Unkerlanter soldiers came through heading east. Leudast lost no sleep over that, or over the provenance of the chunks of mutton and chicken in the cookpots. Leudast lost no sleep over anything. As soon as he helped Magnulf make sure the squad was safely settled, he rolled himself in his blanket and plunged into slumber almost at once. He did not expect to wake till the rising sun pried his eyelids open.

But the first eggs fell out of the sky when morning twilight was barely beginning to stain the eastern horizon with gray. Now he heard dragons' cries, fierce and raucous. The beasts swooped low above the Unkerlanter encampment, dropping their eggs and then gaining height once more with thunderous wingbeats. Some came close enough to the ground to flame before they flew higher. More flames sprang up from tents and wagons they set afire.

Leudast seized his stick and started blazing at them, but the sky was still so dark, he had no good targets. Even with a good target, he knew a footsoldier had to be lucky – had to be more than lucky – to bring down a dragon. He kept blazing anyhow. If he didn't, he had no chance at all to bring one down.

An egg burst close by him, knocking him off his feet and rolling him along the ground like a pin in a game of sixteens. He knocked over a couple of other soldiers, too, just as a well-struck pin would have done, though not enough to gain a good score. They shouted and cursed, as he did. Men were screaming, too, at the top of their lungs.

Some of those screams burst from the throats of wounded men. Others were shouts of anger or, more often, horrified astonishment: "The redheads!" "The Algarvians!" "King Mezentio's men!"

They've got a lot of cursed nerve, hitting us first, Leudast thought. The ground shook beneath his feet as another egg burst nearby. *We were supposed to hit them first, catch them by surprise.*

That hadn't happened. It wasn't going to happen, not now. Remembering how his officers said the Algarvians liked to fight, Leudast had a sudden nasty premonition of what was likely to happen next. "Prepare to receive attack from the east!" he shouted to his squad and anyone else who would listen. "The redheads will be hitting us with foot and cavalry and those stinking behemoths, too!"

"Aye, that's the truth!" No one who knew Sergeant Magnulf could mistake his bellow. "That's what those cursed Algarvians think efficient fighting's all about. Now that the dragons have knocked us cockeyed, they'll send in the men on the ground to try and flatten us."

Here and there in the madness – which did not cease, for Algarvian dragons kept on pounding the encampment – officers also tried to rally their men. But some officers were killed, some were hurt, and some, with action upon them, turned out to be worthless. Leudast watched one run for the west as fast as he could go.

He had no time for more than one quick curse aimed at that captain's back. Then more eggs started falling on the tents. These were smaller than the ones the dragons carried, which meant the Algarvians had already got tossers over the border and into the part of Forthweg Unkerlant occupied. Leudast shook his head. No – the part of Forthweg Unkerlant *had* occupied.

A wild shout came from sentries posted east of the camp: "Here they come!"

"Come on, you whoresons!" Leudast yelled. "If we don't fight the redheads, they'll kill all of us." Even if his comrades did fight the Algarvians, King Mezentio's men were liable to kill them all. He chose not to dwell on that.

Now, instead of reaching for his stick, he grabbed his shovel off his belt and dug frantically. He had no time to make a proper hole from which to fight, but a little scrape with the dirt he'd dug thrown up in front of it was better than nothing. He lay flat in the scrape, rested his stick on the dirt parapet, and waited for the Algarvians to get close enough to blaze.

And then Colonel Roflanz, the regimental commander, shouted, "The attack must go on as ordered. Forward against the foe, men! King Swemmel and efficiency!"

"No!" Leudast and Magnulf yelled it together. Both of them had seen enough combat to know Roflanz was asking to get himself slaughtered, and everyone who followed him, too. The men in their squad, or the two or three of them close enough to hear their corporal, held their places. But far more men followed Roflanz. He was their leader. How could they go wrong if they followed him?

They found out. It did not take long. Algarvians on behemoths blazed them with heavy sticks at ranges from which they could not reply. Other behemoths bore light egg-tossers. Bursts of sorcerous energy flung Unkerlanter soldiers aside, broken and bleeding. And the behemoths themselves, armored against footsoldiers' weapons, lumbered forward and trampled down King Swemmel's men. The

Algarvians swarmed into the holes torn in their ranks.

Leudast almost started blazing at the first men he saw running back toward him. With the new-risen sun shining in his face, they were hardly more than silhouettes. His finger was already halfway into the blazing hole when he realized the men wore long tunics, not short tunics and kilts.

"Fall back!" one of them shouted, stumbling past his position. "If you don't fall back, everything's lost. Powers above, if you do fall back, everything's lost, too." Away he went, at least as fast as the captain who had incontinently fled when Algarvian dragons started dropping eggs on the encampment.

Magnulf said, "If the redheads make us fall back, I'll do it. But I'm cursed if I'll run away just because some coward tells me to."

"Aye, by the powers above," Leudast said. There – there ahead of him were men in kilts. He blazed at them. They went down. Maybe he'd hit one or two, maybe they were battlewise like him, and knew enough to make themselves smaller targets. Either way, he whooped. "We *can* stop the whoresons!"

But the Algarvians, when they met steady resistance, did not try to overrun and overwhelm it, as any Unkerlanter force would have done. Instead, they flowed around it, and soon were blazing at Leudast and the other steady Unkerlanters from the flank as well as the front.

"We have to give way!" Magnulf shouted then. "If we don't, they'll get behind us in a minute, and then we're dead." When he retreated, Leudast went with him. Leudast didn't want to move back, but he didn't want to die, either. As far as he was concerned, for the moment survival and efficiency were one and the same.

Count Sabrino whooped with glee. He whacked his dragon with the goad. The great, stupid beast screamed fury at him. But then it dove on the Unkerlanter column on the road outside of Eoforwic. The Unkerlanters started to scatter, but it was already too late. Sabrino's was not the only dragon falling out of the sky. His whole wing of dragonfliers plunged toward them.

When he saw five or six Unkerlanters tightly bunched, Sabrino whacked the dragon again, in a different way. Flame burst from its jaws. He heard the soldiers shriek as he flew by just above their heads.

He didn't whoop then. Savoring the enemy's anguish might have been all very well for the Algarvian chieftains who'd toppled the Kaunian Empire, but listening to footsoldiers burn brought combat to a level too personal for his taste.

And then, off to the north, he spied a different sort of target, the sort of target of which dragonfliers usually but dreamt. For this campaign, the mages had given him a crystal attuned to his squadron and flight leaders. He spoke into it now: "Look, lads! Another Unkerlanter dragon farm. Shall we go pay them a visit?"

"Aye!" That was Captain Domiziano, sounding as fierce as any Algarvian chieftain from the ancient days. "If Swemmel's men *will* give us presents, they can't be surprised when we take them."

The whole wing swung toward the dragon farm. Sabrino laughed under his breath. The Unkerlanters had intended to take Algarve by surprise. They'd moved strong forces very close to the front. But King Mezentio had had plans of his own, and now the Unkerlanters found themselves on the receiving end of the surprise they'd intended to give.

They weren't responding well, either, any more than Forthweg or Valmiera or Jelgava had when Mezentio's men struck them. There ahead, coming up fast, was a dragon farm whose dragons, on this second day of the attack, remained chained to the ground.

With a great roar, Sabrino's dragon put on a burst of speed. Dragons had no sense of chivalry or fair play whatever. When they saw foes helpless in the ground, all that filled their tiny minds was killing them. Sabrino's problem was not to urge his mount on, but to keep the dragon from flaming too soon and from landing to rend the Unkerlanter beast with its talons as well as burning them from above.

Unkerlanter fliers and keepers ran this way and that, trying to get a few dragons in the air either to oppose the Algarvians or simply to flee. They had little luck; Sabrino's wing flamed them with almost as much gusto as his dragons gave to destroying their winged, scaly counterparts.

By the time the wing had made several passes above the dragon farm, it was as dreadful a shambles as Sabrino had ever seen. By then, his dragon could produce only little wheezes of flame. It still wanted to go back and do some more killing. Sabrino had to beat it savagely with the goad to get it to fly away from the Unkerlanter dragon farm.

As long as it could see enemy dragons on the ground, it was ready to attack.

But, fortunately, it was, like any dragon, too stupid to own much in the way of a memory. After Sabrino had finally persuaded – and there was a splendid euphemism – it to leave the dragon farm, it flew on toward the east without a backwards glance. Sabrino, on the other hand, did look back, not for one more glimpse of the battered foe but to find out how the men and beasts of his wing had come through. He spied not a single hole in the formation. Pride filled him. The great force King Mezentio had built for revenge was performing exactly as its creator had intended.

Once Sabrino had made sure of that, he looked down to see how the fight on the ground was going. Pride filled him again. Here was the same pattern he'd seen in Valmiera. Wherever the Unkerlanters tried to make a stand, the Algarvians either used behemoths to pound them into submission with eggs and heavy sticks or went around them to strike from the side and rear as well as the front. And the Unkerlanters would have to retreat or surrender or die where they stood.

Some – quite a few, in fact – chose to do just that. No one had ever said the Unkerlanters were cowards: no one who'd fought them in the Six Years' War, certainly. But many Valmierans had been brave, too, and it hadn't helped them any. King Mezentio and his generals had outthought them before they outfought them. The same drama looked to be unfolding on the plains of eastern Forthweg.

Every once in a while, the Unkerlanters would hole up in a village or a natural strongpoint too tough to be easily taken. Then, again as in Valmiera and Jelgava, the dragons would come in, dropping eggs on the enemy, softening him up so the men on the ground could finish him off.

When Sabrino's wing came spiraling down to land at a hastily set up farm in what had been, up till that morning, Unkerlanter-occupied Forthweg, the keepers shouted, "How's it going? How are we doing, up ahead there?"

"Couldn't be better," Sabrino said as he slid off his dragon once it was securely chained to a stake. "By the powers above, I really don't see how anything could look finer. If we keep going like this, we'll get to Cottbus almost as fast as we got to Priekule."

The keepers cheered. One of them took a chunk of meat, rolled it in a bucket full of ground cinnabar and brimstone, and tossed it to the dragon. A snap, and the meat was gone. The dragon ate greedily. It had worked hard today. It would work hard again tomorrow. As long as it got enough food and close to enough rest, it would be able to do what was required of it.

"Eat, sleep, and fight," Sabrino said. "Not such a bad life, eh?"

One of the keepers looked at him as if he'd lost his mind. "What about screwing?"

"A reward for good service," Sabrino answered easily. "That'd pull 'em into the army, wouldn't it? 'Serve your kingdom bravely and we'll put you out to stud.' Aye, they'd be storming to join up once they heard that." He laughed. So did the keepers. Why not laugh? The enemy fled before them.

Captain Domiziano came up. "What's so funny, sir?" he asked. Sabrino told him. He laughed, too. "Can I quit and join up again?"

"Up till now, my dear fellow, I haven't noticed you having any problems finding a lady – or, in a pinch, merely a woman – who was interested, or at least willing, when you were," Sabrino said.

"Well, that's true enough," Domiziano said complacently. "The hunting was better when we were on the eastern front, though. Those Valmieran and Jelgavan wenches acted almost the way the ones in the historical romances do. Most of the Kaunian women here won't give us the time of day, and half the Forthwegians are built like bricks.

"It won't get any better," Sabrino said. "When we break into Unkerlant, they'll be even dumpier than the Forthwegians."

"My lord count!" Domiziano said in piteous tones. "Did you have to make me think in such doleful terms?"

"What's so doleful about breaking into Unkerlant?" Captain Orosio asked. He'd come up too late to hear how the conversation started.

Domiziano needed only two words to fill him in: "Homely women."

"Ah." Orosio nodded. He looked west. "You had better get used to it, my dear comrade. Not even the powers above, I shouldn't think, can keep us from smashing the Unkerlanters once for all. You can watch them crumble as we hit them."

"They're trying hard to fight back," Sabrino said, giving credit where he thought it due. "They may even be fighting back harder than the Kaunian kingdoms did in the east. The Jelgavans just quit once we got the jump on them; they had no use for their own officers. The Valmierans did a little better, but they still haven't figured out what hit them."

"Do you think the Unkerlanters have, sir?" Orosio asked, his eyes wide.

Sabrino considered the day's action, the column flamed on the road and the dragon farm caught with its animals still chained to the ground. A slow smile stole across his face. "Now that you mention it, no," he said.

Orosio and Domiziano both laughed and clapped their hands. Domiziano said, "We'll be in Cottbus, burning King Swemmel's palace down around his crazy ears, before harvest time."

"Aye." Captain Orosio nodded again. "He's going to have a lesson in what efficiency really means." He paraded around very stiffly, as if he were afraid to make any movement not prescribed for him by some higher authority.

"You look like you've got a poker up your arse," Sabrino said.

"Feels that way, too." Orosio relaxed into a more natural posture. "But go ahead and tell me it's not how Unkerlanters are."

"I can't do that," Sabrino admitted. "Can't even come close. They're the sort of people who wait for permission to come through on a crystal before they blow their noses."

"And they haven't got enough crystals to go around, either," Domiziano added.

"Makes things easier for us," Orosio said. "I'm in favor of whatever makes things easier for us."

"What I'd be in favor of right now is some wine and some food," Sabrino said. "Our dragons are stuffing themselves" – he glanced back to where the keepers tossed more gobbets of meat to the great beasts – "and I want to do the same."

"I'm sorry, sir, but brimstone and cinnabar give me heartburn," Domiziano said with a grin.

"What would the back of my hand give you?" the wing commander asked, but he also grinned. Aye, grins were easy to come by in an army moving forward. Sabrino looked toward the west again. Faces would be long in the Unkerlanter encampments. He hoped they would get longer, too, in the days ahead. In a low voice, he murmured, "The tide is flowing our way."

"Aye, it is," Captain Orosio said. For his part, he looked toward the tents set to one side of the dragon farm. He was grinning, too. "And it looks like supper is finally flowing our way."

Supper, plainly, had been foraged from the Forthwegian countryside. Sabrino gorged himself on crumbly white cheese, almost preserved with salt and garlic, olives even saltier than the almonds, and breads with wheat and barley flour dusted with sesame seeds. Had anyone back at his estate presumed to serve him such a rough red wine, he would have bitten the luckless fellow's head off. Here in the field, he drank it without complaint. It might even have gone better with his simple fare than a more subtle vintage would have done.

As he ate, the stars came out. The Gyongyosians made them into powers, powers that could control a man's destiny. Foolishness, as far as Sabrino was concerned. Powers or not, though, they were beautiful. He watched them for a while, till he caught himself yawning.

He sought his bed without the least embarrassment or the least desire for company. If young Domiziano had the energy to look for a companion and to do something with her once he found her, that was his affair. Sabrino needed sleep.

Some time in the middle of the night, Unkerlanter dragons dropped eggs not too far from the dragon farm. Sabrino woke up, cursed the Unkerlanters in a blurry voice, and fell asleep again. The next morning, the attack went on.

EARTHLIGHT

A SELECTED LIST OF FANTASY TITLES
AVAILABLE FROM EARTHLIGHT

The prices shown below were correct at the time of going to press. However Earthlight reserve the right to show new retail prices on covers which may differ from those previously advertised in the text or elsewhere.

☐ 0 6710 1605 9	Escardy Gap	*Peter Crowther & James Lovegrove*	£5.99
☐ 0 6710 2261 X	The Sum Of All Men	*David Farland*	£6.99
☐ 0 7434 0827 6	Brotherhood of the Wolf	*David Farland*	£6.99
☐ 0 6710 1787 X	The Lament of Abalone	*Jane Welch*	£5.99
☐ 0 6710 3391 3	The Bard of Castaguard	*Jane Welch*	£5.99
☐ 0 6710 1785 3	The Royal Changeling	*John Whitbourn*	£5.99
☐ 0 6710 3300 X	Downs-Lord Dawn	*John Whitbourn*	£5.99
☐ 0 6710 2193 1	Sailing to Sarantium	*Guy Gavriel Kay*	£6.99
☐ 0 6848 6156 9	Lord of Emperors	*Guy Gavriel Kay*	£16.99
☐ 0 6710 2191 5	Beyond the Pale	*Mark Anthony*	£6.99
☐ 0 6848 6041 4	The Keep of Fire	*Mark Anthony*	£9.99
☐ 0 6710 2192 3	The Last Dragonlord	*Joanne Bertin*	£6.99
☐ 0 6848 6051 1	Dragon and Phoenix	*Joanne Bertin*	£9.99
☐ 0 6710 2208 3	The High House	*James Stoddard*	£5.99
☐ 0 6710 3749 8	The False House	*James Stoddard*	£5.99
☐ 0 6710 3303 4	Green Rider	*Kristen Britain*	£6.99
☐ 0 6710 2190 7	The Amber Citadel	*Freda Warrington*	£5.99
☐ 0 6710 2282 2	Into The Darkness	*Harry Turtledove*	£6.99
☐ 0 6710 2189 3	The Siege of Arrandin	*Marcus Herniman*	£5.99
☐ 0 6710 3719 6	The Twist	*Richard Calder*	£5.99
☐ 0 6710 3720 X	Malignos	*Richard Calder*	£6.99

All Earthlight titles are available by post from:

Book Service By Post, P.O. Box 29, Douglas, Isle of Man IM99 1BQ

Credit cards accepted. Please telephone 01624 675137,
fax 01624 670923, Internet http://www.bookpost.co.uk or
e-mail: bookshop@enterprise.net for details.

Free postage and packing in the UK. Overseas customers allow
£1 per book (paperbacks) and £3 per book (hardbacks).